FATE KNOWS NO TEARS

Mary Talbot Cross grew up in the United Kingdom and took a degree in French language and literature at Aberdeen University in Scotland. She arrived in Australia in 1991 and began researching and writing about Australian history under her given name, Jennifer M.T. Carter.

She lives in Burra, South Australia.

Also by Mary Talbot Cross

The Foundling: A tale of the Burra Burra Mine (1998)

Fortune's Fool: The road beyond Eureka (2001)

By Jennifer M. T. Carter

Painting the Islands Vermilion: Archibald Watson and the Brig Carl (1999)

Eyes to the Future: Sketches of Australia and her neighbours in the 1870s (2000)

The title of this book and the quotations within it are taken from the published works of 'Laurence Hope':

The Garden of Kama (1901)
Stars of the Desert (1903)
Indian Love (1905)

FATE KNOWS NO TEARS

A novel of passion and scandal in the days of the Raj

Wakefield Press
16 Rose Street
Mile End
South Australia 5031
www.wakefieldpress.com.au

First published 1996
New edition published 2009
This edition, with included Acknowledgement, published 2026

Copyright © Mary Talbot Cross, 2009, 2026

All rights reserved. This book is copyright. Apart from any fair dealing for the purposes of private study, research, criticism or review, as permitted under the Copyright Act, no part may be reproduced without written permission. Enquiries should be addressed to the publisher.

Cover designed by designBITE, Adelaide
Typeset by Wakefield Press

ISBN 978 1 86254 785 8

Wakefield Press thanks
Coriole Vineyards for
continued support

Contents

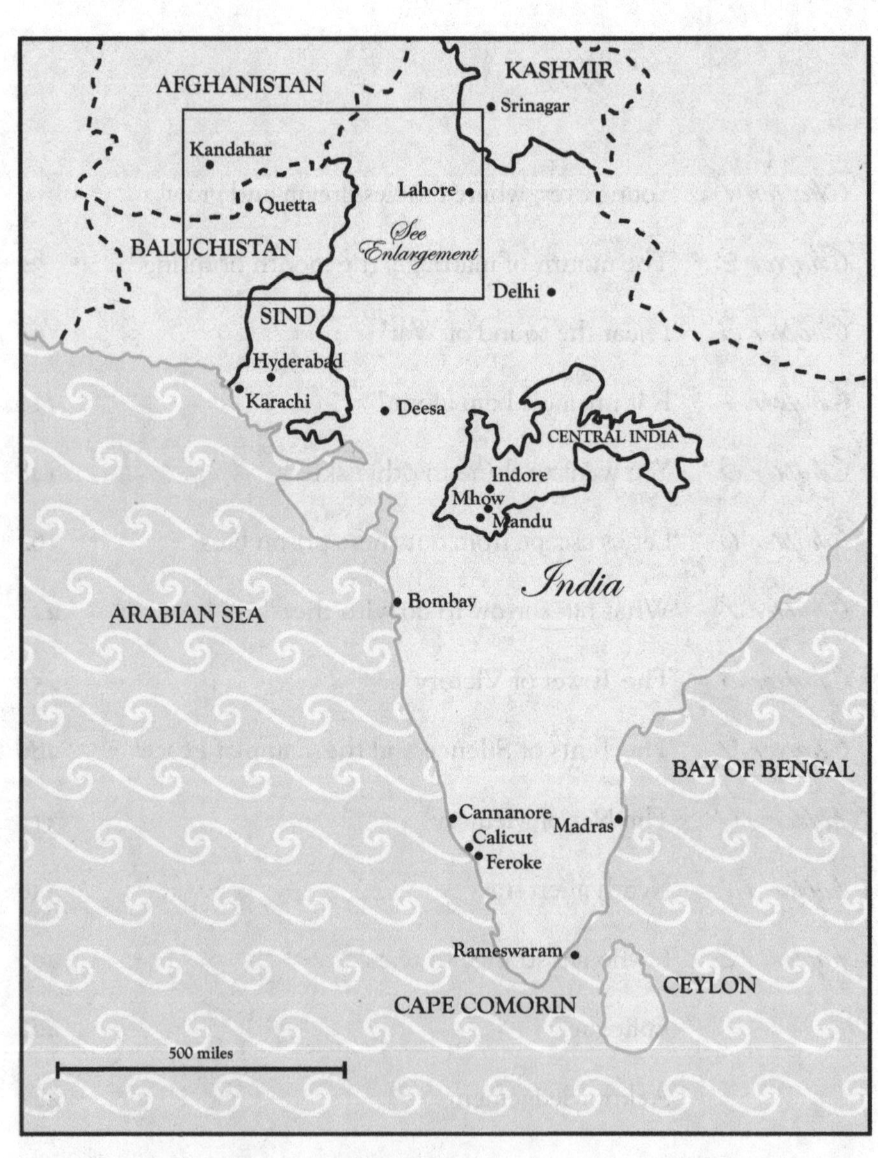
AFGHANISTAN
KASHMIR
Srinagar
Kandahar
Lahore
Quetta
See Enlargement
BALUCHISTAN
Delhi
SIND
Hyderabad
Karachi
Deesa
CENTRAL INDIA
Indore
Mhow
Mandu
India
Bombay
ARABIAN SEA
BAY OF BENGAL
Cannanore
Madras
Calicut
Feroke
Rameswaram
CEYLON
CAPE COMORIN
500 miles

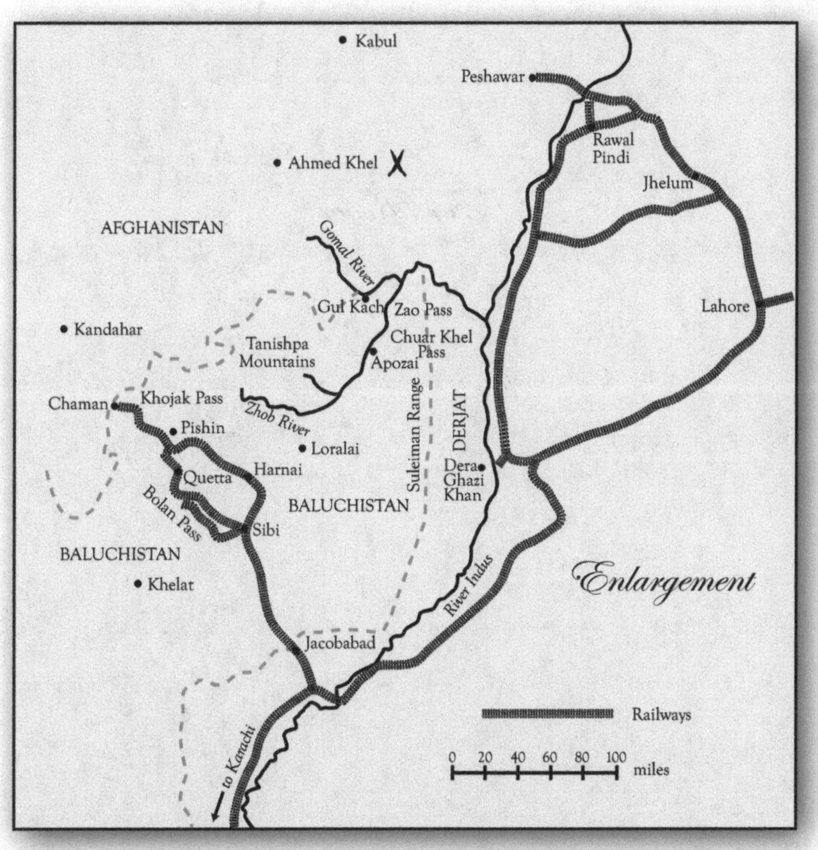
Kabul
Peshawar
Rawal Pindi
Ahmed Khel
Jhelum
AFGHANISTAN
Gomal River
Gul Kach
Zao Pass
Lahore
Kandahar
Tanishpa Mountains
Chuar Khel Pass
Apozai
Chaman
Khojak Pass
Zhob River
Pishin
Loralai
Suleiman Range
DERJAT
Harnai
Quetta
Dera Ghazi Khan
Bolan Pass
BALUCHISTAN
Sibi
BALUCHISTAN
Khelat
Enlargement
River Indus
Jacobabad
Railways
0 20 40 60 80 100 miles
to Karachi

For Roger

1

'Young eyes, where fancies dream and grow'

KARACHI: APRIL 1886–APRIL 1889

'Damn—oh, *damn*!' If the first exclamation had been muted, the second was loud enough for the man in the reading room adjoining the library to raise his head. He looked across at the girl who had followed him into the building some ten minutes before. Even from there he could detect a most unbecoming scowl on her face as she gazed up at the shelves that were obviously quite beyond her reach. Amused, he watched as she cast her eye around in an attempt to solve her dilemma.

Suddenly the short slight figure darted into a corner and returned with a stool. Putting it down with a bad-tempered thud, she climbed on and reached up for her quarry. With no more success than before. Undeterred, she hauled two vast tomes from the bottom-most shelf and placed them on the stool.

It simply would not do, thought the observer, as his amusement gave way to concern, and quickly he crossed the passage to her side. Intent upon her task, the young woman failed to detect his approach and at the sudden sound of the pleasant voice beside her enquiring, 'Perhaps I might be of assistance?' she gave a start and would have fallen, had a firm hand not steadied her and helped her safely down.

She glared at her rescuer before collecting herself enough to thank him for his help. 'I'm sorry,' she said in an unexpectedly deep little voice, 'but you startled me, you know.' She smiled up contritely at the tall man who now released her arm. Had he heard her swear? she wondered, and felt herself blush slightly. The handsome hawk-like features were inscrutable and it was quite impossible to tell. 'It's such a nuisance being so short, with everything always out of reach,' she explained, in case he had.

'It must be,' he agreed sympathetically, returning her smile from his far superior height, and from habit scrutinising the face before him. It could not be classed simply as pretty, for the features were too strong and full of character for that, but it was certainly striking.

'Now, what exactly were you after?' he enquired, twinkling grey eyes meeting the frank blue gaze that was summing him up in turn.

'Captain Burton's *Sindh*—it must be up there, on the top shelf. The librarian said so—before he disappeared.' The petulant tone returned to her voice as she exclaimed, 'Oh, why does Burton have to begin with a B?'

'I don't suppose he had any more choice about that than you do over your lack of inches,' this with lips twitching. 'Here you are.' The long arm reached up and removed a book with ease. 'However, you might find this easier to deal with—in every respect,' the stranger continued, bending down and taking a second book from a far lower shelf. The girl looked at him, then at Ross's *Land of the Five Rivers and Sind*, and grinned despite herself.

'Meaning, I suppose, that Burton is difficult to grasp in more ways than one. Thank you, but I think I'll try him anyway.'

She took the books he offered her, the generous mouth curving in a smile that again transformed her previously sullen face, then without another word she turned and went off in pursuit of the elusive librarian.

A most unusual young woman, concluded the man who had come to her aid, watching her stride away, a purposeful little figure with a wealth of bouncing honey-gold hair ill-confined at the neck by a bright blue bow. Then with a slight frown on his face he went back to his newspaper.

Once outside, the girl blinked at the sudden contrast between the gloom of the Hall and the harsh bright light of daytime Karachi. Then, tucking the two volumes firmly under her arm, she began the long walk home.

It wasn't just books that were out of reach, she thought gloomily on the way, it was *everything*. They had been here six months now, and she still found herself regretting Lahore. Karachi with its brash newness, set incongruously between desert and sea, was no substitute for the ancient stronghold of the Moghuls with its glorious reminders of a golden age long gone. At least in Lahore she had managed to slip away into the bazaar for hours at a time, alone or with Izzie, and savour the real India—until Mother found out and insisted on curtailing her freedom.

The *real* India. What exactly was that, anyway? In Lahore she had plied the tired and jaded civilians from the outlying Punjabi stations with an endless stream of questions, for surely they of all people would know? And the answer was always the same: India was heat, dust and poverty. One did one's best against overwhelming odds—and then one went home to one's well-deserved retirement and tried to forget.

'But there must be more?' she would ask, perplexed. And they would smile and move on, leaving her unsatisfied. Where was the mystery, the magic, the pulse of this ancient land she had read about and yearned to discover for herself? She had felt some of it brush past briefly in Old Lahore, and beckon from the native bazaar, but here in Karachi it was lost again in the humdrum nature of her life.

Somewhere, she thought, as she gazed towards the distant horizon, somewhere all the answers must lie waiting, and somewhere in this vast country there must be someone who knew. Adela Florence Cory sighed and not for the first time in her young life lamented the fact that she had been born a girl.

She could have taken a *tonga* but that would have got her back far too soon. Not that she disliked the bungalow which was now the family home; on the contrary, she loved the old house with its deep verandah and cool high-ceilinged rooms. And the roof terrace she had found on the very first day and made very much her own. What did it matter after all that the house was on the unfashionable side of town?

To Adela that seemed a distinct advantage, since from her rooftop eyrie she could look northwards out across the desert to the hills of Baluchistan. *Baluchistan* ... For the young girl of twenty-one the very name conjured up a whole new world of dreams, a world she liked to imagine full of romance, wilderness and warriors, of blood feuds to the very death. Well, the truth was likely very different, she supposed: there was a whole regiment of Baluchis in the town, drilled to perfection by their European officers, and they all seemed pretty tame.

Remembering her mother's alarm at finding that the barracks were just down the road from their bungalow, and her frantic warnings to her daughters as a result, Adela Cory grinned.

After a while she had cleared the European lines, with their limestone houses standing square and solid in equally unimaginative compounds. It was all so grey and *boring*! She kicked savagely at a stone in the road and stubbed her toe. She swore. By the time she left the Bunder Road and turned into the driveway to her home her bad temper had returned, and even the sight of the brilliant flowers in her mother's impeccable garden failed to lift her mood.

She reached the entrance and reluctantly went inside. In the drawing room, its homely effect heightened by Persian rugs on the flagstone floor and cushions scattered with gay abandon over chairs and divans, her mother was reclining on a sofa, an unopened book on her lap, and her elder sister was playing softly at the piano. Her father must be in his study. Then the girl's eyes narrowed.

'Where's the brat?' she demanded, for her younger sister was nowhere to be seen. Fanny Cory smiled vaguely at her daughter.

'Annie Sophie, do you mean, dear? She was here a moment ago. Isabel, have you seen her?'

Isabel shook her head, then rose in alarm as Adela swept out, a determined tilt to her jaw and a ferocious expression on her face. She went straight to her room and was in no way surprised at what she found. Annie Sophie Cory looked up with a start of guilt from the paper she was reading and quickly jumped to her feet.

'And just what do you think you're doing?'

Adela was outraged at the sight of the plump intruder reading the poetry she had been working on before going out. 'I've told you before, you little wretch, this is my room and you're not to come in! Now, give me that!' She snatched the verses away. 'I've warned you often enough,' she continued. 'You're coming with me to Father!' So saying, she dug none too gentle fingers into her sister's fleshy arm and dragged her along behind her.

By the time they reached Colonel Cory's sanctum the ready tears were flowing down Annie Sophie's cheeks. Adela, white-faced and furious, rapped at the door and marched in without waiting. The short stocky figure of Arthur Cory was standing at the window, looking out. Slowly he turned and surveyed his two younger daughters. What was it now? he thought wearily. Since Annie Sophie had returned from school in England there had been nothing but trouble, trouble nearly always of her own making. And, it seemed to her father, nearly always directed at Adela.

'Father,' that young lady was saying now, almost too angry to speak, 'will you please tell this—this *creature*—to keep out of my room and leave my things alone, or I'm afraid I shall probably kill her.'

Cory eyed them calmly; he didn't believe the threat but the frightened culprit obviously did. 'Leave it to me, Adela.' Steady eyes of the same intense violet-blue as his daughter's looked back at her from a face framed by greying hair and a neatly trimmed beard and moustache, now more white than red. What she saw in Cory's expression was enough to satisfy the girl: quickly she retrieved her books from her room and went up to the roof. And there her family thought it politic to leave her.

'And tales they told me of his deeds in war'

A few days later Adela returned to the library. Not for her the delights of the Gymkhana Club where Annie Sophie would have happily spent all her time. It was a popular venue for young ladies with its dancing, tennis, badminton and concerts, but Adela had no wish to chaperone her sister, or to suffer the attentions of the young men who frequented the place as well—youngsters starting out in business, as well as subalterns from the various regiments stationed in the town. They were all more than willing to be sociable, but she found their conversation tedious and much preferred her own company, or that of a good book. So the two volumes on Sind were quickly devoured and she decided to go back for more.

Again she met with difficulties.

'Oh dear,' she muttered, 'I suppose I shall have to get used to this, but why is there never a librarian on hand to help?' Without thinking, she looked over to the reading room and there he was again. The tall stranger looked up from his newspaper, saw her, and immediately came to her aid.

'We seem to be making somewhat of a habit of this,' he told her. What an engaging smile he had, she found herself thinking; it quite dispelled the severity of his features, and softened the effect of the steely blue-grey eyes. 'How was Burton?'

He remembered, then. 'Interesting—but indigestible in places. You were right.' The bright head nodded emphatically.

The stranger laughed. 'And what are you after this time?' he asked.

'I wondered if they had his translation of *The Arabian Nights*,' she replied, but he doubted it very much indeed. He had seen some of the work himself and thought it quite the last thing that Karachi would offer its young female population for entertainment. His amusement must have shown and when Adela looked at him, perplexed, he felt he should explain.

'I believe it's not considered quite the thing for young ladies,' he informed her gently.

She raised an eyebrow and asked him why.

'Well, you see,' he went on, 'it's a literal translation of some very frank writing, and you would probably be shocked.' His expression was serious, but laughter lurked deep in his eyes and the girl felt she was being patronised.

'I don't shock easily,' she assured him.

No, thought her companion, looking down at this diminutive young woman with the disconcertingly frank violet gaze, no, I don't suppose you do. 'Besides,' he added, 'your parents certainly wouldn't approve.'

'My father doesn't mind *what* I read,' replied Adela, crossing her fingers behind her back as she told the lie.

'Oh, and who is your father?' By now the man was intrigued. 'I'm sorry,' he said instantly, 'I don't mean to be rude. Perhaps I should introduce myself, as we seem to keep on meeting—my name is Malcolm Nicolson.' He held out his hand.

'And I'm Adela Cory,' and she held out hers in return.

Nicolson held it for a moment in a firm warm clasp as he considered the name and her face. 'Your father wouldn't be Colonel Arthur Cory, by any chance? The editor of the *Civil and Military Gazette* in Lahore?'

'Why, yes,' Adela's interest was aroused. 'Do you know him?'

So that was why those startling eyes had seemed so familiar, and the set of the head. Nicolson realised he was still holding her hand and released her. 'Your father and I met there during the recent war,' he explained. 'Is he in Karachi, then?'

'Yes,' she said. 'We live here now. Father runs the *Sind Gazette*.'

'And you were in England when I met him.'

'Yes, I didn't come out till the spring of '81. I was at school.'

She would have been. Indeed, she looked little more than a schoolgirl now.

'All the excitement was over by then, of course.' Miss Cory grinned irreverently as she remembered her father's unbounded enthusiasm for the advance into Afghan territory. 'I suppose you were in the thick of things—' With an unconsciously appealing little movement, she put her head to one side and considered the military nature of his moustache and bearing.

'Yes, I was a little closer to the action than your father,' Nicolson agreed, 'but generally speaking I was somewhat less enthusiastic!' He found himself smiling back as he remembered the peppery little colonel and the fiery editorials of the day.

He would certainly call on her father, he said, before his leave was up, and with a slight bow he returned to his newspaper. But much to the young woman's disappointment, he did not come to the bungalow, but found Arthur Cory at his office off Macleod Road one afternoon before leaving town to rejoin his Baluch regiment, many hundreds of miles away on the border with Afghanistan.

Like many another officer in the Bombay Army, Colonel Malcolm Hassells Nicolson, newly appointed to the command of the 3rd Baluch Battalion, chose to spend his periods of leave in Karachi's pleasant seaside climate and soon he became a frequent visitor to the Cory home.

His first visit just before Christmas was unheralded, and Adela was alone. She had hardly given him a thought since their two earlier meetings—unless it was to regret the absence of a helping hand at the library shelves—and she looked at him with interest. Today the colonel was wearing the rifle-green jacket and the plain red trousers of the Baluchi officers she often saw about the town; his helmet with the green *pugri* made him seem taller still and he looked thoroughly and splendidly the soldier. For the first time she noticed a scar on his chin which heightened the effect.

'You were about to go riding,' he observed. 'I mustn't keep you, Miss Cory.'

She had seen him ride up, and said on an impulse: 'Father will be back later, Colonel Nicolson. Why don't you join me?'

There was no trace of coquetry about her invitation and he accepted. In the weeks that followed they often rode out together, developing an easy companionship as the girl plied him with questions about the area he had come to know and love so well. He found her easy to talk to: she wanted to know everything about her surroundings, and her questions made him look at them afresh through her young and eager eyes.

As he told her of Baluchistan and life in the Afghan hills she watched him quite unselfconsciously, with those great violet-blue eyes wide open, and her lips slightly apart, drinking in his every word. Sometimes her expression would slowly change to one of incredulity as he told her some unlikely tale, and she would force him to confess his deception. Then her spontaneous laughter would ring out and, shaking her head in mock despair, she would swear never to take him seriously again.

It was all very flattering, the colonel told himself, and she was certainly attractive enough to turn a man's head—a man, of course, less dedicated to his profession than he.

It was unfortunate, reflected Adela on the evening Colonel Nicolson first came to dinner, this way Mother had of parading her unmarried daughters like a merchant displaying superfluous wares. She looked up and saw the colonel observing her, and for one disconcerting moment she wondered whether he could read her mind.

Isabel took refuge behind her spectacles at Malcolm Nicolson's greeting and smiled a little shyly before he turned to Adela and then to Annie Sophie. They were a striking trio, so similar in colouring and height, concluded the soldier, as he took each girl's hand in turn. Isabel was very like Adela to look at, a little taller perhaps, but lacking her sister's almost arrogant self-assured bearing, while the youngest girl was newly arrived in India, he understood, and seemed little used to adult company.

I do wish she would stop wriggling, was Adela's irritated thought as Annie Sophie played with the sash on her dress, or twisted a gingerish curl around her finger while she waited for the formalities to end. Whatever must Colonel Nicolson be thinking? The colonel in fact hardly noticed, but over dinner he discovered that Adela was not the only Miss Cory possessed of an enquiring mind. The talk turned to Afghanistan and the war that had ended some five years before. That Nicolson seemed reluctant to talk of his experiences did not deter Annie Sophie in the least for she was fascinated by the man, and determined to find out as much about him as she could.

'Did you fight in the Afghan War, Colonel Nicolson?' she asked, looking at the scar on the strong jaw. He seemed rather uncomfortable at the question but nodded, saying he had been at the action at Ahmed Khel in 1880.

'What did it feel like?' The girl's eyes were shining.

'I was afraid.' The soldier's reply was blunt. 'And so was everyone else, unless he was a fool.'

His interrogator looked disappointed. 'I'm sure that's not true!' she exclaimed, gazing at the colonel in open admiration.

'My dear Miss Annie,' he replied, 'the sight of three or four thousand madmen charging down a hillside, armed with *tulwars*, knives and pistols, and bent on death—yours or theirs, it doesn't matter which—is enough to put the fear of God into anyone. And at such moments, I can assure you, nobody thinks of being a hero.'

His tone was light-hearted enough, but as he paused and looked around the table Adela noticed the man's right hand and the unusually long fingers gripping the bowl of his glass. The knuckles gleamed white in the lamplight and, fascinated, she waited for the crystal to shatter.

'Fighting is always a dirty business, if at times a necessary one,' the colonel went on, 'and an army should exist primarily to keep the peace and save life, not take it.' The thin fingers relaxed and Adela no longer held her breath, turning her head towards her father who was nodding in support.

'Most civilians,' Nicolson went on, 'think of soldiering as a glamorous occupation, but it's nothing of the kind. A soldier's existence is demanding and often solitary and to my mind he's better off without a wife. Many young ladies are dazzled by a handsome uniform, marry, then realise—all too late, unfortunately—that army life is not for them.'

He looked around the table again, then gave a self-deprecating little cough. 'I'm sorry, it's a bit of a hobby-horse of mine, I'm afraid.'

Adela agreed silently that it certainly was; how often in their conversations had the colonel not laid the blame for all the ills of the Afghan Frontier on women and their wiles! Her mouth curved in a faint smile.

Fanny Cory, watching her second daughter's reaction to the colonel's emphatic pronouncement, felt a profound relief. The warning, if warning there were, was not for Addie, then.

'Father, what exactly was the colonel talking about at dinner? He seemed rather upset.' Adela had come upon her father alone the following morning after breakfast.

Colonel Cory looked at her shrewdly. So she had noticed. Well, he told himself, his daughter might as well learn something of the man who was taking up so much of her time. 'There's more to Malcolm Nicolson than many people realise,' he began.

Adela's raised eyebrow invited an explanation, although she already suspected as much.

'He was with Sir Donald Stewart during the occupation of Kandahar, officially as a Brigade Major—' Arthur Cory looked at his daughter. Perhaps he should stop there, but her enthralled expression urged him to go on. 'General Stewart was in the city for months, relying on Afghan informers for news of enemy strength, disposition, strategy, and so forth. Eventually he decided the only way to get reliable information was to set up a Field Intelligence system of his own.'

Adela grinned. 'I suppose he discovered that the natives made everything up to keep him happy.'

'Something like that—And anything really worth knowing was sold to the highest bidder, which often wasn't the Government—*our* government, anyway, which is not renowned for its generosity in these matters. Adela,' Cory went on seriously, 'I shouldn't be telling you this. You must not repeat it.'

'I shan't say a word'—she grinned again— 'not even to the colonel.' She guessed that Nicolson had been one of General Stewart's spies, and now she discovered that, with his appearance and fluency in at least three frontier languages, Malcolm Nicolson could easily pass as a native—and had done so on many occasions. She sensed there was even more to learn about the man, but her father chose not to enlighten her.

'But working in disguise must have been even more dangerous than fighting openly in battle, surely?'

'Oh, Nicolson's no coward. And what you saw last night, Addie, was the result of anger, not fear. He risked his life over and over again, and when he brought back a warning about a body of hostile tribesmen some several thousand strong massing up on the hills, quite separate from the main Afghan army, he was ignored. They moved parallel with our forces for miles along the foothills, whipped up to a frenzy by their mullahs preaching a holy war, and when at last they attacked, my dear, it was all hell let loose—'

'And that was what Colonel Nicolson was talking about last night,' breathed the girl.

'Yes.' Under his daughter's rapt gaze Colonel Cory warmed to his theme. 'They swept down in waves at Ahmed Khel, four thousand or more *ghazi* fanatics ready to die with Paradise their prize, rushing through the cavalry ranks, on towards the infantry and forcing them back in disarray. At last the officers managed to rally their men and save the guns, at the cost of stab wounds and sword slashes from hand to hand combat—' Adela looked a question and Cory nodded '— but the Afghans came off worse. They left a thousand dead on the field and took perhaps another thousand bodies away. We lost a few—not many, thank the Lord—but it could have been a rout, had the infantry not held. And *that* is why the colonel is still so angry, Addie—because of unnecessary risks and unnecessary waste of human life.'

'Friendship is sweet, and Love is sweeter still'

Adela hadn't realised that Christmas could be such fun and for once she went quite willingly to dances and concerts at the Club. True, the subalterns were just as boring, but colonels, she found, were not. She would often glance away from her partner of the moment to surprise Malcolm Nicolson's look of amusement as he watched her, and her attempts to keep a polite distance between herself and any young admirer. It was as if he knew exactly what she was thinking and was daring her to laugh out loud.

One evening he joined the company late and smiled a greeting to the girl across the room. Her response was so warm that the young lieutenant dancing with her, envious that Miss Cory should bestow her favours on another, followed the direction of her gaze. 'You know Colonel Nicolson?' He was surprised.

'Yes, he's a good friend of my father's.'

So that was it. The young man relaxed. 'He was in my regiment, you know,' he informed her. 'We were sorry to lose him.' The tone was almost proprietorial. 'He was wonderful with the Baluchis. Any problem and he would always do his best to help. And they would do anything for him. Anything.'

The lieutenant paused, and then memory got the better of him. 'I owe him a great deal as well—' Adela looked at the boy more attentively and waited; he was obviously wanting to speak. And what he told her made her see the colonel with different eyes.

That he should be brave in the heat of battle was understandable—that after all was his job. That his strong views about his profession, coupled with a hint of mystery about his past, made him fascinating to talk to, she was the first to admit; and that he should be at ease with ladies and such good company, at his age was not at all surprising. But that he should be compassionate … Perhaps from her knowledge of the man that was to be expected too.

She listened as the boy told her of his arrival in India, and how the overspending and the mounting debt to native moneylenders had led him to almost suicidal despair—until the colonel's quiet intervention had brought him peace of mind. 'He said he would thrash the living daylights out of me if I got into trouble again—and I guess he meant it!' The lieutenant grinned as he recollected the friendly cuff over the ear that had accompanied the words and the return of his IOUs. 'He said I could pay him back when I was able. And I have,' he added proudly. 'Miss Cory, I owe that man my life.'

He looked over at Nicolson, the light of hero worship in his eyes, and that moment more than anything else stayed with Adela long after the colonel headed north once more.

As spring advanced, Adela ventured further from her home. Sometimes she took the family's smart new carriage and drove out towards Hawkes Bay and the beaches to the west of the town. But never alone.

'It's all very well wandering through the town as you do,' her normally indulgent father pointed out, 'all you need do is raise your voice and shout for help if there's any trouble. Yes, yes,' he went on impatiently, 'I *know* there never is, but out there it's quite another matter. The place could be deserted—anything could happen to a woman on her own. No, I'm sorry, Addie, there's no point in arguing; promise me you will always take a *syce*.'

Adela was used to disagreeing with her parents, but on this subject and faced with her father's concerned and determined expression, she had no choice but give her word. Armed with her sketchpad and notebook, and always accompanied by a groom, she would sit for hours looking at the sea, or inland to where marshes gave way to sand dunes, and sand dunes to desert, and to the wide horizons beyond. And her thoughts would idly turn to Colonel Nicolson stationed somewhere in the distant Baluchi hills.

One day, some months later, Fanny Cory paused at the door of her husband's study. She watched him perusing the documents on his desk and slowly shook her head. He was in the grip of another enthusiasm, that was obvious. In Lahore it had been *The Russian Menace to the Frontiers of Empire*, here it was—what? *The Karachi Port Trust*? Or *The Railway Question*? Suddenly she made up her mind.

'Arthur,' she said in a determined voice, 'we need to talk.'

The greying sandy head was raised and the colonel peered at his wife over his spectacles. 'Talk about what, Fan? Can't you see I'm busy on tomorrow's editorial? The Viceroy will be here in a few months' time and I want to make sure the town is well aware of the issues for his consideration.'

'All that can wait,' Mrs Cory said sharply. 'There are more important things—things nearer to home.'

Arthur Cory's gaze softened as he gave his wife his full attention. Time and India had not dealt kindly with Fanny, he concluded. She was still comely, but at fifty-two the bright hair had faded, and the lines on her face were accentuated at that moment by worry.

'Sit down, dear,' he said immediately. 'Tell me what's wrong.'

Mrs Cory plumped herself down in a chair and looked over at her husband. 'It's the girls, Arthur. I'm anxious about them.'

'Not all of them, Fanny, surely? Isabel's no trouble. In fact she's a delight. I sometimes wonder how I managed at the paper without her.'

'She *is* twenty-four, and still unmarried,' sniffed Fanny, 'but, no, you're right. I've no real concern about her—it's the others.'

'Oh?' enquired Cory. 'And what have they been up to now, I wonder?' He sounded amused for he believed he knew what was coming next. And to some extent he was right.

Annie Sophie, like Adela before her on *her* return to India, had taken to exploring the bazaar. The colonel was well aware of the fact that his youngest daughter might go to the office with Isabel but often got bored and drifted off towards the native quarter on the opposite side of Macleod Road. He could well understand her fascination and the heady effect of the vibrant colour and activity of the native town—it had been the same for him years ago: the busy stalls laden with pots, brass vessels, jewellery, and food; the jostling crowds; the foreign tongues … No wonder the girl was enthralled. She was sensible enough, though, and—unlike Adela—far too concerned with her own wellbeing to take any risks.

Fanny took a deep breath. 'Well, Arthur,' she said, 'I want you to forbid Annie Sophie to go to the bazaar. You told Addie and she obeyed—eventually. Annie Sophie needs to be told as well. Her behaviour is quite—quite *unseemly*.'

Cory showed some surprise. Fanny sounded unusually passionate. 'She's been going there openly—with one of the young coolies. And it always seems to be the same one. Arthur, for heaven's sake, it's got to stop!'

Upon reflection the colonel agreed, but in doing so put forward a word in defence of his youngest daughter. 'She'll probably say it's in furtherance of her art, you know. She does so want to be a writer.' Cory had once had serious aspirations in that direction himself and he gave a tolerant little smile. 'And you must have noticed that her every action is calculated to a degree. Oh no, Fanny, my love, Annie Sophie will do nothing foolish, of that you may be sure. Whereas Adela—' and his voice became noticeably tender, '—there's such feeling behind everything she does. Her heart will always rule her head.'

'And that's why Adela concerns me most,' said Fanny, coming to the point at last. 'Arthur, I'm worried about her. Truly worried.'

'Oh,' asked the editor, 'why? She seems perfectly happy to me.'

'She is,' went on her mother, 'but she's seeing far too much of Colonel Nicolson.'

Cory gave his wife a quizzical look. 'I should have thought that would have delighted you, my dear. He's a charming man, after all. And most eligible.'

Fanny pursed her lips. 'And *I* should have thought *you* would understand,' she replied in exasperation. 'Especially after that pronouncement of his the first time he came to dinner.'

'Oh *that*,' said Colonel Cory. 'Don't let that worry you, Fanny. I shouldn't think it means a thing. These frontier men are all the same—full of fine words until they find themselves at the altar!'

'It sounded to *me* as if he meant it! And now here he is, back for two weeks' leave, and he seems to be spending most of it in this house, and with our daughter, and—' the words came out in a rush, '—she's going to fall in love with him, Arthur—I know she is!'

'She could do worse,' commented Cory. 'He's a very fine fellow. I've always thought so.'

'And a confirmed bachelor! He's well over forty—although I grant you he doesn't look it—and he's hardly likely to change his ways.' Fanny now appealed to her husband's common sense. 'Arthur, I don't want her to be hurt. He's monopolising her, and she's not meeting anyone else—and all he does is treat her like a younger sister. Or like a younger *brother*,' she added, upon reflection. 'Oh dear, it's so unfair!'

Cory smiled. 'Our daughter seems perfectly happy,' he repeated. 'She likes the man's company, he likes hers, and quite frankly, Fanny, I'd rather she spent the time with him than roaming around on her own. Don't you worry about a thing, my dear.'

But Fanny did, although there seemed no cause: Adela showed no signs at all of succumbing to the dashing colonel's charms.

'Ah, Youth, confiding and unwise!'

'Good afternoon, Miss Cory.'

Adela looked up from her sketching. Malcolm Nicolson was on horseback and she had been too engrossed to hear him approach. His face was in shadow, and the sun had turned his light-brown hair to burnished gold. She shaded her eyes to see him better; he was smiling down at her and she felt herself responding.

'May I join you?'

'Of course, Colonel.' Adela gathered her scattered belongings together to make room on the rocks beside her. Nicolson dismounted and walked his horse to where her carriage was waiting, and tied it to a scrubby tree.

'Your *syce* seems to be asleep,' he remarked on his return.

'Is he? Well, you can hardly blame him, I suppose; I must have been here for ages.' She looked at her sketch critically: it was still not quite right.

Nicolson sat down and looked at her work. She was talented, he thought, although there was a certain insouciance about her work that some might criticise.

'There's something missing, don't you think?' she asked. It seemed perfectly fine to him, and he said so. 'No—' she scrutinised the drawing again. 'I know what it is—it needs a figure—*there*.' She pointed to the middle distance and then considered her companion. 'Would you mind very much, Colonel Nicolson, if I asked you to go over there for a moment, then I could sketch you in? It won't take long.'

Obediently Nicolson complied with her request, and followed her instructions until he was standing exactly where she wanted. It was a long time since he had taken orders in quite this way, he reflected, and idly watched the golden head bent over the paper until she looked up at him again.

'Thank you very much,' and Miss Cory smoothed back a wayward curl. 'You can come and sit down again if you like, I've finished.'

Before doing so he asked if she was quite sure that was all she required. She smiled back at him, unabashed. 'I suppose that these days you're not used to people telling you what to do. People try to tell me all the time, I'm afraid.'

From the little he knew of her he guessed her to be a young woman who liked to go her own way. 'But I suspect you don't always listen.'

'I do sometimes,' she admitted. 'For example, Father makes me bring Mahomed Khan whenever I come out here,' and she pointed to the sleeping *syce*.

'Well, he wouldn't be much help at present if you needed him.' The groom had not stirred once.

'But *you* are here,' Adela smiled engagingly up at her companion.

'You know perfectly well what I mean, Miss Cory! Karachi is a busy port and people come and go, and out here it's very lonely—'

'You sound just like my father!' she replied and went on lightly: 'He's afraid that someone will throw me over their saddle and carry me off to the hills.'

And it wouldn't be half as much fun as you seem to think, my girl, thought the colonel grimly, as unpleasant pictures came to mind. A silence fell and he thought he had offended her so he stared out to sea, watching the boats as they headed for Kiamari and Manora Head.

After a while he realised that she was sketching him, and her silence was simply the result of concentration. He was aware of her sideways glances as she worked but obligingly he kept still and said not a word. She was, he thought, quite unlike any young woman he had ever met. And her father was absolutely right to be concerned—such an open and trusting manner could easily be taken advantage of. All in all, he concluded, there was something refreshingly natural about Adela Cory. And that, he told himself, was why he enjoyed her company so much.

'You've finished?' Her pencil had stopped moving across the paper. 'May I move?'

'I'm so sorry,' Adela was contrite. 'I thought you were miles away and hadn't noticed or I would have stopped sooner.' She held her work out to him. 'What do you think?'

It was a very good likeness. She had captured the clean lines of his profile: the strong, almost aquiline nose and the firm curve of his mouth. Only his expression seemed different: not at all severe, but rather the expression of a dreamer. 'Do I really look like this?'

'Not usually. You look quite stern at times—except when you laugh and smile, of course,' which he often did with her. 'But just now you seemed so far away. What were you thinking?'

He had no intention of telling her! 'I was thinking how pleasant it was out here, and how peaceful,' was all he said and after a moment he added, 'I wonder if I might have the sketch—to send to my sisters in England? Would you mind?'

'Of course you must have it,' came the immediate reply, although Adela was a little disappointed. She would have liked to keep it for herself.

'I felt the soul within me shaken'

At the beginning of November Lord Dufferin, the Viceroy, set out from Simla on his autumn tour. There was huge excitement in Karachi as the townsfolk waited for the great man to honour them with his presence. The Chamber of Commerce prepared petitions to advance the interests of the business sector, the ladies acquired new dresses, and the *Sind Gazette* poured forth fulsome praise on the man deemed to hold the future of Karachi in his hands.

There was a military band playing when the Viceregal train arrived and the troops were out in force, lining Macleod Road in Lord and Lady Dufferin's honour. The young Corys waited some distance away, the better to see the carriage as it passed.

'There's Colonel Nicolson,' squealed Annie Sophie, gesticulating wildly. 'He must be here with his regiment. Doesn't he look absolutely splendid?'

He did indeed, sitting ramrod straight in the saddle, as Adela glanced briefly over in his direction. Then she turned away to look for Lord Dufferin and his much younger wife. As the couple passed down the thronged road the crowd pressed forward for a better view. His lordship, every inch the aristocrat, with flowing hair and a full moustache, peered back through his eyeglass and seemed delighted with his reception. At his side Harriot Dufferin permitted herself a gracious smile, acknowledging the resounding cheers that met them as they passed.

Gradually Adela became separated from her sisters and was caught up in the crush. She was borne forward inexorably until she found herself near the front of the serried ranks of spectators, yet it was not the noble pair that caught her eye but the figure of a small bewildered Indian child, who had squirmed his way through a forest of legs and skirts to stand there all alone, directly in the path of the advancing carriage. It came on at a stately pace and showed no sign of stopping. Was she the only one who saw the boy? Was she the only one who cared? All eyes were fixed on the beaming face of authority as, ignoring exasperated grunts and stifled exclamations, Adela Cory unceremoniously elbowed her way free and ran out into the road.

The horses bore down upon her, and iron-shod hoofs threw up dust in her face as she groped forward blindly for the child. Then in a sudden flash of green and scarlet a hand dragged her clear and the carriage passed, its occupants quite oblivious to the drama. Rubbing her smarting eyes, Adela squinted up at her rescuer.

'Are you always so reckless, young woman?' asked Malcolm Nicolson in rough rebuke. 'You could have been killed!'

'Never mind about me!' she retorted. 'What about the boy?' Her mouth was full of grit and her voice little more than a croak. 'Is he all right?'

'Here,' said the colonel and thrust a wriggling bundle into her arms. 'You'd better deal with young India! My services are required elsewhere.' Then, leaning from his saddle, he retrieved her hat from where it had rolled away in the dust, and with one swift movement set the less than pristine item deftly on her head. The warm admiration in his eyes as he did so quite belied his earlier tone, but the girl didn't notice, so intent was she on the child.

'I've no idea where he lives—' she began, but Malcolm Nicolson forestalled any possible protest by wheeling his horse around and setting off in pursuit of the Viceregal carriage. As he did so his smile broadened to a grin, for behind him young India had obviously filled his lungs with air and was wailing unremittingly for his mother. Miss Cory should be able to cope with that.

Miss Cory gazed after him for a moment, then settling her noisy charge more comfortably on her hip, 'Come along, young man,' she said, 'let's get you home—wherever that is.'

'Adela! There you are! Where on earth have you been? Hurry up and get ready or we'll be late!' Isabel looked at her sister in exasperation. They had lost her in the crowd hours ago, and it was almost time to leave for the Ball. The Viceregal Ball that everyone had been talking about for months. 'Mother is furious with you.

Come on!' and Isabel grabbed her sister's hot and sticky hand and dragged her off to her room.

Adela bathed and dressed in a dream. She had spent the afternoon in the native quarter with the grateful Indian family who had quickly claimed her errant charge. They had pressed their hospitality upon her, and Adela, discovering for the first time the real, the true India, had savoured the experience to the full. She would have stayed even longer had she not suddenly remembered the evening that lay ahead and politely but precipitately taken her leave.

An excited Annie Sophie was going to her first grand ball. She fussed and fidgeted and hopped from foot to foot, while Isabel helped the latecomer put the finishing touches to her toilette. Adela had refused absolutely to wear white like her sisters, insisting on a blue that almost matched her eyes and Fanny, her earlier irritation set aside, was forced to admit that Addie looked very well indeed. A simple pearl necklace around her slender throat set off the smoothness of her skin to perfection, and her thick hair swept up to the back of her head and fastened with pearl pins made her seem taller. For once, thought her mother with satisfaction, her unruly daughter looked poised and all of her twenty-two years.

'You're quite lovely, Addie,' said Isabel, gazing in admiration at the transformation that had taken place while Annie Sophie, itching to be gone, sniffed enviously as she looked at Adela's slim figure and the soft swell of her bosom, and said nothing.

The ballroom was crowded and festooned with garlands and lights. It's all very grand, thought Adela, still in a daze from the rush, and I don't think there's anyone here that we know. The orchestra struck up from the gallery and soon, what with the noise and the heat, the girl was uncomfortably aware of the spicy food she had eaten that afternoon, her head was beginning to spin, and she was wishing she had stayed at home. She was standing on her own in a corner when Annie Sophie sought her out; the younger girl was positively bursting with excitement and looked her disappointment that Isabel wasn't there as well.

'I've been talking to Maisie McHinch,' she said. 'And do you know what she's just told me about Colonel Nicolson?'

'I can't imagine,' said Adela dryly, wishing her sister would go away and leave her in peace.

'Well, Maisie McHinch told me that Colonel Nicolson once crossed the tank out at Magar Pir—over the crocodiles' backs. And he never fell in!'

'Obviously—or he wouldn't be here now. *Is* he here now?'

'Yes, he's over there.' Annie Sophie pointed.

Adela looked across the room.

'Isn't it a wonderful story! Do you think it's true?'

But Adela was no longer listening. She was looking at Malcolm Nicolson as he talked with fellow officers directly opposite her on the other side of the floor. The dancers drifted past her in a blur of confused colour, but all she could see was the colonel.

'Addie, *Addie*—' Annie Sophie gave up and went back to her friend. At that moment Nicolson looked across the room and his eyes met and held Adela's. He smiled. She put her hand to her head, feeling the need for air. She must get out. Blindly she turned to go, feeling trapped among all these strangers.

'Adela.' A steadying hand was on her arm, supporting her and guiding her to one of the anterooms that looked out over the gardens. The sky was bright with stars that quite eclipsed the lanterns in the grounds, and the air was fresh. She pressed her head against the cool stone until the feeling of nausea should pass.

Malcolm Nicolson looked at the girl as she leaned against a column. 'I think you ought to sit down,' he said. Her pallor frightened him and he thought she might faint. He took her to a seat then, 'That's better,' he observed, as the colour returned to her cheeks. 'How do you feel now?'

Adela looked at the man standing before her and with a sudden chill she recognised her fate. How could she have been so blind? For better, for worse, for as long as her life might last, she would love this man and no other. She forced herself to reply in an even tone: 'I feel perfectly well, thank you. You're very kind.'

Nicolson was still looking at her intently, as if to reassure himself that she spoke the truth. 'I suppose you've had too much excitement today, one way and another,' he remarked, thinking of their earlier meeting.

He must never suspect quite how true that was!

'I've certainly had too much to eat,' she informed him with a disarming frankness. 'And a very great rush to get here on time. It's all my own fault,' and she explained everything that had happened since they had last seen each other in McLeod Road. 'But Young India is fine,' she concluded with a smile, finding it easy after all to meet her companion's gaze.

She was delightful, thought the colonel. 'I was hoping we might dance later,' he said. 'If you feel up to it, of course.'

Adela nodded her consent, too happy to speak.

'Unfortunately,' he continued, 'it appears to be suppertime. Perhaps,' and he tried unsuccessfully to prevent a slight smile, 'perhaps under the circumstances you would rather miss that tonight.'

They walked in the gardens instead, and when the dancing began again he suggested they go inside. 'Lord Dufferin is obviously intending to dance with every lady in the room,' he told her, 'and you must not miss your turn.'

Adela pulled a face and paused under a tree festooned with lights. Her eyes glinted with malice as she replied, 'I'd actually rather not dance with him—even if he asked me, which I rather doubt!' Feeling she owed her companion an explanation she continued, 'I'm afraid I think him rather a fool, a fool who's undone all the good of his predecessor.'

'Ah,' said the colonel, comprehending. 'So I'm talking to one of the rare partisans of Lord Ripon!' She sensed rather than saw his smile. 'You favour an India for the Indians, I take it? Unlike your father. And the majority of Europeans.'

Adela gave an emphatic nod. She had argued endlessly and pointlessly with her father in Lahore over Lord Ripon's liberal schemes for the Empire, but nothing, she determined, should spoil this precious interlude. 'I refuse to argue with you, Colonel Nicolson, it's far too glorious an evening,' and she drew in a deep breath of the jasmine-scented air.

'And I wouldn't dream of arguing with *you*, Miss Cory,' he answered gravely, confident that the darkness hid the amusement in his eyes—and his admiration for one who dared speak out against the latest darling of the Raj. 'Perhaps we might dance instead. Though you will find me a very poor substitute for a Viceroy, I fear.'

She found him no such thing, and Fanny, watching them dance one dance after another, sighed happily. After such a public display of interest, she told her husband in triumph, surely an engagement must be imminent.

'Love is only a dream'

Once the excitement was over, Adela seemed much the same as usual and said little to anyone of the evening she had spent. Annie Sophie did not ask and Isabel, who had thoroughly enjoyed herself, had seen Addie dancing almost every dance and been glad. Too far away for most of the time, and too short-sighted, to see the enraptured expression on Adela's face as she looked up at her partner, she felt no cause for concern.

If Mrs Cory had hoped for news of an engagement to the colonel then she was doomed to disappointment. And if afterwards she felt alarm at what now seemed to be the compromising nature of Nicolson's behaviour, she said nothing of that to her daughter. For the next few days the talk in the Cory household was of nothing but 'The Ball' and then it became a thing of the past. Christmas followed and was in many ways an anticlimax, apart from passionate arguments between Adela and her father on the subject of rising Indian aspirations. But all that was forgotten when, with the New Year, came the news that the 3rd Baluch Battalion was to be stationed in Karachi. Adela's heart leapt at the prospect of seeing Malcolm Nicolson again.

The colonel had travelled north more preoccupied than usual, his thoughts full of a young lady dressed in blue, who had put out her hand at parting, thought for a moment, and then said seriously: 'Colonel Nicolson, may I ask you something?'

He wondered what was coming—with Adela Cory it might be anything. He waited and then laughed out loud in delight at the sheer unexpectedness of her question.

'Did you really walk across all those crocodiles at Magar Pir?'

'Well,' he said after some reflection, 'you could say that I did, and then again, you could say that I didn't—' and with that she had to be content.

Try as he might in the following weeks, Nicolson could not forget Adela's radiant face, and dancing through his dreams she came back to haunt him time and time again. After many nights of fitful sleep he came to a decision: if, when next he saw her, Miss Cory showed any inclination towards him, then he would put his principles aside and ask her to be his wife. But, as he was a proud man and would not risk rebuff, the colonel determined to speak only if he could be certain of success.

When his regiment was posted to Karachi early in the year he called on Adela. She was pleased he was back, he could tell, and her manner was every bit as friendly as before, but little did he realise how hard she was trying to keep the delight out of her eyes and her voice. For Adela Florence Cory had determined that this man who disapproved so strongly of marriage must not suspect her true feelings: she would keep his friendship at all costs.

Thus the two of them, so very much in love, both kept silent, and slipped back into the old easy relationship of before.

'What's wrong, Mother?' Fanny was upset, and Isabel had noticed.

'It's your sister and Colonel Nicolson—I'm so concerned.'

'Why?' asked the uncomplicated Isabel, failing to understand. 'He was here yesterday and they seemed very happy together. What's happened?'

'*Nothing* has happened,' exclaimed Mrs Cory, 'and nothing ever will, I can see that now!' and she gave vent to all the frustrations of the past months while Isabel listened with a sympathetic ear.

'Your father won't do anything, and what can I say? The colonel always behaves like a gentleman—it's just that he doesn't want her for himself and fails to realise that Addie never sees anyone else! How will she ever find a husband?'

Isabel, who in the line of her work saw many people, had never had a proposal of marriage and did not feel the loss in the least, nonetheless appreciated her mother's position. Malcolm Nicolson was a most attractive and unusual man, and Adela with her taste for adventure and romance could easily fall in love with him. Isabel determined that the colonel should not be allowed to hurt her.

'Is your father in, Miss Cory? I thought we might go to the Sind Club together.'

Isabel looked up and saw Malcolm Nicolson. How fortuitous, she thought. She told him that her father was out on business, and said she would give him the message. 'But before you go, Colonel,' she added, 'perhaps we might have a word?'

'Of course,' he replied. He liked Isabel and was soon to find that she shared Adela's forthright manner.

'Please sit down.'

Nicolson took a seat opposite the desk that Isabel for the past few months had occupied as assistant editor of the *Sind Gazette*. Her office was small and tidy and he was sure that she was every bit as efficient as she appeared. She was efficient now as she tackled the problem that had kept her awake for much of the night.

'It's about Adela,' she said gravely.

His eyes filled with concern. 'She's not ill, is she? She was perfectly well when I saw her yesterday.'

'Exactly, and I want her to stay well. Colonel Nicolson, tell me, what exactly are your intentions towards my sister?'

Nicolson was taken aback at her bluntness. Before he could reply, Isabel went on: 'Surely you must see that you're monopolising her, Colonel—you may even be compromising her. It seems very unfair that you spend so much time with Addie—when you've made your views on marriage so very plain.'

Yes, thought Nicolson in sudden realisation, it must seem that way to Isabel—and to everyone else. Yes, I can see that I've been unfair. He gave a wry smile before responding. 'Perhaps I should say in my defence that none of this appears to worry your sister. She sees me as a friend—simply as a friend.'

Poor Isabel, knowing no better, agreed. 'But she should be given the chance to meet someone who could be more than that to her, don't you think?' she went on relentlessly. 'There are plenty of young men in Karachi who would be delighted to marry her, I'm sure, but she never meets them.'

Nicolson was silent as he gazed at the earnest bespectacled face opposite. So Adela didn't love him, then—and her sister surely should know. And, even if she were to fall in love with him later, Isabel was right—he could see that too—a marriage to someone of her own age would be far more suitable. No, he would not see Adela alone again.

Lost in his thoughts, he left Isabel's office and quite failed to see the youngest Miss Cory who had stepped back smartly from the door as he opened it and gone over to the window. She had listened to every word and there was a satisfied smirk on her face as she watched the tall dejected figure walk away.

'Come back, come back! I want you only'

'Colonel Nicolson doesn't come to see you any more, does he, Addie? Even though he's stationed in Karachi now.' Annie Sophie was in the drawing room as her sister came in from the garden.

'No, he doesn't,' Adela said, shortly. And then she was arrested by the expression on her younger sister's face. 'What is it, you little wretch? Why are you looking so smug?' She went up to the girl and seized her arm.

'Let go, Addie, you're hurting me!'

'I'll hurt you even more if you don't tell. What is it?'

'Let me go, Addie, and I'll tell you all about it.'

Annie Sophie was smiling; she had been looking forward to this for a very long time. Now she would get her own back for all the snubs Addie had given her over the years.

Looking at her sister's gloating face, Adela waited. It was months since she had last seen Malcolm Nicolson alone, and had spent long hours wondering how she might have offended him but could think of nothing. Perhaps—and the thought filled her with a terrible sadness—he had found more pleasant companionship elsewhere.

He had dined with the family once or twice and had treated her with the same friendliness as usual. Once after dinner, when Arthur Cory had been holding forth on the latest commercial developments in town, Nicolson had caught her eye and winked, and she had rejoiced in the brief complicity between them—but that had been all. And now this little brat seemed to have the answer.

'Well,' she prompted, 'tell me.'

Annie Sophie took her time. 'It was in March,' she said—it was now October—'I went to see Izzie at the paper. I do sometimes, you know. Well, when I got there, Colonel Nicolson was in her office. I don't know why, I expect he wanted to see Father, although I think he likes Isabel, too. What do you think, Addie?'

'Get on with it!' Adela hissed.

'I didn't like to go in, they were having such a good talk, so I waited—'

'And you just happened to overhear what they were saying, I suppose.'

'That's right,' the younger girl said happily. 'They were talking about you.'

'And just what were they saying about me?'

'Izzie said—Izzie said that Colonel Nicolson should leave you alone because you didn't love him, and that you should be given the chance to marry someone else. Or something like that,' she finished weakly.

Annie Sophie had never seen her sister so angry—although she had often given her cause—and felt more than a little frightened. But this time, glee mingled with her fear. If only she could be there when Addie confronted Izzie!

'I'm sorry, I didn't know. How *could* I know you loved him? You never said.'

That was true.

'And it didn't seem fair that he should always be here, when he wasn't going to marry you. I didn't want you to be hurt. Don't you see? I did it for the best, truly I did.'

Adela looked at Isabel. She no longer felt the fury that had caused her to burst into her room unannounced ten minutes before. She now knew everything, and she understood the very real concern that had prompted her sister's actions.

'I believe you, I really do,' she said. 'And I'm not angry any more. *But you don't understand*—I knew he didn't love me and there wasn't any hope, but it didn't matter—as long as we stayed friends. And now that's all over and I have *nothing*. What am I going to do?'

There were no tears, Isabel was relieved to see, but the bleak expression she was to surprise on her sister's face from time to time in the coming months was even worse. Arthur Cory saw it too, and he wondered whether his wife hadn't been right after all. But he kept his thoughts to himself, and if Fanny noticed anything amiss with Adela, then she too kept silent.

'This is no time for saying "no"'

Christmas that year was a sad one for Adela Cory, and with the dawning of 1889 came the news that the 3rd Baluchis had been posted to Hyderabad, one hundred miles away to the north of Karachi. Colonel Nicolson did not call to say goodbye, and when she saw the hurt on her sister's face Isabel cursed herself yet again for her well-meaning interference.

One morning in March she saw an opportunity to make amends. *The following gentlemen*, she read in a notice for the paper, *are to serve as a Committee for the purpose of examining candidates in the Baluchi language:—President, Colonel Nicolson, Commandant 3rd Baluchis*. The committee would be convening on Monday the eighth of April.

So, thought the assistant editor of the *Sind Gazette*, in ten days' time Malcolm Nicolson would be back. Not that it would do any good, she suspected, but she could at least warn Adela.

'What's that you're looking at, dear?' Arthur Cory was standing in the doorway, wondering what had caught his daughter's attention.

'Nothing, Father,' she replied. 'Colonel Nicolson will back here on the eighth, that's all.'

'Nicolson—' Cory said slowly, as he considered Isabel's words. 'Why yes, we haven't seen him for months. Perhaps we should invite him to the house—it would be good to see him again. Better still, I'll ask him to stay— What do you think, eh?'

Isabel thought it was almost certainly a very bad idea. 'Perhaps Colonel Nicolson might prefer to keep to his usual arrangements,' was her only comment.

'Nonsense—can't see that at all, myself.' Cory made up his mind. 'I'll leave a message for him at the Club when he gets here and tell him he's expected—he'll be delighted, I'm sure,' and unable to argue with her determined parent, Isabel was left feeling that matters were completely out of hand.

When her husband told her to expect a visitor Fanny Cory didn't mind at all: she no longer saw Malcolm Nicolson as a threat. It must be a year now since he stopped visiting her daughter, and while she didn't know why, she was only too pleased that he had.

Annie Sophie for her part awaited developments with delight: this was far better than anything she could have hoped for. She had been disappointed that there had been no falling-out between her sisters over Isabel's intervention, but at least she could watch their embarrassment when Colonel Nicolson arrived. If he came, of course, for she was by no means sure that he would.

And Adela hoped he wouldn't; it would be far easier—for them both—if he stayed away.

As chance would have it, Cory was in the Sind Club when Nicolson arrived on the day before his meeting, and he saw the head bearer hand over his note. Frowning, Nicolson was about to send a polite refusal when the short purposeful figure bore down upon him.

'My dear fellow!' exclaimed Adela's father, shaking his hand, 'it's good to see you. I see you have my note. You'll stay with us of course?'

Of course he would, Nicolson realised, and not only because the editor was obviously determined that he should. How, after all, could he resist the temptation of seeing Adela again? The months had dragged for him, too, and he only hoped she was happy.

'Thank you, sir,' he replied. 'I should like that very much indeed.'

'Come along to the house whenever you like, we're all expecting you. I'll be back later—just make yourself at home. Mrs Cory and Annie Sophie won't be in, but Adela will look after you,' and well satisfied with himself and the turn of events Arthur Cory took himself off.

Best get it over with quickly, thought his guest, while they had the place to themselves. He wasn't sure how he was going to explain his sudden and prolonged absence but he would worry about that later. All that mattered was to see her again and hope he was forgiven.

Adela was waiting in the drawing room when the colonel was shown in. She had wanted to run away and hide all afternoon, but her father had made it clear that she was to receive their guest in everyone else's absence. Father really has no idea of what's been happening, she said to herself, and now here we all are about to be embarrassed—she would have laughed if she hadn't been so close to tears. Instead, she forced a cool smile to her lips and held out a hand in welcome.

He was looking well, she thought, as if he hadn't missed her at all. She felt a sudden pang. 'Good afternoon, Colonel Nicolson,' she said, 'I'm the only one here, I'm afraid. Everyone else is out.'

'I know, your father warned me. I saw him in the Club.' He took her hand briefly.

And you still came, as if nothing had happened, as if you hadn't abandoned me for months—suddenly Adela felt an anger she knew to be irrational. Malcolm Nicolson had stayed away for her own good, but she had missed him more than she would ever have admitted, even to Isabel. And now here he was, and she could think of nothing sensible to say.

'Would you like tea—or something else?'

'Thank you, no,' and an awkward silence threatened. 'We might go to the Gardens,' suggested the colonel. It was neutral ground and it would be easier for them both, and there they could talk without fear of interruption. To his profound relief, the young woman agreed.

The Gardens had come on greatly in the three years since the Corys' arrival in Karachi. The trees no longer seemed like shrubs; they had grown tremendously, even if some of them were bent at alarming angles due to the wind off the desert. Awkwardly, among the maturing parterres, Nicolson began to explain his behaviour.

Sensing his embarrassment, Adela's anger faded and she interrupted. 'I happen to know you spoke to Isabel about me, Colonel Nicolson.'

'I see.' There was a silence. 'Did she tell you?' he asked after a while, giving her a piercing look from grey eyes that were suddenly unfathomable.

Despite herself Adela gave a little smile. 'Not really,' she said, 'I suppose it's rather like your crocodiles, if you remember—she did and she didn't—but I did find out. Six months later.'

Six months of unhappiness and many more since then. Nicolson looked down at the young woman's set face, and guessing only a little of what she had endured led her to a bench beneath a shady casuarina tree.

'Oh, how I wish Isabel had left things as they were,' she sighed.

'Why, Adela?' He sat down beside her and resisted the temptation to take her hand.

'Because then you would have kept on coming to see me. I've missed you, Malcolm,' she said simply. It was the first time she had ever addressed him by his given name, but he hardly seemed to notice, so intent was he on justifying his behaviour.

'Your sister pointed out how selfish I was being, and so I decided—very reluctantly—to withdraw from your life. Believe me, it was the very last thing I wanted.'

His look was so tender and so concerned that Adela decided to tell him everything. After all, she had nothing more to lose and this might be her only chance. 'What Isabel didn't know, and what she *couldn't* tell you, Malcolm, is that I do love you—and that I've loved you for a long, long time.'

At first Malcolm Nicolson was too taken aback to speak. In the silence brought on by shock he noted that she was thinner, and her face had lost all trace of childish lines. She was almost beautiful. His voice, when at last he was able to answer, was full of soft reproach. 'You hid your feelings extremely well; too well in fact, my dear—'

Adela failed to understand. 'I had to, didn't I?' came the retort. 'I knew the very last thing you would want was for someone to fall in love with you—you told us so, that night at dinner—don't you remember?'

Indeed the colonel remembered, and he cursed himself and his fine pronouncements. 'But I changed my mind—people do, you know,' he told her. 'You made me change,' and this time he did take her hand and felt the fingers tremble in his. 'Adela, I intended to ask you to marry me last spring, when I came back to Karachi. But I didn't know you cared, and so I let the moment pass.'

'You love me, too—?' A look of joy transformed her solemn face as realisation dawned, and she leaned towards him.

Malcolm Nicolson would have kissed her then—but he was finding all too late that the Government Gardens, Karachi, were not the ideal spot for a tête-à-tête. It was Sunday afternoon and perambulating couples filled the walks, passing their bench at frequent intervals and casting curious glances at the man and girl sitting there, unashamedly holding hands.

'Yes, I love you, I love you very much—but there's something else I must tell you.' He cleared his throat and took her other hand as well. 'Something Isabel said—'

'Drat Isabel!' said her sister impatiently, freeing her hands. 'She's said quite enough, one way and another!' She moved closer, and he caught a faint scent of jasmine from her hair.

He swallowed and with difficulty continued: 'I'm forty-five, nearly forty-six, and you are twenty-three—'

'Twenty-four the day after tomorrow,' she informed him, as if the extra year would make all the difference. 'Lots of people marry older men, if that's what's worrying you,' she pointed out, and named a few, including Lord Dufferin himself.

'Ah, the contemptible Viceroy. So he has some virtue after all,' murmured Nicolson, his eyes alight with amusement and with hope.

'Don't laugh!' Her face was serious. 'Are you going to let age come between us?' she asked. 'Now? After so much wasted time? I've spent a whole year of my life thinking of no one but you—and I tell you, Malcolm Nicolson, that if *you* don't marry me, no one else shall either!'

The colonel looked at the indignant little face raised to his, the blue eyes bright with unshed tears, and decided he had never seen anything lovelier—or more resolute.

'Then,' he conceded, 'I appear to have no choice,' and disregarding the passing strangers who averted their eyes in shocked disapproval, he drew her close at last and kissed her eager lips.

'So might my arms embrace my Heart's Desire'

'If I walk around here once more,' Adela giggled, 'I shall be able to do it blindfold!'

But what was the alternative? If they went back to the bungalow, they would no longer be alone. Here they could walk and talk, at least, although the lack of privacy was irksome. Though perhaps that was just as well, thought the colonel, glancing down at his companion. He saw on her face that same glowing look he had noted at the Viceregal Ball all those months before, but which, in his blindness, he had quite failed to recognise. Now like Adela earlier he was lamenting the waste of time, and it occurred to him more than once in their seemingly endless circuits of the Gardens, that this enchanting girl could have been his wife long since.

'I suppose you will want a splendid wedding at Trinity Church?' he asked. 'Most young ladies would.'

'I'm not *most young ladies*!' came the quick retort.

Very true, thought Nicolson, or you would not have bewitched me so— 'Your mother certainly will,' he pointed out.

'Then we won't tell her till afterwards!'

He laughed. 'Sweetheart, is that what you really want?' and his voice was suddenly serious.

'Of course it is. You don't want a grand affair either—do you?' The thought that he might appalled her.

No, he assured her truthfully, that was the last thing he wanted.

'Then let it be soon,' she whispered, 'as soon as possible.'

Dinner was not in any way the embarrassing affair that Annie Sophie Cory had hoped for, as she watched them all carefully. Earlier, Colonel Nicolson had greeted Isabel in a friendly fashion that quite dispelled any awkwardness between them, and though he didn't look at Addie much, they seemed on good enough terms. What she didn't know was that Malcolm Nicolson was forcing himself to give his attention to the whole family, and not simply to his future bride.

He talked with the greatest of civility to Mrs Cory, to Isabel seated opposite him, and to the youngest girl at his side, but was only too aware of Adela at the far end of the table sitting on her father's right. Her bare shoulders glowed so smooth and warm in the lamplight that he had to force his eyes away, and for once he found himself grateful for Annie Sophie's determined efforts to hold his attention.

The ladies left the gentlemen to their port and Isabel was playing the piano in the drawing room when they joined them. She would have stopped, but Nicolson asked her to continue.

'You play beautifully, Miss Cory,' he told her. 'Do go on.'

Isabel blushed at the compliment, suddenly very shy indeed. The colonel was so handsome, and his voice so pleasant. Strange, she had always found him rather forbidding, but tonight, somehow, he was different. 'I'll play,' she finally agreed, 'but only if Addie will sing.'

Her sister pulled a face; the last thing she had intended tonight was to draw attention to herself. 'Very well,' she said reluctantly, and took her place beside Isabel at the piano. There, the lamps were augmented by candelabra and as she sang the soft glow of the flame caressed her bosom, throat and hair. Nicolson had chosen his seat well and was glad his face was in shadow for, as he watched and listened, he felt his desire for Adela Cory intensify.

He had known her for almost three years, he supposed, and in that time they had enjoyed a friendly uncomplicated relationship. But that was over: the friendship would remain but now there would be more—far more. The one kiss they had exchanged had been enough to seal their fate, but not enough to bring him peace of mind. And the little witch must know, he realised, for she was looking in his direction as she sang of love. Words of love delivered in a low, melodious voice, words which promised everything. He found himself smiling in rueful amusement and when the evening was over and he said goodnight, he raised her hand to his lips and chided her softly for her cruelty.

The family noticed nothing although Annie Sophie wondered in the days to come why Addie looked so happy; after all Colonel Nicolson had hardly spoken to her at all.

Alone in his room, Malcolm Nicolson stood by the window, looking over the moonlit garden where Fanny Cory had worked wonders, and as a scent of *moghra* wafted to him on the evening breeze he was reminded of the Gardens where he had walked that afternoon with Adela. Adela … Adela whom he had thought lost to him forever. He imagined her sleeping nearby and felt a great longing.

He must have been standing at the window for over an hour, staring at the stars shining so coldly in the midnight sky, when he heard the door to his room open. He turned quickly although he knew whom he would see. Even so, he was unprepared for the reality: Adela in a simple white nightgown, tied with ribbons at the throat. Adela, her hair loose, and looking like a child. But no child would smile at him like that.

'You shouldn't be here,' was all he said.

'I know,' she replied, and pulled the door quietly to behind her.

Physical love was not quite what Adela Cory had expected. In fact, her lover soon realised, she hadn't really known what to expect at all. As Malcolm Nicolson held her in a close embrace he felt her confidence turn to confusion, and then with understanding came tears. And after the tears, reassurance, and finally a smile.

'I'm sorry, darling but there was no other way.' He stroked her hair and face with sensitive fingers.

'Then why be sorry?' came the logical little voice.

'Next time will be different.'

'I know,' she said, and he felt her relax against him.

'Why don't you sleep a little?' and Malcolm drew her close within the circle of his arms. She settled there and as she listened to the regular sound of his breathing and the steady beating of his heart it seemed to the young woman as if a long desolate journey had come to an end. Another journey was beginning but she would never be alone again.

She stirred in her lover's arms and gave a sigh of deep content.

'Not sleeping? You're not going away already?' The arms tightened around her.

'Oh, Lord, I'll have to, won't I? Before Rachel brings early morning tea. I hadn't thought of that!' Adela tried to wriggle free but the arms refused to let her go.

'It seems to me, Miss Cory, that you rarely think at all. And I'm very glad.' Nicolson kissed her gently. 'Now, go to sleep. I promise to wake you before dawn.'

'And then I'll have to go—'

'Yes, unless you want to give up all idea of a secret wedding, my girl!'

Another thought struck Adela. 'Malcolm, you're leaving tomorrow.'

'Today.'

'Today.' Her voice was sombre. 'When shall I see you again?'

'I don't know. I'll be back for you soon,' and the colonel was as confident as he sounded. 'As soon as I possibly can—in two or three weeks, a month at the latest—and then we'll be married.' He kissed her again.

'But how shall I know when?'

'You won't, if you want it to remain a secret. How much notice do you need to get married, anyway?'

'None!' came the prompt reply and they both laughed.

On the morning after Nicolson's departure Isabel came into her sister's room with a small package in her hand.

'It's for you, Addie. And it's not from me. You appear to have a secret admirer—one who knows it's your birthday. It was delivered a few moments ago by a Baluch orderly.' Isabel's look was sharp but she went away without another word.

Curiosity soon got the better of her and when she returned Adela was wearing a heavily ornamented bracelet of native design.

'That's pretty,' Isabel commented, 'it looks like Hyderabad silver. Hyderabad—' Her eyes narrowed. 'Something's happened, hasn't it?' she said. 'Do you want to tell me, or shall I guess?'

'It's from Colonel Nicolson.' Adela stretched out her arm for her sister's inspection. 'We're going to be married. Izzie, I'm so happy.'

'And you haven't told anyone. Why?' Isabel looked and sounded perplexed. 'You know how much Mother would love the chance to make a fuss—and how much she wants one of us to give her an opportunity.'

Adela nodded. 'I know. And I couldn't bear it! Can you imagine me with Annie Sophie as a simpering bridesmaid?'—she pulled a face and Isabel giggled—'and all those people staring. Izzie, I simply couldn't.'

'So what are you going to do instead?'

'Oh, we'll go to the Registrar's, I suppose, and tell Mother and Father afterwards.' She shrugged then, 'Isabel,' she said, as a sudden thought struck her, 'you don't mind, do you?'

Isabel didn't care at all, provided her sister was happy, 'But when will it be?' she asked.

Adela shrugged again before replying: 'I don't know—as soon as Malcolm gets leave. Ages yet, probably.'

Isabel doubted that; she felt that now the colonel had made up his mind to take a wife he would waste no more time than was absolutely necessary. 'Don't you be too sure, Addie,' she warned. 'He'll be here sooner than you think.'

'I do hope so. I'm so happy, I could die!'

'I shouldn't, if I were you,' her sister said dryly. 'It would be terribly disappointing for the colonel—now that he's committed himself at last!'

'You do like him, don't you, Izzie?' Adela's tone was anxious.

'Yes. Very much.' Then Isabel's face fell. 'And so does Annie Sophie. She's going to be absolutely furious!'

2

'The month of marriage, the month of spring'

KARACHI AND HYDERABAD: APRIL–DECEMBER 1889

C*olonel M.H. Nicolson, Commandant 3rd Baluchis (Hyderabad), has been granted 2 weeks' privilege leave of absence from 19th April to visit Karachi.* As she read the notice waiting for the *Gazette*'s next edition, Isabel Cory felt a sudden pang. Eleven days after leaving, Malcolm Nicolson was coming back for her sister, and their own close companionship would soon be over.

As Friday wore on she watched her sister grow more restless and the two of them would check the paper yet again. Finally Adela jumped to her feet saying she simply had to get out of the house for a while before she went quite mad. 'Tell Malcolm I've gone out to the Pir's tomb in the desert—and, yes, I promise to take Mahomed Khan!'

It was good to be free of the house, despite the heat and dust. Adela pulled her veil over her face then rode so hard and fast that the anxious *syce* warned the miss *sahib* that the ground was uneven, that there were dry stream beds, and that she should take more care. For her horse's sake, he added, knowing the English might risk their own necks but never an animal's.

The girl slowed down as he predicted, yet the dust still gusted up about them as they crossed the flat terrain. Adela stared around her. She had never come this far before. Barely a tree to break the monotony until the desert merged with the hills. Far in the distance shone the Hab River, thin and silver in the heat haze, and in the mountains beyond, the groom told her, was his tribal homeland.

'Then why live on the plains, Mahomed Khan?' she asked in wonder, and blinked at his willing answer. 'It was a blood feud,' he explained, and his grin revealed gleaming teeth. 'I killed two men. I cannot go back.'

Adela swallowed. Here she was, miles from anywhere, with a double murderer ... Yet her father probably knew and thought him a capable protector of his daughter's honour. Which brought Miss Cory's thoughts back to her lover. Where was he? Had he called at the house? Had he called at all? Perhaps, she decided, perhaps they should go back and see.

As if in answer, the tribesman pointed. 'If the miss *sahib* will look, someone is coming. I think it is *Nikelseyn sahib*.' He turned to her and smiled.

Adela blushed beneath her veil as it occurred to her (and for not the first time), that it was impossible to keep secrets in India—from the Indians, at least. She made out a lone rider heading their way who indeed proved to be the colonel. The two men exchanged a few words, then the *syce* rode off while Malcolm approached her without a word of greeting. As their horses circled each other, with hers tossing its head in an alarming fashion, he came nearer and seized the reins.

'That horse of yours needs firmer handling,' he remarked as he quickly brought it under control. 'And so, my girl, do you!' His voice was grim. 'Do you realise the terrible time I've had tracking you down? Isabel said you knew I'd got my leave, and this is how you welcome me—by rushing off to the desert to hide!'

Chastened, Adela said nothing.

'Our friend was telling me just now that you rode well—if somewhat recklessly. Sweetheart,' Malcolm Nicolson said earnestly, as they turned to go back, 'were you trying to break your neck before our wedding?'

So that was why he was angry. The words of explanation came rushing out, so relieved was she to see him smile at last. 'I'm sorry, Malcolm. I've been so restless, not knowing when you'd be here, and when I did know, I could hardly believe it. It was so difficult to sit still and wait … I felt I was *stifling*.'

'I know, I know,' the colonel's voice softened. 'And believe me, I do understand.' He pulled up at a small grove of tamarisks, dismounted, then helped her down. 'Well, I'm here now,' he said, his hands resting lightly on her waist. 'So, my impatient little wife, how are you?'

As her lips parted to answer, he brought his mouth down fiercely on hers and when at last he released her, her eyes were dark and enormous in a face from which all colour had fled. She was trembling. He kissed her again but gently. 'I'm not going to make love to you, Adela. I want to, but not here, not like this.'

Adela whispered something that he couldn't hear and moved away.

'Now, listen, darling,' and his voice was serious. 'Did you mean it when you said you needed no notice to get married?'

Adela met his gaze and nodded silently.

'Good,' said the colonel. 'Is tomorrow too soon, then? I have a special licence,' and he laughed as she threw herself into his arms. 'So you haven't changed your mind.'

'Of course not!' Adela retorted emphatically. 'What time tomorrow, and where?'

❧

She was late. The colonel was already in the reading room as his bride hurried in, holding on to her hat. He smiled at her haste, but said nothing.

'I'm sorry, I'm sorry,' she said, breathlessly. 'I was ready ages ago, really I was, but I didn't want to get here first, and in the end I had to rush! Malcolm, I'm truly sorry—'

'Don't be. They do say it's the bride's prerogative, after all.' Somehow he had managed to find a small posy of stephanotis and he pressed the girl's fingers round it in reassurance. Malcolm Nicolson considered the flustered little figure with infinite tenderness, as, moved by his thoughtfulness, she buried her face for a moment in the fragrant blooms. Then she looked up and took his arm.

The registry office was dark and stuffy, and the marriage registrar was already waiting with his clerk. He made no attempt to smile, although he knew the bride by sight and the bridegroom rather better. Instead, he thought of his good friend Arthur Cory—and his surprise when his daughter broke the news. Registrar Crawford cleared his throat and tried to hide his disapproval. Turning from the impassive officer to the flushed young woman, 'Shall we begin?' he asked.

Till death. Adela's voice broke as she promised herself for ever to the tall man at her side. The plain gold band slipped onto her finger and he gently squeezed her hand. From a great distance she heard the registrar pronounce them man and wife and she drew a shuddering breath. Nicolson gave her a look of quick concern and she managed a tremulous smile. *No nerves, he has no nerves at all*, she found herself thinking. 'It's nearly over,' he whispered and kissed her on the forehead, then gently on the lips. And then they were outside, blinking in the sudden brilliance.

'Well, it's time to own up, I suppose. Will your parents be at home?' Now the colonel sounded nervous. 'Yes,' she told him, feeling a perverse satisfaction at this belated sign of human frailty. 'Izzie said she'd make sure.'

'Ah, the admirable Isabel.' Malcolm's gaze lingered on the youthful figure of his bride who was wearing a cream silk skirt and a lace blouse of matching colour. 'You're looking particularly fetching this morning,' he went on, 'and such a smart confection—I thought you hated hats?' His tone was teasing.

'Izzie said I had to wear one.'

'Well, it's nice to know you sometimes listen to advice!' She laughed up at him, but then he continued quite seriously. 'Now, listen to me, Adela. Your parents are going to be surprised—and your mother almost certainly upset as well. I know you want to get away from your home as soon as you can—but perhaps we should be patient?' She pouted, but he took no notice. 'I'm sure they will want us to stay, and I think we should humour them a little. A day or two wouldn't make any difference, now would it?' He had no wish to argue with her in front of her family, he added.

To his relief, after a moment's reflection, she nodded. 'You're quite right, of course,' she said. 'We mustn't rush away. But two nights, at the very most!'

'Agreed. Come on, then. We'd better go and confess!'

It was easier than either expected. Annie Sophie looked out at the sound of the hired carriage and started to her feet in some surprise. 'Why, here's Addie,' she exclaimed and she's got Colonel Nicolson with her. I wonder where *they've* been!'

The girl's pale eyes suddenly narrowed as a horrid suspicion filled her mind. Whatever was her sister doing wearing one of Izzie's hats, and carrying flowers? She frowned but said nothing.

The couple came into the house and stood rather uncertainly at the entrance to the drawing room, then Malcolm Nicolson put his arm around Adela and drew her forward. 'We've something to tell you,' he said, looking at her parents with a proud half-smile on his face. 'Mrs Cory, Colonel Cory, a short time ago your daughter did me the very great honour of becoming my wife.' He paused to let the news sink in before adding, 'We're both very happy—and we hope you'll be happy for us, too.'

Arthur Cory was on his feet immediately. He shook his new son-in-law's hand vigorously while Fanny, extremely pale, advanced more slowly.

'I would have liked to show you off to the world, Adela, I expect you know that.' There was a slight catch in the older woman's voice. 'But I understand your reasons, my dear—even if I can't say I approve of them,' and she hugged her warmly before holding her hand out to Nicolson with a smile.

And then Cory was with Adela. 'So, daughter, you're off my hands at last.' Something in his voice made her look at him sharply: the lips beneath the trim, disciplined beard were curved in a satisfied smile.

'Father,' she asked him slowly, 'did you know?'

The blue eyes so very like her own twinkled mischievously. 'I suspected, and in my own small way I think perhaps I helped—?'

'Oh, Father,' she whispered, 'I didn't believe such happiness was possible,' and then his arms were around her, holding her tight.

'Times of pleasure let no man grudge'

The days before Adela left were bitter-sweet for Isabel. They had shared so much since the family circle had been irrevocably broken, when the two of them were sent to school in England all that time ago.

Six-year-old Addie had been heart-broken, wearing herself out with weeping, swearing never to forgive her parents, and turning to her sister in her desolation. Eighteen years later, Isabel still had a vivid recollection of the little girl's face pressed against the window pane, watching her mother and father walk away, the tears running down her cheeks in melancholy imitation of the rain outside. She had not been crying for them, but for India—India, which had already insinuated itself into the very heart of her being.

For a while the older girl had been the centre of Adela's world. It was Isabel who comforted her when she woke up sobbing from dreams that refused to come true; Isabel who consoled her after richly deserved punishment; Isabel who understood that her naughtiness was the result of frustration and despair.

Later, at home, it was Isabel who kept her impetuous sister in check while laughing at her capriciousness; Isabel who would collapse helplessly at Adela's wickedly accurate mimicry of local worthies; Isabel who would hold her breath in horror at Addie's daredevil antics then try to put things right; Isabel, always Isabel ...

Well, all that was over. Adela Cory was a married woman now, and Isabel could rejoice in her sister's happiness. But Malcolm Nicolson was taking her away and nothing would ever be the same again.

Annie Sophie's thoughts of Adela were rather less kindly and in a way it was Malcolm Nicolson's fault. He had always been civil in giving the youngest Miss Cory the attention that she felt she deserved (but very seldom received), and in his company the chubby girl, whose slightly spotty complexion betrayed an over-fondness for sweets, could forget she was barely out of the schoolroom. But in the case of his wife's sister the colonel's capacity for putting people at their ease was to prove a double-edged sword.

Annie Sophie fumed as she slowly came to terms with the marriage of a man she would have dearly loved for herself, and she concentrated her fury on Adela. At school she had managed Addie very well. Most of the time. Though sometimes, her hands smarting from a caning, Addie had suspected treachery and pulled the little girl's ringlets viciously in an attempt to make her confess. Annie Sophie might be a sneak but she was no coward—and Adela went away unsatisfied, openly vowing revenge but clearly impotent. And the younger girl, ever subtle in her methods, quietly continued to make her sister's life as unpleasant as one small person could. But in India it had been different.

Here Addie had everything. Addie's hair was luxuriantly blonde while hers ... Annie Sophie tossed her own gingery locks in disgust. Addie's eyes were a compelling violet, her own were a vapid watery blue. Addie's figure was slender, although she ate like a hog ... Addie Cory was the colonel's wife. Annie Sophie scowled. It was too bad. She took herself off to see Maisie McHinch who always understood.

'Oh, dear,' sighed Mrs Cory, as she watched the last of her family go off to bed. 'It's been a long, long day.'

'But not quite long enough, eh, Fanny, my love?' her husband smiled.

'What on earth do you mean by that?'

'Well, you still didn't manage to talk to Addie on her own, did you? Despite all your efforts.'

'No,' admitted Fanny, with another sigh, it had been impossible. Try as she might, the young woman had tried even harder. 'And now it's too late—'

'Yes,' said Cory cheerfully. 'Too late to scare her with the perils lurking behind the bedroom door.'

'Arthur!'

'Come on, Fanny, Nicolson's no one's idea of a monster! Far from it.' He had seen the effect the colonel had on all his daughters and suspected that Fanny herself was not totally immune. He glanced at his wife shrewdly and she had the grace to blush. 'She'll have to find out for herself, Fan, and that's that.'

Besides, there had been something about the proud carriage of Adela's head as she had left the room, and the way in which she had acknowledged her husband's hand on her waist that led Cory to believe that any words from Fanny on the subject of matrimony would have proved quite superfluous. He chose not to share his thoughts with his wife, but went on: 'And I've never seen a lamb go more willingly to the slaughter, have you? Unless it was yourself?' Fanny blushed again, although the sudden laughter in her eyes answered the glint in his. 'There—you see how foolish you're being.'

Mrs Cory smiled at her husband gratefully, completely reassured, and raised her lips for his kiss.

'Annie Sophie doesn't seem at all happy with her new brother-in-law.' Husband and wife were alone at last in the room the colonel had occupied once before.

'It's not you she doesn't like—it's me. She never has.' Adela walked over to the door leading to the verandah and looked out over the garden. Her voice was deliberately matter of fact.

'Oh? Why?'

'It goes back to when we were at school in Richmond. Please, darling, I really don't want to spend my wedding night talking about *her*.' She didn't look at him. She was more upset than he had realised and Nicolson changed the subject.

'Some people might consider that your wedding night was two weeks ago. Have you forgotten already?'

'No, of course not.' Her voice held the suspicion of a smile.

'Adela! Will you stop looking out of the window and get ready for bed!' He was half undressed himself. She ignored him.

'Malcolm, do come here!' she said, in sudden alarm. 'I think there's someone out there in the garden. Look!'

He went to her side but could see nothing. His deft fingers quickly undid the fastening of her dress and it slipped to the ground in the faintest whisper of silk. 'You're imagining it, darling. Come to bed.' He began to kiss the hollow between her neck and shoulder, but she was not to be deterred.

'There was someone this morning—outside the Registrar's—didn't you see him? He was there when we went in, and he was still there when we came out.' Before, she had thought herself mistaken. Now she was certain. 'An evil-looking Afghan, with a dreadful scar on his cheek. Could it be him?' She turned around, but his reaction was not at all what she expected.

'Malcolm Nicolson, I do believe you're laughing at me!'

'Not at all!' but he quite failed to hide his amusement. 'I'm afraid that's a good friend of mine you're describing so unkindly. Mahomed Akram, why I've known him for years!' Nicolson stepped into the verandah despite his wife's futile gesture to stop him. 'I would trust him with my life—*and* yours,' he added, as a man came out from the shadows. He salaamed, they spoke for several minutes, then the watcher disappeared.

Nicolson lingered in the verandah, lost in thought, and now it was his wife's turn to show impatience. '*Malcolm*!' her tone was insistent but he didn't seem to hear.

When he did return it was to find Adela waiting in the moonlight, all ivory and gold, like some image crafted by a master hand long dead. Neither of them moved. Then with a smile she slowly shook her head and her hair fell free about her breasts. The spell was broken and love began to weave a magic of its own.

Colonel Nicolson was awake early. Thirty years in the Indian Army had trained him to make do with very little rest and he looked at Adela still sleeping beside him like a child, her hair spread out over her pillow and much of his. This time there would be no need for her to creep back to her room: she was his wife, and he was discovering her to be an enchanting admixture of child and woman, innocence and instinct.

As he watched her tenderly she muttered something. She turned towards him and the temptation to make love to her again became too strong; he began to rain soft kisses on her face. She half opened her sleepy eyes and looked at him dreamily.

'Wake up, wake up, little violet eyes,' he coaxed.

'Violet,' she murmured, 'Violet ... Why, that's a pretty name,' and with that she nestled against him and closed her eyes once more.

Amused, her husband let her sleep, but 'Violet' she remained.

✥

'Where are we going?' she kept asking throughout the following day and all he would answer was an enigmatic: 'Be patient and wait until tomorrow.' *Tomorrow*—the true beginning of her married life, for it was all very well being Mrs Malcolm Nicolson, but she was still under her parents' roof and aware of their indulgent gaze.

Annie Sophie watched them too, but rarely spoke, and Malcolm, seemingly impervious to any undercurrents, chatted away to his sister-in-law quite naturally as if totally unaware of her antagonism.

She wants us to be unhappy, Adela realised. From that moment she knew that reconciliation was impossible, and she no longer tried.

That evening at dinner Annie Sophie Cory announced that she no longer wished to be called by her given name. 'If Addie can change her name to *Violet* as seems to be the case—' she included her brother-in-law in the malevolent look she directed towards her sister '—then I want to be called *Vivian*!' she declared.

Everyone looked at her in interest, but only the new Mrs Nicolson presumed to enquire the reason for such a momentous decision.

'Well,' the aspiring writer informed her, 'I hate being called Annie Sophie—it's totally unsuitable for an intellectual. Besides, I think it's horrid!' She looked around at her family defiantly.

'No, no,' said Adela with a very sweet smile, 'I really think you should keep it. Do you know, it suits you down to the ground!'

Colonel Cory, long time keeper of the peace between his younger daughters, hid a smile, while Malcolm Nicolson shook his head at his wife in mock despair—there were times, he was discovering, when her love of devilment quite outweighed all other considerations. Adela grinned back. She saw no need for diplomacy: tomorrow they were off!

The would-be Vivian Cory maintained a dignified and injured silence throughout the rest of the evening, but from that moment her dislike of Violet Nicolson strengthened into hate and it was with mixed feelings that the family saw the couple off next day: relief, regret, envy—all were in the air.

Foreboding too.

Isabel, quite desolate, found herself whispering to herself: 'Oh, Addie dear, be careful. You've given your heart, don't give your soul as well—' for there was something about the intensity of her sister's love that frightened her.

'Mine the Blue Distance'

The little party headed north. Four Afghans on horseback, three laden baggage camels, and a woman in the long white tunic and red baggy trousers of her kind, riding respectfully to the rear. The monotony of the land they crossed was sometimes broken by a ruined sandstone tomb, its pillars and carved capitals slowly crumbling in the desert air. Small lamps flickered in some, but those who had lit them were nowhere to be seen, and it seemed to the young woman that they could well be the only five people left alive in an enchanted world of silence. A world where the desert light held a sorcery all its own—where distances became distorted, stones became mountains and the far horizon mere moments away.

One of the horseman turned back and her reverie was broken.

'Are you all right? You're getting left behind.'

'And you're forgetting about me already!'

The colonel had the grace to look guilty. 'I'm sorry,' he said. 'Old habits die hard.' He gave his wife a searching glance before asking, 'How do you feel, at this very moment? Tell me.'

Violet Nicolson took a deep breath, looked at the vast open spaces around them and the hills beckoning in the blue distance, and her answer came from the heart. 'I feel free, wonderfully free, and I wish this could last for ever!'

She had gone into their room earlier that morning only to receive a tremendous shock. Expecting to find her husband, she saw instead a figure in the white tunic and trousers of a tribesman standing by the verandah. Her first thought had been that it was Malcolm's Afghan, returned for some secret purpose of his own, but although his back was to her and she couldn't see his face, this man was taller. Suddenly she felt a terrible fear. The figure turned slowly towards her and she froze to the spot, unable to do anything but stare back in silence.

Keep calm, Violet told herself. Don't scream and he probably won't hurt you. Her mind was racing; she thought of the tales she and Isabel had scared each other with as girls, about men such as this; she tried to remember whether she had shut the door.

Steeling herself, she began to inch backwards. The door was closed, she found, but there was a table to the right. She remembered the heavy brass lamp it held and reached out, fingers groping frantically behind her. If the man moved any nearer, she would throw it.

The lamp wobbled, as if about to fall. Dear God, where was Malcolm? Oh, why wasn't he here when she needed him?

Malcolm … the man stepped round the bed and came towards her. Her hand gripped the lamp at last and she waited, curiously nerveless, to see what would happen next. The Afghan came closer still and Violet raised her arm, only to hesitate a fraction. Her eyes narrowed, and the stifling wave of panic slowly subsided as she took a closer look. The loose garments emphasised rather than hid the powerful shoulders, and the eyes glinting at her from under the folds of the turban were strangely familiar too.

Then she giggled as the lamp was removed gently from her grasp and put safely back on the table. 'So you would brain me, would you, wife?' and Malcolm's arms were round her, and his laughing eyes held hers. 'I didn't mean to frighten you. But when you didn't recognise me, I'm afraid the temptation was too great.'

'I suppose you wanted to see what I would do,' and Violet sat down on the bed, her knees suddenly weak.

He sat down beside her. 'I expected you to scream. Darling, why didn't you?'

She touched the vicious Afghan knife at his waist with a tentative finger. 'I thought you might cut my throat,' she said simply. 'And why are you dressed like that?'

'Guess,' said her husband, pointing to a pile of clothing on the bed. 'They're for you. Where do you think we're going?'

She hardly dared hope. 'Into the desert?'

'And further—I'm taking you into the hills.'

Even the news that for safety's sake they would not be alone did nothing to lessen her delight, and when the tearful goodbyes were over Colonel Nicolson's Afghan and two others were waiting for them. Everything for the journey was piled high on the backs of three supercilious-looking camels whose collective air of condescension quite failed to match that of her husband's faithful friend. Tilting her chin defiantly and vowing that she would under no circumstances be intimidated, Violet Nicolson met the dark eyes that held hers balefully, and did not look away. Malcolm watched the silent exchange, guessing much of what was in the mind of each. Given time, all would be well, he hoped. If not, he decided regretfully, the Afghan would have to go.

It was strangely liberating to ride astride for the first time in her life, her skirts abandoned and readily forgotten. The going was easy at first and when they reached the Hab River, 'Get down,' said the colonel, 'I've something to show you.'

Taking his wife's hand he led her towards the water. A river it might be but there had been very little rain and they found only a succession of fairly deep pools, some connected, others not. In one of them Violet could see several dark rocks, nothing more, and she wondered why on earth they had stopped.

Suddenly one of the rocks moved, and Violet jumped. 'It's a crocodile,' Nicolson said with a chuckle, and now she could see that it was.

'Was it *here*—' she wanted to know, 'was it here that you ran across the crocodiles?'

'No, but this looks very like Magar Pir used to, years ago. The priests didn't shut them up in those days—it was about twenty years ago—and they roamed about all over the place. And it wasn't intentional, either—though the story has got round that I did it for a bet. No, I was out walking with the regimental doctor and I saw what I thought was a rock in the water, just like that one over there.' He pointed and the rock yawned obligingly. 'I jumped on to it and when I found out my mistake I couldn't get back, but had to keep on going. Unfortunately all the other "rocks" started moving too, but I made it to the other side. Although I believe I aged considerably in the process.'

He chuckled again as his wife frowned, wondering whether to believe the story or not.

'It's true,' he assured her. 'If you ever meet Dr Morton, you can ask him.'

Violet looked at the water as it slowly stirred into life, and shivered—there were some things about her husband's past that she really preferred not to know.

They veered north-eastwards towards the Kohistan Hills and by late afternoon the terrain grew steeper and more rocky. Violet had never ridden so far in her life, and although she was too proud to admit it to herself, to her husband, and to the sardonic Afghan at his side, she was exhausted.

She was almost dozing in the saddle as her mount amiably made its way forward in the wake of the two men ahead, and Malcolm Nicolson, who was deep in conversation with his companion, quite failed to realise when his wife began to lag behind. The camel drivers who followed at some distance saw, but took no notice—in their opinion the woman was in her rightful place.

The shadows were lengthening and playing over the outcrops when the accident happened. In a sudden startled movement Violet's horse reared up, dislodging its rider who fell to the ground to lie crumpled against a rock. At the sound of her cry the two leaders looked round and came cantering back. What they found appalled them: a black cobra, sunning itself in the last of the afternoon's warmth, must have struck out at the passing horse and even now, thwarted, was preparing to strike again.

'Don't move!'

There was little chance of that. Violet Nicolson, dazed and too weary to react, lay still, her eyes almost level with the cold eyes of the snake. *So this is how it is to die*, she thought, watching in frozen fascination. *But at least I have known the best.* She closed her eyes and waited. When the hiss came it brought no pain.

When Violet opened her eyes again, Malcolm was kneeling beside her. While he held her in silent concern she looked beyond him to where the headless cobra twitched in the sand, leaving senseless patterns in the dust. Nearby stood Mahomed Akram, calmly wiping the curved blade of his knife.

'It was you,' she whispered. 'Dear God, I thought it was the snake!' The girl began to laugh, a wild laugh verging on hysteria and tears.

'Violet, stop it!' Nicolson's hands gripping her bruised shoulders brought her back to reality, and the laughter ceased as abruptly as it had begun.

She had lost control of her horse, and for that she was to blame. She could admit as much. But still she would not explain why, for it was not in her nature to make excuses. Malcolm realised this, just as now—belatedly—he recognised her weariness and blamed himself totally for what had happened. But his main concern was to get his wife to a safe resting place before darkness fell, and although her pale miserable little face tugged at his heart, he knew they must move on before reaction set in; before she lost her nerve completely.

'Mount up, Violet.' His voice was more unfeeling than he intended. As he helped her to her feet, she stared in disbelief. She might be lying there dead and she needed comfort ... She bit her lip and looked from the cold face to where her little mare was waiting patiently. The last thing in the world that Violet Nicolson wanted was to climb into the saddle. Here on the ground she was in control, up there she would be at risk. The irrational fear gripping her made movement impossible.

'Get back on your horse, Violet.' The colonel's voice brooked no disobedience and she moved away. The mare whickered as she approached, and nuzzled her. For a moment the young woman pressed her face against the animal's flank and desperately fought the impulse to burst into tears. Here was the comfort she had failed to find elsewhere. Then, aching in every limb and gritting her teeth against the pain, she hauled herself up in silence.

Staring straight ahead, refusing to look at any of her companions, she failed to see the glance Mahomed Akram exchanged with her husband, and his faint nod of approval, and when Nicolson moved off at her side she ignored him.

'Violet, look at me. Please.' The tone was quite different. 'I had to be brutal, darling, believe me. Would you have done it otherwise?' She bit her lip and said nothing.

'Sweetheart, the alternative was to truss you on a camel, like a sack of gram.' Now despite herself she managed the faintest of smiles. The colonel breathed a sigh of relief: thank goodness she understood.

'Delightful Days that dance away too soon!'

As the sun began to set they reached the bank of a shallow watercourse. Beyond the sandy stretch and protected by a rough overhang, opened the narrow gorge through which the stream headed south from high up in the mountains. Purple shadows slid across the scattered stones and slowly the water turned to gold. Somewhere on the other side a jackal howled, and far away on the Indus plain another took up the cry.

Nicolson dismounted. 'We're going to camp here,' he told his wife. 'You can get down now.'

But Violet ruefully shook her head. 'I really don't think I can, Malcolm, though I'd certainly like to. Perhaps we should have stayed with Annie Sophie,' and she forced a cheerful smile as he lifted her down. 'Nothing she could do would quite match this!'

She tried to move and stifled a groan. There was no word of complaint—and no word of the snake. Malcolm Nicolson looked at his bride in admiration. 'You'll feel better in the morning,' he assured her, although he had his doubts.

After a simple meal washed down by cold clear water from the stream, Violet Nicolson leaned against the smooth boulder at her back, drinking in the unfamiliar desert sounds. She drew a deep breath of contentment. She was worn out, she was aching all over, but she was alive and with Malcolm; she had never felt happier. Night had fallen and the jackals were howling again. She tried desperately to keep awake, but her eyelids were too heavy. Soon her head drooped onto Nicolson's shoulder and she slept. The colonel gently disengaged himself and walked over to their tent with an armful of blankets. Then he came back for his wife.

He stayed and watched her sleeping for a while, then he and his old companion talked long into the night under the blazing canopy of stars.

'Come on, sleepyhead—time to wake up!' The voice sounded disgustingly cheerful. Violet forced herself up onto one elbow, grunted, and looked around. The light under the canvas was muted, but outside it was bright and clear. The air was warm and her husband was watching her from the opening of the tent.

'And how are you feeling this morning?'

Violet moved cautiously towards him before answering: 'What I *can* feel feels terrible!' She put out a hand for help and he pulled her to her feet. 'And you told me I would feel better today!'

Malcolm's answering smile was sympathetic. 'I was wrong,' he said. 'Tomorrow you will feel better—I promise.'

That morning early the Nicolsons left the party and walked up into the gorge. It soon become little more than a cleft in the rock and for the young woman, totally unused to such surroundings, it was fast becoming a cold and alarming experience. How Isabel would have hated this! Violet looked up to the small triangle of light that was all she could see of the sky, and thought of her timid sister. She didn't like it much either, but she kept her misgivings to herself.

'Are you all right?' Nicolson asked from some way ahead. 'Just keep on going as you are. It's not much further.' He slowed down a little and she dutifully followed, mechanically putting one foot after the other, keeping out of the stream bed as best she could, and hoping it would soon be over. Just as she thought she could bear no more, 'We're here,' said Malcolm and they emerged from the gloom onto a plateau.

To three sides there were lofty limestone outcrops but before them—nothing. Nothing, thought the speechless Violet, but the most amazing vista imaginable: arid plains stretching far below, broken here and there by narrow winding river beds.

'Baluchistan, the gateway to India.' Nicolson reached for her hand. He pointed out the ancient invasion routes to the south and west, and far away, he told her, over the great ranges which rose line after line in the hazy blue distance to the north, beyond the furthermost mountains, lay Afghanistan. And beyond that, the Russian steppes.

The young woman gasped. At last she understood.

'Yes. I think you can see now, my little Violet, why your father is so obsessed with the defence of India. And why he is so frightened of Russia. He, and others like him, would have us take more of Baluchistan than we already have.' Colonel Nicolson's voice was grim. 'Over there is Quetta'—he pointed to the north again—'at the head of the Bolan Pass.'

'And you were stationed there.' She turned to him eagerly. 'Oh, tell me what it's like.'

'It's cold,' he said flatly, 'and deep under snow in winter. In summer it's infernally hot, and believe me, sweetheart, it's not much better in autumn.'

'And in the spring?'

'In the spring?' his voice lightened. 'In spring it's quite wonderful—carpets of flowers at your feet when you ride in the hills. Tulips, irises, hyacinths. And violets—' Malcolm Nicolson laughed down into his wife's eager face. 'Violets like you—so sweetly scented you might think yourself in heaven,' and he caught her up and swung her round and round in his arms, until she was quite dizzy.

When he set her on her feet again, Violet leant against him, then collapsed onto the grass helpless with laughter. She looked up at the clouds and peaks still circling madly overhead, and then she closed her eyes. Soon she seemed to sleep. Nicolson lay beside her, searching her face avidly as if to commit its every curve and line to memory. Her expressive mouth was gently smiling, a child's smile, confident and trusting, and the colonel felt a sudden pang as he thought of the years that stretched ahead.

Dearest girl, don't ever change, came the silent plea, and to his God he prayed: *Let her always love me*. And staring up into the blind vault of heaven he prayed most fervently of all: *Let nothing spoil her, or break her spirit—and let nothing ever harm her*.

Then he too closed his eyes and neither of them moved until a shadow crept over the sun and a breeze sprang up, a chill little reminder that the days were short and they had a way to go.

As she looked back sadly on those magical early weeks of marriage, Violet thought the glorious sense of freedom lost for ever. Days in the saddle, her loose garments caught by an errant breeze; deep blue midnights lit by frosty stars; cold desert nights warmed by her lover's arms—how could she forget? And how could she bear to remember?

It was over, and they had been back in Hyderabad a day. Alone in her bungalow Violet Nicolson had never felt more miserable in all her life. She had known it was coming to an end, but had not realised until too late how precious each moment had been. And then suddenly it was over.

'We head east tomorrow,' Malcolm had said one morning in his matter of fact way.

'So soon?' She felt her heart sinking.

'We've been away over two weeks. My leave is almost up.'

Of course he had to go, back to Hyderabad, back to the cantonment—back to the regiment. He sounded almost glad, thought the girl. Whereas she felt—what? Anticipation, or was it something worse? All evening the thought kept coming back to haunt her, and finally she faced up to the truth: they were heading east, where an ordeal she dreaded was waiting. She felt a gloom descend, a gloom that threatened to spoil the two days that remained.

On their last night the Afghan sang to them. Violet did not understand a word but no one needed to tell her it was sad—the haunting repetitive melody matched her mood exactly. Mahomed Akram's voice was unexpectedly pleasant and as she listened Violet forgot the ugly scar, watching instead the expression in the dark distant eyes. The man had a soul, she realised in surprise, and the soul of a poet, at that.

Afterwards it was easy to thank him for his music, easier than it had been to thank him for saving her life. Then, he had brushed off her stammered thanks, haltingly expressed in his native Pushtu, with the usual fatalistic words: 'It is written,' as if her life were of no consequence at all, but tonight the gaze he rested on her was glowing and his smile was warm. He's glad it's all over, she decided, and turned away to the tent.

'What was the song about?' she asked Malcolm later.

'It's a lover's lament.' He drew her close under the canvas. 'He would have plucked the stars from the sky for his lass to make a necklace … As I would for you, my little love, had I the power.' She pressed against him. 'Go on,' she urged.

'He would have scattered rose petals over the ground as a couch for his mistress—' Violet sighed pleasurably at the thought.

'But—the song goes—she scorned him, him and his hopes and his passion. When she left him, the sweet green turf sufficed her for her slumbers and he chides her for her cruelty. Darling,' and suddenly Nicolson held her so close that she could hardly breathe, 'you won't ever leave me, will you?'

'No, no,' she whispered, 'I promise, I promise—'

'What is it?' he asked a moment later, sensing a change in her mood.

'Oh, I don't know—I'm being silly, I suppose, thinking of the unhappy times, after you went away —' and more besides.

'Yes,' he agreed, 'now you *are* being silly. This time we're going back together.' The reminder hardly helped, and Violet fell asleep to dream of cantonments, the pining lover—and his lost lady, lying in her resting place beneath the grass.

The next day her mood of the night before had lightened, even though soon they were crossing the Indus plain and making for Kotri on the west bank of the river. It was strange to mingle with the crowds in the busy, bustling town after the emptiness of the hills and desert. There were women shrouded from top to toe in all-enveloping burkas; and unveiled Sindi women in baggy trousers and brightly embroidered vests. On the river, boats plied past piled high with grain, and bare-chested fishermen in their fragile-looking craft pulled in their shining wriggling catch. Her shawl over her head, Violet hurried after the tall figure of her husband, but soon she stopped to stare, and when she looked round for him again he had gone. Jostled by the crowd, wondering what to do and trying to keep calm, she turned with a start as a hand gripped her elbow. The Afghan's face was leering into hers. 'Come,' he said in Urdu, 'we must not keep the colonel *sahib* waiting,' and he led her to where Nicolson stood, looking out at the river.

'Ah, there you are.' It sounded as if he hadn't missed her at all.

'Why did you go so fast?'

'Why did you stop?'

'You knew I had stopped—and you didn't wait?'

'I thought I would teach you a lesson!'

'*What!*' she glared at him in sudden fury. And all he did was laugh.

'Hush, hush,' he said. 'No self-respecting Mohammedan wife would dream of berating her husband in public. Behave yourself, Violet Nicolson, or I shall have to beat you when we get home.'

Home … As they went aboard the ferry the gloom descended like a pall.

'A little Love and some Forgetfulness'

Watching the landing stage approach, the colonel's bride became increasingly nervous and she wished she might remain on the boat forever. Once ashore she looked about her in apprehension. Only three miles down this pleasant tree-lined avenue lay the old town of Hyderabad, and somewhere within its confines was her husband's cantonment. Suddenly she was frightened.

Nicolson inspected his wife's white face, and motioned to Mahomed Akram to leave them for a moment. 'What's up?' he asked gently. He thought he knew.

'I'm scared.' Honest as always, Violet owned up. 'Tell me what to do, Malcolm,' and her hand plucked at his sleeve in panic. '*Tell me how to behave.*'

'My dearest girl, you will simply be yourself.' The look he gave her was as reassuring as his voice. 'And I shall be proud of you—more than proud.' It obviously wasn't enough; she was still looking at him with wide dark frightened eyes. But what more could he say? He tried.

'Darling, I mean it. Be your usual adorable self. Oh, I know some of the women will be put out that you don't fit their idea of a colonel's lady—but don't you dare change your ways for them!' He had made her laugh. 'Now, Mrs Nicolson, are you ready?'

The two Afghans followed by the woman set off towards the town. Should they have made a more conventional entry? Perhaps, conceded the colonel, but it was too late to do anything else now. And this, he still believed, was an easier way to break the ice.

They passed the Native Infantry barracks where Colonel Nicolson was recognised. He acknowledged his men but didn't stop. The presence of a woman drew no comment. They must suppose I'm with Mahomed Akram, thought Violet glumly, but almost immediately the Afghan disappeared.

Word soon spread that Nick was back from his leave and was not alone. 'The old boy's got a native woman with him!' said a subaltern. 'What do you think he's going to do with her?' 'The same as any one else would, I imagine,' replied another, and the ribald laughter could still be heard as the couple passed the officers' bungalows and stopped outside the mess. The officers assembled on the verandah steps looked at the ill-matched pair and then at one another, until Malcolm Nicolson chose at last to speak.

'Gentlemen,' he said, in a voice which rang with pride, 'allow me to present my wife.' Relishing the moment, he held out a hand to the figure beside him. When Violet turned towards him uncertainly, the shawl slipped from her head and the stunned silence, if anything, deepened. For the young men recognised the girl the colonel had danced off her feet in Karachi, and as she returned her husband's smile they thought her prettier than ever.

Mrs Nicolson was forced to spend the next day alone. Colonel Nicolson was back in harness catching up, so she was left to her own devices. Her clothes and the few belongings she had chosen to have sent up from Karachi had arrived and tidying them away was a matter of minutes. This done, she looked around the bungalow which was now her home, and even to her fairly spartan eye the place was sparsely furnished. That wouldn't concern Malcolm, she reflected wryly—he was probably hardly ever here!

The bed in their room was wide and low, there was a carved rosewood table to one side, and a few rugs scattered over the floor. The dining room had a table and six chairs, nothing more, and it had an unused feel about it. She turned away into the drawing room which was hardly better. It held one armchair, a bookcase full of books, and large cushions tossed about in a desultory fashion over more brightly coloured Afghan rugs. A bachelor's den, the sort of room she might have chosen for herself in the same circumstances—but for a couple? She shrugged—after all, Malcolm had hardly had time to prepare for his marriage.

She drifted outside into the verandah. The compound beyond was dusty and barren and Violet felt a sudden pang of homesickness for Fanny's well-ordered beds and fragrant flowers and shrubs. There was one lonely-looking pink oleander in a corner and she walked over and broke off a few stems to take back with her into the house. An indignant *mali* appeared from nowhere to protest.

'Very well then,' she said, surprising him with her knowledge of Urdu, 'provide me with flowers!' She indicated the neglected area with an imperious sweep of her hand and stalked back into the house. Great was the young woman's surprise when an hour later the gardener brought her a bunch of dusty-looking yellow roses, obviously purloined. Oh dear, thought Violet with a pang of guilt, that's *not* what I meant at all; she accepted the offering nonetheless, and was grateful for it.

The servants were hovering when she went inside again, but she didn't know what to do with them. It seemed safer to tell them to carry on as usual until Malcolm came back. He had left early before she was properly awake and she found herself drifting aimlessly until his return. We must talk, she decided in desperation—surely he doesn't expect me to spend my days like this?

No, Colonel Nicolson expected no such thing; he was simply too busy to think about his wife, and his preoccupation with his duties to the men under his command caused the first cloud to loom on the horizon of his marriage.

Late in the afternoon he returned to find Violet curled up in the armchair, reading one of his books. He kissed her on the cheek and she smiled up at him, happy at the thought that now at last they would have some time together.

'I wasn't sure what to order for dinner,' she told him apologetically and Nicolson gave a start. He had quite forgotten to tell her that he was expected elsewhere. Guilt sharpened his voice as, 'I'll be eating at the mess,' he said. 'They want to welcome me back.'

'Oh, I see,' was Violet's only comment. She tried valiantly to hide her disappointment and the colonel felt guiltier still.

'I'm not sure when I'll be back—probably quite late.' His voice was still abrupt.

'I understand,' Violet said, and turned back to her book so that he should not see the tears in her eyes.

He left and she ate a lonely supper, trying desperately hard not to care. After all, he didn't seem to mind, so why should she? It was a miserable and angry woman who took herself off to bed, and who lay curled up in a tense and sleepless little ball until her husband returned in the early hours. She heard him come in, undress and get into bed. She said nothing.

'Violet,' he whispered, 'Violet, I know you're awake.' She was far too still, and she never slept like that. 'Darling, I'm so sorry, I didn't mean to hurt you. I quite forgot to tell you about tonight.'

He felt her stir a little. 'I came away as soon as I could.'

She moved again.

'I know you're angry with me—and I deserve it. You *are* angry, aren't you?'

'Yes, I am,' came the muffled reply.

He drew her to him and began kissing her face and hair. He could feel how tense she was. 'I'm sorry,' he said again, and began to stroke her back with gentle sensitive fingers. He felt her gradually relax and press against him.

He kissed her mouth, tenderly at first and then more passionately. His hands caressed her breasts until he heard her moan with pleasure, and then he stroked her belly and her thighs. His lips and hands became more and more insistent until Violet felt herself being drawn down and down into a dark vortex of intense and frightening sensation. At first she struggled to get free, but could not and then would not escape, until her whole being was suffused with an almost unbearable feeling of light and joy. For a long time afterwards she lay in her husband's arms and he held her close until the trembling stopped.

'I love you, my little one,' he whispered, and then she fell asleep.

She was vaguely aware of him leaving in the morning, when he leant over to kiss the drowsy blue eyes looking up at him. 'Go back to sleep, sweetheart,' he told her, 'I'll come home as soon as I can.' So she got up late, drifted around the house and compound, and went back to her book.

Malcolm, as good as his word, returned before two o'clock. 'Have you eaten?' he asked.

Violet realised in surprise that she had quite forgotten about tiffin. 'No, I haven't.'

'Good, neither have I.'

They sat down opposite each other and as she remembered what had happened the night before, Violet suddenly felt shy. When they had both finished, 'We need to talk,' said Nicolson. 'Yes,' she replied, and they both stood up.

He took her arm and led her towards their room. 'We'll be more comfortable here,' he said, thinking only of the spartan furnishings elsewhere, and was amused at her response.

'No. No—' she said, and drew back. If they were to have a serious talk she wanted it to be somewhere where he didn't have all the advantages, and she told him so outright. He smiled and took her to the drawing room instead.

'We'll have to get some other chairs, I suppose. Meanwhile—' He sat down in the only armchair and pulled her onto his lap. This was hardly any better, thought Violet; no wonder he was laughing at her.

'Now, tell me, sweetheart; what did you do this morning?'

'Nothing really.'

'Well you can't go on like that, can you? You need to go out.'

She looked at him seriously for a moment, then replied, 'So what do *you* suggest?'

'Well, sleepyhead, you can get up when I do, for a start, and go for a good long ride to clear the cobwebs away. What do you think?'

She nodded.

'But I won't let you go on your own. You do realise that, don't you?'

Violet nodded again; he had been afraid she might argue and he felt a great relief.

'You will always have a *syce* with you, or Mahomed Akram will take you—if he's around.' (The Afghan had been elusive since their return and Violet didn't know whether to be sorry or glad.) 'I'll come home in the afternoons whenever possible, and we'll have the evenings, too, and we can ride together. Unless we entertain, that is—' he surprised the smile on her face as she looked at the chairless state of the room, and smiled back '—or are entertained. They'll be after us soon enough. But sometimes I'll be at the mess.'

This time it was a shadow that he saw.

'You have to understand, darling. Some evenings I shall be expected to dine with the other officers. It can't be helped.' His voice was gentle but firm. He had warned her, after all, about army life.

'Of course I understand,' Violet said, 'truly I do.' In the silence that followed they both remembered how hurt she had been. 'And did you have a pleasant evening?' Her voice was light and friendly.

'Yes, I did, as a matter of fact. They ribbed me a lot about getting married, of course—but that was only to be expected, what with my "pronounced views", as you put it!'

'And then I suppose you all played silly games?'

He knew she was teasing him, but he gave her a keen look all the same. 'And what would you know about that, pray?'

She laughed. 'Oh, the subalterns in Lahore were fairly indiscreet—you'd be surprised what they gave away.' It would depend on who was asking the questions, he suspected. 'Well, did you?' she repeated.

'I escaped before it got too bad,' was all he would admit, before asking a question of his own. 'You were very annoyed with me, weren't you, when I got back?'

'It's all over now,' she told him with a kiss.

'Sweetheart, I hope it was all over before you went to sleep,' he murmured, and as he watched he saw the hot colour flood her cheeks. 'No, no,' he went on softly as she tried to hide her face against his chest. 'Look at me,' and he made her meet his gaze. 'You mustn't be afraid of your feelings—or ashamed of them either. Ever. Do you understand what I'm saying?'

'I think so,' she whispered, the colour slowly fading away.

'You are a perfectly normal healthy young woman—and I thank God for it. Violet, don't ever change.'

'Thy wife awaits her coming child'

She was glad of his words in the weeks to come, for soon the regiment went off on manoeuvres. There was a British regiment stationed in the barracks further to the north and they too had gone away into the hills. While the Nicolsons had been allowed to settle in undisturbed after their return, now Violet found herself left alone to face the relentless attentions of the station's other European ladies.

From the moment the news had broken, they had felt immense curiosity on the subject of Colonel Nicolson's new little bride, and her appearances in church on Sundays at her husband's side had made them more anxious than ever to make her acquaintance. Violet was well aware of their stares and pretended not to notice. The women were far worse than the men, she decided. They were like so many vultures waiting to swoop on their prey.

And swoop they did, almost before the colonel was out of sight. Invitations to tea, invitations to supper—inexperienced in the art of giving convincing excuses, his wife was obliged to accept them all. These occasions all seemed to follow a certain pattern: talk of their families, of the children exiled for their own good to England, of their husbands—and then the heads would all turn towards Violet expectantly.

'And how are you finding married life, Mrs Nicolson.'

'I'm settling in nicely, thank you.'

And this was all she would say, finding their repeated questioning on the subject quite impertinent. It soon became obvious that such a reply was not enough: these women were bored, and spent much of their time in gossip. Well, they're not going to gossip about *me*, she thought, defiantly. They talked about their husbands in a way that appalled her, and referred to the unpleasant nature of 'having to do their duty'—and that as infrequently as possible. Again they would look at the young bride.

This is horrible! I will not put up with any more! she decided after the fifth such experience, and thereafter was either *too unwell* to accept invitations, or *out* to all callers. She rose earlier than ever in the mornings to ride without being seen, and went to her bed later at night, for already she was too used to having Malcolm beside her to be able to sleep well with him away. So when the colonel returned after an absence of almost two weeks he was shocked at his wife's appearance. As she threw herself ecstatically into his arms, he was all too aware of the faint blue smudges under her eyes and the pallor of her cheeks.

'What's happened to the golden girl I left behind?' he asked with no little concern. 'Haven't you been sleeping at all?'

He, for his part, looked lean and taut, and better than Violet ever remembered seeing him. '*You* look wonderful,' she observed. 'You obviously haven't missed me in the least!'

'Have I not?' and he hugged her to him. 'But you haven't answered my question. Why are you looking so tired?'

'I've met the *memsahibs* of Hyderabad,' she declared in lugubrious tones that brought a sympathetic smile, and explained how she had managed latterly to avoid them. 'Malcolm, they're dreadful—like a flock of vultures! I've had to tell so many lies to keep away from them, before they picked my bones quite clean! Oh, I'm so glad you're back. Now you can protect me!'

There was a difference about her, Nicolson thought, as they lay side by side in bed. He pulled back the sheet and looked at his wife. Her belly was as flat as ever but her breasts seemed fuller. Violet shivered as he slowly ran his hands over her body. 'What is it, Malcolm?' she asked. 'Why are you looking at me so seriously?'

'How are you feeling, darling?'

'Wonderful!' and she stretched like a little cat.

He laughed. 'No, do you feel well—generally speaking, that is?'

'Of course I do—I've just missed you, that's all.'

'I was wondering,' he went on tentatively, 'whether you might not be pregnant?'

'Pregnant? Of course I'm not pregnant!' and he laughed at how positive she seemed. Yet, as she lay beside her husband in silence, Violet's mind was racing. She supposed she might be pregnant—she hadn't given the matter any thought—but it was perfectly possible. She tried to count the days, and failed. Dear God, she prayed, don't let it be true. I don't want to have a baby—not yet, anyway. *Please don't let it be true*!

In July they went to Karachi where the colonel was to chair an Examining Board. His wife looked the picture of health again, he thought with satisfaction, as he helped her into the train; blooming in fact. Throughout the journey Malcolm Nicolson once more found himself wondering.

It was strange to be back, thought the former Adela Cory as she surveyed her old room which was virtually unchanged; strange too that she would be sleeping here with a husband. Malcolm looked around with equal interest.

'And you told me how spartan my bungalow was—what a little fraud you are! This is like a convent cell!' The walls were bare, and there was almost no furniture. There was also a strange aura of peace. He turned back to his wife. 'I feel like an intruder. Are you sure you want me to stay?'

Violet had been watching him, a little smile playing on her lips. 'Do you know how often I would lie awake thinking of you?' She shook her head in disbelief. 'And now here you really are! Perhaps you should pinch me to show I'm not dreaming—'

'I could do better than that,' he suggested playfully, pulling her into his arms and kissing her throat and then her lips. As he did so a surreptitious hand began to remove the pins confining her heavy tresses.

'No! Not now!' Laughingly she pushed him away. 'They're expecting us to join them. Whatever would they think if we're late?'

'I'm sure they wouldn't mind waiting … just a little,' and he kissed her protesting mouth. 'Very well,' and at last he released her, 'but you'd better tidy your hair!'

'Oh, Malcolm, you wretch! It will take ages.' Groaning, Violet sat down in front of the glass and inspected the damage. He might have persisted in his seduction, even so, but grey eyes met exasperated blue in the mirror and read her silent plea. Good-humouredly, Nicolson settled down on the bed to wait.

Left in peace, his wife removed the rest of the pins, stuffing them into her mouth while she twisted and coiled the luxuriant ropes of hair and tried to bully them into place. It was going to take some time. Colonel Nicolson watched idly and began to reflect upon his wife's possible condition.

'How long since we were married, darling?' he asked her from the bed.

Violet, her mouth full of hairpins, muttered something and made a helpless little gesture so Malcolm worked it out for himself. Over eleven weeks. And ten days before that they had slept together. And in all that time she had not been forced to deny him once. Of course he had gone away for a time, but that was well over a month ago ...

'What were you saying, darling?' Violet Nicolson applied a final pin with a vicious jab and at last gave her husband her full attention. She knew perfectly well what he had asked, and where the question was leading, and she had no intention of talking about it now.

Confronted with her fierce expression, that normally most intrepid of men decided to wait until bedtime. Better still, he thought, he would try to have a word with his mother-in-law during the evening. He had noticed Fanny's speculative eye while remarking how well her daughter was looking. And how Violet herself had pretended not to understand.

Mrs Cory, he suspected, would not be so easily deterred a second time.

It was good to be home and be Addie again for a while, thought Violet, especially as Annie Sophie wasn't there. 'She's over at the McHinches,' Isabel explained. 'It's Maisie's birthday—and she promised to go and stay for a few days.'

Violet raised an eyebrow—a few days seemed a little excessive for such a minor celebration—but she sent up a silent prayer of thanks to her Maker, nonetheless. The short stay would be all the pleasanter for her sister's absence. But any feeling of peace was dispelled the next morning

'Marriage certainly suits you, Addie.' After breakfast Fanny drew her daughter into the garden and sat her down on the bench under the casuarina tree. She eyed her up and down before continuing, 'You look quite radiant. Do you think—?'

'No, I do not!' Violet interrupted emphatically.

But as her son-in-law had hoped, Fanny was not to be put off lightly.

'But how are you feeling, dear? Really?'

Violet gave a snort of exasperation. 'Why does everyone keep asking me that? Can't you see how well I look? Isabel said something just now, *you've* asked me—and Malcolm never stops!'

'Doesn't he, dear?' Fanny was intrigued. So her son-in-law hadn't just been making an idle observation then, the night before. 'You look to me,' remarked Mrs Cory, who in addition to rearing three daughters had buried two infant sons, 'you look to me as if you're expecting a child.' She watched her daughter and waited.

'Oh, Mother, I can't be!'

'*Can't be*, or *don't want to be*?' Fanny observed shrewdly. There was no answer. 'When did you last have your courses, Adela?'

Her daughter looked uncomfortable. 'I don't know. I don't usually bother to keep track, I just know when I'm starting.'

'Well, now that you're a wife perhaps you should take a little more notice. Think!'

Violet thought. 'Not since we were married,' she finally admitted.

'I see,' Fanny said in triumph. 'That's two and a half months then—' Or maybe three, Violet thought gloomily, although she was not prepared to own as much to her mother.

'Very well,' Fanny told her horrified daughter, 'tomorrow, when Malcolm's at his Board, you and I are going to the doctor. And don't argue.'

The following morning, when Lieutenant-Colonel Bainbridge, the civil surgeon for Karachi, had finished his examination, he asked to see Fanny alone.

'Mrs Nicolson is definitely pregnant, Mrs Cory, two or three months pregnant. Now, I don't think there will be any problems, but you never can tell with someone as narrow in the hips as your daughter. It's her first baby, of course, so we can't be at all sure how she'll cope. Perhaps you'll have a word with her husband, though.'

'Of course, Colonel. You'll tell Adela yourself that there might be problems?'

'I don't think there's any point in worrying her at this stage. A word of warning nearer the time, perhaps. But I'll certainly give her the happy news right away.'

Violet said not a word on the way home and her mother was so excited that she didn't notice. When they neared the drive Violet hissed, 'Now don't you tell anyone else until I've told Malcolm. Please, Mother, promise!'

'Of course, darling, I wouldn't dream of it,' but Fanny found it very difficult and the watching Isabel guessed.

She went into her sister's room and found her sitting despondently on a cushion by the window. 'So, we were right, weren't we?' she said.

Violet looked at her. 'Yes,' she said wearily, 'you were right. Oh, Iz, what am I going to do?'

'Do? *Do*? Why, you going to have the baby, of course!'

'I don't want to have a baby. I'm too young.'

'Well, you should have thought of that before!'

Violet scowled.

'Has Malcolm any idea of how you feel?'

'No. He suspects I might be pregnant, but we haven't really talked about it.'

'No, I don't suppose you have! *Don't think about it, and it will go away*—that's you all over!' Isabel sat down beside her sister, and looked at her earnestly through her thick spectacles. 'Well, you'll have to talk about it now, and my guess is that Malcolm will want a baby very much! And if I were you, I'd say I felt the same. And you *will*, I know you will.'

There was a silence.

'Oh, Addie, don't be so silly. I know it's a shock—but it shouldn't be, should it?'

Violet gave a little smile as she considered the question. 'No, I suppose not.' She made up her mind. 'Very well, Iz. I'll do as you say.'

Nicolson found her in the garden. 'Your mother said you were out here. She seems very excited for some reason. Do you know why?' The look he gave her was keen.

'Yes. Mother took me to the doctor this morning. Malcolm, you were right and I am pregnant.' Suddenly Violet felt very humble—and very selfish. Nicolson's face was alight with happiness, and *she* would have denied him this joy ...

Carefully the colonel put his arms around his wife and drew her close, and when he looked at her his eyes were full of pride. 'My own wonderful, clever girl,' he said and kissed her on the brow.

'Not so very wonderful—and not clever at all. Just very, very, silly,' and Violet Nicolson burst into tears.

'Of love and labour, toil and strife and pain'

Before they left, Fanny had a long talk with her son-in-law and passed on the doctor's warning. The result was a conflict of wills between the colonel and the colonel's lady, a conflict that neither won—nor lost—one in which Malcolm Nicolson tried to impose certain restrictions on his wife.

'No more riding from now on,' he told her on their return, and he sighed as her chin predictably lifted in defiance.

'Oh, Malcolm, please—' She so loved the early morning gallops before the summer heat began to strike. The dew on the tamarisks, caught in the first rays of the sun as the golden ball of light appeared above the horizon; the call of the birds flying across the pink clouds at dawn; the feel of the wind in her hair ... Must she give this up?

She used every weapon at her disposal, but her husband remained unmoved by her pleas or by the angry little face scowling up at him. 'I'm sorry, Violet,' and he was adamant. 'You have to be sensible, and that's all there is to it. I can't risk you having a fall. No—it doesn't matter how competent you are, accidents do happen. I'm sorry, darling, it's only until the baby is born—a few months only, after all.'

Only until the baby was born—to Violet the months ahead seemed a life sentence. 'It's all very well for you!' she argued. 'You won't have to stay cooped up here all day.'

'And neither will you. I'll take you out early before I go to work. And in the evenings. In the carriage.' But he could see she was not to be easily placated.

'I can't see that it's necessary yet. Later when I'm fat and ugly, yes.'

'Mrs Nicolson,' he said, and Violet was infuriated by the laughter in his eyes, 'how could you ever be ugly? But you will certainly get a lot bigger. And I shall love you all the more as a result!'

'Malcolm, I don't see why I can't go on riding for a little longer. I'm not an invalid and I don't want to treated like one—or like a child.'

'Then don't behave like one! It's for your own good, surely to goodness you can see that for yourself.' He was finding her attitude tiresome and his face grew stern.

For a moment she glared back and then her eyes dropped meekly.

'Promise me you'll do as you're told, Violet.' He realised his mistake as soon as the words were out. She fixed him with a long level look from eyes that were almost black. And she said nothing.

Malcolm Nicolson left the house feeling less than happy and there the matter rested.

It didn't occur to the colonel that his wife would defy his wishes, and she rode out openly every day for a week. One morning she emerged to find Mahomed Akram standing beside the waiting groom.

'Malcolm isn't here,' she informed him and hoped he would go away.

'I know.'

They looked at each other for a moment, the colonel's wife and the colonel's devoted friend, and Violet realised that it was her he had come to see. 'You'd better come in,' she said ungraciously, and he followed her inside. She invited him to sit. He preferred to stand. She stood too, wishing he would get it over with and go.

But the Afghan was in no hurry to speak. Instead, his eyes wandered round the room, taking in the changes that this small yellow-haired woman had made to his friend's surroundings. As they did so Violet watched the ruined hawk-nosed face, its left brow puckered by the scar that started at the temple, furrowed the cheek and finished at the chin. The left eyelid dragged a little, but the eye itself was whole, and glinted at her like its dark fellow as he gave her his full attention at last.

'Why do you go against *Nikelseyn*'s wishes?' As always, he addressed her in the Urdu he knew she understood perfectly.

Violet's first inclination was to tell him to mind his own business, but she refrained—he probably did think it was his business. Anyway, she told herself, it was an interesting situation: he resented her, and to be honest, she was no fonder of him.

'What exactly do you mean, Mahomed Akram?' she enquired in a perfectly civil voice

'*Nikelseyn* does not wish you to ride. At home with my people, disobedient wives are beaten.'

'Even when they're carrying a child?'

Mahomed Akram looked her up and down dispassionately, and Violet found it impossible to take offence. He was probably assessing her value as a brood mare, she thought cynically. The Afghan countered with a question of his own.

'Why do you risk your life and the life of his son?'

Violet raised an eyebrow, but did not point out that the child was as much hers as her husband's—and had every chance of being a girl. 'I don't believe there is a risk,' she countered. 'Mahomed Akram, why are you saying all this?'

'*Nikelseyn* is my brother and you are my brother's wife.' The Afghan sighed and shook his head. 'I cannot understand why he chose you. You are too small and I do not consider you strong enough to be a mother of men.' Violet hid her smile: she had been right. 'But,' and the deep voice softened fractionally, 'I know my brother has taken you as the wife of his heart. So I say to you: do as he asks—for his sake, if not for your own. He truly fears for you.'

Violet thought for a moment. 'Is that the truth? Malcolm is afraid?'

Mahomed Akram nodded impassively. 'But he will not tell you.' He went to the door. Turning, he asked, 'What shall I say to the *syce*?'

'Tell him to go away. He won't be needed again.'

Violet sat down. What a pity, she thought as she went over the exchange, that she couldn't share it with Malcolm. She was still sitting there when her husband came in unexpectedly and immediately took in the fact that she was dressed for riding.

'And just what were you thinking of doing?' he demanded, his face like thunder.

She stood up. 'I was intending to go out,' she answered peaceably, 'but—' He gave her no chance to finish before he seized her arm.

'Is this what you do the moment my back is turned—go sneaking off against my express wishes?'

'I've never sneaked anywhere in my life! I've been riding all week, if you'd only taken the trouble to look.'

'God in Heaven, woman!' he exploded. 'What does it take to make you see sense?'

'Very little, as it happens. Please let me go, you're hurting.' Her voice was quite calm. 'It's all right, darling,' she told him, as she rubbed her smarting wrist. 'I've already decided that my riding days are over for the moment.'

The relief on his face was reward enough for the sacrifice she was making. 'So what made you change your mind?' he asked after a moment, for it certainly hadn't been anything he had said.

She answered him with a question of her own. 'Malcolm, you wouldn't have seen Mahomed Akram just now, by any chance?'

'Why, yes, he said you wanted to see me. Did you?'

Violet smiled. 'Of course. Always. But I didn't send any message. For some reason, Malcolm Nicolson, your Afghan friend has started to interfere in your affairs.' Her smile deepened as she told him something of what had happened. 'And he seems to think you a very poor judge of horse flesh, by the way,' but the remark failed to produce an answering smile. 'What is it, Malcolm?' for he was frowning, and she remembered something else the Afghan had said. 'There isn't any problem about me having this baby, is there? Something I haven't been told?'

Nicolson looked at his wife and sat down with her on his lap. He decided not to frighten her: she was having enough difficulty coming to terms with her condition as it was. 'The only problem will be if we keep fighting over what is and isn't good for you,' he said. 'But we seem to have solved that—between the three of us—' His fingers stroked her cheek for a moment. 'Violet,' he went on, 'I know you thought I was being a tyrant, but I wasn't trying to take away your freedom. You did that yourself. When you came into my bed.' She gave a start of surprise. 'And, when I welcomed you, I surrendered mine.'

'I hadn't thought of it like that,' she said at last, in a subdued little voice.

'I don't consider that giving up my freedom has diminished me in any way at all,' he went on. 'If anything, it has made me stronger. Because there are two of us, joined in love. But,' and he looked deep into her eyes, 'if anything should happen to you, and I lose you, then I become weaker than I ever was before. And my life is no longer worth living. Do you understand?'

'Yes, yes,' and her voice was choked. *You are the wife of his heart.*

'So if I want to protect you, then surely that is my right? Especially now, when you are vulnerable. Can you understand that, too?' She nodded, her eyes spilling over with tears.

'Now,' he said gravely when he had comforted her, 'I'm playing truant and I really should get back. May I go?'

'Lost with a grief beyond the saltest tear'

'Malcolm, perhaps you and I should come to an understanding.'

'Oh, and what kind of an understanding do you have in mind?'

Three months after Violet's capitulation, Nicolson had no reason to feel wary, yet he looked down at her with a little frown. 'Well?' he repeated.

'Well,' said Violet, in a tone of amused exasperation, 'supposing we agree that I won't break into little pieces, even if you do treat me as a normal human being from time to time—what do you think?'

He gave a short laugh. 'Am I really as bad as all that?' he asked

'I'm afraid so.'

'Very well—I'll try,' and he followed her into the drawing room which now boasted several chairs, and where the night before they had entertained several of his junior officers—young men who had preferred to sprawl on the floor as usual, much to Violet's chagrin and her husband's amusement. A thought suddenly struck him. 'Why is it all right for young Jacob and Southey to fuss over you, and not me?'

Violet sat down carefully. 'Don't you see?' she asked, touching her visibly swollen waist. 'Now they think of me as your wife and the mother of your child—' for the first time she felt a glow of satisfaction at the idea—'and they'll never want to flirt with me again.'

'Perhaps you're right,' but he sounded doubtful. He sat down at her feet and looked up into her face. 'Have they been flirting with you, then?'

'You're not jealous of them, are you?' she asked. She was laughing at him. He didn't laugh back. 'No, of course they've not been flirting,' she said quickly. 'Don't be silly! They might have wanted to—in the beginning—but I soon put them in their place!'

He relaxed a little as her steady eyes met his.

'Don't ever doubt that I love you, Malcolm Nicolson,' she told him earnestly. 'I swear to you by our unborn child that nothing on this earth could hurt me more.'

The new regime he had imposed proved unexpectedly delightful. They rose early to drive to places she had never seen before, and she felt as close to him and as precious now as she had in the very early days before his work had claimed him back. He showed her the graves of General Napier's men where they lay buried row upon row among the red oleanders at Miani, and he told her how the British infantry had *stood thick as standing corn, and gorgeous as a field of flowers*, and how they had carried the day with glory.

Violet had read of the battle for Sind in one of his books and her husband's account failed to impress her. 'That's all very well', she retorted, 'but why must the British always be so greedy? Why can they never leave well alone?'

Colonel Nicolson kept quiet. There was a certain gleam in Violet's eye, and he knew from experience that when his wife went on a verbal rampage she required no answer.

'*A very advantageous, humane and useful piece of rascality*—that's what Napier called what he did,' she went on. 'He provoked the Sindis into a fight, so that he could beat them and steal their country. What was the point in getting even more desert for the Crown?'

'You love the desert,' Malcolm reminded her.

'Yes, but it doesn't make any difference to me if it's not part of the British Raj!'

'But this particular piece of desert is strategically important.'

Violet snorted. 'That's what they always say! It's just an excuse!'

'And Napier did do a lot of good, afterwards—' Nicolson ventured cautiously.

'The British always say that too! They marched into the Punjab as well, didn't they, because it was nearer Afghanistan, and then issued all kinds of self-righteous proclamations which they had no means of enforcing— *Thou shalt not burn widows*, for example, *nor kill thy baby daughters*. We all know how successful that's been!' Her face was flushed.

'You're enchanting, do you know that? All heart and feeling—I suppose you still want to hand over India for the Indians to govern for themselves?' He was teasing her and she rose to the bait.

'I most certainly do! The British have had it long enough!'

'You're British yourself, remember.'

'Yes, but I don't *feel* British. Do you?'

He had never given the matter any thought, and told her so.

'I mean, you've been here since you were sixteen, Malcolm; India's your home. And I feel as if I've never been anywhere else; I've been back here seven years and it's as if I've never been away. I belong here and so do you.' She looked at him approvingly. 'I don't think of you as British at all.'

'Perhaps that's just as well,' he said.

They often drove out to the north of the Old City. There, they wandered slowly hand in hand among the royal tombs and watched them turn to gold in the early morning sun.

'I love it here,' said Violet. 'It should be sad, but it isn't.' She touched the baking weathered brick and her fingers ran lightly over one of the kingfisher-blue tiles. 'They're so beautiful. Perhaps they built them for the living, not the dead.'

'Don't you think that's always the case?' Nicolson replied, suddenly sombre. 'Don't go to any such trouble for me!'

As time went by and September drew to a close Violet walked less, content as she grew more ungainly to sit and watch sunrise and sunset from the carriage. And Malcolm was glad. Violet six months pregnant, he noted with relief, was not as fiercely independent as she would have him believe—and he was, after all, allowed to fuss.

They were returning home one morning when she suddenly gripped his arm. She was deathly pale and there were pearls of sweat on her brow. 'Will you ask the *syce* to go a little faster?' she whispered.

'What is it?' he asked, and yet he knew.

'I began having pains just before we started back—I didn't say anything because I thought they would go away. They did when I had them once before. But this is worse.' She stifled a cry. 'Oh, Malcolm, hold me—it hurts, it hurts so much.'

She lost the baby and she very nearly lost her life. The regimental doctor told her husband to expect the worst, but he refused to listen. Major Dr Masani, who would never have admitted as much in public, was heard to say in private that the colonel's single-minded devotion had saved his wife.

'The man simply wouldn't let her go,' he said, shaking his head in disbelief. 'He sat with her through it all, day and night. He held on to her hand and forbade her to die. God knows how she heard him, but it worked—don't ask me how, but it worked!'

In the weeks that followed, Malcolm Nicolson came to feel that perhaps he had lost his wife after all. Physically she recovered, but she wandered aimlessly through the bungalow like some pale forlorn little ghost. He knew she was grieving, but then wasn't he? She hardly spoke during the day and when at night he reached out to comfort her she retreated from his touch. And he never saw her shed a single tear, which was perhaps what worried him most. Finally, at his wits' end, he wrote to Isabel in Karachi.

His sister-in-law replied immediately: 'Don't let her brood too long, or it will get to be a habit. Try shocking her out of it—what you say or do, I leave to your imagination. It may not work, but good luck anyway!'

It was precious little to go on in the way of advice. What could he say that would break through the hard shell she had built around herself? How could he cut her to the quick? He hated the very idea of being brutal, but faced with Violet's apathy he seemed to have no other choice. Malcolm Nicolson thought long and hard and one afternoon he steeled himself to confront his wife. 'Violet, my dear, I think you should go back to your parents.'

She looked at him with lack-lustre eyes from the chair where she was sitting, her book open but unread.

'You obviously don't want to be with me, so I'm sending you away.'

At this she got to her feet. 'But my place is with you,' she said in a dull voice.

'Is it,' Malcolm pursued relentlessly, 'is it really? My dear girl, you've done nothing but stare out of the window and sigh for the last five or six weeks— I thought perhaps you would prefer to go away.'

'No,' she whispered, as the words began to register. 'No. I want to be with you.' She got to her feet and moved a little towards him.

'Do you indeed?' The colonel gave a harsh travesty of a laugh. 'Then all I can say, Violet, is that you have a very strange way of showing it!' He forced his eyes to be hard and unfeeling, but still she did not break.

And then the words came of their own accord, from his very heart. 'I've needed you, Violet Nicolson, and where have you been? The child had two parents, after all, not one! I've been grieving as well as you, and you've been too wrapped up in yourself to notice—or to care.' His voice broke a little but he managed to finish. 'No wonder I think you can't love me any more!'

The last words pierced the icy barrier of indifference, and Violet stared at him in horror as the enormity of what he was saying sank in.

'That's not true, you know that's not true! Oh, dear God, what have I done?'

She fell to her knees and hid her face in her hands. Then to his great relief he heard the racking sobs as the healing tears began to fall, but still he did not move, hardly daring to believe it could be over. At last she raised her ravaged face and held out an uncertain hand. 'Forgive me, please forgive me—' Then she was in his arms, crying, pleading …

'Hush, hush, dearest. Of course I shan't send you away. And of course I know you love me!'

It was over. She had come back to him. Later, in November, they went away for ten days and by the time they returned all wounds appeared to be healed.

'Intriguing danger, as in days gone by'

One morning in mid-December Violet tackled her husband on a subject that had long perplexed her. 'Who is Mahomed Akram really—some kind of a spy?' She asked the question in all seriousness. Nicolson put down his cup and considered her for a moment before answering. 'What makes you ask that, all of a sudden?' he enquired.

'Well, he comes and goes all the time, disappears for weeks on end, and when he turns up again you both go into some mysterious kind of a huddle—for hours sometimes.'

Only yesterday, for example, the Afghan had loomed up from behind one of the Talpur tombs to give her the fright of her life. Wandering off on her own, she had watched the two of them from a distance, their heads bowed together in earnest conversation.

'He's no more of a spy than I am!' came the unsatisfying answer.

'And that's meant to reassure me, I suppose? I have my suspicions about you too, Malcolm Nicolson!' So saying, Violet got up from the table, lightly dropping a kiss on her husband's head as she passed his chair. He caught her hand, to release it as suddenly without speaking.

That night at supper they were joined by two senior officers from the regiment. In deference to their hostess the talk during the meal ranged over general topics, but when the plates were cleared Violet rose as usual to leave the men to their talk. This evening, however, Malcolm added his voice to the polite protests of their guests.

'No, darling—stay. Though perhaps we'd all be more comfortable next door.' He turned to his colleagues: 'My wife has bullied me into getting more chairs—and she positively insists that you use them!'

Violet laughed in protest, but her two guests needed no persuasion. 'This is absolute bliss, Mrs Nicolson,' said Major Simpson. 'You've no idea how much this man has made us suffer over the years, isn't that so, Sievwright?' The captain agreed, and he too settled back in unaccustomed comfort. They drank their coffee and sipped their brandy and Violet, sitting back a little from the group, watched them: the thickset Simpson, with his bluff weather-beaten features, Sievwright looking like a younger version of his commandant, and the colonel himself, face half in shadow, listening to the light-hearted conversation while his long fingers played with the stem of his glass. He seemed to have forgotten she was there.

Yet, as she made a move to leave he put out a hand and detained her. 'No, darling, don't go,' he said. It would be as good a way as any of her learning what was afoot over the border, after all, and moving his chair a little nearer hers, Nicolson began to talk of the legendary Robert Sandeman and his work in Baluchistan.

Since her marriage Sir Robert's name had cropped up often enough amid talk of his work among the hostile southern tribes. He must, thought Violet, be an amazing man, a mixture of her father's aggressiveness and a very real amiability—for was his method of peaceful conquest not known as the *Forward Policy*? And his method worked. In the last fifteen years amazing progress had been made with very little loss of life. Sandeman had tamed the slippery Khan of Khelat and brought peace between him and his followers, and established the Agency of Baluchistan where he now ruled—or so it seemed to Violet—like some tribal chief himself.

She followed the present discussion intently, and gradually realisation dawned as to why her husband had wanted her to stay. Robert Sandeman's attention had turned to the north of Baluchistan, a place of mountains, rivers, narrow passes and hostile tribesmen. His affable approach had been successful—so much so that the year before, the chieftains of the Zhob valley had begged him to take their land under Government protection. Never one to let such an opportunity pass him by, Sir Robert had decided to take the matter in hand.

'It would be a dashed clever move,' Major Simpson was saying. 'Don't you think so, Nick?'

'Oh, certainly,' replied the colonel. 'Sandeman's nobody's fool. He went up and saw for himself: control of Zhob would give us control of the western entrance of the Gomal Pass—and we all know what that means—'

'*I* don't,' Violet pointed out. If she was to stay, then she would take part—whether they liked it or not.

Her husband turned, smiled, and took her hand. 'No, I don't suppose you do; I'll explain. The Gomal Pass is where two important routes from Afghanistan converge, one from Kabul and north and east Afghanistan, one from the west and Kandahar. Do you see?' She nodded. 'Now,' the pleasant voice continued, 'every year at the start of the cold weather, caravans move through the pass down onto the plains of India, bringing things like dried fruits, indigo, copper, piece goods, and so on—and every year those caravans are attacked. Control of the pass would put an end to all that; do you understand?'

Violet was not her father's daughter for nothing. 'Oh, yes,' she said immediately, 'I understand perfectly. But protecting the caravans is only a part of it, isn't it? It would also give the army a whole new route into Afghanistan—just think of the time you would save if you were ever silly enough to go back to war with the Amir!'

There was a surprised silence and then Nicolson laughed out loud. 'You must forgive my wife's cynicism, gentlemen—but *entre nous* I think we can agree that she's almost certainly right; the Government of India is hardly renowned for its disinterested behaviour, after all!'

Later, in their room, the conversation continued. 'Does all this mean what I think it does?' Violet asked. She was sitting brushing her hair while her husband watched her from the bed.

'And what do you think it means, now that you've become such a strategist?

No, I'm not teasing you. Tell me, I want to know.'

She turned from the mirror to watch his reaction. 'Well, no matter how marvellous Sir Robert is, he can't do all this on his own, can he? If Zhob does become a protectorate, then there will have to be new army posts, won't there?' He nodded. 'And there could still be trouble—not everyone may want to be protected after all—' He nodded again. 'So where does that leave us? Or more precisely, you and your regiment?'

'I really don't know, darling, we'll just have to wait and see.'

She got into bed, and sat there, still thinking.

'Sweetheart, there really isn't any point in worrying about it,' he told her. 'I just wanted you to be prepared, that's all.'

'Prepared for what?' her voice was sharp.

'For a period of separation—if it ever comes.' He pulled her down beside him. 'Violet, I've been asked to go down to Karachi—to meet Sandeman. He's an old acquaintance from the war and my Quetta days; we'll have a lot to talk about.'

'I'm sure you will.'

'Why don't you come, too? It would be a chance for you to see your family before Christmas.' He paused.' And I want you to see another doctor.' He felt her stiffen.

'Why? Major Masani said it was most unlikely I would have another child, and I believe him!'

'Darling, he might be wrong. Surely it wouldn't hurt to see someone else?'

'It might—what if someone else said it *was* perfectly possible, and we waited and we hoped, and nothing happened? No, Malcolm, it's over. At first I didn't want the baby, and now I'm being punished— I refuse to think about it any more.'

He got out of bed and lit the lamp. 'Now, just you listen to me, Violet Nicolson,' and his voice was very stern. 'We went into all this before, when we were away. I thought I'd got this nonsense out of your head. Look at me!'

She raised her head and her eyes were clouded. 'I feel I've let you down,' was all she said.

He came back and sat beside her. 'How often do I have to tell you that it doesn't matter? I nearly lost you. I thought you were going to die and take all the love and laughter with you—and I knew I wouldn't want to live on alone. I need you, Violet, my dearest wife—and you are *all* I need. Will I ever make you understand?'

3

'I hear the sound of War'

MAY 1890–DECEMBER 1890

Colonel Nicolson stood in the bedroom doorway and eyed his wife in silent amazement. 'Violet Nicolson, what on earth have you clarted over your face?' he asked at last, in a voice where amusement mingled with more than a little distaste.

'*Clarted*—What a wonderfully primitive-sounding word, Malcolm!' she replied, a smile of welcome splitting the greenish mess that totally masked her face. 'I didn't realise you still clung to your Highland roots.'

'What is it?' he repeated. 'It looks disgusting!'

'It probably is.' Violet's voice was complacent. 'It comes from the native bazaar and it promises eternal youth.' She wiped the ointment off and leaned forward to squint at her complexion. 'Hmm, I think I was cheated. I look just the same.'

'You'll never grow old, my darling.' They had been married over a year and to the colonel's admiring eyes his wife if anything looked younger.

'Never grow up, you mean!' she retorted.

'That too, I hope.' Malcolm came over to where she still sat frowning into the mirror, and bent over her. He wrinkled his aquiline nose. 'You certainly smell different,' he remarked, for a strange musky scent lingered on her skin.

'It must be this. It's something else I found in the bazaar.' Violet picked up a jar, opened it and held it out. 'Don't you like it? It makes me feel quite *Eastern*.' The midnight eyes glinted at him in the glass before she turned and put her arms around him. 'What do you think, Malcolm?' Her robe slipped from one shoulder showing more than a little of a perfectly rounded breast.

'I think you as tempting as any houri from Paradise—I also think we should get ready for our guests,' and he smilingly disengaged himself. 'I hope you can get the names right this time!' he added, as Violet pulled a face, for while his wife had a remarkable facility for remembering her servants' names and the names of their families (down to the fifth or sixth generation), she could only ever refer to her European acquaintances in Hyderabad as *Mrs Assistant Sessions Judge*, or *Mrs Deputy Collector*—or whatever the lady's civil status required. Violet responded with a laugh. 'I'll try,' she promised, and with that Malcolm had to be content.

'How often do you go to the native bazaar?' he asked casually while they were dressing.

'Quite often. Don't worry, it's perfectly safe.' He was sure it was. Not, as Violet thought, because she went disguised in native clothes and her Urdu was fluent, but because she was the British commandant's wife. 'Nobody can tell I'm European,' she went on airily, and he didn't like to disabuse her. Besides, such sorties gave her something to do.

'And what does Mrs Chief Surveyor of Hyderabad's Canals and Waterways think of your exploits, do you think?'

Violet giggled and pulled another face. 'Is there one?'

'Probably. Darling, I know you don't ever worry about what people think, but shouldn't you care just a little?'

'Why?' He was fastening her dress and, although he couldn't see her face, that one word and the way she said it should have spelled a warning.

'Well, it's a small community and you women should stick together—for mutual support.'

The moment he finished Violet spun round. 'Like in the army, you mean? All thinking the same regimented thoughts, doing the same things, at the same time? Perhaps we should all wear uniforms?' Her mouth was set in a grim line. 'Malcolm, I don't like them, or their values. You know that'—he did—'I'm quite prepared to feed them, and be pleasant as required, but don't ask me to be friends. Perhaps it's a pity there aren't any army wives here, we might have more in common'—from her expression she obviously doubted it—'but you've indoctrinated your officers too well for any of them to want to marry.' She made an apologetic little gesture. 'Darling, these women all think I'm an eccentric—but after everything you've said in the past, do you really want me to change?'

Nicolson felt no need to answer. During dinner he had plenty of opportunity to observe his wife and she was everything she promised. She listened attentively, asked the right questions, remembered names ... But as she encouraged her guests to talk, he noted how from time to time her own opinions crept insidiously into the conversation, seemingly innocuous but covertly outrageous, so that their guests were bound to ask later whether little Mrs Nicolson had really said what she had, and if so, had she meant it? He watched the light of devilment dancing in her eyes, and once or twice he shook his head, warning her to stop.

'You're quite wicked, Violet Nicolson,' he told her, when the last visitors had taken their leave and they were getting ready for bed. Violet gave him a broad smile. 'I know.'

'And I'm probably the envy of every man in this town as a result.' He watched as she removed the last of the pins from her hair and peered at her face in the glass. 'Darling, I've been thinking—'

'Oh?'

'Of course I don't want you to change. I like you the way you are. Loving, witty, charming, beautiful—'

Violet preened herself and reached for the native unguent.

'—even if you do smell like a woman of the streets!'

She threw the heavy jar at his head, he dodged, and they both broke into laughter.

His wife's visits to the Old City were the least of Colonel Nicolson's worries. Several times over the past year he had been called away to Karachi and had chosen to leave Violet behind. In his absence she had continued her early morning rides out to the Talpur tombs, but with one of his young subalterns instead of the groom. She found young Charles Price endearing; he was a probationer with the regiment and he was also, she reflected wryly, probably the only one of the younger officers who had never regarded their colonel's wife as an object of lust. It was better now, she conceded, but with none of them could she have enjoyed anything approaching the friendship she had with this boy; he was a few years younger, and treated her very much as an older sister and confidante.

Her husband tolerated the relationship and it wasn't that that worried him. Rather, it was a certain restlessness about her ever since the loss of their child, and which manifested itself in the reckless way she rode. He sympathised with her need to get out and away from the cantonment, and hours spent among the native shops of Old Hyderabad seemed preferable to the risk of her breaking her neck. He tried not to check her, but at times concern got the better of him and he attempted to issue a stern rebuke.

'Come with me more often then,' she countered one day.

'You know that's not always possible.' And could he control her if he did?

'You don't mind me going with Charles then?'

'Of course not. But—' and the steely eyes fixed her until she squirmed a little uncomfortably, 'I don't think you should challenge young Price to any more races. You put the lad in an intolerable position—he can hardly refuse, after all.'

Violet reflected. Malcolm was right, of course. But she was reluctant to give up her fun.

'How do you think he'd feel if he had to tell me you'd broken your neck?'

Nicolson persisted. 'Besides,' he continued, smiling now, 'I believe you usually win—I really can't have my junior officers demoralised in this way!'

'If I agree—' she began, but the expression on her husband's face recalled the arguments they had had the year before and she swallowed. 'Very well, Malcolm,' she said instead, 'I promise to be more careful.'

'Good girl,' and he gave her a little hug.

'Darling,' Violet slipped her arm in his and looked up at him lovingly. 'Darling, why don't I come with you when you go to Karachi next week? It would be nice to see the family again.' There was something in her voice that made him suspicious, and something about her disarming smile. 'You are going next week, aren't you?' she went on.

'Yes—'

'So I can come with you?'

'Violet, this sudden desire to be reunited with your loved ones does you credit, I'm sure, but,' and the look he sent her was quizzical, 'there's more to it than that, I suspect.'

She nodded her head and her eyes began to shine. 'It's not just Karachi, is it? You're going off somewhere secret. Perhaps to see Sir Robert Sandeman?'

Nicolson gave a start. 'How on earth did you know?'

'I didn't. I guessed. When I found your Afghan clothes in that shocking old portmanteau you insist on taking every time.' She often slipped in a note or a verse for him to find, and once she had come upon the garments. 'Let me come with you, Malcolm. Please. I could be your brother.'

He shook his head.

'Your son?'

'No, Violet.'

'Your lover?' This with an irrepressible twinkle. He laughed.

'Certainly not! I'm sorry, darling, but like oil and water, business and pleasure simply do not mix.'

There was no point in arguing when he spoke like that, so she reluctantly abandoned the idea. How lucky he was, to be able to slough off one identity and assume another so easily. To throw off the shackles of convention, and for days or weeks at a time.

He surprised the wistful look in her eyes. 'It isn't all fun, you know. It does have a serious purpose.'

'The invasion of Zhob?'

'I don't think Sandeman would approve of the word *invasion*, but yes, darling, you're right.' He decided he owed her an explanation. 'You know there was a durbar in Apozai to proclaim the Protectorate? And that the whole valley was included in the arrangement?'

'Yes, just after last Christmas. And then Sir Robert rode through the Gomal Pass, despite warnings of possible ambush. And got to the other end in one piece. He must have been relieved about that—personally, I thought it very foolhardy.' She glanced at her husband impishly before adding: 'Much more foolhardy than racing Charles Price!'

'Sandeman had an escort of six hundred tribesmen which probably helped,' Nicolson commented dryly.

'And now he holds the key to Afghanistan!'

There was a slightly mocking edge to her voice, but Nicolson let it go. 'Anyway, Violet,' he continued, 'there's a lot of work to be done, raising tribal levies to protect communications and so forth, and I've been involved in that. It's all going pretty well so far.'

'So far?' Her voice was sharp.

Lord, what a talent his wife had for seizing on a seemingly innocent phrase and worrying at it like a dog with a rat. 'Well, as you said before, darling, not everyone wants Her Majesty's protection. Trouble is brewing, I'm afraid.'

'And you're to be part of the brew.' Her eyes were as bright and alert as a terrier's.

'Probably.' The colonel didn't seem at all put out at the thought and later set off for his train in the best of good spirits. Overcoming her resentment—and an urge to challenge Lieutenant Price to the longest race of his young life—Mrs Nicolson invited Major Simpson to afternoon tea and charmed him into telling her all he knew about Northern Baluchistan in general, and the mysterious valley of the River Zhob in particular.

'The train that will bear me from you'

As Violet Nicolson had predicted, not all those newly gathered under the motherly wing of the Queen-Empress wished for her protection. Kakar bandits to the west of Baluchistan, and disgruntled Shirani tribesmen to the east continued to wreak havoc in the region. Thus Sir Robert Sandeman, KCSI, Governor-General's Agent and Chief Commissioner in Baluchistan, determined in his wisdom that those responsible for such breaches of the peace should be brought to heel forthwith.

In August 1890 in its summer capital of Simla, the Government of India came to a decision: a punitive force was to be sent to Zhob under Major-General Sir George White, KCB, VC. And—her husband told Violet with some trepidation—the second in command was to be Colonel Malcolm Hassells Nicolson.

Violet's reaction to his news took the colonel by surprise. 'Well,' he said, as she hugged him, 'I thought there would be wailing and gnashing of teeth, instead of which you treat me as if I were a conquering hero!'

'I'm sorry, darling. Break the news to me again and I promise to be more Biblical, if that's what you'd prefer?'

Nicolson grinned and shook his head. He was relieved when his wife continued, 'I'm so proud of you, Malcolm. It's wonderful news.'

'I thought you didn't approve of British imperialism, Mrs Nicolson?'

'I don't! But this is different, don't you see, because it's you?'

Her husband didn't see at all, but was happy she was taking it all so well. 'I'll be away for quite a while—you do understand?'

Violet nodded.

'And we'll be leaving soon—'

She hadn't expected this. 'How soon?' Her voice was a mere whisper.

'In four weeks.'

She bit her lip. 'And how long will you be gone?'

'I really have no idea; weeks, maybe months, who knows? If Chief Dost Mahomed gives himself up fairly soon, as Sandeman hopes, the first phase could be over very quickly; if not, it could take all winter.' There was no point in sparing her the worst, he thought, as he went on: 'And if the Shiranis hole up in their mountains, the same thing applies. I'm sorry, that's all I can tell you. What, still no gnashing of teeth?'

'What would be the point?' she asked him. 'It doesn't make any difference what I feel—and it would upset you if I made a fuss.' She shrugged and tried to smile. 'I'll manage!'

She wasn't sure how, but she would worry about that later, when she had to—and not before.

A few days before he was due to leave, Malcolm joined his wife in the garden. 'What will you do while I'm away?' he asked

'Oh, much the same as usual, I suppose. I shall bully the *mali* into doing something with this desert,' and she pointed to the dust bowls that passed for garden beds. 'He's so hopelessly lazy! Do you think I have any chance of success?'

Malcolm looked at her tenderly. 'Darling girl, I'm sure you could do anything you set your heart on.'

'And then I thought I might go to Karachi—but I shall have to wait, shan't I, to see how things go? Malcolm, you will write to me? Then I shan't feel quite so lonely—' Her lip trembled a little as she spoke.

'Of course I will,' he assured her, 'there'll be some postal system or other, there always is. And you must write to me—do you promise?' He knew from

Isabel's complaints that Violet was a dreadful correspondent.

'I promise,' said his wife solemnly.

And so Saturday 28 September, the day of parting, dawned.

'I don't want you to come to Kotri, Violet. We'll say our goodbyes here—it will be better.'

'Better for you, perhaps, but not for me!'

Her husband found himself giving way. 'Very well. But I don't want any tears at the station.' He felt he was making a mistake, but the smile she gave him seemed worth it. He put his arms around her. 'I'm going to miss you, darling.'

'I don't believe that for a minute,' she replied wistfully. 'I've been watching you—you can hardly wait to go! But I don't blame you,' she added immediately, 'I'm sure I would be the same. Perhaps I should have been a man.'

'Absolutely not!' replied Malcolm, kissing her again and again.

Kotri railway station that evening was abuzz: native officers were purposefully supervising the loading of the *matériel* and five hundred and fifty *sepoys* in their green and scarlet uniforms swarmed everywhere. I'm by no means the only one feeling miserable, thought Violet Nicolson; little groups of soldiers, wives and children stood huddled together, taking advantage of the last minutes to say their farewells. When her own husband left her for a moment she felt the crowd pressing in on her, stifling her, and then he was back. He led her to the train.

'Come inside for a moment—you'll be better out of the crush.' So she climbed in behind him. 'That's better,' she said, as she leaned against the door. 'I thought I'd lost you!'

If only this moment could last for ever, she thought. If only she didn't have to say goodbye.

'You can't stay long,' Nicolson warned; they could both hear the engine getting up steam. 'You'll be all right?' This for the umpteenth time.

'Of course.'

The engine whistled again. 'Darling, you must go.' He bent and kissed her fiercely. 'Now, go!' and he pushed her gently towards the steps.

'Damn!' she exclaimed, as she started to move, 'my sleeve is caught.' She felt the train give a little lurch and she plucked at the offending braid with anxious fingers. Which only seemed to make matters worse.

'Let me,' said her husband, who could sense her beginning to panic, but his attempts to free her were no more successful than hers. 'I'm afraid it's well and truly caught in the latch—I'm sorry, darling, you'll have to take off your jacket and get out quick—the train's beginning to move—'

'I'm wearing a dress,' she pointed out.

'Ah,' he replied, and tried again. By the time he had freed her it was too late.

The train was gathering speed and he would not let her jump. 'I knew you should have stayed at home,' he said with a rueful shake of the head. Violet smiled back, feeling no such regret at all.

⁂

He put her into an empty compartment at the far end of the carriage. 'Stay there,' he told her, 'I'll have to tell the others what's happened or they'll think I've done it on purpose—Don't go away, Violet, don't even move!'

Violet smiled happily: there was, after all, nowhere to go. When the colonel returned he looked happier. 'They all think it's a great joke,' he said. 'Pulled my leg, of course, but laughing at me has helped.' The younger men were nervous, he explained. 'Now,' he went on, 'there's the problem of what to do with you. The train will stop for refuelling, but I don't want you hanging around in the middle of the night waiting for the next passenger train to come along.'

'I can look after myself.'

'I know, but I should worry—so you must let me be selfish! No, I've decided, you'll have to come on with us to Harnai, and go back down with the train.'

'When do we get there?'

'Tomorrow afternoon—and then we shall really have to say goodbye!' He looked at her sharply. 'You're enjoying this, aren't you?'

'Yes,' she assented readily, 'so why don't you relax and enjoy it too?'

'Later,' he promised. 'There's too much to do at the moment,' and once more he left her to her own devices.

Before long the colonel's wife had a visitor. 'Welcome aboard, Mrs Nicolson!' Violet looked up; it was Lieutenant Price.

'May I join you?'

'Of course. Sit down, Charles.'

The lad sat down opposite her. 'Beastly bad luck for you—being stuck on the train like this,' he said.

'I'm leaving you at Harnai.'

'Yes, Colonel Nicolson told us.' He fell silent, his fingers twisting nervously.

'Is it the first time you've been involved in something like this, Charles?'

He nodded.

'You must be scared, then.'

He looked at her but said nothing.

'I know *I* would be,' she continued. 'It would be silly if you weren't, the first time, don't you think?'

The boy looked at her in surprise.

'Once you know how you're going to react, it must be so much easier—and if you're frightened, you won't take silly risks, and then you won't put other people's lives in danger as well as your own. And I'm sure no one is scared for long—' After a moment he managed a smile.

'Thank you, Mrs Nicolson. It was just that Jacob and the others seem so confident.'

'Don't you believe it! They're just better at hiding their feelings!'

He stayed talking for a while and then the colonel returned. 'Off with you, young Price,' he scolded, 'I want my wife to myself!'

The lieutenant grinned and went back to his peers, feeling a great deal happier.

'What was all that about? I came back earlier, but you were deep in conversation.'

'He's nervous like the rest of them, but he won't admit it to anyone.'

'To anyone except *you*. Well, he looks all right now, but I'll have a word to make sure. Don't worry, sweetheart, I won't let on you told me,' and Nicolson changed the subject. 'I suppose you're hungry—you usually are! Here, I've brought you something,' and while she ate he told her what he had arranged: 'Mahomed Akram will take you back from Harnai. Oh, yes,' he told her, 'he's here; I've just been talking to him. In fact, he thought you should stay!'

Nicolson laughed at the very idea but Violet didn't join in. 'In his tribe the women all fight alongside the men, and he seemed to think you should do the same. He was quite disappointed when I told him you were going back to Hyderabad.'

Violet looked at her husband with quickening interest. 'Was he indeed?' she murmured. She and the Afghan had come to a civil understanding over the past year, and she was interested to hear of him taking her side. She bent her head and, while appearing to concentrate on her chicken wing, thought long and hard about what she had just learned. Later, when Major Simpson and Captain Sievwright joined them she listened with interest to their plans. The regiment would march out from Harnai immediately and would join forces with the rest of the expedition outside the town. The Field Force would set off as soon as possible after that. The going would rough and hostile, and in places they would have to make their own roads through the mountain passes. As she looked at the three of them, Violet saw how they all relished the prospect; whatever the junior officers were thinking, these men were ready for the worst.

Next morning she woke to the hills beyond Sibi rearing into the eerie light of dawn. She held her breath as the train plunged into sheer-sided defiles perhaps a thousand feet in height, to debouch onto desolate plains where there were boulders and gravel in abundance, but where trees and shrubs were rare. A solitary horseman appeared from time to time, as if etched on the horizon; others stopped by the track to stare at the belching monster as it thundered past.

'How does anyone manage to live here?' she asked.

'With difficulty. But you'll see that Harnai is very different.'

And so, after mile after mile of flat monotony, they reached an open valley. Green irrigated fields stretched out around them; vine-festooned willows grew by the watercourses; children played beside the flat-topped houses. Harnai itself was little more than a busy village, where women clad in loose indigo-blue tunics and trousers raised excited unveiled faces as they watched the train pull in and shudder to a stop.

'This really is goodbye, you know. I have to go.'

Husband and wife looked at one another, with so many words left unspoken.

'No,' said Malcolm, gripping her shoulders, 'you mustn't cry. Goodbye, my dearest little wife,' said the colonel, and drawing her close he kissed her eyes and then her lips.

'I love you,' she whispered back, and from the carriage window watched him walk away. He did not look back.

Suddenly an unearthly screeching rent the noonday air as the pipers of the 3rd Baluchis prepared to lead the regiment out to camp. Violet Nicolson walked from the station to watch her husband ride off at the head of his men and stayed looking long after he was out of sight.

'*Nikelseyn mem?*' It was the Afghan. 'The train will be leaving soon.'

At the sight of her husband's friend Violet's forlorn expression slowly changed and the idea that the colonel had unwittingly planted the night before, and which had been growing ever since, came to fruition. Mrs Nicolson made up her mind. 'I'm not going back. Please don't try and persuade me. I can't go back, Mahomed Akram. Not now.'

The man's savagely scarred face showed no surprise, but the look he gave her seemed to search her very soul. The pipes were no more than a distant mournful wail and the drums had faded away to nothing when finally he spoke.

'My people believe that all that happens is God's will. You were meant to follow the colonel *sahib*, for so it is written—here,' and he touched her forehead lightly. 'That is your *kismet*, your fate, to go wherever he leads.'

Violet found herself shivering, although she wasn't cold. 'Will you come with me, Mahomed Akram?' she asked.

'It is written,' he said again, a grave smile upon his face, and she remembered that she owed this man her life.

'Hither and thither, in search of love'

'It's all right, Juma Khan, I'll finish off. You can go.' Malcolm Nicolson's feelings, as he dismissed his orderly, were almost as bleak as the *sepoy*'s face. We're both homesick, he thought, and the feeling for him, at least, was an unusual one. Eighteen months spent day and night in the company of an irreverent blue-eyed hoyden had changed him beyond recall, and if Violet were here, he supposed, she would point out that it was surely a change for the better!

He rummaged around in his kit for the things he needed for the night and his questing fingers came across a folded paper. His face lightened into a smile. So she hadn't forgotten. He struggled with his boots, then brought the lamp nearer to see that she had covered one page in her bold generous hand. The colonel settled down on his camp bed to read.

As he did so, his mind was taken back to that night a year and a half before when they lay together under a purple sky, listening to a lover's lament—she captivated by the music, and he by the face increasingly denied him by the capricious flames of the dying fire.

Yet it wasn't Mahomed Akram's voice that he was hearing, but the curiously husky yet melodious tones of the girl who, even now, was being carried further and further away:

I would have taken Golden Stars from the sky for your necklace,
I would have shaken rose-leaves for your rest from all the rose-trees.

But you had no need; the short sweet grass sufficed for your slumber
And you took no heed of such trifles as gold or a necklace.

There is an hour, at twilight, too heavy with memory
There is a flower that I fear, for your hair had its fragrance —

Oh, Violet, Violet. Malcolm Nicolson lay back on the bed and closed his eyes. He was human, after all, and he was paying the price in full. It was some time before he could bring himself to read to the end:

I would have squandered Youth for you, and its hope and its promise
Before you wandered, careless, away from my useless passion.

But what is the use of my speech, since I know of no words to recall you?
I am praying that Time may teach, you, your Cruelty, me, Forgetfulness.

Underneath she had written: *What are the stars, now you have gone? Remember me*! How could he forget? He recalled the brave little face raised to his as they said goodbye earlier that day; Violet gallantly striving to control the tears brimming up in her glorious eyes; biting her lip, then summoning the faintest of smiles. His golden girl … But she was safe, safely on her way back to Hyderabad where she would patiently await his return. He closed his eyes and at last he fell into a deep sleep.

The colonel would have slept less soundly had he known the truth. His wife too was sleeping, but curled up on sheepskins hardly two miles away.

The next day the regiment completed its preparations on the outskirts of Harnai. Violet Nicolson, for her part, was in the small back room of a mudbrick house in the centre of town, where, with the utmost patience, Mahomed Akram was showing her how to wind and rewind a length of white cloth into a substantial turban, while a pretty soft-eyed woman looked on and laughed.

'No, no, it must be secure. *Thus*. And you wear it so, to protect you when the dust storms blow,' and he showed her, so that all but her eyes was masked. These were dancing with mirth. Both the Afghan and the woman (whom he had introduced simply as 'a friend') shook their heads at her, for he continued with a warning. 'You must never speak if anyone can hear—they will know you are not what you seem,' he instructed. 'Never look at anyone eye to eye'—for he well knew the frankness of her gaze—'blue eyes are not unknown, but eyes like yours are rare.' Violet nodded, serious now, for she was beginning to understand the importance of the masquerade.

'I shall tell everyone that you are ill—*here*,' and the Afghan tapped his head. 'People will respect you, and leave you alone, for that is our way. I shall say you are my son.'

Violet nodded again and looked down at her disguise in approval. The tunic and trousers were those of an Afghan boy, and fitted her—in so far as anything so loose and baggy (and comfortable)—could be said to fit. She smiled in contentment. She would follow, she assured her husband's trusted friend, she would keep up. She would remember everything he told her.

'It will be difficult,' Mahomed Akram warned her. 'I understand,' she said.

She also understood that Malcolm Nicolson would be furious when he found out what she had done—but, she told herself, stifling a slight qualm, she would worry about that later.

For three days and nights Violet Nicolson followed her husband. Wakeful nights on inhospitable ground as she tried in vain to sleep, counting the brilliant stars until fatigue at last overcame her; days of discovery as the flat terrain of the Harnai valley gave way to slopes and sparser vegetation. They met few travellers, and when they did, the man and boy on their sturdy Baluchi mares, with the camel following behind, raised only a passing interest.

At first Violet and the camel had eyed each other warily, and the long serpentine neck would arch as it snorted in disdain, but they were thrown together, like it or not, whenever Mahomed Akram stopped to say his prayers. Then Violet would take the nose string, give a little tug, and she and the beast would move away. In time she reached a guarded understanding with the great supercilious creature—as she seemed to have done with Malcolm's Afghan friend. And the days were spent in a companionable silence, broken only by the gentle tinkling of the camel bell as the dromedary padded staunchly behind them over unmade sandy tracks, and through the dust and the hot dry wind that never seemed to die away.

On the third day they came to the head of the Zhob valley. In a village on the way the Afghan learned that the expeditionary force had divided into three, and that the second column was under Nicolson's command. On the fourth day Violet had her first sight of her husband. They had been climbing noticeably for hours, and from high above a ruined hamlet Violet looked down on the last of his column trailing snake-like into camp. Malcolm was easy to spot, and the young woman's heart leapt as she saw him emerge from a group of men; someone a head or so shorter was with him. '*Sinjeman sahib*,' said the Afghan in a voice of some awe, but Violet's eyes were only for the man she loved.

'Should we go down now?' she asked.

What he replied she never knew for, to a chorus of blood-curdling yells, a terrifying horde of tribesmen intent on murder came pouring through the valley. In lines of six or so, firing volleys of shots from antique *jezails*, they swooped down on the camp, their shields of horn and vicious *tulwars* flashing in the sunshine.

Violet would have gone to Nicolson then, if only to share his fate, but the Afghan gripped her arm and stopped her. 'Wait!' he said with a grin, sitting back in his saddle to watch as the tribesmen rode into camp unchallenged, and hurled themselves from their wiry-looking mounts. They thronged round the political agent and the colonel until both men were lost from view.

'They are here to pay their respects *to Sinjeman sahib*,' explained Mahomed Akram, and Violet no longer held her breath. As she watched, a semblance of order was restored among the gesticulating crowd below, and Sandeman strode back to his durbar tent to receive his guests. It was hardly, realised Mrs Nicolson, the moment to make her presence known.

The chance was lost, the column moved off, and they followed in its wake. They headed north-east into the very heart of Zhob where the nights became bitter. Hugging her sheepskin coat about her, the young woman slept fitfully in the cold, and woke to mornings crisp with frost, when the hills stood out in harsh and glassy silhouette against the brilliant ice-blue sky.

The column filed through the pass leading down to the Khaisor plain, and they followed in its wake. The rocks rose sheer to either side, channelling the cruel blast that beat about her head, and her ears rang with the pain. Turban and *push-teen* offered scant protection now, from a wind intent on paring her skin in strips down to the very bone.

The track grew narrower as they came on through the pass, and increasingly precipitous. To look down made her giddy, and she could hardly bring herself to trust the stouthearted Baluch mare. At last they were forced to dismount. The Afghan went first. The horses next. Then came Violet leading the camel.

How it could have happened she did not know. There was a flurry of stones, then the camel baulked and kicked out in all directions, forcing her back against the rock. The rope was dragged out of her desperately clinging hands, and the beast was gone. A series of crashing sounds marked its progress down the cliff, and, after a moment's silence, came the screams: first one then another and another—ear rending, heartbreaking. Fists in her ears, Violet tried to block them out to no avail.

The Afghan was with her in seconds. There was no need to explain: her agonised face, and the sounds—piercing still despite the frenzy of the wind—told him everything. Wordlessly, he handed her the horses' reins and slipped over the cliff-side, disappearing from view even before she thought of telling him to stay. After an eternity, the screams were cut off as suddenly as they began. And then passed two eternities more. Unnerved, first by the screams and then the silence, Violet Nicolson waited, full of fear for her companion. Just when she had given him up for lost—this man for whom she suddenly found she cared—Mahomed Akram reappeared as silently as he had gone, looking none the worse for wear. And with him, the saddlebags. Sobbing with relief, she took them from him and watched him scramble back to safety.

'Come,' was all he said. She followed as before, and as she trudged along behind him she sent a grateful prayer to whatever power had saved his life.

From time to time, Mahomed Akram looked back at the slight figure, beaten and buffeted by the gusting wind. More than once they were forced to shelter against the flanks of the patient beasts, and as he became aware of the girl's failing reserves of strength, he became increasingly worried. 'We must go on, *Nikelseyn mem*,' he urged her. 'It will be better in the valley—there we will camp, and you can rest.'

At last they reached the valley floor. Down by the river Mahomed Akram helped his charge dismount and set about patiently rubbing her frozen hands and face. Feeling returned, bringing with it excruciating pain and tears to her eyes, and the weals raised by the camel's rope began to smart. Violet Nicolson forced a smile of thanks to her wind-cracked lips, then: 'I think it's time to surrender,' she said. 'I don't imagine Malcolm will send us back, do you?'

'Cold steel is very cooling to the fervour'

Sixteen miles down river, Sir George White and his headquarters' force rejoined Sir Robert Sandeman and the second column, and brought the mail with them. Malcolm Nicolson opened a letter from his wife but frowned when he saw it had been posted from Hyderabad the day before he left. It was the only one. The fervent declarations of love and devotion did little to dispel his disappointment, and it was a quiet man who joined his colleagues for the evening meal.

Sir Robert sensed the younger man's preoccupation. 'Not bad news from home, I hope, Nick?'

'No news at all, really, Sandey,' the colonel replied despondently, 'but I suppose it's difficult to get the letters through.'

Sandeman, who was responsible for the system and saw to it that it worked—and worked extremely well, at that—said nothing and the talk soon turned to Dost Mahomed's son. Intelligence had come in that the outlawed Bungal Khan had deserted his eagle's nest, high in the mountains above the Tanishpa Pass, and was now at large with a gang of his tribesmen.

'God alone knows where he is,' said White, annoyance writ large upon his angular features. 'We'll try and flush him out by burning the villages he uses; that might just do the trick. But whether he goes north or south after that is anyone's guess.'

The two columns set out for Tanishpa at dawn next day, and when the woman and the Afghan reached their deserted camp in the early afternoon, they were too late to claim protection. The village with its trees and ruined houses might seem safe enough by day, but what danger might not lurk at night? Somewhere, thought Violet Nicolson, surveying the valley that stretched before them, and the mountains beyond, somewhere to the north were Tanishpa and the army.

All too belatedly she was aware of the great danger she was in, and she was at last more than ready to face up to her husband's anger.

⁂

It was unfortunate that after his treatment at Sir George White's hands, the renegade Bungal Khan turned south, not north. It was even more unfortunate that he and some of his band of two hundred men came face to face with the colonel's wife below the Tanishpa Pass.

Mahomed Akram saw them coming first. 'Show no fear,' his voice was urgent. 'Remember, I shall tell them you are my idiot son.'

Terrified, Violet forced herself to follow him. She heard the Afghan talking, talking—and she could not understood a word. She dared not look up, and made no protest when a hand took her bridle and her horse was wheeled around. With a sick feeling in her stomach she realised that they were being taken away from safety, back in the direction from which they had come.

'What news of Bungal Khan?'

'We didn't catch him, sir,' the young lieutenant of Bengal Lancers answered ruefully. 'But we have four prisoners, and a good number of camels, bullocks and donkeys.'

General Sir George White swore out loud.

'And I've heard, sir,' continued Lieutenant Chesney, quite unperturbed by his chief's show of temper, 'that he surprised a party of our grass cutters near the camp and carried one of them off with him.'

White swore again. Losing Bungal Khan was something he could rectify in his own good time, but the captive's life was in immediate danger. 'Very well, Lieutenant,' he said, 'leave it with me,' and he strode off to consult with his second-in-command. Shortly afterwards two parties set out, one to reconnoitre to the north, the other heading south to search for traces of the Kakar chief below the Tanishpa Pass.

Violet Nicolson could only guess what her companion had told the leader of the band. The small sharp-featured man had listened, and his keen, hooded eyes had looked at them for a long, uncomfortable moment. But they were still alive and unharmed, so whatever the Afghan had said must have been convincing, and now they were prisoners in a sizeable village where the villagers, who had welcomed the outlaws with all the food they possessed, were waiting anxiously for them to leave.

They stayed, and as the shadows lengthened it became clear that they were going to spend the night among their reluctant hosts. At some point late in the afternoon a frightened-looking man was brought in and dragged from a mule, protesting feebly. He was buffeted about the head, his warm coat dragged from off his shoulders, and then he was tied unceremoniously to a tree. Violet did not know what the band intended to do with him—or with them—but at least *they* had been fed. Meantime, she made herself as inconspicuous as possible, crouching by Mahomed Akram's side and not daring to speak.

In the evening the tribesmen crowded round a fire. Someone shouted out and Mahomed Akram stood up and nudged Violet with his foot; she crawled after him, hoping that this was what he intended. She felt the welcome warmth of the fire on her body, and resisted the temptation to stretch out her hands to the flames. Then her companion began to sing. The men stamped and shouted their approval, demanding more, and at last Violet dared to raise her eyes.

Now in shadow, now in light, Greek gods and grizzled prophets sat around the fire, listening intently, and as she watched in fascination one of the number suddenly stared in her direction. Then stared again. She dropped her gaze, until at last the singing and the laughter died away and Mahomed Akram stood up and hauled her to her feet. Someone took hold of her, and they were both pushed towards a tree and tied up near the other captive.

Violet could still see the fire where the men talked on. The same young man who had watched her before watched her now, and she began to feel more and more uneasy. 'One of them keeps looking at me,' she whispered to the Afghan. 'Do you think he knows I'm a woman?'

'No, *Nikelseyn mem*, he thinks you are a boy—' She gasped and Mahomed Akram cursed himself for saying anything at all.

Gradually the fire died down and the Kakars drifted away in all directions to sleep. Violet was too frightened to close her eyes, but at last sleep came to her as well. When she woke she saw that the tree beside her was deserted; their fellow captive had somehow slipped his bonds and fled.

The small party of Bengal Lancers ranging south the next afternoon came across the fugitive grass cutter who was weak from fright, cold and hunger, and they wasted no time in taking him back to camp. There he told his tale: of how he had been captured by the fearsome Bungal Khan; of how they had taken his warm clothing but failed to find his knife; and how he had been so desperately anxious to escape that he had not risked freeing the Afghan who was a prisoner too, lest the idiot boy with him make a noise and rouse the camp.

Malcolm Nicolson listened carefully to the tale, asked many questions, then consulted with his commanding officer. 'I think they must have been at that Kakar village we passed on the way north. They may have already left, but it's worth a try, don't you think, sir?'

'I do indeed, Nick. Make any arrangements you think fit, and go to it!'

A party of fifty Baluchis under Lieutenant Price, whom the colonel considered ready to be blooded, and twenty Bengal Lancers under a native *jemadar*, set out at dawn the next day in search of Bungal Khan. The outlaws hadn't moved; having lost four of his own to fire and powder, this pleasant village of some fifty houses pleased the chieftain very well, and he was loathe to leave. Let the *feringhis* go further north, he thought; they will soon tire. Until then, there is food aplenty here, and entertainment too.

So for a second night Mahomed Akram sang his frontier songs, while Violet Nicolson suffered nightmares, waking and sleeping, under the brooding gaze of a lustful thug. She was rubbing her newly freed wrists and ankles next morning and hoping for food, when the punitive party approached the village. As silently as possible, Charles Price's men made their way over the rocks and thorny scrub, and the outlaws, only just waking after the noise and merriment of the night before, were taken completely by surprise. The sheep and goats gave the alarm, for Bungal Khan, confident to the last, had posted no sentries at all, and his men had barely time to reach their horses before the Bengali *sowars* rode into the village to the covering fire of the 3rd Baluchis.

With a cry of delight Violet would have started to her feet, but her companion pulled her back and forced her flat. The rifle fire was murderous and she made no further attempt to move. As she was lying there, someone grabbed her arm and she half rose, thinking the Afghan had changed his mind—only to shrink back as her admirer's leering face thrust itself close to hers. When she tried to pull free, the grip on her arm tightened like the jaws of a trap.

Mahomed Akram leapt to her rescue, only to be met by a savage blow to the throat. He fell to the ground and did not move. At that, Violet sank her teeth into the hand that was holding her, but fared no better—with a howl of pain the outlaw struck her hard in the face with the other. She staggered under the impact of the blow, and for a moment she was half stunned, yet as he dragged her to his horse her head began to clear. Frightened she certainly was, but more than that she was enraged; struggling to free herself, pushing at her captor in desperation, her hand came in contact with the knife he was wearing at his waist.

Without taking time to think, Violet Nicolson seized it and plunged it into his body right to the very hilt. When she tried to pull it out, the man gave a grunt and fell forward, taking her with him and pinning her to the ground. She lay helpless beneath him, while bullets scuffed the dust around her and whined over her head, and, as the life-blood soaked into her tunic, the young woman wondered if she would ever again be free.

How long she was there she had no way of telling, but at last she sensed footsteps and the corpse was pulled away. She raised a frightened face to see Mahomed Akram bending over her. He was alive, then! Without a word, he dragged her after him, ducking and weaving across the village square, to take refuge among the sheep and goats while the soldiers finished their work.

At length an exhilarated Lieutenant Price returned to take possession of the spoils. The outlaws had all made off—bar a couple who wouldn't be going anywhere ever again—but at least he had something to show for his trouble, and there would be fresh meat and to spare for the troops that night. At the side of the square he came across two disreputable-looking Afghan tribesmen crouching for shelter behind the terrified livestock; they were both filthy and the younger one, he noted with some repugnance, was quite foul with blood.

'Were you two prisoners of this bunch, then?' Price asked in passable Pushtu.

Mahomed Akram nodded; Violet said nothing. She did not understand what Charles was saying and avoided the young man's scrutiny. He would recognise her soon enough and in no way was she ready for explanations yet.

'You'd better come back with us,' said the lieutenant. 'Can you walk?'

The Afghan looked at his companion who was on her feet and looking deathly pale. 'Yes, we can,' he replied, changing to Urdu so that Violet could understand, 'but perhaps the *memsahib* had better ride—our horses are over there.' He pointed.

Price looked over to the horses before the full import of the words struck him. A white woman! Good God, what would Old Nick say about that? He looked at the lad more closely. There was no point in trying to conceal her identity further so, 'Good morning, Lieutenant Price,' said Violet, in the voice he knew so well, although it was huskier than usual from all the excitement.

The young man stared in amazement. 'Good heavens!' he exclaimed. 'It's Mrs Nicolson! Oh my Lord, the colonel is going to have a fit when he hears about this!'

'I know,' said the colonel's lady. 'Will you tell him, or shall I?'

Then she fainted.

'That I came to you was written by Fate'

The Lancers returned to Tanishpa first. Colonel Malcolm Nicolson was in his tent but emerged at the hubbub of sound that greeted their arrival.

'Well?' he asked.

'He got away again, Colonel *sahib*,' the *jemadar* told him.

'Any casualties?' the colonel asked sharply, thinking of young Price, whose first experience of action this was.

'None of ours, Colonel *sahib*, but we killed two of theirs.'

'I see. Any prisoners?'

'Two, I think' said the *jemadar*, doubtfully.

'What do you mean, *you think*?'

'Well, Colonel *sahib*, one was an Afghan and one was a woman—a *white* woman.'

Nicolson was shaken by the news. He thought rapidly and then ordered: 'Get the grass cutter—the one that was taken—what's his name?'

'Mazallah, Colonel *sahib*.'

'Get him,' snapped Nicolson, and stalked back to his tent. The grass cutter duly appeared and the colonel began his interrogation all over again. 'Describe the two Afghans,' he ordered.

The grass cutter thought long and hard. 'The man had a scar,' he said.

There was nothing unusual about that, thought Nicolson, despite a certain suspicion forming in his mind. 'And the boy—what was *he* like?'

'He was an idiot,' came the reply.

'What did he look like?' came the patient question.

'I did not see, Colonel *sahib*. His face was covered.' Mazallah could tell that more was required and went on: 'He was small in stature.' Perhaps that would satisfy the colonel *sahib*. It did not.

'Did they speak together?'

No. The boy was an idiot, Mazallah repeated.

'Not at all—even at night, when no one was around to hear?'

Mazallah thought again; well yes, something had puzzled him—he tried to remember. 'The man spoke once,' he recalled at last. 'But all I heard was *Nikelseyn*. Your name, Colonel *sahib*,' the grass cutter added helpfully.

Mazallah smiled at his interrogator; Malcolm Nicolson glowered back.

Violet grew more silent and thoughtful as they neared the camp and hardly listened to what Charles Price was saying, while the youthful lieutenant began gleefully to anticipate the sensation he was about to cause: returning thus with the colonel's wife was something his peers could never hope to match! When they arrived back some considerable time after the cavalry, Nicolson was waiting, his humour black. He had strong suspicions as to the identity of the man and the woman, but of course he might be totally wrong. He spoke first to his men and praised their work, and left them to dispose of the livestock. Next he turned to the lieutenant.

'Make your report, Lieutenant Price, and be quick about it!' He listened with only half an ear, however (although later—much later—he made a point of taking the lad aside and commending him for his work). He dismissed him as soon as he could and, knowing his worst fears about to be confirmed, turned to the remaining pair.

The Afghan dismounted with an enigmatic smile as the colonel took hold of his wife and hauled her off her horse. She staggered against him as she reached the ground, but there was no reassurance in the iron grip that steadied her briefly before the folds of turban were wrenched away from her face.

'Look at me,' he ordered, and reluctantly she raised her eyes to meet the icy glare. There was no comfort to be found there either. Rarely had she seen her husband so angry, and never before with her. 'So I was right!' he said furiously, and turned back to his friend.

'It's not his fault,' Violet came stoutly to her companion's defence. 'It was all my idea—I made him come!'

'I doubt that very much,' said Nicolson grimly, knowing that his old friend did nothing against his will. Ignoring Violet, he addressed the Afghan in his own language.

'That's not fair, I can't understand what you're saying to him!'

'Perhaps, young woman, that's just as well!'

'Mahomed Akram, tell him you're not to blame—' she appealed.

'*Nikelseyn* knows the truth, *memsahib*—even if he will not admit it!' and with that enigmatic utterance Mahomed Akram left them.

'Just you come with me,' and Nicolson dragged his wife towards the tent. 'I've no intention of arguing with you in public. No one knows you're here as yet, thank goodness!'

'I think you might be wrong about that, Malcolm,' she remarked, for already there was a hum of excitement as scarlet and green figures began to huddle together, *pugris* nodding vigorously as they began to spread the news.

'Damn,' said Nicolson and he pushed her inside.

Once she regained her balance Violet looked around, interested despite herself. She had never been inside a campaign tent before; it was quite large, she thought, with plenty of room for two. There was only one low camp bed, of course, but the ground would do for her—by now she was quite used to doing without even the minor comforts of home.

Nicolson looked at his wife who looked back without flinching, outwardly unrepentant but inwardly quailing, and determined to brave it out. She had compromised her husband—she could see that now. What woman had ever had the effrontery to do what she had done? Her face was pale and her eyes enormous as she waited for the storm to break about her head.

For once in his life Malcolm Nicolson was unsure of what to say or do. He had been prepared to be furious—he *was* furious, he reminded himself—but now that Violet was standing safely before him, his overwhelming feeling was one of relief. She was safe and all he wanted to do was to put his arms around her—but in the circumstances it hardly seemed appropriate, and the soldier in him struggled with the lover.

Violet decided to break the silence. 'I suppose you're worried about your dignity and your position?' His anger was rekindled by her jibe. 'Of course I'm not!

Violet, do you never think! You might have been hurt, you might have been killed—' Horrified, he belatedly noticed her *kurta*, and the dark stain on her breast.

'You *are* hurt!' he exclaimed, reaching out to her. If only I were, she thought, he might find it easier to forgive me. 'It's not my blood—' she began, and sat down, suddenly weak at the knees and unable to continue.

Nicolson's anger returned in full force. 'Good God, woman,' he exploded, as a thought suddenly struck him, 'what am I going to do with you for the rest of the expedition?' And with that, not trusting himself further, he stormed out of the tent and went to seek advice.

❖

'I hear Mrs Nicolson has joined us,' said Sir Robert Sandeman, to whom the colonel had gone with his troubles.

'Yes,' said the latter, glumly.

'You don't seem too pleased about it. Man, anyone here would be delighted to be in your shoes!'

'Perhaps.'

'You don't agree?'

'I suppose I do, but there's General White.'

'Ah, yes—Sir George. I expect he'll be as mad as you are, and with far more cause. And how *is* your wife, by the way—or didn't you stay long enough to find out?' Sandeman's blue eyes twinkled with amusement.

'She is well. But covered in blood—blood she assures me is not her own.'

How very interesting, thought Sir Robert. 'But she wasn't near the fighting, was she?' he asked.

'No, young Price said he found her and her companion hiding in among the sheep and goats.'

'Now, that was probably worse,' and Sandeman gave a hearty guffaw. Nicolson failed to join in.

'The lassie's had a few adventures, Nick, by the sound of it. You should be proud of her, you know.'

'Proud—when she's gone against what she must have known would be my wishes?'

'Ah yes, man, your wishes— How long have you been in the service now? It must be over thirty years ...' Nicolson nodded. 'You'll be pretty set in your ways, then.' The colonel frowned but said nothing. 'And how long have you been married—a year, two years, is it?'

'Eighteen months. Why?'

'So the lassie's still got a mind of her own— Well, well. Is that really such a bad thing? Would you have her do your every bidding, then?'

'No,' the colonel said slowly, 'no, I wouldn't have her change—but I'd prefer her safe in Hyderabad, that's all ...'

'Out of the way and not interfering with your work? I see.'

A silence fell. Well, well, thought Sandeman. Nick wasn't the first man faced with the choice of love or duty, and he wouldn't be the last—the circumstances were unusual, of course, but the fellow would have to work out things with his spirited young wife as best he could.

'When were you last in England, my friend?' he inquired after a few moments.

Again his fellow Scot managed to surprise him. 'Not for many years, Sandey. Why?'

'Well,' said Sir Robert, a broad smile spreading across his ruddy face, 'when I was there three years ago, wives were busy running away from their husbands. Not after them, like yours!' He paused to let his words sink in. 'Now off you go and leave George White to me.'

Her hands locked about her knees, Violet Nicolson sat awaiting her husband's return. Now that she was safe at last a desperate tiredness had overcome her. She closed her eyes but still she could see a grinning bearded face, a face where angry surprise succeeded lust as steel jarred against bone then slid on unchecked to its goal. She looked up in relief as the tent flap drew back and Malcolm reappeared.

'So,' she said in a valiant attempt at light-heartedness. 'Am I to be shot at dawn, or are you simply going to beat me for disobedience?'

'It looks like someone's been doing that already.' Nicolson sat down and looked at his wife properly for the first time. Her cheek and jaw were beginning to show the signs of a very ugly bruise, and she winced as he gently touched her face.

'What happened? Are you going to tell me?'

She shook her head. 'No, not now. I don't want to talk about it yet.' Her face was haggard in appeal and Nicolson did not insist; she would tell him when she was ready, and he was prepared to wait till then. He slipped his arm around her shoulders and Violet relaxed.

'I was half expecting you, you know,' he told her, 'after the Lancers got back with a tale of a white woman and an Afghan.'

She summoned up a little grin. 'So I suppose you prowled around for hours, *nursing your wrath to keep it warm?*'

'Something like that,' he admitted. 'It was a shock, when I supposed you back in Hyderabad—although you sent me no letters.'

Feeling a stab of remorse for the disappointment he must have felt, 'I'm so sorry about that, darling,' she said.

The laugh he gave hid a degree of exasperation. 'You're sorry about that, but not at all sorry for the upheaval you're about to cause! That, Violet Nicolson, is quite typical of you! Come on,' and he pulled her to her feet.

Outside, she took stock of her surroundings. They were on a wide plateau, hemmed in on three sides by mountains and dominated by one sharp peak. That must hide the fortress Charles was talking about, she thought; the few stone-built thatch-roofed houses at its base seemed deserted.

'They'll be back,' said her husband. 'They won't have gone far. Come on,' he repeated, taking her hand to hurry her along, oblivious to the eyes that watched them. They followed the little stream that served the camp, then turned aside into a little gully. 'Good,' said Nicolson, 'this will do,' and he stopped in a clearing where stunted juniper trees hung on precariously among the boulders and ferns. A pool overhung by a leafy carob tree had formed among the moss-covered rocks.

'In you get,' the colonel said heartlessly, 'You stink like a herd of goats!'

The chill pure water of that sunless spot cleansed her of the dead man's blood, but the memory refused to leave her. She was shivering on the bank, dressed again, when Malcolm pulled her to the ground beside him. She gave a little protest but his movements only became more urgent. She lay there, remembering the weight of another body and the attendant horror. Thank God it was over quickly. He looked at her then, and quite misunderstood the wounded gaze of her darkened eyes.

'I'm sorry,' he said curtly. 'But you'll have to understand. There'll be no time for dalliance from now on.'

'Where death was cruel and danger rife—'

Juma Khan was waiting at the tent when they returned, looking as unhappy as Violet felt. She went inside, leaving the orderly to talk to her husband, and then she heard them walk away. She sank onto the cot with a sigh. *Oh, Izzie,* she found herself thinking. *I suppose you would say it's all my fault and it serves me right. And so it does—but even you couldn't tell me what to do!*

Nicolson woke her roughly. 'Women's clothes,' he said. 'From the local *malik*'s wife. Juma Khan got them for you—at some considerable cost, I may say.' She pressed the soft stuff to her cheek for a moment, then changed into the baggy trousers and long indigo tunic he handed her. She looked at him gratefully, relieved that the masquerade was over.

'I'm glad you didn't give yourself a haircut,' the colonel observed dryly as she freed her hair and shook it over her shoulders.

'I thought about it. But I didn't have scissors and Mohammad Akram wouldn't lend me his knife—' her voice broke off and a bleak expression washed over her face.

'Darling, whatever's wrong?'

'Nothing, nothing at all, truly. What time are we seeing Sir Robert, did you say?'

Nicolson allowed the blatant change of subject to go unchallenged. 'As soon as you're ready,' he replied, and watched intently as with trembling fingers she began to plait her hair into one long shining braid.

Some time later Violet was examining the Governor-General's Agent in Baluchistan equally keenly, and with no little surprise. She had expected a lean rapacious frontiersman who sank his teeth into new territory like a wolf into unsuspecting sheep, yet here was a short, stocky individual in his middle fifties, with reddish hair and inclined to plumpness.

Shrewd blue eyes assessed her in return. He and Lady Sandeman had often wondered what kind of a woman had managed to bring Malcolm Nicolson to heel, and here she was! Looks alone wouldn't have done it, he concluded, although she surely was a bonnie lass. Nor would her obvious adoration—she was by no means the first girl to fall in love with the gallant colonel, after all. No, it had to be more.

Under gently probing questions put in a rich Scots accent the story of her adventures gradually emerged—a story that her own husband had as yet failed to fathom—and Robert Sandeman began to recognise in Violet Nicolson a spirit and a toughness that made her a fitting mate for his old colleague and friend.

'So you looked up, and there they were, all around you? You must have been gey scared, lassie.'

'I was, but Mahomed Akram didn't seem at all afraid.'

'So what happened next, lass?'

'Well, Bungal Khan gave us the nastiest look I have ever seen—until I was reunited with my husband, that is,' and Violet, who was recovering rapidly under Sandeman's admiring gaze, sent Malcolm a cheeky grin. 'He's only a little man, but he has such presence. No one dared argue with him, and when he told his men to leave us alone they obeyed, but you could tell they weren't happy. I think they meant to kill us when they moved on from the village.' She was quite matter-of-fact about it, which only added to Nicolson's feelings of horror.

'Of course, Mahomed Akram told them he was a harmless minstrel and that I was his dolt of a son.' The irrepressible smile twinkled again for a moment. 'That was the really difficult part—I couldn't understand what they were saying and didn't know what to do, and of course I wasn't supposed to look at him, so when Mahomed Akram kept kicking me I was never quite sure what he meant—'

'Were they rough with you, my dear?' the Scot asked gently, eyeing the vivid bruise on her face.

'No, not at all, Sir Robert. When they knew he could sing they had a use for him, and they left me alone as well. He kept them quiet for hours, he has such a beautiful voice,' said Violet, 'and watching them all round the fire, I quite forgot where I was until—' Her voice trailed away as she remembered one who had watched her in his turn, and whose eyes were now closed for ever.

'Until what, Violet?' prompted her husband, who had seen the shadow momentarily cloud her face.

'Until they decided to go to sleep,' she finished lamely. 'You know the rest: Lieutenant Price came riding to the rescue this morning—and here I am!' She smiled brightly at her audience and refused to say anything more.

And for some reason you fainted—and that's not like you at all, thought her husband, who had seen the lieutenant again for a few more words. His eyes lingered speculatively on her swollen discoloured jaw. Tomorrow, he decided, he would insist on a proper explanation.

Violet slept heavily until the small hours of the morning. And then she had a dream. In it she once more knifed her attacker and they both fell to the ground; but this time, when the Afghan set her free, she did not rise but lay there helpless, watching a disembodied hand drive the blade into her own flesh time and time again.

She sat up, wild-eyed and trying not to scream. Malcolm woke immediately.

'What is it, Violet? What's wrong?'

His voice startled her, so tight was she in the nightmare's grip. 'I've had a dreadful dream,' she said at last. 'It was so horribly real—'

He could feel the sweat drenching her body. 'Do you want to tell me about it?' he asked her, and held her as in a halting voice she told him the whole story.

Oh, Violet, Violet, he thought, all this need not have happened—but at least she was unharmed. He rocked her in his arms like a child as she turned to him for comfort. 'You're safe,' he said later, when the crying stopped. 'He would almost certainly have killed you when he found out he'd been cheated—you do realise that, don't you?'

'Yes,' her voice was subdued.

'And he may well have raped you first—so try not to have any regrets.' She muttered something. 'And for heaven's sake,' he finished, 'don't go wandering off too far on your own while you're here—you might not be so lucky another time!'

❧

General White arrived the next afternoon and Sir Robert proved as good as his word. Sir George frowned a little as Sandeman broke the news of his second-in-command's revised domestic arrangements, but to Malcolm Nicolson's relief more pressing matters soon took his superior's attention. Violet meanwhile had thought it wise to make herself scarce. She retraced their steps of the afternoon before and leaning back against the carob tree, she gave herself up to her thoughts, pleasant and unpleasant.

In two weeks she and Mahomed Akram had come over one hundred miles, one hundred miles of narrow tracks, and sometimes no tracks at all, across plain and plateau and windswept passes. She was here at last, in the land beyond the hills that had so tantalised her as a girl, the hills that had always seemed to beckon her on.

And it was a journey not only in time and space. Violet Nicolson had learnt one of its secrets already: that it was a cruel unforgiving land where the weak and the reckless did not survive—a land that had taught her to kill.

She heard but did not watch the headquarters' column arrive, and made her way back to the camp a long time after. Malcolm was not at the tent, but Juma Khan was hanging around glumly outside. She spoke to the young man who seemed more than willing to talk, and half an hour or so went by before she realised. At the end of it the lad went off in one direction and Mrs Nicolson in another.

When she returned, her husband was waiting for her. 'Juma Khan's done a bunk,' he told her and Violet tried to look surprised. 'He was pretty homesick, and we're not all that far from his village—relatively speaking, that is. I suppose,' said Colonel Nicolson, 'it was all too much for him. Perhaps your turning up was the last straw.'

His wife murmured that perhaps it was.

'It's odd, though. He only joined up because of a family feud but I should have thought it unwise for him to go back as yet.'

'Oh? He can go back, then?' The young woman feigned surprise.

'Yes, it's different with the Baluchis, darling. With Afghans, a feud goes on for generations, until all the males are dead and only the old women remember what triggered it off in the first place. But in this case, a hefty fine to the *malik*, and it's all forgotten.'

With that Nicolson hurriedly got to his feet and looked in his kit. He swore. 'He's taken my money, damn him. And here I was thinking he was as honest as the day!'

He was more concerned over his poor judgement of character than anything else and Violet thought she should own up. 'Malcolm,' she put a conciliatory hand on his shoulder. 'Darling, why don't you sit down?'

'Sit down? I have things to do,' and the colonel moved towards the opening of the tent.

'Please stay.' Violet took his arm and he allowed her to lead him back, already half suspecting what she was going to say. One look at her was enough. In the overly candid gaze meeting his there lurked the merest hint of a smile. 'Darling—'

'Yes?' he raised a quizzical eyebrow.

'I'm afraid the only thief around here is me. We had a long talk, Juma Khan and I, and he told me how much he wanted to go home, and why he couldn't. So I gave him what I had left over from the journey to Hyderabad—'

'You mean the journey you didn't quite finish.'

'Yes,' Violet resumed quite unrepentantly. 'He thought it would be enough for the chief, but I gave him your money too, to be on the safe side.' She put her head to one side and considered her husband. 'I really thought you wouldn't mind, seeing how concerned you always are for your men's welfare.'

The colonel caught hold of her none too gently. 'You haven't been here for five minutes,' he exclaimed, 'and already you're threatening to disrupt the smooth running of this campaign!' but his grey eyes were gleaming with an amusement he was trying vainly to suppress.

'Yes,' agreed Violet equably. 'You appear to have lost an orderly and gained a wife. I hope you're not sorry?'

Nicolson burst out laughing. Not at all, he assured her. He only hoped that General Sir George White would agree it was a fair exchange.

'The weary day's laborious pace'

'Mrs Malcolm Nicolson?' The question was a mere formality, for who else could this young woman possibly be?

'General Sir George White?' countered Violet. There was no mistaking the commander of the Zhob Field Force either—although with his slightly hollow cheeks and beak of a nose, the thin balding man in his mid-fifties looked more the schoolmaster than the soldier. 'Would you care to join me, General?' She gestured to a boulder by her side.

'Thank you, if I'm not intruding,' he replied, equally formally.

Violet stifled an inclination to giggle. These niceties were more fitting to a cantonment drawing room, surely, than a hillside pool in the wilds of a hostile country. She waited. Her husband's commanding officer had certainly not come upon her by chance.

White sat down carefully, and stretched his long legs out before him. 'You're a considerable distance from home, my dear.' This in the same politely conversational tone.

Violet decided to take the bull by the horns. 'Home is where the heart is, Sir George. Or don't you agree?'

'Ah.'

'You mustn't blame my husband for my being here, you know.'

'No?' White's first inclination had been to do exactly that, until Sandeman's quiet but firm intervention on Colonel Nicolson's behalf had forced him to delay his verdict.

'No.' Violet stared unblinkingly at the leader of the punitive expedition and spoke up intrepidly in her husband's defence. 'That wouldn't be at all fair, you see. Malcolm had absolutely no idea I intended to follow him. How could he, Sir George? I didn't know myself!' She smiled a little in recollection as she added, 'He was absolutely outraged when I turned up. I suppose you've heard all about that and how I got here?'

'A little.' But it would be interesting to hear her version. Like Sandeman before him, White began to question her, and like Sir Robert he came to the conclusion that here was a most remarkable young woman.

'So this was all the result of an accident, you say?'

'Initially yes, Sir George. But my Afghan friend sees it as the hand of Fate—my decision at Harnai too. But that, I prefer to think, I made of my own free will. I suppose,' and her tone was suddenly wistful, 'you're angry too, and you're going to send me back?'

White looked at her. She still bore the marks of the blow Sandeman had told him about, and the bruise was now a dramatic blue, black and green.

'And if I did, Mrs Nicolson, you would go?'

'Of course. I've compromised Malcolm's career enough, I imagine. He always says I never look before I leap, and this must be a prime example.' Violet Nicolson bit her lip and lowered her vivid gaze.

'You appear to have paid the price of your impetuousness, my dear young lady.'

'This, you mean?' Violet tentatively touched her face. 'Yes, I suppose I have. But I don't think I'm likely to run into Bungal Khan again, do you? I'll leave whenever you say, Sir George.' She smiled at him cheerfully, although she could not quite hide that the prospect of the return journey through the mountains appalled her.

The general cleared his throat. The stalwart soldier, holder of the Victoria Cross, and a veteran of several wars, found himself warming to this brave little person who had undergone such hardship to be with her husband.

'No one would be inhuman enough to send you back from here, Mrs Nicolson, and certainly not me!' he assured her, patting her hand. 'Though why you think Zhob so fascinating, I really cannot think!'

The answer to that was apparent soon enough. Colonel Nicolson, looking for his wife, came across her in animated conversation with his chief. He coughed, and the couple looked up—Violet with pleasure and Sir George a little guiltily.

'You've caught me playing truant, I'm afraid, Colonel, but it's been a while since I've had such charming company. And never on campaign! I absolutely forbid you to send Mrs Nicolson away, do you hear?'

The colonel looked at the general over Violet's head, and not altogether happily. George White calmly returned his gaze. 'Until Apozai at least,' he added. 'We'll review the situation there.'

Apozai. It was hardly an oasis, but it seemed one to the task force when they reached it eleven days later. And the hospitality afforded them by the 34th Bengal Pioneers in their newly constructed mess was verging on the Olympian when Malcolm Nicolson left the party early to go back to his wife. It was no surprise to him when Mahomed Akram appeared silently out of the shadows surrounding his tent.

'All is well, my friend?'

The Afghan touched his arm briefly. 'All is well, brother,' he replied, before he took himself off.

'Is that you, Malcolm? I hope it is.' Violet's voice issuing from the depths of her sleeping bag was muffled and exceedingly sleepy.

'Yes. Go back to sleep, little one.'

But Violet, barely awake, was determined to be civil.

'Did you have a nice dinner in the mess?'

'Yes, thank you, darling.'

'And a rollicking time afterwards?'

'Perfectly so, I thank you, sweetheart.'

'I'm glad.' The little voice fell silent. Reassured that all was well with her world, Violet Nicolson had gone back to sleep.

Sleep did not come as easily to the colonel. The whisky he had drunk served to make his wits sharper, if anything, and he lay awake confronting the problem that faced him. What to do about his wife?

He had warned her that the march would not be easy, and that she should not expect concessions. She had promised to keep up and she had. Some days he had hardly seen her, leaving her to fend for herself. And she had managed. She had scrambled down steep mountainsides, and through the narrowest of defiles, and whenever they reached a flat valley bed she had breathed a sigh of relief, only to realise despondently that it was all to do again. And over her the whole time hung her husband's threat that if she failed, he would leave her behind at Apozai—*Even if you do manage to twist Sir George round your little finger again, Violet, do you understand?*

She had understood and she had not looked for praise—which was just as well, thought Nicolson a little guiltily. Sandeman, he remembered, had taken him to task quite early on. What was it he had said, with that way he had of smiling when he was at his most severe? *You're being too hard on your lassie, Nick. Man, she's here whether you like it or not, and she's trying to make the most of it—and so should you!*

And Violet had thought the same. The colonel smiled in the darkness as he remembered how she had confronted him on the day of a sandstorm, when he had thought he had lost her for good. She had been separated from them through no fault of her own, and when he finally found her she had spoken out stoutly in her defence, forestalling him in everything she thought he might have wanted to say. Only to find him smiling ruefully when she stopped at last to draw breath.

'You thought I'd be angry, did you, Violet?'

'Aren't you?'

'No. Not any more. Sandey told me off! He thinks I'm too hard on you, for some reason.'

His wife had raised an eyebrow, but said nothing.

'Am I too hard on you?'

'I'll survive.'

'And what exactly do you mean by that?'

And she had told him in no uncertain terms: 'Look, Malcolm, I know you think I'm a nuisance—*dalliance* apart, I know you think I'm in the way.' The sarcasm appeared quite lost on her husband so she continued. 'Well, I have no intention of going away, and I *will* cope, and I *will* keep up, and I shan't give you any excuse at all for getting rid of me!'

And therein lay the problem. He was enjoying her company more than he cared to admit. And the moments of dalliance, as she chose to put it, were very precious and all too rare. No, his comrades would be carousing until the early hours and there would be a few thick heads in the morning, but all he had wanted was to come back to this scrap of a girl, who was getting thinner and more exhausted by the day, but who never complained and always had a cheery smile for him, no matter what.

'But I *don't* want to get rid of you,' he had told her then, and he didn't want to now. But … After a few days in Apozai where Sandeman had business with the chiefs, they would be heading east into the highest part of the Suleimani

Mountains, and winter was coming on. And there could be fighting. She should stay behind and rest in safety. But in whose care?

⁂

In the event, the matter was taken out of his hands.

'There's trouble ahead,' said Sir George the next day. Intelligence reports confirmed that the Shirani tribe was in outright revolt, and the commander viewed the prospect with relish. This after all was what they were here for, and it had been a damned tame show to date.

Nicolson listened to his chief's prognostication gloomily. Not that he wouldn't mind a bit of action, himself, but there was Violet to think about. Not for the first time, he cursed her reckless nature.

Sandeman watching him, sensed his dilemma.

'What's the matter with you two?' White demanded, looking from one man to the other. 'Oh, I know, Sandey, you hoped you could persuade them to come into the fold without a fight, and you still might, my dear fellow, but you, Nick, what's got into you?'

'I'm sorry, Sir George, it's the question of what to do with my wife: I don't want her in any danger. Perhaps she should stay at Apozai?'

White snorted. 'Apozai is hardly any safer, in my opinion. Where would she stay? Who would keep an eye on her? Have you thought of that?'

Malcolm Nicolson had. There were no white women in the place, and after the boisterously convivial evening he had spent in the officers' mess, he could think of no one he would happily entrust with the welfare of his wife.

'No, Nick, you'll have to take her with you. Besides, if you left her behind, she'd probably follow!' The general gave another snort of amusement and walked away.

'Oh, Masters, you who rule the world'

Violet sat in the sunshine near the tent: it was good to know that tomorrow there was no need to move on from Apozai, nor the day after. She had been cold, weary, and wet and now it was over—for the moment. She settled herself against a boulder, closed her eyes and after a while she slept.

A shadow falling across her face woke her. 'Good morning, Charles,' she said. 'The colonel's not here; he's over at the Political Camp.'

'I know, Mrs Nicolson, I've come to talk to you—if you don't mind, that is?'

'Of course not, sit down. How is everything?'

'Wonderful. You were right—you know, what you said four weeks ago.'

'Is it only four weeks, Charles? It seems like a lifetime, don't you think?' Lieutenant Price nodded. He looked fit and happy, thought Violet, quite unlike the nervous-looking lad of the train. 'So it's all working out well, is it? Tell me about it,' for she guessed he wanted to stay.

And he told her many things she had been too tired or anxious to notice for herself, and things she couldn't possibly have known and which Nicolson hadn't thought or wanted to tell her: how men from the King's Own Yorkshire Light Infantry had climbed up to Bungal Khan's fortress and blown it up; how some of the Khan's men had surrendered; and how a fanatic had been hanged for attempted murder at Apozai, only the day before.

'And we're to parade before Sir Robert the day after tomorrow,' the lieutenant concluded.

'A show of strength, you mean? So that the tribes will know it doesn't pay to resist the British Raj?'

'That's right, Mrs Nicolson.' Price totally failed to detect the irony in her voice and Violet decided it wasn't fair to tease him—especially as he didn't understand.

She chose not to watch the parade and march past. What was the point of it all, anyway? Was control of the Suleimani Mountains so very vital? Would any foreign power ever be mad enough to invade India through the wastes of Baluchistan? They would have to conquer Afghanistan first, an even worse prospect for any foreign invader. But the local chiefs were impressed by the display of military might, and she supposed that was what really mattered. It was clear that Sir Robert had them eating out of his hand: they were all there to watch—all save the dissident Largha Shiranis. And Sandeman fully intended to deal with them as well.

At five-thirty in the morning of the first day in November bugles rent the early morning air with notes of purest silver and half an hour later the second column of the force marched out of Apozai. A barrier of barren limestone rock confronted them to the east, traversed at intervals by near inaccessible gorges—through which Malcolm Nicolson and his men were ordered to create a military road. It seemed impossible, and anyone but Robert Sandeman might well have conceded defeat. What if the only conceivable path lay along the bed of a stream which burrowed its tortuous way through the very heart of the mountains, a bed which was narrow and partially blocked by rock? The Scot gazed up at the awesome conglomerate cliffs and the water falling from a height of sometimes twenty feet and listened to no excuses.

'Take as long as you have to,' he said firmly, 'but do it!'

The impossible took only a week—a week in which Violet wrote to Isabel at last:

Dhana Sar, Thursday 6 November, 1890—We are camping on a stony plateau at the entrance to the Chuar Khel Dhana, surrounded by steep hills covered in olives and acacias. The nights are very cold. The gorge is virtually blocked in places but Major Garwood of the Royal Engineers is working miracles. Malcolm expected things to be bad and he hasn't been disappointed! Sir Robert is anxious to waste no time—he is desperate to talk terms with his Shiranis before Sir George tries sterner tactics—but even with working parties spending hours at a time in the icy water, progress is very slow. The noise of the blasting is terrible, and afterwards ramps have to be made, and the bed of the stream filled up with stones. The animals are the real problem: we lost several camels on the way here, poor beasts, but everyone seemed more concerned about the fate of the stores— Some of the Shiranis have surrendered but their chief Murtaza Khan has taken off even deeper into the hills, hence Sir Robert's haste— Tomorrow Captain Sievwright and Lieutenant Price are to go through the gorge with 100 of Malcolm's Baluchis, to make sure the road is clear, and we should soon be on our way. We are well, and Malcolm has forgiven me. What a lot there will be to tell you when I see you next—

When would that be? wondered Isabel, when the letter reached her a remarkably short time later. Her sister was living in a different world these days, a world she could barely imagine. She hardly envied her, but Annie Sophie did. The youngest Miss Cory, while loving home comforts to excess, fancied she loved the colonel even more, and would willingly have changed places with his wife.

While the work was going on Violet Nicolson had plenty of time to think. She pondered on the British place in Baluchistan—were they as welcome as they chose to believe? There was still resistance in the hills, though further to the east. And there would, she imagined, always be Mahomedan fanatics, willing to die for their cause.

The hanging of the *ghazis*—there had been more than one, as she was to find out—came up quite casually in conversation one night at dinner in Sandeman's Political Camp. When Nicolson began to explain she interrupted: 'I know about it already; Lieutenant Price told me.'

She sounded quite aggressive and Nicolson looked at her in surprise. 'Did he know that his body would be burned,' she went on, 'or did he die expecting to be buried?' It was important for her to know and Major Garwood, the force's chief engineer had the answer ready.

'The second *ghazi* would certainly have known, Mrs Nicolson, for we'd already burned the first!'

'There were two of them?' she asked the engineer.

'Why, yes, Mrs Nicolson, the one who killed a Hindu coolie near the Cavalry lines was hanged on the twenty-first. The other one tried to kill an officer going home on sick leave, and he was hanged on the twenty-seventh. Yes, indeed, he would have known what was going to happen, for sure!'

'You sound very pleased about it, Major.' There was nothing in Violet's voice to warn Garwood of trouble.

'Of course,' came the satisfied reply, 'We have to teach these black devils a lesson, don't you know?'

'No, I don't know!' Violet's voice was indignant. Nicolson looked across quickly, caught her eye, and shook his head slightly. He knew his wife and could see she was ready for a fight.

Sandeman was observing the exchange with interest. 'So what are your objections, my dear? Do tell us. I'm sure we all want to know.'

Violet turned to the engineer and Nicolson groaned inwardly. 'So, Major Garwood, you think hanging teaches everyone a lesson?'

'Of course—an eye for an eye, a tooth for a tooth—that sort of thing, you know. Like the Bible says.'

'But why *burn* the body afterwards—surely there's no need for that? The offender is dead and you've made your point by then, I imagine!'

'Why, it acts as a deterrent! These beggars are less likely to go in for this kind of thing if we take strong measures.'

Nicolson hardly dared look at his wife as the engineer explained what she already knew: 'They believe they won't get into Paradise if their bodies are burned, not buried.'

'So you not only kill them but first, deliberately, take away their hope of heaven?' Outraged, Violet was past caring whether she caused offence or no. 'Does the Indian Government wage war on the soul as well as the body? It seems horribly pointless and vindictive to me—and hardly likely to gain you any friends!'

The passionate outburst was followed by absolute silence. Garwood looked at his adversary and found himself smiling somewhat apologetically. Before he could answer, however, a third voice intervened.

Richard Bruce, the commissioner responsible for regulating the Derajat territory they were crossing, had joined the force earlier that day. 'In my opinion, gentlemen,' he interjected quietly, 'Mrs Nicolson is absolutely right.'

Violet looked across gratefully as the thin, sharp-featured man went on: 'And you are by no means alone, my dear lady, I can assure you. Many of us believe that it is unworthy—at the very least—to take advantage of an enemy's beliefs to achieve our aims. And to expect approval from our Christian fellows, to boot!' The civil servant fell silent.

Major Garwood cleared his throat. 'I'd never thought of it like that,' he conceded. 'What about you, Nicolson?'

'Well,' said Malcolm, 'in fairness to Sir Robert, who represents the British Government in Baluchistan, I should make it clear that he always leaves these matters entirely to the discretion of his officers. I think I'm correct in saying that?' He looked across the table and received nods of confirmation from both Sandeman and Bruce.

'For my part,' he went on, weighing his words most carefully, 'I have to say that I believe hanging to be a fitting punishment for murder. Like my wife, however,' and he paused to look pointedly at Violet whom he knew to be watching and listening intently, 'I also believe that to punish a man a second time—by using his religious beliefs against him—is quite wrong. Although I would go even further than she has, by saying I think such a course of action to be nothing short of obscene!'

'I hope that satisfies you,' he whispered to her at the first opportunity, 'you've absolutely terrified Garwood, poor fellow. He'll probably never recover.'

By the evening of 8 November the column had all come safely through the Chuar Khel Dhana Pass. Despite the working parties' best efforts it hadn't been easy, but the task was finally completed. And so, they learned as they emerged at the other end, was the rest of the expedition's business.

'So it's all over,' Violet said. 'Just like that.'

'That's right,' confirmed her husband. 'Sir George has been busy all week accepting the submission of the Shirani chiefs.'

'Just like that,' she repeated, 'without a proper fight?'

'I believe you're disappointed! No, it wasn't *just like that*, but it was fairly peaceful as it happens. The key to success in something like this—in Baluchistan, anyway—is to win over the chiefs, and the rest will follow.'

'Rather like camels.'

'Yes.' There was laughter and something more in Malcolm's eyes. 'You're absolutely right, but don't let Sandey hear you; he thinks a little more finesse is involved!'

'So what happens now?'

'Sandeman will hold a durbar up at Kurrum tomorrow to confirm the surrender and terms—and the men will get a rest.'

'And then we all go home?'

'On the great lone hills in the storm-filled weather'

'There you are! I've been looking for you everywhere.' Nicolson smiled down at the urchin tucked away out of the wind, a collection of warm copper-coloured stones at her feet. 'I've had enough for today. We all have,' and he flopped down beside her. 'What have you been doing?'

'Scribbling, thinking, looking for these— You know, enjoying not having to rush,' and she held out one of the pebbles for his scrutiny. It was the nearest Violet was likely to get to admitting she had found the going hard, and Nicolson assessed her appearance critically. She was looking better and had put on a little weight.

'Are you warm enough? It's much colder up here.'

'I'm fine, thanks,' and she burrowed deeper into her thick embroidered *pushteen*. 'Is it going to rain again, do you think?'

On Tuesday 18 November the Zhob Field Force split for the last time and the lucky ones went back to Quetta. Nicolson's Baluchis had not yet finished their work, however; they were to blast a way through the Zao Pass, further to the north, and the only one who wasn't disappointed was a young woman reluctant to return to the disapproving stares of Hyderabad. Mahomed Akram had gone as well, and while eternally grateful to the Afghan, Violet Nicolson was relishing the prospect of having more of her husband's company.

'How much longer will it take, do you think?' she enquired casually.

Malcolm shot her a shrewd glance. 'The longer the better, eh?'

'Something like that.' Violet hugged herself happily—if it was anything like the Chuar Khel Dhana, this latest road was going to take a very long time …

'Aren't you tired of all this cold and wet?' he asked her.

'Not at all!' She stretched out her legs, and surveyed the grubby trousers she was wearing. 'You cannot imagine, Malcolm, how free these make me feel. After wearing petticoats all my life.'

Nicolson admitted that, true, he had no idea. 'But you can't stay like this,' he warned. 'This will come to an end soon enough.'

Violet pulled a face. 'I know. And I shall miss the freedom—the anonymity.'

'You've hardly been anonymous, woman!' Unobtrusive, yes. Undemanding, certainly. Otherwise, somehow, he would have found a way of sending her back.

'But no one has minded my being here,' Violet pointed out triumphantly, as she snuggled close. 'Perhaps,' and she looked up at her husband through her thick lashes, 'perhaps I can come with you next time, too?'

The colonel had no intention of this particular situation repeating itself, but faced with the full force of Violet's persuasiveness, he thought it better to change the subject. 'Look,' he said, 'I've something for your collection.'

'Goodness, a shell! How did it get here?'

' It's a fossil. Once upon a time all this area was at the bottom of the sea.'

'So it's even older than the mountains.' Violet held the long, spiral shell with reverent fingers. 'And it's as beautiful. Darling,' she vowed extravagantly as she tucked it safely away, 'I shall keep it forever!'

Walking back to the camp arm in arm, 'Aren't you just a little bit tired of making roads?' Violet asked him.

'No, not if it's going to serve a useful purpose.'

'And is it?'

'Yes, if troops are to be deployed here in future.'

'And if they're not?'

'Well then, I shall have had a very good time—hard work, exercise, fresh air. Because,' Malcolm added with a boyish grin, 'despite what you may think, sweetheart, I'm thoroughly enjoying myself, like you!' It was true: wet and dirty and probably tired, there was a carefree, happy air about him that Violet welcomed. She also welcomed his willingness to talk.

'I suppose you could say that road-making runs in my family,' he went on. 'My father did the same work in Central India.'

'But it wouldn't have been at all like this, would it? It must have been terribly different. Think of the dreadful heat, for one thing.'

'You're right,' he agreed, for in Zhob the mid-November weather was beginning to change. The clouds were starting to close in on the mountains, and with them came a cold intermittent rain.

'Tell me about your father, Malcolm. What was he like?'

'Darling, to be honest, I can hardly remember—I was only six or seven when he died. He had retired by then, and we were living in Boulogne: my parents, my sisters, my brother and me.'

'You have a brother?'

'He was two years younger than me. He was invalided out of the Indian Marine and died when he was twenty-nine. Poor Edmund … India has dealt harshly with our family,' Nicolson continued. 'My father died long before his time as well. Do you know, Violet,' and he sounded surprised at the realisation, 'my mother has been a widow for over forty years. We should go back to see her.'

Perhaps they should, but it was not a plan the younger Mrs Nicolson felt inclined to encourage.

⁂

The weather grew dark and increasingly cloudy. The showers became heavier and more frequent. On 26 November they reached Gandari Kach, the flat open area at the mouth of the Zao defile. And a forlorn, dismal place it was too, thought Violet, taking cover while the colonel went off with a party to reconnoitre as far as he could inside the gorge.

'Aren't the tents here yet?' he asked his soaking wife on his return, and she shook her glistening head. 'Well, you can't stop here,' he said, as a few pebbles rattled down to fall at her feet, and he pulled her out from the inadequate shelter of the overhang into the driving rain. 'This conglomerate is dangerous stuff. We've been dodging rockfalls all the way back.'

He was frowning as he looked around him. 'Yes, I'm afraid the whole lot could come down at any time—that's why the pass is blocked. And if we ever get it clear,' he added, 'the work will probably all have to be done again some other time.'

'So why do it in the first place?' she asked, laughing into her husband's glum face.

The rain stopped overnight, and work began in the morning under a baleful threatening sky. A long narrow path was being blasted through the rock a mile from the opening when the heavens opened with renewed vigour. The sappers abandoned the ramp they were constructing and hurried back to the entrance. On the way they were overtaken by a party from further up the gorge, some twenty men in all, *sepoys*, camel drivers and camp followers, all pushing past them in their haste to find shelter. Behind them came Nicolson and the engineer in charge.

By now the rain was lashing down in sheets, and the twenty men huddled in the very spot that Violet had chosen the day before. When Nicolson emerged in his turn he saw them immediately. 'Get away from there!' he yelled, gesticulating wildly as he ran towards the cliff. For he could see what they could not—a boulder beginning to slip high up on the face above them, its imminent fall heralded by a shower of smaller stones. 'Get away!'

None of them heard, so busy were they laughing and talking, but Violet did, and came out of her tent to see what was happening. As she watched in horror, the whole cliff began to slide forward, slowly at first, with one boulder falling to be followed by a second, then quicker and quicker, gathering momentum. One after another, great slabs came crashing down, and with them came blood-red clay and short-lived dust.

The sound of the fall reverberated round the camp, the uncanny silence that followed broken only by the colonel's incisive orders and the faint cries of the buried men.

Frantic hands clawed impotently at the massive pile of mud-stained rock, but soon the muffled voices died away to nothing.

'Can nothing be done?' Violet asked in a shocked whisper.

'We'll get in through that.' Nicolson spoke with a confidence he was far from feeling, as he pointed to two great boulders and a tiny gap between.

'Is it safe?'

'Safe enough,' he said. There had been no further rock falls for some minutes. He stepped forward purposefully, but the gap in the rock when he reached it proved too narrow for the colonel's broad shoulders, and too narrow for all the others who tried.

'Malcolm, let me try.' Violet put a gentle hand on his arm.

Despite himself, Nicolson considered his wife's slight boyish frame, then emphatically shook his head. 'No, it's out of the question. Violet, no!'

She refused to give up. Lieutenant Price, himself covered in mud from his own attempts to succeed where his colonel had failed, listened to Mrs Nicolson's low passionate voice urgently pleading for the right to risk her life: 'You tried, Malcolm, now let me. Please, darling— Look at me. I'm the only one who has any chance at all. *Someone may still be alive—let me try while there's still time.*'

Blue eyes held grey for a moment and Colonel Nicolson made up his mind: 'Very well,' he said and let her go.

Then began the waiting. Price stood beside him, neither man daring to speak. Around them stood the equally silent Baluchis, not a man among them who had not lost a brother or a friend in the rockslide, not one who had not resented the pale-haired *mem* from the start of *Nikelseyn*'s marriage. Violet had been right all those months before: there were no secrets in India, and after each argument between the couple, after every dispute, the *sepoys* had hoped the troublesome *mem* would be sent away for good. Not that *Nikelseyn* had changed in any way towards them—he remained as fair and compassionate as ever, but his life was no longer his own—nor, more importantly, was it totally theirs. Watching the drawn features of the man they considered their father and their mother, they tried to understand the nature of his feelings—and why the *mem* should put her life at risk.

It did not take long to squeeze and squirm her way into the darkness. Only Isabel would ever be told the full horror of the journey that followed, as, blind and fighting claustrophobia, she groped her way forward, encountering crushed limbs and the smell and feel of blood. There was no other movement, and the bodies beneath her apprehensive fingers all seemed lifeless. She strained for the sound of breathing and the warning rattle of pebbles. Nothing. Behind her, she could see a faint glimmer and as her eyes became accustomed, she made out more light coming from her right. She inched towards it on her hands and knees and then she heard the moan. One man at least was alive, then … and she crawled towards the sound.

There was enough light to show exactly where he lay. She removed the smaller rocks from his chest but it would take someone stronger to shift the rest. The worst of the fall must have caught the others, but if she stepped over this one survivor there was almost enough room for a man, or men, to stand.

Moving backwards by the way she had come, Violet attempted to gauge the distance. At first it was impossible to turn and when she did, that one heartening sliver of light beckoned her on and became brighter. She heard several voices, Nicolson's among them, and the sound almost unnerved her. *What if I'm trapped; what if I'm going to die here?* She threw herself against the rasping surface of the rock, twisting sideways, resisting the impulse to panic … Then she was free …

Bruising fingers gripped her shoulders for a moment as Nicolson pulled her to her feet. Quickly she told him what she had found, and paced out the distance to where she reckoned the injured man was lying. And then he left her.

Muddy, grazed and bleeding, Violet stood there, not wanting to watch, not daring to look away. '*Nikelseyn mem*,' the voice came from behind her. She turned. It was Malcolm's forbidding new orderly, proffering a blanket. Another *sepoy* held out a pannikin of steaming *chai*. Gratefully, she accepted both, warmed more than anything by the sudden unexpected feeling of belonging.

The sappers removed the injured man, and another who was dead. As they prepared to go back in for the other bodies, the cliff came down again and nearly took the rescue party with it. It was pointless to continue until the weather cleared, so at last Malcolm Nicolson allowed himself to look to his wife.

He found her exactly where he had left her, with a group of his Baluchis hovering protectively, their presence—he suspected—preventing her from bursting into tears. He was wrong. Violet was totally calm as she watched him approach, his gait weary and his ashen face that of a very old man. Without protest, he let her take his arm and lead him away.

What could you say to a man who blamed himself for twenty deaths? Who sat with his head in his hands, refusing comfort? 'Malcolm, there was nothing you could do. Why blame yourself? You could do nothing.'

'I failed them. They were my responsibility.'

'You got them out. Now they can be buried.'

He did not reply.

She tried again. 'If they had died in a fight, then perhaps it could have been blamed on your tactics. But, for heaven's sake, Malcolm Nicolson, not even the Indian Army can take control of the weather!'

He looked up at that. She was quivering with frustration. 'I'm sorry, of course you're perfectly right—and no one could have done more for them than you. Will you come with me now to see what can be done for Amir Allah?'

It took another two days to get the Zao defile open, another two days for the injured man to die. Amir Allah clung stubbornly to life until the evening of the second day, when Nicolson fought his way back through another torrential downpour to tell his wife that at last the Zao defile was open.

As he came into the tent where Violet and the dying man's brother were keeping their silent vigil, the dying man, whose rasping breaths were increasingly shallow and irregular, seemed to recognise his colonel. Nicolson stepped forward and took the cold hands in both of his. The man's lips moved slowly once and moments later he died.

Violet bowed her head then rose to her feet with a sigh. The *sepoy* leaned forward to close his brother's eyes, and then he turned and spoke to his commandant's wife directly.

'He will never forget what you did,' Nicolson told her. 'He is a Moslem, of course, and accepts it as God's will, but thanks to your courage his brother will receive a proper burial. Both you and I know how much that means to one of his faith.'

Violet touched the man's arm in sympathy and went outside. Taking a deep breath, she loosened her hair and raised her face to the torrential rain. It helped a little.

'We're going through tomorrow.' Nicolson gave her the news at last. 'Where we're going and for how long, I don't know. But I do know we're staying in Baluchistan. We'll be getting further orders at Apozai—and then I'm sending you to the Sandemans in Quetta.'

4

'Is it my fault I am alone?'

BALUCHISTAN: DECEMBER 1890–MARCH 1893

Arthur Cory treated his office at the *Sind Gazette* rather like his personal club. Here he received old friends who dropped by, perhaps after a trip to England and before making their way north to the Punjab and Baluchistan by train. Or local worthies like his doctor or his lawyer, or Alexander McHinch, who had grown rich on the back of the prawns and oysters he packed in ice and conveyed north in containers to Lahore. The room was larger than Isabel's and lacked its order. Whereas Isabel could reach for any item she wanted and know she would find it in place, Arthur Cory's files and papers took on a life of their own, moving from bookcase to desk to floor as the day progressed. Yet, as if by magic, there was always a corner by the fire, with its two armchairs and plumped-up cushions that remained free of clutter and ready to welcome a passing guest. The colonel's room was lined with bookcases and cabinets; only three framed pictures beside the window broke the lines of shelves and cupboard doors. Cory never tired of pointing them out to his visitors. They were, he had explained to his banker only the day before, the work of his three daughters; understand the pictures, Colonel Cory said with a smile, and his friend would understand his girls as well.

The first, in fact, was a sampler. From a distance it was a riot of colour, full of life and with a certain wild attraction. Seen at close quarters it was obvious that the needlewoman had quickly lost both the pattern and her patience, to produce a frenetic tangle of puckered knots. Embroidered in the corner were the initials *A S C* and the date, *1878*, a year that had seen Annie Sophie abandon her needle for good. Next to it hung Adela's pencil portrait of her father, dashed off in minutes and bearing a dazzling likeness to the sitter. When Isabel answered her father's call she approached his desk and stood under her own creation, a watercolour that Cory had pointed out to his visitor with particular pride. Quiet and meticulous in its detail, its beauty was evident only when examined closely.

Cory looked up briefly. 'Take a seat, my dear,' he said. 'I won't be a moment.' Isabel removed a pile of books from a high-backed chair and sat down. Cory put the finishing touches to his latest editorial on Baluchistan, then set it aside. 'I've just received a letter from your sister,' he told her. 'And she has enclosed one for you.' He didn't hand it over immediately but took up a single sheet of paper instead and perused it. 'It seems that Adela has been with Sandeman in Quetta for a fortnight,' he explained. 'That is, Sir Robert Sandeman, the Government's representative in Baluchistan, the man behind the Zhob Expedition. You remember, Izzie.'

Isabel who, despite the newspaper's main preoccupations, had no interest in politics at all, tried to look as if she did. After all, the Zhob campaign had been highly successful. More importantly, Colonel Cory had capitalised on his son-in-law's participation to such an extent that the *Sind Gazette* had more subscribers than ever before in its short history.

'I knew Sir Robert in Lahore,' Cory removed his spectacles, distracted for the moment, 'during the late Afghan conflict.' Isabel did her best to hide a smile, for whom had her father *not* known? 'Adela's in good hands.'

'Shouldn't she be in her husband's, and not causing trouble for somebody else?' came the sharp response. Isabel knew that once the news had come through from unofficial sources that Adela was not in Hyderabad but had run after Nicolson, her father had been worrying continually. He looked older, overtired and crumpled; even the office seemed more out of control than usual. Not for the first time she cursed Adela's recklessness—and Adela's husband for his indulgence of it.

'Come now, my dear. We both know she behaved very badly and that Nick was simply not to blame. But that's over. She's safe, thank the Lord, and Nick will join her as soon as he can.'

'I understand it's been snowing in Quetta for days,' Isabel remarked. 'Cooped up, with nothing to do but wait for Malcolm to come and fetch her—imagine how she'll be hating *that*! In a way it serves her right for all the trouble she's caused. Do you know, Father, I believe he was glad to get rid of her and I can't imagine he'll be in any hurry to have her back! Although I suppose they'll be here for Christmas as usual?'

'No, she and Nick won't be coming to Karachi for Christmas *or* New Year. Your mother, of course, will be extremely disappointed when she hears.'

'So am I,' Isabel acknowledged. 'And I imagine you are, too. But possibly not Annie Sophie,' she added dryly.

The colonel allowed himself a slow smile. 'Do you know, my dear, I believe I'm rather relieved. Like you, I find keeping the peace between my two younger daughters rather tiresome! No, I imagine we shall invite Mr and Mrs McHinch—and Maisie, of course—and ...' here he looked at Isabel quizzically, 'I thought we might ask that nice Mr Tate from the Punjab Bank to join us. What do you think?'

'Is there a Lady Sandeman?' Isabel asked quickly, to divert her father from what she imagined to be another of his matchmaking attempts. She supposed the Resident must have a wife, or even her brother-in-law would have had to observe the proprieties and send the culprit back to her parents.

'Yes, she's Sir Robert's second wife,' Cory told her. 'He lost his first, and two of his children, years ago at Dera Ghazi Khan. It was far too remote a place to fetch a doctor, you see. It would have broken a lesser man, but he pulled through and devoted himself to Baluchistan instead.'

And to 'The Forward Policy', reflected Isabel. No wonder her father admired him so much. All afternoon Adela's letter waited at the edge of her desk, unopened. At last the assistant editor of the *Sind Gazette* completed her day's work and began to read what turned out to be many pages written in Adela's bold undisciplined hand. Much as she loved her sister, Isabel felt that in this unseemly episode Addie Nicolson had gone too far in her devotion to her husband, and any discomfort she was feeling at the moment—about which Isabel found herself reading at length—simply served her right! Sometimes, it seemed to Isabel, she was living her life secondhand, through her sister, and that the only males she would ever know with any degree of intimacy would be her brother-in-law and, of course, her father. Practical and levelheaded, she had never allowed herself to regret her lack of adventures and there was nothing about Adela's present eagerness to leave Quetta (which was 'dull', 'boring', 'tedious' and, finally, 'unbearable') and go back to Zhob that sparked even a scintilla of envy. 'If I don't get away soon, I shall die!' As Adela confided how close, in fact, she had come to dying in the rockslide of the Zao defile and her near terror at the prospect of being entombed alive, her mouth full of dust, her nostrils filled with the smell of corruption, perhaps, thought Isabel with a certain disloyal satisfaction, the vagabond had been punished enough.

In Quetta Helen Sandeman was looking forward to her guest's departure with almost as much desperation as her guest. 'It's not that Mrs Nicolson is not being perfectly pleasant. It's just,' and Lady Sandeman, a comfortably built motherly woman in her late forties, searched for the right words, 'it's just that she's so *distant*, as if she doesn't really hear what I'm saying. Or as if she does hear, but doesn't care!' she finished with a rush.

'Oh dear,' came the only reaction.

'Yes, and there are so many things I want to ask her! About what happened to her, and what the colonel said when she turned up out of the blue, oh, you know, Rob—all the things you mentioned but said I should ask her myself. Well, I *have* asked her and she won't say a word! It's as if she thinks I'm being nosy!'

'And, of course, you aren't ...' The Resident's affectionate gaze rested on his wife. 'She won't talk about Nick behind his back, you know. And she feels no need to talk about herself. It will be different when he gets here, you'll see. That I can promise.'

'And that's another thing!' Lady Sandeman exclaimed. 'She sits by the window, looking out across the snow and when anyone comes, she springs to her feet and runs to the door as if it could be him. She must know he won't get here for a week at least!'

'Earlier than that, I suspect. If I know my old companion, he'll be just as anxious to see his wife!'

Helen Sandeman gave a little sniff. What men saw in Violet Nicolson she could not fathom. 'Oh, dear,' she said as an appalling thought struck her. 'What if Colonel Nicolson doesn't come for her at all?'

'No Rival like the Past'

The next morning it stopped snowing at last and Violet could bear her confinement no longer. Wrapped in her Afghan coat and with a bright scarf wound about her head, she wandered aimlessly through the Residency grounds, her mind drifting over recent events. She had parted from Malcolm at Harnai with a brief caress, a sigh of relief from the colonel and—if she were honest—one from the colonel's wife. Then he had marched off without a backward glance, and she had hurried away with Lieutenant Price to take the train. When Malcolm arrived they could begin to make their plans, she thought, and she would escape what had begun to feel like a prison. For the first time since the Sandemans met her at Quetta station she felt almost happy.

The house was out of sight. Violet could no longer make out the line of the driveway. The shrubs all looked like one another and she supposed that she was lost. She shrugged. What did it matter? On a sudden impulse she bent and began to make a snowman. She straightened then bent once more, so lost in the act of creation that she failed to hear the crunch of virgin snow behind her. Malcolm Nicolson had arrived days early as Sandeman had predicted.

Quelling a wave of irritation that Violet was not there to greet him (in all fairness, how could she have known he was coming?), he exchanged niceties with his hosts before inquiring as to the whereabouts of his wife. She had been easy to find and he watched her undetected for several moments, until she straightened one last time to place a twig in the travesty of a face and stood back in admiration. Suddenly she squealed in surprise.

Brushing the snow from her neck Mrs Nicolson wheeled round in delight. *He was here* and it was not the reunion she had so looked forward to, yet so much dreaded, under the curious eyes of strangers. 'Shame on you, Malcolm Nicolson,' she scolded as he walked towards her. 'To take a lady by surprise, and you an officer and a gentleman!' She bore not the least resemblance to any lady of his acquaintance, her husband ventured, smoothing back the wayward tendrils from her glowing cheeks as she pressed against him wantonly to receive his kisses.

'I see you still prefer your native wardrobe,' he remarked as they made their way back. 'Once the trunks from Hyderabad arrive I suggest you start dressing like an Englishwoman.'

'I suppose you think Lady Sandeman doesn't enjoy being with someone who appears to have gone native,' she retorted. 'Well, I've been here a fortnight and she's not said a word!'

'Then, as you've been here a fortnight,' and Malcolm's tone was perfectly pleasant, 'you should know that Helen Sandeman is one of the most broad-minded women you're likely to meet. No, my dear wife,' and he pulled her to him possessively, 'if you must blame anyone, blame me.'

'You?'

'Yes, me! I want to see you in dresses with full skirts and a fitted waist. With your shoulders bare and glowing in the lamplight.'

Violet felt her hackles rising. She had no wish to be dressed as some object, as some doll for a man's delight—even if that man was her husband and she hadn't seen him for two weeks and yearned for his embraces. 'As you looked when you sang to me that evening in Karachi. If you remember?'

'Very well, Malcolm,' she responded meekly. 'I promise. As soon as the boxes arrive ...'

The Nicolsons' possessions arrived one day after the colonel, yet that evening, too, Mrs Nicolson sat down to dinner wearing a deep blue, exquisitely embroidered Afghan tunic, one of several acquired after prolonged haggling while waiting for the train at Harnai. 'I'm afraid,' she told Lady Sandeman, 'your ayah did her good work for nothing—all those dresses so beautifully pressed, and all far too big for me at present!' She smiled triumphantly across at her husband.

'I shall be fattening Violet up in time for Easter, if not for Christmas,' Nicolson was not in the least put out. 'And I'm taking her to Bombay for a few weeks' leave—to do some shopping.' He looked at his wife, whose smile became a little rueful. While she had won the battle, she suspected that Malcolm was more than likely to win the war.

To Helen's satisfaction Colonel Nicolson proved more forthcoming than his wife. 'Violet is a woman of many talents,' he confided. 'Why, at one point she masqueraded as a sheep, or was it a goat? And at another she managed to control the most recalcitrant camel.'

'Really? Do tell us, Nick.' The tale was new even to Sir Robert, so Nicolson proceeded to paint a vivid picture of the dark and damp of the Chuar Khel Dhana Pass, where Violet had intervened out of pity for a frightened beast. The colonel's whimsical turn of phrase and shameless exaggeration could not hide the very real danger. When the leading camel had baulked at a narrow sandbag bridge across the raging river water, no amount of cursing could make the creature budge, he explained, and the smell of fear threatened to spread panic through the rest. 'But my wife rose beautifully to the occasion,' Nicolson went on. 'She coaxed it across the bridge, even though one false move, one kick, would have seen them both in the water—and the camel's problems doubtless solved for good.' The bantering tone was dropped as he added quite needlessly, 'I was extremely proud.'

'He certainly didn't say so at the time—all he did was offer me a job as a camel driver!'

'Perhaps you might prefer donkeys?' Robert Sandeman suggested when the laughter died down. 'Have you ever seen the local beasts?' he asked. 'They slit their nostrils at birth to help them breathe when they carry heavy loads in the mountains.'

'Then I'm surprised they don't do it to their women as well. Or perhaps they do?' Violet enquired caustically. 'They appear to do most of the carrying and they look extremely tired and old, although some of the ones I've seen can't have been any older than me.'

Lady Sandeman gave a dry laugh. 'I know exactly what you mean, Mrs Nicolson—the men so handsome and the women so careworn. It seems to be a characteristic of this country.' She and Violet nodded, in complete sympathy for once.

'Yet the girls are beautiful,' added Sir Robert. 'It seems to be marriage that does all the damage. Although,' and he raised his glass gallantly in tribute, 'the ladies present are obvious exceptions!'

'They say that Afghan women are very beautiful, too,' Lady Sandeman gracefully accepted the tribute. 'Is that true, Malcolm? I believe you spent many months in Kandahar—and of course Rob was in Afghanistan for some of the late war as well. There must have been a good many broken hearts when the army finally left.'

It was lightly said but the two men's eyes met and held. 'Yes,' Nicolson said at last. 'Some Afghan women are truly very lovely.'

Neither man said another word and the older woman realised she had committed some kind of *faux pas*. Sensing her husband's discomfiture Violet intervened before the silence could deepen. 'Wasn't Sir Robert Warburton's mother an Afghan princess?' she said quickly. 'And isn't it interesting that nobody seems to mind about *that*, even though other attitudes towards such marriages have changed? Why, the white women of Hyderabad are quite *ghastly* about avoiding Indians—they think it's all a question of showing the flag, but I'm sure they really do more harm than good!'

'Well, well, Nick,' Sandeman said when the two men were left alone to their port. 'I'm sorry about that. Your lassie noticed, of course.'

'Of course she did—and changed the subject, too. In fact, for someone whose tact equals that of a sledgehammer she did extremely well. But I'm bound to hear more of it later.'

He did. His wife's reluctance to leave the fireside and join him in their bed boded ill for the colonel, and when she looked up from prodding at the glowing embers to ask: 'Who was she, Malcolm?' Nicolson sighed, and prepared himself for the inevitable raking over of memories that must surely follow.

'Come here then and I'll tell you.'

Violet rose to her feet and walked towards him slowly. With her hair falling about her shoulders she looked very young and exceedingly vulnerable. Her eyes were clouded with apprehension and at the bedside she hesitated, as if no longer welcome. Nicolson reached out and took her hand in a warm firm clasp.

'Well, where shall I begin?' he asked as she settled down beside him.

'Why not at the beginning?' she suggested glumly. 'It seems as good a place as any.'

She probably wasn't going to give him any help at all, Nicolson decided, but there he was wrong.

'It's something to do with Mahomed Akram, isn't it? That's why you and he are so close.' Violet frowned in concentration as she tried to remember everything that had puzzled her in the past, and as she did so, Malcolm Nicolson compared his wife with another girl, long dead. How different they were. One tall, dark, stately, and meek in nature, with eyes of a soft, deep, amber hue, and the other, small, impetuous, strong-willed, and whose passionate violet eyes flashed sometimes ice and sometimes fire. Nicolson drew the warm little body close within his arm.

'Who was she, Malcolm?' Violet repeated.

'She was everything my wife is not, and never could be. No, no, sweetheart,' he chuckled as she tried unsuccessfully to free herself and his arm tightened round her, binding her fast. 'And you,' he went on, 'are everything I hoped she would be, but wasn't.' Intrigued at that, Violet stopped struggling. And as she lay passively against him, Malcolm told her of the siege and occupation of Kandahar; of the rich Afghan families who put their own interests first, their country's second; of one family in particular, whose son he knew—had known for years.

'Mahomed Akram.'

'Mahomed Akram Durani. Who spied for General Donald Stewart.'

'Like you.'

'Like me. His family welcomed me into their home. There seemed no harm, no harm at all ...' The mellow voice she loved so well trailed away into silence as she waited expectantly. 'There was a daughter, too.'

Of course, there would have been. She could almost see her: one of those gentle doe-eyed maidens who fetched water from the well, sensuous, graceful, appealing—until time and weather reduced their skin to wrinkled hide. But this one had been rich, protected; she was unlikely to have grown ugly so soon, if ever. 'What happened to her?' Violet's voice was subdued.

'She watched me, from behind the lattice of the women's quarters, and one morning as I passed her in the yard, she raised her veil.' Violet felt him shrug. 'What do you expect happened? She was beautiful, fresh with the dew of youth—and I was fool enough to fall in love. And she returned my feelings. Or so I believed.'

Try as she might, Violet could detect no trace of bitterness in her husband's tone.

'There was a kind of madness in the air throughout those long, long months in Kandahar and I would have married her if her family had consented, but we left in April 1880, her brother and I, with General Stewart's brigade.' He paused then continued, 'It was after the fight at Ahmed Khel.'

'Mahomed Akram was there, too?' Violet traced the scar on Malcolm's face with the lightest of caresses.

'He saved my life, and the same blade marked us both. I was lucky, he less so.' Nicolson kissed her wandering fingers and gave a rueful smile. 'He is truly my brother—in blood, if in no other way. When I was free at last to return to Kandahar she was gone, married without protest to a man she did not love. She died ten months later bearing his child. And the child died with her.'

The voice was still matter of fact, the face devoid of expression, but now there was a trace of pain. 'It was a long time ago, my darling,' Malcolm said at last, 'a barely lingering memory—nothing more. I have other memories now.' Violet swallowed her tears as he added, 'some are bitter, some immeasurably sweet. And *all of them* are of you.'

'In the softest silk is our sister dressed'

The next morning, although it was snowing heavily again, the colonel and Sir Robert went to District Headquarters where Nicolson was due to discuss plans for his future with Sir George White. Their wives, who had abandoned their own proposed visit to the town, stood at the Residency window for a while, watching the great flakes drift down to settle on the garden.

'This is quite normal for us up here, you know. It stops for a short while then it begins again. We can always guarantee a white Christmas for our guests!'

'I haven't seen such snow since I was little—and even then it was never anything like this. We stayed with my grandmother in London for the holidays and the snow was cleared away immediately. It always seemed such a shame, but here I must admit I feel a little differently! Lady Sandeman,' diffidently Violet changed the subject, 'there's something I'd like to ask you now, if you wouldn't mind ...'

Helen smiled as the younger woman explained her problem and offered her assistance immediately. The two women spent the morning closeted together and by tiffin were firm friends. When Sir Robert returned to the Residency he found his wife and their guest on first-name terms at last, laughing and talking as if they had known each other for years. He was delighted, for if things turned out as he intended, they would be seeing far more of Malcolm Nicolson's wife in the days and months to come.

'Aren't you ready yet?' Malcolm Nicolson made no effort to hide his annoyance. 'You knew the Whites were coming to dinner and I heard them arrive ten minutes ago. Really, Violet, what's got into you? You never take as long as this!' Especially when it was simply a matter of pulling a tunic over her head, he thought in exasperation.

'Darling, you go on.' From her dressing room Violet sounded quite unperturbed. 'Tell them I'll only be a minute.'

'Very well—I just hope you mean it!'

Malcolm Nicolson presented his wife's excuses and was engaged in conversation when she at last made an appearance. He was standing with his back to the door and did not realise why such a silence had fallen. He turned and stared as Violet paused and looked at him from the doorway.

Dressed in the gown she had worn at the Viceregal Ball in Karachi, a gown that left her shoulders bare and hugged her tiny waist, with the elaborate coils of her coiffure emphasising her slender neck, she held her husband's gaze for a moment. Then, gloved hand outstretched, she regally advanced towards him. A mischievous little smile played upon her lips as she saw the effect she was having. Helen, who with her maid had helped create that very effect, watched the colonel, while he in turn watched his wife.

'Violet Nicolson is a very clever young woman, and Malcolm is a very lucky man—and I only hope he knows it!' was Lady Sandeman's opinion when, at the end of a most successful evening, she and her husband retired to bed.

Christmas for the Corys was by no means the dismal affair that Isabel had feared. The McHinches were engaged elsewhere but John Tate had accepted with alacrity. Five years a widower, he missed the company of women and he bestowed his friendly smile and handshake first on Isabel and then on Annie Sophie. The younger girl simpered and then did her best to monopolise the family's guest; her older sister, who had always found Mr Tate so helpful in matters of business, took the opportunity to study the banker at her leisure.

Annie Sophie rattled on and, like Nicolson before him, Tate appeared to give the girl his full attention. He was about the same age as her brother-in-law, Isabel decided, but shorter and lacking his vitality. Where Malcolm Nicolson had the face of an ascetic and the harnessed energy of an athlete, John Tate, while by no means fat, had the comfortable build of a man who would never run while he could walk, never ride where he could drive. 'I'm going to be a writer,' she heard her sister announce. 'A novelist, I think, and I'm going to write all sorts of wonderful stories about India. Addie has inspired me—that's my other sister, Mr Tate, the one who ran off with an Afghan!'

'That's not true, Mr Tate, as I'm sure you know. Annie Sophie has far too vivid an imagination.' Isabel quelled her sister with a fearsome look and passed the banker a dish of roast potatoes.

Cory's artistic analogy had not been lost on Tate. After dinner, he put aside his glass of port, and stood up. 'Do play for us, Miss Cory. And I shall turn the pages.' Brooking no refusal, he held out an arm and gallantly led Isabel to the pianoforte. 'I do so love music,' he told the company, 'and the chance to hear an accomplished musician, alas, has been so rare.'

Although she played unerringly as usual, under the gaze of her companion's intent brown eyes Isabel was flustered. To her relief, Annie Sophie soon clamoured for her turn and, still blushing, she was able to retreat to a corner of the drawing room. Tate followed and drew up a seat beside her. 'You play most charmingly, Miss Cory,' he whispered. 'And you look most charming tonight, if I may say so. That soft grey colour suits you admirably. Or is it mauve?'

Isabel stared in fascination as the banker's fingers, square and spatulate where her brother-in-law's were long and sensitive, reached towards her. For a moment he stroked the rich velvet encasing her upper arm. 'Handsome, most handsome,' he murmured, leaning forward, and in her confusion afterwards, Isabel wondered whether he had meant the fine material of her garment, or herself.

'Cholera, Riot, and Sudden Death'

Gul Kach was bitterly cold and completely belied its name as 'the place of roses', yet as Violet hugged her coat around her she did not mind in the least. She had taken it for granted that Malcolm would want her to go back with him to Zhob. Instead, he had done everything to dissuade her, but had stopped short of compulsion. Instead, he taught her how to load and fire a revolver. Now she was here in this isolated outpost high above the Gomal valley where caravans, laden with all kinds of goods according to season, filed through from Afghanistan down to the Indus plain. Neither of them had any regrets. She felt no need for the company of women, and was content to read, write, be of any help she could, and wander within the limits laid down by her husband. Charles Price was no longer there, and Violet sometimes wondered why he, and not another of the lieutenants, had been sent to an even lonelier post. She preferred not to dwell on the lovelorn look he had given her in farewell, hoping she was mistaken, but Malcolm had been quite blunt.

'The lad's been in love with you ever since he rescued you from Bungal Khan's clutches.'

'Oh.'

'He'll get over it. Especially now he's with Seivwright's detachment in Mogul Kot. He'll be far too busy to think of you out there!'

'Malcolm, you're not jealous, are you?'

'Of course not. But I don't want to watch him making a fool of himself over my wife. It'll be good for him to get away—and he knows it. He'll have a fair bit of responsibility, after all.'

'And he'll forget all about me, I suppose.'

'Precisely.'

There was, it occurred to Violet Nicolson, a latent ruthlessness about her husband, especially where she was concerned. She wondered idly what he would do if he ever thought he had real cause for jealousy. Meanwhile, on the subject of jealousy, there was something she wanted to ask her husband, and she was prepared to bide her time.

❧

'Darling, who is Mrs Steel?' Malcolm Nicolson blinked at the unexpected nature of the question and stared at his wife in the gathering dusk. 'Now where did you hear that name, I wonder?'

'Sir George mentioned her at dinner one night when we were in Quetta. I meant to ask you afterwards, but I forgot.'

Violet's presence in the rudimentary camp at Gul Kach above the Gomal River, although against the colonel's better judgement, had been a comfort and a delight for weeks, and the intrusion of a third in the person of Mrs Flora Annie Steel was as unexpected as it was unwelcome.

'Who is she?' she repeated. 'The general said she was the only woman he could think of who might have done as I did, and followed you to Zhob.'

Nicolson's mouth twitched in amusement. 'Were those his exact words?' he enquired.

'No, not quite. I think what he actually said was that she would have probably have managed as well as I did—had she been there.'

'I see. I think I prefer the second version.'

'Who is she, Malcolm?' Violet was not to be deterred. 'You still haven't answered my question!'

'She's someone I've known for twenty years or so. Her husband retired last year and I believe they're living somewhere in Scotland.' There was just enough light for him to see Violet raise an eyebrow.

'Was she a married woman when you met her?'

'Very much so! She was married at twenty and she proudly refers to herself as a *baby bride*.' Violet snorted and her husband went on quickly: 'She married her cousin who was in the civil service out here, and I've always thought she scared him to death, poor fellow.'

'And does she frighten *you*?'

'Not a bit!'

'And where did you first meet this Mrs Steel?'

'In a hill station—Mussourie or Dalhousie, I can't remember where exactly.' He smiled at Violet. 'It wasn't a hill station romance, if that's what you're thinking, her husband was there at the time.'

In India that didn't necessarily mean a thing. 'I see,' she said.

'Do you?' Malcolm raised a quizzical eyebrow in his turn. 'I hope you're not going to be jealous of Flora Steel, my dear. That would be too ridiculous! What else did Sir George have to say?'

'Not much. Except that she was one of the kindest women he knew.'

'Yes,' agreed the colonel, 'she's kind, and practical, and can't bear waste of any sort—and that includes waste of human beings.'

Violet was a little disconcerted by the sudden warmth in her husband's voice.

'Do you know, darling, she talked George White out of resigning his commission when he was a major—he'd been in the service for years without further promotion—and look at him now, commanding Quetta District!'

'Would I like her?' Violet was sure she wouldn't.

'As you're unlikely ever to meet her, it doesn't really matter one way or the other, does it?' Malcolm Nicolson leaned back against the camel bag that served as a cushion and shut his eyes, indicating to his inquisitor that as far as he was concerned the matter was closed. Flora Annie Steel, he thought as the silence deepened. She had not crossed his mind for quite some time. He really should inform her of his marriage.

Patrols checked the valley daily, and several times a week bands of traders passed through without harassment. How long this state of affairs would last was another matter. The Amir of Afghanistan saw his frontier increasingly under threat, and from Britain, a so-called friend, at that—a friend who was closing in on him little by little; creeping slowly and surely towards the walls of his great cities of Kabul and Kandahar—and he was agitating for the border dispute to be settled for once and for all. Negotiations were already under way to do that very thing and there was talk of the army's withdrawal from the border post of Gul Kach.

'Once the tribes get to hear of what's in the air, there could be trouble,' the colonel warned his wife. 'If they think we're leaving, they might just decide to help us on our way!'

'Surely not, darling.' Violet put out a reassuring hand. 'Aren't they all loyal to Sir Robert?'

'I'm not talking about the ones on our side of the valley.' Nicolson's face was grim as he ignored her gesture. 'The Amir has plenty of cronies further to the north!'

Yet it remained quiet in the following months and the colonel's gloomy predictions proved unfounded. So one morning in March, when there was the first hint of warmth in the winter air and when the patrols were due to go out along the Gomal River, Nicolson succumbed at last to his wife's pleas and with very few misgivings took her with him into the valley. As luck would have it, when they were on their way back they came under attack from a large group of Waziris ranging south from their tribal heartland, intent on mischief and spoiling for a fight. Perched like vultures on the snow-covered crest opposite, they began to fire down on the patrol.

Yelling to his men to run for cover, Colonel Nicolson dragged his wife after him towards the shelter of the tumbled boulders hard up against the cliffs on their side of the river. The ambushers had chosen well: in one of the narrowest parts of the valley the Baluchis were easy prey. The deadly rain of metal ricocheted off the rock face behind them and no one dared move. They crouched there listening to the rumble of dislodged boulders crashing into the river only yards away, some of them bounding up the bank towards them. There was no hope of retreat; injury—if not death—seemed certain. There was no sense of panic: the soldiers under attack were out of the ordinary, and trained by an extraordinary man. Now and again a *sepoy* would cautiously raise his head to risk a shot, ignoring the whine of lead and the splinters of rock. The colonel did the same. When the patrol had been pinned down for over twenty minutes Nicolson spoke to his wife.

'Now listen carefully, Violet. We've no chance at all of getting away and the ammunition can't last much longer. I want you to take this.' It was his service revolver, fully loaded, and a pouch of bullets. 'When they come down to finish us off, shoot any of us who are still alive. Do you understand?'

Violet gasped. 'How could I possibly do that? Malcolm, are you mad?'

But when he told her in terse yet in graphic detail exactly what the tribesmen—and their women—did to enemy dead, and to any man unfortunate enough to be found living, she could see that he was perfectly sane and that she must find the strength to do what he demanded of her. Huddling back in silent misery and leaving him free to shoot, Violet Nicolson waited for the end. As a woman he said she would be spared—and had torn off her *pugri* to reveal her hair—but she had no intention of becoming any Afghan's whore, and she would save one bullet for herself if she could.

As the bullets screamed about their heads and the great rocks continued to tumble into the river, the shots from the beleaguered patrol became increasingly spasmodic. At last the ammunition ran out and they ceased completely. With the silence came a great whoop of triumph from across the narrow valley.

'They'll come for us now—there has to be some kind of a path.' Sure enough, half a mile away or less a black line of figures could be seen painstakingly making its way down over the slippery snow-covered conglomerate towards the river.

'Isn't there time to get away?' she asked, but Nicolson silently pointed to the devastation caused by the loosened boulders. There was no way even the fleetest of foot—nor even a horseman—could pick their way through and escape. *Was it for this that she had survived the hazards of Zhob? Or was this what Mahomed Akram had meant by* kismet, *her destiny always to follow her husband?* She thought of what these men were intending to do to Malcolm, the mutilation, the cruel dismemberment, and felt an urge to vomit. Then Colonel Nicolson rose to his feet and drew his sword. At a word his *sepoys* did the same. She could not understand what he added, but to her amazement first one man, then another, then all of them erupted into a great burst of uninhibited laughter. *Of course he would die on his feet with a laugh on his lips, at the head of his beloved Baluchis.* And once her husband had done his duty by the regiment, then the time would come for her to do hers ...

For one last time, Violet Nicolson drank in the glory of the mountains that soared above the Gomal Pass, telling over the bullets in the small pouch as she did so, *please God, let there be enough*. And something caught her attention. Along the cliff face opposite, just below the icy crest, little puffs of white were rising. Cracks appeared at intervals then ran together. For a moment the cliff hung suspended, then as Violet stared she saw it slowly slip. A roar filled the narrow defile as the loosened snow slid down with an ominous rush, taking earth and rocks with it as it gathered momentum. The Waziris were swept up and swallowed in its path. When all was silent again, Violet approached her husband. As she returned his revolver and bullets, he saw that his wife's hands were steadier than his.

If Malcolm Nicolson thought her composure remarkable he was both right and wrong. It took several weeks for the brittle facade of invulnerability to splinter, and for much of that time the colonel was absent, sharing his knowledge of the frontier with government surveyors and officials. When he returned it was April, and he brought with him the Indian Government's order that the regiment withdraw and abandon the lonely outpost to the biting winds for good. There had been no further attacks from raiders; no enemy swept down on the small collection of tents. Instead, fever stalked the sentry pits by night and death came all the same. The victim it claimed was Rahmat Allah, whose brother Violet had once tried so desperately to save at the Zao defile. Since his brother's death, the *sepoy* had never spoken to her (he spoke no Urdu and she no Baluchi) but his smile had warmed her on the chill winter mornings and she considered him a friend.

The colonel was surprised at her reaction. After the affair of the pass he believed her well beyond extravagant shows of grief such as the one he witnessed now. 'He would have accepted it as God's will, or Fate, if you prefer,' her husband said, in an effort to console her.

'And you,' she suddenly snapped. 'How do *you* see it, Malcolm Nicolson? Fate, the will of Allah, a stiff upper lip—God in Heaven, am I the only person in this country who knows how to cry?'

He made no attempt to stop her as she pushed past him blindly, and he watched her go, hands thrust deep in pockets, kicking at the stones in her path, to return an hour later, smiling sheepishly and her eyes red with weeping. 'I'm sorry, Malcolm,' she said. 'I was upset.'

'And you still are. Of course you are. But this is India. It happens all the time; you should be used to death by now.'

Violet stared at him with disbelief. '*Used to death?*' she echoed. 'What have I seen of death to get used to it? A child stillborn; a man I knifed—who may or may not have killed me first; men crushed beyond recognition or choked to death on mud ... If I had had to shoot you all, one by one, perhaps I would have got *used to it* by the end!' She began to laugh wildly. 'I suppose fever is an almost normal way to go. Or cholera ... *Here today and gone tomorrow*—I'll *never* get used to it—I *don't want* to get used to it, I don't want to forget! I want to feel grief, not become hardened to it like you!'

'*Darling, don't.*' He caught hold of her and shook her. When she was calmer he answered her rebuke. 'Of course I feel grief, but in order to survive out here you can't afford to give way. My dear, you are young, sensitive, you take these things to heart, and I honour you for it. But don't let death exact too great a toll.'

He tilted her chin so she was forced to meet his gaze. 'Life has to go on. That may seem hard—it may even seem trite—but it's true. Otherwise everything we value would come to a standstill.' He watched with approval as she made a visible effort to pull herself together, and by the time Sir George White and his party arrived for the final inspection the colonel's wife was perfectly composed.

'The Flower of Khorassan'

Spring embraced the Gul Kach plateau. The roses from which it took its name were coming into bloom. Soon their pink and white petals would fall on Rahmat Allah's lonely grave and the great, fragrant bushes would be his only companions. The 3rd Baluchis packed up and again they marched on Apozai, and it was there that Colonel Nicolson said his farewells. After his leave, he would not be returning to his old regiment; he had been selected to raise another, for specific service in the Protectorate of Zhob. The 24th Baluchis would be reconstituted in June, or July at the latest, if all went according to plan. Nicolson faced the challenge with his usual quiet confidence and saw no reason why it should not.

It was a golden time. For two months he and his wife were free to roam the flower-bedecked highlands of Khorassan, and Violet's waking thoughts and deepest dreams were of the tales Malcolm told her of this ancient land and its people. As they followed the Zhob along its rocky course no one challenged the tall hawk-faced Afghan and the youngster at his side, or thought to question the travellers' right to hospitality in village or lonely hillside camp. They watched the sun over the Suleimani Mountains turn the snow to blood in its dying rays, and afterwards when the stars came out in the clear night sky, none matched in brilliance the eyes that dwelt on the colonel's face. Violet Nicolson had married him for love alone, knowing nothing of his life as a soldier. Now no woman could know more, but there was so much more about him to discover.

'Malcolm, do you believe in Fate?'

'Goodness, what a question! And at this time of the night too.' Nicolson turned over towards Violet and prepared to listen. 'Whatever makes you ask?'

It was all the answer she was going to get, at least for the moment. She was used to his way of answering one question with another until he sensed the lie of the land, but at least this time he was prepared to humour her. Contentedly she lay back, and looked up at the spangled heavens where a shooting star fell to oblivion as she watched.

'Well, I was thinking—'

'I know.'

'Malcolm, do you think all this was meant to be? The way we met, fell in love and nearly lost each other. The way I came to Zhob, even.'

'No, I'm afraid I don't.' The colonel sounded unimpressed. 'If I hadn't met you in the library at Karachi, I would have met you at your house. I hardly see your wretched little sister as an instrument of Fate, though I suppose *she* might, and if I remember correctly, you eventually took matters into your own hands—with a little help from your father. Am I right?'

'But what about the train?'

'Yes, I might grant you that. But coming on to Zhob was your decision, surely? You came of your free will.'

'Mahomed Akram said it was my *kismet* to follow you.'

'Darling, for all his western allegiances Mahomed Akram is a follower of Islam, and it suited him perfectly to tell you that. Why, I had the devil's own job to persuade him to take you back to Hyderabad in the first place, so of course it suited him to blame Fate when you wouldn't go! And it suited you as well! Unfortunately for you both, I failed to subscribe to a similar belief, if you remember?' She did. Vividly. 'I'm sorry, sweetheart. I may have made the East my home but I still believe in free will and personal responsibility.'

He could sense he had failed to convince his wife. 'If, as you seem to believe, we are pawns in some vast cosmic game of chess, let me ask you something.'

'What?'

'Was my selection to raise the 24th a random chance, or was it, perhaps, in some small part due to merit?'

'Malcolm, that's not fair!' Violet sat up, indignant. 'You're the only one who could do it! You know how much you deserve the honour!'

He chuckled. 'So Fate had no part to play? You can't have it both ways, you know. Either we have no responsibility at all, or we create our own opportunities. Whether we get our just deserts, or no, is another matter. Now, can I go to sleep?'

But she wasn't finished with him. 'Malcolm?'

'Yes?' Ever patient, the colonel turned to her again.

'You do believe in God?'

'In a compassionate God, yes. One who allows us to make our own mistakes, and then forgives us. Now go to sleep,' and he kissed her gently on the brow.

⁂

At first their wanderings appeared to have no purpose, but gradually the sheep tracks were left behind and they veered west to join the military road.

'All roads lead to Quetta,' Violet observed.

'Yes, but we shan't be staying long. We've work to do.'

'Work? What kind of work? I thought you were on leave.'

'I am—officially. Unofficially I'm off to the northern frontier to recruit for the new regiment. And you're coming with me. If you would like to.' He squeezed her hand as he sensed her excitement. 'You've always wanted to see beyond the far horizon; now here's your chance before the official recruiting parties take over. I don't suppose you ever thought of anything like this, eh?'

'Never. Not even in my wildest dreams.' She took her eyes from his face and looked about her. Suddenly she knew that this was where she truly belonged. *Home is where the heart is*. She had said it once before and now she meant it more than ever. This land was theirs, from the river swollen by the melted winter snows to where the road they were following disappeared in the far distance. Theirs, the stony slopes rising gently from the plain then ever steeper to the pinnacles above. A barren land, where soon the glorious flowers would die, their beauty shrivelled with the grass in the hot summer sun. A land she knew to be demanding, relentless, unforgiving, cruel. But they were here, now— Avidly she breathed in the faintly scented air.

'When I die, I shall come back here. They can keep their seven heavens of emerald, pearl and—oh, I forget the rest! Just give me Baluchistan ...' and she flung herself from her horse and buried her face in the flowers.

'Don't think of leaving me yet.' Laconic as ever, Malcolm Nicolson dismounted. 'We've far too much to do. Now—what do you think about camping here, over by the wild olives? We're in no hurry, are we?' His dexterous fingers slowly unwound the ample folds of her *pugri*, while his blue-grey eyes steadily held hers. Then he loosened her plaited hair, combing it free with attentive fingers. With his hand resting lightly on her waist he led her to the grove. 'The people of Khorassan attribute great powers to what they call the *sinjit* tree,' he told her. 'Even the most reluctant maiden becomes compliant when a man coaxes her into its shade.' Nicolson smiled down at his wife who turned away briefly to one of the olives with its thorny branches and profusion of shimmering silver leaves. It didn't look at all magical to her, she said.

'Smell this.' He held out one of the small fragrant yellow blooms.

'It's beautiful,' she admitted, 'but even so, it hardly seems enough; whatever they say.'

'You are too cynical by far, my wife. For all you claim to be a poet!'

Violet grinned. 'Sometimes, Malcolm Nicolson, you sound just like Izzie!'

'I shall take that as a compliment. Anyway, I'm told the perfume really works,' and he drew her down beside him.

Distracted completely by the mention of Isabel, Violet pushed back her hair and sat up again, voicing a thought that had preoccupied her on and off for weeks. 'Goodness, do you think Mr Tate proposed to Izzie under a tree like this? I can't imagine her accepting otherwise, can you?'

In village after village the colonel talked earnestly to the *maliks* who listened courteously and entertained the couple royally. Sometimes they slept in the villages, sometimes in the rest houses Government was beginning to provide, and always the errant pair worked their way nearer and nearer to the still undetermined frontier with Afghanistan. By the end of May, when they reached the small frontier station of Loralai, Violet Nicolson had seen more of Baluchistan than any other European woman and probably native women, too. Some fifty miles southeast of Quetta, Loralai was to be their home for the next six months and recruits poured in daily. Kakars from the Loralai district and Pishin were used to service with the Raj; the Afridis from the north as well. Most of these recruits were likely to stay. None of the disaffected Afghans from over the border were strangers to fighting, either, and the prospect of being paid for their favourite pastime would probably hold them to the regiment indefinitely. The true Baluchis, Malcolm explained, were almost as likely to desert; they were farmers, by tradition, not fighters.

'Come seed time and harvest they'll be gone!' he told her. 'Life at Loralai won't be for them.'

Would life there be for her? It could be a dull enough place for anyone, but how would his young wife cope? Perhaps, he suggested tentatively one day, perhaps she would like to learn Pushtu? In a formal way, he said, from lessons.

Violet eyed the papers he had just tossed onto the dining-room table. They were the notes she had urged him to make for her during their travels north of Quetta, and in and around Pishin. Notes of the songs and the tales they had heard in lonely villages by campfires at night. Notes he had made for her with the greatest good humour, delighting in her interest in things that were dear to his own heart. And there they all lay, scribbled down randomly in a mixture of Pushtu and English.

'Well, what do you think?'

'What do I think? I think it's a plot on your part to keep me out of mischief. Could I possibly be right?'

The look she gave him was so piercing that he was forced to laugh. 'There's some truth in that, I must confess, but think of the benefits—for you as well as for me!'

'Persian, Pushtu, Baluchi, Brahui—' she counted them on her fingers. 'How did you come to learn so many languages, Malcolm? I know you all have to learn Urdu—but what about the rest?'

His reply to such a question was typically laconic. 'In the Indian Army, my love, a bachelor has but two options when it comes to recreation—the third has long since been frowned on—' Violet grinned; she had seen more than one old British bungalow with generous women's quarters. 'Nowadays,' Malcolm Nicolson went on, 'a single man can choose between pig-sticking and hunting, or learning a language. I chose the latter. A book at night makes for infinitely better companionship than a row of trophies on the wall.'

'Then you must have had a lot of time on your hands! Come on, darling, there has to be more to it than that.'

'A little perhaps, but we're talking about you, not me. Will you let me teach you?'

Violet smiled happily. 'Of course.'

'There is no risk'

All was quiet in the new Protectorate of Zhob and in the east beyond the Suleimani Mountains. There was no further need for punitive expeditions to snake their slow unwieldy way through the narrow passes. The villages destroyed by the Field Force were gradually rebuilt, the fines all duly paid, and the tribesmen settled down into the law-abiding ways of the Sandemanian system. In December the regiment moved to Sibi, north of the plain Violet had once glimpsed briefly from the train, an undistinguished place in the valley of the Nari River. Sibi was loathed for the bitterness of its winters and the infernal summer heat, yet it guarded the Bolan Pass and was essential to the defence of Quetta. Rarely a morning or an afternoon went by without one or more of Nicolson's young officers dropping in on some vague pretext or other, and the colonel did not seem to mind. Lieutenant Price remained with the 3rd Baluchis but Lieutenant Jacob was adjutant of the 24th. He was the most frequent of their visitors, and Violet was not long in seeing that the older officers, unless invited, rarely called at all. Nicolson had no hesitation in telling her why.

'Unlike Jacob, you see, they don't approve of my methods. In this kind of country, and with these particular men, I've found that simple drill is almost irrelevant. Being able to march long distances in the heat or cold, and shooting accurately when they need to, is much more important. Others don't agree. They also think I'm too sympathetic, that I trust my men far too much, and that there aren't enough parades—apart from that, we get on well enough!' He gave a short dismissive laugh.

In the event, it was at one of those very parades that Malcolm Nicolson's faith in his *sepoys* almost brought about his death. Violet heard of it indirectly when Claud Jacob came by one morning, white and visibly shaken. At first she thought nothing of it, simply sat him down, gave him tea, then in a motherly kind of a way asked him what was wrong. The adjutant looked at her unhappily, uncertain whether to answer her question or not.

'Something's happened, hasn't it?'

'It's Colonel Nicolson,' Jacob admitted at last.

'What about the colonel?' Violet's voice was sharp and she started to her feet. 'What's wrong with him? Come on, Claud, I need to know!'

'One of the recruits tried to kill him on parade. He's all right, Mrs Nicolson, truly he is—' Jacob would have detained her but she had already gone, forgetting to take a coat and almost running in her haste to reach the parade-ground. Halfway there she met her husband coming away.

'Goodness me, Violet, whatever's wrong? You look quite distraught!'

'Are you all right? What happened?' Clutching his sleeve frantically, she searched the tranquil face lit with its usual reassuring smile.

'Calm down, Vi. Nothing's wrong at all.' Quite unperturbed, Colonel Nicolson slipped his arm through hers and walked her quickly back to the bungalow, where Lieutenant Jacob was pacing up and down in the realisation that the little he had said was certainly far too much.

'Ah,' said his commandant, 'now I begin to understand.' He looked from the lieutenant to Violet, and back again. 'And what exactly have you been saying to upset my wife, young man?'

Jacob simply grinned sheepishly and went away without a word.

'Malcolm, Claud told me that someone tried to kill you. Is that true?' Violet's distress was evident and he led her to a chair.

'Yes, but he didn't make a very good job of it, as you can see,' he said calmly. 'His heart wasn't in it. Sit down and I'll tell you, if you really want to know.'

'*Of course I want to know*!'

'Apparently he was sent to join the regiment by his mullah, with instructions to kill me—'

'A *ghazi* —' breathed Violet. 'Darling, how awful!'

'A very half-hearted one, as it turns out,' Nicolson assured her. 'He found he enjoyed regimental life, so he put off his attempt as long as he could. I think the mullah must have got at him again and this morning he went for me with his bayonet—'

'Who stopped him?' The question came out in a croak.

'I did. With that stick you always tell me is so ridiculous. I knocked the bayonet out of his hand and told him to get back in line—and, fortunately for him I suppose, he did.'

Violet's eyes moved involuntarily towards the great oak staff her husband carried as his sole defence. She always thought it ridiculously inadequate but she was wrong: that morning it had saved his life.

'What will happen to him now?' she asked.

'He'll stay. I told him that since he'd eaten the regiment's salt, he owed his duty to us and not to his priest. He'll probably turn out the best of the bunch!'

Violet shook her head in disbelief: once again, he had come so close to death and could brush the experience aside so lightly, make a joke of it even. Some days later she returned to the subject. 'Was he an Afridi—the man who tried to kill you?'

'No, he wasn't. Darling, you seem to be obsessed with that particular tribe—why?'

'I suppose because they're such a dreadful lot. Nobody likes them, do they, not even the other Afghans. And certainly not Mahomed Akram.'

'They make excellent fighters though—when they care to stay.' He gave her a quizzical look. 'Who's been telling you about Afridis, Violet? Was it Mahomed Akram?'

'Oh, no, he's far too discreet. Not that I haven't asked him. No, actually it was Isabel. Annie Sophie has told her all sorts of things. It's her latest research, she says, for the book she's writing.'

'Oh?'

'It's about a white woman who goes off to live with a Pathan in his village.'

'Well, it does happen, you know, it's not just us men who find the Afghans attractive.'

'*Touchée, mon colonel,*' Violet acknowledged the thrust. 'Is it true then—what they do to unfaithful wives?'

'Well, they kill them, if that's what you mean, after cutting off their breasts. I must say your sister has some very odd ideas of what to put in her book! I suppose that came from her?'

Violet nodded. 'Yes. What brutes they are!' and she shivered.

'Don't waste your sympathy on the women, Violet. Surely I don't have to remind you what the women do to injured soldiers, and how they mutilate the dead?' Nicolson's voice was harsh. 'They know what to expect if they commit adultery!'

'Do you condone that kind of punishment, Malcolm?' There was a silent challenge in her eyes.

'I neither condone nor condemn. It's the custom, and in the army we're instructed never to interfere with anything like that.'

'General Napier did in Sind. He told the Hindus to stop burning widows and killing baby girls—*he* interfered.

'That was a long time ago; we do things differently now.'

'So you would never interfere? Even to prevent a death? A woman's death?' She was appalled, for it seemed counter to everything she knew of her husband's nature.

'Not if that death was for a recognised offence—no.' He was implacable, and Violet looked at the severe lines of his face and said no more.

'But Vengeance has a savour all its own'

Only the colonel's young wife took the trouble to explore the abandoned fort. The view of the northern mountains from the ruined guardian towers brought consolation for Sibi's dreariness. Palest pinks from the snow-topped mountain crests at dawn; rich ruby reds from the crags in the early morning sun; dramatic peaches and purples from the dying afternoon—Violet Nicolson brought these and many colours besides into her bungalow. Bright rugs, cushions, and embroidered quilts in every room bore witness to her determination to be cheerful. Dressed in warm woollen tunics of vivid blues and reds, she rode the plains with Malcolm or Mahomed Akram, and whenever they encountered solitary horsemen they would stop to chat and pass the time of day. The Marri tribesmen of the area were dedicated gossips, and whether passing the mud huts of the scattered villages or the dark camel-hair tents pitched among the stunted scrub, the strangers were recognised and pressed to stop and talk and drink the sweet green tea favoured by the tribes.

To Violet, the men with their bushy black beards and the long ringlets of which they were inordinately proud became a source of fascination. They called themselves 'tigers', Malcolm told her, and were always harping on about their warlike past. She saw that for herself. As they told their tales their strange, honey-coloured eyes would flash fire, and they would finger their swords and their shields as if longing for those bloody days to return. 'Sandeman has got them to make peace with their enemies,' whispered Nicolson, 'but they miss the inter-tribal warfare, and even now they'll fight their rivals on any pretext at all.' It was easy to believe.

None of the women dared raise their soft dark eyes to look at the colonel or his

Afghan companion for fear of being punished. They had no say at all in the choice of a husband and once married, they could be the victims of idle chattering tongues who, if believed, could bring about their death. Violet was dumbfounded—what kind of life was this? She had given herself in love to a man she respected, freely and without reservation, and she could imagine no other way. And although she was now a married woman, she considered herself no man's chattel. Her interest in the tribesmen became tinged with more than a little distaste.

The couple often rode over the plain to the south of Sibi. To the fanciful Violet it seemed a landscape made in Hell, where some giant hand had been at work, piling up rocks and sand and clay, intending one day perhaps to return and finish the act of creation. This monstrous work, she said, bore silent witness to the world's contempt, and yet it held a strange allure. One Sunday just before Christmas, they were overtaken by one of the sudden dust storms that could blow up at any time of year, and which turned night into day within seconds. The howl of the wind made communication impossible, so the colonel seized the reins of Violet's horse before he lost her in the murk. They had passed an outcrop, he remembered, that Violet thought resembled a gigantic stranded whale, so he made in that direction. The rock loomed up almost before they knew it, and they dismounted to take shelter as best they could, cursing the spiny vegetation that met their questing hands as they groped their way forward in an attempt to escape the unforgiving sand. By now it was as dark as night—darker even. Malcolm held Violet to him, protecting her face from the swirling dust, and she drew comfort from the steady beating of his heart. After a while came the sound of other horses. Nicolson answered the voices that hailed them and pulled Violet to her feet. 'They're Marris,' he told her. 'They're taking us to shelter.'

It was a village. Not that she could see much, but she could hear voices, sounds of activity, restless horses; all in some kind of a courtyard beyond a narrow archway, to which they were admitted after a great deal of animated discussion. 'I'm afraid we've arrived at an awkward moment, and they won't let us go until it's over.'

'Until *what* is over?'

'I'm not sure yet. The laws of hospitality mean that they won't deny us shelter during the storm, so that's something. Anyway, you're off to the women's quarters. I'm staying here.'

Violet wasn't wanted there either. Usually on these occasions a dozen or so pairs of dark inquisitive eyes would examine her. Someone would offer her water to wash with, and a scented tea to drink. Women of all ages would sit close to their strange visitor, buzzing with interest while they touched her bright hair from time to time, their bracelets jangling in her ears. Violet looked around her. The lamp-lit mud-brick room was not so different to theirs in Sibi, but unlike hers in Sibi this room was filled with a feeling of almost tangible dread and sorrow. Even the children were mute and kept their distance.

She squatted down uninvited as near to the doorway as possible, and waited for some kind of sign that it—whatever it was—was over outside, and that she was free to leave. Suddenly the curtain over the doorway was drawn aside, and a wrinkled old woman hurried in. She was in obvious distress and her breathless words came tumbling out, so anxious was she to tell her news. While she was addressing the others, Violet took her chance. By the time the crone spotted the unwelcome visitor, it was too late to stop her. Violet darted down the passageway and out, to where the gusting sand had subsided. Now she could see the courtyard she must have crossed earlier. Buildings surrounded it on three sides; there was a gateway in the wall on the fourth.

At the gate horsemen shouted and gesticulated. Inside, men on foot conferred with a tall figure dressed in a long coat of rich green brocade. The chief, she supposed. A voluminous white turban made him taller still, and from its folds long oily ringlets escaped almost to his waist. The eyes beneath the turban were angry, and the mouth set in a cruel, imperious line. He glanced in her direction and almost immediately Malcolm came to her. She gripped his hand in relief. 'What's going on?' she asked. 'Why all this?' and she indicated the seething mass of noise.

'You shouldn't be here, you know. I suppose you escaped. Well, now you'll have to stay and see it through,' he said grimly. He pointed to a corner of the yard where a white-faced woman, little more than a girl, stood between two men, each of them holding her by an arm. They seemed to be waiting for something. 'She was caught with her lover a short while ago—that was what all the fuss was about when we arrived. They're her husband and her brother and they are about to see her punished.'

'Punished? You mean they're going to kill her?'

'Yes. They'll kill her lover too, when they find him.'

Violet felt quite ill. 'Can't you stop it? No,' and she remembered what he had told her. 'No, of course you can't. Malcolm, I won't stay here—I have to go. Ask for our horses and take me back to Sibi!'

The colonel shook his head. 'I'm sorry, darling, I'm afraid there's nothing to be done. We'll just have to stay.'

'But she looks so young. So frightened. Malcolm, is there no hope for her at all?'

'None. They don't want her blood on their hands, so they'll make her hang herself from the nearest tree.'

Violet was horrified. 'You mean that none of these—these *monsters*—is man enough to do the job himself? They're disgusting! No,' and she slapped off his hand impatiently, 'don't even think of stopping me; I'm going to her—*now*!'

Cursing under his breath Nicolson followed in hot pursuit. Violet in her headlong course was impossible to stop; and no one tried. The fearsome-looking tribesmen, in fact, were at a loss as the slight figure of the *feringhi* elbowed her way disrespectfully through their ranks. They knew she was *Nikelseyn sahib*'s woman and that it would be unwise to touch her, so they gave way before her and to *Nikelseyn* who followed. Let *him* punish her as she deserved ... Thus unimpeded, Violet made directly for the far corner.

'Tell them to let me speak to her.' The glacial tone of her voice brooked no denial and the colonel spoke briefly to the sullen pair. One man stood aside and let Violet approach.

'Tell her I'm her friend, and that I'm going to stay with her.'

Nicolson spoke again.

'And now you can tell these brutes to go away. Please, please do as I ask, Malcolm,' and this time she was pleading rather than demanding. Protests at the colonel's words meant nothing; in the end both men withdrew, and at last Violet was able to embrace their frightened, weeping prisoner. Silent and helpless, Nicolson watched his gallant wife who alone had dared to intervene, and despite all his previous affirmations, his chivalrous heart was revolted by what must follow. It was a small and stunted tree, that makeshift gallows, itself clinging desperately to life, but tall enough to do the job required of it. Waves of nausea threatened to overcome the colonel's wife as she saw it was a *sinjit* tree. *Bring here the maiden of thy desire, In my scented shade to rest, And be she cold as bitterest snow—*

'Violet, come away now, don't watch!' Malcolm took her other arm, but she shook him off.

'I have to stay. Surely you understand I won't abandon her now!' Murmuring words of comfort Violet stroked the woman's head, and her arm was round her still as she went unresisting to her death. Close to the gnarled trunk of the wild olive, Violet Nicolson looked on unflinching while the unknown woman attached the rope and breathed her last, and afterwards, when they were safely out of sight of the village, she knelt among the thorns and vomited again and again.

No amount of water could remove the bitter taste of what she had witnessed. Head bowed, hands clenched into fists, the angry little figure sat hunched at the table in her bungalow, thumping the wooden surface in complete and utter frustration as she relived the hopeless moments.

Nicolson made no move towards her: he was her husband, but above all he was a man, and he sensed quite rightly that in her present mood all men were anathema to his wife.

'They killed her! They killed her for wanting to choose for herself. She wanted to be free and now she's dead! God in Heaven, Malcolm, when is it ever going to change?'

Nicolson rashly ventured a reply: 'Things *are* gradually changing—for Englishwomen, at least. You're being given more and more freedom, all the time.'

Violet jumped to her feet at that, and glared at him across the table. 'How can you say that, *how can you*? We're all born equal, men and women; we're all equally free! How can you talk about *giving* me what is mine by right? Freedom isn't something to be doled out, in ever increasing amounts, like the monthly housekeeping! I thought you of all people would understand—'

Totally nonplussed, the colonel looked at his wife. She looked back and a heavy silence fell, broken at last by Violet.

'I'm sorry, Malcolm. Of course you don't deserve any of that. You'll have to forgive me.' Shoulders bowed, she turned away wearily and went towards their room. He reached her before she got to the door but still he didn't dare touch her.

'I didn't realise you felt so strongly—about *all this*—' he wasn't sure what to call her impassioned declaration.

'Neither did I.' She sighed. 'And I can't expect you to understand.' She moved towards the door again.

'My dear, I'm trying very hard.' He rested his hands on her shoulders, gently, just enough to make her pause. 'Freedom brings with it its own restrictions and responsibilities—do you understand that?'

Violet looked at him then, and after a while she nodded. 'I think so.'

Nicolson smiled, and kissed the top of her head. 'Then go free, little bird,' he said, and stepped aside to let her pass.

'The hearts of his friends are as cold as the Tirah snows'

When Violet Nicolson did not spread her wings and test her newfound freedom in any spectacular way her husband wasn't sure whether to feel disappointment or relief. Life in Sibi continued much as usual, and no outsider would have detected any difference, but differences there were. Mrs Nicolson no longer looked at her husband for approval where she might have done before, but showed confidence in her own judgement—which usually proved as sound as his. As the sole arbiter of her own behaviour, it amused the colonel to see that his wife was every bit as hard on herself as he had ever been; he had been right in what he had told her—

with freedom had come responsibility. His smile became more rueful when he realised that she was still as outspoken as before. Indeed, she was less inclined than ever to suffer fools gladly. But the charm remained, and more than one hot rebuke was tempered by the warm look that turned a hapless victim into a willing slave. And, most importantly of all, after almost three years of marriage Malcolm Nicolson found his wife every bit as enchanting as ever.

At Christmas the colonel and his wife held open-house and did their utmost to make the season a joyous time for everyone. Their bungalow was filled with Nicolson's young men, who all missed their families and loved ones in varying degrees. Christmas the previous year in Quetta had been a more formal, albeit jolly affair. Here, everyone sat on the floor, talking and singing till the flames died down, late into the night.

Alone at last, Nicolson threw a log on the dying fire and settled down with his arm around his wife. 'Another year nearly over. I wonder what 1892 has in store for us all.'

Violet leaned against him. She said nothing as she gazed absently into the flames. *They* might be looking forward to the days ahead and Isabel had arranged a date for her wedding at last, but there would be no new beginning for Rahmat Allah nor for the girl she had tried to help. 'Death, always death.' She spoke aloud, and although appearing to answer his question, her mind was far away.

Nicolson felt a sudden chill. 'I must have more of the Highlander in me than I thought,' and he forced himself to laugh. 'I felt just then as if someone were walking on my grave.'

Violet remembered the failed attempt on her husband's life, and gave a little gasp. 'You imagined it, darling,' she said immediately. 'Look, the fire is nearly out, no wonder you're feeling cold. It's very late: perhaps we should turn in.'

The New Year began promisingly enough: the recruits were shaping well and the town was looking forward to the horse fair which was famous throughout the frontier. A grand durbar was due to follow, presided over by Sir Robert Sandeman, the Agent to the Governor-General in Baluchistan.

'The population doubles or trebles at this time of the year. It's amazing, you'll see. They come from all over, Afghans, Duranis, Waziris, your friends the Afridis … There are some very dubious characters among them, too, I have to say.'

Violet looked at her husband. Determination to honour their pact was obviously preventing him from saying what he really wanted. 'I won't go anywhere without you,' she promised, and Nicolson heaved a sigh of relief.

February came and Sibi filled with strangers. The bazaar was crowded with horse traders; tribesmen began to arrive for the fair and the feasting, and the tribal sports that followed the durbar.

The Sandemans were to stay with them and Violet began to grow excited at the prospect of seeing them again and going on to Quetta with the regiment afterwards. But the Agent and his wife did not come on the appointed day, nor did they come on the next. Then the stunned town heard the dreadful news: that *Sinjeman sahib* was dead; struck down by fever as he tried to bring peace to a remote little state in the south.

Nicolson brought Violet the news. She caught her breath at the sight of his devastated face, and listened in silence to what he had to tell her. She managed to control her grief for the man who had been her friend as well as his, and put her arms around her husband as he sat at the table, his head in his hands. She could find no words to help him, this soldier who had seemed inured to death. When at last he looked up, his cheeks were wet with the tears he made no attempt to stem.

'Helen was with him when he died. He was ill for over a week, and she nursed him to the end.'

'Then that will surely help her in the days ahead,' said Violet, hoping if not totally believing her own words. 'Where is Helen now?'

'Still in Las Beyla. She'll be in Quetta when we get there, and then she's going back to her family in Ireland. Violet, I simply cannot believe he's dead. He was so full of life. He had so much to offer this country …' and Malcolm Nicolson's voice broke.

'His work will go on.' Violet drew his head against her breast in comfort, and shared his anguish silently as he mourned the passing of his friend. Poor Helen Sandeman, it was such a cruel loss. But as a second wife, who had lived most of her life elsewhere, she had never really been a part of India. Otherwise, how could she go away and leave her husband lying here in a foreign soil? Violet thought of that kind and generous-hearted man buried in a lonely desert grave, and she, too, began to weep.

The great outpourings of grief throughout Baluchistan continued for weeks after Sir Robert's tragic passing. Some of the mourning had been extravagant, but nonetheless sincere for that. The *maliks* gathered in Sibi all the same, intent on paying tribute to the absent figure they described as their 'shepherd'. If that were the case, then some of the flock were only masquerading as sheep, reflected Mrs Nicolson. And she wondered how long they could be kept under control. Colonel Nicolson had greater confidence in Sir Robert's influence—even from beyond the grave—and he told her she would be proved wrong.

'We'll see,' was all she had said. 'Meanwhile, who takes over as Agent?' But did it really matter? They were on their way to Quetta, and without the friendship of the Sandemans it would not be the same. Malcolm was seeing the men get settled; some had never been on a train before and their reactions had varied between interest and alarm. While the colonel did his rounds, his wife was left to her sorrowful thoughts as she gazed out of the carriage window.

'Violet. Darling—'

She looked around as her husband's voice reached her at last. 'I'm sorry, Malcolm, I didn't hear you come in. I was miles away.' He sat down and took her hand.

'Try not to be sad. Think of the good things. Look, we're coming into Harnai—do you remember when we said goodbye here before I went to Zhob?'

He always asked her the same question, at the same place. She nodded, knowing that this time he was trying to lift her spirits.

'Would you follow me again, knowing what you do now?'

This was a question he hadn't asked before, and she reflected long and hard before replying. She thought of the cold, the wet, the uncertainty, the danger. No, she wouldn't want all that again! The train came to a rattling stop, and she remembered the feeling of desolation as the tall figure strode away down this very platform, knowing she wouldn't see him again for months, if ever. Nicolson watched the serious little face, and the series of emotions it expressed while she considered her reply, and then she gave him an apologetic look.

'I'm sorry, Malcolm, but yes, I'm afraid I would!'

He laughed, put his arm around her, and kissed her soundly. Lieutenant Jacob, who was about to join them, hesitated before returning to his companions; his question, he decided, was unimportant and could wait.

Quetta in the evening sunshine, with no Sir Robert Sandeman to greet them; no, it wasn't the same at all. The hustle and bustle of the troops pouring onto the platform took the young woman's mind off the absent figure for a while. Then there was the luggage to disentangle, directions to give, and she was off to their quarters leaving Malcolm and the others to organise the troops. The cantonment in the upper part of town was thriving. The poplars planted in the early days of British occupation gave the military lines the appearance of a lush green oasis, and the cantonment was taking on an increasingly permanent air. Violet raised her eyes to the great encircling mountains, beyond which lay the source of all threats, real and imaginary, to the might of the British Raj. All roads lead to Quetta, she had said the year before, and it was true.

She passed the old unpretentious Residency, then drove past its successor—still in the early stages of construction but destined to be much finer. Well, the Sandemans would never live in the house they had so enjoyed planning. The gloom threatened to overcome her again.

Pull yourself together, Violet Nicolson, she told herself sternly. *This will never do*! She arrived at the house set aside for their use in the cantonment, a bungalow almost identical to the one they had left in Sibi: the same domed roof, the same number of rooms, almost the same number of cracks in the walls, and surely in the very same places! She forced herself to laugh. Well, the rugs and wall hangings she had insisted on bringing would stand them in good stead, if only it didn't rain too much. She had heard horrific tales of buildings such as these, built of mud bricks and baked in the hot summer sun, which reverted to their natural liquid state in times of heavy storms. Well, she wouldn't let herself worry about that now, there was far too much to be done.

She gave instructions to the coolies to dispose of the crates and trunks, rolled up her sleeves and set to work. When her husband appeared much later there was a semblance of order about the place; the lamps were lit, the rugs were down and the bed was made.

He looked around appreciatively. 'Why, you've got it looking like home already! So what do you think?'

'I think it will collapse with the first real downpour—or the second, if we're lucky!'

'Then we have at least until August,' Malcolm said cheerfully. 'Good.'

'Just as the dawn of Love was breaking'

Isabel was to be married to John Tate in May and Violet had no intention of attending the wedding.

'Come on, Violet, I really think you should go—it will give you a chance to see your family. You've not been to Karachi for over a year.'

'I know and it doesn't matter.'

'Your parents miss you.'

'Look, Malcolm, they sent me away for years and years. One more can be nothing to them.'

Nicolson thought she was being unduly hard but did not say so. Violet rarely talked of her school years but he guessed she had not been happy. She made a futile little gesture with her hands.

'I begged them to take me away, but they wouldn't listen. I hated that place—they knew, and did nothing! They said it was for the best—I suppose that's what parents always say when they haven't got an answer. So, I stayed. I must say I was extremely badly behaved, and I got Izzie into trouble, too.' Violet grinned suddenly as she remembered the midnight forays, the petticoats caught on branches and torn on brambles. 'I can't imagine her getting married, can you?'

'So you keep saying. Well, *I* can. She'll be extremely happy and John Tate will value her every bit as much as she deserves. So why won't you go her wedding?'

'Oh, she doesn't need me. I would much rather stay here, with you. You're not trying to get rid of me, are you?'

'Of course not.' But Violet's manner continued to perplex him. 'There's something else,' he said at last. 'Something you're not telling me. Some other reason why you want to stay.'

'No, I don't think so,' and again she sounded defensive.

'Oh, come on, darling. There has to be. You and Isabel are so close—you must want to be there to see her happy!'

Violet hesitated before replying. 'It's silly, I know, but I don't think I should leave you, that's all.'

'For heaven's sake, Violet, I'm old enough to look after myself!'

'Maybe I'm superstitious, but anyway I'm staying!'

'Why superstitious?' Nicolson was intrigued.

'Well', she said reluctantly, 'I went away once before, and it was a mistake. I shan't do it again.'

'You've never left me—I've left you!'

'Not you—someone else, a long time ago. And he died.'

'I see. You think it might happen again, to me, is that it?'

'No, of course not. But I don't want to take the risk.'

Malcolm Nicolson studied his wife. Her eyes were suspiciously bright. 'What a silly little thing you are,' he said. 'Tell me about him—would you mind?'

'If you really want to hear. He was in the army, too. I didn't know him very well at all, but he was different to all the others—you know, the other subalterns in Lahore. Izzie said I was silly to grieve so when he died, and you will probably think so, too. But he cared about me—I know he did.'

So was that what Isabel had meant? *Don't let her brood too long, or it will get to be a habit*. 'Tell me more,' was all he said.

'You have to understand what Lahore was like—what I was like. I was eighteen, no, nineteen—isn't it strange how things get so much dimmer, although it was only ten years ago? I cannot see his face, or hear his voice, and yet I can remember everything he said.'

'Not strange at all,' he told her with a smile. 'I have my ghosts, too, remember.'

'We saw a lot of Rudyard Kipling. He was our age and he worked for Father on the paper. And although you wouldn't think it now, he was such fun, and he gave the most wonderful parties!'

'I've heard he had a great sense of self-importance, even then, and a cruel sense of humour,' Malcolm Nicolson observed. 'And that people were glad to see the back of him when he went back to England.'

'That's true, of course, and that's where John Reynolds comes in. He didn't think much of Rudyard's behaviour either—and he didn't think much of mine, because you see, I was even more ghastly than Annie Sophie.'

Brutally honest as always, Violet told her husband what she had learned from the much older Lieutenant Reynolds: that it wasn't fair to take advantage of being a woman and behave arrogantly in public when the other person couldn't possibly retaliate—that there were far better ways of being remembered; that she was intelligent and pretty and vivacious, but that it was the quieter Isabel that people preferred to spend time with—for Isabel was good-mannered and showed interest in what other people thought and said, and with Izzie they didn't have to be on guard against a cutting tongue …

'Good Lord.' Nicolson was impressed. 'And *you listened* to all that?'

Violet nodded. 'He really was the sort of person you listened to—you tried to do what he said because it was so absolutely right. We went away to the hills in the hot weather, and all the time we were there I tried to change. I was so proud of myself, and I knew he would be, too. And then, when we got back, I heard that he had died of cholera. I was so unhappy, I wanted to die as well.'

'And it went on and on, like after you lost our baby?'

'Yes. Until Izzie had enough.'

'What did she say?' Nicolson wondered if Isabel's technique had in any way matched his own.

What did she say? Violet remembered every word. *You're only nineteen, for heaven's sake. Are you going to wallow in misery for the rest of your life, or are you going to pull yourself together? Do you know, you remind me of the old woman in* Great Expectations*—the one you always said was so silly—the one you said should have eaten the wedding cake and stopped moping! Well, Adela Cory, you're becoming just like her! Don't you think it's time to stop before we all get sick of you?*

'So I tried. It wasn't easy, but it wasn't as hard as I thought. And I recovered. As you know.'

'Would you have married him, had he asked you? *Did* he ask you?'

Violet wasn't ready with an answer. 'What is it they always say, Malcolm?' she countered lightly. '*Lieutenants must not marry; captains may marry; majors should marry; and colonels must marry* … If we had known each other better, perhaps we would have liked each other less. Anyway, no, he didn't propose.'

'He sounds a remarkable young man. You listened to his advice, and you never listen to mine!'

'I was very young then—now I know better. And I'm going to stay here, with you, and that, my dear husband, is that!'

❧

Robert Sandeman's dignified black-clad widow, the only female friend Violet had made as an adult, returned to Quetta briefly, then went away for good. Violet attended Isabel's wedding in Karachi after all, escorted by her husband, and when it was over she felt she had lost Isabel as well. It had been a quiet affair in the registry office since neither bride nor groom—unlike the bride's mother—wanted a fuss. The change in Isabel was marked. Her smile was sweet and not acerbic. There was less bustle about her: her movements were slower, more dignified. She was prepared at last (as her brother-in-law told her sister later) to allow herself to be *cherished*.

'*Cherished?* The man's *besotted*! Look at their house, why, he's completely refurnished it for her—*and* he's bought her a new piano, shipped all the way from London! And did you see how he looked at her—as if she was the most beautiful woman in the world!'

'And that's exactly as it should be. And so she is—to *him*. Would *you* like a piano, Violet?' and he was relieved to see her laugh.

Violet missed Helen Sandeman, she missed her sister's letters. Mrs Tate was too busy with her new life and her old work at the *Sind Gazette* to write to Quetta often, so Violet immersed herself in her studies, and even the colonel, who knew the keenness of her mind, was surprised by her rapid progress. Never one to be shy, she practised her newly acquired linguistic skills on the native officers, who good-humouredly allowed themselves to be subjected to her almost daily interrogations. On his rare appearances even Mahomed Akram did not escape, and at night when the lesson was over, Violet would sometimes read her poetry aloud. She still accompanied the colonel on his sorties whenever she could, and if left to her own devices might go to the Quetta Institute to find a book or a newspaper—the Institute where the ladies modestly read in one room, the gentlemen in another—but other than that she preferred her own company.

'I get enough exercise as it is,' she told her husband, forthrightly explaining her refusal to take part in the badminton and amateur theatricals, 'and I've had enough of acting a part, one way and another. I intend to be myself from now on,' she warned him, and meant it, although Malcolm did manage to persuade her to go to the infrequent dances. She enjoyed Quetta but, as she told her husband, society would have to accept her on her own terms, or not at all. And eventually society did. There were few white women in Quetta, and one as amusing as young Mrs Nicolson was not to be ostracised—and she *was* the station commandant's wife, and so friendly with Sir George and Lady White … In the end, invitations to the Nicolsons' quarters were sought after. True, you could never be sure what you would be getting to eat, or when it would be served—she was so dreadfully *lax* with the servants—but the conversation was witty, the colonel charming, and his unconventional wife was never boring. Besides, when Mrs Nicolson could be bothered she would sing charmingly to her guests and play the banjo with panache (if not totally without mistakes).

'You never fail to amaze me, Violet,' the colonel said after her first performance, when their guests had left. 'Whenever did you learn to play?'

'Ages ago, at school, they made all us "Indians" learn. *It's so much easier than a piano in the jungle, don't you know?*' and she mimicked the music-teacher with whom, among others, she had carried on a running battle. 'I borrowed Claud's banjo, and I've been practising.'

It was news to the colonel that young Jacob played as well. 'How do you find these things out, Violet? They seem to tell you all their secrets and I can't think why!'

'Because I keep things to myself, *that's* why! They trust me.'

'And they don't trust me?'

'Of course they do! But there are some things they'd rather tell a woman.' Confidences about love affairs, broken hearts—Violet Nicolson dealt with them all, as well as she was able. But she wondered how she would cope with Malcolm when his regimental life was at an end. In little over a year she would have to find out.

'The golden time is over'

Malcolm Nicolson and his wife gazed about them, standing high on the very edge of Empire. The yellow sands of the Afghan plain stretched for mile upon endless mile to meet the rolling desert wastes far off to the west. The air was clear, and the mountains sharply defined against the crystalline blue of the sky. The wind penetrated their sheepskin coats, but they were oblivious to any discomfort. 'I love the mountains,' Violet said quite unnecessarily. 'Even at Simla you could imagine yourself close to God.'

'I didn't think that was why people went to Simla,' Nicolson observed. 'I thought it was all picnics and politics. And flirtations.'

Fanny had flirted, that was true, and her daughter had looked on in embarrassment until she had found how easy it was to escape. She told Malcolm how she had walked amongst the pines and giant rhododendrons, or had spent hours gazing at holy Himalaya. 'Doesn't it make even you feel small and unimportant, up here, among all this, almost in the clouds?'

Malcolm Nicolson, who had not felt small or insignificant since obtaining his captaincy in October 1869, had to disagree. 'But I shall certainly miss all this when I relinquish the command. There's something special about the frontier,' he explained, 'an excitement, a tension that you don't get anywhere else—and I've been here all my life. My heart will always be here, wherever we go.' He said nothing more, and lost in thought, he seemed to forget that Violet was with him.

'And you really have to leave?' She was watching him in concern.

'Oh yes, the regulations are quite clear: after seven years' regimental command, you go; and it makes sense, when you think about it. In the old days the colonels hung on forever, till they could hardly get into the saddle—or out of it, for that matter. So the army brought in the seven-year rule.'

It made no sense at all to Violet. Her husband would be fifty in the June of the following year, and apart from the grey in his hair looked not a day older than when they'd first met. He was as fit and as lean as ever, and delighted in the hard physical demands made upon him.

'What will you do, Malcolm? Father retired when he was only forty-seven.'

'Your father was rather a special case, don't you think? Enough private funds to buy into a newspaper, for example—'

'Yes, that's true. Isabel and I used to wonder about that. We made up all kinds of stories—loot from the Mutiny, that sort of thing. Ridiculous, really.'

Perhaps it wasn't as ridiculous as all that, reflected Cory's son-in-law. 'I'm not retiring, Violet,' he said. 'Besides, what would I do? I'm a professional soldier.'

'So—what will they do with you?'

Her question made him laugh. 'Well they won't shoot me, if that's what you're worried about, and I don't think they'll put me out to pasture quite yet, either! No, the word is that I'll join the General Staff. And that means, Mrs Nicolson, that you will be a general's wife at the ripe old age of twenty-eight. How does that appeal to you?'

'It doesn't!' and she pulled a face at the very idea.

Malcolm laughed again briefly. 'I didn't think it would!'

Violet tried to put all thought of leaving out of her mind. She rode and wrote and read, but time moved on relentlessly and before she knew it, was almost autumn. The regiment was shaping well and it looked like being ready to take its place in the British Line sooner than expected. Nicolson had decided that when that time came, he would relinquish the command early, and take the long leave that had been accumulating over the months and the years. It would, after all, only be fair to his successor.

If only she had given him a child, a son to delight in … But she had miscarried again, in the early stages of the pregnancy, and had said nothing to her husband.

And warned her ayah to say nothing either. This time it was Dr Masani who gave her comfort.

'You have *not* failed your husband, Violet, my dear, and he would be the last man on earth to think such a thing! And perhaps, you know, he would prefer to have you to himself.'

Violet looked at the doctor who, like Claud Jacob, had followed the colonel to the 24th. 'But last time he grieved every bit as much as I did.'

'Last time was last time. What did he say to me, after the patrol was so nearly wiped out? Yes, that's it—he said that you and he were now "handfasted by danger, as well as by your marriage vows". I thought it an odd expression, but I understand what he meant. As a couple your experiences have made you inseparable, why, you appear even to think as one! A child, however much you loved it, would surely change all that?'

'I see. Of course our life would change, and perhaps I wouldn't want that. I'm not likely to know now, though, am I?' Violet gave Masani a wistful little smile, for he had told her that in his opinion she would never carry a child to full term, and might never conceive again. 'I can bear all that, but how can I be sure that Malcolm feels the same?'

'How much do you remember about the last time, Violet?'

'Nothing. Perhaps I was drugged.'

'I don't suppose Nick has ever told you the whole story?' She shook her head. 'And he never will, probably. I'd done all I could for you, you see, and it simply wasn't enough. As you rightly said, I gave you morphia and was resigned to let you slip away. But he's a stubborn man, that husband of yours, and he wasn't prepared to let you go.' The doctor cleared his throat. 'For hours he sat beside you, willing you to live. He reminded you over and over again of a promise it appears you made early on in your marriage. A promise never to leave him—'

All through the night Malcolm Nicolson had fought with Death, and in the morning, grey with exhaustion and drenched with sweat, he had been rewarded.

'Somehow you must have heard his voice pleading with you, for you certainly came back to him.'

Violet made no attempt to stop the tears coursing down her cheeks. *How often do I have to tell you that it doesn't matter about the baby?* Malcolm had said. *I thought you were going to die and take all the love and laughter with you—and I knew I wouldn't want to live on alone. I need you, my dearest wife—and you are all I need.* Now at last she could believe him.

Hand in hand, the colonel and his lady walked through the snow to the church on their last Christmas Day in Quetta, and as she looked at the memorial to Sir Robert—a handsome window with angels and shepherds in the fields—Violet managed to retain her tears. But when the hearty voices raised their hymns to heaven in celebration of the infant Christ, her own voice broke at the thought of her children and her other dead, those she had loved and those who were virtually strangers. *The Lord giveth and the Lord taketh away*, but the name of the Lord was not blessed—or at least not by Violet Nicolson. From that moment on, she trusted only in the man at her side and the love they had for one another. Malcolm Nicolson, his patrician face serene as he joined in the responses of the congregation, might still believe in a compassionate Almighty Being but, as far as his wife was concerned, God too was dead.

They went for long, hard rides in the winter hills and returned, exhilarated and exhausted, to sleep a dreamless sleep. Or they would sit at some village campfire, under the blazing vault of heaven, listening to songs and stories late into the night. Violet wrote feverishly of what she had heard: poem after poem of lost and unrequited love, of cruelty, of despair. She had found a kind of comfort in her writing, but when 1893 dawned and the time of departure came inexorably nearer, nothing could console Colonel Nicolson for the imminent loss of the Baluchi hills, and the regimental life so close to his heart.

5

'You went to shine in other skies'

INDIA: APRIL 1893–APRIL 1895

For his work in Baluchistan Malcolm Nicolson was created a Companion of the Bath. Word reached him in Srinagar, courtesy of a news clipping dispatched there by Colonel Cory. The official notification caught up with the Nicolsons in Karachi, along with that of his promotion: at the end of October 1893 Brigadier-General M.H. Nicolson would take command of Deesa District, three hundred miles north-west of Bombay City—and many hundreds more from his beloved frontier.

'It's small,' Arthur Cory told Violet, 'but it's a start. I always knew Malcolm would do well, my dear. Ever since Zhob I've been telling your mother that he was a rising star in the firmament.' Violet pulled a face at such extravagance. Now that her father had a second son-in-law in the person of the local bank manager, she sincerely hoped he would set rather less store by the first.

Good as it was to be with her parents, the reunion with Isabel gave her the greatest pleasure of all. For all too short a time they were girls again, reliving the past until the present claimed them. 'Mother tells me they're moving out to Clifton Hill next month. Fancy them actually doing it, after all these years of talking—I suppose it's because of Annie Sophie. She has such a desire to be fashionable …'

'*Vivian*, please,' and Isabel Tate's eyes twinkled wickedly behind her spectacles. 'She got her way about that too, you know, the moment Malcolm took you away!'

'So, how *is* the brat?' Since arriving the night before, it had been easy for Violet to avoid her younger sister.

'Abominable! Like you used to be—but with less than half your charm! In fact, with no charm at all,' and Isabel frowned. 'She's nearly twenty-five and Mother and Father would love her to get married—but who would have her?'

'I can't imagine. Well then, they'll have to get rid of her some other way,' and Violet gave an impish grin. 'Perhaps they should send her back to Grandmother Cory in London; she always doted on her, if you remember. Then they can eat cakes and get fat together. What do you think?'

The two sisters looked at each other. 'That's a very good idea,' Isabel said slowly. 'But who's going to suggest it?'

'I will. And if it doesn't work out, Annie Sophie—Vivian, I mean—can always blame me!'

Isabel laughed. 'Don't let's talk about her any more,' she said. 'Tell me, how was Kashmir?'

Not that she needed to ask. The unaccustomed stream of correspondence from her sister, with its determined cheerfulness dealing only with generalities, had told Isabel Tate all she wanted to know. Her brother-in-law had parted from his regiment with the utmost reluctance, no doubt, and had probably undergone bereavement every bit as real as Violet's when she lost her babies. And Violet, Isabel concluded with her usual insight, must have suffered as much from Malcolm's withdrawal as he had done earlier from hers. But her sister's glowing looks now, and the quiet pleasure with which Malcolm talked of his CB and the news of his promotion, confirmed that her brother-in-law had come to terms with the end of one life and the prospect of another.

How was Kashmir? Violet considered the early weeks on board the houseboat; weeks of guarding her tongue and weighing her every action, of drifting through the lotuses whose tight green buds beckoned like fingers inviting her to drown her sorrows in the lake. But then, resolutely putting all that behind her, 'Oh, you know, Izzie,' she said with a shrug, 'the sun shines, the people smile, and you drift on aimlessly for days and days at a time ...'

'It doesn't sound like either of you to me!' Isabel retorted, but letting the evasion pass. 'And what about the Moghul gardens, and Shalimar Bagh. Are they as beautiful as everyone says?'

'They absolutely defy description.' This time Isabel could not doubt her sister's sincerity. 'You should ask John to take you, and see them for yourself.'

There was none of the charm of a Moghul garden about Vivian Cory. Self-opinionated, and the continuing despair of her parents, just as she had been jealous of one sister before, so was she envious of the other now. Not of Isabel's marriage—in her eyes John Tate and his solid respectability bore no comparison to the charismatic Nicolson—but of her role at the *Sind Gazette*. For Miss Cory wished to write. Indeed she had *already* written tales she wanted to see in print; tales she wished Isabel to publish. Tales that her sister had rejected out of hand.

'She thinks she's another Kipling, darling. Isabel says she's terribly rude about Anglo-Indian society.'

'Just like him—and you,' observed Malcolm, who was helping Violet dress before dinner. He dropped a kiss on his wife's bare shoulder.

'Oh no, much worse than me,' she assured him.

'Then Isabel has cause indeed to worry!'

'What are we going to do with her, Malcolm? I suggested she go to our grandmother in London—indefinitely, if not for ever—and Isabel thinks it's rather a good idea.'

'I agree. But you'll have to make her believe it was her own idea, or out of sheer perversity she'll refuse to go!'

'Izzie tells me you're busy writing these days.' That evening at dinner Violet looked at her younger sister with what she hoped was a friendly expression, only to be rewarded with a scowl.

'Then I don't know why she bothered. She won't have anything to do with it!'

'I can't think why.' Violet failed to catch her husband's eye and went on. 'I should have thought she'd be glad of anything—if only for the sake of a change.'

Oh dear, thought Nicolson. That isn't going to help. 'What I think your sister means, Vivian,' he said, intervening quickly before the young woman had time to take offence, 'is that Isabel might find your work too sophisticated for Karachi. To be appreciated, you know, writers often have to look away from their own home towns, which can be provincial in the extreme.'

'Well, that's certainly true of Karachi!' The petulant little face looked at her brother-in-law with sudden interest: perhaps he was more sympathetic towards her than she imagined. 'There is absolutely nothing here for people like me—it's so incredibly boring, Malcolm, you've no idea! If only I could get away ...'

To Violet it all sounded terribly familiar, and for a moment she felt a certain fellow feeling. 'Yes,' she heard herself saying, 'I do know what you mean.'

'I don't want any sympathy from *you*, thank you very much,' snapped Miss Cory. 'It's all very well for you—you and Malcolm are always on the move.' Her pale eyes narrowed. Her sister looked so happy and fulfilled.

'Travel *is* very stimulating, of course,' and Nicolson gave the young woman his understanding smile. 'You must have enjoyed your time in England and on the Continent immensely. How long have you been back in India?'

Violet watched Vivian Cory count on her plump little fingers and sigh, 'Eight years. Eight whole years.'

'It *is* a long time,' General Nicolson agreed. 'Things must be constantly changing back in England. What a pity you can't see it happening for yourself.' He turned to his wife and his eyelid drooped slightly. 'I'm sure *you'd* like to visit

London again, wouldn't you, my dear.'

Violet responded exactly as he hoped. 'London?' she exclaimed. '*London*? Good heavens, Malcolm, it's a *ghastly* place, and the last place on earth I would choose!'

Clumsy, perhaps, and only a small contribution to her husband's strategy, yet it sufficed. By the time the Nicolsons were ready to leave for Deesa, Vivian Cory had announced her intention of visiting her grandmother. And had received her parents' wholehearted blessing on her plans.

'Too high for service, as too far for love'

A whole new world awaited the Nicolsons, too. The cantonment at Deesa sprawled along the riverbank three miles north-east of the native town. Even so, here on the edge of the Rajputana desert, colours, sounds and smells assailed their senses, and impinged upon their daily existence in a way that at first seemed crude and offensive. Used as they were to the stark simplicity of the Baluchi mountains and the muted shades of the plains—where sunrise and sunset alone brought life and colour, and where two or three horsemen sighted on the horizon constituted a crowd—Deesa to the new arrivals presented a teeming throng of garishly dressed and frenetic humanity.

Malcolm had warned of heat and insects. And never-ending dust. So gloomy a picture had he painted, in fact, that the gracious bungalow, with its flourishing garden (which had clearly benefited from the iron hand and sharp tongue of the previous general's wife) came as a welcome surprise. Once again Violet had nothing specific to do with her time—for she had no intention of seeking out the few European women in the district. Recalling the earliest days of her marriage, she determined not to make the same mistakes again and kept herself busy. Malcolm would leave her to her own devises at six and meet her again at one. In his absence she rode, and explored the town and its environs. She looked, questioned and learned, and, as before in Hyderabad, she felt the insidious East renew its fragrance-laden spell. It was a pleasant enough existence, but she felt pampered and indulged all the same.

May brought the hot weather and Violet was forced to abandon her daily sorties. When Malcolm returned from his office she would search his face anxiously, knowing he felt the heat as much as she, and dreading to find signs of the fever that lurked in the native town and which she knew he had suffered before. At tiffin one day Nicolson commented on his wife's listlessness. 'Why don't you go up to Mount Abu?' he suggested. 'It's no distance away, after all, but so much cooler. I think it would do you no end of good.'

'No, I'm perfectly well, darling, really. If I promise not to get irritable or lose my temper, will that do instead?'

'Now, once upon a time that would have seemed a marvellous bargain! But you've changed, I've noticed. You're much more docile these days.' She smiled at that, but let it pass. 'Yet there must be plenty of things here in Deesa to anger you.' This time he received an answer.

'Perhaps it's the fatalism of the East,' she ventured. 'Perhaps I've learned the wisdom of not trying to interfere. Perhaps I've realised that change must come from within, and it's a matter for the Indians themselves. Who knows?' And perhaps it *was* only the weather, she thought, *or perhaps I'm simply growing up*. 'I'll leave it to Annie Sophie to change the world,' she added lightly.

'She's begun then, has she? Has she written?' It seemed unlikely.

'No, I've heard from Isabel. Our sister, she tells me, has become involved with some literary group that's revolutionising London, and is having a wonderful time—or so she says!' Violet spoke lightly, but Nicolson's answering look was keen, for a thought had suddenly struck him. 'You're not wanting to be over there yourself, are you?' he asked.

'Darling, I do not want to go to London, especially with Annie Sophie at large! No, you're probably right—it's just the heat, and I must learn to accept it, like the Indians. *It is written*, as Mahomed Akram always said,' and Violet gave a sigh.

She had thought it strange, in the first place, that the Afghan had come south with them, so far from his tribal homelands. He had seemed happy enough in the alien surroundings, until two months earlier when he took his leave, first of his erstwhile companion and then of his companion's wife. Violet had been alone. The gaze from the coal-black eyes was as impenetrable as ever, yet when the Afghan made his farewells she sensed that this time he would not return. She felt a sudden pang of anguish and impulsively put out her hand. Mahomed Akram had hesitated. Then ignoring centuries of tradition, he took the young woman's hand in both of his. He addressed her in words too swift and intense for her to follow, and then he was gone.

Gradually Violet's sorrow became less acute, and then only a dull ache to be revived at moments like this. 'Malcolm, why did he go?' she asked. 'Why has he gone for good?'

'Is that what he told you?'

'No. But it's true, isn't it?' She had to wait a long time for an answer.

'When we married,' Nicolson said at last, 'I was afraid that you and he wouldn't get on,' and, to be sure, Violet remembered all too well the sullen looks that had met her, those first mornings of their married life. 'It was natural he should resent you—we were like brothers, after all, and there you were, suddenly come between us. But you won him round, without even trying, simply by being yourself. Otherwise I would have told him to leave—didn't you realise?'

Violet shook her head. There was so much she didn't see, her husband thought. 'So he accepted you. First through duty, then through friendship.'

'But why go after so long?'

'Do you remember the snake? The *second* snake, I mean, here in our compound?'

'How could I forget?' Violet shivered at the memory of walking through her perfumed garden and all too late hearing the Afghan's cry of warning. Of looking down to where the purplish speckled body of a krait hissed and writhed under her heel, the head unable to strike—and she unable to escape unscathed. His intention obvious, Mahomed Akram had moved forward swiftly, only to be checked by the woman's desperate appeal.

'*No! Wait!*' and the urgency of her next words brought her husband running. 'Malcolm,' she called out, 'I'm in the garden. Bring out the long scissors! *Oh, darling, hurry, please!*' And then, with a hand that hardly shook, she bent and cut the deadly snake in two. A moment later she was safe in her husband's arms.

'He would have died for you that day, sacrificed himself for you and died happy. But you had no need of him and he finally understood it. So,' said Malcolm Nicolson, 'he came and told me he was returning to his people.' Malcolm watched as comprehension at last dawned upon her face. 'Yes, he loved you and loves you still, I've no doubt.'

'You knew how he felt?' Violet's voice was subdued.

'Yes, of course. He made no secret of it to me.'

'*And you didn't mind?*' Violet thought of the hours she and the Afghan had spent alone together.

'He honoured you, he honoured our friendship, and he accepted the hand of Fate—why should I mind?'

'*And I never knew ...*'

'It was better that way—the friendship never soured, the memories pure ...' Tenderly Nicolson kissed her stricken face. 'Never forget him, that is all he would ask. In the name of Allah the Compassionate, the Merciful, he would want you to remember all that has passed between you. Remember him, Violet, as he will always remember you, the "unattainable woman" of his songs.'

'I too have waited, parched and worn with pain'

May advanced with no sign of the monsoon. The general's wife spent more and more time indoors, alone with her thoughts and her verses. Despite the punkahs, and the wet *kuskus tatties* hung over windows and doors to cool the stifling air, more often than not Nicolson would return to find her stretched out on the bed in her shift, her body soaked with perspiration. At last he decided to act.

'I'm off next week on inspection,' he announced. 'And you're coming with me. I'll arrange for somewhere for you to stay at Mount Abu. It really is much cooler up there, darling, so no arguments this time, please.'

Violet was suffering too much to be ruled by superstition. Instead, she meekly packed a bag and made no protest when she was left behind at the little hill station in the company of kindly strangers. She remained there one night and a day, long enough to toil her way up the rough narrow mountain path that led to the four Jain temples nestling among mango trees beyond the town. She approached the first, removed her leather boots and went in.

Row after row of exquisitely carved white marble pillars, chiselled into patterns intricate as lace, met her eyes. No priest approached her and she was alone in the silence and the light. Stockinged feet on cool stone, she reflected on the impassive posturing figures that for centuries had gazed down blindly on a never-changing world—a world of uncomplaining peasants toiling in the heat for scant reward. How long she stood there, she did not know, and when at last she left, it was with a feeling of inner peace and a sense of her own good fortune.

She thanked the hosts who had entertained her so briefly and made her way down by rail to Palanpur. From there she finished her journey to Deesa by *ekka*. Late in the evening the pony cart deposited her at the bungalow, where she found Malcolm Nicolson prostrate with fever and too ill to recognise his truant wife. Her ayah welcomed her return with relief. She and Nicolson's native orderly were tending the patient and clearly they did not see eye to eye.

'How long has the general *sahib* been unwell?' Violet enquired, taking in the fraught situation between Hindu and Muslim immediately.

'Two days, *memsahib*.'

Two days, and still the fever hadn't broken … Quickly Violet collected rugs and blankets—all too few in this place that was still as hot as hell—and piled them, as the Brahuis did, over the unconscious figure on the bed. And then she watched and waited. If Malcolm wasn't sweating she most certainly was, and how she longed to tear off all her clothes!

Go away, she willed, *go away*. But the orderly stood his ground, and for once Violet found herself cursing her husband's ability to arouse such devotion in his men. Wiping away the drenching sweat as best she could, Violet continued her silent vigil and the Muslim waited with her. Sometimes Malcolm lay so still she thought he must be dead already, and sometimes he tossed and turned, muttered deliriously, or tried to rise, fighting their restraining arms or seizing them in a grip of iron. At midnight on the third day the fever broke, and at last she knew her husband would not die. She brushed her soaking hair back from her brow and smiled wearily.

'Bring water—tepid water,' she told the maid and sent the man off to fetch quinine. Once, while she was sponging his sweating limbs and body over and over again, Nicolson opened his eyes and recognised her.

'You shouldn't be here,' were his only words before he lapsed into a peaceful sleep. Gratefully, Violet sank to oblivion on the floor beside his bed.

'Well, well,' said Malcolm Nicolson, as a bright little figure entered the room where he lay propped up by many pillows. 'You go to Mount Abu an Englishwoman and you come back an Indian. Why *did* you come back?' He tried to sound severe, although his home was a haven of happiness since the return of the diminutive harpy who, with bare arms and midriff set off by folds of bright blue cotton, stood over him now, hands on hips, demanding that he eat.

'I didn't realise you were such a tyrant.' Malcolm managed a laugh before his voice took a serious turn. He looked at her drawn features and the shadows under her eyes. 'You're exhausted, aren't you, darling, and good heavens, did I do that?' He touched the unsightly finger marks on her bruised arm.

'Yes, but it doesn't hurt,' she assured him. 'Isn't it odd that you should have had such strength then, and hardly any now?'

'Fever is a very strange thing, you know. Lying there helpless, I had dreams that would have made you blush, yes, even you, my little wanton,' and he lightly stroked the bruises, hoping she would understand and once more find it in her heart to be patient. 'I'm so glad you came back,' he said. 'How did you know I needed you?'

'I can't say that I did.' Violet was perfectly honest. 'I was in the temple and it was so peaceful that I felt almost as if I was floating away, as if nothing could hold me back— I can't explain properly what it was like, but I felt I was shedding all my imperfections. Then I found myself thinking of you and I knew my place was here, no matter the heat and discomfort, and I knew I could stand it, after all. Don't laugh at me,' and she looked at Malcolm rather uncertainly.

'I wouldn't dream of it, sweetheart,' and he took her hand. *Piety, liberality, gentleness and penance*, he thought. As guidelines for someone earnestly seeking self-improvement, those followed by the Jains could hardly be bettered. 'There are Jain temples here in Deesa as well,' he told her. 'Did you know?'

'I thought you would be wearing your new sari.' Up and about again Malcolm Nicolson came in and kissed his wife. He knew she had intended going to the bazaar after her now daily visit to the temple, but wasn't at all surprised when she shook her head.

'I decided not to get one,' she replied.

'Oh? Didn't you see anything you liked?'

'Oh yes, they were wonderful— I just changed my mind, that's all.'

The general looked after his wife as she took his helmet and jacket from him and walked towards the door.

'I suppose you gave it away, like the last one.'

Violet said nothing.

'My dear girl, you can't clothe all India, you know—and you can't feed it, either.' (Although he knew she tried.)

'But your attempts at housing aren't going too badly,' and from the verandah he indicated the dozen or so figures making themselves at home near the compound outbuildings. 'Or are they all the *mali*'s relations?'

'You don't really mind, do you, Malcolm? It seems the least I can do.'

Nicolson was amused. 'Would it make any difference if I did? No, Violet, I don't mind, but I do think we've reached our limit as far as the compound is concerned, don't you? As for the rest, what you do is your own concern, but if you won't clothe yourself, then you must allow me the pleasure. Do you agree?'

Once this had been a bone of contention, but now Violet simply smiled and nodded—only to add a moment later, 'But nothing too extravagant, mind. Remember, I'm only your wife!'

'I sit in the shade of the Temple walls'

As the longed-for clouds built up and thunder pealed in the distance, the general's wife stood in the open and waited for the first drops of the monsoon rains to fall. They came intermittently at first, and then in solid sheets, ending the heat that had increased inexorably day by day, driving Europeans perilously close to the edge of reason. With the change in the weather, normal life resumed, and before long General Nicolson was called away for several days. He left his wife sleeping like a child, and when she awoke he was already well on the road to the outlying stations. A letter came for him that afternoon. Its blurred postmark declared it to have been posted somewhere in Scotland many weeks before. It was addressed to Colonel Malcolm Hassells Nicolson, and had been forwarded from Quetta. There it lay, waiting for him on a little rosewood table near the door, and each time she passed it Violet was consumed with an almost irresistible feeling of curiosity. She picked up the envelope several times, and turned it over and over in her hand as if by constant scrutiny it would yield its secrets. The handwriting was a woman's, of that she was convinced, and in some distant recess of her mind there lurked a memory that refused to surface, try as she might to make it. As the afternoon wore to a close Mrs Nicolson became increasingly restless. Sitting on the edge of the formal pool in the centre of the compound, her bare feet dangling in the water, she tried to think. When had they talked about Scotland? Who had he said lived there? It had all been terribly vague, *he* had been terribly vague ... She had asked him about someone, yes, she had asked him about ... now, who on earth was it? The answer still refused to come, and the sound of the fountain seemed to stifle thought. On the evening that Malcolm was due to return, she told the ayah where she was going, and set off to meet her husband on the road from Palanpur.

Some time later General Nicolson was startled at the sight of a pale wraith advancing on him from a lonely wayside temple, and both he and the orderly with him instinctively reached for their revolvers. 'Good Lord, Violet, what are you doing here?' he exclaimed as he recognised his wife. Before she could reply, he told the man to go on ahead. 'I might have shot you!'

'Nonsense, darling, you'd never shoot a woman—and you don't believe in ghosts! I just thought I'd walk out and wait for you here. It's perfectly safe,' and Violet waved in the direction of the little shrine behind her. 'I've been talking to the priest—he's been telling me all kinds of tales.'

'I can imagine,' her husband said dryly. 'Well, are you ready to come with me now, or shall we go in and listen to some more?'

'No, of course not, let's go home!'

He reached down and pulled her up behind him. 'Now,' he said, before they started back, 'why don't you tell me why you're really here.'

'I told you—I just felt I wanted the walk.' She made her voice as light as she could but Malcolm wasn't fooled.

'Violet Nicolson, you're a very poor liar, even when I can't see your face! Come on, tell me.'

'Well,' and Violet hugged him tightly around the waist, 'there's a letter for you, sent on from Quetta. It's from Scotland and I've been trying to remember who you said lived there, and for the life of me I can't.'

'So you came all this way to meet me, out of sheer curiosity, and there I was, thinking it was for love!' Flora, he was thinking, it had to be Flora. What on earth did she want? To congratulate him upon his marriage? Or was there something more?

'*Malcolm*!'

'I'm sorry, darling, it must be from Mrs Steel. You remember, Sir George White's old friend.'

'Your friend, too,' Violet observed shortly, suddenly remembering everything he had told her about the civil servant's wife, and trying to stifle her jealousy of a woman she would never meet.

As Malcolm Nicolson entered the weathered stone building shaded by sacred peepul trees and set in a tangle of lantana and vivid creepers, he understood once more the appeal the temple held for his wife. It had puzzled him at first that an energetic creature like Violet should choose to spend hours in such surroundings, until he too felt its serenity settle about him. He realised then that her restless nature had possibly found what it needed: an undemanding place of silence, where she could attempt to come to terms with the changing circumstances of her life.

She had travelled far in the five years of her marriage. It had been both a physical and a spiritual journey, sometimes almost too difficult to bear, and here in the Jain temple at Deesa she had clearly found peace. He spied her now, sitting hands round knees at the base of one of the carved pillars, facing the figure in one of the several shrines. Malcolm looked from the staring black marble features to Violet's equally expressionless face. The curve of the lips was just as solemn, but when she saw him her slow warm smile of welcome made him quicken his step.

'You've gone *jungli*, General Nicolson,' she observed.

'So have you, *madame la générale*.' He touched her outstretched fingers and sat down beside her. They made a strange couple, he was in his Afghan clothes and she in her sari, but none of the monks drifting silently past took any notice. His transformation made sense, thought the general's wife: removing military boots, belt and sabretache at the temple steps would be an irritating process. Nicolson's solution to a practical problem was (as always) equally practical, but when it came to problems of a domestic nature he had learned to be cautious.

'Are you ready to come back, do you think, or would you rather stay?'

'Let's stay a little longer, please. Look at that face, Malcolm—so old and so wise. When I sit here everything seems possible, after all.'

'What do you mean by *everything*?'

'Oh, things I'm not very good at. Self-control, for one thing—governing my thoughts and actions as I should. Being sorry when I haven't. You know, everything they teach here in the temple.' Violet looked at her husband apologetically and they both thought of the previous evening, when the letter from Scotland had upset her so much and she had lost her temper.

Nicolson squeezed her hand. 'Come on,' he said, 'let's go home.'

'Have you written to Mrs Steel yet?'

'Yes, before I came to find you.'

'What did you say to her?'

'I thanked her for her good wishes—I thought you would want me to begin with that,' for it had been a rather frosty letter from his old friend, who was obviously put out, not only by the fact that he was married at all, but that he had been so long in telling her.

'And then I said we would be delighted to have her visit when she came out to India in the autumn.'

Nicolson refrained from looking at Violet, so failed to see her pull a face.

'I explained that we were no longer in Quetta, and suggested we might see her in Bombay if she didn't want to come on here. We'd be able to take a couple of weeks' leave and rent somewhere on Malabar Hill, and she might welcome a rest after the journey out from London. What do you think?'

Violet thought all the way across the *maidan* and was still thinking when they reached the bungalow. 'Of course you will want to see each other,' she said agreeably, as they went inside. 'I don't suppose it matters where. You'll have so much to talk about after all this time. But you won't need me to be there, surely?' She looked up at him through her lashes with a little smile. 'Why don't you go to Bombay by yourself?'

'That's very generous of you, Violet. If I didn't know how much you dislike Bombay, I would say *noble*, even,' and he laughed at her injured expression. 'However, Flora plans to go up to Lahore after she's seen us, and I really do think she will want to visit us here.'

But Mrs Steel had no wish to go to Deesa. Perhaps she didn't want to see Violet Nicolson running her own household as the commanding general's wife; perhaps she thought the general would have more time to devote to her elsewhere. Perhaps (like Violet) she hoped that Malcolm Nicolson would travel to Bombay alone. But for whatever reason, Mrs Steel chose to be reunited with her old friend in Bombay. And a reluctant Violet was to be present when they met.

'I want you there,' her husband insisted. 'Besides, what would Flora think if I failed to introduce my wife?'

Violet couldn't have cared less what the older woman thought, but gave an answer despite the rhetorical nature of the question. 'She'd probably think that you'd married a native woman, and didn't dare produce her in public.' A sudden thought struck her. 'Very well, Malcolm,' Mrs Nicolson said meekly. 'Of course I'd love to come.'

So relieved was General Nicolson at his wife's easy capitulation that he didn't think to question the nature of the smile hovering about her lips.

'Bring forth the Bride for her Lover's Delight'

Several more letters were exchanged during the following months, leave was arranged for mid-October, and on the nineteenth of that month Flora Annie Steel returned to the India she had left five years before. General Nicolson was there on the quayside to meet her, and together they drove through the old town and up to Malabar Hill.

Violet was waiting for them, a vivid splash of colour in front of an equally vivid house. As the carriage came into the drive, Mrs Steel's eye was drawn initially to the pink, coffee and cream bungalow, set (she confided to her diary) like some gigantic ice cream in a riot of roses and bougainvillea. It would all seem rather vulgar, she added to herself, if it weren't in Bombay—and rented by her friend. And then the inquisitive gaze took in the still figure waiting under the portico.

Only when the carriage stopped and Malcolm came round to help her down, did Flora Steel see that the woman in the purple red-bordered silk sari was white not black, and realise that the garland of marigolds and tuberoses held out in little, henna-painted hands was intended for her. She looked into merry, deeply violet eyes the like of which she had never seen, and heard a low, musical voice bid her welcome. This, she realised with a shock even before the general had time to make the introductions, must be Malcolm Nicolson's wife.

The two women, both of a height, eyed each other curiously. Violet saw a rather dumpy woman in her late forties, with faded fluffy fair hair, rosy cheeks, and light blue eyes in a round and capable face. The small mouth was set in an expression of disapproval and then it spoke: 'Thank you for the garland, my dear, but I don't think I'll wear it. If you don't mind.'

Unabashed, Violet took it back from the reluctant hand of her guest and decided to wear it herself. 'Do come inside, Mrs Steel,' she said brightly, 'I'll show you to your room. I expect you'd like to freshen up. It's this way, if you would follow me.'

As General Nicolson's young wife walked into the house the silk folds floated around her, and the languid sway of her hips and the scent of the flowers around her neck combined to give Flora Annie Steel an impression of her hostess that the following week did little to dispel. Violet Nicolson, she concluded, was one of those dangerously sensual females who held a man in thrall with their bodies and not their minds … Poor Malcolm, how tired he looked, and how she pitied him.

The object of Mrs Steel's pity looked on in amusement as the two women—so very different in some ways, yet so alike in others—endeavoured to be civil. Flora was outspoken in her opinions and, given the slightest encouragement, held forth on any subject under the sun. No encouragement, he knew, would come from Violet, his wife. Sitting in silence while Mrs Steel pontificated, her hostess made valiant efforts to curb her tongue; she pleated her sari or played with the petals of a flower and gazed longingly at the garden as she did so. And all the while her guest's opinion was being reinforced: that little Violet Nicolson had not a serious thought in her pretty sex-ridden head.

As long as Flora doesn't talk about the status of Indian women or ridicule self-rule for

India we should get by, thought General Nicolson, as he endeavoured to keep the subject general or on matters from their common past. His tactics proved successful: Violet's thoughts drifted far away and she paid no attention, or she would excuse herself and wander into the garden. Or go to bed early while the two old friends talked of mutual acquaintances and times past far into the night.

It gradually emerged that Mrs Steel's visit had more than a social purpose. She was, she informed her hosts one morning over breakfast, intending to write a grand novel about the Indian Mutiny. And to do this she must conduct a programme of research. And gain impressions of everything she could while she was here. Violet wondered why this should be necessary—surely, with twenty years spent in the country already, impressions should be plentiful enough? Yet dutifully she accompanied Flora on her sketching expeditions, and sat and watched as the pencil flew and notes were taken and comments made—and listened to interminable accounts of the day's doings over the evening meal at night.

Mrs Steel, it also transpired, was an expert on housekeeping and cuisine. Thank heaven, then, she didn't come to Deesa, thought Violet in relief, as she listened to endless criticisms of the cook. At least *here* I don't have to take complete responsibility for what appears on the table. She caught Malcolm's eye and he winked; he must have been thinking the very same thing.

'Why don't you write a book about all this, Mrs Steel, you know so much,' and Violet gave her guest the sweetest of smiles.

'Thank you, my dear; when the novel is finished, my publisher thinks that I should.'

Touchée, my girl, thought General Nicolson, hoping that his wife would leave it at that. Time and again he had seen her open her mouth to speak and think better of it, and to his relief this was another such occasion.

'Do tell us about your "epic", Flora,' he intervened quickly, before Violet should change her mind. 'Have you worked out the plot yet?'

'Only sketched it so far, Malcolm—I must collect my impressions first. I'm going north, as you know, back to Kasur where Henry and I were stationed'—this last for the younger woman's benefit—'and I shall live there as a native woman, as will my heroine, up on the rooftops.'

'Goodness,' breathed Violet, 'what a wonderful idea.' There was no hint of sarcasm in her voice at all, and she looked at her guest with sudden respect. 'All on your own, too, Mrs Steel.'

'Of course. For absolute authenticity, I shall have to. And then I go on to Lahore.'

'Violet was brought up in Lahore. She knows it well,' Nicolson told his friend, seeing a chance both to capitalise on his wife's awakened interest in their visitor and to bring the two women closer. It worked: Violet found the older woman less tedious than she thought, and Mrs Steel for her part, watching the now animated face opposite and finding the girl to be unexpectedly witty and intelligent, was forced reluctantly to revise her earlier opinion of Malcolm Nicolson's bride.

It was with mixed feelings that she took her leave of the Nicolsons a week later: intense regret at parting with the man who had made her so very welcome, and relief at being free of the young woman whose love was so obviously returned. As the train pulled out of the Victoria Terminus she stood and watched them, standing close together on the platform waving, and it was not only the prospect of a long stay among strangers that made her feel lonely.

'So that was your Mrs Steel,' said Violet, as the couple turned away. 'I wonder if she'll write her masterpiece.'

'I'm sure she will. She's someone who always gets everything she wants.'

Not quite everything, thought Violet Nicolson with no little satisfaction, taking her husband's arm as they walked to their waiting carriage.

'I cannot escape. What are the Stars to me?'

In November Malcolm Nicolson was gazetted major-general and advised of an imminent move further south. 'It's wonderful news for you, darling,' Violet said warmly, hiding her misgivings. 'And when do we leave?'

'In April.'

Five months, then, before the general assumed command of a far larger district in Central India for a period of five years. It was a prestigious appointment—the kind of appointment people hoped for, and very rarely were given. Malcolm watched his wife carefully, but could detect nothing but pleasure on her face.

'Darling,' he warned, 'you must make the most of the time we have left—things will be very different when we get to Mhow.'

Violet took his words to heart. She treasured every moment of the quiet time before they were caught up in the official life that loomed ahead. Sometimes in the evenings she walked out to meet her husband as before, sitting so quietly on the temple steps that the little striped squirrels forgot their fear of the stranger and slipped down from the peepul tree to play awhile at her feet. Grey doves fussed in the branches above her and somewhere in the distance peacocks screamed. Lost in thought and dreaming dreams, she sat almost motionless until she heard her husband's horse.

They rarely entertained, preferring to spend the twilight hours driving along the empty roads, and lingering in the garden after supper to watch the flying foxes cleave the darkling sky.

'I hate the thought of leaving this.' Violet turned to Malcolm and he caught a faint scent of *moghra* from his flowers in her hair.

'I know but you mustn't fret. Look up, sweetheart. Some things will never change.' In the purple sky the stars shone bright and constant, and low on the horizon Violet saw the wondrous Southern Cross. 'Of course there will always be glorious Eastern nights like these,' she admitted. 'But what of the *days*, Malcolm, what of them?'

General Nicolson shared her apprehension. He had many preoccupations, but mainly he thought about his wife. There would be things expected of her that he supposed he would have to insist upon, and it had been a long time since he had dared do any such thing. 'I can appreciate what Christianity has in common with Eastern religions,' she said, when he tentatively broached the question of weekly attendance at church. 'Generosity; compassion; love of your neighbour; doing good; turning the other cheek—I know all that. But what's gone wrong here, Malcolm? Oh, not in Deesa. I'm sure everyone is very nice—I just haven't had anything much to do with them, that's all. Here in *India*, I mean. People smile nicely and worship together in harmony on Sundays. Then they stab each other in the back all through the week! I've absolutely nothing against Christianity,' she assured her husband solemnly. 'It's simply Christians I find I cannot stomach!'

Oh dear, thought Malcolm Nicolson, whenever he remembered how deadly serious she had been. There could well be trouble ahead, and for once in his life he preferred to leave the problem alone.

6

'Let us escape from out these prison bars'

MHOW: APRIL 1895–DECEMBER 1897

The Nicolsons arrived in the Central India Agency on an intensely hot afternoon towards the end of March 1895. The importance of the Mhow Command, and of its new commander, was reflected by the size of the party waiting to greet them. As the train pulled in, the entire District staff stood at attention before moving forward as one. General Nicolson stepped onto the platform first, and as his wife stared down at the sea of grinning teeth, she felt something akin to despair. Malcolm's arm reached out to support her—or was he preventing her from running away? Violet smiled mechanically and shook hands with these oh-so-formal officers who all looked the same. How would she ever remember the faces, let alone the names? Then mercifully only one of them was left.

'I'm sorry,' she said. 'What did you say, Lieutenant …?' She looked vaguely at the young man who sat opposite her in the carriage. He was saying something she felt too dizzy to hear.

'Elkington. I'm to be your husband's aide-de-camp, Mrs Nicolson.' The boyish clean-shaven features were creased in a frown of concern. 'I was just saying we haven't far to go to your quarters. You must be exhausted.' The general's wife looked pale, and he'd been afraid she might faint in the crush.

'You're very kind, Lieutenant Elkington.' She was weary but this time Violet's smile was sincere. 'Yes, it was a long journey.'

A journey that she'd had no wish to make, but at last they were here, and that (as Malcolm would say) was that. Five years to be spent on this sunburnt plain, with not a hill in sight. And Malcolm—what was *he* thinking? Her husband's face, serene and interested, offered no clue at all.

'Here we are then,' the ADC's voice was hearty, 'the General's Bungalow. Pretty grim, I'm afraid, but it's probably the only roof in town that doesn't leak!

That may mean nothing to you now, Mrs Nicolson, but just wait till the monsoon starts in June!'

Violet surveyed her new home. Square and whitewashed, balustrades at attention like the District staff, it was much like any other bungalow she'd been in, but bigger. The reception room was cool, and she looked round for somewhere to sit. The only furniture was made of cane and she hesitated to use it. Mhow, thought Violet Nicolson in her present jaundiced mood, probably harboured not only regiments of European and Native troops, but also their equivalent in white ants and other destructive insects.

'Why don't you sit down while I organise some tea,' Robert Elkington suggested. 'The chairs are perfectly safe,' he added with a grin, as if reading Violet's thoughts. 'I tried them all out earlier.' Without waiting for a reply the slightly built lieutenant left the room, while the general, a good head taller and certainly heavier, lowered himself gingerly into a seat. Then the Nicolsons looked at one another.

'He appears very capable,' said Violet.

'With tea parties, perhaps. I'll reserve judgement on the rest.'

The young man did not linger and, revived by the tea, Violet began to explore. She found more cane furniture in the shadowy depths of the verandah, and, outside, a compound shrieking with an impossible mix of colours. Her spirits rose at the cheerfully vulgar display and she made her way back to her husband in one of the bedrooms.

'Well,' he asked, 'what do you think?'

The room was large, with the usual high ceiling and small windows near the roof; there was a dressing room for Malcolm, and a bathroom for them each. 'It will do very nicely, I suppose,' and she eyed the square Indian bed frame, and the webbing interwoven from head to foot and from side to side. 'I take it this one is the best?'

'I mean Mhow.'

'Ah, *Mhow* …' Violet's temporary elation was quickly forgotten. 'Malcolm, however are we going to survive?'

Over the next few days, Violet organised her household and got to know her servants' names while remaining vague about her neighbours'. She arranged the rugs and cushions that had followed them faithfully from Baluchistan to Deesa and bought more in the native bazaar. She filled the house with lantana from the compound and met Malcolm with a cheery smile each day when he came back from District Headquarters.

Callers came. One or two to begin with, but when word spread that the new commanding general's wife was *interesting*, the trickle became a flood, and each time Violet was treated to a virtual monologue on the rites and rituals of Mhow. She learned what was done, and when, and how, and why. The Mhow Club, the Tent Club. Mhow Week in December and another one in February. The hot weather, the cold weather, the rains ... Violet listened politely to explanations of them all. They were such a happy little community, she was told.

'Oh yes, Mrs Nicolson, you may be sure that we all pull together.' Showing the flag, as they put it.

What did they do with dissenters, Violet wondered. Hang them from the flagpole too? She forced a smile to frozen lips as the visitors looked around, assessing her belongings, assessing *her*. And later, in a huddle over tea at the Club, had she known it, they shared their impressions of little Mrs Nicolson. Rather withdrawn, they thought, not at all like the general. Now wasn't *he* charming?

I have to get out, thought Violet after two weeks of such visits. *I need to breathe. If I don't get away, I shall choke on the odour of sanctity*. She told Malcolm.

'Of course you must,' he readily agreed. 'And I'll come with you!' So the two of them rode out at dawn the next morning, both in Afghan clothes.

Violet had been wrong. There *were* hills, odd little hills like pimples on the plain which stretched before them for mile upon endless mile, broken by dry watercourses and trees, and by fields of opium poppies showing bright against the rich black loamy soil. To the south of the cantonment rose the Vindhya Hills and beyond them the line of the Western Ghats.

'Over there,' and the general pointed vaguely eastwards, 'there are teak forests. And waterfalls. And a spectacular pass. I'll take you as soon as I can get away,' he added as his wife looked longingly at mountains that spelt freedom. 'We'll go,' he assured her, 'once it all calms down.'

Violet inclined her head. She knew exactly what he meant—and exactly what would come of this latest promise. He was busy during the day at Headquarters and in the evenings he was entertained in the mess. It was natural that he should wish to get to know the officers of the European and Native regiments, but when he came home he slept in his dressing room so as not to disturb her, and was away again in the early morning. Sometimes, it seemed to Violet, they scarcely spoke all day.

'I'm surprised you played truant this morning,' she said tartly. She had heard it all before and waited in vain.

'Oh, I sent word to Elkington, telling him to hold the fort today. He'll cope—and it would hardly be a disaster if he didn't. I'm sorry, darling, I do know how you feel.'

They dismounted and stood looking towards the east.

'We don't get much time together, do we?' he continued, 'but because tomorrow is special we'll dine at home alone.'

She looked surprised.

'It's your birthday! I do believe you've forgotten!'

'Thirty years old already,' and Violet pulled a face. 'Perhaps I'd prefer to forget!'

'Well quit of the world and free'

In May, as was customary, many of the wives retreated to the hills, a situation which brought Violet relief from their attentions, if not from the heat. The temperature rose steadily to one hundred degrees and above, and she did not venture far. Instead, she fretted the hours away indoors, trying to write and feeling that her head would burst. She had one visitor. Mrs Dwyer the chaplain's wife, a stout lady of middle years, felt the heat even more than she, and would have been far better off in the hills. The distressed matron foundered like a beached whale on an inadequate divan while Violet plied her with cool refreshing drinks. After all, the Dwyers' bungalow was very much hotter than theirs, thought her reluctant if good-natured hostess.

'She'll move in, if you're not careful,' Malcolm Nicolson warned, when the visits became more and more frequent.

'Not she!' retorted a young woman who was beginning to understand Mhow to perfection. 'Once the others start drifting back, she'll be reminded of what I really am. She'll start noticing the smell of brimstone and then she'll leave me in peace. Still, she's not as bad as some of the others, I suppose.'

Sure enough, with the onset of September Mrs Dwyer's almost daily visits ceased. There was something a little *pagan* about Violet Nicolson, she confided to the adjutant's wife on that lady's return from her Himalayan haven, especially when she wore those native clothes—and bare feet, too! Admittedly, the general's floors were made of stone, but the scorpions, my dear! Mrs Nicolson simply didn't seem to care. When the pews in Christ Church, Mhow, began to fill again, the chaplain's wife went back to smiling at Violet in the vague, slightly disapproving way taught her by her Christian sisters.

Freed of the house by the change of season, Violet discovered a new world beyond the British lines, where no one else from the cantonment seemed to go. Forests whose luxuriant thickets hid Hindu shrines and statues. Streams, high waterfalls, and deep ravines, where black water swollen by monsoon rains splashed and bubbled against the backdrop of the looming Ghats. Violet rode out in the cool of the morning, sometimes with her husband but more often with a groom. Mhow, she decided—as she filled her lungs with the good fresh air and looked towards the distant mountains with not a soul in sight—Mhow might not prove so bad after all!

She returned from her outings refreshed and with a healthy colour, and Malcolm, who would gladly have gone with her every time, never grudged her the freedom denied him. He was looking weary, and—to any eye less critical and loving than his wife's—older than his fifty-two years. There were bouts of fever too, when Violet nursed him tirelessly until the worst was over.

The Nicolsons presented a united front to the world, and by the time all the exiles returned it was a world where the women were equally united—in their approval of the husband and disapproval of the wife. Mrs Nicolson (it was obvious to the ladies) shone in the company of men and had entertained vast numbers of them during the hot weather. That General Nicolson had been present too, and that the dinner parties had been at his instigation not hers, was not mentioned by the coven that collected at the Club. Mrs Nicolson must be put in her place, they decided, as soon as an opportunity arose.

An opportunity did not arise, however, for Mrs Nicolson disobligingly fell ill. It began with a terrible headache brought on (she said later) when a parcel sent by Isabel disgorged a book bound in a virulent yellow cover. 'I should have known from that alone that I was going to be sick,' she told Malcolm when the crisis was over and she was well enough to talk. 'Isabel told me to read our sister's story, and when I'd finished I began to feel dreadful. Have you read it yet?'

'No. I've been too busy looking after you.'

As Violet drifted in and out of consciousness, she had been aware of the cool hands on her forehead and the patient blue-grey eyes watching over her. Then the fever had returned, bringing with it strange thoughts and fancies, a raging thirst, and dreams. 'Was it you who cut off my hair?' That at least was no illusion.

'Yes. You were dangerously hot and the doctor said it should go. I offered to take responsibility.' Malcolm's look was anxious as he asked: 'Tell me if you really mind.' He handed her a mirror somewhat apprehensively.

Violet gazed at her reflection. She resembled a thin, hollow-cheeked child. The heavy tresses were gone and the roughly cropped hair already showed a tendency to curl. When he asked, 'Are you sure it doesn't matter?' he was relieved to hear her laugh.

'Come and sit down.' Violet patted the bed with a frail-looking hand.

'I never really understood fever before,' she said. 'To be cold yet sweat, and to ache so much, and then to be so hot—and all at once sometimes. Poor Malcolm, you have it so often these days.'

'And for once it's my turn to look after you.' He ruffled the curly head leaning against him. 'Now, where's that book you were talking about?'

She pointed to a small table, and Nicolson fetched the offending item in its solid yellow and black binding. He checked the list of contents. '*Theodora. A Fragment.* Is that the piece?'

'Yes. Read it.' Violet flopped back against the pillows, suddenly exhausted.

'Just as well it's only a "fragment" if this is what it does to you!' Violet managed a weak chuckle. 'And what a pseudonym to choose!' he remarked. 'Victoria Cross, indeed! Annie Sophie must have known it would cause offence—which is why she did it, I suppose.'

Violet watched her husband through half-closed eyes. Occasionally he would smile and, 'Good heavens,' he might murmur. 'So Theodora is an heiress,' he said at one point, 'who will lose her fortune if she loses her virginity—or has my Latin let me down after all these years? Well, well,' and he looked at his wife, 'Annie Sophie has an interesting idea there. Writing as a man, too—and a man obsessed, at that. Your little sister may go far.'

'The further the better!' a tired voice muttered from the bed beside him, and Nicolson stood up.

'Rest now, sweetheart,' he said, bending over to kiss her brow. 'I'll come back later and tell you what I think about Theodora and her goings-on. I just hope I don't end up with fever too!' Violet smiled weakly at the sally and then she fell asleep.

❧

Mrs Nicolson was a long time in recovering. She seemed to have no energy, wanted no visitors—not that many were forthcoming, the general soon realised—and preferred to sit by herself in the garden, reading, writing, or simply sitting with a faraway look on her face. Deeply concerned, he sought medical advice. Surgeon-Colonel Maunsell, the chief medical officer for Mhow and Deesa, listened to him carefully.

'Should I call in and see her, do you think?' he said at last. 'We're old acquaintances after all.'

'I think Violet might suspect a plot,' Nicolson replied, 'but yes, I'd appreciate it if you would.'

So Maunsell called at the bungalow and Violet greeted him with a look of enquiry in her eyes. 'I'm delighted to see you again, Colonel. Is this a social visit, or did Malcolm ask you to come?'

Maunsell smiled down at her. 'Your husband thinks you're taking too long to recover, my dear. What do you think, yourself?'

'I've never had fever before. I don't know how long I'm supposed to take,' she countered. 'I tire easily, but I suppose that's to be expected. Malcolm says I was quite ill—ill enough, anyway, for you to suggest a haircut!' When she smiled she looked more like an urchin than ever. 'What do you think of my new appearance?'

The doctor looked at the intelligent face surmounted by its shock of short bright hair. She was trying to change the subject, he suspected.

'You'll be setting a new fashion in Mhow,' he told her, 'once you're out and about again.'

Violet grimaced. 'I'm not sure that I want to—get out and about in Mhow, I mean. I feel happier here, in the house and the garden. Anything else seems just too much of an effort.'

When Maunsell asked Violet to show him the garden she rose to her feet immediately. As she walked with him through the compound the doctor watched her carefully. She showed no signs of fatigue, even though they were outside for quite some time. *There's nothing wrong with you physically, young woman,* he decided, *but I'm not too happy about your state of mind.*

'Your wife needs stimulation, Nick.' Maunsell had carefully thought over what he should say. 'And for some reason she seems to have lost her self-confidence. I can understand her not wanting to go out in society at present. That isn't much to her taste at the best of times, is it? But not going anywhere at all—now that *is* strange, and from what I've seen of her, quite out of character. Either she should go away for a while …' He paused and looked at Nicolson enquiringly.

'She won't. I've asked her already.'

'Then is there anyone you could ask to come here—a friend, a relation, perhaps?'

Isabel, thought the general. *I'll ask Isabel!*

'Yes,' he replied instantly. 'Violet has a sister in Karachi. I'll write to her today, although she's probably too busy.'

'I, the cast out, dismissed and dispossessed'

Alarmed by the thought that her sister might once again have lapsed into a state of black depression, and moved not so much by what her brother-in-law had written in his letter as by what he left unsaid, Isabel did not hesitate one moment. Of course the paper could manage without her, said Colonel Cory instantly, while his wife fussed endlessly about Isabel undertaking such a tedious journey on her own.

But Mrs Tate had come to the same conclusion as Mrs Nicolson many years earlier: there were no secrets possible from one's Indian servants. Whatever was waiting at Mhow, Isabel had no intention whatsoever of tittle-tattle being carried back to Karachi.

'John's friends the Turners will meet the boat at Bombay, and they'll see me onto to the train.' She would come to no harm in a first-class carriage, she reminded her mother, and the Turners had offered a servant to deal with her luggage and the bedding, and brave the crowds at the numerous railway stations to organise her food. 'Really, Mother, things have advanced since you followed Father all over Northern India!'

She listed some of those improvements, especially in the matter of sanitation, and Fanny had to be satisfied with that.

Contrary to his every inclination, John Tate hid his feelings about their imminent separation. He made no attempt to dissuade Isabel, and publicly supported her story that the two sisters wished to see each other again after such a long time. Only afterwards did Isabel realise how much her absence had meant.

Days of weary travel by sea and on the Great Central India Railway had ill prepared her for what she found at the bungalow in Mhow. The general's wife had no signs of the invalid about her. On the contrary, Addie Nicolson looked the picture of health, and far too comfortable for someone who had caused so much upheaval. *Cocooned*—yes, that was the word! Each of the servants hovering, ready to attend to her every whim! Only when Isabel noted how tired and drawn her brother-in-law was looking, did she concede that indeed there must be a great deal wrong.

'Oh yes, John,' she told her husband, when the couple were reunited in Bombay four weeks later and settled into a suite at one of the city's finest hotels, 'Malcolm was delighted to see me, but of course—as I told him—I only ever hear from him when there's a crisis!'

Tate stood at the window, watching the boats plying to and fro across Back Bay. He had lost weight during the absence of his wife and when he asked wearily, 'And what was the crisis this time?' Isabel's resentment against the Nicolsons reignited.

'One entirely of their making! Addie wouldn't say anything at first, but she appears to have annoyed all the officers' wives—or most of them, anyway—because she refuses to conform. She dresses differently, and will have nothing to do with what she says are nasty little clubs where they gossip and invent rumours—'

'But she is the commandant's wife, surely, and the ladies expect her to mix?'

'I know, I know, but that sort of thing has never carried any weight with my sister! Adela Nicolson is the most uncompromising person I know—fair play and honesty are her guiding values, and she's made it clear that she's found precious little of either in the cantonment. No wonder those women don't like her! She has always tried set the world to rights and now, I'm afraid, she's paying the price. She had no callers to speak of all the time I was there. Why, when I arrived, she wouldn't even leave the compound! Now, what was it she said by way of an excuse? Oh, yes—that Malcolm managed so well without her; that he was always getting invitations to dine, and he enjoyed himself whether she went with him or not.'

'I see. I cannot help wondering, dearest, why General Nicolson called upon you, instead of dealing with all this himself.'

Isabel shrugged.

'I imagine he would have, if he'd realised what was going on. The trouble is that Malcolm is the centre of Addie's universe, something I've always thought unhealthy, by the way ... Why, you and I have our work and friends as well as each other, but she has no one else. So when things go wrong she doesn't want to bother him, and *he's* too wrapped up in his own concerns even to notice. He gets on with his job—even if his heart isn't really in it—and then escapes on regimental manoeuvres and that sort of thing whenever he gets the chance. Why, I do believe she sees more of his ADC!'

Isabel pictured Robert Elkington with his thickly waving dark hair and merry brown eyes. The lieutenant, so near the general's wife in age, was undoubtedly attractive—in a coltish kind of a way. In many ways, she thought, and not for the first time, it was a good thing after all that her sister was still obsessively in love with her husband.

John Tate, who cherished every moment of this, his second chance of happiness, was also unable to fathom how Malcolm Nicolson could neglect his vital young wife. Remembering the period of bleak despair following his bereavement, he suddenly found himself in total sympathy with his sister-in-law.

'So Adela is left on her own for much of the time,' he said, with feeling, 'and has been brooding over her troubles. And making them appear much worse, I imagine, than they really are.'

'That's it exactly! But I managed to convince her that she was able to cope, as she always has done in the past—and I also reminded Malcolm most forcibly of his responsibilities.'

She stood up and joined Tate by the window.

'So, John, dear,' she said, slipping her hand into his, 'I really do think it was worthwhile my going.'

And next time, she resolved, *the Nicolsons would have to sort out their problems for themselves!*

When Malcolm and Violet Nicolsons waved goodbye to Isabel, each of them in their own way was feeling relieved.

'So, darling, she's on her way back to her husband.'

Despite the well-simulated regret, there was something about Nicolson's expression that earned him a calculating look from his wife.

'I shall miss her, of course,' she answered, 'but I feel as if I've been spring-cleaned from top to toe with not a cobweb left! It's a wonderful feeling in some ways, but I'm glad it's over. You're glad, too, aren't you?' she said bluntly.

'To be perfectly honest, yes. Of Colonel Cory's three redoubtable daughters I think Mrs Tate might possibly be the worst!'

'What about Annie Sophie?'

'Ah, yes, "The Fragment" and Miss Theodora ...'

'What did you think of it?' Violet sounded amused. 'You never did tell me.'

'Well, to be honest, the pompousness reminded me of your father and the passion was just like you! And the whole piece was unconvincing—as if the writer didn't know what she was talking about.'

Malcolm Nicolson went on to say a good deal more about Annie Sophie. Then he asked, 'How ever did she get involved with these *Yellow Book* people, in the first place?'

Violet shrugged. 'Who can say? She's over in London on her own and goodness knows what she gets up to—Grandmother Cory never could control her, even when she was little. I can't say I care terribly much, and I imagine you care even less! Anyway, Malcolm, what did you and Izzie talk about last night? She said it was all very frank. I suppose that means she made you feel uncomfortable for some reason.'

It was strange how marriage had changed Isabel; in the past Violet had easily dominated her elder sister, but now Isabel was very much more forthright and self-assured. *Don't accept everything Addie says at face value*, she had warned the general, when her homily was at an end. *She will never make demands on you, you must surely realise that by now—so just don't take advantage*!

'What exactly did she say?' Violet persisted.

'Nothing that you need worry about,' and Nicolson, still smarting from his sister-in-law's home truths, refused to say anything else.

'She reminded me of how I used to be,' Violet remarked.

'Of how you still are,' he corrected gently. 'Just scratch the surface—'

'—And there's a termagant beneath. Is that what you mean?'

'Not at all,' he contradicted firmly. 'There's an independent woman who speaks her mind—and is ready to take the consequences. By the way, sweetheart,' he added, 'what's been going on in Mhow, while I've been so engrossed with my own affairs?'

She was surprised by the sudden question. 'Nothing,' Violet answered. 'Nothing. Really. Nothing I can't handle now.'

Strengthened by Isabel's visit, Violet Nicolson once more took her place in society: she fulfilled her commitments as the commanding officer's wife, was considerate to her guests, and accompanied her husband wherever and whenever required. But while being perfectly civil, she remained as aloof as was humanly possible and the level of antagonism continued to rise. Nicolson, more attentive these days, noticed something of what was going on but what could he do? Did he want to do anything? No, he decided. The bird must continue to fly free—if there was a risk of a broken wing, then sobeit.

'Deep in the jungle vast and dim'

Violet resumed her morning rides and afternoon drives. Her days were her own, and she wandered further and further from Mhow, taking her sketchbook with her. She and Malcolm had gone to Simrole Pass with Isabel, before she left. They stayed in the *dak* bungalow and it had not been at all to her sister's taste.

'But it's sheer luxury, Izzie,' Violet had insisted. 'We've a roof over our heads, a hot meal—even if it is a tough old chicken—*and* a bed. What more could you want? You should have come with me to Zhob!'

The rest house overlooked a great ravine, and in the pass itself basalt pillars of immense height and size could be glimpsed through the bastard teak. Nearby there were clear streams and water holes. And all around the house, trees and dense vegetation provided deep cover for animals and birds.

'Tigers, Iz, just imagine, prowling round the bungalow at night—'

Nicolson shook his head disapprovingly. 'Don't take any notice, Isabel,' he advised. 'Sometimes your sister's sense of humour is quite misplaced.'

'I know, believe me!' and Isabel laughed off Violet's comments. But she refused to go far, all the same, and as she kept to the narrow tracks she wondered what lay hidden in the tall sere grass and brittle scrub that grew on either side. Violet felt no such qualms, and after her sister's departure she returned to Simrole Ghat time and time again. Until, that is, the Tent Club joined her and the air reverberated with the sound of shots and triumphant cries as antelope and blackbuck fell to the hunters' guns, and ducks were blasted from the sky in a sudden storm of feathers.

'I hope the tigers eat you—every single one,' she muttered, covering her ears in a vain attempt to block out the hideous din. She took refuge in the mud-brick village, where the children told her of a temple and a ruined fort where none of the *sahibs* went.

Down the winding dusty track she rode until she came to a shallow ford, and then across and up into the scrub where the stunted teak grew ever thicker. After a mile or so the path divided, and she took the left-hand fork. The narrowing track plunged down through a stream then up into a grassy clearing on the other side. The dry leaves crackled beneath the horses' hooves, and behind her the scowling groom complained that the *jungli* was an evil dangerous place. Violet only laughed and the man was still grumbling when she came to a halt and dismounted.

'Look, Pir Mahomed, isn't it wonderful here?'

The groom sniffed by way of an answer. Another infidel shrine, he thought, what was so good about that? But the *memsahib* was pleased so what was the point of arguing? He dismounted in turn and sprawled on the grass to wait.

Thick trees enclosed the clearing, thinning a little where the stream fell away over a steep waterfall into the gorge below. Others stood out starkly against the horizon and surely, there in the haze, was the outline of a fort. Violet looked about her with a contented smile and spared only a glance for her companion before heading off.

At the far end of the glade was a simple Hindu temple, made of white stone and standing some twelve feet high. Its four twisted columns were touched with red, and met in scalloped arches to support an open jade-coloured dome. From a brass vessel suspended within came the constant drip of falling water. Violet approached over the grass and dried-up leaves, and as she removed her shoes she looked around her for the priest. Even so, the tall orange-clad figure slowly unwinding itself from the shade of a holy fig tree caused her to start in surprise. It bade her sit down on the steps and Pir Mahomed, who sat watching with his back against a tree beside the stream, grunted and closed his eyes. He knew what to expect and it would probably take hours.

Oblivious to the villagers who joined them and the women filling *chattis* at the steps of the small tank, Violet Nicolson sat and listened to the priest. The Maharani Ahalya Bai had built the shrine, he told her, a *most* benevolent and charitable royal lady. Here he paused while Violet obligingly produced a handful of coins. The saintly queen had also built the well, he continued, and the pure water never failed. Other stories might have been forthcoming but all of a sudden there came the sound of a disturbance. Violet looked up with a frown.

On the fringes of what was now a crowd, her Muslim groom was gesticulating wildly and shouting in response to taunts from one of the Hindu villagers. She called him to her and the crowd parted to let him through. They muttered ominously as he passed and Violet began to feel alarm.

'Fear nothing, lady,' said the priest. 'No one will harm him in the holy presence.' He stood up unhurriedly and addressed the man who was still abusing the groom. 'Brother, brother,' he called, 'save your breath and save your curses. This man is human—surely that is punishment enough!' He laughed and everyone except the groom joined in.

'I don't know what caused it,' Violet told her husband later. 'Perhaps he wasn't at fault, but I was frightened. If they'd attacked him, what could I have done? No, I can't take him there again.'

'But they didn't attack him, and you certainly can't go alone as you seem to think. I'm sorry, Violet, but as you told Isabel,' and Malcolm gave a little smile, 'there are always prowling tigers! Don't worry, I'll find you someone else.'

When Mrs Nicolson next went to Simrole Tank she had with her a splendid Sikh borrowed from one of the Bombay regiments. The sight of Hira Singh, Malcolm assured her, would put the fiercest beast to flight. Extremely tall, with a bright blue turban and black moustache and beard, the Sikh was good humoured and long-suffering, besides. Which was just as well, thought the general, as he waited patiently in the evenings for his wife's return.

'A strange and a wayward thing'

'Mhow Week starts on Sunday,' Malcolm Nicolson noted. 'Yes—it's always the third week in December. There'll be an invasion, I'm afraid. Officers from other regiments, petty princelings, all here for the polo and the hunting.'

'How horrid! I suppose they'll want to go out to Simrole.'

'Yes. So you can stay here, and help me entertain the ladies. What do you think?' It was a casual sounding suggestion, but Violet knew it was more than that.

'Very well,' she sighed. '*Noblesse oblige*.' She knew she didn't sound very noble, and it had to be done—and the following February as well. 'What else goes on?' she enquired.

'Oh, concerts, dances—one in fancy dress, I believe.'

'Really?' Her glum face brightened. 'That sounds fun. Shall we go?'

General Nicolson looked at his wife's suddenly mischievous countenance and thought it might be better to stay at home. 'Perhaps,' he conceded at last. 'If you promise to behave.'

Violet readily gave him her word and, wearing one of her demurest gowns and not in masquerade at all, she conducted herself perfectly at the fancy dress ball. Her bright curls were gleaming—and so too were her eyes as she remembered her afternoon's escapade.

It hadn't been easy to persuade Lieutenant Elkington to lend her one of his uniforms, and even more difficult to cajole him into accepting one of her outfits in return. Not for the dance, she had told him, but for a little fun beforehand. 'Go on, Robert, *do* say yes.'

When Mrs Nicolson looked at him like that the young man found it impossible to do anything but agree.

❧

General Nicolson's afternoon proved by no means as enjoyable as his wife's. Pestered for hours by the second-rate secretary of a third-class maharajah over trivial details that were the province of his ADC, when he finally traced Elkington to his own quarters he was stopped dead in his tracks. He took in the situation immediately—and he knew exactly whom to blame.

Lieutenant Robert James Goodall Elkington, RE, a few dark locks escaping from one of Mrs Nicolson's prettiest Kashmir shawls, and wearing a floral gown topped with a wrapper that her husband knew she detested, was sitting on the cane settee in the reception room, convulsed with helpless laughter. Violet herself was parading up and down before the young man, talking and gesticulating energetically, and when her husband paused silently on the threshold her back was to the door. The general's eyes flickered from the lieutenant to the slim figure of his wife. With her short hair and seen from the rear she could have been a boy. The uniform suited her, and as he surveyed his wife's shapely legs in Elkington's neatly fitting trousers General Nicolson's forehead creased in an exasperated frown.

He coughed, and came into the room, the maharajah's secretary still in hot pursuit. Elkington, suddenly sober, shot to his feet and Violet turned around. At the sight of her husband and his companion she covered her face with her hands. But if Malcolm had expected some sign of shame then, the sight of the brilliant eyes spilling over with mirth as they peeped through her fingers soon dispelled any such hope. After a moment, and with a look of apology towards her fellow-conspirator, Violet Nicolson rushed from the room, leaving the young man to cope as best he could.

When she returned clad in a more conventional manner the Indian gentleman had gone, but not before exchanging a few halting civilities with the Nicolsons' young 'guest', introduced tersely by the general as a friend of his wife's who was on a regrettably brief visit to Mhow.

Nicolson looked at his wife in silence and then he addressed his ADC. Anger faded as he eyed him up and down. 'Attractive as you are in a gown, my dear Robert,' he finally managed to drawl while keeping his face straight with an obvious effort, 'your uniform fits you better. If you're sure you've finished with it, Violet, you'd better let him have it back.'

Once they were alone, Malcolm Nicolson tried to take his wife to task. 'Whatever were you thinking, darling? Thank goodness the secretary didn't realise—think of British prestige!'

Violet did as he suggested, but then giggled unrepentantly. 'Didn't Robert look splendid?' Nicolson's lips twitched a little. 'And what did you think of me?'

Malcolm reflected. 'All I can say, my dear,' he said after a moment, 'is that I'm heartily thankful I caught the pair of you in time. I take it you were all set to share your fancy dress with Mhow?'

Violet chose not to answer. After all, enough people had seen them drive through the cantonment and Malcolm would find out soon enough. He did. At the fancy dress ball the talk was of very little else. If Violet Nicolson had roused antagonism among her fellow wives before her appearance that afternoon, her most recent exploit made the young woman seem doubly dangerous. After a little good-natured ribbing, Elkington's part in the affair was soon forgotten, but the memory of Mrs Nicolson lingered on. Shocking, said the senior officers in public, keeping their disquieting thoughts to themselves; scandalous, agreed their wives. The junior officers were openly of the opinion that the general's wife had looked quite stunning.

'Do you mind?' Back in their bungalow and all too late, Violet considered her husband's feelings. Malcolm gave her a long considering look. Did he mind? In the short space of an hour that afternoon she had turned the cantonment upside down, and it was still reeling from the shock.

'I can understand why you did it,' he said slowly, 'and I sympathise with how you feel. I know you feel suffocated in Mhow—I do myself—and presumably you're prepared to take the consequences. A woman who is attractive, and disruptive with it, will never endear herself to her own sex, after all.'

Violet opened her mouth, but before she could reply Malcolm continued. 'You didn't think, did you, what a hornet's nest you were about to stir up when you put on young Elkington's clothes. And you didn't think of Elkington, either. I can't imagine he was overly anxious to join you?'

Violet hung her head as she thought belatedly of the young man's career. 'Will it make a lot of difference to him?' she asked.

'Who can tell? Not with me, certainly, and probably not with Mhow. No, I'm afraid you're the one they'll be after!'

Violet bit her lip. 'You once told me that freedom brought its own responsibilities. I forgot, Malcolm, and I'm sorry. Sorry about Robert, anyway, not about anything else.' She began to chuckle as she remembered the consternation mingling so comically with recognition as, on horseback and astride, she had escorted her own carriage and its occupant round Mhow.

Malcolm sighed. How could he be annoyed for long with this irrepressible creature? He ruffled the bright mop of hair and her smile deepened.

'I prefer you as a woman,' he told her. 'Do *you* mind?'

'Philosophy of Morning'

Everyone else was on holiday for Mhow Week, so why should the general go to work? Malcolm Nicolson laughed as he disentangled himself gently from the soft and clinging body of his wife. It was dark. He couldn't see her face but imagined it flushed from sleep.

'No, you little anarchist, I won't be tempted! If you want my company, you can get up too. Come on, lazybones, let's go and see the sun rise over Bercha Lake!'

The road was still in darkness as they rode out past the British lines. Once or twice they were challenged, then recognised and given a cheery good morning as they continued on their way. The *maidan* was a scene of bustling activity, and in the flickering lamplight figures hurried to and fro, their distorted shadows playing on the canvas of a hundred tents. It was the princes' encampment: some were staying in their own palaces at Indore, but the rest were here and had brought the trappings of state with them.

'They've come for the polo?' Violet exclaimed. 'All this—just for a game?' Malcolm Nicolson sensed his wife's scorn. 'Why didn't they bring their private armies and fight in earnest? It could hardly be more trouble and surely it would be more fun?'

'You don't come out here much, do you?' Malcolm asked, when they reached the lake. Backed by the dark outline of Janapao Hill, the great reservoir and its still waters attracted many visitors from the cantonment, which partly explained her dislike of the spot. But this morning in her husband's company Violet's feelings were different. The uniform blanket of night was lifting and wispy trails of light—so many delicate roseate fingers—were stealing across the heavens. Dark clouds loomed black, purple, and then umber as the sun began to rise, and bands of yellow, crimson, and purple-red streaked the muted green of the sky. To the silent Violet it seemed as if some great celestial fire was raging overhead.

Up on the hill beside the lake they dismounted and looked back to Mhow and the plain where the lamps still flickered. The silence was broken at last by Violet. '*East is East and West is West, And never the twain shall meet*. Do you think that's really true, Malcolm, or has Kipling got it wrong?'

'Is it true?' she repeated, when Nicolson remained silent. Was he thinking of his Afghan maiden?

'Yes,' he said slowly, 'I'm sure it's true. What made you come out with that all of a sudden?'

Violet pointed to the rajahs' tents that seemed to form some kind of a bridge between the world of the Government of India and India itself. 'The princes aren't representative of India at all, are they?' she said. 'They're really half

British—just think of the Resident's reception last night. It was dreadful to see them aping English ways. Except Holkar, of course,' and she gave an appreciative chuckle. The corpulent Maharajah of Indore never made concessions to his British masters, and he and the general's wife had found an instant rapport. In fact, her conversation with the head of the Indore ruling family had been the only pleasant part of an evening when the worlds of East and West had managed to meet briefly, smile, touch fingers, then move on.

'They had nothing to say to me, Malcolm, nothing at all. But then, they're not used to talking to women, are they, only to bedding them. And a European woman must seem rather intriguing by way of a change.' She paused as she remembered the lascivious stares that had come her way. 'To be perfectly fair,' she continued, 'what are they supposed to think? You dress us up for formal occasions—perhaps undress us would be more accurate—' and she shot a provocative glance at a husband who refused to be provoked. 'You encourage other men to handle us in public, albeit to the sound of music, and then throw a fit if a native princeling presumes to take advantage! His Highness of Indore apart, *of course* we had nothing to say to one another, and I felt too embarrassed for words.'

'Is that why you vanished for hours on end?' He hadn't mentioned before that he had noticed.

'Yes.'

One handsome self-assured potentate, all jewels and dazzling aigrette, had proved the final straw. Violet escaped to where the fountains were playing, and where the sounds of a distant waltz drifting through the gardens seemed preferable to first-hand inanities and *sotto voce* innuendoes.

When the evening drew to a close and his wife still hadn't reappeared, Malcolm went in search of her. Following the lines of little oil-filled jars, their wicks flickering in the fragrant breeze, he headed for the furthermost part of the grounds. This would be where he would go, he reasoned, if he were an amorous oriental intent on seduction. Halfway there he met Violet coming back, quite unruffled and smiling serenely. And alone.

'Hello, darling, were you looking for me?' She slipped her arm into his and came close. 'Isn't it romantic, Malcolm—just look at that glorious moon!'

'You'd better come inside,' was all he said. 'We have to say our goodbyes.'

'Did you think I had stolen off with an admirer?' she asked him now, turning her back on the busy camp below. 'And was that why you behaved so badly last night?' Her delighted laughter rang out at the memory of the silent return from Indore and the tempestuous lovemaking that followed. 'Malcolm Nicolson, I do believe you were jealous!'

There was enough light now to see his sheepish smile, and looking at his wife, whose eyes were filled with tender amusement, the general had to admit the very notion was absurd.

'Never mind the princes,' and Violet returned to the matter that still preoccupied her. 'What of the real people, Malcolm, the ordinary people on both sides? Can we ever be part of one another?'

She was not representative of her race; neither, supposed Nicolson, was he, but he let that pass. He could tell that the answer she wanted was 'yes' but he had to disappoint her.

'Darling, how can it be possible? I've spent years on the frontier among the Afghan races and to some extent you could say I understand them—but I could never be *of* them. Their history and culture and ours couldn't be further apart. We can agree on some things—what you might call the rules of the game we play up there, for example—but our outlook is quite different. We each have one God whom we would consider compassionate and merciful,' here he patted her hand for he knew she did not necessarily agree, 'but thereafter we differ. The Christian would see himself as master of his fate; the Muslim cannot. We've talked about all this before, don't you remember?'

Violet sighed as she remembered a starlit night years before in Khorassan and sensed what would follow.

'Whereas a man from another culture might have fought me for your love,' Nicolson continued gravely, 'Mahomed Akram went away, as God's will decreed. *That* is the difference, Violet. Hindus are what concern you most, I suspect, and the very same thing applies. Could you face life with the fatalism that they do? No, of course you couldn't—you feel impelled to act, to bend events to your will. How else are you and I together, after all?'

She had to smile at that.

'Hinduism is the result of centuries of accepting the role of caste—a conditioning process abhorrent to our Western eyes. How can we ever understand its complications, let alone try to change it? That fatalism is why, my little love, India will never come to rule itself.'

Violet felt moved to protest. 'No, Malcolm, you're wrong—and if you believe that, then you're subject to the same kind of conditioning as they are! It will take time, of course it will, but it will happen. It *must* happen—'

'But not through the actions of European do-gooders like the Besants, Humes and Nortons!'

'Why ever not? There are plenty of Indians ready to lead once they are shown the way—the ones educated in England, for instance. Whose hopes are frustrated as soon as they come home. It's starting, Malcolm,' and her voice rang with confidence. 'One day no one will be able to stop it!'

She believed every word, and as he looked the years seemed to slip away, leaving behind a passionate girl full of the clear convictions of youth. Did his wife not realise that the highest castes would dominate in matters of government too—as they already did in religion?

'Do you know,' he told her, slipping an arm round her slim shoulders, 'one of the few pieces of advice your father has ever given me was never to talk politics with his daughter. Darling, we must agree to differ,' and he gave her a little hug. 'All I *will* say is that Hinduism is a vast philosophy. I suspect that you may be guilty of selecting whatever facets appeal to you, and disregarding the rest. Like so many other Europeans.'

Violet flinched. What was it a district judge from the *moffussil* had said to her long ago in Lahore? Something about her seeing Indian life through Western eyes. And possibly misunderstanding everything as a result. And now Malcolm was saying it too.

'You're probably right,' she was forced to concede. 'But I shall keep on trying to learn and understand, whatever you say—surely there can be no harm in that?'

'So green a place in this bitter land'

There was generally a mass exodus from the cantonment after Christmas when people went to camp in more natural surroundings. Malcolm Nicolson waited to hear their plans and then he made his own. But he was popular if his wife was not. Once they learned that General Nicolson was off to the ruined city of Mandu, high on the Malwa plateau some fifty-five miles distant, others decided to join him—and, of course, Mrs Nicolson.

Before long, matters were quite out of hand. Lieutenant Colonel and Mrs Stokes; Captain and Mrs Edwards; Captain Davidson—in some way or another Violet had antagonised them all.

'How could you do this to me, Malcolm?' she cried in disbelief. 'I'll die, I know I will!'

'Nonsense. The place is huge—there'll be plenty of room for us all!'

In that case, thought Violet, there was room for another, and she persuaded Robert Elkington to join them. Then she told Malcolm what she had done.

'I see,' he said with a frown. 'I suppose this is your way of redressing the balance? I did ask him to come, you know, but he said he was off to Ujjain. For some reason he must have decided that Mandu by elephant was preferable, after all,' and to Violet's relief his grave expression relaxed into a smile.

'We're going by elephant?' she squealed. 'How wonderful! Do you think that will put Mrs Stokes off—and Mrs Edwards?'

'Absolutely not—why, nothing at all would deter them.' Violet had been afraid of that. 'Anyway, we'll have horses till we get to Dhar, and we don't have to travel in a party before then, so cheer up, darling, it won't be too bad.'

And, Violet found, it wasn't. Far away from Mhow everyone seemed more human, and what with the challenge of climbing onto the elephants, and the laughing and joking that went on while they did so, the ice was broken. By the time the lumbering beasts left the gentle, wooded slopes and began to climb the steep escarpment that guarded the fortress of Mandu, the ladies had visibly thawed.

Once the glory of the Malwa plateau and now ruined and desperately overgrown, the fort presented a study of light and shade within its walls: sunbathed grey stone buildings with shadowy interiors; glistening tanks and lowering jungle; mosques and deserted pavilions and broken, creeper-covered stones. The mahouts took them through the Delhi Gate past the small village where their bullock carts were waiting, and where dark, staring children watched the strangers move on to the very centre of the abandoned city. Bougainvillea and lantana blazed brilliant purple and orange against the perfection of a cloudless azure sky, and somewhere *moghra* bushes bloomed modestly unseen, exhaling all the timeless fascination of the East. The glittering expanse of Mandu's great lake stretched beyond. With its profusion of blue water lilies and lotus leaves, the lake was the obvious place for a camp and the little party chose a spot by the furthermost shore.

In the midst of the activity that followed Violet caught Malcolm's eye and easily read his thoughts. Never had they camped like this, and in such company! Leaving the *khansamar* to organise their tents, and putting Lieutenant Elkington in overall charge, they slipped away.

'A very good idea of yours, to bring along young Robert; he can make himself useful for once!'

'Malcolm, that's not fair. He's always useful!'

Nicolson agreed, adding that for the next few days he would be particularly so—as a buffer against their companions.

Walking in strict formation, Lieutenant Colonel Stokes and Mrs Stokes and Captain and Mrs Edwards followed the Nicolsons on their late afternoon stroll. They went with them to see the palace perched on the very edge of the precipitous Malwa cliffs. They inspected what was left of the queen's bathroom and living quarters. They perambulated the delicately domed watchtowers at each end of the terrace. Then, satisfied, the quartet marched off noisily in step, the women discussing the plumbing and the men arguing over logistics.

'They've gone before the sunset,' Violet said incredulously. 'Why didn't they stay?'

'I suppose they've seen many a sunset in their time,' Malcolm remarked. 'By now one must look very like another.'

'You don't feel like that, do you?'

'No, of course not.'

How could he, when each time his wife gazed spellbound at the glory of the heavens, and caught her breath in awe? The sky was already flushed with pink when he drew Violet past a little pillared pavilion to the very limits of the fort. At the rampart's edge, sheer cliffs dropped away some thousand feet to a broad and fertile valley.

'Look, there's the Nerbada River, do you see? That bright thread you can just make out in the distance. My father spent his service days out there, as Superintendent of Roads.'

'So your work in Zhob was rather like his.'

'More difficult, if anything', he told her. 'The road through the Zao defile is nearly finished, by the way.' After a moment's silence he went on. 'India killed him, too,' he said sombrely. 'Oh, I know he didn't die out here, but it killed him all the same—the heat, the fever—as it killed Simon, my brother. We Nicolsons don't seem to live to make old bones.'

Violet knew little of Malcolm's family, apart from the fact that her husband was the product of a second marriage; now she was hearing too much.

'Malcolm, *don't*!' she protested.

'I'm sorry. It's just strange that I should end up here, of all places, that's all, and it set me thinking. Your father would know the area too. Wasn't he in Central India during the Mutiny?'

'Yes,' Violet said dryly. 'And to hear him talk, you'd think he'd relieved Lucknow single-handed—on all three separate occasions!'

They both laughed, the dark mood was broken, and they made their way to the deserted palace colonnades and empty tanks on the other side of the terrace.

'How splendid it must have been in Mandu all those hundreds of years ago! Think of the court with its pageantry and music! The Afghan king took a local Rajput bride, did you know, even though he wasn't a Hindu.'

Malcolm sat down on a step and prepared to hear all about it.

'Rup Mati—that was her name—gave up everything to be with the king who was extremely persistent in his attentions. Her father threatened to poison her to defend the family honour, but she escaped. And then,' Violet heaved a dramatic sigh, 'Baz Bahadur tired of her, and seemed to forget her very existence.'

Malcolm hid his amusement. Here, he suspected, was another of his wife's lost causes, another instance of man's inhumanity to woman.

'Poor Rup Mati sat here, gazing down at the silver river, and felt her heart slowly breaking. While below in his own palace, her lord caroused with his women and drank the hours away. Oh, how she lamented over their lost love and all she had sacrificed for his sake, and when he heard her beautiful voice coming to him on the evening air he relented and came back.'

'And they lived happily ever after, I trust,' although from the enjoyment Violet was getting from the story it hardly seemed likely.

'They should have, but one day the Moghuls came with an army to attack Mandu, and the king fled like a craven, leaving his queen behind. Rather than bring shame upon their love and submit to the conqueror's lust, she swallowed powdered diamonds and died.'

Violet sighed again, this time almost contentedly.

'Have you noticed, Malcolm, how the women always kill themselves when this sort of thing happens? Poor Rup Mati—wed at fifteen and dead at twenty-one! Baz Bahadur, on the other hand, enrolled in Akbar's army and lived to a ripe old age, which I must say seems rather unfair!'

How Western she was in her story telling, thought Malcolm, and how incurably romantic. Although it was, he agreed, the perfect spot for lovers. They made their way back to camp as darkness was falling, to find great events afoot: Mrs Edwards had seen a tiger!

'I suppose they glared at each other and Mrs Edwards won. She's far fiercer than the captain—I'm surprised you haven't enrolled her in the army.'

'In that case, you would be nothing less than a field marshal! Mrs Edwards is a charming lady—if a little narrow in her outlook. Whereas sometimes, Violet Nicolson, you have no charm at all!'

Back in their tent Malcolm had informed her that they would be changing for dinner and Violet was still scowling at the thought. 'The fact that you and I don't share the same ideas as anyone else doesn't matter,' he explained. 'Here we'll have to conform.'

'Well, I've packed nothing formal, so I can't!' This, on a triumphant note.

'Then what a good thing I did so on your behalf.' Malcolm grinned. 'Come on, darling, we shouldn't keep everyone waiting.'

Over dinner the talk turned to tigers, and the two bachelors were full of ideas for a shoot. 'Where exactly did you see it, Mrs Edwards?' Robert Elkington asked.

'It wasn't all that far away, actually. There's a tower across the lake—you can see the dome from here, but not at this moment, of course,' and Mrs Edwards gave her neighing laugh. 'There was the most gorgeous blossom, Lieutenant, rather like a horse chestnut and a wonderful creamy-white, growing just off the track nearby. I simply had to take a closer look, don't you know?'

Violet stifled a yawn and wished there was something else to eat.

'Anyway,' the domineering voice continued, 'I heard a sound in the undergrowth. I took no notice to begin with—it might have been a horrid little Bhil hunter, or one of those ghastly holy men—but then it came nearer. Then those awful yellow eyes were staring at me. And I saw the whiskers—' Mrs Edwards paused for effect.

It must have been rather like the captain returning from a night in the mess, thought Violet, and she struggled to stifle a giggle. 'And then it went away. I can show you where it was, Lieutenant, if you like.'

'It will be miles away by now,' Violet observed. 'It was probably as scared as you.'

'Oh, no, my dear Mrs Nicolson,' Captain Edwards assured her proudly. 'Nothing frightens my wife. In fact, she's bagged a tiger or two in her day.'

And still might, thought Violet, for the light of slaughter in the older woman's eye was quite remarkable.

'You're not going after this one, are you, Mrs Edwards?' she asked.

'No, but Captain Davidson and Lieutenant Elkington thought they might try for it tonight.'

Violet turned to the two young men. 'And how do you propose to do that, gentlemen?'

'Oh, the usual way,' Davidson said airily, as if it were an everyday event. 'We'll get a goat from the village, tie it to a tree—a mango, don't you think, Elkington—and then we'll each climb another tree and wait.'

'Poor old goat,' remarked Violet, 'it hardly seems very sporting. I always thought hunting tigers took a lot more nerve! I've got a far better idea,' and she paused, a wicked gleam in her eye. 'Why don't you wait on the ground yourself, Captain Davidson—although there's no need to tie yourself up, of course—and then see what happens? That would be much more fun for all concerned, and fairer too!'

There was a silence before Mrs Stokes laughed. 'What a capital notion! No hunting, then, gentlemen, unless you accept Mrs Nicolson's rules. Agreed?'

Violet smiled at her unexpected ally, and the tiger continued to prowl at will.

'Don't you go wandering away on your own tomorrow, Violet. I take the tiger seriously, even if you don't!'

Malcolm Nicolson looked across to his wife's camp bed, where she lay watching him.

'I wouldn't dream of it, darling!'

'I'm not so sure of that.' Violet's thoughtless tendency to wander off still caused her husband a great deal of concern. 'Stokes and I are off shooting for the pot in the morning, and perhaps you'd like to go sketching with the ladies?'

'Perhaps.' And then again perhaps not, for Violet's idea was to avoid them like the plague. She didn't think that either woman would be anxious for her company and she was right. They were perfectly friendly, but they didn't include her in their plans. In the event, she spent the next morning alone with Robert Elkington. The lieutenant caught up with her as she headed off early in the direction of the village.

'You're not going by yourself, are you, Mrs Nicolson? I don't think that's safe. May I come with you?'

'Yes, of course.' Belatedly Violet remembered Malcolm's warning, and this should placate him. She strode out with the young man beside her, both observing a companionable silence until she spotted a half-ruined building. Mournful and desolate, it was caught among the strangling roots of the banyan tree that had grown up around it.

'I'd like to stop and sketch this, do you mind?'

With a silent apology to its occupant, Violet sat down on a nearby Muslim grave and set to work, while Robert Elkington made himself comfortable on the ground nearby.

Now and again Violet spoke to him without taking her eyes from her sketch. 'You should go and see Rup Mati's pavilion in the sunset, Robert,' she said after a while. 'It was amazingly beautiful last night.'

'I don't think I shall, Mrs Nicolson. Sunsets aren't much fun on your own.' His tone was wistful enough for Violet to put down her pencil and give him her full attention.

'You're not sorry you came, are you?'

'Oh, no, not at all! You mustn't think that! I'm having a wonderful time.'

'Good,' and Violet returned to her drawing.

The time passed quickly as the young man wove his fantasies about her golden head. All too soon Violet looked up with a smile and held out her sketch for him to see.

'I think that's all I can do for the moment so perhaps we should go. The hunters are probably back by now and I'm hungry, aren't you?'

But it was not the pangs of hunger that Elkington was feeling. He was about to speak when a sudden rush of grey foiled him. One of the dozen or so small monkeys that had been chattering in the trees around the ruin had darted down and caught hold of the pad.

'Oh no you don't, my friend!' Violet hung on to her work and shook the animal free. It jumped onto her shoulders, chattering in displeasure, and buried its paws in her hair. 'Ouch!' she squealed as it gave a hearty tug. 'Robert, please help me!'

It had all happened so quickly, but now the startled lieutenant rushed to her aid. He seized the furry little body and gently prised the tiny paws apart. Then he lifted it away and tossed it back into its tree. Violet's eyes were still closed.

'It's gone now, Mrs Nicolson,' and he lightly touched her arm. She opened her eyes. 'Thank you for rescuing me,' she said. 'I don't think I could have managed on my own.'

The look she gave him was so warm and she was so close that for a moment he forgot himself. He was still touching her as he began to speak: 'Mrs Nicolson, Violet, before we go back to the camp, there's something I must tell you.'

'No, Robert, I'm sure there isn't.' The voice interrupting his was kindly but firm. 'Don't say anything that you might regret later. We're good friends, you and I, and it would be a pity if anything changed that, don't you think?'

Lieutenant Elkington had to be satisfied with that, and Violet stayed close to her husband's side for the short time that remained.

'From the heart of the dark Bazaar'

Over the weeks and months that followed Robert Elkington struggled to forget that Violet Nicolson was a woman of flesh and blood, with wonderfully soft hair faintly smelling of jasmine, and at last he was able to put her back on the pedestal where he realised she didn't belong, but where it was far safer for them both for her to be.

General Nicolson was too perceptive not to notice that something was wrong with his aide but it was left to Violet to enlighten him.

'He thinks he's in love with me. That's all.' Violet shrugged.

'That's no small matter, then. I *know* I'm in love with you, and it's the most important thing in my life.'

'You don't tell me very often,' his wife chided gently. 'It usually takes some near-disaster to make you own up.'

'Is this a near-disaster, then?' He sat down and drew her onto his lap.

'No, of course it isn't. And I'm only telling you now so that you will leave poor Robert alone, and stop asking him well-intentioned questions that can only hurt.'

'So how did you discover his feelings?' he asked. The tone was light but his eyes held a glint of steel, and she felt him relax only when she told him what had happened at Mandu.

It all made sense, Nicolson thought, looking back. The young man had returned from the expedition subdued, to go about his duties with his customary efficiency but with rather less enthusiasm than usual.

'He'll get over it—they always have.'

Nicolson was forced to laugh at her cool pronouncement. Yes, they always did, these young officers of his who were dazzled by his wife. But for once he hadn't noticed it happen—a measure, he supposed, of his preoccupation with his work.

Some wives, neglected as she undoubtedly was, looked to other men for consolation but not Violet Nicolson. As the wedding month of March progressed many Indian families included Violet in their celebrations, and Malcolm Nicolson could see that in India itself he had a far more seductive rival than his callow ADC.

'Of course I want to go to their weddings, although I can't understand why they invite me,' Violet said, when yet again he returned to the heady scent of jasmine and a sari-clad figure still garlanded with blooms.

'I can,' he replied, for what did it matter that society viewed his wife as another of those eccentrics that Anglo-India threw up from time to time? Violet, he knew, would never turn away from a needy human being, whatever their colour and creed. The present invitations were a simple way of showing gratitude for numerous kindly acts: consideration towards the servants, the comfort given a crying child in the native bazaar, practical help offered a hungry family—kindnesses Violet kept to herself but of which her husband was fully aware.

'Thirteen is so very, very young to marry. I wonder if that little bride has any chance of being happy?'

'Who knows? She will certainly accept everything that comes her way with no questioning at all. And look ahead and plan for her children's weddings. Unlike your own mother, Violet, who was thwarted not once but twice! How is Fanny, by the way?'

'Goodness, I'd quite forgotten Isabel's letter! Now wherever did I put it?' Once it was found and opened she shared anything she thought might interest him: 'Uncle Heneage Griffin has sold the mine in Colorado—Mother will be so pleased if he's decided to go back to England, now that poor Uncle Clifford's dead. Perhaps he'll visit us here—Everyone's well—Karachi is expanding, so that makes Father happy, of course.' Her eyes suddenly narrowed and she read on in silence. 'I don't believe it!' she said at last, sitting down with her hands to her face.

'What is it, Violet? Not bad news, I hope?' But his wife wasn't grief-stricken, simply amazed.

'It's Annie Sophie.' Of course, who else could produce such an effect? 'She's had a book published. Isabel will send it on when she's finished. It's called *The Woman Who Didn't.*'

'Didn't what?'

'What do you think? Although she nearly did, apparently—Izzie says it's rather *fast*. There are all sorts of strange women in it—one plays a banjo, she says, and smokes a cigar.'

'At the same time? You should try.'

'Malcolm, it's not funny!'

'Well, you should reserve judgement until you've read it. It's possibly very good.'

But it wasn't. At least Violet didn't think so, and Malcolm thought that the fragment of 'Theodora' had been punishment enough. 'You can read me bits when I can't sleep,' he suggested, but failed to produce even the suggestion of a smile.

'Oh, Malcolm, where is it going to end,' his wife wailed in exasperation. 'Where on earth is it going to end?'

⁂

One Sunday at morning service in Christ Church Violet saw a woman she hadn't seen before. She was in her late twenties or early thirties, and her face when seen in profile was aquiline and strong, very northern, and seemingly carved from rock.

'Granite, rather like granite,' she told Malcolm afterwards. 'But most handsome, don't you agree?'

'I don't spend my time in church staring at strange women,' he replied. 'Getting you there and hoping you'll behave is enough. But,' and he reflected, 'you probably mean Mrs Arthur Jacob. Her husband is a captain in the 20th Hussars. They've only just arrived. They're Scottish.'

'I must call on her,' agreed Mrs Nicolson when he suggested it in the hope that Mrs Jacob's company might prove congenial. But predictably Violet did no such thing.

General Nicolson was right to be concerned about his wife. As Isabel had told her husband, he was often away on cold weather manoeuvres and inspections. When he returned he would notice how unrested and pale his wife was looking, for, while the days of separation presented no great problem, she found the solitary nights a trial. Then, she prowled around the house or in the garden, or would toss and turn in her lonely bed finding sleep impossible. Simrole was quiet again. The sportsmen had gone and Violet returned to spend many an hour on the temple steps, or by the village well. The road she took almost daily made its way through the opium fields, and one day the myriad pink and white and purple blooms suggested a solution for her uneasy spirit. It was so simple. The next time Malcolm went off, she removed one small pellet of opium from his fever supply and dreamed the night away. She wouldn't do it too often, she told herself, but often enough to ensure an uninterrupted sleep—just now and again. He need never find out.

The hot oppressive weather returned all too soon. Weddings gave way to funerals, and each day brought a relentless reminder of death: the keening sounds of a funeral, smoke drifting up from the burning ghats, vultures circling the Parsi Towers of Silence. She stayed at home, lying listlessly on her divan all day with the punkah creaking erratically overhead, until towards the end of June the liberating rains poured down, cooling the air and releasing the imprisoned Violet from her self-imposed confinement. Riding along the Simrole road one morning the Nicolsons met Mrs Arthur Jacob out riding with a groom. Malcolm hailed the woman cheerily, she answered with a gay wave of the hand, and they went their separate ways.

'You've not called on her yet, have you?'

'No, there really hasn't been time.'

There had been plenty of time if she'd wanted to brave the short journey from their bungalow to the Jacobs', thought General Nicolson, but now perhaps she'd do something about it. In the event, it was Captain Jacob's wife who called one morning when Violet was on her own.

She was shown into the drawing room and once there she blinked. That Mrs Nicolson was unusual—eccentric, even—she had been warned. But to what extent, she had in no way been prepared. The general's wife received her visitor reclining upon a broad colourfully draped divan. In a rich magenta sari, and with each of her arms adorned with a heavy silver bracelet, she was scarcely less vivid herself. Mrs Jacob blinked again as she noticed the woman's feet were bare, apart from a silver band about each ankle, and that her toe nails were painted red.

'Won't you take a seat?' Violet Nicolson's voice held a poorly disguised trace of amusement. Violet Jacob looked around—where was there to sit? There was one armchair at the far end of the room, but it seemed hardly polite to distance herself so far from this intriguing little person. There was another divan nearby so, disposing her skirts carefully about her, she sat down cautiously in the manner of her hostess.

'With your shoes off it's even better.'

The attractive voice, so unexpectedly deep, sounded even more amused as one Violet gazed at the other, neither sure of what to say.

'I really suppose I should have visited you ages ago, Mrs Jacob. This business of etiquette is all terribly tedious and confusing, don't you think? The order of precedence, and so forth—' Mrs Nicolson's carmine lips parted in an engaging smile.

She could afford to think like that, thought Captain Jacob's wife. She was, after all, first in the pecking order. My goodness, what unlikely material for a *Burra Mem*—just wait till she told Arthur about her visit!

'Would you care for tea, Mrs Jacob?'

'*Tea*? The offer seemed such a terrible anticlimax,' Violet Jacob said to her husband later. 'I thought that at the very least she would offer me bhang! She's such an interesting woman, Arthur,' she went on, 'and so *oriental* looking—apart from her colouring, of course. I'm sure she was wearing kohl—her eyes looked quite enormous.' Remembering the sensual mouth, the bared midriff and the curve of the languid silk-swathed limbs Mrs Jacob added: 'She really wouldn't have been out of place in a harem.'

'Oh?' remarked her husband. 'General Nicolson doesn't strike me as being a pasha. Was he there?'

'He came in before I left. He wasn't a bit surprised at what she was wearing and I imagine he encourages her. I didn't stay long after that—I suddenly felt I was dreadfully *de trop*.' Her aristocratic features softened as she recalled the look Malcolm Nicolson had given his wife, and how he had gone to her immediately to take her hands and kiss the fingers lingeringly one by one. He had spoken to the caller pleasantly, saying she must come back soon and visit them both, and before she had realised it she had said her goodbyes and was on her way home.

'So Mrs Jacob called on you instead? You must have given her quite a shock!'

'Yes, but she took it very well, considering. And you didn't manage to embarrass her either, with your extravagant greeting—I wonder what she thought of *that*?' Violet's darkened eyes glinted as she spoke.

'I've more than a suspicion that she knew exactly what I had in mind, and that's why she left so quickly.'

'Oh?' Violet asked idly. 'And just what *do* you have in mind, Malcolm?'

He laughed. 'I'm going to change,' he said, and went towards the bedroom. Violet followed him and stood with her back to the door, watching him undress. She caught her breath at the sight of the muscular shoulders and chest, the slim hips and the strong thighs. He was so beautiful … Her head began to swim and she felt faint from the intensity of her feelings. Nicolson looked up and saw her. He held out his arms in invitation but she could not move. He was a great distance away—far out of reach.

'I worship you,' he heard her whisper. 'You are my God—' She swayed and leant against the door. He was there in a trice, and she would have knelt at his feet. He gripped her arms and when he looked into her face, what he saw there frightened him.

'We are equals, you and I,' he told her fiercely, '*equals*. I want none of this Hindu nonsense, Violet, do you hear?'

She watched his lips move soundlessly as his hands tightened like a vice.

Gradually she became aware of the silver biting into her flesh, and her head began to clear. 'I'm sorry,' she murmured after what seemed an eternity. 'What were you saying?'

'Come and lie down; you'll feel better in a moment.'

Once on the bed beside her, his mind was empty of his earlier intentions. Her sari was soft against his naked body as she lay compliant in his arms, but love-making was the last thing on his mind.

What was happening to his wife? Slowly, insidiously, India seemed to be drawing her deeper and deeper under its spell, making a mockery of her earlier fight for freedom, her desire for equal rights in a world of men. He would, decided Malcolm Nicolson, take her away for a while, away to the healing hills perhaps, anywhere far away from these mysterious influences that threatened to steal her soul.

But he did not get the chance. A severer than usual bout of fever struck him down and he took weeks to recover fully. To the general it seemed a blessing in disguise: Violet nursed him devotedly as before and, as before, her total absorption in his wellbeing and the need to deal with the frequent callers took up all her time.

Malcolm Nicolson sat in the garden as his strength returned, thinking of the problem that had earlier occupied his mind. Violet seemed quite her old self again, he thought happily, as she took total charge of his convalescence and treated him like some recalcitrant child when he went against her wishes. Perhaps there was no need to go away. And where would they have gone? His mind wandered as he considered all the possibilities.

England, he thought after a while, how long had it been? He couldn't remember, but it was fourteen years since Violet had last visited the land of her birth, and like him she showed no desire to return. He shook his head; they should go back, if only to see his mother and prepare themselves for his eventual retirement. He was fifty-three, too young for such thoughts, of course, but, as he had remarked to his wife, India took its toll of men like him and it was as well to be prepared.

Violet was horrified when he suggested that they spend a long leave in England in the coming hot weather. He reminded her that they both had relations there whom they hadn't seen for years, but the argument carried no weight. And because there no longer appeared to be any urgent need to get her away from the place, General Nicolson allowed his wife to carry the day.

'Some unknown way, beyond, above'

During his illness Malcolm Nicolson had had ample opportunity to watch his wife and his ADC together; they enjoyed an easy relationship again, he concluded, and their mutual concern for his welfare had done wonders towards healing the younger man's supposedly broken heart. Violet Jacob called more often when General Nicolson resumed his duties, and Robert Elkington called less.

The captain's wife, like Violet Nicolson, had pronounced views on everything under the sun and a keen and enquiring mind but, unlike her namesake, she never allowed her heart to rule her head. Nicolson encouraged his wife to see more of her, and to his relief she did. She went riding with Mrs Jacob and accompanied her on sketching trips, although she did not share her passion for botany. A flower, to Violet Nicolson, was a beautiful thing that might make your senses swoon with pleasure from its colour and its scent. Take the time and trouble to paint it—never!

In the end she achieved a degree of friendship with the Scotswoman, who had a dry sense of humour and seemed to share certain of Mrs Nicolson's views on military life. True, the woman had too many friends in high places (at the Indore Residency, for example) for Violet to feel totally at ease, yet sometimes the spirit of mischief took control of her tongue and she would give wickedly accurate impersonations of people known to them both. Violet Jacob would laugh, but whether she kept such wickedness to herself, who could tell? And did it matter if she didn't?

Over Christmas that year Mrs Jacob discovered an old school acquaintance staying at the Residency in Indore. Marian Doughty was one of those intrepid single English ladies who travelled the world alone, and when Violet met her at the Jacobs' she took the vagabond to her heart. Probably, Malcolm could not prevent himself from thinking, because the young woman was only a bird of passage.

Miss Doughty had been charmed by a prolonged stay in Kashmir, had made copious notes of her experiences, and had brought back with her transcriptions of several native songs. 'But, alas, Mrs Nicolson,' she lamented, 'I cannot understand one word …'

Malcolm was present when Violet took the papers she was offered and glanced at them politely. 'Goodness,' he heard her say after a moment, 'I can understand some of this! Look, darling,' and she handed them to him, 'doesn't it all seem familiar?'

They exchanged a glance and a smile and when Violet turned back to her guest, her face was quite animated.

'Shall we translate them for you, Miss Doughty?' she suggested. 'I might even, if you like,' and her voice was diffident, 'attempt to render them in verse.'

Marian Doughty was delighted. She would have liked to take the translations away with her when she left for Bombay and England, but she lingered for several months, and once the sense of urgency was gone Mrs Nicolson allowed herself to be distracted by other matters. Thus, when she said goodbye to the traveller in April 1897 Violet still had only promises to offer. Until, that is, General Nicolson prevailed upon his wife to fulfill her obligation. It kept her busy while Malcolm was away for long hours at a time. She worked late into the night, and when she retired the remedy for sleeplessness was close at hand—in a small flower-painted papier mâché box she had brought back from the Vale of Kashmir.

Once her self-imposed task was finished, Violet again succumbed to the pull of India and plunged deeper and deeper into her exploration of the Eastern way of life. As she became more knowledgeable, she yearned to understand something of Hindu philosophy. She had been brought up in the tenets of the Christian faith and had cast that faith aside in Quetta; now there remained a void demanding to be filled. Metempsychosis, *maya* ... That the lower castes of Hindu society (and those with no caste at all) should be sustained by a belief in reincarnation went without saying; that the present world was *maya* or simple *illusion* was impossible for a European grounded in the everyday to swallow. *Reality* was what lay *beyond* this world, her teachers told her, and as Violet Nicolson struggled to come to grips with the concept she would have liked to discuss it with her husband.

Malcolm Nicolson, however, was facing up to a totally different kind of reality that left him no time to spare for his wife's latest preoccupation. News came filtering through from the Afghan border in the early summer of 1897 that the tribesmen were up in arms, and that the frontier was likely to go up in flames. The Olympian beings on the lofty heights of Simla ignored the portents, but Malcolm Nicolson believed them, along with other old frontier hands.

'No, not Baluchistan as well,' he said in answer to Violet's stricken enquiry, 'Sandeman's work is safe, but everywhere else there'll be trouble, mark my words if there's not.'

The grim prediction came true. By the end of August, embers that had been smouldering for years were fanned into an almost uncontrollable blaze. Goaded on by their mullahs and the Amir of Afghanistan, fanatical Pathans swept through the Khyber Pass yelling jihad, drunk on the prospect of Paradise and the taste of the infidels' blood. Mhow breathlessly awaited the outcome of events on the North-West Frontier of India, and each day General Nicolson came home with a dismal face. Over the dinners the couple were obliged to give and attend, there was endless doom-laden discussion of this latest uprising. To Violet it all seemed so boring and pointless. It was the same old story, she thought: complacent belief in its own superiority creating another near-disaster for the British Raj, and nearly producing another 'epic of the race' for Malcolm's friend Flora Steel to write about.

❧

What might have been a lonely time was mitigated by her burgeoning friendship with Violet Jacob and the two women often visited Indore together. Mrs Jacob's interest in India existed only on a superficial level but one evening, after visiting the Residency, Mrs Nicolson took her companion to a party in the native town.

'What an interesting experience!' Mrs Jacob exclaimed afterwards, as they returned to Mhow in a tiny train on the branch line from Indore. 'However did you meet that banker and his family? They live so deep in the native bazaar!'

Violet smiled but did not reply.

'And those women with the enormous pearl nose rings—my dear Mrs Nicolson, I thought I would *die*!'

It had been a strange evening, the general's wife conceded, but to have been invited to the banker's home in the first place was remarkable. She told herself that Mrs Jacob had behaved extremely well, considering: the women's quarters had been clean but extremely stuffy, the smell of burnt sugar and cardamom overpowering. That, rather than what she saw, could well have caused Mrs Jacob to expire, but curiosity—and her determination to communicate with a row of silent ladies in saris—had carried the day. Of course, Violet Nicolson observed, all that tinsel and gold and silver paper everywhere made the rooms look rather *tawdry* but, as she reminded Mrs Jacob, it was to celebrate the festival of Ganesha.

'That fat little fellow with the elephant head is the protector of business affairs, you know, as well as being the god of learning. There are hundreds and hundreds of others.'

'However do you remember which is which?' the Scotswoman asked, for Mrs Nicolson was so very knowledgeable about all the native customs and all the Hindu gods (as well as being enviably fluent in Urdu). 'I suppose each person would have their particular favourite?'

As Violet Nicolson swayed to the rhythm of the carriage a strange little smile played upon her lips. 'Why, of course,' she said. '*I* have chosen the Lord Krishna—or perhaps,' and the smile took on a dreamlike quality, 'I should say he has chosen me.'

Mrs Jacob glanced at her sharply. What on earth did she mean by that? And whatever was she saying now?

'The Lord Krishna so enjoyed female society during his time on earth,' said Mrs

Nicolson. 'The sacred texts, of course, teach all about it.' This time there was more than a hint of humour in the violet eyes.

'But aren't those writings … *indecent*, Mrs Nicolson?' Mrs Jacob asked, surprising herself by the question.

'Because they describe sexual acts so graphically, is that what you mean?' and her companion's candid gaze never faltered. 'It all depends on one's viewpoint, surely? I don't think them in any way indecent,' continued the general's wife. 'After all, someone who has abjured the flesh might well believe my marital behaviour to be improper—or yours, for that matter. But it's not improper, is it?'

By now the blue eyes were fairly dancing with amusement. The Jacobs had a small son, yet it was difficult to imagine the tall somewhat angular figure seated opposite locked in the throes of passion.

Mrs Jacob sensed she was being challenged. She remembered the first time she had called on this outspoken woman, and how she and her general had so obviously wanted to be left alone. 'You may be correct about the writings, I grant you,' the Scotswoman replied with a steady look. 'I haven't read them. But not many people would agree with you.'

In mid-October both Violet Nicolson and Violet Jacob returned to Indore to attend more festivities, on this occasion in honour of the Hindu goddess Durga. Mrs Jacob, together with Mrs Edwards and Mrs Thompson from Mhow, watched from the back of a painted elephant (thoughtfully supplied by Indore's maharajah) while General Nicolson's wife chose to mingle with the crowds in the teeming city streets. She took the same train as the other ladies, but only Mrs Jacob might have detected her among the Indians who boarded at Mhow, dressed as she was in a vivid magenta sari carefully draped to cover her hair. And of course, she travelled to the city in an overcrowded third-class bogie.

As part of the regal procession headed by Maharajah Holkar on his sumptuously caparisoned royal elephant, the three European women surveyed the scene from the back of their own rather more modestly decorated beast. They peered rudely into first-storey verandahs as they passed, and commented loudly on the women leaning out and gazing back. The whole of Indore's female population must be crammed in there, thought Amy Thompson, for there were no black women loose in the streets that she could see.

No, she was wrong: there were a few, from the lower castes, she supposed, and there were a couple of them down there now, to the forefront of the crowd. Good heavens! Mrs Thompson gave a start and clutched the side of the howdah as she stared at the upturned faces; could one of them be Mrs Nicolson? She turned to her companions for confirmation. When she looked back the woman in the purple-red sari was half turned away, smiling up into the face of a handsome young Indian, who had her by the arm and was returning her smile. She must have been mistaken, surely? It couldn't possibly be General Nicolson's wife!

Mrs Jacob had seen more of the incident than Mrs Thompson. As the pressure of the throng pushed Violet Nicolson towards the feet of their elephant, the captain's wife caught her breath in horror. She saw the ayah utter a silent scream and reach for her mistress in vain, and she watched a young man thrust his way to Violet's side and pull her to safety. She saw Violet smile her thanks and then Mrs Thompson said something, distracting her. It was all over so quickly and by the time she looked back the general's wife had disappeared.

Violet shrugged off the near-accident. 'Say nothing to the *Burra Sahib*,' she warned the ayah. Malcolm was so touchy these days and she had no intention of having her freedom curtailed. It was a furious young woman, therefore, who listened to her husband as he prepared to leave her yet again.

'You are not to go to Simrole while I'm away,' he instructed his wife, 'or anywhere out of sight of Mhow. I absolutely forbid it, Violet. And for once you will listen.'

'But why, Malcolm?' She was almost spitting with rage. 'You've no right to tell me what to do—I'm not a child, for heavens sake!'

Nicolson chose to ignore her outburst. 'There could be danger outside the cantonment and I need to go away with my mind at rest.'

'What danger, Malcolm? The trouble is on the frontier, hundreds of miles away!'

'It could spread here soon enough—we're not doing too well up there, and plenty of people are delighting in our defeats. And it's only forty years since the Mutiny, after all.'

'Darling, that's ridiculous. As if anyone here would harm *me*—they'd hide me like Mrs Steel's "Kate" in that novel of hers!'

'Must you treat everything as a joke? I'm deadly serious about this, Violet,' and Nicolson's voice was cold as ice. 'Give me your assurance, my dear. *Now*.'

When she raised her rebellious gaze she saw that his face was quite pale. 'Very well,' she replied. 'I shall stay within sight of the cantonment. You have my word.'

Her tone was as glacial as his, and later she watched him ride away, desolate at the coolness of his farewell.

Violet's face haunted the general all the time he was gone. He knew he had put things badly, so anxious had he been to gain her consent. He returned earlier than expected sixteen days later, eager to be reconciled with his wife. She was not there.

'Great sins are written against thy name'

The days dragged during Malcolm's absence, and unless she took the drug the nights were impossible. She raided his store of opium time and time again and found herself depressed and irritable as a result. There was nowhere to go and no one to talk to. Whenever Violet Nicolson walked round Mhow she could almost have sworn that women turned away. She told herself it was her imagination but she began to feel vulnerable. If only Malcolm would come back, she thought; at least no one ever snubbed her in his presence.

One day by the bandstand, she came across a crying child. It was little Billy Russell who had fallen and skinned his knees. She knelt and put her arms around him, comforting him with soft words and offering him a bonbon. He smiled up at the kind lady through his tears and was whispering his thanks when there was a rush of skirts and the boy was snatched away. Violet was nearly knocked over but managed to keep her balance and slowly straightened.

'I'll thank you to keep away from my son, Mrs Nicolson!' Mrs Russell's eyes were narrowed in dislike. 'I don't want him catching anything from those blacks we all know you're so fond of!' The outraged woman turned and stalked away, carrying the frightened boy who had renewed his sobs.

Speechless and uncomprehending, Violet looked after her. She had been made to feel a leper by a woman she had never harmed. God, how she hated this place! Slowly she made her way back to the bungalow and there she shut herself in her room and wept.

As the days went by and she relied more and more on an opium-induced sleep, Violet came to view her surroundings with increasing detachment. Mhow was a nest of hypocritical vipers—even the men were dominated by their wives and disliked her heartily. She convinced herself she did not care and, denied her visits to the gentle shrine by the Simrole stream, she went instead to the temple in Mhow.

She listened to the bells, the tom-toms and the braying calls to worship, and watched the Brahmin priests at their work. And as she did so, she realised that by no means was everyone welcome there, either. The lower castes were turned away, while outcastes never dared approach. In her newly found objectivity Violet's heart went out to them all, for she also knew what it was to be considered unclean. What kind of religion was this, anyway? What justice was there in a system that condoned the degradation of women; that banned people from its temples? Whose interests did the system serve?

Well, she knew the answer and Malcolm had been right. What hope was there for India when the mass of its great population was sentenced to some kind of cosmic treadmill, bearing in uncomplaining silence the hardships of this life in the hope that the next one would be kinder? And what real chance did they have of *that*? Who conditioned them to put up with injustice and poverty in the first place? The answer was always the same—the priests and the priestly caste with their convenient notion of *maya*.

What was the point of a soul reborn? she asked herself in despair. There was only one life—one precious life, to cherish and make the most of in the hope of leaving a legacy for the next generation. And what had she achieved? What had she to show for her thirty-two years on earth? She had no child, and she had succeeded in alienating the one person she valued. With Malcolm lost, what reason was there left for living?

As her mistress became more and more introspective, her maid, Noona, hid the opium. It made no difference, for Violet terrified her into giving it back. Violet only left the bungalow at night and took to driving down the Simrole road, glad to turn her back on Mhow but (true to her promise) returning before the lights of the cantonment quite disappeared. Sometimes she rode out towards the lake. Hira Singh had returned to his regiment and she took the surly Pir Mahomed instead. One evening Violet refused to tolerate any more grumbling. She dismissed the man with a torrent of sharp words and went on alone as far as Janapao Hill. Halfway up she dismounted and looked down over Mhow. The princes' encampment was long dismantled but the cantonment lights shone ever bright and smug. *East is East and West is West*—and she belonged nowhere. She sat down and buried her head in her hands.

How long she was there she didn't know. When she looked up again the moon was out. The illuminated path stretched away to the top of the hill and, as if mesmerised, Violet Nicolson followed. The summit was further than it seemed, and when she rounded the last bend she paused to catch her breath. She heard singing and followed the sound. There, in front of the brightly shining temple, thronged Hindus from Mhow and hunters from the hills. Tribals and low castes must have gathered for a fair, she realised, and they were drunk—horribly drunk—on some country-brewed liquor that they were drawing from great earthenware *chattis* lying about on the ground.

One of the men heard her. As she turned to go he looked in her direction and for a moment they stared at one another, the man too surprised to move. He must think I'm a ghost, a *churel* dead in childbirth, and Violet nearly laughed. Then others saw her and she would have run away, but they came at her too fast. They closed in on her with the speed of the hunter and began to feel her clothes and touch her hair.

She was reminded of Mandu but there was no Robert Elkington to help her here. The mouths jabbered words she couldn't understand, and the fingers picking and plucking at her clothing became more persistent. A hand lingered then gripped her arm, and she saw the expression on the dark features change from idle curiosity to lust.

Violet stifled a scream and managed to wrench herself free. Tripping and stumbling, she ran down the path as fast as her shaking legs would take her. Mercifully she did not fall, but slipped and slid her way safely back to where she had tethered her horse. She had heard no sounds of pursuit, yet someone had got there first and was waiting.

'Violet darling, I'm back.' Malcolm Nicolson called to his wife several times and when she did not come to meet him he frowned. It was past ten o'clock. He turned apologetically to Major Thompson. 'My wife must be out. Stay and have that drink anyway.' But the major, anxious to get back to his own spouse, declined politely and went on his way.

Nicolson called Noona, who shook her head. No, the *memsahib* had no engagement; she had gone out riding. *So late and on her own*? He was relieved to hear the woman say that his wife had taken the groom. But what was she saying now? Pir Mahomed had come back without her? When was that? Oh, never mind! Cursing, the general hurried over to the stables and shook the sleeping *syce* awake.

His own horse was still saddled and he overtook the major on the road. Where the devil was Nicolson off to now? Thompson wondered, then he shrugged; it was, after all, none of his business. When he got home and told his wife, Amy Thompson thought she might just have the answer.

While the Thompsons were discussing the state of the Nicolsons' marriage Malcolm made his way slowly up Janapao Hill. Both he and his horse were tired and he was relieved to see Violet's mount by the side of the path, patiently cropping at the wind-burnt grass. But where in God's name was his wife? He dismounted and looked around him. She could have been anywhere. As he was debating what best to do, he heard the sound of someone running downhill towards him and coming to a sudden halt.

'No, no, I don't believe it …'

Violet's voice was little more than a croak as she sank to her knees on the path, a stitch in her side and desperately out of breath.

Malcolm hurried forward.

'Don't touch me, don't touch me,' she pleaded, and without looking up she recoiled from his outstretched hand.

He raised her to her feet and then, 'Violet,' he said gently, 'it's me. Sweetheart, it's me. Who did you think it was?'

She looked into her husband's face and for only the second time in her life Violet Nicolson fainted.

Malcolm Nicolson got Violet home and tried to make sense of what had happened. She would say little, and once she was asleep he tackled the maid. Slowly he pieced together some kind of a story. For one thing, his wife had been taking opium to help her sleep.

She had needed none tonight. He, too, was exhausted, but he refused to give in until he discovered what had been going on in his absence.

'How often does my wife take opium?' he asked Noona. Every time the *sahib* went away, he was informed. But never when he was home, the ayah could swear to that. I couldn't be so sure myself, thought the general in despair. What of the nights he spent in his dressing room alone?

The *Burra Mem* had become depressed, the maid went on. Something had happened one day in Mhow. She had come back and stayed in her room for hours, crying. Since then, Noona told a frowning Malcolm Nicolson, she had refused to see anyone who called—including Jacob *mem*. She had even been unkind to Noona. At that, Malcolm Nicolson was forced to give up and he went to bed a very worried man.

Violet was still sleeping when he left for work next morning. There were dark shadows under her eyes and her cheeks were hollow.

'Leave her be,' he told the ayah, and patted her shoulder in an attempt to reassure her. 'Don't worry. You've done all you could.' For she had told him of Violet's rage when she had discovered the opium was missing, and he sympathised. But the little Kashmiri box was in *his* pocket now, and there was no way his wife was going to browbeat *him*!

Violet awoke in the mid-morning, bathed, and made an effort to look her best for Malcolm when he returned for tiffin. She looked critically in the mirror and pinched her skin with vicious fingers to bring some colour to her cheeks. *He was back*!

And then she remembered how they had parted all those days before, and the ice in both their hearts. It had been her fault, and last night she hadn't even said she was sorry, simply clung to him for comfort in the knowledge she was safe. When Malcolm Nicolson entered the house at noon his wife was waiting for him with an uncertain smile on her face but he didn't hesitate. He caught her to him, only to release her a moment later. Good as it was to be home, he wouldn't relax until he knew what had been going on while he was away.

'Well,' he said after they had eaten, 'are you ready to tell me what happened?'

He had been wondering all morning. All Violet would say the night before was that she was unhurt and that no one had attacked her. She had repeated it obsessively until he accepted her assurances and let her sleep.

'I don't know where to start,' she finally admitted.

'Why not begin at the beginning?' and he produced the delicate little box. He set it on the table and opened it. 'Opium is an evil, darling, no matter how beautiful the dreams. It turns illusion into reality, and reality into nightmare—' Her eyes seemed enormous, either from the drug or from what he was saying.

'No more opium,' he told her, 'not when I'm away, not when I'm here. Never. Promise me, Violet.'

She promised but not without a protest. 'I *did* see everything so plainly. It was as if I understood at last, as if the clouds had cleared away and I could understand India. Malcolm, *I really understood*.' And she had few delusions left, he soon realised. 'The idea of caste repels me,' she told him, 'but I love the country and the people. Is that so very strange?'

He refused to be distracted.

'What happened last night on Janapao Hill, Violet?' he asked again, and this time received an answer.

'It was my fault, totally my fault. I came upon a country fair with those little Bhil hunters from the jungle and I watched for a while. When I turned to go, I was seen. They looked at me as I looked at them—we were objects of curiosity to each other. They came up to me and felt my clothes, my hair— And then they realised I was a woman.' She looked at him steadily before adding: 'It would be wrong to blame them for what might have happened next.'

'They were drunk, I take it.' Nicolson's voice was equally matter of fact.

'Yes, and I was frightened. But they didn't follow me.'

'They might have.'

She shook her head. It was over. She was safe. She would forget. 'You came home early—I'm so glad. But I was afraid you would call out the army to hunt them down, and they don't deserve that.' She reached for his hand but he failed to notice.

'Why were you there in the first place, Violet?'

Dear God, would his questions never stop?

'I wanted to get as far away from Mhow as possible, while keeping my word to you,' she said enigmatically.

What on earth had he made her promise? At last Nicolson remembered. 'Darling, you have a very literal mind—I'm not certain I meant quite that,' he said with a short laugh, before returning relentlessly to the attack. 'Why was it so important to get away?'

'As you said—it must have been the opium. Malcolm, I don't want to talk about it.' And try as he might, she refused to say more.

'A plea to cancel a thousand lies'

The next morning Malcolm Nicolson met Major Thompson and stopped to have a word, but the major, who was sporting a noticeably blackened eye, muttered an excuse before hurrying away. Wondering for an instant what could have happened, Nicolson turned to the pile of papers waiting on his desk. He was about to tackle them when Robert Elkington came in.

'These require your signature, sir.' He had yet more papers. The general groaned. They could wait—there were more urgent matters to attend to.

'What's up with Major Thompson? Do you know?'

'I believe he walked into a door last night, sir.' Hurriedly the lieutenant put the papers on the desk and his hands behind his back. But he was not quick enough.

'Is that so? A door called "Elkington", was it? Or did the same door skin your knuckles, Lieutenant?'

The young man didn't answer.

'Oh, come on, Robert. I can't have my officers fighting!'

'No, sir, of course not.'

'What was it about? Come on, man, I need to know.'

Elkington shifted uncomfortably from one foot to the other under the piercing gaze from eyes he had known to show compassion. There was no trace of compassion in them now and reluctantly he gave an answer.

'It was about Mrs Nicolson, sir.'

'What about my wife?'

'It was in the mess last night, sir, after you went home. Major Thompson repeated something Mrs Thompson said.'

'Oh? And what exactly was that?'

'I told him to shut up, sir—he was a little bit the worse for wear—and when he left soon after, I followed him outside and hit him.'

'Nobody saw you, I trust?'

'No, sir.'

'But everyone heard what he had to say, I suppose?'

'Yes, sir, I'm afraid so.'

'And what *did* he say, Lieutenant? You still haven't told me.'

Elkington didn't want to, but the gimlet eyes gave him no choice.

'That Mrs Nicolson has a lover. Sir.'

The general raised an eyebrow. 'Was that all he said?'

God damn it, thought the squirming ADC, *why can't Old Nick let it rest?* 'A native lover, sir. And that that was why she was always disappearing when your back was turned.' Thompson had gone into details, and under the general's insistent gaze Elkington repeated them all.

Nicolson listened impassively. 'I see,' he said when the young man had finished. 'And what do *you* think?'

This was easier, thank the Lord. 'That it's utter nonsense—we all think that, but it's the women, sir, they started the rumours in the first place. They don't like Mrs Nicolson, I'm afraid, for all sorts of reasons, and especially since she reminded them that we are all equal in the sight of God. Some of them treat their servants very badly, you see, and she found out—'

'And waded in with her usual diplomacy, I suppose?'

Elkington grinned despite himself. 'Yes, sir.'

'Very well, Robert. Thank you for telling me. Now I've work to do, if you don't mind.'

As he appended his signature to page after page of minutiae, Malcolm Nicolson found himself haunted by a small, persistent voice that told him over and over again that there was no smoke without fire. That the women were vicious, he did not doubt, but the sheer enormity of the suggestion must have some basis in fact. He tried not to listen to the tiny voice but it would not go away. The clouds of scandal that had been looming on the horizon for so long had broken over their heads at last, and he intended to find out the cause.

'So there we have it, Violet. Now you know what's going the rounds at Mhow at present—that my wife has taken an Indian lover.' Tiffin was over, the dishes cleared and General Nicolson had outlined briefly what Lieutenant Elkington had told him. 'Have you nothing to say?' and he waited for his wife's response.

'In my defence, do you mean?' she retorted. 'Is this a court martial? Well then, it's not true and I deny every word! Malcolm, you don't believe it, do you? You *can't* believe it—'

She was on her feet, facing him across the table, gripping the back of her chair till the knuckles of her hands shone white. Nicolson looked back at her indignant face. Of course he believed her, he said, but Mrs Thompson had been so certain of what she had seen.

'And what exactly did she see, pray?' Violet's question cut the air like a knife.

'You at *Dussehra*—in a sari, and laughing with an Indian in the streets of Indore City. He had his arm around you—'

Violet was enraged. 'Is that all?' she spat. 'The woman is perverted if she thinks that makes us lovers! Are you sure she didn't see us coupling in the street, as well? Malcolm, I've never seen the man before—or since. He came out of the crowd and saved me from being trampled under the feet of an elephant. I thanked him, and then he was gone. Ask Noona if you don't believe me, she was there. Or would you really rather believe Amy Thompson?' She stopped and waited.

Malcolm stood up, never taking his eyes from her face. It was such a simple explanation and he believed every word. He was too happy to speak, but Violet took his silence for condemnation and slowly moved towards the door, defeated.

Suddenly she remembered another incident, and all at once everything became clear. *I'll thank you to keep away from my son. I don't want him catching anything from those blacks you're so fond of.* Violet repeated the words out loud and turned to face her husband.

'Mrs Russell said that to me one day when I tried to help young Billy. I couldn't understand why—but now of course I do. They've treated me like a leper ever since then. Is that what you think, Malcolm? I was sure you of all people would believe me, but obviously I was wrong.'

Her eyes filled with a deep sadness as they lingered on the beloved face, and when she spoke again her voice was low and resolute.

'Malcolm,' she said at last, 'I've brought you nothing but embarrassment since the day we married. I shall understand if you ask me to go away.'

'*No*!' The spell was broken and Malcolm spoke, 'No! I do believe you. I've never doubted you.'

He reached her and took her hands. 'Violet, believe me, I'm sorry. Truly sorry. Say that you forgive me, please ...'

Could it really be so easy? Violet Nicolson felt near despair. She had apologised, now so had he, but what would follow? Good intentions lapsing into neglectfulness as before—was that what she wanted?

Malcolm waited as she bit her lip in an attempt to keep back her tears. 'Violet, *please* ...'

'Of course I forgive you,' she said at last. 'But what of the rest?' Her voice was as frozen as her expression. 'Shall I leave—before I totally wreck your career?'

His career! What did that matter? The thought of losing his wife shocked Nicolson into baring his soul.

'What other people think is their affair. You are my life's blood,' he told her, pressing her hands to his heart. "Without you *this* will fall silent. Now do you understand why you have to stay?'

His officers gave Malcolm their full support but Violet's life was as difficult as ever, for Mhow's women were different. At heart they might not believe the rumour either, but they wanted to, and that made all the difference. It was human nature, Nicolson supposed. And human nature couldn't be changed, although young Elkington had taken matters into his own hands and tried. And so had Arthur Jacob's wife. The Scotswoman had done all she could to counter Amy Thompson's claims. After all, as she told everyone, she had been there too and she knew what *she* had seen. But Mrs Thompson's version was much more interesting, so that was what most of the ladies preferred to believe.

The general went about his business as usual and at first his wife refused to leave the compound. 'I've had enough,' she said, when he suggested it. 'I'm sick of it all. Let me stay here.'

'It's not like you to run away and hide,' he observed. 'But if that's what you really want, very well.' He shrugged and walked away.

The next day, to his immense satisfaction, his wife went out alone—not very far, but far enough to proclaim her defiance. Shortly after, when Maharajah Holkar held a great ball at his Lal Bagh palace just outside the city, both the Nicolsons attended. With the eyes of the gathering on her, the general's wife greeted one enemy after another, wan but still defiant and head held high.

The maharajah watched it all from his dais. He had no patience with Englishwomen who were always interfering and causing trouble. General Nicolson's wife on the other hand was different: she was delightful and unaffected, and her laughter was unforced. When she came to pay her respects to Indore's portly ruler, Shivaji Rao Holkar broke with tradition. He left his glittering throne and walked forward to shake her hand in the European fashion. He engaged her in conversation for some minutes, then summoned a good-looking scion of the royal house to escort her to the ballroom. Let her desiccated English sisters make something of *that*—if they dared!

It was a conspiracy, thought Violet Nicolson, in a daze, for she was not left alone for a moment. One partner after another claimed her—men she hardly knew, as well as the young officers from Mhow. Whirling her around the magnificent colonnaded ballroom, they showed their solidarity with the general by dancing with his wife. And showed their solidarity with her.

Robert Elkington hovered in the background and watched protectively until at last he could claim her for their waltz.

'I believe you hurt your hand, Lieutenant,' Mrs Nicolson remarked, as the hand in question took her own. 'I do hope it's recovered.' He assured her that it had. 'That was a very silly thing to do, Robert,' she chided, but softening the words with an affectionate smile. 'Don't make a habit of it, will you?'

Elkington grinned back. He did not think there would be any need, he told her, and he held her as close as he dared—until the music faded and General Malcolm Nicolson came to take possession of his wife.

He led her outside and there, in the ghostly light shed by the many lanterns, he gave her his full attention. The pearls about her throat heightened the translucence of her skin, while the gown of heavy cream silk emphasised her slightness. She looked pale and insubstantial, ethereal almost. He caught his breath, and touched her bare arm as if to reassure him she was in fact flesh and blood. He walked her to the end of the terrace, where the steps led down to the wooded banks and dark waters of the Sarasvati.

'I know how difficult you find all this,' he told her. 'But look down at that river, Violet. For thousands of years that river has been flowing past this spot. And it will be flowing still when you and I are long forgotten, and our troubles forgotten with us. What does it matter, after all, what a few misguided people think?' He raised her fingers to his lips and held them there, looking deep into her eyes.

It was a great disappointment to Amy Thompson, coming out to take the air with her spouse and finding the general's wife caught up in a close and passionate embrace, to recognise General Nicolson himself one moment later.

'I'm afraid you've caught me *in flagrante delicto* again, Mrs Thompson,' Violet heard herself saying, as Malcolm released her and she pinned back a straying lock of hair. 'Another delicious rumour for you to spread around Mhow, I shouldn't wonder! Good evening, Major Thompson. I do hope your eye is better.' Then Mrs Nicolson swept regally back towards the palace.

'For this is Wisdom'

Entertainment succeeded entertainment in the winter months at Mhow. Dances, concerts, dinner parties— Violet's head was swimming as the endless round went on. Malcolm watched her anxiously. She was behaving in an exemplary fashion, apart from her one lapse at the palace—and who was he to blame her for that? But he wondered how long it would be before her nerves gave way. And there was still December Mhow Week to come.

He found an unexpected ally in Mrs Jacob, who hailed him one day as he was returning home and stopped to have a few words. He rebuked her for no longer coming to call, in a jovial kind of a way, and she answered him more seriously.

'Your wife doesn't encourage callers these days, General Nicolson. I suppose you know that?'

'I do. And I also know why. But you, young lady, are different. Come for afternoon tea tomorrow—you *and* your husband. Violet will be delighted to see you!'

Mrs Jacob doubted that very much, and there she was wrong. Suddenly ashamed of having shut this woman out, Violet smiled warmly and tried to explain. Mrs Jacob waved her words away with an impatient hand. 'Show me the garden,' she said, slipping her arm through Violet's, and they went outside.

The two women walked along the raised walks where it was difficult to tell where path ended and garden began. It was, thought the captain's wife, quite as undisciplined and charming as her hostess. 'Is this where you met the snake?' she asked.

'Goodness, I wonder who told you about that? Malcolm, I suppose—I've quite lost count of the number of times he's dined out on that story. No, it was somewhere else.'

'You must have been terrified!'

'I was, but afterwards I realised that the poor creature was probably more frightened than me. I had no choice but to kill it, and it really was very beautiful. I wasn't alone, of course—and that made all the difference.' *Where was he now, the faithful Mahomed Akram? On his own still, with a woman—or dead somewhere up on the Frontier?* She realised that her visitor was watching her curiously and went on quickly: 'Malcolm came rushing out with the scissors and saved the day. But I've never liked wearing really long skirts since then—they do get in the way so.'

Violet Jacob had often noticed the neat little ankles. So had the rest of the ladies—and made unpleasant remarks. 'How very sensible, Mrs Nicolson,' she said. 'There are so many snakes in Mhow!'

'And not only in the gardens—you've noticed that as well?'

They were still laughing when their husbands joined them. Malcolm looked approvingly at his wife whom he hadn't seen so relaxed for weeks; Mrs Jacob's company obviously did her good. That there was a hint of hysteria in Violet's laughter he didn't suspect until the following night.

The Inspector General of Cavalry was visiting Mhow and was invited to dinner. The Jacobs, among others, were there, but none of them outshone General Grant, a man of vast proportions known to the cavalry and everyone else as 'The Rogue Elephant', and whose booming voice quite matched his girth.

The two Violets left the men to their after-dinner brandy and escaped to the drawing room, thankful of a little peace and quiet.

'He's staying in Mhow for weeks and I'm so grateful you and Captain Jacob could come tonight, it helps spread the load a little.' Violet giggled. 'What on earth does he look like in the saddle?'

What horse could take the weight? And what about their furniture? When General Grant lowered himself onto a sofa half an hour or so later his hostess held her breath. All would have been well, she supposed, had the curtain been left hanging in its proper place. But caught as it was across the end of the sofa, a catastrophe was bound to follow. It was too late to warn him and she could only watch in horror. With a misplaced confidence the general planted his ample posterior onto the seat beneath and brought the curtain rail crashing down upon his head. And onto Mrs Jacob's.

A stunned silence followed. Then first one startled red face and then another emerged from the dusty velvet drapes.

'Good God, Nicolson,' exclaimed an amused Rogue Elephant, ruefully rubbing his pate. 'I was warned to expect just about anything if I dined under your roof, but I didn't reckon on the roof falling down on top of me! Man, do you always try to murder your guests?'

They both looked so comical as they struggled to get free, and Malcolm and Arthur Jacob in their efforts to untangle them seemed only to make matters worse. Violet began to laugh. Everyone joined in, and only Nicolson realised that his wife was in danger of losing control.

'Why don't you go and find a servant, darling,' he suggested, 'then we can fix the rail properly. We can't have General Grant thinking we do this every time we have people to dine!'

Violet left the room, glad to have the opportunity to conquer what she herself knew threatened to become hysteria, and by the time she returned order had been restored.

There were a good few evenings to be got through before they could relax alone together, thought Malcolm Nicolson, And none of them likely to be as genial and carefree as this. Violet was under far more strain than he had realised—if only she could get through to Christmas.

She no longer roamed the countryside alone or with a groom. People would talk, she said, voluntarily condemning herself to days without exercise—unless Malcolm was free to go out with her himself. Sometimes she went out with Mrs Jacob but that lady was much in demand, and she felt she had no right to make claims on one she had so recently shunned. Robert Elkington's services as escort she firmly declined.

He had come gallantly to her defence already, and caused comment enough; someone would see them together and who knows what talk might follow? So Violet thanked him, gritted her teeth, and slowly fought her way back towards respectability. And all the while she was boiling with impotent rage. Rage at Mhow, rage at poor Malcolm—why, sometimes in her helplessness she felt she hated him for keeping her there. Why should she have to fight? Why couldn't she be herself? Her anger gave her the will to go on: Christmas, she told herself, keep going until Christmas. But after Christmas, *what*?

Malcolm came in one afternoon after the Mhow Week festivities were over to find Violet asleep on the very sofa that had brought disaster on their guests. She had been writing and must have dozed off over her work. It was the draft of a poem and one or two lines caught his attention. As he read a little more he frowned. What on earth was going on in her mind? Her face was relaxed and worry-free as she slept, her lips curved slightly in a smile. What was she dreaming now, his golden girl? He watched her until she stirred, opened her eyes and saw him standing there. Her face lit up in welcome and she moved to make room for him.

'Tell me how you are today,' he asked.

'I'm fine,' she told him. 'I've been writing, as you see.'

'I know. I've read a little—do you mind?'

She hadn't meant him to see it, but shook her head. 'Of course I don't mind. I have no secrets from you.'

'Then tell me how you are—truly.' For hadn't Isabel said that her sister would always say she was 'all right' or 'fine'—even when she wasn't? Violet did not answer straight away and perhaps she did not intend to, so Nicolson looked at the paper he was holding in his hand. 'You've called it "The Teak Forest", I see. We'll go back to Simrole soon and camp. Shall we?' When she nodded her assent, he read aloud to her some of the words she had written in passionate complaint:

> '—*And under your kisses I hardly knew*
> *Whether I loved or hated you.*
>
> *But your words were flame and your kisses fire,*
> *And who shall resist a strong desire?*
> *Not I, whose life is a broken boat*
> *On a sea of passions, adrift, afloat.*
> *And, whether I came in love or hate,*
> *That I came to you was written by Fate*
> *In every hue of the blood-red sky,*
> *In every tone of the peacocks' cry*—'

He read no more but put the poem aside to subject her to an unblinking scrutiny. 'Do you mean what you've written here, Violet?'

She looked back equally seriously. 'Darling, I love you—you know that.'

'Yes, I know. I know it very well. It's the rest that worries me. Are you really a broken boat drifting down some great, sad river? Is that how you see your life? Tell me, Violet Nicolson, I need to know.'

'Well then—yes!' He was her friend as well as her husband, and the need to confide was suddenly overwhelming. 'You see,' she explained, and the words came out in a rush, 'I don't know what to believe any more. I was always so sure of myself and happy to condemn others, knowing I was right. But what if I'm the one who's wrong, Malcolm? Perhaps women are meant to be passive and accepting of any treatment? Here to serve men and see to their needs? And what if these women in Mhow are right, and their standards of behaviour are correct, and mine are wrong?'

Her fingers were plucking at the pleats of her skirt in the nervous gesture that was becoming a habit and Nicolson's hand reached out and forced her to stop. She looked at him, eyes wide in supplication. 'What if I'm the only one marching out of step? Malcolm, I've been asking myself whether there isn't something wrong with me? Why am I so very different?'

She was tired, she was bored, she was depressed; she had lost faith not only in her God but also in herself. Malcolm Nicolson understood. He also understood that she was begging him for help. 'Dearest girl, there is nothing wrong with you at all. *In any way*.' But how was he to convince her, this woman who had brought laughter into his life as well as untold disruption and infinite love?

'You're not including our physical relationship in this litany of woe, I trust?' asked the man who had spent all his adult years in India, and who, as uninhibited as any oriental, could spell out the joyous nature of their lovemaking—sometimes languid, sometimes passionate and demanding, shameless even, but full of courtesy the one for the other. 'Well, are you?' he repeated when he had finished.

He had startled her into laughter. 'No, no, no, of course not!'

'Good. Then we don't have to worry about that, at least. As for the rest—' Suddenly Malcolm Nicolson found himself remembering his conversation with Robert Sandeman in a northern valley long ago, when his fellow Scot had advised him to cherish his wife's independence of spirit.

'Sweetheart, you are not alone,' he told her firmly. 'There is no one like you in Mhow, I admit, but what you feel about injustice and freedom is felt by other people too, women—and men—here in India. There perhaps aren't very many, but they exist. And there are plenty of them elsewhere, of that you may be sure.'

If Violet was to be convinced, and regain her self-confidence, then she had to meet others of her kind. Not here, where society was hidebound and inward looking, where her spirit was constantly being bruised, but far away where women were speaking out and making their voices heard. He wanted her back: the rebel, the virago; the champion of causes that did not necessarily have to be lost. She needed to be stirred and stimulated in totally different surroundings. Malcolm Nicolson acknowledged that he might find it an uncomfortable experience, but he was prepared to take the risk.

'I'm taking you to London,' he told her. 'Then you will see exactly what I mean.'

7

'What has sorrow to do with thee?'

ENGLAND: JUNE–AUGUST 1898

As soon as the demands of Mhow Week ended Malcolm Nicolson began to make his preparations. He received leave to return to England the following May for a period of eight months and booked a passage to London, writing to inform his mother of his proposed return. But how exactly did he intend to fulfill his fine promises to his wife? Each time he put the problem aside he was confronted by memories of Isabel taking him to task unmercifully; Isabel reminding him that his duty towards her sister was as great (if not greater) as that he owed his country and his Queen. Small as she was, his sister-in-law had made him feel even smaller.

A solution to his dilemma was not long in coming. Flora Steel's Indian Mutiny novel, *On the Face of the Waters*, was now in print and a signed copy arrived for General Nicolson in time for Christmas 1897. Violet, who read it first, found the novel gripping. She also found the contents fair. Malcolm agreed on both counts and wrote to congratulate his friend. He also told her of his plans.

When his letter arrived at Flora and Henry Steel's Highland home in Aberdeenshire, Mrs Steel preened herself at the general's words of praise and immediately sent a reply. 'So you're off to England!' she wrote. 'You surprise me, Malcolm, I must say. You were always so set against going back.'

'It's for Violet's sake,' Nicolson explained in his next letter, deciding to open his heart to one of his oldest friends.

'Yes, I can see she's a bit of a rebel,' Mrs Steel duly answered. 'It doesn't always pay, of course. Society in India doesn't forgive indiscretions easily.' Although, she added, she had enjoyed a few clashes with convention herself. 'But then, I'm tougher than your Violet, I imagine. She'll do better in London—as you say, she won't be the only one of her kind.' Mrs Steel stifled a sniff as she penned the words. 'Anyway, Malcolm, leave it with me. I'll tell my friend Blanche you'll be in London in June. If you let me have your address, she'll introduce your Violet to a few people. Mostly literary folk, I take it that's the kind of thing you'd like. By the way, is her sister still there? The one who calls herself Victoria Cross?'

Malcolm Nicolson decided to take Violet to his mother's home first. 'It's high time you and she met,' he said. And my sisters are anxious to get to know you. After nine years of marriage they must all wonder if you really exist!'

It was a lot longer than nine years since Nicolson had seen his family, and his wife had no wish to make their acquaintance at all. The years of polite notes exchanged annually at Christmas had suited her very well; she already knew all she needed to know about the Nicolsons.

Yet she didn't argue. At Tilbury docks she simply watched Malcolm take charge of everything: the luggage, the telegram and the railway tickets. She would have preferred to stay in London for a few days, but a visit to Northamptonshire was a small price to pay for the blessed freedom from British India.

When the couple arrived at the small village near Oundle where her mother-in-law had lived with her daughters for many years, Violet was forced to change her mind. Malcolm's mother, an erect eighty-one-year-old matriarch dressed in sombre black with a cap of the local lace on her snowy-white head was there at the station to meet them. She suffered Malcolm's somewhat restrained hug with a dignified smile, and extended a mottled hand to his wife. Then she stooped from a great height to brush her daughter-in-law's pale cheek with cold dry lips. The greeting from Mary and Caroline Nicolson—it was impossible to tell whether they were older or younger than Malcolm—was equally distant.

They were so tall, these Nicolson women! Under the cool scrutiny of three pairs of critical eyes Violet felt insignificant, uncertain, and suddenly apprehensive. She watched Malcolm catch up his sisters in his arms and kiss them heartily. They laughed and began talking all at once, while Violet, quite forgotten on the fringe, struggled with a familiar urge to gather her skirts and run away. The urge was still there when they reached the family home, a plain two-storey Georgian house built of dove-grey limestone. The walls were almost two feet thick, as if designed to keep the world out and the inhabitants in.

A cloistered calm prevailed inside Scorrybreck House where no one talked in anything above a whisper. The downstairs rooms were furnished with heavy furniture, of a vaguely French design belonging to a long-gone era. The walls were hung with an old-fashioned dark green paper, and the matching green curtains at the windows were worn and dingy. Violet longed to throw them wide to let in the cheery sunlight, but only dared draw one aside a fraction when her mother-in-law wasn't looking. For a brief moment she stared out at the garden. Its glorious early summer beds were bright with disciplined colour, and the sweeping circular drive was bordered with vast rhododendron bushes already well in bloom. She would, she vowed, spend as much time as she could away from this dreary mausoleum, this house where the aura of celibacy could almost be cut with a knife.

The next day, the rain lashed relentlessly against the windowpanes and obliterated the view of the grounds. Denied her chance of escape by the fickle English weather and virtually ignored, Violet contented herself with watching her husband's mother. Mrs Nicolson sat enthroned in a great wing chair surrounded by cushions, with her feet on an embroidered footstool. There, she was administered to as if it were her right—her *divine* right. She never lifted a finger unless absolutely necessary while, over the course of the long morning and an even longer afternoon, neither Mary nor Caroline Nicolson were allowed to stay seated for long. In the long years of her widowhood Malcolm's mother must have trained her daughters to anticipate her every need, to the extent that one or the other was always fetching something for their aged parent or making a tender inquiry as to her comfort. No wonder the widow looked so *young*: her daughters' looks and youth had been sacrificed on the altar of their mother's wishes, their passions too. Violet was horrified at the realisation. How they must envy their brother's wife her status, and resent her.

But when the rain cleared and a watery sun struggled through the clouds, Violet found she was totally wrong. There was no resentment in the way her sisters-in-law insisted on showing her the high-walled garden and the *potager* where neat rows of vegetables awaited their fate. There was no resentment in the way they pointed out the soft-grey stone church and the Old Hall, the home of the local squire. They shared their favourite walks along the River Nene, where osiers and aspens grew, where water hens swam and where villagers in their flat-bottomed boats went fishing for eels. 'We love it here,' they confided shyly, 'and we so hope you will come to love it too.'

They beamed approval on her as they told her of their brother's letters, when they had first known that Malcolm—so committed a bachelor—had fallen in love. Their mother had been doubtful, but they had known. Known from the first, before he had, even, when he had sent home her sketch. Did she remember? Would she care to see it? Linking arms with their new sister, they took her back inside to where the drawing hung splendidly framed in the narrow panelled hall, and commented on the fine aquiline profile so very like their own.

They had had their dreams of marriage, these gentle kindly women, dreams stifled by their mother. Major Nicolson might be dead, but the family had stayed together. Except for the boys—their father had destined *them* for India and his widow had honoured that pledge. When Simon Edmund died aged twenty-nine there was all the more reason to keep her girls beside her. She declined Malcolm's invitation to his sisters to join him in India, and discouraged the suitors at home who became more and more infrequent with the passing of the years. And Mary and Caroline Nicolson had become women and then old maids, with all the opprobrium those words evoked. Little by little Violet pieced the story together, and as she did so, her wariness of her mother-in-law deepened to firm dislike.

'My father died in Boulogne when Mother was the same age as you are now. He was fifty-seven. She's been widowed for almost fifty years,' Malcolm told her. 'Always wearing black, still mourning him after all this time. Isn't it amazing?'

It was, the thirty-three-year-old Violet agreed—if it were true (although she kept such reservations to herself). Fifty years a widow. Fifty years of waking alone, sleeping alone, *of being alone*—the very thought appalled her. And how could Mrs Nicolson have endured two bereavements with such obvious serenity if she had truly loved her husband and her son? Her face should be marked with grief; there should be signs of loss, surely, even now. There was no memento of Malcolm's brother or of the major anywhere in the house that she could see—unless her mother-in-law's bedroom was a shrine to the men long dead?

One day when the old lady was entertaining the curate to afternoon tea Violet dared to peep inside. With its whitewashed walls and bare floorboards, it was the austere room of a mother superior, even to the crucifix above the single bed. There was not a picture in sight of anyone—living or dead. Feeling both guilt at her deceit and triumph at being vindicated, Violet Nicolson joined the company downstairs.

The widow observed Violet with equal interest. Naturally, she had always wanted her son to marry. And have children. But he had clearly made a most unsuitable choice—one had only to look at her daughter-in-law to tell. She was far too narrow in the hips, and no wonder she was unable to breed. Malcolm should have thought of that, of course, but from the way he kept touching her he was obviously besotted.

His father would have been the same, thought old Mrs Nicolson, if he had not been shown the merits of self-control. There was nothing so disciplined about her son's wife, that was obvious. Her daughter-in-law was pretty, granted, but there was a more than a touch of wildness there. You had only to look at the over-bright eyes and the flushed cheeks and the dishevelled locks when she came in—wet and muddy, more often than not—from her endless tramps over the countryside. The lace on the immaculate cap fluttered as the old lady shook her head.

'What is the use of caring?'

'I hadn't realised that England was still so feudal. Look at it, Malcolm. Rows of tied cottages, the squire owns all the village, he even chooses the vicar—'

'It reminds you of India, does it? There are Brahmins here too, is that what you're saying?'

'Something like that, yes.' All those labourers coming out when the squire passed by, doffing their caps while their wives bobbed a curtsey—it was positively mediaeval.

'I take it you don't approve, Violet, even though the squire here obviously cares about his tenants.'

'You're absolutely right. Of course I don't approve! I wonder if Sir Henry exercises his *ius primae noctis*?'

'Of course he doesn't! And I forbid you to mention any such thing when we dine there tomorrow, even in jest!'

'Is he married, Malcolm? He's so good-looking. What a waste it would be—no wife, and no village maidens to deflower on their wedding night!' Violet sighed deeply and peeped impishly at her husband through her lashes. Nicolson gripped her hand, striding out so that she was obliged almost to run to keep up. This left her with no breath for talking and he was glad of the silence. Violet in this mood worried him; she was beginning to feel bored and he hoped the rest of the visit would pass without incident.

Sir Henry, it transpired, did have a wife, a pleasant woman much the same age as his own—and she owned a bicycle. Quite how the conversation had taken that turn over dinner General Nicolson did not know. But he knew well enough that the machines had fascinated Violet ever since she had seen one or two intrepid young women weaving their way skilfully through the London traffic.

It would be the perfect means of locomotion, she kept saying during their daily walks. It was so flat here on the edge of the fens and she could easily learn. Malcolm, she would beg, her great eyes adding force to the plea, couldn't she try, just once …? He always refused—not that he would willingly deny her anything, but he had the public weal at heart. And now here was the little minx persuading Lady Browne to lend her a bicycle, and Sir Henry was supporting her request. It would be delivered next day, they assured her, and she was to treat it as her own. Malcolm Nicolson groaned.

The following afternoon Malcolm and his mother took tea on the terrace overlooking the garden, and every so often Violet passed by below on her borrowed bicycle, looking up at them both with an exuberant smile. She was doing very well, thought her husband. Only a few spills to date, no bones broken and, most importantly, no one else involved—the general found himself beginning to relax. Violet was quite without fear, and in consequence was now completing her circuits more and more quickly. Perhaps, it occurred to Malcolm, he should take his mother inside before she became quite dizzy at the spectacle.

'Your Violet has so much energy. And I have to say she seems so very young, Malcolm dear. Hardly suitable material for a *general's wife*, I would have thought,' Mrs Nicolson went on.

Her son frowned at the reproving tone. 'She wasn't a general's wife when we married, Mother,' he pointed out.

'Of course she wasn't, dear. But I'm sure you know what I mean.' The widow, herself a general's daughter, gave a slightly pained smile.

'I agree with you, Mother, Violet is not a suitable wife for a general. But she tries very hard. And that is why she is having so much fun now. I, for one, am delighted to see her so happy.'

For she was happy—this was the Violet who delighted in something as unsophisticated as a shell; this was the Violet who had bombarded him with snowballs in the course of a Quetta winter; this was the Violet who had a child's infinite capacity for joy. She passed them again. Malcolm smiled and waved; then his heart was in his mouth as she returned the gesture—with both hands—and the bicycle wobbled alarmingly. She recovered her balance, as he supposed he always knew she would, and he watched her go. Then he turned back to the old lady.

'In fact, Mother,' he added, 'I'm no more suitable material for a general, and if I didn't think those contraptions so confoundedly dangerous, I'd be down there with her myself!'

He watched his wife complete another circuit, then putting down his teacup hurriedly and muttering an apology he ran down the steps, taking them two at a time, for he had seen what Violet couldn't see: Mr Timms the curate, coming up the drive with a confident stride as Violet swept equally confidently round the curve to meet him.

The coming together was both inevitable and brief. When Nicolson reached them the curate was lying prone among the rhododendrons to one side, and Violet was trapped in a large bush to the other. Between them lay the bicycle, its wheels still spinning forlornly. At first glance none of the three appeared to have suffered any harm. Violet would have to forgive him for seeing to her victim first, decided Malcolm, as he proffered both a helping hand and his apologies to Mr Timms.

'Not at all, not at all,' murmured the long-suffering curate. 'My fault entirely, of course.' It usually was, or so his wife told him, and this time—though he couldn't see how—it surely was as well.

'Are you all right, dear lady?' he asked, as he helped Violet from her leafy bower. Violet was trying hard not to giggle as she assured him that she was. He had looked so alarmed as she bore down upon him; he had truly remarkable reflexes for a man of the cloth, and the way in which he had leapt to safety had been a triumph in one so portly. Her lips twitched as she watched him dust himself down and straighten his clerical collar.

'I'll see to Mr Timms, Violet,' Malcolm told her firmly. 'Perhaps you should return the bicycle—at once.' He could forgive her the accident, but not the urge to laugh at the gallant little man.

Violet understood why she was being punished, and accepted the suggestion in silence. She cycled all the way to the Old Hall, handed over her steed with a frank explanation as to why she had decided to keep it no longer, and, feeling extremely sorry for herself, started out on the long walk back. The Brownes had offered her their carriage but she declined: anything to delay going back to dismal Scorrybreck House. She lingered in the village where the schoolchildren were just coming out at the end of the day. Sitting on a stone bench by the church she watched the earnest faces of some, the relieved expressions of others, but all of them whole and healthy. If her children had lived, what would they have been like? Would she have had a son, like that scamp over there tormenting his small sister, or a little girl, like the child who was staring at her with eyes so like her own? She gave herself a shake.

As she walked back along the darkening lane she quickened her step. It wouldn't do to be late for dinner, which everyone took so early here in the country. Malcolm came to meet her well before the iron gates of his mother's home were in sight. 'You've been a long time,' was all he said, as he took her arm. No word of rebuke, just a quick glance at her face. She was looking forlorn, more than the loss of the bicycle would warrant, so something must have happened. He would wait and ask her later.

In fact, what he told her in their room after dinner brought the light back to her eyes. He had decided they would return to London earlier than planned, and if the changed dates did not suit her grandmother, then they would stay in a hotel. They would come back before they left the country, but for the moment they had been here long enough.

'I take it you agree?' he asked.

Violet nodded emphatically. 'We've upset your mother's routine, or at least I have. She's tried not to show it, but I know. And,' she added forthrightly, 'I'm not the wife she would have chosen for you, Malcolm. I'm sure we both know that.'

'Then I'm glad she had no say.' Violet looked happier now and Nicolson asked her: 'Why were you so upset before dinner?'

'It wasn't about the bicycle,' she said defensively.

'Of course it wasn't. Mr Timms is fine, by the way. I walked with him down the drive on the way to meet you—he was rather nervous about going on his own for some reason, and kept muttering about *Jehu driving furiously*, or was it *driveth*? But otherwise he was quite all right. So, how are *you*?' He returned to the attack.

'Me?' Violet gave a wan smile. 'I stopped by the school and saw the children. I couldn't help thinking, that's all.'

There was no need for her to say more. 'Darling, you're still young enough to have half a dozen children,' and Malcolm hugged her.

'I don't want half a dozen, just one would be enough,' and Violet's lip trembled. 'I can accept being barren—what a cruel word that is—but not the way your mother looks at me. With pity and more than a hint of disdain. I'm glad we're leaving early.'

Poor Violet, poor little woman. Try as he might, Nicolson could not convince her that to him her continued good health was all that mattered. She would see things differently in London, he told himself, and he would make sure she had no time at all to brood.

'For sake of thine own content of mind'

After a little under two weeks in Northamptonshire, the Nicolsons settled into the elegant terraced house on the corner of the quiet street in Pimlico, where Violet's grandmother had been living since the death of her barrister husband. To Caroline Cory her granddaughter was a child still, if a far happier one than the girl she remembered. It took the elderly lady a little while to get used to the fact that Adela was married, and that her tall good-humoured husband was a general, no less. She peered at them both over the top of her gold-rimmed spectacles when she thought they weren't looking, and shook her head.

Mrs Cory withdrew to her sitting room soon after their arrival, giving them the use of another, larger, parlour. 'No, no, my dears,' she said when they protested, 'this is your home for as long as you want. You must feel free to invite anyone here that you wish, and to have a little privacy too.'

The year before, her sitting room had proved a useful retreat. Then, young Annie Sophie had been staying and Caroline Cory had been only too delighted to escape from the motley crew of young people that often assembled in her house in Cambridge Street. 'Writers' the girl had called them and she supposed that some of them were, but even so it had been a relief when her youngest granddaughter's enthusiasm for literature waned, and she used the proceeds from that dreadful book she had written to take herself off to America to visit her Uncle Heneage Griffin.

And now Addie was back to turn her home upside down again! Mrs Cory knew exactly what to expect. She would throw back the curtains and let in the light; she would pester the cook for all her favourite puddings; she would make the house ring with her laughter as she clattered up and down the stairs. Her grandmother's comfortable if somewhat monotonous routine would be disrupted in a thousand different ways … With a delighted smile on her plump little face, Mrs Cory settled back in her chintz-covered chair and waited for the disruption to begin.

❧

'Come on, darling, up you get! It's past seven o'clock!'

'Is that all?' Violet turned over, intending to go back to sleep, but a ruthless hand pulled back the eiderdown and she was left shivering in the cold morning air. It might be June, but there was no 'hot weather' to contend with here in London; perhaps it would be wise to get up and dress before she caught her death of cold. 'You've been out already?' she asked, as she thought about moving. It was so very early.

'Of course. You forget I'm usually up hours before this—and so are you! Come on, Violet, we've lots to do!'

'Nothing will be open yet,' she wailed and reached for the covers again.

'Breakfast,' he said. 'Can't you smell the bacon?' Used to living in a country where the pig was reviled and never reached the table in any form, Nicolson coaxed a reluctant Violet from her bed with the formula that had never failed him yet in England. It did not fail him now.

After breakfast the couple set off on foot and Malcolm slowed his pace to suit hers. And everywhere they went Violet wanted to stop and look. It was if she had never been in London before, for she saw the city with new eyes—eyes that weren't blurred with resentful tears, eyes that weren't yearning for bluer oriental skies. For she knew it was only for a time, this separation from the East; meanwhile she would soak in what experience she could, and learn what was going on in the world of educated women.

It was strange that in this her husband should act as guide. 'First,' he said, 'you should read. Find out what women like you are writing.' And he took her to the London Library in Saint James's Square where, for the price of a modest subscription, she was free to browse among the shelves for as long as she wanted and borrow whatever she wished. 'You'll have no problem reaching—look, there's a set of steps,' he told her. 'I'll be back in an hour.'

Stack after stack of books confronted her, but where to begin and what to look for? Violet Nicolson shook her head in delighted disbelief and forced herself to think. When Malcolm returned exactly sixty minutes later she was in the reading room, the sunlight from a large window playing about her bowed head like a halo. She looked up. 'I'm in heaven,' she sighed happily. 'Or it's the nearest I can ever hope to be!'

Malcolm sat down beside her and removed a smudge of dust from the end of her nose. 'And what have you found?' he asked.

'It was difficult to find anything at first. I wanted books by women—modern women—about modern women. I asked the librarian and he didn't seem to know. So he gave me the catalogue and I found this.' Violet was clearly excited. 'It wasn't at all what I wanted, but I couldn't put it down.' She handed the book to her husband.

'*Hafiz*. Hardly modern—and, of course, a man.' He looked at the title page. 'Translated into English verse by Gertrude Bell,' he read out. He opened the volume at random, and his eyes quickly scanned a page:

I cease not from desire till my desire
Is satisfied; or let my mouth attain
My love's red mouth, or let my soul expire,
Sighed from those lips that sought her lips in vain.
Others may find another love as fair;
Upon her threshold I have laid my head,
The dust shall cover me, still lying there,
When from my body life and love have fled—

No wonder Violet was thrilled! Here were free renderings of Persian thought, translated into verse only the year before by another woman—a link with the translations she herself had done for her own interest, and for Miss Marian Doughty. He glanced at the publisher's name: William Heinemann. *Heinemann*? Now, where had he come across that name? He was about to ask Violet but the librarian was hovering, ready no doubt to point to the large notice enjoining *SILENCE* on all. 'Come on,' said Malcolm. 'It's time to go.'

Violet would have liked to borrow the book, but it would take time to fill in yet more forms, she supposed, and Malcolm was always in such a hurry. She sighed, unwillingly relinquished her treasure, and followed him out into the bright daylight, across the leafy square, past the statue of some mounted monarch or other (he wouldn't let her stop and look) and on towards the bustle of Piccadilly. Nicolson had noticed several booksellers while he was conducting his own particular business earlier, and in the second one they entered he found what he wanted and presented it to his wife.

'Your own copy of the Hafiz translations, darling, to read at your leisure.' He pressed it into her hands and her obvious delight transferred itself to him. They chose a host of other books and on the way home she fingered the brown paper parcels, thinking of the pleasure they would give her in the months to come, when all this was over and they were back in Mhow.

Soon Violet was lost in a world of her own: a world where women felt desire and expressed it without shame; where women yearned for adventure and sensation and their actions set them free. Malcolm was right—she was not alone and women were writing openly of these things. Did they really know, or did they simply dream? What a paradox it was that through something as old-fashioned as marriage she had found the equality and freedom that other women craved—none of them would believe her if she tried to explain.

Hours later she put her book aside and gazed down over her grandmother's garden. Flooded with late afternoon sunlight and brimming over with flowers, it reminded her of India, that land of life and death, despair and hope; a land inextricably linked to her lover. Whispering his name, Violet lay back against the cushions and closed her eyes.

When she opened them again, he was with her in the room, and the air was heavy with the scent of roses. He had raided the garden. 'Malcolm Nicolson, how did you dare?' she exclaimed in horror. 'Grandmother will have your head on a platter for this!'

'Not she,' he smiled back. 'She helped me cut them. Your grandmother and I understand one another perfectly.'

It was true; they were fellow conspirators in a plot to make her happy and Violet protested only half-heartedly. It was so bad for her to be spoilt, but how she enjoyed it! When Nicolson stooped and kissed her, and tucked a yellow rose in her hair, Violet caught his hand. 'What about you, darling? Have you had a good day?'

General Nicolson had forgotten the charms of the city and how, for someone on leave from India with time on his hands, London in the season could be a very pleasant place indeed. 'Yes, indeed,' he replied, as Violet made room for him beside her, 'I lunched with Alfred Sinclair at the Army and Navy Club. You remember—I introduced you on the boat.' Changing the subject, he handed her an envelope. 'This came for you earlier. I wonder who it's from.'

Violet did not recognise the handwriting either and tore it open impatiently.

'Oh, dear,' she said after a moment. 'It's from a Mrs Montague Crackanthorpe who is "at home", it appears, on Thursday afternoons from two-thirty to four. She wants to meet me—I can't think why! Malcolm Nicolson,' and Violet looked at her husband with intense suspicion, 'has this anything to do with you?'

'I've never met the woman,' he answered truthfully. 'Tomorrow's Thursday, so you'd better accept and see what it's all about.'

She pestered her grandmother. Yes, the name was familiar, the old lady said, and the address was certainly a most respectable one. Hadn't one of Annie Sophie's friends had a similar name? Perhaps it was his wife? And Caroline Cory added her encouragement to the general's.

'The Moghra flowers, so sweet, so sweet'

Outside Number 65, Rutland Gate, Knightsbridge, the rain beat down, laying the dust in the street and forming great puddles. Violet was alone with her hostess in the drawing room and, given the weather, was likely to remain her only caller. Blanche Alethea Crackanthorpe looked at the young woman seated opposite. So this was Vivian Cory's sister and the wife of Flora Steel's Indian general.

The rich golden-brown hair caught back at the nape of a slender neck emphasised a most determined jaw; the lips were full and sensual, the nose strong, the eyes lively and expressive. It was, in sum, the face of a woman to whom passion was no secret, a woman who, she imagined, was physically fulfilled. (Blanche, no stranger to the joys of the flesh herself, could recognise the signs.) She could also understand why Flora had been so put out at meeting Malcolm Nicolson's wife, and had come back from her visit so depressed.

'Do have another cup of tea, Mrs Nicolson.'

Violet scrutinised her hostess while she busied herself over the teacups. Mrs Crackanthorpe must be in her early fifties. Her profile was patrician with a hint of melancholy about the lips. She was slight, elegantly dressed in purple silk, and displayed all the self-confidence bestowed by unlimited wealth.

'We have a mutual friend, you know.' Blanche Crackanthorpe paused as she put the Dresden teapot back on its silver stand. 'Flora Steel suggested I meet you.'

'Did she, indeed?' murmured Violet, trying not to squirm under the sardonic gaze. *Damn you, Malcolm Nicolson*, she thought furiously, as her teeth met in a piece of walnut cake, *you arranged this*!

'She's an old friend of your husband's, I believe.'

'I believe so too,' Violet replied, as soon as her mouth was quite empty. 'We met in India. Once.' And the visit had been no great success. Nor was this one likely to be, if her hostess kept harping on about Flora Annie Steel.

'Have you children, Mrs Nicolson?'

She must surely know the answer to that if she'd been discussing her affairs with Mrs Steel. 'No.' Violet's voice was flat.

'And is that by accident or from choice?'

'I'm not sure I understand what you mean, Mrs Crackanthorpe.' Violet almost glared at her hostess. 'I lost two children during pregnancy—by accident, if you wish to put it that way. I have not chosen to be childless. In fact, I didn't know that choice could have anything to do with it.' She replaced her exquisite teacup none too gently in its saucer.

'Ah,' murmured Blanche, not at all put out, 'you are not as modern as I thought. So you know nothing of Malthusian principles, then, and the theory of population control?'

When Violet confessed her ignorance Mrs Crackanthorpe changed the subject. 'I met your sister Vivian several times,' she continued, and again the younger woman felt her hackles rise. 'She knew my late son. Poor Bertie—' and Blanche's gaze rested on the photograph of a wide-eyed child on a table by her side. 'He was so brilliant, such a fine writer. He drowned in the Seine, eighteen months ago. But I can feel him with me still—' A long elegant bejewelled hand caressed the elaborate frame while Violet shivered. She would, she decided, take her leave as soon as was politely possible.

'I knew them all, of course, the contributors to *The Yellow Book*—your sister included. And if I may say so without causing offence, my dear, she was quite the shallowest of a rather unusual set of young women.' Blanche sat back and waited for her words to take effect.

Goodness, how very outspoken! Violet was quite disarmed. Perhaps she need not be in too great a hurry to go after all. 'Why, you don't offend me in the slightest, Mrs Crackanthorpe,' she answered warmly. 'I thoroughly agree with you, in fact, and my knowledge of my sister must go far deeper than yours.'

The two women looked at one another in perfect sympathy.

'And do you write, too?' asked Blanche.

Violet hesitated. 'Yes,' she admitted, 'yes, I do. I write poetry inspired by my life in India.' Mrs Crackanthorpe was now the only person, other than Malcolm and Isabel, and, of course Marian Doughty, who knew, and she wondered whether she hadn't made a mistake in speaking. In fact her words seemed hardly to register at all.

'India is such a terribly sensual country, I always think,' said Violet's hostess, ignoring what she had just been told. 'Not that I've been there myself, of course, but I imagine that the climate heightens the senses most wonderfully—would you agree?'

Whatever did she mean? 'I've lived there all my adult life—I really couldn't say, Mrs Crackanthorpe.'

'Ah. People who visit India tell me that the nights are delicious, that the perfume hangs heavy on the air, that it makes one feel so very *romantic*. Are they right, do you think?' The intense dark eyes did not leave the younger woman's face for a moment as she waited for an answer.

Violet laughed and decided to be equally frank in her turn. She probably wouldn't be invited back (which she was beginning to think would be rather a pity) but it was time to call a spade a spade.

'Are you asking me whether the English indulge in sexual relations more frequently there than they do in a colder climate?' Blue eyes held brown quite steadily. 'I doubt it, Mrs Crackanthorpe! It's usually far too hot, for one thing; for another, people are often ill. And frequently, of course—the English being no more monogamous in India than they are elsewhere—the partner of one's choice might not be immediately available.' Violet paused. She certainly had Mrs Crackanthorpe's full attention now, but if her hostess thought she was going to discuss anything other than generalities, she was mistaken. 'I suppose,' she continued, 'the scent of *moghra*—that's a most delicious type of jasmine, Mrs Crackanthorpe—coming to you on the evening breeze when the day's work is done can bring a sense of euphoria with it, but then so can a whisky and soda! And in ninety-nine cases out of one hundred, euphoria dissipates at the bedroom door—or so I should imagine. For the reasons I stated earlier.'

There, that had probably done it! Violet felt it was time to leave.

'How refreshing you are, Mrs Nicolson! Women are usually so very reluctant to talk about sex.'

'It's a very private matter, don't you think? I certainly do,' and Violet stood up.

From a first floor window Blanche Crackanthorpe watched her visitor cross the street. The rain had stopped and she must have decided to walk part of the way. What an interesting creature! Suddenly Blanche wanted to know whether the Nicolsons were of the ninety and nine sad cases, or did they perhaps constitute the one hundredth? Flora Steel had sniffed while referring to her old friend's marriage, but had failed to make that clear.

'How did you get on in Knightsbridge? You did go, didn't you?' Violet had given Malcolm a cheery wave from the corner, but there was no knowing where she had gone after that.

'Oh, I went all right.' Suddenly, in her eagerness to tell him of her visit, Violet decided to ignore the part her husband must have played. 'Malcolm,' she exclaimed, 'Mrs Crackanthorpe thinks of nothing but sex!'

'Then I imagine you and she dealt extremely well together!'

'Sometimes, Malcolm Nicolson,' Violet commented, 'you're a perfect pig!' and threw a cushion at him. Grinning, he caught it before it hit a particularly ugly piece of ruby glass.

'A contradiction in terms, surely?' he said. 'Now, darling,' and he sat down and pulled her onto his lap, 'tell me about sex. And Mrs Crackanthorpe, of course.'

Violet related her afternoon, ending by saying, 'I don't think she'll invite me back, do you?'

'I'm sure she will, and she'll probably want to take a look at me, as well.'

Malcolm Nicolson was right. The very next day an invitation arrived for dinner at Rutland Gate the following week and the Nicolsons accepted.

'Bacon agrees with you.' Malcolm turned Violet towards the mirror. 'You're putting on weight in the most delicious places—look.'

'Whatever do you mean?' She stared at her reflection critically. She could see no difference—but then she didn't want to.

'If you continue to eat six rashers at breakfast you'll soon be as plump as your grandmother. But never as good-natured—' for his wife was scowling as he laced her into the corset she detested and hardly ever wore. The cream silk dress she was so fond of, altered by her grandmother's dressmaker to bring it a little more up to date, was pulled over her head and fastened. Violet had categorically refused the expense of a new gown, and now she studied her reflection. So did her husband.

Most of the skirt's fullness was gone, and her bosom swelled appealingly from the low-cut décolletage; the much-maligned corset made her waist dramatically small and her narrow hips seem wider. When she walked about the room the gown swayed below her knees in a most alluring way—as did her hips above. Watching her, Nicolson's eyes narrowed at the thought of the evening ahead. Men had been attracted to his wife before, but never had she been dressed like this. And here he was about to parade her in public and expose her to all kinds of temptation, to all kinds of advances from men more sophisticated than he. Suddenly he felt a fool.

'What is it? Darling, what's wrong? If you're feeling unwell again, then tell me.' Malcolm had had a few unpleasant twinges the day before and Violet was still alarmed. The dinner engagement at the Crackanthorpes' was, she pointed out, quite unimportant.

'No, no,' he was quick to assure her, 'I'm perfectly all right. The only problem we have is you—do you think you can manage?'

'I'll try, but you may have to carry me!'

It was a good thing his wife was naturally athletic, thought the general as he helped her into the cab, watching as she seized the handles firmly and hauled herself aboard. That she had to hitch up her skirts to do so was noted by an appreciative cabby, but conscious of her companion's fierce glare the man's eyes did not linger, nor, when they reached the stuccoed terraces of Rutland Gate, did he dare question the only moderate size of the tip.

'Come on, then.' Violet laughed up into her husband's serious face as they approached the handsome portico of Number 65. 'Let's find out whether it's to be a dinner party or an orgy—with a bit of luck it will be both!'

'Of curious, twisted thoughts that men call "mad"'

It was a dinner, a most respectable dinner, a dinner served on delicate porcelain supplemented by silver, crystal, and elaborate epergnes—a dinner of which Mrs Nicolson could eat only a little since her corset was so tight. So she drank instead, not too much, just enough to give her courage to get through the evening, for at the sight of such sophistication she suddenly felt gauche and provincial.

Montague Crackanthorpe kept an excellent cellar, her husband informed her afterwards and she believed him, but all she cared at the time was that the wine she was drinking gave her a comfortable glow in her stomach, replacing the sick feeling that was there before.

Seated on Crackanthorpe's right, she listened to her host while her eyes rested on Malcolm. He was at the far end of the table next to his hostess who, clearly charmed, was making every effort to entertain him. Violet refused a delicious-looking pudding and took another sip from her glass.

She turned back to Crackanthorpe who was now talking to the company at large. With his sleek black hair and marble brow, there was a sinister air about him. Full red lips provided the only colour in a cold clean-shaven countenance. She forced herself to concentrate.

'We're thinking of calling it the Eugenics Society,' he was informing his other neighbour, '"eugenic" meaning "well-born", of course.'

Of course … Violet's mind once more began to wander.

'Our aim would be to promote all that is superior in mankind, ensuring that the progeny of superior strains outnumbers that of the inferior.'

Violet blinked and listened more carefully to the slightly pedantic voice.

'We believe that the quality of modern society will be improved only by concentrating on its more intelligent members.'

A murmur of approval spread around the table.

'We believe that all those below average intelligence should be eliminated—' there were further sounds of approbation '—and that only by doing this can a race be kept physically and mentally healthy. The right to breed must therefore be strictly controlled.'

'And who will do the controlling, Mr Crackanthorpe?' Violet spoke into a sudden silence. 'You? Me? No,' she corrected herself quickly, 'not me, of course—I'm only a woman and know nothing of these things. But who will make the decisions? The poor have more children than the rich, so will the rich have the right to decide how many children the poor should have?'

'Exactly, Mrs Nicolson, you understand our position perfectly.' Montague

Crackanthorpe beamed his approval and Violet felt quite ill.

Malcolm looked down the table at his wife. The deep little voice had caught his attention and he had heard everything she said. He listened, as did everyone else, as she continued: 'And if a couple were below average height, then they would be discouraged from having children too—all for the good of the race?'

'Quite so, my dear lady.'

'Even though their children could just as well be tall?'

'That is a chance we would not care to take.'

'And if a couple were below average intelligence, the same would apply?'

Crackanthorpe nodded.

'Even though they might possibly produce a genius?'

'Come, come, my dear lady, that is hardly likely.' With that, the barrister gave a scornful laugh.

Enjoying Crackanthorpe's cellar if not his views, General Nicolson settled back to listen. Crackanthorpe's wife noted the proud smile that played about his lips as he twirled the stem of his wineglass in long fingers and listened. Blanche listened too: she had heard Montague propound his ideas often enough before, of course, but this was the first time she had ever heard them challenged by a woman.

'Would you then, Mr Crackanthorpe, control the numbers of the lower classes, so that there were enough of them to serve the needs of the higher—enough and no more? Enough *farm labourers*, for example, enough *street cleaners*, enough *fishermen*, and so forth. Enough *carpenters*, shall we say? No one to deviate from his parents' calling, and the undesirables to be weeded out before birth— Is that right?'

'In Utopia, my dear young lady, yes,' said her host. 'But we are far from being there—yet.'

Violet began to dislike the man intensely. He was patronising her—for her sex, and for her comparative youth. And he was so sure he was right. She on the other hand knew that he was wrong. This form of social control was evil—far worse than anything that existed here or in India. There was no pretence of religious belief in what he had been saying—it was a cold and calculated form of evil such as she had never dreamt existed. How could she possibly keep silent?

It was the *yet* that did it, Violet told Malcolm afterwards, and the slow smile that accompanied the word.

'I'm afraid I can't agree with anything you say, Mr Crackanthorpe.' Violet's cheeks were flushed and her bosom heaving with indignation as she cast caution completely to the winds. 'It goes against everything I've been brought up to believe in: equality, the right to life, natural justice—!' She stopped and defiantly drained her glass.

At her end of the table Blanche Crackanthorpe hid a smile; for once her husband was at a loss for words and she found the situation piquant in the extreme. But enough was enough. 'Ladies,' and her magisterial gaze swept the table, 'ladies, shall we leave the gentlemen to their port?'

Silently addressing one particular *Jewish* carpenter whom she denied existed—and who probably wasn't listening if he did—Violet Nicolson got to her feet. Please let me make a dignified exit in this ridiculous dress, she prayed, and she moved towards the door.

Silence fell. The outspoken young woman was handsome and she was intelligent; as they watched her leave—a short seductive figure in a gown that fitted her in places like a glove—more than one gentleman would gladly have put Crackanthorpe's theories of procreation to the test. Nicolson was aware of the effect she was having. By God, he thought furiously, if any man here makes any kind of a jest about her, I'll kill him with my own bare hands!

The port circulated. Crackanthorpe stood up and raised his glass. 'Gentlemen, the Queen.' Perhaps the thought of the stout and doubtless flatulent Queen-Empress kept the company from comment on her spirited young subject; perhaps it was the presence of the fierce-looking servant of the Crown who happened to be the young lady's husband. For whatever reason, the talk moved on to less controversial matters, and General Nicolson forced himself to relax.

'Well done, Violet—I may call you Violet, I hope? And you must call me Blanche. My husband can be so very *pompous* at times.' Mrs Crackanthorpe laughed, and, with the exception of Violet Nicolson, the women joined in. Pompous he might well be, dangerous he certainly was. Violet felt angry and disgusted. She desperately wanted Malcolm to come and take her home.

She looked towards the door seconds only before it opened silently to admit Malcolm and the others. It was as if she knew, thought the watching Blanche, as if she sensed his approach. Their eyes sought each other out immediately. He came to her side and kissed her hand, and shortly afterwards the Nicolsons took their leave. They were, decided Mrs Crackanthorpe, looking after them, that elusive one couple in a hundred.

Malcolm was silent on the way home, and silent still when they reached Cambridge Street. Mrs Cory had retired and Violet would have dearly liked to follow her example—she felt most uncomfortable and wanted to remove her stays—but she went into the drawing room, determined to find out what was wrong with her husband. Malcolm followed. 'What is it, darling?' she asked. 'Something's wrong. *Is* it that pain again?'

He looked at her and gave a short laugh. 'No, that's gone. For good, I hope.'

'Then I've embarrassed you by speaking as I did. I'm sorry.'

'No, sweetheart, you didn't embarrass me in the least! But I'm afraid I almost embarrassed you.'

'Really? How very intriguing—' When had that ever happened? 'Tell me how,' she urged.

'I will,' he said, 'but not here,' and he led her to the stairs. 'You looked quite lovely tonight,' he told her when they reached their room. 'And I was proud of everything you said. Here, let me help you.' He began to unfasten her dress. It was easier somehow to explain when she wasn't looking at him. 'But every man who was listening desired you—I could see it in their faces—and I'm afraid it made me very angry.' He fell silent.

The gown slipped to the ground with what seemed a deafening rustle. Violet turned to face him, and at the sight of her half-naked body Nicolson resumed his confession. 'There wasn't a man there who wasn't imagining you as you are now,' he told her, tracing the outline of one smooth enticing breast with a finger.

'But you are here, Malcolm, and they are not,' Violet's eyes were unusually grave.

'I felt like a savage; I wanted to kill them for their thoughts.'

'It must have surprised them to discover a woman with a mind as well as a body, don't you think?' and Violet laughed her sweet musical laugh before her face became serious again. 'Look, darling,' she put a hand on his arm and felt how tense he was, 'the conversation took an unfortunate turn, and that's all there is to it. You shouldn't mind.'

She turned her back again. 'Will you please unlace me?' she asked. 'I can hardly breathe.'

As he did so Nicolson gasped at the marks left on her flesh.

'You see,' she remarked evenly, as she slipped her nightgown over her head, 'being an object of lust is painful for me, too. Perhaps you should remember that next time— Or are you planning to keep me in purdah from now on?'

'You think I'm being ridiculous, don't you?'

'A little.' A younger Violet might have seized the opportunity for yet another confrontation on the subject of female dress—after all, he had chosen the gown in question and sanctioned its later modification—but tonight she merely gave a wise little shake of her head and looked at her husband earnestly.

'Malcolm,' she said, 'all these men will ever do is look at me—and you know that very well. I noticed nothing because the only man in the world I care about is you. I need your love, and I need your good opinion. And above all I need your trust. Do I have it?' The look she gave him was tender and amused—and confident.

'Of course you do!'

'Good. Now let me tell you a secret: I know exactly how you felt.' She sensed his surprise. 'How do I know? Because I feel the same way when you talk with another woman, as you did tonight, a woman who is more poised than I, more controlled, more dignified. When I see women look at you with a smile in their eyes, an invitation even, then I know how you felt this evening. Tall, elegant women dancing with you fill me with a particular envy and rage, especially if they are dark— Shall I go on?'

There was no need. They finished undressing, put out the light and got into bed. Violet was soon asleep but Nicolson's thoughts kept him awake until the early hours of the morning.

'What have you learned?'

In the days that followed their evening in Knightsbridge General Nicolson made it his business to find out more about his hosts. That Montague Crackanthorpe was a brilliant barrister, it appeared was common knowledge. The man was also an Oxford Fellow and counsel to the university court. To some, the great wealth he had inherited from a second cousin (at the small cost of changing his name from Cookson) made him worth cultivating. The Crackanthorpes' marriage was generally agreed to be both a social and a personal success. So it was a great pity that Violet's instant dislike of the husband was matched by Malcolm's wariness of the wife. There were no more invitations to dinner, but Violet continued to visit Blanche Crackanthorpe. At Rutland Gate she met a great variety of women, women who spoke their minds and who were listened to, and argued with, all with the greatest of good humour. Women who were devoted wives and mothers, other women who weren't; single women who earned their own living and demanded the right to vote … Violet's head filled with the new ideas put there by her hostess and her hostess's cronies: Suffrage, Socialism, Fabianism, Theosophy—the words all tripped lightly from her tongue. As long as there was a basis of logic Violet Nicolson gave each new theory her full attention, if not necessarily her allegiance. It probably wasn't the hot bed of revolution it sounded, reflected her husband, quelling his initial feelings of alarm, and Violet was safer there than wandering around London on her own.

She propounded the latest theories, not only to him but to her grandmother and Colonel Sinclair too, and they all listened to her obediently while, bright-eyed and excited, she talked late into the night. It was new and yet it wasn't new, this credo she was shaping. This ideal world she was forming was no less Utopian than Montague Crackanthorpe's, but it was full of compassion and love and no little common sense. Violet sifted through the mass of ideology, and what remained were the beliefs she had always held, now no longer blurred and indistinct but gleaming like grains of gold in the bottom of a prospector's cradle. Ideas that were not unique but shared with others, and it was this knowledge that she was not alone that restored her faith in herself and the human race.

For that Nicolson knew he should thank Mrs Crackanthorpe, but he still could not warm to the woman. For one thing she had a disturbing interest in spiritualism; thank goodness Violet had laughed that off, otherwise he would have felt obliged to intervene. His wife's attendances at meetings of the Theosophical Society alarmed him less. The English felt a keen interest in the Orient, he knew, and since Violet believed it could only help India's cause she followed Blanche into dreary half-filled halls, more fascinated by the people than by the message they had come to hear. The message of reincarnation she had heard before. And rejected.

As she moved around the city, Violet Nicolson gave her full attention to the world of modern London. There were so many women in the streets, not only out shopping (although there were enough of those, goodness knows) but going to work in offices and shops, earning their own living and in no way dependent on the male. It fascinated Violet to see them. She met some of them at Theosophical meetings with Blanche; the idea of equal treatment for the masses may have drawn them there in the first place, but Eastern mysticism made them return. India was so full of glamour and appeal, they said, how fortunate she was to live there! She did not disabuse them with tales of filth and disease, but looked at them a little enviously herself. For to Violet Nicolson—the kept woman—their lives were far more glamorous than hers. She shrugged off the beginnings of discontent for, after all, no one else had what she possessed.

Her husband watched her comings and goings with interest, and as she recounted her days to him he marvelled at her energy. She kept what she called her 'ridiculous' clothes for formal occasions, and wore her 'comfortable' garments when out and about on her own. 'I'm an individual,' she insisted, 'I don't need to look like everyone else.'

There was no danger of that, thought Malcolm Nicolson. Unlike most women of her class, she scorned frills and flounces; her skirts were unfashionably full and enabled her to walk everywhere possible. Soon she knew London far better than he, and there seemed to be no bookshop or library that evaded her notice. She still yearned for a bicycle but it was no use: her husband refused to be swayed. There were things called *automobiles* in London now, he told her, dangerous horseless machines with four wheels that would mow her down without stopping; he had seen them going at frightening speeds. No, Violet, he said for the umpteenth time, a bicycle was out of the question. It was a pity, but there it was. So when she visited Mrs Crackanthorpe she took the tramway.

Forthright in her opinions though she was, the barrister's wife did not share her husband's controversial views or Violet would not have gone back. Blanche entertained many well-known writers and others starting out on the path to fame, but Violet Nicolson met very few of them. Great novelists like Thomas Hardy and Henry James were mentioned but remained unseen. That was another pity. She had admitted to writing poetry but she had obviously not been taken seriously. It was hardly surprising, she supposed—she wasn't sure herself how seriously she *should* be taken.

Blanche Crackanthorpe wrote. Magazine articles, mostly, and when Violet began to read one of them she realised why her friend had handed it over with such a sardonic smirk. *Sex in Modern Literature* was a forceful analysis of recent trends, and it soon became apparent that her own sister was one of the writers under attack. Mrs Nicolson made herself comfortable among her grandmother's cushions, and continued. *Theodora* was mentioned by name and her sister's technique of writing as a man seen as revolting, especially when identifying herself with him *at one of his baser moments* …

Oh dear, thought Violet, does Blanche think I'm like Annie Sophie? Is that why she doesn't want to see my work?

'Of course it isn't,' Malcolm assured her. 'She's probably forgotten what you said. And how could she possibly take exception to anything you've written? She talks of the *Real* and the *Ideal* being of equal importance—look, here,' and he pointed to the place—'one complements the other; the body needs a soul. Annie Sophie seems to have forgotten that, but you most certainly haven't.'

'Cold-blooded vice and careful sin'

When Alfred Sinclair went north to visit relations Malcolm Nicolson did not miss him for long—the Army and Navy Club was always full and he was never short of company. One morning a tall thin clean-shaven man in his mid-forties approached him. There was a military air about him, although he was wearing civilian clothes.

'May I join you, General Nicolson?'

Malcolm looked up at the sound of the cultured voice. 'Of course,' he said affably, putting his newspaper aside. 'I don't believe we've met.'

'John Lister Kaye,' said the stranger, holding out his hand. 'Delighted to meet you. May I get you a drink?'

'Thank you, but no, it's a little early for me.'

Lister Kaye settled himself in an armchair opposite and the two men were soon in easy conversation. He often reappeared after that and one day he invited the general to lunch at the Guards' Club. 'It's just down the road from here. Perhaps you know it, General?' It was an unnecessary question; he had seen him there, and had enquired as to his identity. General Nicolson, he learned, occupied one of the top posts in the Indian Army.

In cultivating him, it was not the soldier's fellowship Lister Kaye was seeking—he had far too many casual acquaintances as it was. Over an excellent meal of good solid English fare, Lister Kaye effortlessly turned the conversation to the East. 'China, General,' said the man Nicolson now knew to be a baronet, 'have you ever been there?'

No, Malcolm admitted, he had been no further east than India. Sir John had suspected as much. 'A fascinating country, I'm told,' he said. 'But our time there is running out. China is the country of the future.'

'Is that so?' murmured Malcolm. 'I believe the British will remain in India for a few years yet—for the rest of my active service, anyway.'

He smiled and the conversation drifted on. Sir John had been in the Royal Horse Guards and told tales of his time with the regiment—he did not say how brief a time that had been—and with Malcolm capping them with stories of his own, there was a great feeling of *bonhomie* in the air when the two of them parted.

The next day an invitation came for Violet: Lady Lister Kaye requested the pleasure of Mrs Nicolson's company for afternoon tea at 17 Bolton Street, Mayfair. 'It's for tomorrow! Oh Lord, Malcolm, do you think I should go?'

'Yes, of course you should. It will do you good to meet a real lady!'

Violet's eyes became mere slits. 'And what do you mean by that, pray?' she enquired.

'Nothing,' he grinned. 'Send a note and say you would be delighted.' He would escort her there himself, he said, on his way to meet Sir John, and he would collect her later. There really was no hope of escape, so Violet reluctantly agreed.

The next afternoon she was shown into a large room furnished with elegant eighteenth-century pieces. One wall was devoted to Wedgwood plaques, and water-colours, another was completely covered by a Flemish wall-hanging of decidedly overweight nudes. There were exquisite vases on the mantelpiece and tables, and precarious-looking *jardinières* spilling over with ferns. Her feet sank into the moss-like carpet as she moved over to the window. It was all, thought Violet Nicolson, just a trifle *too* grand.

Almost immediately a door opened at the far side of the room and a woman came in. Several inches taller than Violet, and dark-complexioned, her features were heavy, sullen even, but when she smiled, as she did now, her face was transformed. She came forward, her hands extended in welcome. 'I'm so pleased to meet you, Mrs Nicolson,' she said in a noticeably American accent. 'Johnny talks about your husband so often.' And had insisted she get to know the general's wife. Unwillingly, Natica Lister Kaye was now complying with his request—as she always did. The two women who shook hands were in striking contrast, one so dark and one so fair. And both were unsure of what to say.

'Are you enjoying London, Mrs Nicolson?'

She was.

'You've been here before, I expect?'

Yes, her father's mother lived here, and she and her sisters had been educated in Richmond. Had Lady Lister Kaye been in England long?

'For seventeen years, Mrs Nicolson, but I go home to the States quite often.' As often as possible in fact, and her husband couldn't stop her as she had money of her own.

Violet said she had an uncle in America. Did Lady Lister Kaye know Colorado?

Her hostess laughed. Oh, no, she said. She was from Louisiana, and her family from the island of Cuba.

So that accounted for the woman's sultry looks. How interesting, Violet said politely. She preferred a warmer climate herself.

Before the stilted conversation ground completely to a halt, an animated exchange came from the hallway. Seconds later the door was flung open, to admit a blonde tornado followed closely by an outraged butler.

'Stevens, you silly old thing,' the newcomer tossed over her shoulder, 'there's absolutely no need to announce me. My sister knows perfectly well who I am!'

But I don't, thought Violet. Who on earth was this expensively dressed woman who stalked over to inspect her with bright brown eyes. 'So who are you?' the stranger asked in an attractive drawl. 'I'm the Duchess of Manchester—the *dowager* Duchess, thank God—but you can call me Consuelo.'

'I'm Mrs Malcolm Nicolson and my husband, I'm happy to say, is very much alive.' Mrs Nicolson gave the dowager an engaging grin before adding, 'Please call me Violet.'

'Well, Natica,' pronounced the duchess, turning to her sister, 'I must say I like your guest's style. Where did the two of you meet?'

'Johnny met General Nicolson and thought I might like to meet—Violet,' replied Natica Lister Kaye.

'I see— Well, Violet, it's just fine to meet you as well!' The widow smiled and held out her hand. The younger woman shook it firmly and Consuelo Mandeville, *née* Yznaga del Valle, widow of George Victor Drogo, the late (and evidently unlamented) eighth Duke of Manchester, sat down beside her on the chesterfield. The hitherto stilted conversation then took a livelier turn.

When the general and Lister Kaye joined the trio some two hours later, the tea cups had long been replaced by sherry glasses, and formality had been tossed out of the window. It was odd, thought Violet, in the brief moment between the men's entrance and her introduction to the baronet, how the talking suddenly died away.

Noting her flushed face, Nicolson greeted his wife and then John Lister Kaye took her by the hand.

'Mrs Nicolson,' he said, and he gave a slight bow, 'I am delighted to meet you. Your husband has been singing your praises.'

Then the man was a liar, came Violet's immediate response. Malcolm would never do that to a stranger—and rarely to anyone else. 'And all of it exaggeration, I'm sure,' she replied smoothly.

'May we join you, my dear?' Lister Kaye turned to his wife.

'Of course,' murmured that lady, who seemed to have shrunk a little. Intrigued, Violet shot a glance at the dowager duchess. Consuelo Manchester was watching her brother-in-law between narrowed lids. The touch of malevolence in her expression was hardly noticeable, perhaps, but to Violet the contrast seemed marked—for the lively forty-year-old had been bubbling over with mirth and high spirits only seconds before.

Consuelo soon recovered her good humour. Violet would have listened in fascinated dismay to the widow's brash interrogation of her husband, but Lister Kaye's voice producing the usual social inanities forced her to give the baronet most of her attention. Some might call the man handsome, she imagined, but for her his features held something of the vulpine—they were predatory, and the mouth was cruel. The smile playing on the thin lips at present failed utterly to reach his eyes, eyes of a murky grey like the waters of a sunless highland tarn. Violet repressed a shiver, and she found herself wondering why Malcolm spent so much time in his company. Perhaps Sir John had more charm and warmth when in the confines of his club; was he perhaps what was known as a *man's man*?

It amused Johnny Kaye to know he was being assessed. The general's wife was not what he had expected; she was considerably younger than Nicolson, for one thing, and she was very much shorter. He preferred tall brunettes himself, women with a touch of hauteur. Still, he reminded himself with a secret smile, all cats were grey in the dark. This little thing wore her heart on her sleeve, you could tell that from the way those great blue eyes looked at her husband, and it might, he reflected idly, be amusing to seduce her. At some later date, of course, for it certainly would not do to prejudice his dealings with General Nicolson just at present.

'I think perhaps we should leave, Violet.' Malcolm's patience with his transatlantic inquisitor was wearing thin. As they left Bolton Street behind them Violet too gave a sigh of relief. There was a strange atmosphere in that house ... She hadn't realised it before, but the moment the baronet appeared the temperature had seemed to drop several degrees. Yes, it was good to get away.

Mrs Crackanthorpe laughed when she was told of the encounter. 'Violet, my dear, you must remember that the dowager Duchess of Manchester is an American and says exactly what she feels.'

'But Blanche, she sounded glad the duke was dead!'

'And that shocks you, does it, my dear? Is it the feeling itself, or its frank expression?'

'Both.'

'An Englishwoman perhaps wouldn't be so unguarded in front of a complete stranger, but if she had been married to that brute, who knows? Consuelo Manchester has had the most terrible life—' and Blanche treated her guest to some of the details.

When the recital was over Violet expressed her sympathy with the woman she had earlier condemned, and Blanche Crackanthorpe gave another laugh. 'She must have known what she was up against. Any unmarried English peer who goes to America, goes there for a wife, a wealthy wife. And Americans are dazzled by a title—we all know that! She made a bargain, although better or worse than her sister's, who can say? Mandeville, as he then was, got some much-needed cash and *she* got a coronet. That it was such a very poor bargain, all the same, was her misfortune. How could she have known he was quite as bad as he was?'

Violet's eyes opened wide as her friend explained.

'Drink, drugs, music hall actresses, debts, bankruptcy, fraud— But she would probably say that it all worked out well in the end. After all, she's a duke's widow with plenty of life in her yet.'

That, agreed Violet, was certainly true.

'My dear girl, if you think everyone marries for love then you are naive in the extreme. I did and so did you, but we are very much the exceptions. Most women,' Blanche Crackanthorpe asserted, 'marry for security, status, children, or to escape being called old maids. Love may be in there somewhere too, if they're lucky. These days, you know, some couples set up house *without* the benefit of clergy. And very healthy it is, in my opinion—and proof of a far greater commitment to one's chosen partner.'

Violet's jaw dropped. It wouldn't happen in India, she said. Of course it wouldn't, Mrs Crackanthorpe agreed. Anglo-Indian society would never condone such behaviour. Anglo-Indian society exemplified British hypocrisy at its most rampant, for *it did* condone adultery—provided it was discreet, of course. Adultery was more open here in England, she informed her listener. If the Nicolsons were going to be mixing with the upper classes, then Violet had better be warned. 'Will you still be here at the end of the season, do you think?' she enquired.

'Which season do you mean, Blanche?'

Mrs Crackanthorpe made no attempt to hide her amusement. How very unworldly her young friend was proving to be. 'Will you be here in August when the *London* season is over? Everyone leaves and goes off to the country—I mean the aristocracy, of course. Because if you are, and if your husband is still friendly with Sir John, then no doubt you will be invited to join the Lister Kayes at their country estate.'

Violet thought that might be nice; London was already getting very dusty and it was only the end of June.

'I don't know about *nice*, my dear; it would certainly open your eyes.' Eyes she had noticed opening wider and wider in the course of the afternoon. '*Musical beds*,' pronounced Blanche Crackanthorpe with relish. 'A favourite pastime of the British aristocracy, and one for which you should go prepared. It's considered acceptable behaviour, you see, come nightfall, for a husband to go in one direction and a wife in another—provided one doesn't lose one's way in the dark.' Sometimes there were nasty surprises, she added, with her throaty chuckle.

When Mrs Nicolson returned to Cambridge Street her head was spinning. Suddenly life in Mhow seemed very uncomplicated and almost sane. She tried to explain why she would prefer not to meet the Lister Kayes again but Malcolm listened to her impatiently. Sir John was different, he assured her. His approach to life was measured and serious; he had a vast experience of business. In fact, said General Nicolson, he was most impressed with everything about his new acquaintance.

'Scent of fur and colour of blood'

So the Nicolsons saw more of the Lister Kayes, not less, and were gradually drawn into society in their wake. There were musical evenings, for example, especially at the de Greys', when Earl de Grey drifted through the soirées organised by his wife with a slightly vacuous expression. Reputedly the best shot in the country, his lordship was a man of the outdoors and he found it difficult simply to sit down and concentrate—like many of those present. Sir John, whose love of music appeared genuine, and the tall stately Lady de Grey were different. They always sat together, and it was only after she had attended several such occasions that Violet noticed the baronet's supple fingers slowly stroking the inside of his companion's arm, and the feline smile on the countess's painted lips. Gladys de Grey, she concluded, was every bit as interested in sport as her husband, but the noble lady preferred to stalk her prey through the jungle of society salons.

Violet's dislike of the baronet, which hitherto she had told herself was irrational and unworthy, deepened with the realisation, and she suddenly understood why Natica Lister Kaye always looked so sad. But how was she to explain it to

Malcolm? He said sternly that what she thought she might have seen was none of their business, and that a man's private life was just that—private. When she pointed out that a man who cheated on his wife was just as likely to cheat on a business partner Malcolm was unimpressed. What did she know of such things, he asked. She countered by saying that she believed she knew quite as much as him, but that only made him angry.

The general blamed Mrs Crackanthorpe for Violet's tedious attitude. She had been listening to tittle-tattle relayed to her by a woman with far too much time on her hands, and she was imagining things as a result. All in all, sighed General Nicolson after their heated exchange, he wished his wife would go to Knightsbridge less often.

As a certain coolness developed between the couple, Violet's dislike of Lister Kaye increased. Malcolm spent longer at the club, evenings as well as days, and it was obvious to his wife that he was becoming more deeply involved in the baronet's schemes. What they were she did not know. It saddened her that Malcolm chose to tell her so little and she refused to ask—for she had been rebuffed enough already.

When Colonel Sinclair returned from Yorkshire at the beginning of July and called during one of Malcolm's frequent absences, he was welcomed like an old friend. Soon Violet found herself confiding her misgivings. Sinclair told her the little he knew of Sir John Lister Kaye. The baronet lived near Wakefield, he believed, and had a large estate and an interest in coalmines.

'Malcolm seems so taken with him, I don't know what to do. They talk a lot about China—or they used to—he doesn't discuss things like that any more. In fact, Alfred,' Violet added with a pathetic little smile, 'these days we don't talk very much at all.'

Sinclair patted her hand; he could see she was on the verge of tears. 'Is Kaye the only man Nick has met since I've been away?' he asked.

'No, Sir John has introduced him to several others, either at the Guards' Club or the Carlton. He's a member of both.' Sinclair nodded. Both clubs were a little beyond his means. 'Alfred,' she asked, 'what do you know about the Earl of Wharncliffe?'

'Wharncliffe? Why, he's one of the richest landowners in England, I should imagine. A lot of his money comes from coal, I believe—and he was chairman of the Great Central Railway for a time. Violet,' and the colonel's voice was reassuring, 'if the Earl of Wharncliffe is in on any of Kaye's schemes there shouldn't be anything to worry about. Is he?'

'I really don't know. But we are dining at Wharncliffe House tomorrow,' here a new note of complaint entered the young woman's voice, 'and Malcolm has insisted I buy a new dress.'

Her companion laughed. Why indeed go to unnecessary expense to impress some stranger she didn't give tuppence for? Violet Nicolson considered that people should be judged by merit alone, and it was interesting, thought Alfred Sinclair, that Nick—on this occasion, at least—did not share her views. 'You mustn't worry,' he told her. 'I've known your husband for much longer than you have, my dear, and I've never seen him make a fool of himself.'

There was a first time for everything, thought Violet glumly, and immediately felt extremely disloyal.

But Malcolm Nicolson was not about to make a fool of himself—he was far too cautious for that. His savings were important to him and the idea of adding to them was attractive. What Sir John said about China made sense. Now that the war with Japan was over, China's rulers were beginning to appreciate the importance of such things as mines and railways—as the British had in India after the Mutiny—and Britain had a vital part to play. 'Believe me, Nicolson, I know,' said the baronet. 'Trust me.'

The general wanted to, but despite his confident statements to his wife, he too was beginning to have his doubts. Malcolm Nicolson had certainly noticed Lister Kaye's musical companion, and the magnificently proportioned Countess de Grey was an outstandingly beautiful woman. Stunningly dark with glowing black eyes under heavy brows, the countess was tall and graceful. Her cat-like walk exuded sensuality. She was, mused General Nicolson, just the sort of woman that his wife envied in her weaker moments, and after Violet's revelations he watched her ladyship more closely. Within a very short time he came to the same conclusion as his wife: Lady de Grey and the baronet were lovers. And Lady Lister Kaye was fully aware of the fact. *Could* you trust a man who so blatantly cheated on his wife?

He was sorry he had quarrelled with Violet. The new dress had been meant as a peace offering, but all it led to was a renewal of hostilities.

'I don't want to go,' she declared vehemently. 'I'm sick of Mayfair, I'm sick of Bolton Street, and I'm sure Wharncliffe House will be every bit as frightful! I just want to be myself, Malcolm—that's why I'm here, or don't you remember?'

She was certainly being herself now, he thought; her fists were clenched and wilfulness was written all over her angry face.

'You might enjoy it,' he suggested. 'Wharncliffe's wife is a most interesting woman, and a great patron of the arts. They both are.'

'Oh? I thought we were going to talk about coal. And possibly China.'

'Violet, please be reasonable.'

'I am being reasonable—very reasonable. I'll go—' *Thank goodness for that*—'but I don't need anything new!'

In the end the general's cold civility wore her down, so that when she could bear no more she agreed to go back to her grandmother's dressmaker in the Haymarket. For her gown Malcolm chose a heavy black silk.

'I've never worn black in my life!' A few embers of rebellion were still smouldering but they were swiftly stamped out.

'It will suit you.' And it did.

Malcolm helped her dress for the evening in silence. She stood in front of the mirror and studied her reflection approvingly: she appeared taller and very elegant. Nicolson studied her, too. Her skin seemed even whiter against the black silk, and suddenly he remembered the first time he had seen her shoulders bare like this.

'Darling, I'm so sorry—' It had been weeks since his voice had sounded so tender. He turned her to face him. 'Sweetheart, don't let's fight any more. *Please*—'

Violet looked up at him, resisting the temptation to cry. He had won, she had given in; he could afford to be magnanimous. 'I'm sorry, too,' she said and raised her cool lips for his kiss. All of a sudden she felt homesick for India.

She had seen Wharncliffe House before. It was only a stone's throw from Bolton Street, and it dominated Curzon Street. The later additions hadn't quite managed to spoil the quiet charm of the original Georgian building and, set back in its own tree-filled grounds, the white-stuccoed house seemed a veritable oasis.

Since she had unburdened herself to Colonel Sinclair, Violet Nicolson had found out more about the Earl of Wharncliffe. He possessed vast tracts of Yorkshire, Cornwall, and Scotland; he owned coalmines. He was a member of the Conservative party. He was a friend of the Prince of Wales. He shot grouse. He was probably unpleasant, she concluded.

The drawing room at Wharncliffe House was much larger than the Lister Kayes' and less cluttered. That was fortunate, reflected Violet, since it was extremely crowded. The Wharncliffes' dinner parties were obviously not of the intimate kind. She stayed at Malcolm's side and searched for someone she knew. Her hostess said a few words of greeting before she drifted away and then, inevitably, the baronet appeared at Malcolm's shoulder and Violet was left on her own.

As she looked from the face of one stranger to another in despair, a painting on a far wall caught her attention. It was the life-size portrait of a European woman in oriental dress. Gauzes, damasks, brocades—she wore them all with considerable panache. Violet thought of her own loose-fitting tunics and baggy Afghan drawers left behind in India and gave a sigh of regret.

'Isn't she splendid?' came a voice at her side and Violet quickly turned. The man whose silent approach over the opulent carpet had startled her looked quite splendid himself. He was a little above average height, and his craggy face was surmounted by a leonine shock of steel grey hair. He must have been in his late sixties.

'I was thinking how very *comfortable* she looked,' Violet replied enviously—the woman had obviously thrown away her stays. Her companion, guessing perfectly what she was thinking, gave an uninhibited laugh.

'It's a portrait of Lady Mary Wortley Montagu,' he explained, 'a very modern lady for her time. She ran off with her husband to get married, then ran away from him years later.'

'My husband appears to have run away from me,' Violet observed dryly but it suddenly didn't matter. 'Lady Mary Wortley Montagu—didn't she introduce vaccination against smallpox?' she asked. 'And didn't she try it out on her own baby first? I've always thought how brave she was to do that.'

'Yes, we're very proud of her in the Wharncliffe family. Perhaps I should introduce myself: Edward Montagu Stuart Granville Montagu-Stuart-Wortley-Mackenzie at your service.'

'Goodness,' she exclaimed. 'How do you manage to remember all that, your Lordship? I'm Adela Violet Florence Nicolson—that's just a little bit easier, don't you think?'

They exchanged an amiable smile. She must be the Indian general's wife, thought the Earl of Wharncliffe. Lister Kaye had wanted them all to talk business, but with Mrs Nicolson asking him such interested questions about his venerable ancestress, he decided such matters could easily wait.

How fortuitous, thought Sir John Lister Kaye, as he watched them. Mrs Nicolson seemed quite taken with Wharncliffe and he with her and that could only help his plans. His cold gaze moved on. General Nicolson was talking with Lord de Grey, but the baronet could see no sign of the statuesque Gladys. He shrugged. His relationship with Lady de Grey, while of many years standing, was by no means exclusive. She had other interests, and so, sometimes, did he. When he failed to spot the countess he looked back to the general's wife.

He had sensed her coolness from the start and it worried him not at all. He also realised that he had come between her and her husband, and it amused him to see the couple, once so united, now in no small way estranged. Black suited the woman, he decided—it emphasised the marble whiteness of her flesh. She seemed cold, icy even, but beneath the ice might well hide fire. One day soon, the baronet promised himself, he would give himself the pleasure of finding out.

Gladys de Grey came up and lightly touched his sleeve. 'You'll be wasting your time with Mrs Nicolson, Johnny my lad,' she remarked. 'Of all the women in this room, you've picked the only one impossible to bed! Take my advice, and leave her alone. She likes your wife *and* she's in love with her husband—which, my darling, makes her an impregnable fortress. Even for your undoubted charms.' Her eyes mocked him as she moved away, which made her lover all the more determined to attempt the assault.

After dinner the ladies left the gentlemen to their brandy and cigars—and possibly their coal. Violet was feeling a little light-headed. She did not belong in this company, and neither did Malcolm, though he was making a better pretence of it than she.

The women divided into two distinct groups: one around the determinedly blonde Lady Wharncliffe (who at over sixty had not a grey hair in sight) and another around Lady de Grey. Politeness and inclination would have drawn Violet towards her hostess, but Gladys stood in her path.

'Do join us, Mrs Nicolson,' she insisted, and when she touched her arm Violet resisted the impulse to recoil. The woman's dark eyes reminded her of a snake and her perfume was heavy and decadent, but oh, thought the diminutive Violet, she was so very lovely. Mesmerised she joined the little group, and listened to gossip about who was sleeping with whom, and who wasn't, and why. Blanche Crackanthorpe had been so very right to warn her, and at the earliest opportunity Violet slipped away.

The Countess of Wharncliffe patted the sofa on which she was sitting and Violet sat down beside her. 'I've never visited India,' said Susan Wharncliffe with a welcoming smile, 'do tell me about it. I've always wanted to go, but there never seems to be time.' Her tone was wistful. She had time; it was Edward who was busy. His days were always full with meetings and business; she filled hers with embroidery, and flower-arranging, and smoking cigarette after cigarette. The countess lit one now.

The acrid smoke reminded Violet of other sharply contrasting smells, and she found herself talking to her hostess of India. Her voice took on a dreamlike quality as the heavy heat of the poppy fields came back to her, and the chill of distant mountains. The pink of lotus buds, the browns and yellows of the plain, and, oh, the poignant beauty of all those ruined tombs quite overgrown with roses … With a start she remembered where she was. 'I'm so sorry, Lady Wharncliffe, do forgive me. I've been talking far too much.' Violet bit her lip and blushed.

'Not at all, my dear,' her ladyship had been listening with fascination. 'Why, you have the soul of a poet!' *The soul of a poet* … she had said the same of Mahomed Akram in the dear dead days of long ago. Suddenly Violet felt the hot tears burn her eyelids and she desperately wanted to go home.

The gentlemen returned, most of them still huddling together intent on business. Violet distinguished the tall figures of her husband and Lister Kaye among them. They were obviously going to be involved for quite some time and she gave a little sigh. The countess heard her and felt an instant sympathy. Edward would be in there somewhere, too.

However to Lady Wharncliffe's surprise the earl came over and joined them. 'Mrs Nicolson has been telling me about India,' said his wife. 'Edward, the East is so fascinating.'

'And *I've* been telling Mrs Nicolson about Lady Mary. We have an edition of her letters in the library, young lady. Would you like to see it?'

Lady Wharncliffe nodded her encouragement and Violet smiled in delight. 'I should like that very much, Lord Wharncliffe. Thank you.'

Lister Kaye watched them go, and then turned his attention back to the general.

In the library Wharncliffe handed Violet a handsome leather-bound volume. 'Here you are, my dear,' he said. 'Edited by my grandfather in 1837.'

Violet caught a few words here and there as she carefully turned the pages. She would have liked to read the letters one by one, but soon the earl was proudly showing her his favourite books. After a while the door opened and the butler came in. 'There's a telephone call for you, my lord. Will you take it here?'

'Thank you, Howard. No, I'll take it in the study,' and Wharncliffe turned to Violet. 'Do stay as long as you want, my dear,' he said. 'I'll tell your husband where to find you.' So she sat down at a desk near one of the great windows that overlooked the darkened grounds and began to read. Like herself, Lady Mary had mixed with Eastern women, though perhaps, reflected Mrs Nicolson, her ladyship's experiences had been a little more disconcerting:

> *The lady that seemed the most among them entreated me to sit by her, and would fain have undressed me for the bath. I excused myself with some difficulty. They being all so earnest in persuading me, I was at last forced to open my shirt, and shew them my stays; which satisfied them very well, for, I saw, they believed I was so locked up in that machine, that it was not in my power to open it, which contrivance they attributed to my husband.*

Violet laughed out loud: she must tell Malcolm. As if on cue, the door opened to admit a tall figure. She put the book down, and went to meet him as he was turning to close the door. 'Darling,' she exclaimed, 'I'm so glad you've come. There's something I want you to see.'

'Is that so,' drawled the man she so detested. 'Then I'm glad I'm here.'

Violet gasped. She moved towards the door but the baronet barred the way. 'Let me pass,' she said coldly.

'My dear Mrs Nicolson, why such haste? We've not spoken all evening.'

'I can't think that we have anything to say, Sir John,' and Violet repeated her request.

'Come, come, my dear lady, I'm sure we could find a great deal to talk about.' The baronet took a step towards her, a leer on his pitiless face. As his eyes looked her slowly up and down then returned to linger on her bosom, Violet felt as if she were being stripped naked. The man's intention was obvious: he had only to turn the key in the lock and she would be at his mercy. The walls of the library were thick, and the drawing room was at the other end of a very long corridor ... No one would hear her cry for help.

She forced herself to think. What had she seen on the desk where she had been reading, something both practical and pretty? Yes, now she remembered, and she knew what she would do to escape.

'There's no way out over there,' he laughed, watching her hurry over to the window, and he certainly wasn't prepared to see her walk slowly back. Had she decided to submit? He would have preferred a little more of a contest, but nonetheless he was beginning to feel a thrill of anticipation at what would surely follow.

'Stand aside, Sir John, or I promise you'll be sorry.'

Something glinted in the subdued gaslight, and he laughed when he saw the paperknife she was holding. 'You're being absurd, my dear. You'd better give that toy to me or someone may get hurt.'

'You're absolutely right,' said Violet Nicolson coolly, 'and it won't be me.' Her hand was as steady as her voice as Lister Kaye reached out towards her. The baronet's confident smile changed a grimace as the slender blade bit viciously into his palm, and he gave a grunt of pain.

Violet darted behind him and opened the door, pausing only to remove the key. Then she was safely outside. It took only a moment to lock the door, take a deep breath, and walk away.

Once in the drawing room she made her way through the crowd to where Gladys de Grey stood watching her. 'Sir John seems to have locked himself in the library,' she told the woman with a composed smile which deepened as she handed over the key. 'Perhaps you would like to join him?'

She found Lord Wharncliffe talking to Malcolm and thanked him. The letters were quite remarkable, she said. She would like so much to show them to her husband, but not, perhaps, tonight. In the background someone was singing; it was late and people were beginning to take their leave. Violet was suddenly very tired. Malcolm felt remorse at having neglected her all evening, but exciting things were afoot and, when he told her later, he was sure she would understand.

'Well, Johnny Kaye, the little colonial got the better of you, did she?' Lady de

Grey found the baronet pacing up and down in the library, cursing broadly. She looked at the hand wrapped up in his handkerchief, and her smile broadened as she saw the spreading stain.

'So it's not only your pride she injured! Come, come, my dear Johnny, you must be losing your touch— Even savages expect a modicum of finesse.'

'Damn you, Gladys, and damn her, too!'

'I think you should be thankful that Mrs Nicolson showed so much restraint. Whatever did you do, Johnny?' The Countess de Grey laughed her silvery laugh, and for the moment Lister Kaye found himself hating her. Nothing, he had done nothing, that was the really damnable thing. Or perhaps—and he suddenly recalled the expression in his victim's eyes—it was fortunate. Violet Nicolson had, he realised, shown a very great restraint indeed; for a moment he had expected the knife to slide between his ribs.

Lady de Grey examined the deep cut at the base of his thumb. 'She's probably spent her adult years fighting off the entire Indian Army,' she observed. 'Don't try it again, my lad. Next time you might not be so lucky!'

Lister Kaye scowled. He needed no such advice from his mistress—he had already decided to leave helpless-looking women well alone.

'Take up your lute and sing!'

Violet said nothing of the incident, for what would have been the use? The man had not laid so much as a finger on her, after all, and Malcolm would say she had imagined it—and be appalled at her response. Lister Kaye's name was rarely mentioned between them now as it was sure to bring discord, and both of them weighed their words carefully before speaking. As a result sometimes they did not speak at all. She waited for Malcolm to tell her what was going on, and when the confidence didn't come she felt deeply hurt. Was it because she wouldn't understand—or because she wouldn't approve—or because her opinion didn't matter? The London season was nearly over and mercifully Malcolm was still uncommitted to the baronet's enterprises—as far as Violet knew.

Spurred into action by the baronet's behaviour, Mrs Nicolson decided to find out more about his schemes. It did not take her long to discover that China was a vast country with untapped resources—virgin ground for French, German and Russian business interests. And that the British Government, never happy to be left behind when foreign competition was involved, was queuing to buy concessions along with the rest. It was, she concluded, a situation guaranteed to bring a smile to the lips of one such as Sir John Pepys Lister Kaye.

She swallowed her dislike of Blanche's husband and one morning took herself off to his chambers in Lincoln's Inn. Montague Crackanthorpe was both surprised and intrigued to hear that Mrs Malcolm Nicolson wished to see him, and as he listened carefully to her earnest questions he found he bore her no ill-will. When she later voiced her concerns for her husband he admired her even more. Giving her all the assurances he could, and waiving any suggestion of a fee, he took her out to luncheon. Two hours later Violet returned to Cambridge Street, determined on a confrontation.

It was late afternoon before Malcolm joined her. When he did, he handed her two envelopes. Violet recognised the writing on one and opened the second whose bold, impetuous characters she had never seen before. As she read its contents she bit back an exclamation of dismay—an invitation from Sir John's paramour to stay at her country home was distinctly unappealing and she had no intention of going. But how could she manage to escape? As Malcolm read a letter of his own her mind was racing, and when he finally looked up she held out the card for his inspection.

'It's from the Countess de Grey. We're invited to Combe Court for the weekend. *Both* of us,' and she shot Malcolm a sardonic look. 'I thought she usually invited husbands and wives separately. I suppose that must mean she has no designs on you, after all!'

Violet had believed the contrary. Malcolm's distant politeness had seemed to intrigue the countess, in the same way as her own even more distant incivility still fascinated Sir John—who, of course, she realised with a sinking feeling, was sure to go down to Sussex as well. Leaving Natica in London. The baronet now sported a thin white scar on his hand while hiding a severely bruised ego, and she was unpleasantly aware of his scrutiny whenever they met. Somehow she must stay behind in London, too!

As she was desperately thinking of solutions, fate, in the unlikely shape of Mrs Henry Steel, came to her rescue. 'We'll have to refuse, I'm afraid,' Malcolm was saying. 'Flora's coming up to town to see her publisher and she suggests we meet for luncheon. I shall write back to say we'll both be delighted.'

At this moment the formidable Flora seemed the lesser of two evils, and when he looked at his wife for her reaction Malcolm Nicolson was gratified, if a little surprised, to see the smile of genuine pleasure that greeted his words. By now all thought of confrontation was forgotten, and so, too, for the moment, was Violet's second letter. By the time she remembered to read it, Malcolm was at his club, and then, with them both caught up in their separate existences, the letter and its contents completely slipped her mind.

Luncheon the following Saturday was surprisingly pleasant. If the literary lioness cast a reproachful glance at her friend for not lunching with her alone, she redressed the balance by producing her publisher, William Heinemann, to partner her at the meal. Heinemann was a small tubby man in his thirties whose dark hair spread thinly over the large round surface of his head. The force of his personality permeated the restaurant, and for all his lack of inches, Heinemann made even Malcolm seem small. His rather high-pitched metallic laughter elicited a response both from his companions and the tables around. Mrs Steel fell unusually silent as the publisher talked of the authors he had discovered.

'Your own books, my dear Flora, are my favourites,' he was saying now. 'There is a quality there that I cannot describe to anyone who has not had the good fortune to read them— *You* have read them, of course, my dear young lady?' and Heinemann turned his glowing gaze on Violet.

Thank goodness she had, otherwise the rather endearing face would surely have crumpled in disappointment—might he even have wept?

'Of course, Mr Heinemann,' she answered, warming to the little man. She looked at him demurely and then down at her plate.

'We also enjoyed Miss Bell's interpretations of Hafiz which you published recently,' Malcolm added. 'They have a very great merit of their own, I think, although they are not, of course, a totally faithful translation.'

When Heinemann replied Violet hid a little smile. She doubted whether he had read the originals, which Malcolm most certainly had. 'Oh, I agree, General,' said the publisher. 'It's very much the case of FitzGerald and the *Rubai'yat* all over again, I imagine—hardly translations at all. So, Mrs Nicolson,' and he gave Violet another warm smile while Flora Steel looked on in silence, 'you enjoyed the poetry, did you?'

'Oh, immensely,' Violet told him with sincerity, for she had already read the Hafiz several times.

'And do you write yourself?'

Violet felt the eyes of her companions upon her, waiting, and even to Malcolm her reply came as something of a surprise. 'I do write a little, Mr Heinemann,' she said. 'In fact, a friend of mine is preparing a book on Kashmir, and she wrote this week to ask whether she might include some of my verses—translations that I did for her last year. And of course I agreed. I'm sorry, darling,' the look she sent Nicolson was full of apology, 'I was going to tell you about Marian Doughty's letter, but we've both been so busy, I forgot.'

Malcolm gave a tight little smile at her explanation and turned his attention back to Heinemann. 'Violet's work is very interesting,' he told him. 'In fact, she has dealt with Persian-inspired poetry in very much the same way as Miss Bell, and with similar feeling, although, of course, Violet's inspiration comes from the North-West frontier of India. I do think she deserves more than a passing mention in someone else's book,' and he looked reproachfully across at his wife.

'I'm sure she does,' said William Heinemann, who, while he might sparkle and shine in company in a somewhat flamboyant way, possessed the same deep sensibility that he thought he recognised in Mrs Nicolson. 'There is an enormous interest in India among the reading public at present, and a very great love of poetry too,' he explained. 'I share both, and when you are ready, do send me your manuscript, Mrs Nicolson, and I'll see what I can do.'

Flora Steel watched in silence as Violet thanked the publisher politely for his interest. The offer, the older woman decided, was engendered by good company and excellent food and would soon be forgotten. Malcolm Nicolson thought differently. He might not be the best judge of his wife's poetry, but William Heinemann—who trusted his own good judgement and was prepared to put it publicly to the test—was quite another matter. And why, after all, should Miss Marian Doughty reap the sole reward of his wife's undoubted talent?

'Well,' he said on their return to Cambridge Street, 'so your work is going to be published.'

'Yes,' replied the unsuspecting Violet. 'Isn't it wonderful?'

'Of course—but apparently not wonderful enough for you to discuss it with me first.'

'*Malcolm*! I've already said I'm sorry and explained.' Puzzled by his tone, Violet asked him why he was so annoyed.

'You didn't think, did you, Violet? Miss Doughty will make use of your poetry in her book. It could well help make it a success.' He ignored Violet's impatient gesture at the thought and went on, 'If it *is* successful, then a share of the royalties might well have been yours.' Nicolson shook his head. 'If you had asked me, I would have explained all this.'

Violet looked at him in disbelief and disappointment. What on earth did the money matter? Her only regret was that the poems, in retrospect, could have done with a little more polish. And what was he saying now?

'Next time, Violet,' and his voice was cold, 'please have the courtesy to consult me before taking any decision of this kind.'

He obviously considered his own omissions to be of no importance, thought his wife, yet he was making such a fuss over this. It was so *unfair*. All at once the hurt and worry of the past few weeks came spilling out.

'And what haven't *you* told *me*, Malcolm?' she demanded angrily. 'What hasn't been important enough for *you* to share? You go out on your own most of the time, and when we do go out together you get into some ridiculous huddle with people you consider to be your friends, but don't consider to be mine. What is it you discuss with them—what are you up to? We used to talk about everything—we never had secrets from each other! Don't I matter any more? I used to be your equal, or so you said—' Violet by now was shaking. She sat down quickly.

Nicolson remained on his feet as she rapidly warmed to her theme: 'Ever since you met Lister Kaye, you've been different, and you've treated *me* differently. I haven't changed, and my expectations are the same, whereas you— You just seem to want someone to make up the numbers at dinner and a body to warm your bed. Any woman would do for that! Well, I can tell you now, Malcolm Nicolson, I refuse to become a cipher like Natica Lister Kaye—if that's what you really want.'

Violet waited for his reply. None was forthcoming. Dashing the hot angry tears from her eyes, she jumped up and ran blindly out into the street.

From her window Mrs Cory watched her go. Poor Addie, she had been restless for some time, and there had been trouble between her and her husband for weeks. After all these years was she only now discovering how very tiresome men could be? The old lady's impulse was to follow her granddaughter and comfort her, but that was for the general to do. She sat back and waited for Malcolm Nicolson to come and ask if she had seen his wife.

'I wish you well; go gather the gold'

Violet pushed open the heavy oak door of the church on the corner. There was no one inside and she walked slowly up the nave. It was some time since she had been in a church, and never in one that was empty. It was cool and lighter than she had expected, and the silence was almost tangible. She looked back when she reached the transept but Malcolm hadn't followed. The afternoon sun was catching the stained-glass rose of the west window and vivid colours were playing on the grey stone flags, but she saw none of it. She turned towards the altar in despair.

There hung the crucified carpenter, agonising eternally for his beliefs. *His* good name was assured. To live and die according to one's creed, surely that was all that mattered? She approached and raised her face to the east window. She was tired of London and its twisted values—values that slowly poisoned the lives of those who lived there, values that threatened to make strangers of them both. Wearily, Violet took a seat in the choir. She had not prayed sincerely for years; indeed, for years she had denied the existence of God, following the liturgy mechanically when called upon to do so, but now her lips moved silently and the words came from her heart.

She did not pray for herself, nor did she pray for her marriage. There was something even more important at stake. Before her eyes was the face of a soldier, a man who was stern but fair, impatient of his own weaknesses but full of compassion for others. It was the face of a man who was respected, a man whose name was revered, a man whom this stay in London threatened to change beyond recall. Violet Nicolson bowed her head and prayed for her husband's integrity as she had never prayed for anything else in her life.

When Nicolson found her, she was leaning back against the wood of the stall, her face frozen as if carved from the same stone as the saints above her head. He had never seen her look so desolate. He came and sat beside her, taking her hand in his. It was frozen.

'Little wife,' he said gently, 'come back with me now. And we'll talk. We'll talk about anything and everything you want. Violet, I swear before God, here in this church that I hadn't meant to shut you out. I was going to tell you, only later—'

'Have you committed yourself to anything yet?' Violet's voice was dull, her eyes lustreless as she turned her head at last to look at him.

'No. And I shan't until we've discussed it. You're so cold, sweetheart, let me take you back.'

So she walked with him down towards the rose window and the door. As they reached it, the vibrant colours danced over the stones and seemed to warm her face. She turned and paused; she looked back up the nave towards the altar. Her lips moved silently and then she followed Malcolm out into the sunshine.

'So what exactly does Sir John want—your money?' Back in their sitting room, the Nicolsons were talking openly at last.

'Hardly that—I don't have that much, and he knows it.'

'Then he must want your backing in some other way—your name printed on a prospectus, perhaps. Is that it?'

Nicolson looked at his wife in some surprise. What did she know about such things? She knew a lot, he soon discovered, and when she had finished he gave a rueful smile. 'I must apologise again,' he said, almost humbly. 'I've underestimated your business acumen completely. And I'm truly sorry I said what I did about Miss Doughty's book. It was ungenerous of me, Violet, and of course I wish her every success.'

Violet touched his cheek. It didn't matter, she told him, and went on to explain what did. 'The important thing, Malcolm,' she said, when she had finished, 'is whether you agree with me? Will you refuse to let your name be associated publicly with this scheme? Let Sir John get his lease from the government if he can, and then attract investors for himself!'

'You're quite serious about this, aren't you?'

'Never more so.' Hadn't she been worrying herself sick for weeks?

'Very well, darling. I'll tell him when I see him tomorrow.'

'He won't give up easily,' she warned. 'Your name among others on any prospectus would lend his scheme credibility, as he's certainly well aware. And that's all people can rely on, with China so very far away.'

'You mustn't worry. I've given you my word. But it *is* a very promising venture,

Violet. There's a fair-sized British community out there, and there's a great future for railways—the Shanghai-Woosung Railway is complete already.'

'But it's only twelve miles long,' Violet pointed out and her husband blinked.

'And there's the Northern Railway, built by British engineers.'

'There was a great deal of trouble over that, one way and another.'

He blinked again. 'But it *is* a success, sweetheart, and other lines to Russia and Burma are under construction.'

If he was hoping to impress her, the attempt failed miserably. 'Where will the Lister Kaye Railway go?' the trenchant voice enquired. 'To Cloud Cuckoo Land, perhaps?'

Nicolson was forced to laugh. 'He's more interested in the mining side, actually.'

'I see. And so are you—aren't you, Malcolm? I can't imagine you finding railways too exciting, after living in India. But not *coal* surely?' Nicolson shook his head. 'What is it, then; is it the idea of gold?' Violet looked at her husband keenly. *Gold*. The fever that entered men's blood and drove them mad, had it affected him, too? Chinese gold in Manchuria and Unsan was enough of a fact for him to believe in a return for his investment, but it was also enough of a chimera to hold appeal for an adventurous spirit.

She was correct. John Lister Kaye had floated the idea of gold when all else had failed, and Malcolm Nicolson had been hooked. 'I meant to invest a small amount,' he admitted, 'you know, just enough to give credibility to my name on his list. It would have been exciting to wait and see—' He looked at his wife somewhat wistfully; heaven knew these days there wasn't a great deal of excitement in being a general.

'You'd have waited a long time and seen precious little in return, if you ask me,' she observed caustically. 'Has Lister Kaye been to China himself?'

'No, not yet.'

'And all your evenings together have been spent talking about the marvellous prospects China has to offer?' Her voice and look were sceptical.

How could he describe the camaraderie he experienced in the clubs? And that, being so used to the company of men, he found it difficult to spend all his time with a woman—however beloved she was? Belatedly, Malcolm Nicolson tried to make his wife understand, about that and about his hopes.

Violet turned away and looked out over the garden as she considered everything he was saying. She would never understand his need for the society of his own sex, she who could do so well without the company of women. But she *could* understand his need for excitement and for dreams—for was she not the same? Soon they would be returning to India, and China was hardly on the way. It was a distant land with strange customs; they couldn't speak the language. The country was immense. It was, concluded Violet Nicolson, a totally ridiculous idea ... Then she found herself remembering the bitter loss Malcolm had felt on leaving the frontier, the initial nightmare of Kashmir, the boredom that had followed since—and everything she owed the man she loved beyond life itself.

'I'm sorry, sweetheart, but that's the way it is,' Nicolson concluded. 'And that's the way I am.' He had done his best, and could think of nothing more to say.

'So you still only want my company at dinner and in bed—?'

He looked at the back of her head anxiously, realising at last how much she had suffered through this latest instance of neglect. But was the fighting not over yet? With a sudden movement she faced him, and the blessed laughter was shining in her eyes.

'You are everything to me, Violet Nicolson, everything, do you understand? Wife, companion—yes, and mistress, too. Have you any objection to that?' His gaze was fierce and his kiss was fiercer still. No, safe again in the haven of his arms, Violet had no objection at all, and she told him so when he let her go and she could speak.

'So you're not angry with me any more, sweetheart, and we're friends again?'

'Yes.'

'And you'll warm my bed tonight?'

'Of course, of course,' she laughed, 'and tomorrow, if you like, we'll go to China!'

8

'The Tower of Victory'

INDIA AND ENGLAND, NOVEMBER 1898–MARCH 1902

After China and weeks at sea, Mhow was waiting. The cantonment seemed so small and the General's Bungalow so terribly ordinary, but that in itself was a relief. Dutifully following Lister Kaye's directions, the Nicolsons had trailed from treaty port to treaty port, and from Pekin to Shanghai, in the face of endless opposition. And yet, while the experience reinforced Malcolm's innate distrust of the Russians, he remained totally optimistic. Never mind commercial competition among the Europeans, he said, and open dislike on the part of the Chinese, Britain had been a presence in China for years, and that counted for a great deal. Violet remained unconvinced. She had enjoyed the little she had seen of so strange a country but her opinion remained the same as in London—the baronet's railway proposition was basically unsound.

'I can't believe we're back,' she told herself repeatedly, circling the tin trunks where everything had been bundled away six months before. 'Did it really happen, or was it all a dream?' She studied one of the bungalow's cane chairs; it appeared as sound as when they'd left it, but then you never could take something like that for granted. At first glance the cantonment looked the same as well, but who knew what changes had taken place in their absence? Mrs Nicolson sat down gingerly and the chair held together. When Malcolm returned the trunks were still unpacked.

'I'm sorry, Malcolm. I simply couldn't face it,' and Violet gave a self-deprecating little laugh. 'I wondered if I'd be opening a Pandora's box, and the same old unpleasantness would come tumbling out and the trouble begin again. But of course, that's silly! I'll make a start this very minute,' and she jumped to her feet. The general looked at her with approval. This was no longer the despairing young woman who had questioned her very existence. There was an air of serenity about her—she had, he concluded, found herself at last.

And he had nearly lost her.

As Violet moved purposefully towards the door Malcolm stood in her way. 'Wait, darling, we should talk. We don't have to stay here, you know,' he went on seriously. 'There are other places available—'

'But I'll be fine. Oh, I know I've treated it as a kind of fortress, to shelter me from the world outside, but that's all over. No, it will do very nicely until we leave—it's almost December, after all, and then we only have another year.' To the confident new Violet Nicolson a year meant nothing.

'How would you like to live in a maharajah's palace?' Malcolm asked.

'It would very much depend on the maharajah, don't you think? Why, are you planning to get rid of me?' She sent him a quizzical look. 'Do tell me what you're up to, Malcolm Nicolson,' she murmured.

'I've just been told that the Maharajah of Dhar died in July.'

'I'm sorry, of course,' Violet said instantly, for she had found the old man charming on the several occasions they had met, 'but what has that to do with us?'

'The heir is only a boy, and he won't be coming to the polo in Mhow for a good few years yet. So that means the guesthouse is empty, and Robert thought we might like to rent it.'

'Darling, we've been there—it's huge!'

'Oh, it's hardly a palace by Indian standards, but you could entertain in style—and who would dare criticise your menus?'

'Flora Steel, for one!' she retorted. 'Have you seen that book she's sent me? It's all about housekeeping. She hopes I'll find it both "informative" and "useful" …' Violet pulled a face.

'Don't change the subject!' The general was up to his wife's little tricks. 'Well, what do you think? Apparently it's fully furnished with everything we could possibly need—'

'I suppose you'd fill the women's quarters with *bibis*—or does it come with concubines as well?'

Nicolson ignored this latest quip. 'Well, are you going to give me an answer?'

Violet pictured the generous compound at the edge of the British lines: the house with its spacious rooms, the marble lattice at the windows, the cool flagged floors; she imagined her bare feet dipping in the courtyard fountain … and then she asked one final question.

'Can we afford it?'

'Yes.'

When Violet Nicolson confronted Mhow a few days later, she met with a surprise. The same narrow-minded women she had left half a year before now welcomed her back. They eagerly accepted the invitations to dinner—and stayed too long. They seemed to want to be friends.

It was strange, she said, how people changed and yet they stayed the same. 'Perhaps,' Malcolm suggested tentatively, 'it's because you've changed as well. You're no longer afraid of them, and that makes all the difference.'

'I was never afraid!'

'No, of course you weren't,' and Malcolm hid a little smile.

The maharajah's guesthouse suited Violet's taste for the oriental. There were none of the dull greens and faded blues they left behind them in the official quarters: orange, red, salmon pink and yellow rioted through the public rooms; vivid blue glass chandeliers and coloured candle-shades diffused the evening light. They used the maharajah's crystal and plate at splendid dinner parties, when Violet marshalled his servants into a credible semblance of order, and when the rooms were adrift with her favourite flowers. Whatever the truth of those earlier days, the general's wife—so poised, so queenly—was afraid of no one now.

'Seeking for golden gain'

At Denby Grange, his heavily encumbered estate near Wakefield in the northern English county of Yorkshire, Sir John Lister Kaye sat in his library, a whisky in his hand and a scowl upon his face. He was staring at the hearth. The fire burning there was meagre and the baronet was thinking about coal. Damnation, he said to himself, the estate must be sitting on miles of the stuff and he could hardly afford to fill the grate! And for once no invitations had been forthcoming to spend Christmas and New Year away from home. Natica was off visiting her blonde bitch of a sister, and Gladys—Gladys was staying with her in-laws, the Ripons, at nearby Studley Royal. But she might as well be half a world away, for all the good it did him. Cursing, the baronet kicked at a half-burnt log in frustration then turned as he heard a discreet tap at the door.

'The mail, Sir John.' The butler proffered a silver salver and silently withdrew. Lister Kaye saw that one of the letters was from India. Nicolson, it had to be Nicolson—now what did he have to say? The general's report proved to be succinct: everything he saw in China bore out what Sir John had told him; trade was healthy in Shanghai and the ports further to the north, and there were ample opportunities for anyone interested in railways. *Of course, Sir John, you know that already. You would be competing with the Russians and the Germans and the other foreign powers, but presumably you have the stomach for a fight.*

Sir John was not at all happy with that phrase. Did Nicolson, then, have his doubts?

Violet Nicolson certainly had hers when Malcolm had told her what he had written—the baronet had given up easily enough with her! 'And what about you, Malcolm?' she asked him. 'Do you want to be part of it, after all?'

'I'm afraid the gold is likely to remain a dream,' he admitted. 'For all his confidence, I can't see Lister Kaye getting a foothold in the Chinese mines. But yes, I'm certainly tempted.'

'I suppose the money would be safe,' she reflected. 'If Sir John fails to get a lease for his railway venture, then he'll have to give it back—is that correct?'

'Yes. The money remains in trust until he gets the concession, or until he gives up trying. I've asked him to let me know how much money has been subscribed to date. A simple enquiry seemed reasonable enough.'

Lister Kaye smiled as he finished the letter. It seemed that the fish had taken the bait and was ready to be reeled in. Everything was going well, he answered by return, and the Earl of Wharncliffe was set to join the venture. If the scheme was good enough for Wharncliffe, it was certainly good enough for Malcolm Nicolson. Confident in his lordship's good judgement, the general arranged for the transfer of several thousand pounds and settled back to wait.

By the time the transaction was completed the earl's judgement, sound or otherwise, was no longer relevant: Sir John laid his hands on Nicolson's money in the same week that Edward, first Earl of Wharncliffe, was laid to rest in his grave. What intentions the dead man had entertained vis à vis China no one knew for sure, and Lister Kaye for one didn't care. It would be some time before the Nicolsons returned to England, and by then he would be ready with some tale to fob them off.

Mrs Crackanthorpe sent them the news that Edward Wharncliffe was dead. He had been ailing for some considerable time, she wrote, and had given up all business interests months before his death in May (of a heart attack) at the age of seventy-one. Violet put the letter aside, a sick feeling in her stomach. She mourned the kindly man who had treated her with such civility, but above all she regretted the guiding hand that would have kept the baronet in check. And surely—and she counted on her fingers—the earl was already ill when Lister Kaye had penned his letter. That night she dreamt she was back in China. On the smooth skin that could have been her own, a dragon began to writhe and twist under the tattooist's skilful hand. Slowly as she watched, it was transformed into a living, breathing serpent. Blue and green, it coiled about her limbs and chest, stifling her, and its eyes—when it reared its head to strike—were the cruel eyes of Lister Kaye.

'The links which stretch out to the Future, with forces of life and of death'

Soon enough Violet succeeded in banishing Sir John from her thoughts. She had other preoccupations nearer home; disrupting her husband's routine was one. 'I thought the mark of a good leader was to delegate,' she told him. 'So—delegate! Instead of letting all this paperwork get you down, give it to someone else—Robert, for example. It will do him good.'

And it's doing you a lot of harm, she thought, examining the tired face before her. Malcolm's healthy complexion had faded already and he looked almost ill.

'It's a tempting thought,' he agreed.

'Then let yourself be tempted! You're such a puritan, Malcolm Nicolson—life was meant to be enjoyed.'

'There's nothing puritanical about you, Violet, I must say,' and Malcolm eyed his wife. The vivid sari she was wearing revealed large areas of soft white skin; the bodice verged on the indecent. Her feet were bare and when she walked there was a jangle of silver, as there was now as she stretched out her hand to him in a lazy feline movement.

'So, will you spend more time with me in future? Come out with me in the mornings, like you used to. Please.'

So the Nicolsons resumed their morning rides, and when they went camping it was not the rough and ready affair of former years, but grander, with uniformed servants and the cook.

'We're getting older,' Violet observed. 'We never needed such luxury before. Do you remember Zhob?'

'Do you remember China?' he countered. 'After China we deserve a little comfort!'

'All those pigs,' she mused. 'Everywhere. Walking, penned up, carried. All that bacon on the move— Oh, I do miss bacon, Malcolm,' and she heaved a theatrical sigh.

'Is that all you miss about London?'

'I think so, yes.' Violet leaned back in the camp chair and studied the night sky through a tracery of branches. 'What about you?'

The answer when at last it came was not what she expected.

'I shall be fifty-six next June, my dear.' Malcolm's voice was serious. 'In July I shall either be promoted or stood down. Mhow could well be my last appointment. I may have to decide what to do with the rest of my life—which is partly why I was so drawn to Sir John's proposition.'

He reached for her hand. 'However much you may try to turn me into a lotus-eater, my love, I am not made to be idle. In London I met men who had ideas, plans for the future. And I realised that I too must plan.'

'Does having a wife hold you back, then?' Violet's voice was scarcely audible. Malcolm gripped her fingers and she winced with pain.

'Of course not, darling, no! It is for you that I have to plan. To provide for you when I'm no longer here.'

'Don't talk about it, Malcolm, please. It upsets me so!'

'We have to face up to the facts, sweetheart. I'm twenty-two years older than you.'

'We knew that when we married and I've never thought of it since. So why must you?' She slipped onto the ground beside him, hiding her face against his knees.

Their voices fell silent and the rustling jungle noises took their place. Why must he think of dying, indeed? Was it because they were back in India where death was so much a part of the everyday fabric of life; or was the pain he had suffered in London a timely reminder of his responsibilities as a married man? Malcolm Nicolson wasn't sure. He stroked Violet's hair with slow movements of his strong sensitive hand. She was so precious—how could he leave her when the inevitable moment of parting came? As if reading his thoughts, she raised her head and her face showed livid in the starlight.

'When we were staying with your mother,' she said, 'I watched her. She and I are very different and I decided that *I* would not be a widow for long. I could not live without you, Malcolm, and I shan't even try!'

Malcolm Nicolson fully understood her intention and made no attempt to change her mind. 'Then,' he said at last, in a voice half choked with emotion, 'please God we have many years before us yet.'

In July word arrived from Lister Kaye—a long letter of self-justification for any delay on his part. But why, Violet thought in exasperation, was the man still holding back when the thrust was so patently forward? Why didn't he get on with business? Was it fear of the strong competition, or was there a more sinister reason? She read the letter again more carefully.

What the man seemed to be saying, for page upon unnecessary page, was that it would be politic to wait: for internal reforms to the fiscal laws affecting export; for the removal of restrictions on inland water navigation; and for foreigners to be given permission to reside in the interior of China for purposes of trade. Many more safeguards were required, Sir John said in conclusion, and all in all he felt he should wait for appropriate trade treaties to guarantee all the above.

Then Violet turned to the independent report he had included of Admiral Lord Charles Beresford's experiences in China. Published in *The Times* of London in May, Beresford's account bore out everything the baronet had said. When she had finished, Mrs Nicolson was forced to concede that Sir John might possibly have a point. So the baronet was simply being cautious, and Malcolm's money was safe.

Only ten inches of rain fell that year. April was wickedly hot. So was May. The Nicolsons celebrated Malcolm's birthday alone together at the beginning of June, and his promotion to lieutenant-general less quietly in July. There was no word of retirement. The heat continued unabated, and Violet Nicolson—lost in her own little world of the intellect—chose not to venture far from home. In September a chance remark from Robert Elkington at dinner one evening brought her back to reality.

'What was that, Robert?' She had been listening with only half an ear.

'I said the monsoons appear to have failed this year, and that's why it's still so beastly hot.' He looked at her soberly before going on: 'Famine has come to the Malwa plateau and people are beginning to die like flies.' For years the rainfall had been low in Central India, he reminded her, and famine had hit the neighbouring states already. Now Indore State was affected in its turn.

Suddenly Violet had no appetite and she pushed her plate away; she should have realised what the lack of rain implied. 'What's happening?' she demanded, looking from Nicolson to Elkington, their only guest. 'What are you doing—what is Holkar doing? You can't let all those people starve!'

'Darling, everything that can be done is being done.' Malcolm told her of the famine carts, the camps that were being set up, the food rations that would be distributed by government servants, but reassurance wasn't enough. Distraught and guilty, for she hadn't been to Simrole for months, Violet insisted that one or the other—or both—should take her there the following day.

Both men went with her. Partly burnt bodies choked the streams around the village while the vultures circled overhead. Jackals, emboldened by the easy pickings, prowled openly through Simrole itself. The burning ghats could no longer cope with the corpses and the stench of rotting flesh was everywhere.

'Can't they be buried, before there's disease as well? Why doesn't someone *do* something?' It was Violet's perennial cry in the face of insurmountable odds, and as usual, when met with silence for an answer, she would have tried herself—but there was nothing she could do, either. Overcome, she turned away from the hollow-eyed men and women sitting in the dust, too apathetic even to stretch out their hands for the obscenity of alms. Above all, it was the children who broke her heart. Whereas before they would have run to her, laughing and calling, now they stood in the dirt, mute with misery, their bellies distended with a hunger they couldn't understand. And she was powerless to help. As she stood by the bloated body of a tiny baby, tears of grief and frustration ran down her face unchecked.

'But the children,' she persisted, 'surely we could help the children?'

'Violet, it's being taken care of. It takes time, that's all. You'll just have to believe us.' Grim-faced and patient, Malcolm Nicolson attempted to reason with his wife. In the end he had to resort to a brutal logic. 'You cannot take them all,' he told her, 'and what right have you to choose who should be given the better chance of life?' He was right and she knew it. Biting her lip she steeled herself to turn away and walked back to the carriage ahead of the men.

Forced to harden her generous heart, Violet Nicolson put her trust in officialdom and once more retreated to her books. Her solitary wanderings were over; these days her adventures were those of the mind. European visitors to Indore found their way to Mhow, to the Nicolsons' lavish table and lively wide-ranging conversation. On these occasions Malcolm Nicolson felt an intense relief—surely the spell India had cast over his wife was broken.

At last the five years' appointment was drawing to a close. The years had changed them both—he aged by repeated bouts of fever, she tempered into a strong and determined woman. How she sparkled now, thought the general, with the pre-Christmas festivities at their height, as she entertained her guests! Who would have believed this wife of his would finish by having Mhow at her feet, the women as well as the men? Had she thought of where she wanted to go in January, when his leave began? he asked her.

'I should like to go south,' she replied without hesitation. 'South to Rameswaram.'

It was certainly south, the general thought in some surprise—almost as far south as anyone could go without wetting their feet, and only twenty miles or so from Ceylon.

'Unless you want to go somewhere else?' Violet asked him belatedly. South would be very nice, he answered meekly. Would she care to make the arrangements herself?

If the prospect of being on their own again from January filled Violet Nicolson with nothing but joy, for her husband it was different. For one thing there was this wild scheme of Violet's. Whatever possessed her? She had done something like this to him once before, he remembered, and in similar circumstances, and, to be honest, he would have welcomed a return to Kashmir. He was a man whose affections and inclinations lay in the North, after all, with the Muslim races, and he felt uneasy at the thought of going further south. More importantly, there was no word of another appointment, and the prospect of years stretching ahead like the blank pages of a book filled him at times with the bleakest of misgivings.

Before that, there were the farewells to be got through—rather like a lingering death, he told himself morbidly; everyone gathering at his professional bedside to see him safely off ... *Mandu!* In his wish to be free of the insincerities surrounding what was almost certainly his retirement the idea came to him unbidden. Suddenly January seemed too far away and, normally the most patient of men, the general couldn't wait. He decided to take a few days away with his wife, as soon as possible and alone. Violet had never known Malcolm to do anything so impetuous, and the memory of their camp at Mandu sustained her throughout the final inspections later, the regimental dinners, and the evenings in the mess that claimed him almost nightly after their return. For she had only to close her eyes to see once more the twilight pavilion of a hilltop fort, where in the fading glow of sunset Rup Mati's magic had embraced them both.

The cantonment saw in the twentieth century together. There were the usual murmurs of delight and disappointment as fireworks flashed across the sky, and a few days later the newly promoted Captain Elkington saw the Nicolsons off at the station where he had met them all those years before. He saluted as the train drew out, then the young man slowly made his way back to the cantonment with the rest of the well-wishers. He felt incomplete and very much at a loss.

'The Night of Shiva'

It was amazing how little the Nicolsons had in the way of baggage after almost eleven years of married life. It shouldn't have taken Violet long to pack, had she not stopped to reminisce over small items of small worth but of infinite sentimental value. 'Do you remember?' she would ask and hand something over with a smile. A rug, a shell, a little painted box ... Malcolm remembered them all and watched them put safely away in a trunk, to be collected in Bombay on their return from Rameswaram where they were going by steam packet, not train. She was in no hurry, she told him. Of course it would take longer that way, but wouldn't it be fun to linger and see something of the coast?

The little they saw of Malabar entranced her, if not him, and she could have stayed for ever, but—she reminded herself—she had a purpose. Before long they were rounding Cape Comorin in what Malcolm Nicolson thought the leakiest old tub in existence, and there they hit the most violent storm he had ever known.

As the mountainous waves crashed against the bows and washed over the deck in merciless succession, the general believed he was about to breathe his last, while his wife laughed in exultation and mocked him for his fears. The wind whipped against her face, blowing her hair into mad disarray, and she rode the storm like some wild elemental being while Malcolm lay prostrate in their cabin, white-faced and expecting to die. And when she joined him there at last she knelt by his side for hours, full of tenderness and remorse.

By Tuticorin General Nicolson had fully recovered, although his pride still suffered. By the time they reached Rameswaram he wished he had been buried at sea. 'You knew about this, I suppose?' he asked, after two days spent in a town swarming with Hindus on pilgrimage. 'You knew there was some kind of festival here, now?' His voice was irritated. Violet noted the fact but made no comment.

'Yes. It starts the day after tomorrow. We've only just got here in time. It's *Sivatri*, darling, the Night of Shiva.'

Nicolson felt no need to enquire further. It was something to do with the wretched *lingam*, no doubt, though why Violet should want to get herself involved he really did not know. He had believed she had got over all that nonsense long ago; it was, he reflected wryly, a very great distance to come to find out his mistake. Apart from them the government guest bungalow where they were staying was empty, which came as no surprise. What self-respecting European would want to get mixed up in this seething mass of ill-washed humanity? Malcolm was still growling when Violet found him.

'Darling, I don't think I've ever seen you in such a foul mood! Whatever is wrong?'

'Take me away and I'll never be like it again, I swear.' He tried to laugh at himself with little success. 'I belong in the North, Violet. I'm completely out of my depth here, you ought to know that!'

'It will do you a great deal of good if you'd only let it! I've always thought that if we hadn't married you'd have turned into a stuffy old colonel—now you're well on the way to becoming a stuffy old general instead! Malcolm, just relax—'

'I'm sorry, Violet, but I can't abide southerners. I've spent my entire adult life among Baluchis and Aghans and they're different.'

'Of course they're different—they're the "martial races", as you soldiers call them. They're always fighting, and they wouldn't know what to do if they weren't. Hindus see life differently, that's all.'

'I simply cannot feel at ease with a people who allow sex to permeate their lives and who actually worship a phallus,' Nicolson grumbled.

His wife burst out laughing. 'You sound just like Mrs Steel! It's the *life force* they venerate, not the *lingam*—and you're a complete fraud, Malcolm Nicolson. There have been times when you have come close to doing that very thing yourself! Shall I remind you?'

'No, you wretched woman, there's no need! But I don't let it interfere with my everyday life.'

'Then perhaps you should. And that's not true either,' she remarked gleefully. 'What about Mandu?'

'All right, all right,' he admitted. 'But that doesn't alter the fact that I feel uncomfortable here.'

'Then I'm truly sorry.' And she was. 'I should have realised, I suppose. As soon as the procession's over we'll go back to Bombay. And you need never come south again.' She was trying hard to keep the disappointment out of her voice as she went on: 'You won't mind if I go to the temple now? No, stay here, darling, you really don't have to come, I'll be perfectly safe. Rest, you're looking tired.'

Another disappointment awaited Violet at the temple: she was not allowed into the *mulasthanam*, the inner sanctum. Anonymous enough in her sari and with the tell-tale hair covered, she might have succeeded in passing as a Hindu, but it would have been a betrayal of trust. So she did not see the *lingam*, the life force, nor could she be present at its ritual anointing with holy Ganges water.

Pushing against the tide of humanity as she turned back, she should have been afraid but strangely wasn't. Had she stumbled she might have been crushed, but some invisible hand seemed to smooth her path, and she re-emerged unscathed into the daylight. She stooped by the tank for the ritual ablution, then came away through the soaring gateway tower. She paused only to look back at the tall pyramid so unlike anything she had ever seen. Malcolm should have come, she thought, in sudden annoyance. How could he be so narrow-minded? Forty years of soldiering in Baluchistan and Sind had marked him in a way she had never suspected—although, if she forced herself to think, there had always been traces of a prejudice she had chosen to ignore.

Nicolson was in a better mood when she returned. He had booked their passage north, he told her; they would be leaving as soon as *Sivatri* was over. He watched the procession with his wife—not that he wanted to, but she had no intention of missing it and he refused to let her out on her own. Thousands of pilgrims lined the streets, and they too waited in the suffocating mass for the triumphal car to appear. First he heard the shrill notes of the flutes, then the gongs and drums and in the distance the temple bells. After a while the separate sounds merged to become one dull persistent beat that throbbed relentlessly in his head.

There was a murmur then a shout as the great tower appeared, rolling on wheels made of solid blocks of stone, some six feet across. It was drawn along by ropes; at each one hundreds of willing sweating men strained to pull the Goddess Devi on her relentless way. If Shiva was creator of life, then she was Earth Mother and the crowd pushed forward to look.

But what was there to see? It was all glittering tinsel and gauze, draped round a form perched far too high above the ground. Nicolson stared almost spellbound, part of him still able to analyse the danger should the car lurch off-course into the crowd, yet part of him caught up in the steady and persistent throb of the drums. It seemed to echo in the pulsing of his blood, the pounding of his heart, and he sensed his Western nature giving way to the insidious lure of the East.

The sudden surge of the crowd thrust his wife against him and he caught her to him for safety. Her eyes and teeth glinted in the torch-light as she laughed up at him for joy. 'The life force!' she exclaimed in exultation. 'Surely you can feel it now?'

She was soft and she was vital; she was eternal Eve. Was it the life force that he felt, this pounding in the blood and this heightening of the senses? Was it this that made him pull his unresisting wife out of the crowd into the temple shade and hold her closer and closer still? Or was it simply lust?

Whatever it had been, Malcolm Nicolson reflected later, if Violet hadn't swayed in his arms and complained of giddiness and malaise, then the rain of mindless kisses would have continued, and would have him led the devil only knew where! He half-guided, half-carried her back to the sanity of their room, and laid her on the bed. Neither of them spoke and he sat beside her till she slept. Next day they boarded the ship equally silently, and turned their backs on Rameswaram—he full of regrets for what had happened on the Night of Shiva, she regretting what had not.

The steamer headed north, and with Cape Comorin uneventfully behind them Nicolson's spirits began to rise. He hardly noticed how little Violet ate and how subdued she was, so busy was he planning the rest of his leave. The sea was smooth as glass and his wife an excellent sailor, so when she became violently ill a few hours from the port of Calicut General Nicolson was understandably alarmed. A word with the master, and they left the ship. He was taking her to the European Hospital to see a doctor, he told her, and they would stay here in Malabar until she was quite recovered.

'Well?' he asked, when she rejoined him after what had seemed an unconscionably long time. 'What did the doctor have to say?'

Violet led him back unerringly to the beach where two hours earlier they had been put ashore. She sat down on a fisherman's upturned boat and looked silently out to sea.

'Well,' he repeated. 'Have you decided to tell me or not?'

'Sit down, Malcolm,' she said and he obeyed. As he slipped an arm around her shoulders she decided to announce the news bluntly. 'I'm going to have a baby,' she told him. 'I'm three months pregnant already. I'm sorry, I should have realised. Mother always said I was far too casual about these things—'

Malcolm greeted the news in silence. Of course he was surprised, thought his wife. It was, after all, something they had stopped thinking about, this possibility of having a child. 'I'm afraid I won't be able to come walking with you in Kashmir after all,' she added as an afterthought and waited for his reaction, forcing her face to be as expressionless as her voice.

The silence deepened. She had miscarried before; there were great risks ahead— What was she feeling? What should he say? 'You are more precious than any child could ever be,' Malcolm said at last. 'I can't forget what nearly happened before—but I can't forget either how it nearly broke your heart. Are you happy, sweetheart?'

At last Violet allowed herself to smile, an infinitely sweet smile that came from the heart and illuminated her features as if from within. 'Oh, Malcolm,' she exclaimed, 'I thought if I went to Rameswaram—as women do, you know, to pray for a child—then perhaps I might conceive. But,' and her laugh was joyous, 'there was no need, no need at all! Oh darling, I'm so sorry to have dragged you there!'

'With my bad temper!' His arm tightened and he drew her against him, pressing his lips to her brow. 'I'll look after you, my little love, and this time nothing will go wrong.'

He spoke with a confidence he was far from feeling, but the look she gave him was full of trust. If Malcolm believed that, then so did she, and this time the baby would not die.

'Love's last reward'

He found them a bungalow, there by the Arabian Sea, for a month or two until she could travel comfortably, and as they waited and wandered the golden sands, and lingered by the salt lagoons of that gentle southern land where all races had somehow learned to live peaceably together, Malcolm Nicolson too came under Malabar's spell.

'Do you believe in magic?' Violet asked him late one afternoon as they walked back along the shore. 'Do you remember the sunset at Mandu and the feeling of enchantment in the air?'

He shook his head and gently mocked her for her fancy—until she told him that it was there the child must have been conceived. And the same enchantment returned as they walked barefoot on the sand and waded through the surf, together and hand in hand. He would never forget her as she was now, the wind gently playing in her hair and softly draping the folds of her garments about her slender limbs: Violet, with little as yet to betray the curves of approaching motherhood, and confidently facing what lay ahead.

If only time would stand still; if only they could be ever thus: the man proud, the woman triumphant, and both of them happy in the certainty that all would be well.

❧

Before she was six months pregnant he took her back to Bombay, to the house they had rented once before on Malabar Hill. With the bay to one side and the ocean on the other, the breezes would cool her and she could rest in the garden and wait. Or so Malcolm Nicolson thought.

'Darling, you can't expect me to sit here and do nothing, surely?' she protested.

'Well, yes, I thought exactly that.'

'I shall go mad! I shall think too much—I shall worry.'

That was very true. She was beginning to look ahead; either she would lose the baby as she had before, or she would have an unsuccessful struggle to give birth. She tried to hide her fear from Malcolm, but he was fearful, too.

One day she came into the drawing room to find it quite transformed. There was a table by the window covered with paper, pens and books. Her books.

'What on earth is all this?'

Nicolson laughed at her surprise. 'It's for you. You're going to start working on your manuscript for William Heinemann.'

'Malcolm, darling, surely you've forgotten all that nonsense?'

'Not at all! Come and sit down.' She did as she was told. 'That's right,' he said in approval. 'Now, where are your notebooks?' He found them at last in the bottom of one of the trunks—faithful friends that had followed her everywhere, but for some time sadly neglected. He fetched them and took a seat opposite his wife. 'Now,' he said, 'what can I do to help?'

'So you *are* serious.'

'Never more so. Why don't you start making a selection and I'll help you copy them out?'

As he read and wrote, Nicolson was fascinated by what the poems revealed. That his wife was many women, he already knew. It was, after all, the myriad facets of her personality that had kept him with her through love as well as duty. For was it not she who would have died of love, and of unrelieved desire? Was it not she who swayed seductively through palaces and courtyards, confident of her ability to hold kings and commoners in thrall? Was it not for him she wrote that there was no breeze to cool the heat of love …? His eyes rested tenderly on Violet's bowed head. Lover and wife, now she was carrying his child—his own love for her had never burned brighter.

The manuscript was still not ready when the first pains struck.

'So soon?' she whispered in sudden dread. 'It's far too early.'

'No,' he told her firmly, 'it's absolutely as it should be. I'll take you to the Sisters now and we'll finish our work here afterwards.'

The hospital wasn't the biggest in the city, but who was to say it wasn't the best? Violet had wanted to be near the shore, to look out onto the water, and this was the one he had found. There, the nuns, quiet gentle women who calmly took control, led Violet to her room, which was light and cool with a verandah leading into the garden. From her bed she could see the sea.

'Malcolm, I'm afraid.'

It wasn't fear of the pain, but of that pain being wasted; she was afraid for the baby—and afraid of death.

'I'll be very near, I promise. Sweetheart, they've said I can stay with you for hours yet.'

'Malcolm, I may die.'

'No, no, little one, don't think of such things!'

He had thought of it often enough, and it must have shown on his face.

'I don't want to leave you—how could I leave you?' The pain in her voice had nothing to do with what her body was experiencing with increasing frequency. He held her in his arms and it seemed to help.

'Malcolm,' she said hours later in the evening, when one of the nuns came to take him away and her voice was almost too low to be heard, 'I'm afraid of the dark and of never seeing the light again. Of never seeing *you* again.'

What could he answer as he gripped her hand and tried to give her strength? He remembered what she had told him one poignant starlit evening and the vow she had made—a vow he had unconsciously echoed in his heart.

'Listen, my dearest love.' He was aware of the hovering nun and his voice was barely audible. 'I shall be with you, no matter what happens. We shall always be together. *Do you understand?*'

He was relieved to see her nod. Yes, she understood what he was saying: he would not let her go down into the darkness alone. He kissed her goodbye and left.

The next morning she was still in labour. No, General Nicolson couldn't see her, the sister said, and it would be better if he didn't stay. It would distress him—and Mrs Nicolson as well, if she thought that he could hear. Why didn't he wait outside?

'Tell her that,' he said urgently, 'tell her I'll be waiting in the garden.'

Thank goodness the man was going to be reasonable—for a moment the sister had thought he would cause trouble and insist on seeing his wife. Yes, she would most certainly give Mrs Nicolson his message, she assured him. She nodded and walked silently away to carry out her pledge.

Malcolm paced the garden paths all day, refusing every tentative suggestion that he eat. Evening found him gazing out over the water, towards a dark horizon where the sun had long since set. How could she still be going through this torment? Why did no one tell him she was dead?

He turned towards the long low building and as if in answer he saw a white figure come gliding over the grass towards him. So it was finished and she was coming to say farewell … The tears welled up in his eyes as he waited.

When she reached him Sister Thomas gazed at him in some concern. He looked as if he had seen a ghost. 'General Nicolson.' Her voice was full of compassion. 'General,' she touched his arm, and he gave a start. 'Mrs Nicolson is asking for you,' she told him.

'He's very small to have caused so much trouble,' said Malcolm Nicolson to his wife who was watching him anxiously.

'You've said that often enough about me too— Darling, isn't he beautiful?'

Nicolson looked down critically at the ugly red face of his son, then he knelt and cautiously touched the baby's tiny fists. 'You sleep like that too, did you know?' and he tried very hard to smile at his wife.

'You're crying,' she said, and reached out to brush away the tears.

'No, I'm not,' and the tears flowed even faster.

Violet looked up at Sister Thomas with an appeal in her eyes. 'My husband is very tired,' she said. 'Could he please stay in the hospital tonight?'

Bless the woman, as if she wasn't exhausted herself! Of course he could stay, replied Sister Thomas. They made a bed up for Malcolm Nicolson in the room next door and only then did Violet allow herself to sleep.

Once Violet was well enough, life caught up with her. There were letters, there was news, and there was her work—abandoned weeks before.

'But what does it all matter?' she asked as Malcolm pressed several envelopes into her reluctant hands. 'I have all I need here with you both,' and she smiled up at him then indicated their sleeping child.

'There's a letter from Blanche—why don't you read it? Come on, darling, the outside world is waiting. You can't ignore it for ever!'

She wanted to, and even more so when she had finished Blanche Crackanthorpe's letter. 'What's this trouble in China she refers to, Malcolm? You've not mentioned anything to me.'

'No, I didn't want to disturb you, with the baby almost due.'

'And what else have you shielded me from?'

'Nothing, sweetheart.'

'So tell me about China.'

There had been trouble for months, he told her, and foreigners had been attacked, singly and in groups, at the instigation of reactionary forces at the Imperial court. All foreign interests were at risk, with foreigners and Christian converts being murdered every day by adherents of a secret society calling itself *The Fist of Righteous Harmony*. The Japanese and German ambassadors had been killed, foreign settlements were under attack, and an international force had been dispatched to protect the legations. Since then the forts at Taku had been stormed, he told her, and the siege of Tientsin raised in July.

'And what about Pekin?' asked Violet.

'The legations were relieved in the middle of August, after a siege of some eight weeks.'

'And now all is well again?'

'Hardly, but the situation is calmer.'

'And Sir John?'

Nicolson had been waiting for the inevitable question. 'It seems he was right to hold back. It's hardly the moment for trade.'

'No, I suppose not.' And to Malcolm Nicolson's relief, his wife left it at that.

'The Flowers upon the Tree of Life!'

Old Mrs Nicolson's expressionless eyes surveyed first her grandson and then her grandson's mother. After a moment she spoke. 'Malcolm Josceline John Sinclair Nicolson. Rather a grand name for such a tiny mite, wouldn't you say?'

'But he's growing every day, Mrs Nicolson, and one day he'll be very happy to be reminded of so many good people.' Violet smiled calmly at her mother-in-law, while feeling anger in her heart. Would the woman never be satisfied? She had produced a grandchild contrary to all expectation, they had brought that child to England, and she had hoped the old lady would be satisfied—but no!

Her own parents had been thrilled and Isabel delighted with the nephew who bore her husband's name. And now, while March blustered and rain beat down upon the fens, and with his sisters away ministering to another ancient relation, General Nicolson was off to London to lay siege to the India Office—leaving his wife alone in Northamptonshire to bear the brunt of his mother's disapproval. After examining her grandson minutely, and checking that he had the correct number of fingers and toes, the old biddy was now criticising his name. Or was it his size? Already Violet was bitterly regretting India.

The moment Mrs Nicolson dozed off in her chair she tiptoed out. She confided her son to his nurse, put on a cape, and made her escape into the wind-swept garden. Looking about her furtively, she scurried down the drive and out towards the freedom of the water meadows. Soon, thank God, she would be off to London too, and this dismal place could be forgotten!

Shortly after returning to Cambridge Street, Violet received a letter from William Heinemann. She had forgotten all about the manuscript dispatched in autumn the previous year and the publisher's invitation to luncheon came as a great surprise. So too was what he had to say.

'Your work is most interesting, Mrs Nicolson,' he told her, once the niceties were over and they were sitting down to eat.

'Thank you,' she said.

'Your husband has read it?' and Heinemann's lips curved in a slight smile.

'Yes, he has. In fact, he helped me copy it out.'

'Ah, that would explain the two different hands. One so much easier to read—though each distinctive in its own way, of course.' He twinkled at her once more and Violet was forced to laugh. 'Malcolm's is the neater,' she confessed, and they ate in companionable silence for a while.

'I should very much like to publish your work, Mrs Nicolson,' the publisher said, over the pudding. 'Do you think your husband would agree?'

'Does he have to?' Violet frowned.

'Given the nature of some of the verse, perhaps it would be wise.'

'Mr Heinemann, this whole idea was my husband's,' Violet pointed out. 'I most certainly would have done nothing without his encouragement—I hope you understand that—and I can't imagine him objecting in any way.'

William Heinemann looked at his guest who had never appeared more the innocent. She didn't follow the drift of the conversation at all, he realised, and he didn't know her well enough to risk putting his reservations into words. He was quite sure, however, that General Nicolson would understand at once.

'Perhaps you would discuss everything we've been talking about with your husband,' he suggested as they parted, 'and let me know what he thinks as soon as you can.'

Alone in their sitting room that evening Violet told Malcolm what the publisher had said. 'Mr Heinemann talked about *the nature of some of the verse* making it desirable I should have your consent before he goes ahead. I don't understand what he means—do you?'

Upon reflection General Nicolson understood only too well. What had seemed pleasant and enjoyable, when read alone in the privacy of their home, might seem little short of sensational when seen on the printed page. While he was mulling this over Violet spoke again.

'He asked what name I intended to use. I said, "Why, Violet Nicolson, of course," and he said I should discuss that with you, too. Malcolm, what did he mean? Have I suddenly become so very stupid?'

'Not stupid, darling, but perhaps a little naive,' and he ventured to explain. 'Your poems express emotions that some readers might find shocking— did you never realise?'

'No. I wrote what I felt, or what I imagined others might feel. What's so shocking about that? You've always told me I'm the same as anyone else, so anyone reading my poetry would understand, surely?'

'They might not understand if they knew that the poetry was written by a woman. In a man such feelings might seem more—acceptable.'

Violet snorted. 'What are you saying, Malcolm? That you don't want me to publish it after all?'

'No, no—haven't I always encouraged you?'

'Then what is it?'

'I'm not happy at the thought of your name being attached to the book.' There. He had said it. He waited for the storm to break, and break it did.

'My name, or yours? What are you afraid of? That I disgrace you in some way? I'm not ashamed of anything I've written!'

'Of course not, but it may not seem fitting in a general's wife.'

'Ah. There we have it! *A General's Wife*,' and Violet's voice was heavy with scorn. 'A lieutenant's wife may publish—and be damned!—but not *A General's Wife*. You're afraid of a *succès de scandale*, and that it will come between you and a future appointment, is that it?' Her eyes sparked at him until he felt no bigger than his son. His son …

'And we have to think of the boy,' he added.

'Little Malcolm? Don't be ridiculous—it will be years before he can read!'

'You know very well what I mean. I'm sorry, my dear, but I refuse to allow you to use the name of Violet Nicolson on the book.'

'You can't—can you?'

'Probably. I hope you won't make it necessary for me to find out.'

They glared at each other as they had so often in the past.

'Very well. I shall call myself *Adela* Nicolson —' Malcolm shook his head.

'*Florence* Nicolson then.'

'No. In fact, it might be wise if you took the name of a man.'

'What? I refuse to do any such thing! You brought me to London two years ago to show me that women can think for themselves, that they can be independent, that they are equal with men—and that it was a wholly admirable thing. You made me proud of myself, you filled me with hope. And now you expect me to turn my back on everything I believe in!'

Instead, she turned her back on her husband, and did not speak to him again all day.

She did not wish to use a pseudonym—it was dishonest and besides, what was the point? Her sister used a pseudonym and people still knew who she was. Annie Sophie ... now no one could accuse *her* of worrying about public disapproval. Several books already, and more were probably on the way, and all selling well—even if her reputation had more holes in it than a sieve. Was that what Malcolm was afraid of? And if not, what *did* he fear? Whatever it was, she told herself glumly, he was hardly likely to discuss it with her now.

She went to find her grandmother, and sat on the floor beside her chair. Caroline Cory looked down affectionately as she listened to the whole sorry tale. 'Someone more famous than you will ever be, Addie, my dear—for all your undoubted gifts—once asked: *What's in a name*? What *is* in a name, dear, after all? If Malcolm has qualms, you must respect them. His good name is worth a great deal to him, and a great deal to you both.'

Violet was reminded of how she had prayed for the integrity of that very name two years before and felt a little ashamed.

Caroline Cory stood up and went over to a glass cabinet. When she returned she handed her granddaughter a silver goblet that Violet had never seen before. 'Look at it, Addie,' and Violet saw there was some kind of a design.

'It's our family crest,' explained Mrs Cory, and her granddaughter looked more closely at the stars and griffins' heads. 'What does the motto say, Addie?' the calm voice intruded on her thoughts.

'*Virtus semper viridis*. Virtue is ever green.' Violet looked up at her grandmother questioningly.

'Malcolm has a right to expect his good name to remain untarnished, don't you think? Honour should be allowed to flourish.'

'Yes,' said Violet slowly. 'It should spring eternal. Like hope.' A little smile began to play upon her lips.

'The world often sees evil where no evil exists,' Caroline Cory went on. 'These are love poems, you say?' Violet nodded. 'Love poems you addressed to your husband?'

'No, Grandmother, not really—or only a few. Some of them are translations of Indian songs.'

'And the others? Did you address them to someone else?'

'No, of course not!'

Mrs Cory gently patted the hot indignant cheek. 'Others may think that you did, my dear. And that is why Malcolm is afraid. He knows how much you love him, and so do your friends and your family, but what of the rest, the strangers, people who make more of the age difference than you do? No, Addie,' the old lady was quite adamant, 'for his sake and your own there must be no name that will link you to him, not even the Christian names you never use. *Now* do you understand? And do you not agree that any name at all will do for your book—and that you should tell your husband as much?'

Violet looked at her grandmother. She was so wise, and it seemed easy to agree to do as she suggested. It was not so easy when General Nicolson came back from dinner at one of his clubs. He was warmly civil to Mrs Cory and virtually ignored his wife.

'Look, Malcolm, I'm sorry.' Alone later, and without her grandmother's encouraging eye, Violet was finding it more difficult to apologise than usual. She stood squarely in front of the tall, silent figure and made herself continue. 'I don't suppose it matters what name I use,' she said ungraciously, 'and if you want it to be a man's name, then all right, I suppose I agree.'

It was hardly a handsome apology, but Nicolson knew it was the only one he was likely to get. And he could see her point of view. 'I'm sorry, too,' he said immediately. 'I know I've upset you. Have you thought about a name?'

'I think so. But it's late. Perhaps we can talk about it tomorrow?'

'No. We'll talk about it tonight. And then we can let Heinemann know what we've decided.'

By the time they went to bed they had reached some kind of reconciliation. But in the publisher's book-lined office next morning the matter still rankled.

'And what of the book's title, Mrs Nicolson? I trust you've decided on that as well?' Heinemann leaned forward eagerly in his huge leather armchair.

'Oh, yes, Mr Heinemann, I most certainly have.' Violet gave Malcolm a sly look before replying. 'I thought that as you two gentlemen seemed so struck with its *sensual* nature, I should call it *The Garden of Kama*—Kama, of course, being the Hindu god of love. Then everyone will know what to expect, and, from what you seem to be suggesting, no one will be disappointed!'

Nicolson raised an eyebrow; the title was something they had quite overlooked in the course of their nocturnal deliberations. But one capitulation from his wife was all he could reasonably expect, he decided, and he made no comment on her choice.

William Heinemann sensed there had been some kind of a conflict between his newest writer and her husband, and was relieved that the typesetting could go ahead at last. All being well, he told them, *The Garden of Kama* would be on his autumn list.

'Fame and fortune and folly and fret'

If Violet's business was concluded Malcolm's was not. He still hoped for news from the India Office but time was dragging on. Meanwhile, he could not be tempted away from London, and the couple was still in Cambridge Street when the social season got under way.

Sir John and Lady Lister Kaye took up residence in Bolton Street once more, and the baronet had several pleasant lunches at his club with the general.

'Sir John was asking after you, Violet,' her husband duly informed her. 'He hopes we will dine with them one evening soon.'

'I don't think I can leave the baby, darling, do you?' It was the perfect excuse—an eight-month-old infant required its mother at the most irregular times.

'I'm sure we could manage something.'

'I don't think I want to *manage something*, as you put it, Malcolm, and your son might not understand.' And that, he could see, was to be her last word on the subject. It was strange, he reflected later, how she managed afternoon tea with Blanche Crackanthorpe so often, nonetheless.

It was not, in fact, the baronet who wished to see Violet, but Natica, his wife. When she heard that the Nicolsons were back, Lady Lister Kaye expressed her delight and her wish to meet Violet again. Since the unfortunate death of her financier brother in April and her inheritance of part of his substantial fortune, Lady Lister Kaye was becoming adept at expressing her wishes—and Johnny Kaye, always short of funds himself, more ready to listen to his wife. When he told her that Mrs Nicolson felt unable to leave her infant son for any length of time Natica was not to be deterred. She ordered her carriage and took herself off to Pimlico.

'Isn't he gorgeous?' she exclaimed upon her introduction to the Nicolsons' son and heir. 'Just look at those little hands, Violet! Do you realise how lucky you are?'

Violet did. Her child was a constant source of wonder, and how she and Malcolm could have produced something quite so perfect she still didn't understand.

'I had a son too, you know,' Natica told her. 'He didn't live long, a few months, that's all. I sometimes think that if he hadn't died, or if I'd been able to have more children, then Johnny and I—' She caught Violet's horrified look and stopped with a smile. 'I'm sorry, Violet. I tend to forget how easily you English get embarrassed.'

'You're not embarrassing me, Natica. I just don't think you should blame yourself for any difficulties between you and Sir John, that's all. I lost two children, and it brought *us* closer together. But it's none of my business, of course.'

She hoped Natica would change the subject, but her visitor was quite happy to talk. 'Johnny married me for my money. Only there wasn't that much at the time, or not enough to settle his debts as it turned out. Johnny does everything in style—perhaps you've noticed?' The laugh Lady Lister Kaye gave was scornful. 'Even his women are on the grand scale—you've seen him with the statuesque Gladys, no doubt?'

It would be difficult not to, Violet remarked.

'I simply cannot understand why women find him so attractive,' the baronet's wife went on bitterly. 'They all end up falling at his feet.'

'Not quite all of them, Natica,' Violet said soberly.

'You mean Johnny—Johnny *tried*—?'

'Yes. In the library at Wharncliffe House two years ago.' Mrs Nicolson gave a grim little smile before adding: 'I hope you won't mind me saying, Natica, that in my opinion your husband has about as much physical attraction as a snake—and very possibly less. I'm sorry if you find that offensive, but it's the truth!'

Lady Lister Kaye burst into peals of uninhibited laughter.

'I've told no one, not even Malcolm,' Violet went on, 'because I dealt with the matter in a rather unusual way and he might not have approved. Perhaps Sir John still has the scar on his hand?'

So that was why Johnny disliked Violet Nicolson so much ... Natica gazed at her hostess in admiration, and was more than ever determined to entertain Violet in her home.

In June another unexpected visitor came to Cambridge Street. Mrs Nicolson was alone when her younger sister called, and she stood up, surprised and uncertain what to say.

'I've come to see my nephew,' Miss Cory announced. 'I've only just heard. How naughty of you, Addie, to keep the news to yourself!'

'It's no secret. Everyone except you must know—and I hardly thought you'd be interested. What is it now, Annie Sophie, seven years since we've seen each other? You're looking well.'

Her sister was looking extremely prosperous too, in a well-tailored close-fitting dark-blue suit. Violet suspected that the voluptuous curves were held in check by the fond embraces of a corset, but the effect was most fetching, nonetheless—to anyone who liked their blondes running slightly to fat.

Sitting down, Miss Cory acknowledged the compliment, with a smile that disappeared almost instantly as she remarked: 'I'd be obliged if you'd remember my name is Vivian.'

'*Vivian*. Yes. I forgot. So you don't call yourself *Victoria Cross* then? Although

I suppose it would be considered a little impertinent.'

Vivian Cory smiled, disclosing perfect little teeth. 'Still as forthright as ever, Addie, I see. I suppose you've read my books—all three of them?'

'I started one of them once—I can't say it was very much to my taste.'

Vivian let her pale eyes run over her sister's unfashionable dress and thick hair caught loosely with a ribbon. 'Ah, yes,' she murmured, 'it always comes down to taste.'

A silence developed.

'So where is my nephew, Addie? I really do want to see him, you know.'

'He's asleep.' And his mother wasn't going to wake him.

'And Grandmother?'

'She's having her afternoon nap.'

'Malcolm can't be sleeping too, surely?'

'No, he's out.'

'And how *is* my dear brother-in-law?' Her nephew was only an excuse; it was Malcolm Nicolson she really wanted to see.

'Malcolm is very well. Stay, and you can see for yourself. He shouldn't be long. I expect we can find something to talk about till then, don't you?'

It wasn't difficult; Vivian Cory was all too happy to talk about herself and her foreign travels—and her Griffin uncle.

'How *is* Heneage?'

'He's busy. Once he's wound up his affairs in the States he's coming back to England for good. Although we shall winter on the Continent, of course.'

'Of course. So you've come back early. Why?' Violet thought there had to be a reason.

There was, and Vivian Cory's eyes began to shine. She was back for the publication of her latest novel, she said, and it would be an absolute sensation!

'Surely that's for the public to decide?'

Vivian looked at her sister pityingly. It would be a sensation, she told her, because of the subject. 'It's terribly exciting, Addie,' and she gave a mysterious smile.

'And probably indecent! Have you thought for one moment of your family, and how they feel about all this?'

'Don't be so stuffy! Who are *you* to pass judgement on *me*? You've upset enough people in your time!'

'That's very true. And I'm sorry. But you're not. You enjoy being in the centre of a cheap sensation, don't you? *Don't you?*'

Before Vivian could reply, Malcolm Nicolson came in. He went to his wife and kissed her before seeing the visitor. He straightened slowly, and brother and sister-in-law looked at one another for a long moment in silence.

He was old ... tall and upright as ever, but with deep lines marking his face and hair turned an iron grey. The great moustache didn't help either, thought Miss Cory, though it was probably obligatory in a general. She looked from her brother-in-law to Addie. Addie so young and fresh-looking to be the wife of this man of nearly sixty—and the mother of his baby son.

Vivian no longer found her brother-in-law so attractive, but the feeling of jealousy remained. Her sister looked so happy; she would give anything to remove that look of smug complacency from her face—and if she ever got the chance, she would!

She didn't stay long. She would see her nephew and grandmother the next time, she promised gaily, and she would bring them a copy of her new book.

'I'm glad you came back when you did, darling,' Violet said in relief, as she watched her sister hail a cab. 'We were just beginning to fight.'

'She hasn't changed much—there's just a little more of her, that's all.' Malcolm was obviously unimpressed with what he had seen.

Violet giggled. 'I thought exactly the same. But wasn't she well dressed?'

That was certainly true, he agreed. Perhaps Violet should ask Vivian the name of her dressmaker?

'But I don't go anywhere. Why would I want new clothes?'

It was the old argument and Nicolson let matters lie, until Violet at last accepted an invitation from Lady Lister Kaye, and she found that none of her dresses would fit.

'I'm not fat!' she said defensively.

'No, of course you're not. You've just changed shape a little. What can you expect?'

'I *expect* I shall suffocate! I certainly shan't be able to eat a thing. Malcolm, I won't go—I look dreadful.'

'There I can't agree. Look at yourself.'

Violet did, and was appalled. Her stomach was flat, and her hips and waist slender, but the rest—it was disgusting!

Nicolson grinned at her reaction. 'You'll be the envy of every woman there.'

'You didn't say there'd be a crowd— Darling, I'm staying here.'

'Nonsense. Come on, or we'll be late.'

Sir John was not looking forward to the evening, either. As he dressed, he examined a small scar on his right palm from time to time, and when his wife asked, 'How did you hurt yourself, Johnny?' the mock concern in her voice made him glance up sharply. Damn it, he thought, she knew.

There was no crowd, in fact, and Natica had chosen her guests with care. The de Greys were there: she thought Gladys might like to share Johnny's discomfiture; the Charles Beresfords who were barely ever civil to each other, to ginger

Johnny up about China and to keep the general amused; and of course the Nicolsons. What a pity Consuelo wouldn't come, but the dowager duchess was mourning her brother, and her twin daughters who had died the previous year, and not even the ill-disguised scowl on Johnny's face as he sat down with Mrs Nicolson beside him could have brought a smile to her sister's tragic face.

The baronet scarcely uttered a word, but while his thin lips savoured the excellent food his eyes feasted on his neighbour's shapely bosom. Violet ate virtually nothing. The man was as bad as ever, she decided, vowing never to set foot in Bolton Street again. Natica would just have to understand!

Gladys de Grey, seated next to General Nicolson, exercised all her considerable charm—how amusing it would be to succeed with the husband when Johnny had failed with the wife. She met with no success. Malcolm Nicolson answered her questions politely (while asking none of his own) and the blue-grey eyes only softened when resting, as they frequently did, on the small figure seated to the right of Lister Kaye.

How terribly boring, Gladys decided after a while—a man who was in love with his wife! The countess, the relict of one cuckolded earl and the promiscuous wife of another, had never understood the attractions of monogamy and she abandoned her thankless task. With a gleaming smile she turned her attention to Admiral Lord Charles who, she had good reason to believe, totally shared her views.

The Nicolsons did not linger after dinner. Looking at Violet's unhappy face, Malcolm thought she was fretting for the baby, and as soon as was polite he took her home. Thank goodness, Violet said to herself as they left. She had done her duty by her husband and faced up to Lister Kaye. But now it was finished.

She was wrong. Other invitations followed, and soon the Nicolsons were known all over town.

It might have been pleasant were it not for Annie Sophie. She had visited her sister again and brought with her a copy of her newest book inscribed: *V.N. from your affectionate sister, Victoria Cross*, and after the young woman left Violet settled down in the garden to read. She fell asleep in the warm summer sunshine after only a few pages and when she awoke Malcolm was there, reading the novel in his turn.

'Hello, darling, I didn't hear you. Have you been back long?' She stretched out her hand to him and he took it absent-mindedly.

'Long enough,' he replied. 'How much of this stuff have you read?'

'Just the beginning. She has quite an eye for Anglo-India, don't you think?'

'And not much of an eye for anything else, if you ask me.'

Nicolson read it with a horrid fascination late into the night and suggested Violet read it next day. 'Well?' he asked, when she put the novel down at last.

The candid eyes looked into his. 'It's horrible. Quite horrible. Malcolm, she said it would be a sensation, and she was right. Whatever will people think?'

'They will think that people in India behave in that way, I imagine.' Malcolm's cool gaze held hers. 'And will you lend your copy to anyone else to read, I wonder?'

Violet remembered the inscription and shook her head.

'Why not?'

'Because they'll know she's my sister, of course.'

'So a pseudonym can be useful, after all?'

Violet sent him a look of intense exasperation. 'Did you make me read that awful book, just so that you could make your point yet again? Oh, Malcolm, surely you don't think my book will be anything like hers?'

'No, but it may well have the same effect. And you *are* writing about the strongest emotion of all. The normal reaction is to look for the source of a writer's inspiration. Who is the heroine based on, people may ask, in your sister's case—and, in yours, who is the mysterious lover?'

'But my inspiration is India!'

'And who do you think would believe that?'

Violet refused to worry. After all, no one could possibly guess the identity of 'Laurence Hope'.

Blanche Crackanthorpe settled back in her chair with a smirk. 'Well, my dear Violet, I think I can safely say that your sister has excelled herself this time.'

'With *Anna Lombard*, do you mean, Blanche?' Violet looked at the thin sardonic face opposite.

'Indeed I do. She has an amazing imagination—unless that is how Englishwomen behave in India, of course. How many of them take native lovers, do you think—and then marry them in secret?'

'None. It's impossible to have secrets in India—and a secret like that would spread like wildfire.' And rumours too, the younger woman thought uncomfortably.

'So what Vivian writes about white women being attracted to natives is quite wrong, would you say?'

'I don't really know, Blanche. Perhaps not. Afghans are extremely striking, physically, but I've never been attracted to them myself, if that's what you're asking. My sister is absolutely right when she says they believe that women have no souls—and I find the thought of being at the mercy of any one of them positively chilling—' She remembered an occasion when she so nearly was, and shivered even now.

'No, it's all extremely far fetched,' Violet assured Mrs Crackanthorpe. 'And for a woman to be in love with one man while submitting willingly to the intimate embraces of another—Blanche, it's too horrid for words!'

'Has Malcolm read the book?'

'Yes. He said very little, except that he was glad Vivian used a pseudonym. And he commented on the fact that she always talked about *old* colonels and *old* generals.'

Blanche hid a smile—yes, she thought, that might indeed strike a nerve. 'People are buying the book by the thousands,' she said aloud, 'whatever you may think of its literary merits. I suppose the ideas *are* very modern—'

'Perhaps.' Violet was not prepared to find even the slightest merit in her sister's work.

'And have *you* never thought of writing, my dear? Your other sister writes too, I believe.'

Violet felt a pang of disloyalty towards her friend as she denied any such inclination. Blanche had obviously forgotten what she had said about writing poetry, and it seemed wiser not to remind her. The lie continued to trouble her, and in November, when *The Garden of Kama* appeared in the bookshops, she found it extremely difficult to keep silent. The book had an olive-green dust jacket and was bound in the same soft colour. Her own verses leapt out at her from the pages, and how she wanted to proclaim that this, too, was her child! But she had given Malcolm her word and, difficult as it was, when the book was the talk of London, she gave no one any cause at all to link Mr Laurence Hope with Mrs Malcolm Nicolson.

In January 1902, worn out by repeated attacks of dysentery and believing he had not long to live, Colonel Arthur Cory made his will. In February he and his wife left Karachi. Entrusting the *Sind Gazette* to his competent oldest daughter, and saying farewell to the town he had done so much to shape, the colonel set his face towards England where he would see his mother and his two younger daughters for one last time.

No one was looking forward to the colonel's arrival more than 'Victoria Cross'. She had puzzled for some time over *The Garden of Kama*, which had been brought to her notice by friends. Was this an authentic picture of the India she knew so well? they asked the author of *Anna Lombard*. She was an expert on the sub-continent, so what did she think?

After reading them, Miss Cory had to admit that the verses were certainly familiar. Oh, not because of the *moghra* and champak flowers—no, it went deeper than that. It was as if she had read some of them before. Not because of any clichés—indeed, for first verses, they were remarkably free of such blemishes. No, it was the *passion* and the *melodrama* she had already met, as well as some of the images. Vivian lay back on her *chaise longue* and popped one chocolate after another into her greedy little mouth as her mind began to wander.

Her parents must be preparing to leave Karachi and she imagined they wouldn't miss it—the place was so *provincial.* Who had said that once? Why, Malcolm, of course; she remembered the advice she had taken so eagerly. And it had all been Addie's doing, she realised now; Addie who disliked her so much, Addie, who had always been unkind. Addie, who had always frightened her a little, especially when she had found her in her room once, reading her verses …

The erstwhile Annie Sophie's eyes narrowed in discovery; *that was it*! Addie Nicolson, who never tired of preaching, so pious and so smug; *Addie Nicolson* had written those sensual verses celebrating physical passion in such a shocking way! Acceptable in a man, of course, but in a woman, and a serving general's wife at that?

Vivian Cory chewed on the last chocolate with particular delight, and then she stood up. She had people to see and things to do before her parents arrived—and she intended to make use of every minute.

'Darling, they've reviewed the book in *The Athenaeum* and they've quoted *The Garden of Kama* in full. Isn't it exciting?' Violet looked up from the journal she was reading and raised her face as usual for her husband's kiss. Today, however, he did not approach but stood watching from the doorway.

'What is it? Something's wrong, tell me.' She quickly got to her feet. 'Is it Father?'

'No, your father should be here at the end of the week. No, Violet, I've come from the Carlton Club where someone has just congratulated me on being the husband of Laurence Hope.' He paused to let the full import of his words sink in.

All Violet felt was relief that the deception was finally over, but Malcolm was obviously taking the matter very seriously indeed. 'I'm sorry if you're upset,' she told her husband, 'but you really shouldn't worry. It's bound to be a nine days' wonder. They'll soon forget—you'll see. Now,' and the poet turned back calmly to the journal, 'would you like to hear the review, or not?'

Violet might have chosen to ignore the gossip but it refused to go away. Each day Nicolson had to endure innuendo and knowing glances, and when his parents-in-law arrived he was almost at his wits' end as to what to do or think.

The Corys' delight in their grandson helped him forget for a while. Little Malcolm at eighteen months was walking strongly and beginning to talk, and he took to his grandfather immediately. He would sit on his knee for long periods, pulling at the still elegantly trimmed white beard while Violet watched with a lump in her throat, filled with gratitude that her father should have been spared long enough to enjoy a happy relationship with the little boy.

One afternoon Arthur Cory stayed in while mother and daughter took the child to the nearby park, and Nicolson decided to confide his worries.

'Oh, yes,' Cory said, 'Addie's told me all about the book and public reaction to it. She's no idea how her identity was discovered, but it was none of her doing—you do realise that, don't you?'

Violet had refused to discuss the matter further after that day, but her husband knew she wasn't at fault. 'I didn't ask her, Arthur; she gave me her word to keep silent and I trust her.'

'Of course. And now you're worried what people are thinking, is that it?' In the manner of those who sense death waiting at their shoulder, Colonel Cory decided to allow himself the luxury of speaking frankly. 'So what *do* you imagine they're thinking, my dear fellow?'

'That she must have had a lover to inspire the verses.'

'Which is absolute rubbish!' Violet's father scoffed at the very idea. 'There's no one on this earth more honest than Adela—which makes life very uncomfortable for us all at times! If my daughter had taken a lover, she would have told you—and faced the consequences. And why would she want one? I know for a fact that she still loves you as much as she did when you married. And I imagine you feel the same about her—or we wouldn't be having this conversation.'

'Yes.'

'So what's a little gossip? Anyone who knows the two of you will know the truth, and no one else matters, surely?' He could see that Nicolson was still looking preoccupied. 'Is there more to it, then?' he asked.

'Yes, and I should have thought of it before.' The general heaved a sigh. 'It's two years now since we left Mhow and I've been hoping for another appointment, but there's nothing forthcoming. I'm afraid that when this business reaches the India Office, my chances will be finished.'

'I see,' Colonel Cory said slowly. 'Well, don't tell my daughter, whatever you do—it would break her heart if she thought she were in any way to blame. But let me say this to you in all seriousness, Nick: the Army in India is finished—or finished as you and I know it. Sweeping changes are taking place and men like you, with your special talents, are no longer seen as necessary. It's tragic, but there it is! They want an army run on British lines, all heartless drill and manoeuvres—what part could you play in a system like that? No,' and the white beard wagged emphatically, 'for you, my dear fellow, it's over, whether you like it or not. You must have seen the changes coming, surely?'

Nicolson had, in Mhow, but had refused to recognise them. 'So what do I do, Arthur? Resign?'

His father-in-law gave a terse laugh. 'Don't jump,' he advised. 'Wait till you're pushed! But think about what you're going to do for the rest of your lives. Are you going to stay in England? Do you intend going back to India? You've decisions to make, both of you. Why don't you take my daughter away and discuss it—and leave my grandson with me?'

It was easy to take his father-in-law's advice, but more of a problem to persuade his wife.

'He's *not* a baby, Violet,' Malcolm pointed out patiently when at first she refused to leave her son. 'He's eighteen months old, two in September, and he'll be perfectly safe. Your parents and grandmother adore him; so let them enjoy him on their own. Your father hasn't much longer; let him spoil the little lad.'

'And you always said that was so bad for him! Oh, do you really think he'll be all right?'

'He has his nurse—she'll keep your parents under control, just as she manages you!'

'So where are you thinking of going?' Despite herself, Violet was intrigued.

'To the North African desert. We'll have the warm sun on our backs and the spring flowers at our feet. What more could we want?'

She wanted her son but, failing that, his father's undivided attention would do very nicely. She told him so.

She was extremely reluctant, all the same, her husband could see that, but it would do her good. If they did go back to India, the separation from their son would be a lot longer than the two months he planned for them at present.

9

'The Tents of Silence and the Camp of Peace'

MOROCCO AND ENGLAND, MARCH 1902–DECEMBER 1903

If Arthur Cory considered Morocco an unusual choice for a holiday, he said nothing. Neither did his daughter. Violet believed Malcolm wanted privacy at last, away from the claims of relations and friends, the endless social round, and the existence of 'Laurence Hope'; that he wanted time to explore and re-discover the joys of a long-lost past. But she was wrong; his interest in North Africa was of quite a different order, and in Morocco, one of the world's crossroads, where East met West amid the mingled smells of oranges and offal, her husband—like so many others in limbo—once again turned his thoughts to trade.

And for this she had left her son …

Before long, however, curiosity got the better of her. In Morocco Violet found a mixture of the mediaeval and the modern that reminded her of China. The same interested parties continued their intrigues, but, whereas in China commerce was subject to tradition and strict codes of conduct and taboos, in Morocco everything was for sale and everyone had their price. Perhaps, reflected Violet Nicolson wryly, that was a time-honoured tradition, too. Was this why they had come to North Africa—to pit their wits as amateurs against men who had spent a lifetime twisting and cheating their way towards success?

Thank God for Walter Burton Harris, the cynical and eccentric local correspondent of the London *Times* who had crossed their path in Tangiers two weeks after their arrival. He invited them to stay at the exotic Villa Harris and once they were there, he said what Violet no longer cared to point out—that Malcolm, as a soldier not a businessman, was more used to the field of honour than the melting-pot of vice. He added that while General Nicolson might be used to the Afghan races, he was certainly not up to the antics of the French.

'They've been nibbling away at Algeria since 1830, General, and they would very much like to acquire Morocco. And the French have a way of getting what they want—in Africa, anyway.' Looking Malcolm squarely in the eye, Harris delivered a warning: 'If you're prepared to fight them, and all the lowdown devious methods they've spent centuries perfecting, then by all means go ahead, General Nicolson. They make better enemies than friends, but as business rivals the French are deadly! Take my advice, man, and keep your money safe.' *And keep an eye on your wife while you're about it*.

'Lace me up *tight*.' Violet was taking more trouble than usual over her toilette and had chosen her smartest gown. She had no intention of looking provincial at Walter Harris's dinner for the French he so delighted in denigrating, nor of being bored when Malcolm left her (as he most surely would) to her own devices.

'I don't need to. You've lost weight.' Malcolm turned her round. 'You're not fretting for the boy, are you? If so, you must go home.'

'A little, perhaps,' she admitted, caressing his cheek briefly. How could he be so kind, and yet so neglectful? 'But I don't want to go back—not yet anyway.' And certainly not until this madness was safely put to rest—for good.

'How do I look?' she asked at last.

'Extremely elegant, my wife, if a little pale.'

Violet searched on her dressing table, found what she wanted, and rubbed a little rouge into her cheeks.

'War paint,' Malcolm was surprised and by no means approving. 'I didn't think decent women used such tricks.' His wife stared at his expression in the mirror, and then with more than a trace of defiance applied a touch more red to her lips. She put kohl on her lower lids, added a few more pins to her hair and finally straightened.

She looked taller. Whether her coiffure would stay in place, her husband wasn't sure—without the help of a maid the arrangement was perhaps a little ambitious, but it certainly gave her height. As did the little heels on her shoes. Away from the bright light on the dressing table the colour seemed less brash. Her face took on mysterious tones, and the East beckoned from her enormous eyes.

Her husband moved towards the door and held it open for her. They did not look at one another, and Violet Nicolson walked through without another word.

If Walter Harris had wished to underline his earlier comments, he couldn't have succeeded better. With their talk over dinner of a railway to link Rabat with neighbouring Algeria, it was as if the Frenchmen had control of the country already! The Moroccans were *so backward*, lamented her neighbour on her left. They feared the railway would do away with the need for camels—as it would, of course, but who cared about that if it meant *progress*? And what an outcry when the Sultan was photographed! These people were so *primitive* in their views … The man gave an affected little laugh.

'It's their religion,' Violet pointed out. 'It forbids the making of any human image. Surely no one should criticise them for adhering to what they believe?' Her low clear voice penetrated the hum of general conversation and when everyone else stopped talking to listen, the man's discomfiture was obvious. The silence added force to her remarks, spoken in attractively accented French. But the attention she received was unlikely to win her friends among the women either, thought her husband, nor was the fact that she looked so very handsome. Despite the artificial colouring she had employed, Violet had a long way to go before she matched that of the *mesdames* gathered in Harris's seaside property that night and she really need not have bothered—they had been in the African sun far too long and, for all their Parisian chic, looked faded and well past their prime.

How his own wife managed to look so fresh after all her years in India, he could never quite fathom, and he watched her afterwards as, with a enigmatic smile on her still red lips, she held a swarm of gallants at bay. She might be resisting what she later termed their 'colonising efforts', yet it simply spurred them on. They laughed at everything she said, and was it only the wine that made her eyes sparkle in response? With a frown General Nicolson forced himself to give his full attention to the desiccated Frenchwoman at his side.

The next day Harris offered them the use of his servants and his tents for as long as they liked. 'Get out of Tangiers,' he urged. 'See the *real* country.' For the city—as he was at pains to explain—was Eastern but not *of* the East as they knew it. Jews, Berbers and Moors might walk the alleys of the Old Town, donkeys, camels and mules laden with goods from the interior might block the Soco Grande and the air might reek with the stench of dung, but only a few yards further away cosmopolitan Tangiers sought to deny the East, and there the values were Western in the extreme.

General Nicolson did not hesitate to take his host's advice. Thoughts of trade were no longer paramount in his mind, and with the minimum of explanation he carried his taciturn wife off into the north African *bled* where spring flowers and ripening grain cast a rich patchwork before them, and where Violet's heavy heart lightened for a spell. The colours were so beautiful, and these rolling plains might have been Baluchistan … Then the reminiscent smile faded from her lips. Malcolm's eyes might scan the far horizons in the hawk-like way she knew of old, but the mountains ahead were unfamiliar and this was no homecoming. There were no campfire songs waiting for them in the blue-grey distance, no mingling with tribesmen in villages where Malcolm was hailed as one of their own.

Here, in the *bled* they were alien.

Yet were they any different to the nomads they passed, or who passed them without a word of greeting? Would they ever settle down, or was she to spend the rest of her days moving restlessly from one group of relations to another while Malcolm pursued his quest for El Dorado? Would their child ever know a home of his own?

Would their old intimacy ever return?

The silence of the desert—*his* silence—weighed upon her soul like lead. Dear God, if only they could go back to the truly golden time! To the days when they had laughed and loved and talked freely in surroundings such as these—when there had been no secrets, no constraints. Violet Nicolson made up her mind: their differences must be resolved here, on neutral ground, and when they reached Fez, the holy city whose *souks* were full of slaves, she found the freedom to speak.

Dressed in Moorish garments, their heads covered by the hoods of cream-coloured *haiks*, husband and wife wandered into a walled sunlit garden set unexpectedly among the Old Town's scholarship and squalor. Banks of irises lined the flagstones of the paths, and from the valley flowering apricots and oranges sent fragrance to them on the lazy morning breeze. Nearby a Persian waterwheel was turning, turning …

Lulled by its perpetual movement and the sound of the ancient refrain, the Nicolsons settled into their no-man's-land of displacement and disguise and Violet felt able to break the heavy silence. 'What patience that donkey has,' she sighed, as the blindfolded beast described its endless circles and the wheel moved round and round, creaking on into eternity, and sending the sparkling water through the deserted garden as it had for centuries past. She turned to the robed figure at her side. The eyes narrowed against the sunlight were still the eyes of a dreamer.

'Malcolm,' she forced herself to ask, 'what are you thinking?' He came back to reality with an effort then he gave her a slow and friendly smile.

'I was thinking how good it was to be back in the South, with the sun on my back and in my bones—and to be honest, I was thinking of Baluchistan.'

'I've been thinking about it too—the flowers reminded me so as we came over the *bled*.'

'We can't go back, sweetheart. It would never be the same.'

'I know,' and she gave another sigh. 'I know. And how I've changed—that girl has gone for ever!'

'Has she? I see signs of her quite often. Although recently all I've seen is a total stranger. What have you been trying to do, Violet?' He knew perfectly well, but all the same he pushed the hood back from her face and forced her to meet his gaze.

She flushed. 'I wanted you—I wanted us—' it was impossible to finish, but she tried, in an attempt at last to clear the air. He listened with a hurt deep in his eyes.

'I've never stopped loving you, Violet, even if I haven't expressed that love in the way you wanted—and the way I've wanted, too. I'm sorry if you thought other men found you more attractive than your husband—' He took her hand and raised it to his lips, too proud, even with her, to admit he was growing older. Instead, he fell back on the perennial excuse—although the Lord knew that was true enough as well. 'Sweetheart,' he said, 'I've had a great many things on my mind for months,' and he hoped that would content her.

It did, and with his explanation came a great sense of shame. She felt small and mean—she *had* behaved very badly. And there had been things she should have noticed, things she *might* have noticed, had it not been for preoccupations of her own. 'And I've spent so much time with the baby—' she said contritely.

'Of course you have.' The tender look he gave her only made things worse.

'And the book,' she went on. 'You were so upset about *The Garden of Kama*. Oh, darling, forgive me, I should have understood.' She had never sounded more remorseful as she continued: 'Malcolm, I'm truly sorry about the other night.'

'So am I,' he told her, and her flush deepened to an unbecoming scarlet. He had rebuked her sternly for her flirtatious behaviour, she had reproached him angrily for his neglect, and a silence had fallen that was only being broken now. 'It was as much my fault as yours,' he admitted. 'I've hardly confided in you lately.'

'You never do,' she answered. 'And I don't suppose you ever will,' for that was how he was. With the final realisation that nothing would ever change him, her eyes spilled over with tears.

'Don't cry,' he pleaded, 'don't cry. There's enough water here as it is!' and she managed a shaky little laugh. 'I don't mind about anything, I don't even care about the book. Not any more. They'll have forgotten all about it by now, so perhaps we should go back?'

Violet thought of her son with longing, and then she considered her husband. He looked so much at ease in his Arab robes and better than he had for months. Much as she loved the lad, the father would always come first. 'No, Malcolm,' she said firmly, 'we'll stay for as long as we planned. But what will you do *afterwards?*' The question she had been dreading to confront came unbidden to her lips.

'I shan't come back here, if that's what you mean? Harris is right, Morocco isn't the place for me.' And it wasn't the place for her. It wasn't simply the French he didn't like: there were other things beneath the surface that appalled his decent, straightforward nature—sordid things he wasn't prepared to explain to his wife.

'And from the look of it,' he went on, 'I shan't be in the Army, either.'

'And you'll mind that very much, won't you?'

'Of course. The Army has been my life.'

'Malcolm, I understand all that. But now it's time to start again.'

'Dearest little Vi, how logical you are, but I'm nearly fifty-nine! Tell me what to do with myself, and I'll do it. I've been looking and found nothing.'

'You have a wife and a son—enjoy them!'

'You make it sound easy, but don't you see? With your writing you have a whole new life stretching out before you; I'm at the end of mine.'

Violet was on her feet in a flash, looking down on him furiously with wonderfully indignant blue-black eyes. 'Don't you ever say that again—don't even think it! I'm here, you have me, that ought to be enough!'

Looking at her, Malcolm Nicolson had to admit that for the moment it was. She was more than any man could manage, diminutive though she was, and so he told her. 'Well, what shall we do?' he asked again, prepared at last to discuss their future. 'We can't live in London for ever—it's not fair on your grandmother, kind as she is—and quite frankly I'm tired of being a gypsy.'

'Find somewhere of our own?' she suggested, hardly daring to hope.

'Have you any idea of what that would cost? At present we don't have the money. Even renting somewhere on a permanent basis would be beyond us.'

Violet hesitated. 'At the risk of introducing a serpent into the Garden of Eden,' she ventured at last, 'what of Lister Kaye?'

'There you have it,' her husband admitted. 'What of Sir John? Whenever I ask about China, he always has an excuse, or some encouraging piece of news to keep me quiet. He thinks that within the year there'll be something positive to report. He even talks of going there himself.'

She snorted and Malcolm flinched. 'That's a very unbecoming habit,' he remarked, 'and lately it's been getting worse.'

Violet ignored him, and continued: 'Malcolm, if anything goes wrong—and it seems to me more likely than anything going right—what will we do?'

'Well, if we want to be independent—and still have enough money to educate the boy—then, as things stand, and unless we suddenly come into a fortune, we shall have to go back to India. We can live very cheaply and I'll find something useful to do.'

'I'd love that,' Violet said, happily. 'Why don't we do that anyway?' Suddenly her beloved India was all too far away.

Nicolson checked her gently. 'Patience, darling, we have to wait. You, of all people, should know that,' and they both thought of her ailing father. India, it might very well be, thought Malcolm Nicolson, and perhaps within the year, but how could he tell his wife that he felt she should go back without her son?

'I would not waste your time for long'

Tired but exhilarated after weeks of following what Harris had dubbed their 'alternative Grand Tour', a journey that in the end had taken them as far south as Marrakesh, the first person the Nicolsons saw on their return to Cambridge Street was Violet's younger sister. As they entered the hall, Vivian Cory came to greet them.

'Well,' she said, 'so the nomads have returned! Have you come to pitch your tents awhile, or will the caravan be moving on?'

Violet refused to be provoked. 'I expect we'll stay,' she said, trying to keep the dislike out of her voice. 'Where is everyone?'

'Father's sleeping, and so is Grandmother. The others are in the garden.'

Violet smiled apologetically and left Malcolm with her sister while she went to find her son.

'How are you, Vivian?' Obviously thriving, she reminded him of a sleek pampered feline, and the enquiry was polite and automatic. His sister-in-law eyed him up and down before replying; what a difference in Malcolm—the desert obviously suited him! The old familiar jealousy bit again.

'I'm well, thank you,' she answered. 'And so are you, I think. Shall we sit down, or are you dying to see your son?'

Of course he wanted to see him, but he would let Violet have him to herself for a few moments without her sister looking on. 'And how is the colonel?' he asked.

'Father? He's well enough, but you might as well know that he and Mother have decided to go to Italy. They've been waiting for you to get back—you've taken so long! And Grandmother thinks this house is too big, now she's getting so old—she wouldn't say so to you and Addie, of course, but she would like to close it down and move back to her Frederick relations.' Vivian gave her brother-in-law a small catlike smile before adding, 'Malcolm, you really should settle down in a place of your own, you know, and let other people get on with their lives!'

'I see.' Of course she was right, but he was glad she had said it to him and not to her sister. It would have spoiled the homecoming for Violet—but perhaps Miss Cory intended him to relay her comments to his wife? He would, of course, say nothing of the exchange.

Violet, meanwhile, bunched up her skirts and ran down into the garden. She found her mother reading on a garden seat, and a stranger patiently throwing a ball to little Malcolm who sometimes caught it, sometimes not, and rarely threw it back. Good-humouredly, the man retrieved the ball from under a rose bush, while the boy waited with outstretched arms.

Would he remember her? At the foot of the steps Violet hesitated. Then she was catching him up and smothering him in kisses.

'Mamma,' he said happily, his chubby little arms wrapped around her neck until he spotted the neighbours' cat and began to wriggle. Reluctantly Violet set him down.

'He kept asking when his Mamma was coming back. He really has missed you, Addie.'

Violet turned to the speaker, smiling ruefully. 'It doesn't look like it. Poor cat.' Then she considered the bearded stranger, whose soft voice reminded her a little of Lady Lister Kaye's. In his fifties, and of medium height, the man seemed strangely familiar and he certainly knew her. '*Uncle Heneage*,' she said at last, 'is it really you?'

'You've changed more than me, my dear,' remarked Heneage Griffin.

'I should hope so! It must be all of thirty years since we last met—it's so good to see you. And Mother too!' Violet hugged them both, and then hoisted her protesting offspring onto her hip before the exasperated cat finally vented its rage.

'How's Father?' Holding her squirming son tightly, Violet turned back to Mrs Cory.

'Not too well, I'm afraid, dear. We're hoping to go to Viareggio soon—you remember, where we were before.'

'Yes, of course. It should be wonderful now, and in winter. It will do Father so much good and he'll get better.' Violet spoke with conviction.

'Addie dear, no.' Fanny put a gentle hand on her daughter's arm. 'Don't raise your hopes. Your father knows he hasn't long and he's quite resigned. Now you're safely home we'll begin to make our plans.' She looked towards the steps and a welcoming smile crossed her weary face. 'Why, here's Malcolm now—Vivian must have decided to stay inside.'

At the end of June the Corys left for Italy and Violet gave way to her grief. 'Don't upset yourself so,' Malcolm said as he tried to comfort her. 'We've known your father was dying for some time. When we went away you knew you might not see him again, remember. And Viareggio will be much better for him than London.'

'But he's far too frail to travel—'

'Nonsense! There's absolutely no need to worry. Heneage is with them, and Vivian is going as well.'

'I'm sure that will make a lot of difference!' and Violet sobbed all the more. Colonel Cory was stronger than she thought, Malcolm told her, and hadn't he always been a fighter? They would go to Italy later in the year, he said, and she would see her father one last time.

'You're far too good to me,' Violet said with an effort. 'We've only just come back, and we're both tired of travelling. No, of course we'll stay here.'

Nicolson gently stroked her hair. She was taking it for granted they were still welcome in Cambridge Street, as they surely were, but it wasn't fair to old Mrs Cory. She must be nearly ninety; another old lady who seemed determined to go on for ever. His mother was now living with her sister somewhere near the sea. They would, he supposed, have to visit soon, despite Violet's reluctance. He bent and kissed her head. *Dear, patient little wife*, he promised silently, *soon you shall have your own home.*

A few days later, the general went to see Mark Grey, the Nicolson family lawyer. He returned to Pimlico with a smile on his face and a spring in his step, to find Violet in the garden protecting the cat.

'Our son is quite fearless, darling. He's going to shoot tigers in India when we go back!'

'He's a bit to grow yet, don't you think?' and Malcolm swung his son onto his shoulders while the child whooped with delight. 'Sweetheart,' he said over the sound of the boy's laughter, 'someone I know is leaving the country for a year and Grey says he'll arrange for us to take over the lease of his rooms. So how would you like to live in Parliament Street? There's a lot of building going on in the area, there isn't a garden, but there's room for Malcolm's nanny and the housekeeper will probably stay. What do you think?'

Violet was delighted. 'You'd so like it, wouldn't you, Malcolm,' she exclaimed, 'and the little one could go to the Park and play with other children before he becomes an absolute monster.' She shooed the pacified animal away and smiled up at them both. Then a sudden thought struck her. 'But what about Grandmother—how would she manage on her own?'

'Why don't you ask her?'

Caroline Cory patted her granddaughter's hand and told her not to worry. Her brother's family had been pestering her to stay for quite some time, and of course Addie must have her own household to run.

The move to Parliament Street went ahead, and summer slipped into autumn on a pleasant wave of picnics in Saint James's Park, parties at Rutland Gate, and a few little gatherings of their own. With the Lister Kayes on the Continent or in Yorkshire, nothing occurred to mar the happiness they felt in their new surroundings.

Violet returned from the park one afternoon, red-cheeked from playing with her son among the falling autumn leaves, to find her husband already at home.

One look at his serious face and she handed the child over to his nurse, took off her coat, and fussed with the cushions for a moment—all in an attempt to delay what she feared Malcolm was going to say.

'I've a letter here from Viareggio,' he told her when she finally sat down. 'Violet, I'm afraid your father is worse and has taken to his bed. He hasn't said anything, but Heneage thinks—and your mother agrees—that he desperately wants to see you and the boy. The doctors reckon he hasn't long, but your uncle is convinced you have plenty of time to reach him. If your father knows you're coming, then he'll have the will to wait.'

'I thought you were going to say he was dead already.' Violet sounded surprisingly calm. 'Of course I'll go. And Malcolm will come with me: he adores his grandfather. What about you, darling? I'll understand if you'd prefer to stay here. I'll have Nanny and I think that between us we could cope with anything. And little Malcolm's so brave—do you know, he tried to pull out a drake's tail feathers this afternoon!' Violet began to laugh, then her voice broke and the laughter turned to tears.

'I'm coming with you,' Nicolson told her fiercely. 'How could you think otherwise? Violet, you mustn't worry—leave everything to me.'

'His eyes that saw the world no more were calm'

Twenty years since she had been in Viareggio on her way back to India from school—how time flew. The place had grown almost beyond recognition, the business of the port overtaken by the pleasure seekers who swarmed to the increasingly fashionable beaches. But the air was just as Violet remembered: fresh off the sea, or redolent of the pinewoods outside the town.

With some trepidation she went into her father's room in the familiar little *pensione* tucked away in its garden behind the Via Garibaldi. Propped up against the pillows Arthur Cory looked wan and insubstantial, and she felt a sharp pang at seeing him so passive—he who had always had such boundless energy. Malcolm had said he was a fighter; well, he wasn't fighting now! The colonel simply lay there, waiting for her—and for death.

'Hello, Father.'

Cory opened his eyes and smiled. 'Addie, my dear, here you are at last!' He gripped her hand with surprising strength. 'Where's the little lad,' he asked. 'You've brought him?'

'Of course, he'll come and see you soon. He's running through the sand dunes for a while—he's been cooped up travelling far too long.'

'Just like you, Addie. Just like you. Oh, how you hated being cribbed and confined! Always wanting to be up and doing—' the old man's eyes were misty with memory.

'Like you too, Father!' Violet said cheerfully. 'Why don't you let us take you onto the terrace?' The air was balmy and it seemed an affront to stay inside. 'It's really very pleasant out there, you know. You'd enjoy it—'

Cory looked at his daughter. He had feared she would not come, and now that she had she was like a breath of good fresh air. He had been in bed for weeks; he doubted if he had the strength to move, but, 'Do you know, Addie,' he said, 'it *would* be good to see the garden again. And to watch the little fellow playing.'

So the days went by and Fanny and Violet sat on the terrace with the dying man, sometimes talking, sometimes in silence. It was a strangely happy time, punctuated as it was by a child's laughter and an old man's recollections. Malcolm joined them when he wasn't with his son, and in the evenings he would spend many a pleasant hour with his wife's uncle, whose soft melodious voice told yarns of American mining towns where fortunes could be made overnight if your luck was in, and lost at the turn of a die if it wasn't. Inevitably the talk turned to China, and Heneage was encouraging. Why, he said, Malcolm could still make good—he and Lister Kaye. In fact, said Violet's uncle, that name was puzzling him—but where he had heard it, and in what context, he simply couldn't remember …

Vivian Cory, for her part, was bored with Viareggio and tired of waiting for her father to die. The busy streets and opulent shops of Florence had long been calling her, but Heneage wouldn't go. Their duty, he insisted, was here, with her parents. And with Addie's arrival nothing changed. They would stay united as a family at her father's bedside for as long as necessary, Griffin told his youngest niece, and the usually biddable uncle stood firm.

It was *Addie*. As Vivian Cory watched her sister take control her eyes grew hard and spiteful. Despite all her efforts to discredit her, Addie Nicolson reigned supreme and Father wouldn't let her out of his sight! And now she had Heneage under her spell as well! And, of course, there was Malcolm—he had no time for his sister-in-law either. It was simply too bad! Sulking, the young woman spent more and more time on her own. She was wealthy, she was chic and sophisticated, she was a famous writer—but here in the family circle she was simply Annie Sophie Cory, with no recognition of her gifts at all. *Anna Lombard* had shocked them all, and yet no one seemed to care about *Laurence Hope*.

She would show them! If they thought her last best-selling novel in poor taste, let them wait till the next was in the London bookshops. Her brilliant career had only just begun!

'Are you happy, my dear?' asked her father.

'Yes, I am, truly—although I'm not in India,' and Violet pressed a gentle kiss on her father's brow.

'You and I have India in our blood, my dear,' said the colonel. 'My mother's family was there at the beginning, you know, and you'll go back, never fear. I would have stayed on until the end, of course, but your mother wanted to come home. Well,' and the old man nodded philosophically, 'it was for the best, and she'll soon be back in England.'

'Father …' Violet wanted to know why he was so accepting—he had always fought so hard against adversity—but it was difficult to ask.

'Yes, Addie, what is it?'

'Aren't you afraid?'

'Afraid of dying, you mean? No, dear, I'm not afraid. There comes a time, you see, when death is welcome as a friend.' The old man paused for a moment then chose his words with care. 'Think of me as a very old clock that's slowly winding down, or whose parts perhaps are wearing out. One day that clock stops—for ever. Its use is over and you put it by with no regrets.' He looked at his daughter serenely. 'I'm tired, Addie, very tired, and soon I shall be ready to go. And when I do, you mustn't be sad. You must save your tears for those who die before their time, my dear. Don't weep for me.'

In January Colonel Cory began rapidly to fail. It was as if he had set himself the goal of one last Christmas with his family, one last New Year. On the fourteenth of January he sank into unconsciousness and Fanny, who had hardly left his side for a fortnight, kept vigil through the night. In the morning Violet insisted that her exhausted mother sleep.

'I'll sit with him, Mother dear. Malcolm or I will fetch you if—if we think you should be here.' She couldn't bring herself to say the words. 'I'll be all right, darling,' she said to her husband when her mother had gone. 'Why don't you and Heneage take little Malcolm for a walk? Perhaps Vivian would like to go with you.'

'Your sister's gone to Florence for the day. She met some Italians yesterday and they invited her to join their party.' Nicolson's expression showed plainly what he thought. 'I won't be long,' he assured her, and she watched him stride away to find his son. Then she returned to her father.

To her surprise, the colonel's eyes were open. When he saw her he made a slight movement with his hand and she went to sit by his side. 'How are you, Father?' she asked.

'I'm all right, Addie,' he replied, and closed his eyes again. He lay there so still that she thought he was sleeping, but his hand reached out and took her own. He was tense, as if he was waiting for something, some signal … What could it be?

Soon her father would be gone, and she realised suddenly that this was perhaps the last opportunity she would have to talk to him alone.

Haltingly at first, and then more easily, she relived the moments of their past, moments when they had laughed together, times when they had raged. He was listening, she could tell. She thanked him for his understanding, for giving her the freedom that she craved; she thanked him for his unfailing love. And finally, holding his hand against her cheek, and leaning over him to be sure he heard, she whispered that she loved him dearly too.

As she did so, she felt his body relax and his breathing change. His face was slowly suffused with a golden light, or was it only the sun rising high over the pine trees and shining into the room? Violet couldn't be sure, for her eyes were filled with tears. As she watched, her father's eyes opened and gazed at her. His lips moved silently then were still.

The clock had stopped at last.

Nicolson found her staring at the peaceful face, her father's hand in hers. She had gently closed the dead man's eyes, and it was difficult to believe that they would never again be open.

'Does your mother know?' He put his arm around her.

'Not yet, I'll go and tell her. Stay with him, Malcolm,' and she rose to her feet and went out.

There was a calm dignity about her where her husband had expected great distress. But there was nothing calm or dignified about the Violet Nicolson who confronted her younger sister on her return much later, arms piled high with parcels and packages.

'How could you think of your own pleasure at a time like this? Father is dead and Mother needs us all.'

'I needed a change,' Vivian was defiant. 'I've been here since June—in case you've forgotten—while you were enjoying yourself in London.'

'I doubt very much that you've spent too much time in Viareggio, Annie Sophie. Oh, admittedly since we've been here you've not gone gallivanting quite so often. What have you been doing in your room all day, you little wretch—writing another frightful novel, I suppose?'

'How dare you refer to my work like that, Addie Nicolson! The whole world knows about *you* and *your* behaviour. Thanks to that book of yours, no one need ask how you spent your time in India! And you were so smug, weren't you, thinking you could keep it all a secret—but I soon fixed that!'

The triumphant look on the younger woman's face was replaced by one of apprehension as Violet realised what she had said. 'So it was *you*,' she breathed. 'You *little snake*!' She took a step towards her sister then stopped as suddenly. What did it matter, after all? 'You wanted to create trouble between Malcolm and me—but it didn't work. And Mother and Father didn't mind, either. Whereas you and your ghastly imaginings cut them to the quick!'

The two women glared at one another, Violet seething with anger that her sister had been the cause of Malcolm's discomfiture, Vivian smarting that her artistry had been maligned—and both silently resolving to have nothing to do with each other ever again. An uneasy truce reigned until after the funeral, and then with no regrets on either side the sisters went their separate ways.

'Soft songs of sorrow and distress'

Violet Nicolson did not grieve extravagantly for her father, but she most certainly grieved. She often thought of Arthur Cory and the sublime manner of his dying. It was, she realised, his final gift to her—a message not to be afraid. And this knowledge helped her come to terms with her loss.

The little family settled back into some kind of routine. Malcolm went to his clubs, although less often in the rain and snow and slush of gloomy London. Violet wrote, played with the child, and told him tales of his grandfather and a far-off, sun-baked land. Alone with her husband in the evenings, she would sit silently by the hearth beside a blazing fire, gazing into the flames and thinking of another kind of heat while beguiling pictures danced before her eyes and called her home.

The Nicolsons were in danger of becoming hermits, or so Mrs Crackanthorpe said when she came to seek her out one afternoon. 'Really, Violet, this simply will not do! Are you pining for your father, my dear? You're looking quite wan—what you need is good fresh air!'

Fresh air in smoky London? It hardly seemed possible. Violet smiled at her friend. 'If I'm pining for anything, Blanche, it's for the southern sun. I'd forgotten how cold England could be!'

'Well, it will soon be spring.' That hardly seemed possible, either. But visits from Blanche—who bore her no grudge for concealing the identity of Laurence Hope—always cheered her.

'So it was your sister who blew the gaff?' The slang expression sat incongruously on her friend's patrician lips when Violet told her.

'Yes, though I still can't fathom how she knew—and I was in no mood to ask. Blanche, *how on earth* did she get involved with the *Yellow Book* set?'

'It was one of those strange quirks of fate, as far as I know, Violet, my dear. She met its editor, Aubrey Beardsley the artist—or his sister, I believe it was, at first. They lived down the street from your grandmother for a time. Aubrey's dead, of course, poor lad, both he and my poor, lost Bertie—' and Mrs Crackanthorpe lapsed into a silence Violet didn't care to break. 'Yes,' Blanche resumed after a while, 'Vivian quickly became Mabel Beardsley's friend and insinuated herself into the circle. The rest you can imagine.'

Dark with malice, Blanche's eyes glinted across at Violet. 'Your sister was hardly an asset, intellectually speaking, but she has a pretty face, you must admit, and she was one of the young ladies John Lane—the publisher, you know—entertained to afternoon tea at his rooms.' Violet raised an eyebrow but said nothing. 'And from the Albany it was just a small step to Vigo Street, the Bodley Head Press—and publication. Your sister appears to be a skilful manipulator of men. Anyway,' Mrs Crackanthorpe added briskly, 'when are you coming back to Rutland Gate? We've missed you. And—' she had saved her own piece of news till last '—you're quite a celebrity, my dear, and for all the best reasons! Your poetry is being sung as well as read, did you know?'

'No, really, Blanche? A woman did write when we were in Morocco, now that I come to think of it—wanting to set some of the poems to music. She must have done it, then, and I can't even remember her name.' Violet Nicolson shrugged the matter off as being of little importance.

'Mrs Amy Woodforde-Finden,' Mrs Crackanthorpe said instantly. 'She's called them *Four Indian Love Lyrics*. And very charming they are, too. Violet, do say you'll come to one of my evenings and play them for us. And sing. It would be such a triumph for me!'

'I'm sure it would, Blanche dear, but I'd rather not,' came the firm reply. 'Why, I'd feel like a performing monkey.' And Violet refused to be swayed.

She did however go out and about again, but she hated the London streets. They were packed with scurrying figures, heads down against the wind and the rain, in too much of a hurry to spare a thought for the beggars huddling in doorways out of the wet. Backs bent and shivering in the cold, they were a silent affront in a Christian land and nobody appeared to care. She cared—and could afford to do so little. It all seemed better in the spring. As the pale sunshine filtered through the burgeoning leaves Violet began to feel warm again. She romped on the grass in the park with her little boy, attracting amused glances from people passing on their way to or from work—and lingering looks from others far more idle.

'Good afternoon, Mrs Nicolson. So this young man is your son?'

Violet looked up then rose quickly to her feet, brushing back the unruly locks of hair as she did so. So the baronet was back in town …

'Yes it is, Sir John.' Clear blue eyes stared steadily into muddy grey as she drew little Malcolm protectively against her skirts. Lister Kaye noted the gesture, but was not in the least offended; it proved that the mother was not quite so indifferent to him as she would have him think—love and hate being two sides of the same coin, after all.

'And how are you, my dear,' his voice was civil. 'And how is General Nicolson? We must have dinner together soon. Natica will write to you.' He raised his hat and left her gazing after him in dismay.

The invitation came and the social round intensified. Violet went out visiting more often in the afternoons and saw far less of her boy. When she came home he was overjoyed, and they played madcap games in what was fast becoming too small a space for a rapidly growing child. When he came upon them unexpectedly one day, Malcolm complained of the noise and chaos and general lack of discipline.

'I'm sorry, darling. You're not usually home so early. And the little one has so much energy. He needs to play.'

'He has a nurse.'

'And I'm his mother—' Violet stared at her husband defiantly. She lifted the boy and carried him out of the room. When she returned Malcolm apologised, and the matter was not referred to again. But Violet remembered—and took care there was no repetition.

If her son was unable to keep still for long, his father was almost as restless. One night Violet woke to find the bed beside her empty and her husband on the prowl, unable to sleep, walking up and down with his face set in a frown.

'What is it, darling? Tell me—'

'It's nothing, Violet. Go back to bed.'

'Not unless you come with me.' Once there, she reached out her arms to him, but he gently but firmly put her away, and she retreated to her own side of a bed that suddenly seemed vast and cold. They lay awake and silent till the dawn.

As spring wore on, Malcolm's mood could change from irritability to affection and then as quickly back again. He might rebuff her one night and approach her with importunity the next; she did not understand his moods and she did not ask for explanation. Instead, she threw herself into preparing the book William Heinemann had recently requested, and which she had decided to call *Stars of the Desert*.

'Lit by the sunlight of a great renown'

Mrs Nicolson was caught up in her own affairs and her husband was caught up in his. Lister Kaye's attentions were more assiduous than ever, and he even carried the general off to Court for the afternoon levées where (supposed his wife) men paraded like peacocks before their Sovereign Lord. Mrs Nicolson had little respect for the fleshy philanderer herself, and pitied his long-suffering consort. Or perhaps Queen Alexandra really didn't mind? Was she like Lady Lister Kaye: indifferent, contemptuous even? It seemed very likely.

The baronet's wife had many tales to tell of what went on in the season, and out. She and her sisters mixed with the highest of high society, and she would gladly have drawn Violet into the rarefied atmosphere as well, but Mrs Malcolm Nicolson's brief moment of notoriety proved more than enough. Let her husband enjoy the glitter of Saint James's—it was certainly not something she craved herself. She preferred to go to Rutland Gate for têtes-à-têtes with Blanche, and on one occasion in June prevailed upon her husband to go with her.

'Mr Hardy will be there,' Violet told him in a state of great excitement. 'Can you imagine, Malcolm, *Thomas Hardy* in person! You will come, won't you?'

She had read the *Wessex Poems* from cover to cover more than once, lingering over some for hours, and perhaps she could talk to the poet about his work, she said. Tom Hardy had written novels too, Malcolm pointed out. He thought she would have wanted to talk about *them*, and his eyes twinkled wickedly.

Violet, who had read several, and had seen far more in them than most—excluding Blanche, of course, and now, it seemed, Malcolm—blushed and said she couldn't possibly talk about them to a stranger, even if that stranger were the author. 'And he probably won't want to speak to me anyway!' she concluded, defending herself against a charge of being unexpectedly coy.

But Thomas Hardy did single her out for attention. He had noticed the pretty young woman earlier, standing across the room with a man he assumed to be her father, but once she was introduced and he knew her for the much-discussed poet Laurence Hope, he would not let her go.

It was flattering to hear her talk of his own poetry in such glowing terms, and to watch that delightful mouth with its slight suggestion of moisture on the upper lip. Blanche always overheated her rooms, even in summer, but with the ladies showing so much flesh—and his eyes lingered a moment on Violet's bare arms and low-cut gown —perhaps it was as well.

She seemed the embodiment of his Elfride, or of his Tess; she was Woman as he had written of her, Woman as she was meant to be—voluptuous and passionate and not afraid to proclaim her feelings. Whether she was one of the new breed of women who determined the course of their own lives, that he could not tell. For a moment his eyes considered the tall, erect figure of her husband, deep in conversation at the far side of the room. An ill-matched couple, some might think, but not he—in his opinion age and youth could deal extremely well together. Hardy smiled then turned his appreciative gaze back to Violet.

'It's such a beautiful piece—a sonnet and one, I think, of four,' she was saying.

'So full of feeling and quiet controlled dignity.'

'Dignity and control, you say?' They were the last things he admired in a woman. Was she *controlled*, he wondered, this wonderfully vital and healthy young creature? No, he thought, or not always—such vibrant sensuality would not allow itself to be denied. He looked at General Nicolson and envied him the enjoyment of his undoubtedly passionate wife.

'Yes,' Violet went on. 'And then the speaker talks of being *Numb as a vane that cankers on its point, True to the wind that kissed ere canker came*—I'm afraid that's all I remember.' Hardy found her apologetic smile quite charming. '*Numb as a vane that cankers on its point*—' she repeated with a sigh, almost forgetting where she was. 'That was what I really found most moving, Mr Hardy. I should be like that if my husband died—with no sense of direction, and my heart and soul all eaten away with grief.'

Hardy, who had almost forgotten what he had written all those years ago, watched the mobile lips and the lustrous eyes, and the rise and fall of her breasts. When Violet paused for breath he leaned forward and took her hand.

'You mustn't let yourself become morbid, my dear young woman,' he said. 'Life is to be enjoyed—to the full. *Carpe diem* or as another sage has said: *The Bird of Time has but a little way to fly*—'

'—*Before we too into the Dust descend, Dust into Dust, and under Dust, to lie, Sans Wine, Sans Song, sans Singer, and—Sans End!*'

'So you know your FitzGerald too,' Hardy commented none too graciously, as he saw another poet take his place. 'But of course—I think I remember seeing a little trace of his Omar Khayyám in your poems, am I right, and in the quatrains, in particular?'

'And the themes, Mr Hardy: Death, Chance, Fate and the inexorable passing of Time—although I believe they are common to all Persian poetry of that period.'

'They are common in every age, Mrs Nicolson. If you have read any of my novels, you will have seen how they have influenced *me*. *Chance*, *Fate*, call it what you will, plays a great part in the life of Everyman—and of every woman, too, I suspect.' He smiled at her warmly as she listened.

Her attention was most flattering, and when Blanche came for him half an hour later Hardy took Violet's hand once more, pressed it gently, and promised to send her a copy of his *Wessex Poems*. Mrs Crackanthorpe would give him her address. And what a pity, he said in parting, that she had chosen not to publish her verses under her own name. 'You could have struck a blow for your sisters, my dear young lady, a blow for equality in this male-dominated society of ours that denies women the right to *feel*. Instead, you chose the name of a man.' Shaking his head in mild rebuke he smilingly took his leave.

'I see you've made another conquest,' Malcolm observed when he returned to her side. 'Your Mr Hardy appeared totally captivated.'

'He was only asking me about my poetry,' Violet said defensively. 'He seemed very interested.'

'Of course he was, sweetheart—interested in everything about you. He would have transported you to Dorset to have his wicked way, if he'd been able!'

'Malcolm, that's ridiculous!'

'Is it? He's no older than me. For Hardy the combination of poetry and an appealing woman must be irresistible.' He looked at his wife, who was still most attractively flushed from the excitement of the encounter, and put his arm about her possessively. And I'm sure he envies me the pleasure of having you warm my bed.'

Violet felt a little put out—she hadn't seen the conversation in quite that light. 'Oh,' she said in disappointment, 'and I thought he was only interested in what I had written. And you,' she said, rounding on her husband, '*Warm your bed*, indeed! You know how I hate that expression! You sound so incredibly arrogant, Malcolm Nicolson!'

Mr Hardy was right, she found herself thinking—she should stand up for herself more often.

'What I held passion and thou held'st lust'

A few days later Violet was walking with Lady Lister Kaye along the paths of Saint James's Park. The late June sunshine was pleasantly warm and the little boy had run on ahead, followed by his nanny.

'Have you really never been to the Royal Opera, Violet?' Natica was saying. When Violet refused her invitation to dine, the baronet's wife had suggested they go to Covent Garden instead.

'I've heard no opera at all. There's not much demand for it in India,' Violet pointed out.

'But you've been in London for several seasons—what a lot you've missed!'

'Have I, Natica?' Violet was not in the least perturbed. 'I think I should find it rather artificial.'

'Sometimes it certainly is,' Lady Lister Kaye agreed. 'But when you're privileged to hear great music and fine voices, it becomes a wonderful experience. You must come with us,' she said. 'The de Greys have a box and we're always welcome to join them with our guests.'

'You don't mind her company, Natica? I find that surprising.'

'Oh, I'm used to it. It was going on long before Johnny and I ever met. Gladys married the Earl of Lonsdale, Johnny married me, and then her first husband died—had the timing been different, they might have married each other.'

'And you would have been far happier, I'm sure.' Violet gave her friend a compassionate glance. 'Well,' she continued on an ironic note, 'I have to admire her staying power—and his. And Earl de Grey's the most! So the countess really loves music?'

'Yes. And so does Johnny. He has a very fine singing voice.'

'Indeed?' It was difficult to credit. 'I'm sorry, Natica,' she said, 'I'm sure it would be very nice, but I don't believe I should accept the countess's hospitality, feeling as I do about her. Besides, I don't think Malcolm would agree to go.'

'Leave your husband to me, Violet,' said Lady Lister Kaye, 'and swallow your scruples—just for once. You'll be surprised how easy it is!'

Nicolson was persuaded, Violet duly swallowed, and the evening of June the twenty-third found them in the Royal Opera House at Covent Garden for a performance of Wagner's *Tristan und Isolde*. At least she knew the story, Violet thought, and perhaps she would remember a little German after all these years. No, it might not be as dreadful as she anticipated.

The Earl and Countess de Grey certainly did themselves proud. Their private box, hardly less magnificent than the rest of the building, was furnished like a comfortable room, with rose-coloured hangings and fine seating. Better still, it was large enough for there to be no need to speak to Gladys at all. Lady de Grey had taken up her seat at the far side, the earl was absent, and Sir John was solicitously removing his mistress's wrap. Good, thought Mrs Nicolson with some satisfaction, it looks as if he's going to leave us in peace.

Natica was to her left and Malcolm beyond, ready to slip outside, she suspected, if it all got too much. What Natica had said to him, Violet did not know, but he had agreed to come to this, the final performance for the season of Wagner's controversial opus.

Violet gazed out over the auditorium. It was crowded, and an expectant buzz of conversation rose up to her from the stalls beneath. Her unaccustomed eyes took in the ivory and gold, from the proscenium arch with its twisted columns to the box fronts ornamented with plaster nymphs, and on up to the low saucer ceiling and the arches to its sides. The ceiling was an unexpected and startling blue, and hung all over with individual pendant lights.

It was all far too ornate. How could anyone possibly forget they were in a theatre? The lights dimmed, and Mrs Nicolson settled back sceptically to wait for the opera to begin.

Gradually and despite herself, she gave herself up to the bittersweet music with its augury of grief, desire and death. The dark deep tones of the double basses and bassoons, the penetrating notes of oboe and clarinet—presaging the doomed lovers sentenced to a yearning without end—stirred in her traces of longing. By the time the Prelude was over Violet Nicolson was entranced.

Perhaps it was the subject. Perhaps she was transported to that time long ago when her own heart was full of painful resignation. She listened and she watched, leaning forward in her chair as the great Ternina sang of her despair:

'Mir erkoren,
mir verloren
hehr und heil,
kuhn und feig:
Todgeweihtes Haupt!
Todgeweihtes Herz!'

Death-devoted heart, indeed, with Tristan lost to her forever. Would they die, would they really drink the poisoned draught? Violet watched Isolde's face and imagined the poison stealing through her veins. No poison, this, it proved, but the birth of uncontrollable desire—no death drink, but an elixir of love. And only death could now assuage the longing.

Tristan! *Isolde*! Able no longer to deny their love, the doomed couple gazed at one another. Trembling, they embraced and mouth hungrily met mouth.

And then the lights went up. Violet blinked and swallowed. Momentarily bemused, she looked around to see Malcolm smiling at her side. He hadn't left, then? Taking her arm, he led her to the back of the box and its smaller anteroom, away from the immediate glare.

'You're enjoying it, aren't you?'

'Oh, yes, tremendously! How about you, Malcolm? It's not exactly to your taste, I imagine.' She looked at him in amusement.

'I've been watching *you*, Violet, which is always to my taste.' For a while, enraptured as she was by the music and the myth, his wife had become the tragic Irish princess—and Malcolm Nicolson had been enchanted in his turn.

'The conflict between Love and Honour, Malcolm—what a dreadful dilemma!'

'Not at all. I would choose honour and you—you would choose love. Not a dilemma at all—for either of us!'

'Sometimes, Malcolm Nicolson, you can be terribly stuffy.'

'I know, you've told me before. Often.' They smiled at each other affectionately, then turned to talk to Lady Lister Kaye until the curtain rose on the second act.

'Tristan du, ich Isolde, nicht mehr Tristan!'
'Du Isolde, Tristan ich, nicht mehr Isolde!'

As she listened to the naked passion of the love duet, Violet felt faint. *Ewig eine, ohne Ende*. No names, no parting, always one—forever. If only it were true ... To go down into the dark night together, what greater bliss could there be?

The tears came to her eyes as Tristan kissed Isolde on the brow and turned to face the traitor's sword.

'Here's my handkerchief,' said Malcolm obligingly, 'you never seem to have one when you need it.'

Violet took it and blew her nose. 'I suppose you think it's a glorification of adultery, General Nicolson?' she asked him.

'Not at all, she probably wasn't married, only betrothed—if that. It's no good, Violet, I'm too stuffy to be provoked,' and smiling, he turned away to speak to the Charles Beresfords while Violet withdrew a little, happy to be left to her thoughts.

'Well, Mrs Nicolson,' said Lister Kaye, joining her now she was alone. 'What wonderful music, don't you agree?' He smiled at her pleasantly, and Violet found herself relaxing. At last, she thought, at last we can have a reasonable conversation.

But then the baronet added: 'Wonderful music, that is, to accompany the ideal coupling—'

To his delight Violet gave a little gasp.

'What a wonderful concept, my dear lady,' he continued, 'to experience night after night of unslaked desire—seemingly satisfied, only to be renewed and satisfied again. Now, wouldn't that be bliss indeed?' His eyes were a little warmer than usual as he observed the deep colour he had summoned to her cheeks.

'That would very much depend, Sir John. In some circumstances it might seem a terrible punishment!' Violet's eyes glinted malevolently and he could not mistake her meaning. 'Perhaps,' and she smiled up at him sweetly, 'perhaps you are confusing desire with unbridled lust, with no place for the heart and mind at all? I can think of nothing worse than that, Sir John.'

Her lip curled and she turned away. Nicolson heard nothing of the exchange but he did see the expression on her face. And on Lister Kaye's. Frowning, he moved over to his wife while Gladys de Grey took her place at the baronet's side.

'So you're still lusting after our little poetess, Johnny? It *is* a purely physical union you're after, I take it?' The countess had heard and enjoyed every word of the exchange. 'Though *pure* is perhaps not quite the word to use! Forget it, my lad,' and she tapped him smartly on the arm with her fan. 'Mrs Nicolson has eyes only for her ageing Tristan and it's quite touching. Beautiful even.'

For once Lady de Grey was not sneering. There was something about the younger woman's devotion that she envied, and the countess rarely envied a soul.

❧

The pure notes of the shepherd's pipe caught at Violet's throat with their poignancy and then they died away. She watched as the third act of the drama unfolded, was there with the lovers, a part of them, as the *Liebestod*, the Love-Death, rose, softly at first, then swelling inexorably, to reach its climax with a mighty crash of sound. Milka Ternina's voice soared triumphantly as the mystic union was at last achieved. Lost to the world, Tristan and Isolde had found each other, and Nature had claimed them as her own.

Smiling, the princess sank onto her lover's breast—and the opera was over.

The audience rose to their feet as one and the enthusiastic drawn-out applause gave Violet time to compose herself. Malcolm was at the far side of the box, where he had moved to watch her better. He had told her the truth. Opera was not at all to his taste, and the principle pleasure for him that night had been to see his wife's delight, and the total immersion of her sensibility in the sights and sounds and emotions of this new experience.

After a while he became aware that his were not the only eyes resting on her glowing face. Johnny Kaye's thin lips might be smiling slightly as he listened to the music, but that smile deepened as from time to time he turned his head to look at Violet. When the last faint sounds of applause had died away, it was Sir John who moved swiftly to her side and placed her wrap about her, and she did not even notice. Still transported by the music, she did not notice either as the baronet's fingers brushed her skin, lingering a little on her shoulders and her back, caressing even.

She might have been oblivious, but Malcolm Nicolson was not, and he felt a hot tide of rage possess him.

'Damn the man,' he thought furiously. 'He has taken my money and now he wants my wife!' At last jealousy spurred him on to do what common sense should have dictated long ago—tomorrow, he promised himself, tomorrow Lister Kaye should tell him the truth.

'The Sands of Truth'

By the next day the white heat of Nicolson's anger had turned to ice, but the fire returned when the morning post brought a letter from his wife's uncle, who at last remembered why the name Lister Kaye was familiar.

Gathered piecemeal over the years, and centring on America's golden west, Heneage's was a long story. Mining, he wrote, stopped in California in 1884, and the following year there had been a scheme afoot to sell off part of the Sacramento valley. The valley in question had always been a mixed blessing to its farmers, Heneage continued. Flat and fertile it certainly was for the most part, but subject to annual flooding and periodic drought. The detritus from the mines made matters worse by raising the river levels all year round, and during the annual floods the Sacramento swamplands became a great inland sea. But, of course (said the Englishman who was promoting their sale in 1885) if levees were built to hold back the floodwaters, the harvest from the salvaged land would be enormous. *Trust me*, he urged the ex-miners desperate to earn a living; he had farmed in the valley himself and he should know.

Had this Englishman also known, Heneage Griffin speculated, about the levees that were already in existence upstream? That they would channel the waters and force them further south to the former swamplands, causing certain damage and even loss of life?

The promoter's manner had been persuasive. There was a great demand for grain worldwide, he said, and investment would pay, and pay quickly. So the erstwhile miners trusted him, and only later did they learn the truth. Some of them paid for that knowledge with their lives. Others moved on to Colorado and found work at Griffin's Seven-Thirty Mine outside Georgetown. The Englishman was some kind of a titled fellow, the disillusioned men told their new employer, and he went by the name of Lister Kaye.

'Either this Lister Kaye fellow was a fool in his choice of land, or an unmitigated villain,' Heneage Griffin's letter concluded. 'The name is unusual, but it could have been a relation and not Sir John himself. Perhaps we should give him the benefit of the doubt?'

There was no doubt at all in Malcolm Nicolson's mind. He opened the bureau, flung the letter onto a pile of papers, and went out.

'Well, there you are,' Sir John explained when Nicolson ran his quarry to earth in the Carlton Club in Pall Mall. 'I've been unable to make much headway and the expenses have been enormous. All subscribers must share the loss, I'm afraid. I'm so sorry, General,' the baronet concluded, not looking in the least repentant, 'but that means that you should expect no return at all for your investment. Things may look up, of course—I'm planning a trip to China later in the year to see for myself—but I'm afraid that as things stand at present the venture, to all intents and purposes anyway, should be considered at an end.'

So it was over. Nicolson felt nothing but relief. Now there were decisions to be made, and he must break the bad news to Violet. Lister Kaye looked at him curiously. Were there to be no recriminations then, no outpourings of rage? He felt a reluctant respect for the man whose savings he had most probably lost, and whose wife he certainly coveted.

'I must be incredibly unlucky,' the baronet confided, when Malcolm brought up the matter of the Sacramento scheme. 'I suffer these setbacks quite often, but still I try again. It's a case of "cleaving to hope", I imagine—although perhaps in the circumstances, my dear General, that is an unfortunate phrase and you must forgive my flight of fancy. How *is* Mrs Nicolson by the way?' and he gave his vulpine smile. It was only then that he saw the general's grey eyes blaze with anger and he felt a sudden fear.

Resisting the temptation to take the man by the throat and shake him like a rat, Malcolm Nicolson squared his powerful shoulders, turned his back and silently left the club. He went straight to Parliament Street where he found Violet reading by the window. She listened until the serious voice fell silent and then her reaction was very like his own.

'I'm glad we know at last,' she said. 'Now we can forget all about him. Poor Natica—it was such a lovely evening.' She sighed. Then a thought struck her, and she made up her mind to confess. 'I think this may be all my fault,' she told him.

'Your fault? Whatever do you mean?'

Nicolson listened as his wife described her encounter of five years before, and then he gave a slightly bitter laugh. 'If you had told me then, I wouldn't have listened—we had our differences at the time, if you remember? No, sweetheart,' and he gave her a swift kiss, 'if anyone's to blame, it's me and my wish for a quick profit.'

'Malcolm, why did you choose today of all days to confront him?'

Should he tell her the whole truth? In the light of her own revelation he decided not. 'I had a letter from Heneage this morning,' he said, 'telling me where he'd heard of Lister Kaye.'

'Really? Where is it?' His eyes turned towards the bureau and Violet was on her feet in an instant. As she put her hand out for the letter she saw a wad of bills, and an imposing-looking legal document beneath. Puzzled, she retrieved them all.

'You've made your will, I see,' she said slowly. 'You didn't tell me, Malcolm. When was this?'

'About two weeks ago. A few days after my birthday.'

'Was it because you'd reached sixty and you felt you should mark the occasion?' She forced herself to keep her tone light and even. He nodded, and she put the will, unopened, back in its place. Then her eyes turned to the bills she was still holding, all from a chemist and all unpaid.

'Why so many?' she asked, a catch in her voice. Malcolm didn't answer, which gave her time to think. She thought of the nights of broken sleep, the walking up and down, and the fierce look of concentration on his face; he must have been trying to conquer pain. She thought of how sometimes he had clung to her almost in despair.

'You're ill,' she accused. 'You're *ill*, and you've been keeping it to yourself. Oh, darling, I thought I meant more to you than that!'

'You do, of course you do! I wanted to spare you the worry, that's all.'

'And the will—it had nothing to do with your birthday! People only make wills when they're young enough to feel immortal, or they're old enough to die—' Violet's voice rose hysterically as she gripped his arm.

'You're being silly, sweetheart. It's a precaution, that's all it is. I haven't been feeling well and I wanted everything in order. I'm better now, believe me.' His voice was quite matter of fact.

'What's wrong with you, Malcolm? *Tell me the truth!*'

'It's nothing.'

'It's enough to keep you awake at night in agony!'

Nicolson relented. 'Sweetheart, I have what is known as calculus, or gravel. It's formed in the bladder and I'm taking something to break it down, also laudanum when necessary—hence the chemist's bills. It can cause extreme pain or simply mild discomfort, but I'm not in pain for long when it happens,' he assured her calmly. 'Nor does it happen often. I'm only sorry you've found out.'

The straightforward explanation succeeded in calming Violet's fears, then something else occurred to her. 'What needs to be put in order?' she demanded. 'Darling, these are the only bills, aren't they, the only debts?'

'I'm afraid not. Violet, you'd better sit down and listen.'

Horrified, she heard him explain how living on their own was more expensive than he had ever expected, and that the lease was just the beginning. There were the housekeeper's wages, and the nanny's, their own living expenses, clothes for the growing lad—the list went on and on. It didn't occur to Violet to point out that clubs and appearances at Court didn't come cheap either. All she knew was that Malcolm was worried and again she had not been allowed to share.

'You borrowed money from Alfred Sinclair—and from *Mrs Steel*? Oh, Malcolm, how could you?'

'Flora is very difficult to resist.' Nicolson gave her a sheepish look. 'I'm sorry, darling, it was the last time we were at Talgarth.'

'Oh,' said Violet. 'Was it when I came upon you among the rhododendrons and you both looked extremely guilty? I thought—'

Nicolson interrupted with a great shout of laughter. 'I hope you thought nothing of the kind!'

'No, of course I didn't!' Violet's tone was indignant. 'I decided you'd probably been talking about me.'

'We had. About your welfare—should anything happen to me—and then Flora winkled out the story of the bills. And offered me one hundred pounds.'

'Which you accepted?'

'Which I accepted.'

'What are we going to do, Malcolm? We can't stay here, thank goodness the lease is almost up.' After the shock, Violet's mind turned to practicalities.

'Leave it to me, darling, I'm going to see Mark Grey this afternoon.'

While Malcolm went to see his lawyer, Violet visited her publisher. William Heinemann was sympathetic; he had experienced domestic difficulties himself and was quite prepared to help his protégée. Of course she could have an advance on her next book, he assured her—provided she could finish it by the end of July. *The Garden of Kama* was selling well, and he was sure that *Stars of the Desert* would be equally successful. His dark eyes twinkled like stars themselves as he suggested she might care to contemplate a third volume. Feeling a little happier, Violet went back to what would shortly cease to be her home.

'So,' she told Malcolm proudly that evening, 'with the advance, and Father's legacy, we'll have nearly four hundred pounds. We can pay the bills, and Alfred and Mrs Steel.'

Nicolson looked fondly at his wife. Not a word of reproach, and she was laying all she had in the world at his feet. 'I can't let you do it,' he said. 'It wouldn't be right.' And it wouldn't be enough.

Violet looked back steadily. 'When we married it was for richer and poorer, wasn't it, or didn't you mean what you said?'

It was blackmail, he protested, as he sat down and drew her onto his lap. Sheer blackmail. She put her head on his shoulder and closed her eyes. *For richer and for poorer*—the words echoed in her head, to be followed by others more sinister. *In sickness and in health* she remembered herself saying all those years ago, when anything but good health had seemed impossible. Dear God, she begged, with the sad haunting strains of Wagner's *Liebestod* playing once more in her ears, please don't let Malcolm die …

The ragged wounds of desperate grief

Mark Grey invited them to his home; they were his friends, he said, and they were more than welcome to stay. When Malcolm relayed the news, Violet's reaction was mixed.

'How very kind of him,' she said immediately, 'but of course we can't accept. There are too many of us.' She thought of little Malcolm and his nanny, and how the child at almost three was becoming increasingly boisterous.

'I know,' Nicolson replied, 'but I've thought about all that. Malcolm can go to my mother now she's in Brighton—you know how she's always pestering us to let him stay—and he would love the beach. It would be good for him, and it would give you the chance to finish your book. By the time the summer's over, we'll have made our plans and be ready to move on.'

He waited for her to comment but what was there to say? He seemed to have worked it all out—to his own satisfaction at least—and it seemed pointless to raise objections.

'Very well, Malcolm,' Violet replied, 'as you wish. I suppose I should think about packing.' She put her son's things in one trunk and their own in another; one was dispatched to Park Street and the other went to Brighton, with the three Nicolsons following a few days later.

'Well, Malcolm,' Mrs Nicolson's sharp gaze transfixed her son, 'so you've made another unfortunate decision, have you? And this time you've lost thousands of pounds.' The old lady, who prided herself on never having made a single mistake in her long well-ordered life, gave a genteel sniff.

'And what would the first unfortunate decision be, Mother?' Nicolson's eyes did not waver and his voice was cold.

'You know perfectly well, dear. I never thought Violet a suitable wife—and events have proved me right, don't you think!' His delighted sisters might have read *that book* from cover to cover but one or two of her daughter-in-law's impassioned outpourings had been more than enough for *her*!

'I think you're being totally unfair, Mother. Violet is an exemplary wife and mother.'

'Really, dear? Well, you'd be the best judge of that, I suppose.' Her tone indicated quite the opposite.

Nicolson sighed and fidgeted as he had done when a small child. Violet was outside and he longed to join her. The dim room where the smells of lavender and camphor strove for ascendancy was not to his taste at all.

'Now, Malcolm, I have a proposition to make to you, so stop wriggling and give me your full intention!' Nicolson sat up obediently, then smiled and forced himself to relax while waiting for his mother to go on.

'What I propose is this: that you both go back to India. That seems ideal. Ideal for you and ideal for Violet. Especially as living costs there are so much lower. However,' and the old lady paused, 'however, I cannot allow you to take my grandson with you—he is the last of the Nicolsons, after all. He needs a firm and stable upbringing, and that, I flatter myself, your sisters and I can provide. And a little boy needs a healthy climate to grow up in. That, too, we can offer.' She smiled in triumph and waited expectantly.

'With all due respect, Mother, Violet and I will decide where Malcolm goes, and with whom.'

There was a silence. Nicolson had no wish to expose his small son to the rigours of India, but he was not prepared to let his aged parent dictate to him either—until she unveiled the rest of her proposition, and he was forced to reconsider.

'I am prepared to settle all your outstanding debts and pay your passage to India, and advance you a little more besides from your inheritance—and in return, my grandson will remain here with me.'

Not only was it very reasonable, it was the answer to his dilemma. 'That's very generous of you, Mother,' and he thanked her sincerely. 'But,' he added, 'I doubt very much whether Violet will agree.'

'Indeed?' The widow's tone was frosty. 'If you want my opinion, my dear—' he didn't, but it was forthcoming anyway '—I consider you allow that wife of yours far too much freedom. Tell her what we've decided, and let that be an end to it!'

So he put the suggestion to Violet, and she was outraged. 'You can't mean it! If we go back, Malcolm goes with us! That's what I've always intended, and that's what I thought you wanted too.' Although her husband had never said as much, she realised now. 'I can't bear to be parted from him, not now, not ever!'

She ran to her son and snatched him up in her arms, raining passionate kisses upon his bewildered face. She carried him over to his father with tears in her eyes. 'I want India,' she said defiantly, 'but I want him, too. And you. Is that so very unreasonable?'

No, he realised it wasn't, as he took the child from her and sent him to play outside. He wanted India as well. He wanted the year-long warmth to take the chill from his bones. He wanted his family to share it with him. But he genuinely feared for the boy. 'Darling,' he reasoned in his turn, 'you know how children suffer in India. Do I need to remind you how many of them die?'

Violet turned away, trying not to think of the tiny graves at Mhow, their occupants sheltered by the wings of doves and angels. 'I won't let anything harm him,' she said fiercely. 'He will be safe with me, I swear.'

Malcolm put his arms around her. 'I know, I know,' he said soothingly. 'But he'll be even safer here. And soon he'd have to come back to school, anyway.'

It was the wrong thing to say. He felt Violet stiffen and pull away. 'No!' she exclaimed. 'Never! It happened to me and he'll hate us! Or, worse still, he'll forget us—Malcolm, I couldn't leave him behind. Please don't make me,' she whispered, and she leant against him, her face ravaged with despair.

'It's all right, sweetheart, it's all right. Of course I shan't make you,' and he stroked her hair as she sobbed with relief. If they chose the situation well, he said, near a cantonment with a hospital, there should be no need to worry. They would all go; they could just manage without his mother's help if, to begin with, they only paid the more pressing of the debts.

'We could go back to Malabar,' she said excitedly, laughing and crying at once. 'It's never too hot, and we'll be near the sea like we were before. You always said I could have had the baby at Cannanore or Calicut if I'd had to, because there was a hospital— Darling, it would be ideal! You must tell your mother—'

After her interview with her son, old Mrs Nicolson sent for his wife. She motioned to her to sit down and then she began to speak: 'I believe you're creating difficulties, Violet. I understand you wish to decline my more than generous offer.'

Her daughter-in-law sat perfectly still and said nothing, resisting with difficulty the unworthy temptation to tell this interfering old besom to mind her own business and hurry up and die ...

'I think there's something you don't quite understand, my dear Violet.' Mrs Nicolson looked at the expressionless face before her.

'Oh?'

'Yes. Malcolm is not at all well.'

'I know, he's told me, and he's also said there's nothing to worry about.'

'I see. Then he's shielding you from the truth. How very like him that is! His doctors, on the other hand, say that only a reasonable standard of comfort, with no worries of any kind, especially about his son—and in the warmer climate of India, of course—will give him the chance of reaching a ripe old age like his mother.' She gave a smug little smile.

'Malcolm has said nothing of this to me.'

Mrs Nicolson was not at all surprised to hear it. Her son had said nothing to his mother either, but her fabrication worried the old lady not at all. What did worry her were pangs of conscience over her daughters and the spinsterhood to which her selfishness had condemned them both—not that she would have chosen such a forthright word to describe her behaviour. She was well into her eighties now, and might not have long to live. At night a small accusing voice would occasionally speak out disturbing her sleep, and her conscience would keep her awake for long and lonely hours. Providing her daughters with a surrogate child might well be the answer to their problems—and hers.

That her son's wife would suffer in the process seemed a matter of small importance—if of any importance at all. Mrs Nicolson smiled again, for now she knew exactly how to proceed. 'Naturally Malcolm would say nothing to you, my dear,' she countered. 'I'm sure he always tries to spare you the worst. Am I not right?'

Violet nodded mutely. So Malcolm was really ill. And yet at some cost to himself he had been prepared to save her the heart-rending separation that his mother obviously cared nothing about. The old witch disliked her and she hated giving in, but did she have a choice?

Seeing the effect her words were having on her daughter-in-law, Mrs Nicolson warmed to her theme until Violet knew what she must do. With a dull ache in her heart she agreed to everything her mother-in-law wanted—even to her final demand: 'Promise me you will say nothing of our conversation to Malcolm, Violet. You know he wouldn't want to think of you worrying.'

'Of course.' White-faced and determined, Violet stood up and quickly left the room.

True to her word, she said nothing to her husband other than that she had changed her mind. She was sure it was for the best, she told him, but she didn't want to discuss it now or ever. After a few days they went back to London. Mark Grey lived in a quiet street in Mayfair and it was easy to throw herself into her work. *Stars of the Desert* was handed over as promised, and by August Violet found herself wondering what to do.

'You could always start another,' Malcolm suggested, and immediately regretted his words when Violet announced tragically: 'I shall never write another poem. I seem to have no emotions at all. Malcolm, I feel quite dead inside.'

'What you need is India to inspire you,' he said. 'We'll be going back soon.' He hadn't meant to sound heartless, and to his dismay she began to cry, great sobs that racked her body silently. Only when he held her did he realise how thin she was becoming.

'Oh Violet, sweetheart, don't. Darling, don't.' Nicolson felt quite helpless. He said they would take the boy if parting with him was going to make her ill, and she only wept the more. No, no, she told him, it wasn't possible, and she hid her face against his chest, where the strong heartbeat brought her comfort. Malcolm's health must come first, she told herself, as she grew calmer. Nothing else mattered at all.

10

'The Net of Memory'

MALABAR, INDIA: MARCH 1904–JULY 1904

Some weeks later, the studio portraits taken by the society photographer Beresford at William Heinemann's request were ready. Violet had worn the purple sari that had so shocked Flora Steel, and the silver bracelet, the first token of her husband's love. Her head was draped in gauze, the usually expressive mouth unsmiling, the eyes mournful. The dominant mood captured by the photographer was one of tragic introspection.

'Is this really how I look?' Violet asked in dismay and Nicolson studied the pictures. 'Most of the time,' he answered truthfully. 'Yes.'

'Then I'm surprised you've put up with me! Darling, I'm so sorry. Forgive me.'

What was there to forgive?

He suggested they leave as soon as they could—for her sake and his, he said, rather than dragging out the whole business any longer. Did she agree? Yes, yes, she sighed. A fortnight later the last farewells were over, and the Nicolsons were on their way back to India, alone.

Once the boat left Europe, Violet's mourning for her child grew less intense and her husband more outspoken. The little lad was happy, Malcolm told her, and perhaps she should pull herself together. If he had presumed to say as much earlier in the voyage he would have provoked bitter tears, but with Port Said behind them a touch of oriental fatalism settled on Violet's shoulders. Or was she simply tired of weeping?

She began to walk the decks in daylight, where darkness had served earlier to hide the signs of grief. After Suez she sighed less often, and Malcolm Nicolson watched his wife slowly come back to life. With the East in her sights Violet's heart began to thaw—although a chance word, a sudden memory could still revive the fierce pain of parting. One day when her laugh rang out at some ridiculously inconsequential thing the general knew she was beginning to heal.

At Aden a telegram from Isabel was waiting: John Tate was dead. Isabel said little more, and indeed, there was nothing much more to say. A heart attack lasting only a few seconds had wiped out eight years of complete happiness and a lifetime of self-indulgence. One moment the banker was commending his wife's committee work for the Lady Dufferin Hospital, the next he was slumped over the dinner table, his purple face in awful contrast to the pristine white of the cloth. By the time the Nicolsons arrived in Karachi, the banker had been in his grave for several weeks and his now painfully thin, acerbic widow was back at the helm of the *Sind Gazette*.

If Isabel had changed, so had Karachi. It lacked the ancient history of Peshawar and Lahore, and compared with India's great trading cities of Madras, Bombay and Calcutta, the town was a brash newcomer. Karachi's initial progress had been as slow as it was inevitable, but by the beginning of the twentieth century the pretensions of its businessmen were beginning to bear fruit. The town's natural landlocked harbour was now a sizeable port, and the railway had expanded. Under Arthur Cory and then his eldest daughter, the *Sind Gazette* had trumpeted Karachi's merits assiduously, and prospered under the town's commercial rise. While Isabel's tragic bereavement changed nothing of all that, to Violet Nicolson the newspaper lacked *soul*. She watched her widowed sister driving herself unmercifully, and one evening when the two women were alone she put forward a proposition.

'I think perhaps Malcolm and I might stay in Karachi, after all,' she said. 'The house is far too big for you, you know. We could keep you company, and I could help you with the paper. Think about it, Izzie. There's plenty of time.'

The suggestion was totally unexpected and Isabel was shocked. She had no intention of turning her house into a shrine for her dead husband, but this was the home that she and John had made together and the thought of sharing it permanently with the Nicolsons was most unwelcome. For one thing, Addie—in Addie's inimitable way—would turn the house upside down to suit her own tastes; she would disrupt the servants' routine. And then she would probably try to impose her ideas on the *Gazette*. To be fair, it was easy to understand Karachi's attraction for her sister, as old memories were revived—but *no* to anything else!

When Mrs Nicolson brought the subject up again a few days later, Isabel Tate was ready. She felt her sister's expectant gaze upon her, and unwittingly adopted the strategy employed by another, malevolent, widow. Thus she was able to refuse without causing lasting offence.

'What do I think about you staying?' The eyes behind the pebble lenses did not blink. 'I think it would be a dreadful mistake!' she said bluntly.

'Why?' Violet's voice was aggressive.

'I'll tell you why! It's all very well for you—Karachi is where you and Malcolm fell in love and where you first were lovers. It's special for you, and that I can understand.'

Isabel's voice softened only briefly.

'But remember, Addie, Malcolm's memories go back further than yours—nearly thirty years further. He's always been a soldier, active and purposeful, and now there's nothing of that left. How do you think he feels? Oh, he wouldn't tell you—you're enjoying yourself far too much, and he wants to make amends to you for taking you away from your son—but I can see it, even if you can't! It's tearing him to pieces inside.'

'But they make such a fuss of him in the regimental mess.'

'Of course they do! Malcolm Hassells Nicolson is a legend in Karachi. Colonel Nicolson of Zhob, Nicolson of the 3rd and 24th Baluchis—they've even resurrected the crocodile story, and the one of how he used to hop around the top of the church tower.'

'He's never told me about *that*.'

'Of course he hasn't, it's far too ridiculous!'

Isabel dismissed her brother-in-law's eccentricities scornfully and went on.

'Addie, all that's beside the point. They're happy to entertain him now, but the novelty is bound to wear off. One day he'll be like those circus freaks that are fascinating for a while and then rather boring—until finally you don't notice them at all. Meanwhile, Malcolm will be yearning for a past he can't reclaim and will turn into an embittered old man.'

Violet stared at her sister, whose sight was getting weaker, but who remained as perceptive as ever. She thought of how Malcolm had taken her to Hyderabad, to the 3rd Baluchis, where the time had flown by among old friends and familiar faces. But Isabel had opened her eyes. His memories had been bitter-sweet, then, and that was why they hadn't stayed longer … and what would Karachi do to Malcolm in the end?

When at last she spoke, she sounded thoroughly shaken. 'Izzie, of course you're right. So tell me what to do.'

'Do I really need to?' Relieved at the swift success of her argument, the normally undemonstrative Isabel gave Violet a hug. 'You intended to go back to Malabar, didn't you?'

'Yes. But I thought I—we—could be happy here. I was wrong. You've made me see that. Thank you, Izzie, dear,' she squeezed the widow's hand. 'How is it you're so wise and I'm so blind?'

'It's easier for outsiders. It always is. Tell Malcolm *you* want to go, *insist*—otherwise he'll stay here for your sake. And you'll end up by regretting it—you as well as him.'

'My Paramour was Loneliness'

The boat put in at Cannanore, fifty miles north of Calicut, where there was a cantonment and a sizeable town. At Malcolm's suggestion they disembarked. They would stay for a few days, he said, before going further south. There were plenty of untenanted bungalows these days, he told her, what with the cutbacks to the army, and he was sure they would find somewhere within their means.

When, out of courtesy, General Nicolson called on the commanding officer of what once had been the military capital of Malabar, he was warmly received—in southern India the name 'Nicolson' was a name like any other, but a general was a general, after all. So, instead of lodging modestly at their own expense, the Nicolsons were pressed to make unlimited use of the quarters reserved for visiting dignitaries. Alas, said the commandant dolefully, nowadays such visitors were very rare.

The General's Bungalow at Cannanore was a flat-roofed garden-house dating back to the far-off times when Dutch and Portuguese merchants vied with the British for the local maharajah's favour. Roomy, cool, and elegantly furnished, it overlooked the sea. There was no beach, only cliffs, and the waves crashed against the rocks many feet below. The air was balmy, the breeze a delight, but it was not at all what Violet had envisaged. Malcolm's 'few days' became several weeks, and rather than see more of her husband, as time went by she saw less, for the affable General Nicolson proved a most agreeable addition to the regimental mess. He tried to explain and she tried not to feel aggrieved.

When Malcolm abandoned her night after night and returned later and later, Violet's resignation turned to anger, and anger to concern. For what had his mother said? That Malcolm should limit his social activities; that alcohol in more than moderate amounts would put too many demands on his constitution … Violet's lip curled—the old biddy should see him now! *And it was going to make him ill.*

'You really should be wearing a hat, you know. The sun is deceptively mild.'

Violet started; she had quite failed to see the woman approaching along the cliffs. She smiled back at the speaker who was a few years younger.

'You're new here, aren't you?' the latter continued. 'I don't think I've seen you before.'

'My husband and I are on our way south, and we seem to be staying far longer than we intended.' Violet's voice was bitter. 'We meant to go to Calicut, you see. We've been there before and we wanted to go back.'

'Yes, it's a beautiful place,' the stranger agreed. 'Cannanore is so very *regimented.*' She gave a cheerful laugh. 'Of course, it would be, wouldn't it? When I came here first, I thought of all the wonderfully *straight lines* in the cantonment—British lines, native lines, strict lines of behaviour that must never be crossed. You know, all that sort of thing.'

She laughed again and Violet listened with increasing interest.

'My husband says I'm far too much of a rebel—he's a great believer in goodwill to all men, you see, and turning the other cheek. But then he would be—he's the chaplain!'

She didn't look like a chaplain's wife, thought Violet, unconsciously comparing this merry young woman with stolid Mabel Dyer at Mhow. She wondered what she was going to say next.

'But I'm afraid I can't agree,' the pleasant voice resumed. 'The meek may inherit the earth in the long run, but a little less meekness might get them there all the sooner!'

'How very true,' Violet said thoughtfully. 'Do you know,' she added impulsively, 'you remind me so much of me when I was younger. Now I'm afraid I'm in danger of becoming far too meek myself!'

She smiled somewhat ruefully. Then the chaplain's wife went off in one direction and the general's wife in another.

A little less meekness ... why even Thomas Hardy had thought her too compliant! A *little less meekness*, Violet reminded herself in the coming days as she sought an opportunity to confront her husband, but it was easier said than done. Malcolm was thoroughly enjoying himself, and there seemed to be no hint of the old trouble at all.

It was an odd regime that brought relief by being thus ignored, and Violet found herself thinking more than once that the odd unpleasant twinge or two would do her cause no harm. These feelings were followed by ones of guilt, which only served to heighten her sense of loneliness and utter futility. Besides, she told herself over and over, it was difficult to confront someone who was very rarely there!

It was not until Malcolm failed to return to her bed at all one night that Violet's patience finally gave way.

He came in the following morning looking rested and relaxed. 'I'm sorry about this,' he said, and she found his manner irritatingly offhand. 'I fell in with an old acquaintance and I quite forgot the time. I walked him back to the guest-house and, since you're usually asleep these days when I get in, I thought I might as well stop the night down there. Darling, it won't happen again.'

'It shouldn't have happened even once!' she snapped. I've been worrying myself sick about you, Malcolm Nicolson! I was awake all night, thinking you might be unwell and in the hospital.'

'Don't exaggerate, Violet, please. Why should I be unwell?'

'According to what I was told it's highly likely—you're not supposed to drink to excess, and I don't imagine you were drinking only soda water with your friend!'

By now Nicolson was looking at his wife intently. 'Darling, whatever are you talking about? Who told you all this?'

Violet remembered the promise made to a frightful old woman and bit her lip, but when the full force of the general's piercing eyes was brought to bear on her white face she found it impossible to keep silent any longer.

'It was your mother,' she finally admitted, 'and I really shouldn't be breaking my word.' She looked at him miserably.

'*My mother*—I see. What else did she have to say?' His voice was so angry that Violet flinched. 'Come on, darling,' he repeated, but this time gently, 'tell me what else my mother said.'

Violet told him in enough detail for him to understand: the old lady had frightened his wife into giving up her son, and to do so had woven a web of lies. Which Violet had believed at the time, and which she still believed.

For weeks she must have been worried to distraction while gallantly keeping her pledge. He could have said there and then that his mother had lied, and that she had cheated them out of their child, but why should Violet be tormented further by knowing her sacrifice to be unnecessary? So he said nothing and Violet got to her feet.

'I'm tired of all this,' she said, and the desperate weariness in her voice shook him more than anger would have done. 'I didn't come back to India to spend my days—and nights—alone. I renounced seeing my son grow up so as to be with his father, and I'm beginning to feel it was a dreadful mistake.'

The look from the great eyes was almost impersonal as she continued: 'I thought you needed me more than he did, but that doesn't seem to be the case. If *you* don't need me, then I'm going back before *he* forgets me, too. Perhaps you should decide what you really want.'

A sound of wheels came from the drive outside and Violet picked up an old carpetbag in which she had crammed the few things she deemed necessary.

'I'm going now,' she announced. 'There's a train to Calicut in an hour and I'm going back to where we were happy. I'll wait one week, Malcolm, and if you haven't come by then, then don't come at all for I'll be gone. I've left you a note.'

She nodded towards a small blackwood table by the window where a sheet of paper stood out in mute accusation, then she turned to go out.

'No!' Nicolson was beside her, holding her back.

'You're hurting me, Malcolm,' she said in a dull voice, but his vice-like grip did not slacken.

'Don't leave, Violet,' he said. 'Please wait. Say you'll wait and I'll come with you tomorrow.'

He was deathly pale, and she was puzzled to see compassion in his eyes, rather than guilt.

'Stay with me tonight,' he pleaded, 'and we'll travel down the coast together.'

Her brain was numb and she no longer felt the pressure of his fingers. 'Very well,' she said at last, forcing herself to think. 'I'll tell the *gharry wallah* he won't be required.'

He freed her and watched her walk outside. She did not return.

He found her at last far beyond the garden bounds sitting in the old familiar pose, hands locked around her knees as she gazed at the distant ships on the horizon. She did not turn her head.

'I read your note,' he said. 'Darling, forgive me. I'll never hurt you again, I swear.'

'Don't swear to anything, Malcolm Nicolson,' she said grimly. 'I expect you will, and I expect I'll put up with it when you do.'

'For one awful moment I thought you'd thrown yourself over the cliff!'

Now Violet looked at him and shook her head with a bleak little smile. 'How could I do that?' she asked. 'I couldn't even have gone back to England without you, but would *you* have come to Calicut?'

'Of course, my silly Violet!' He got up and pulled her to her feet.

By the time they reached the house she was shivering uncontrollably. The brandy he forced on her made her light-headed, and it was not long before she fell asleep. It took Nicolson no time at all to pack, and when he had finished he went out into the verandah and gave himself up to his thoughts. One way and another, he reflected sombrely, the Nicolsons had done very badly by his wife. Poor Violet, she was trying to do her best for him and the little boy, and in the process was being destroyed. If his mother was to blame then so was he, for Violet should never have been left alone night after night with her memories.

When she reappeared he led her to a seat. 'I hope you're feeling better,' he said gravely.

'Malcolm, I don't feel anything at all,' and she gave him a pitiful travesty of a smile. 'Just desperately tired.'

'Then we'll go somewhere where you can rest,' he said. 'What exactly do you want us to look for? Do you have any idea at all?'

'What do I want? I don't know. I suppose I should feel guilty at taking you away from all this,' with a shrug she indicated the gracious rooms behind them, 'but I'm afraid I can't. I don't mind where we go,' she told him, 'as long as you're beside me at night and in the morning—' Once it wouldn't have seemed a lot to ask, now it seemed too much. '*But only if you want that, too.*'

'Oh, darling, of course I do! What shall it be, then? A river-boat or a fisherman's hut? A tent perhaps, or something a little more European? Or shall we wait and see what tomorrow brings?'

He tried to keep his tone light-hearted, but he could see her hanging on to his every word, clinging to even the most whimsical idea as drowning men clutch at straws. For he knew she meant exactly what she said—anywhere at all with him would do. The realisation made Malcolm Nicolson feel extremely humble.

'A simple want; so easily allayed'

When he saw the tall figure pause at the garden gate and look his way, the *mali*, who had been sitting in the shade doing nothing, was galvanised into action. The *memsahib* demanded flowers but the *sahib* demanded perfection. *Aiye*, *aiye*, groaned the gardener, lamenting the days of idleness he had envisaged, and wondering how long his new employers were going to stay. He began to give the pots at the end of the terrace more attention than they had received for many a year and Nicolson was forced to smile. The man would make the task last all morning and what did it matter? There was no need for any of them to hurry over anything in this quiet little backwater—gone the bustle of London life and gone the pressures of Mhow, long gone.

Beyond the boundaries of the compound the coco-palms quivered in the breeze drifting up from the Beypore River, and near at hand a tangle of golden Maréchal Niel roses scrambled over a garden arch. Nicolson plucked one perfect flower and walked towards the bungalow. Squirrels scampered over the patchy grass ahead of him and one of the little striped creatures, bolder than the rest, darted up the steps to the house. It fled at his approach and Nicolson climbed the steps in his turn. He paused until his eyes adjusted to the sudden dark of the verandah.

Here and there sunbeams slipped past the grass *tattie* screens, dancing capriciously over the books on the table without quite reaching the chair where Violet was asleep. Her muslin gown fell in soft folds to the flagstones and the breeze played with the locks of her loosened hair. He stooped and retrieved a paper that was drifting over the stones, then sat down quietly so as not to disturb his wife.

He looked at her tenderly. Violet's lips were curved in the slightest of smiles, lips that had reproached him only once in Cannanore, before voicing the sweetest of demands. Soon they would have been married fifteen years, he reflected, and ever since that day in 1889, the impatient young girl had been imperceptibly changing, becoming stronger and more self-possessed. Like fine steel she had bent beneath the blows that life had dealt her, if at times she had nearly been broken.

The past three years had been testing for them both, he reflected, and his wife had emerged with considerably more credit than he had. She had kept her integrity and had found a niche for herself in London's literary world while he, quite frankly, had let the city turn his head. It had been bad for his health and worse for his morale, and worst of all it had threatened his marriage. For a while he and this golden girl of his had been in danger of drifting apart, and he had made matters worse at Cannanore. But now, thank God, he had learnt his lesson!

A chance meeting in Calicut, a word of a bungalow for lease in one of the nearby villages, and here they were in Feroke. Violet had taken one look at the isolated house, with its solitary jackfruit tree standing sentinel by the gateway, and, 'It's perfect, Malcolm! Oh, do let's rent it!' she had begged.

For a couple wishing to put the past behind them this part of the coast was a perfect choice, she continued. The few Europeans in the area were too busy earning a living to bother them—apart from the usual civilities that cost nothing and wasted very little time.

Within days Violet was looking better. Her eyes were alive again, and she began to shoo him out of the house, telling him to stop fussing and leave her be. She had things to do, she scolded, so why didn't he go and get his bearings?

Feroke House was on the edge of the village and gave her the privacy she craved. A thickly planted *tope* of coconut palms grew around the house, and beyond the mud brick boundary wall a steep track led to the old fort at the top of the hill. Built in Tippu Sultan's day, it still watched over the seabound reaches of the Beypore River, and often in the late afternoon they made their way up to the weathered ruins. As the shadows lengthened and the soft air took on the luminous quality so special to the East, they would linger like lovers, sharing a silence broken only by the call of ricebirds, watching the waters burn red and gold in the rays of the setting sun.

She had been right: this simple undemanding life was exactly what she needed. He touched her cheek and Violet stirred. The smile deepened when she opened her eyes and saw the rose, and her husband was moved at how easy it was to make her happy.

❧

While General Nicolson went out and about on his own again, his wife returned to her poetry. There was so much to record. So many experiences overwhelmed her daily, and at times, as she confided to Malcolm, she felt at risk of drowning in the flood. It was as if her life had come full circle and she was ready to start again.

One morning Violet sat alone in the verandah. Letters were beginning to reach them; there were several on the table beside her and she held one from Mary and Caroline Nicolson. Her sisters-in-law had spared no detail and Violet could picture her three-year-old son vividly. The child's precocious sayings, his sense of adventure, his little pranks—*so like his dear father*—all were sent unsparingly from the South of England. Violet stifled an impulse to write a letter of entreaty in return, begging the older women to send more, many more details—or did she mean *fewer*, or even *none at all?*

She read the letter once more, her eyes dimmed by tears of guilt as well as longing. She had thought so little of her son these last few weeks, for her preoccupations had been totally with his father. She heard Malcolm calling for her from the garden and brushed the tears away. In a day or two, she told herself, the pain would go.

'Violet! Violet, where are you?' General Nicolson's voice rang out impatiently and she smiled. He would find her. He always did.

'Mail?' he asked, coming in and looking at the table.

She nodded. 'A letter from Mother and one from Blanche. And one from your sisters. Everyone in Brighton is fine, here, see for yourself,' she said brightly.

His eyes quickly scanned the sheets covered with small neat writing. Thank goodness they hadn't thought to send a studio portrait—they must be warned, for that would surely break Violet's heart. 'Good,' was all he said, and then he studied her tear-stained face.

'You're not brooding, are you?'

'No, no, of course not,' she answered too quickly.

'India's no place for children,' he reminded her firmly. 'The lad's far better off where he is.' In her heart of hearts Violet could only agree. It was foolish to think of her son in the care of strangers when the only strangers in his life were his father and herself. Another year or two, and they would see him again and find out if he remembered who they were.

Malcolm didn't seem to feel the loss of his son as she did, she thought, when he swiftly changed the subject. She quite failed to see the anxious glances he sent her throughout the afternoon. Nor did she question why he took her everywhere with him for a while until the letter was forgotten.

He took her through the small village with its three tile factories and steam-curing works. He took her for exhausting walks beside the river. He took her to Calicut, where the dim green gloom of coconut groves gave way to golden beaches and shallow bays hugged by laterite cliffs. But when he proposed a visit to the boatyard at Beypore she laughed out loud.

'Oh, Malcolm, really,' she protested, 'you're a soldier, not a sailor! You know how much you hate travelling by sea!'

Yet once they were there, she fully understood his interest. Wooden sailing ships like these had sailed the Arabian Sea for centuries, laden with Malabar's wealth of spices. For centuries they had maintained contact with the worlds of East and West. They were a testimony to the craftsman's skill and dedication, and possessed exactly the durability and dependability Nicolson had always expected of his men.

Violet stared up at the vast body of a half-completed boat. The deck under its woven awning of fronds was many feet above. 'May I?' she asked impulsively, before, gathering her skirts, she darted up the ladder to see the work close to. Only local teak from the Nilambur plantation was used, the manager explained when he and Malcolm joined her, and absolutely no metal at all. The Uru boats of Beypore were special, and he nodded emphatically, very special indeed.

'They used to look for gold up in the mountains,' he added, 'but do you know, Mrs Nicolson, good timber is far easier to find!'

The slight sallow-skinned man made his little joke and Violet smiled politely.

While Mr D'Souza guided his wife back onto the precarious bamboo ladder, Nicolson lingered. Far below, a small overloaded ferry struggled between the riverbanks but the tantalising blue haze of the Western Ghats was all he saw.

'Gold,' mused the general. 'Gold. *Now, I wonder …*'

'Men should be judged, not by their tint of skin'

One morning at breakfast Malcolm Nicolson put down his cup and addressed his wife. 'When were you thinking of inviting the Walters to dinner, my dear?'

'Well, to be perfectly honest, I wasn't.'

He frowned. 'I'm sorry, Violet. They were kind enough to invite us when we arrived and that's well over a month now. To delay any longer would seem discourteous.'

The finality in his tone made opposition futile.

'Very well,' she murmured, 'I'll send someone over this morning with a chit. Shall we say tomorrow?'

'Excellent,' and Malcolm took another sip of tea.

The Walters were Swiss. Herr Walter ran one of the local tile factories on behalf of the Basel Mission and Violet found him pleasant enough. On the other hand, she had taken an instant dislike to his wife. Frau Walter was one of those capable women to whom childbirth was an easy and regular event. Her ample bosom had provided safe anchorage for a succession of small Walters, all of whom survived.

Every day a well-trained line of children, the boys in white sailor suits the girls in spotless pinafores, made its way from the family bungalow down the single village street. Woe betide any child who scuffed its boots in the fine red dust, or allowed itself to be distracted by a straying dog, or indeed a straying native infant. Eyes darted right and left at their peril.

Although she distrusted all things Indian, Frau Walter did not believe in educating youngsters *at Home*. She said so—often—and Violet soon learned to avoid her tender enquiries about the Nicolsons' only child in England.

Left alone after breakfast, Violet thought about the dinner Malcolm insisted that she give. She would warn the cook when she made her daily inspection of the kitchen at ten, but tomorrow morning would be soon enough for details. They had been served plain and wholesome food at the Walters' so Violet reached for the small dark green volume sent her by Mrs Steel as another 'thank-you' after her stay. Its immodest title *The Complete Indian Housekeeper and Cook* never failed to irritate her and she rarely made use of it, but today she turned its pages seeking inspiration.

'Darling, here's the menu I suggest for tomorrow,' she ventured later. 'I'm sure the cook can cope.'

Malcolm glanced at the paper she handed him. 'Yes, I'm sure he can. The question is, can we? *Hotch-Potch—Bechamel of Fish—Chicken cutlets—Chocolate Shape*—it should certainly fill us up!'

'I used Flora's book,' she said defensively. 'I thought you'd be pleased.'

Malcolm's smile deepened. He understood his wife's attitude towards the dinner party, even if he did not condone it, and he had no intention of interfering with her arrangements in any way. He simply wanted the evening to be a success.

And at first it was. The Indian cook had added his own gloss to the solid European dishes ordered by his mistress, but nonetheless they met with the approval of her guests. Spoonful after spoonful of thick meaty soup was swallowed in quick succession; the anonymous fish was mercifully free of bones. The cutlets vanished with alarming rapidity, along with the carrots, cabbage and potatoes *maître d'hôtel*. Conversation resumed, only to fade with the advent of the 'Shape'.

'How are you settling in, General Nicolson?' Herr Walter took advantage of the lull while his wife helped herself to the farinaceous pudding.

'Extremely well, thank you, Walter,' and Malcolm smiled at his careworn guest. Violet watched her husband, envying the ease with which he dealt with strangers.

'We find Feroke very much to our liking,' he went on. 'I think we've met most of the European community now, although you are in fact our very first guests'—this with a courteous bow of the head towards Frau Walter who glowed in response, her mouth too full for comment.

'And how do you find the Robinsons up at the other tile works?' she asked, once she was free again to speak. 'You know that she isn't quite one of us, of course?' Seeing incomprehension on the faces of her hosts, she explained: 'She was a Miss D'Souza before her marriage and has *Indian blood*'—this in a hushed tone.

'Any relation to the manager at the boatyard?' Malcolm asked, sending Violet a frown of warning.

'His sister,' Walter intervened quickly, wishing his wife would not show her prejudices quite so openly in public.

'He's a fine fellow,' commented Malcolm. 'I've been to his yard several times. Wonderful ships, those Uru boats. Don't you agree, Violet?'

'Oh yes,' she replied, 'and Mr D'Souza is charming. I haven't met Mrs Robinson yet, though. I think I'll call on her tomorrow.'

'I believe you write poetry, Mrs Nicolson.' Mrs Walter looked at her hostess slyly. Violet stared back in amazement, her coffee cup poised midway between saucer and lip. How on earth did the woman know?

She glared accusingly at her husband who shook his head slightly, as surprised as she. Finally she replied. 'Well, yes—I do write a little.'

'My friend in London says you have published two books—about *India*.' Mrs Walter made it sound as if Violet had committed some social indiscretion. 'And you use a *man*'s name, Mrs Nicolson. *Why*?'

Again, Violet was rendered speechless, and Malcolm intervened before she found something to say which he—if not she—would regret.

'My wife, while quite understandably wanting to publish her work, wished to respect my privacy.' The quiet firmness of his words suggested his guest should do the same.

Mrs Walter opened her mouth to ask another question. Her husband caught her eye and she quickly changed her mind. Silence prevailed for a moment, then she turned back to her hostess. 'Mrs Nicolson,' she wheedled, 'we do so want to hear you read one of your poems. Just one—'

Smarting from the woman's insensitive curiosity, Violet went into the drawing room and returned with a copy of *Stars of the Desert* already open in her hand. 'I'm sure you only wish to hear a short piece and I think this one will do very nicely. Its title is *Men Should be Judged*,' she announced, 'although I imagine we might include women too …' She smiled at Mrs Walter, glanced defiantly at Malcolm and then began to read:

Men should be judged, not by their tint of skin,
The Gods they serve, the Vintage that they drink,
Nor by the way they fight, or love, or sin,
But by the quality of thought they think.

It was not long before the Walters made their excuses and left.

The street was quiet when Violet set out late the following morning and the few people she passed greeted her in their usual friendly fashion. The road to her destination swung left out of the village, then turned up a steep track leading to the works. The Robinsons' bungalow was easy to find among the outbuildings. It was small and neat, and the garden was filled with struggling English plants. When would people ever learn that only roses had a chance of survival? Violet shook her head, handed her card to the immaculate servant who answered her ring promptly, and waited.

The door opened again and she was shown into a cool room where a tall, slender woman greeted her. Her quiet, modest manner and dark looks reminded Violet of Natica Lister Kaye, but there the resemblance ended. Ellen Robinson glowed with happiness. They talked for half an hour and when she rose to leave, Violet received a shock.

'Do you know, you're the second visitor I've had today, Mrs Nicolson.' The tone implied that normally Mrs Robinson would have been gratified to receive even one a week. 'Mrs Walter called this morning and she was *so* nice. She's never spoken to me before. And she said such nice things about *you*. I'm so pleased to meet you at last.'

Violet drove home in a reflective mood. There was, after all, plenty to occupy her mind.

'But Love deceived me'

Malcolm Nicolson's own preoccupations with the present were mingled with thoughts of the past. If at night he dreamed about gold, he awoke thinking of his career. It was three years since he had relinquished the Mhow Command, and while he was still on the active list it seemed unlikely that he would receive another appointment. Violet's father had been right—they were all gone, the veterans of Kabul and Kandahar, and the star of a new generation was in the ascendant.

And that was how it should be, he conceded. But he felt young enough to be on his feet from dawn to dusk; the old energy was still present. True, the health problems of recent years caused him occasional discomfort but there had been nothing much for a while. And certainly he would worry Violet with none of it—the poor lass had enough to cope with lately. As for him, there was no point in sitting around brooding. If they were to stay here, then he would need to get to know the district better and find out what it offered.

Malcolm had taken Violet at her word. His purposeful figure became a familiar sight in and around Feroke as he left her to her writing. And soon many of the official and unofficial British working in the area found their way to the Nicolsons' door. And he found his way to theirs. Entertaining in this part of India was a far more relaxed affair than it had been in the north: Violet welcomed the casual passers-by who called in on her husband—and then became invisible for the duration of their visit.

Malcolm often found himself in Ariakode, a pleasant two hours' ride away in an attractive wooded setting. Although there were other small towns in the vicinity also housing European officers and troops and government officials, Ariakode suited the general perfectly. There was plenty of easy shooting should he feel so inclined, while the town's economy was closely linked to the teak plantations at Nilambur.

He felt at home immediately. The community was predominantly masculine, and Henry Wilson, the resident magistrate who had been in Ariakode for over five years and a widower for four, frankly welcomed a new face at his table. The two men quickly became friends and Violet was pleased that Malcolm had found congenial companionship, even at some distance from home.

She would have been less complacent had she known how often the conversations over a peg or two in Wilson's shaded verandah came round to the subject of gold. Vincent D'Souza's casual remark at the Beypore shipyard had stayed with Malcolm Nicolson, and the banked-down fires of gold fever were rekindled. Newspaper accounts of the successful gold fields in neighbouring Mysore caused the flame to burn as brightly as ever it had in those heady days of 1898, when Johnny Kaye had peddled his China scheme over port and cigars in the opulent surroundings of his London club. It would be good to show Kaye a thing or two, mused the general, and the money would certainly come in handy.

When General Nicolson asked Henry Wilson to tell him about Nilambur, the magistrate was only too happy to oblige. Ernad *taluk* was rich in valuable timber, he explained, much of it privately owned. Government plantations had been established in the district as far back as 1842, and teak was floated down the river to Ariakode. In the season, he told his guest, you couldn't see the water for logs. 'We only have a small timber depot here, of course,' Wilson concluded. 'Most of it gets diverted to Kallai.'

'So the teak business is thriving.'

'Indeed it is. You should take Mrs Nicolson up and have a look. There are a couple of public bungalows and Tom Peters, the Forest Officer, would be delighted to show you round. He doesn't get to see many new faces since the gold finally ran out. If there ever was any, that is. Plenty of fool's gold, probably—*and* fools!'

So it was true!

'Tell me about the gold,' asked Malcolm Nicolson, and Wilson once again obliged.

Violet's birthday came and went and April turned to May. The sky was brazen and the ground like iron. The clouds slowly banked up against the Ghats, heralding the southwest monsoon. When Violet returned from a walk in the village one morning she found a letter lying opened on the living-room table. Idly, she picked it up and her heart gave a sickening lurch as she saw the official paper. Dear God, had the summons come at last?

Dear General Nicolson, I am instructed by the Commander in Chief to inform you … With mixed feelings Violet read on. Her husband's *distinguished services to the Government of India* were at last to be suitably recognised; the Commander in Chief was pleased to confer upon her husband the honorary colonelcy of the 3rd Baluch Battalion. The letter was dated the 15th of May 1904.

So the moment had come; the message was clear. The honour was an empty one and Malcolm's military career at last was finished. Violet did not know whether to laugh with relief for her own sake, or to weep for her husband's dashed hopes.

She put the letter down, thinking quickly. Where was he? Where would he have gone? How badly was he taking the news? She ran out of the bungalow, across the terrace, and through the archway. Instead of going on to the main gate she turned left. She hurried along the narrow path, pushed past the overgrown bushes and emerged onto the riverbank.

She looked up and down the beach. Yes, yes, there he was, standing motionless at the water's edge. The tall figure, normally so ramrod straight, was bowed and Violet hesitated. Would he think her intruding, should she go away? Quickly making up her mind, she ran down the stone steps towards him.

'Malcolm—' she began tentatively, only to fall silent. Her husband's face was grey with despair. 'Darling—' Impulsively she took his arm.

Slowly he met her gaze, and the hawk-like eyes, compelling no longer, were dulled by defeat.

'The waiting's over, the old war horse has been put out to pasture.' He gave a bitter laugh. 'Of course, I should have realised—it's been too long. But I *did* still hope, and now it's over.' He turned back to the river.

Violet could say nothing, for the lump in her throat was choking her. Besides, what was there to say? It was true, so damnably true. Malcolm was sixty-one, the army called for younger men. But it was cruel, all the same. She moved closer, wanting to comfort him, hoping her silent presence would be enough.

'Come on, let's walk,' he said, and tucked her arm under his. The silence between them became oppressive, as if the general's anguish weighed down upon them both. Perhaps she should leave him to his grief? For a moment Violet felt a desperate urge to run away—after all, what good was she doing—but her feet had turned to lead. As if aware of her thoughts, Malcolm drew her closer and the feeling of suffocation eased a little.

Soon the bungalow was out of sight. As they rounded a bend in the river Violet caught her breath. There on the damp sand before them was flung the lifeless, broken body of a boy. Violet hung back in horror as the general knelt beside him, but there was nothing to be done—the lad must have drowned up-river. His livid face was torn by rocks or branches, and try as he might Nicolson could not close the blood-caked lids.

He stood up and looked at his wife. 'He's gone of course, poor devil. *His* troubles are over. God, how I envy him!'

Something inside her snapped. She seized him by the arms. 'How dare you talk of giving up, Malcolm Nicolson!' she shouted. 'How dare you even think it! You have many good years ahead of you. Oh really, sometimes you make me *so angry*!'

As she tried to shake him, her own small figure quivering with rage, he looked down at her from his great height and, despite himself, smiled in wry amusement at the picture they must present.

'Oh, how can you laugh about it?' Violet exclaimed in exasperation. 'Really, you're quite impossible!' and she burst into tears.

Malcolm hugged her. 'Oh how I love you, Mrs Nicolson,' he murmured against her hair. 'And what would I do without you to bring me to my senses?'

As they walked home, he comforted his wife and by dint of telling her that all would be well, came close to believing it himself.

He left Violet at the bungalow and took himself off to the police station to report the death. Later he joined her out in the verandah. 'Darling, we need to talk,' he said, and she immediately put down her pen and prepared to listen. 'I think we have to consider all the possibilities before us in the light of this morning's letter.' Violet nodded. 'The question is, do we stay in Feroke on a permanent basis, or do we go somewhere else? I'm talking about India, Violet, of course.'

'Of course—we must stay here for your health.'

It hardly seemed the moment to tell her of his mother's deception, so once more Nicolson found himself postponing the matter. 'With or without my health, India is all we can afford. So is it to be Feroke, or do we move on?'

'Malcolm, what do *you* want?'

'Oh no, this time *you* decide! I've uprooted you far too often and you've followed me without question—now we're going to do what you want for a change.'

Violet sighed happily. She had no doubts at all. Isabel had pointed out the folly of returning to old haunts, and while she might still cherish an ever-dimming dream of a little boy playing on the beach beneath the palms, she knew that was out of the question. But there was still a dream, a dream that *could* be fulfilled. No more polite promenades along the front at Brighton with old Mrs Nicolson and her equally ancient sister; no more dreary English winter afternoons—they would spend the rest of their days in Malabar, with the spice-scented breeze blowing gently as they walked along the shore or by the river.

'I really didn't think you'd take so long, darling. You have the most wonderfully expressive face, have I ever told you?'

'Often,' and Violet touched the hand that stroked her cheek. 'I don't need to tell you what I've decided, do I?'

No, and thank God it wouldn't mean a return to Karachi! 'Tell me all the same,' he urged.

'We'll stay here, then—if you want that too?'

'Yes, indeed I do, but things will have to change. I can't drift along any longer. I must have something to do. Now,' and he sat down beside her, 'I've been making enquiries about Nilambur. No, listen,' as she started, 'you must hear me out. Violet, there is gold up there, I've been shown nuggets. And there were English mining companies up there in the '70s and '80s—'

'So why aren't they up there now?'

Nicolson didn't seem to hear. 'We'll have to go up and take a look,' he said. 'I know how to get a mining concession and Henry Wilson says he'll help speed things up. If it looks promising, I imagine we can start in two or three weeks.'

Violet felt a flash of irritation; why ask *her* to decide when his mind was so obviously made up? Then she recalled that he had left it to her; she had weighed everything in the balance and had made her decision freely. She should be happy that he agreed—for whatever reason! No, that was unfair. She had her poetry, let him have his gold if that was what he really wanted. But, please God, she prayed, let there be no more disappointments.

'If that's what you truly want, darling, then I'll help you all I can. Perhaps we'll find the end of the rainbow, after all.'

Nicolson looked at her suspiciously, but try as he might he could detect no trace of mockery on her gently encouraging face. He breathed a sigh of relief—it had been far easier than he dared hope.

Violet and Malcolm saw little of each other during the next week. Nicolson busied himself with plans for a trip to Calicut, then up the coast to Tellicherry to consult the old records, and on to Cannanore.

'Why go so far?' asked Violet. The memory of the General's Bungalow still rankled, and suddenly she was unwilling to let Malcolm out of her sight.

When he told her that one of the engineers who had worked in the Nilambur area twenty-five years before was still alive and living in Cannanore Violet overcame her reluctance. At the same time she felt she was indulging a small boy, but did it matter? They were both happy with the decision to stay and life, full of surprises, was beckoning them on.

During Malcolm's absence she received a visit from Henry Wilson. The magistrate was down for the day from Ariakode, and when Violet explained the reason for her husband's absence, she wondered why he looked uncomfortable.

'Oh dear,' he confessed. 'I'm afraid I'm to blame for all this. Your husband asked me about gold, I told him what I knew, and this is the result. Personally, Mrs Nicolson, I think it's all a bit of a wild goose chase.'

Violet found herself warming to her middle-aged visitor. 'So do I,' she agreed. 'But I shan't try to dissuade him.'

'Well,' said Wilson, 'he's very lucky you've chosen to take it like this. I've become a bit of a hermit since the death of my wife, and it's done me a world of good, you know, having your husband drop in from time to time. I would hate to cause any trouble. He's a fine man,' he added, 'and I'm glad he's feeling so much better these days.'

Violet was startled. Malcolm had said nothing to her about feeling unwell, and she had noticed nothing untoward. Surely all that was over long ago? She forced herself to carry on a light-hearted conversation with the widower over tiffin and hoped that he wouldn't notice her preoccupation. Just what, she asked herself, had Malcolm been hiding from her this time?

The next two days dragged by and Violet busied herself with letters and household chores. There was linen to be sorted and bags and stores packed for the camp at Nilambur. She looked around the room. Had she remembered everything? She checked she had paper, pencils and books—it was bound to rain a great deal of the time—and her eye fell on the *Wessex Poems*. Kind Mr Hardy to send her this gift, and her intention of repaying his kindness had been quite forgotten in the heartbreak of parting from her son. Well, she had time to remedy that now! She opened her own copy of *Stars of the Desert* at the title page, thought for a moment, then wrote: *Thomas Hardy from Laurence Hope, Feroke, Malabar, 1904*. She enclosed a short note, wrapped the parcel, and strolled down to the little red-tiled post office a few minutes' walk away.

'Mrs Nicolson! Mrs Nicolson!' Frau Walter bore down purposefully upon her.

'I believe General Nicolson is away? You must come and have dinner with us tonight!'

'No, no,' Violet demurred, 'I couldn't possibly.'

'But I insist! The dear general would simply not forgive us for neglecting you.'

He probably would, thought Violet, but with an inward sigh she found herself agreeing. Faced with such determined kindness it was simpler to give in, and, besides, it would help pass the time. At six o'clock her carriage swept into the tile-yard, through the gateway beyond, and deposited her before the manager's flawlessly whitewashed two-storey house with its incongruously bright window boxes. Her hostess hailed her, and Violet allowed herself to be drawn into the deep verandah to take her seat in a well-upholstered rattan chair.

The children were duly paraded for her inspection and then sent off to the nursery with the ayah. Violet said how charmingly well-behaved they were and her hostess beamed and glowed with pride. Herr Walter came in, looking as anxious as ever, and they talked of this and that and the weather until the meal was served and they ate in silent concentration.

'And how is dear General Nicolson?' Frau Walter enquired afterwards. 'We thought he looked a little tired when we saw him last. Has he been unwell again?'

'No, no, not at all,' Violet replied brightly. 'Why, only the other day he was saying he'd never felt better.'

'Good, good,' cooed her hostess, reminding Violet of a plump pouter pigeon, 'but it must be a worry, all the same.'

Violet felt furious. How did everyone seem to know so much more about her husband's health than his wife? *Just you wait till you get home, Malcolm Nicolson*, she thought grimly, as she drove away. *You have a great deal of explaining to do.*

'Many a man has a secret dream'

Malcolm Nicolson was shown into Patrick Grant's sparsely furnished living room in Cannanore, and a slight white-haired figure rose from a chair by the window to greet him. The two men could not have been in greater contrast—one tall, dapper and very much the soldier, the other short and at ease in a crumpled ill-made cotton suit. The engineer shook hands with his distinguished visitor, and invited him to take a seat.

'This is a very great pleasure, General,' he said. 'You'll take a whisky?'

Without waiting for a reply, he handed Malcolm a generous measure and took the armchair opposite. Starved of company, he was in no hurry to find out his visitor's business and Nicolson, too, was content to wait. He took in his surroundings as he sipped slowly, and the maps on the wall claimed his attention most of all. Grant had travelled widely, from the look of it, and he wondered why the man had chosen to settle in Cannanore of all places. Violet would probably have asked outright, but he was not about to do so.

'You'll be wondering what an old fellow like me is doing in a place like this.' Grant read his thoughts with a twinkle in his bright brown eyes. 'Most people do and the answer's simple. I married a Eurasian girl from Goa, and when I retired I decided not to go back to Scotland—you'll surely have noted a tolerance in Malabar you'd rarely find elsewhere. And the climate is kinder here, you'll have noticed that as well. I fancied her chances of surviving the Scottish winters were slight, you see, as well as anything else, but it made no difference in the end. She died all the same, my lassie.' For a moment the old man fell silent. 'Ah well, that's a gey long time ago now, ' he continued with a sigh. 'You'd be a Scot, yourself, General Nicolson, with a name like that?'

'Yes, I suppose I am, although my wife insists that I'm more Indian than anything else! My father's family lived in Thurso; he was a major in the Bengal Army and, I suppose, an engineer of sorts. At least, he ended up Superintendent of Roads in Jubbulpore District back in the 1830s.'

'Is that so? It would have been a hard life, now, making roads in Central India all those years ago, and in that shocking heat.' Patrick Grant nodded. 'But you've made a few roads in your time, too, General Nicolson, I'm thinking. That was a famous trip you made to the Zhob, in 1890 I think it was, and a fair few tons of rock you shifted.'

Malcolm was surprised at the reference.

'Maybe,' he answered soberly. 'But I left twenty fine fellows buried alive in the Zao defile, that's what *I* remember. It was a high price to pay and I often wonder whether it was worth it.'

'But you've not come all the way from Feroke to talk about roads, I'll warrant! Another wee dram now, General, before you tell me how I can be of service.'

Nicolson sat forward in his chair. 'I've heard a lot about the work you did in the mountains, sir, and I'd be grateful for any advice at all you could give me. I've applied for a gold-washing concession near the village of Nilambur, you see.'

'You've gone that far already, have you?' the older man responded with a smile. 'In that case it seems to me you mean to go ahead, whatever I may say! I can see the same look on your face as I've seen on many another! But of course I'll tell you what I know—*and* I'll tell you why we gave up. And maybe I'll be able to change your mind for you before it's too late.'

Malcolm leaned back in his chair again, stretched out his long legs and prepared to listen.

'We found traces of old mines above Nilambur when we started up our own in the early 1880s. The hills are riddled with the workings, but much of the prospecting nowadays is confined to the river bed and you'll have competition, for one thing. Oh yes,' Grant smiled as Malcolm gave a start, 'the Beypore is known locally as the Gold River, and the natives still pan for gold in a haphazard kind of a way. I'd say your best bet would be to get them to work for you and pay them a daily rate.

'Of course I've no idea how much money you're willing to spend—' what was a general's pension worth, he wondered '—but if you want a large-scale operation like ours was, then you'll need machinery to crush the quartz, rather than simply working the alluvial deposits in the banks or beds of streams.'

'I see. So you *did* find gold in the outcrops?'

'Oh yes, it was there all right, but it wasn't easy to get at. It was a long process, requiring a lot of heavy machinery and a lot of manpower, and to be honest it wasn't always entirely successful.'

'It sounds expensive,' ventured Nicolson. 'But it's the only way of dealing with bulk, I suppose?'

'Actually it isn't. There was another company up there at the same time as we were and they didn't fancy the expense we went to. So they used a simpler method favoured in the California rush, and one used in the Australian goldfields too, I believe—two millstones banded together with iron and fixed to a central shaft by a beam. The whole thing is then rotated. It's known as a Chilean Mill and it was used a lot in South American silver mines. Look, the principle is simple enough,' and Grant quickly sketched a diagram on a piece of paper.

'I see,' said Nicolson, getting up to look over his shoulder. 'And bullocks to pull it round the circular trough. Yes, yes, that seems quite possible,' and he resumed his seat.

'In fact,' Grant said slowly, 'I do believe those stones could still be there! About four-and-a-half tons they'd be, about two miles out of Nilambur on the Chellambore stream—they'll be gey difficult to spot, at the rate things grow up there, but you never know. I can't think that anyone would have shifted them, and if you're determined to go ahead it would save you a bit of money if you found them.'

Malcolm nodded in agreement. 'So why did the mining stop?' he asked.

'We overreached ourselves.' Grant was perfectly frank. 'We had to borrow, and when we fell behind with interest payments the bank foreclosed on the loans. It was impossible to go on.'

'So what you're saying, sir, if I understand you correctly, is that to have any chance of success an operation has to be modest. Concentrating on a simple washing operation, perhaps, using pans and cradles and as many workers as possible? What do you think?'

'Well, that would certainly be easier. The main thing is to make the stream water work for you, not against you. And now's the right time of year for that, with the monsoon coming on and the water levels higher.'

Patrick Grant said farewell to his visitor and watched him stride away. He shook his head sagely—there went another man about to waste his time and money. The good Scot in him was appalled at the very thought.

'Think not I scorn the Science That lightens human pain'

Violet decided to take the carriage and meet Malcolm. The road to Calicut was never crowded, but she allowed plenty of time for the eight-mile journey to the railway station. It was pleasant to dawdle and she always enjoyed the sunshine and the scenery. The palm groves grew right to the road and she caught intermittent glimpses of the low huts in their depths. High up in the trees she could see the black toddy pots, and occasionally she caught sight of a practised Tiyah shinning up a trunk to collect his haul of milky sap.

In town, small open-fronted shops were everywhere: jars of coconut oil in one, coils of rope in another, piles of matting encroaching onto the road from another. Coir baskets spilled their mangoes, bananas and jackfruit at the feet of passers-by. The smell of toddy was unavoidable. The missionaries could preach against the evils of the drink till the moon turned blue (the cynical thought came unbidden), but against a government reaping *crores* of rupees in excise duty they would have little, if any, effect! She stopped at a stall to buy tiny packets of spices, then, savouring the smell of cinnamon and ginger, she gave the order to walk on.

At the railway station, lounging natives surrounded by pots, pans, boxes and innumerable small children occupied every possible scrap of shade. The few Europeans paced purposefully up and down the platform, defying the sun. The train pulled in to scenes of utter bedlam as comatose brown bodies came suddenly to life and jostled their way towards third-class carriages, all of them bawling and shoving in the fight to find a place. Violet jumped down and walked quickly towards the head of the train, leaving the din behind her.

She scanned the arrivals impatiently. Yes, there was Malcolm, standing head and shoulders above the other travellers. A boy appeared at his side as if by magic and took charge of his capacious portmanteau. Turning, the general caught sight of his wife. He waved and strode towards her, leaving the lad to keep up as best he could. By the way he hugged her she knew the trip had been a success.

'This is a pleasant surprise,' he said, when he had deftly retrieved his luggage.

'I wasn't looking forward to taking the *gharry*. So, what have you been doing while I've been gone?' he asked, when the carriage turned into Calicut's main street.

'Oh, nothing very much, really. Mr Wilson called yesterday, and stayed for lunch. He'll call again tomorrow, I think he said, or the day after ...'

'What else did you do?' Malcolm prompted.

'Oh, yes, I sent the book I promised Mr Hardy months ago and Frau Walter recruited me for dinner ...' Again her voice faded and she looked sharply at her husband. Had it all been imagination?

'Malcolm, how are you feeling?' she asked.

The question took him aback. 'Very well, why?'

'Well,' she said, despite feeling foolish, 'two of your friends tell me that you haven't been in the best of health lately, and I was surprised,' she didn't say *hurt*, though this was evident from her voice, 'to hear it from them, and not from you.'

'I'm sorry.' Malcolm was instantly contrite. 'It's the same trouble I had last year—it comes and goes. Perhaps I should have told you the last time it happened, but it was weeks ago and I've felt so well ever since. There's no need for you to worry, you know, and perhaps this time I'm really better.' He smiled and patted her hand. 'Let's wait and see. I'll tell you the minute I feel any pain,' he promised. 'There, will that do?'

Violet frowned: she was not a child to be placated.

'Malcolm, I'm serious about this,' she said. 'You must see a doctor, I mean a doctor in Madras or Bombay, someone with experience of these things. *Now*.'

'Oh, darling, no,' and his voice was full of protest. 'There's so much to do. Wait until I tell you what I learned in Cannanore!'

He looked at her adamant face and came to a rapid decision.

'Oh, very well. We'll compromise. Two weeks or so in Nilambur, maybe three, and we can be in Madras by the middle of July. I'll write to my old friend Stewart and ask him to make enquiries. How about that? Will that satisfy you? We can have a bit of a holiday at the same time. Well, what do you think?'

Violet swallowed. He was being so reasonable. Did that mean he thought there was no problem, or did he have real cause for concern? It was impossible to tell. But he *had* agreed to her suggestion. An intense feeling of relief swept over her. Everything was going to be all right.

'I Arise and go Down to the River'

It took less time to get ready than Violet expected. Malcolm insisted on the minimum, as the equipment and stores were to make the first half of the journey by boat to Ariakode where Henry Wilson had undertaken to organise onward transport.

'We can go by river, too, if you like,' he offered with a smile but Violet immediately declined, preferring to go on horseback. The sight of what was nothing more than a large canoe, piled high with boxes and a trunk topped with several large shallow wooden pans did nothing to change her mind. *Alligators* ... Her husband might have kept his healthy contempt for the ugly creatures, but she avoided the lush grasses growing along the riverbanks and eyed every floating log with the greatest suspicion.

She turned away with his gently mocking laughter in her ears, leaving everything in charge of the bearer and the boatman, and both of them to the mercy of the current.

The red dirt road the Nicolsons took was lined with coconut *topes* punctuated with jackfruit trees and rampant pepper vines. The winding miles went by and palms gave way to evergreens and bamboo stands, and somewhere out of sight the river could be heard making its way down to the rice fields and the sea. The air was hot and humid, with a promise of rain to come, and both rode in their own small circle of silence. Sometimes those circles touched briefly, with the exchange of a glance, a word or a simple smile. Time wore on and the silence grew complete. Malcolm was lost in his thoughts and Violet was abandoned to hers, adrift on a sea of overwhelming sensations.

The murmur of a hundred hidden rivulets, a hint of spice from a simple hut; the golden glint of amber flesh, the cloying scent of unknown flowers; the deafening din of a brightly crowded street, the reek of fermenting toddy ... When at last they reached Wilson's house it had become too much, and all Violet wanted to do was sleep. She would have preferred to stay in the travellers' bungalow a little way out of town, but Henry Wilson insisted the Nicolsons stop with him. Anxious to make them welcome, he had filled his home with guests—police, planters, and officers from the cantonment, most of them unmarried—and Violet spent the evening avoiding admiring glances from the younger men, and boldly speculative ones from their elders. Compliments and inanities—Violet had seen and heard them all before—but somehow she found the strength to hide her impatience until at last they were alone, and she was free to seek oblivion in her husband's arms.

She dreamt she was travelling a long and tortuous road. It was late afternoon, and the mist was beginning to shroud her companion who rode ahead. He did not turn, nor did he speak, yet from the set of the head, the breadth of the shoulders, she knew it to be Malcolm. When she would have called on him to wait, the deadly scent of datura filled her nostrils and its ghostly poisoned trumpets brushed her parted lips. She was silenced and he passed from view ...

The next morning she woke as from a drugged sleep, and opened her eyes to see Malcolm leaning over her, smiling. Slowly she realised where she was.

'You've been sleeping like the dead,' he remarked, plumping up her pillows and smoothing back her hair. 'Here,' and he handed her a cup of Henry Wilson's incongruously delicate china. 'If you still feel tired,' he said seriously, 'we'll stay another night. The hills can wait.'

Violet thought of the previous evening, when the coarsely braying laughter of official and unofficial Anglo-India had filled her with a stifling despair. A repetition was unthinkable. She handed Malcolm her empty cup and swung her legs out of bed. 'Darling,' she assured him, 'I feel quite refreshed. And the hills have waited too long!'

Over breakfast Malcolm pronounced himself delighted with the arrangements Wilson proposed. He was just as pleased when Wilson—enthusiasm writ large on his usually anxious features—offered his services at Nilambur.

'There's nothing that can't wait here, and to be honest, Mrs Nicolson,' he said wistfully, 'I should hate to miss out on the fun.'

Violet was familiar with the route to the valley in the Nilgiri Hills. She could even name the tributary streams flowing off the Wynaad plateau to swell the Beypore River. She had been shown the map often enough and then it had seemed straightforward. The reality was different. The track making for the foothills was steeper than she had imagined, and the runnels from the previous rains were set like concrete. Violet's horse stumbled more than once, and for a while she was forced to give her full attention to the nervous beast. Henry Wilson was all solicitude while her husband, for his part, did not seem to notice. Instead he eyed the thickening mists around the mountain tops with growing satisfaction.

The monsoon would come any day now, he told his companions. When that happened, the Chellambore stream would become a torrent—ideal for the gold-washing they were planning. The excitement in his voice was obvious, his manner animated, his eyes alert. He had severely trimmed the great moustache and looked far younger. Violet felt the familiar tug of nostalgia, but the frontier days were gone for good. They must look forward, not back, she told herself. In a week's time it would be Malcolm's birthday, and she hoped with all her heart that the coming year would bring him what he so desired.

The light was fading when the party reached its destination, a sizeable settlement in a forest covering eight-and-a-half square miles. As well as a building proclaiming itself the Nilambur District Forest Office, the settlement boasted a post and telegraph office and a hospital. Several squat European-style bungalows shared a compound in the centre. On three sides of the clearing was forest;

behind a cluster of native-workers' huts on the fourth side rose the teak trees, magnificent and doomed.

The guest bungalows were wooden structures like the rest of the buildings, their stark simplicity relieved by the ornamental fret-work on verandah and eaves. Henry Wilson went to his, and the officer whom Wilson had introduced as Tom Peters followed the Nicolsons into theirs. The two small rooms had just enough furniture for comfort and there was, Peters told them, a hut nearby for Sultan, their bearer, which he would share with the resident cook.

Tom Peters examined them as they looked around. He had heard of the couple's arrival in Feroke, and for all the village's remoteness, rumours had been drifting up from the coast for weeks. Now that General and Mrs Nicolson were here in person, their quixotic quest for gold somehow seemed more natural, and Peters found himself hoping they would stay.

Malcolm supervised the unloading of their luggage and Violet listened to him explaining yet again the finer points of 'cradles', 'riffle-blocks' and 'blankets'. Peters who knew more than a little about the mechanics of gold prospecting listened politely. Then he remarked that the weather was about to hamper their operations. It was a pity but it was, of course, unavoidable.

'The monsoon sets in with a remarkable regularity at this time every year,' he told them. 'Plumb in the middle of June, give or take a day. We've had some of what we call "the blossom showers" already.'

'Don't worry, my dear fellow,' General Nicolson replied airily. 'We've come prepared for rain. In fact, we want it!'

'Indeed, sir,' and Peters, a spare man in his mid-thirties whose blunt features were beaten a deep brown from years spent out in all weathers, eyed the elderly soldier anxiously. 'I wonder if you realise quite how difficult it will be? Two weeks' rain with rarely any intermission—I wonder whether you're prepared for *that*? Anyway, I've arranged for the Tiyah headman to help you tomorrow morning, so just tell me, or Wilson, where you want to go and we'll see he understands. His uncle worked for Patrick Grant, you know.'

Malcolm showed his surprise and Peters smiled.

'Oh yes,' he said, 'everyone knows of your trip to Cannanore, General Nicolson! He'll show you the old workings if you like. But it's up to you, of course.'

'Thirst may be quenched at any kindly river'

Work began in the timber plantation at dawn. The newcomers awoke to the tinkling of elephant bells as the great beasts trampled their way towards the river, and Henry Wilson came tapping at their door to suggest a walk in the forest before breakfast. As they advanced along a tenuous path, he pointed out many fine timber-woods that were without doubt destined for the axe. Almost devoid of foliage, they were waiting for the monsoon, like the strangers, and when it came they would burst into glorious leaf. Until then the overhead boughs were bare, brightened now and then by the gorgeous colours of an orchid, or a flash of bright plumage followed by a raucous call. Sometimes the leaves rustled or a twig might crack, and Violet, mindful of resident tigers, would move a little closer to her husband.

The village headman appeared after breakfast. He was called Padmanabhan and was a tall man of about forty. His long, straight hair was caught in a knot to the side of his forehead and, like the other men Violet had seen—and all the women—he wore a spotless white sarong reaching to his knee and nothing above the waist. Behind him, a small boy of six or so peered round inquisitively at the odd white overdressed *mem*.

Two young Tiyahs joined the group while Peters was explaining where the general wished to begin his search. The large, vicious-looking knives they carried were needed to cut through the rampant undergrowth, he said; it was particularly bad where they were going. As well as leeches, there were snakes, he warned. Everywhere. He eyed Violet doubtfully. In shirt and breeches, and carrying a wooden pan, which she refused to let the child take as well as his own, she looked young, boyish and capable, but to Tom Peters, starved of female company by the nature of his occupation, she was a fragile and vulnerable woman.

'Don't worry, Mr Peters, really,' Violet protested, sensing Malcolm's rising irritation as the man fussed around her. 'I shall be perfectly all right!'

'Actually, Peters, my wife is well-acquainted with snakes,' Nicolson added curtly. 'Why, she trod on one once and cut off its head—I don't think we need worry, do you?'

Resisting the temptation to remind the newcomer that in India snakes were to be worshipped not killed, Peters subsided and the party moved off. The two young villagers took the lead, followed by Nicolson, Wilson, and Padmanabhan with Ravi his nephew. Violet brought up the rear. She pushed her way through the rank undergrowth cautiously, for she was by no means as indifferent to snakes as her husband so proudly proclaimed.

Birds swooped overhead and once or twice groups of black-faced monkeys paused to stare cheekily before darting noisily from view. Every so often, Violet caught her breath at the sight of some glorious flowering bush or creeper and paused to look closer, but as the party gradually gained height she quickened her step: she had no wish to be left behind.

After about fifteen minutes the vegetation grew sparser and Violet caught the sound of running water. When they came to the steep bank of the Chellambore stream the Tiyah villagers stopped and broke into animated conversation.

'Padmanabhan's uncle worked five miles further up from here, among those rocks with the brownish stains,' said the magistrate, pointing ahead to a dramatic outcrop on the skyline. 'That was where Grant's crushing machines operated. His uncle told him exactly where the other company's pump engine and Chilean Mill were abandoned, and with luck we'll be able to find them. Shall we go on?'

They followed the stream and sometimes were forced to walk in the bed itself. Progress was slower, but half an hour or so later the party halted again.

'This is the spot,' Wilson said portentously and pointed to where the tangled vegetation seemed unusually lush. It was impossible to see how the Tiyahs knew for certain—it was, after all, a quarter-of-a-century's growth—but they began to hack confidently at the thick bushes and creepers and suddenly there came a shout. Emerging from a bright mantle of branches and glossy green leaves was the rounded and rusty hulk of the boiler. Nicolson hurried forward. He was just in time to see a shiny black snake disappear into a gaping hole in the boiler's side and he stopped dead in his tracks.

'The Tiyahs will deal with this, they're used to it,' said Wilson, and the half-naked men began hacking and slashing at the thickets. Before long they had succeeded in clearing a large area down to the bank of the stream. Now that she could see exactly where she was treading, Violet entered wholeheartedly into the spirit of the hunt.

'What's that?' she asked. 'Look, over there, at the edge of the clearing—there seems to be some kind of giant stone. Could that be what we're after?'

Closer inspection revealed not one great stone but two, lying cracked and abandoned in a circular stone ditch surrounded by a flat, flagged area scarcely visible through the weeds. It was all that was left of the Chilean Mill.

'You'd never get that going again, even if you wanted to,' Wilson observed. He picked up part of the rusted iron band and Malcolm was forced to agree. The two men turned away and clambered up the hillside behind the headman to look for the mine workings. Once they were out of sight, Violet and Ravi set to work panning for gold.

Before long the little boy grew bored and went off to join the two young men up in the clearing. Equally happy to rest her aching wrists, Violet sat down on a large boulder and gazed about her. The silence was broken only by birdsong. On the other side great rocks veined with quartz sparkled in the sun. Might they really contain gold?

Her gaze travelled down over the vegetation and for a while she idly watched the light playing on the water. All at once a rustle of leaves caught her attention and she looked up. On the bank opposite the still figure of a little man with tightly curled hair was standing among the bushes, listening in his turn. He was, she supposed, one of those aboriginal hunters still to be found in the hills. She held her breath, trying not to move, so how did he know she was there? He turned his head. The eyes in the dark face met hers silently across the water, and for a moment two civilisations met and the world stood still. Then another rustle, and Violet was alone.

Feeling strangely bereft, she moved down into the stream but it was too deep to cross. She picked her way back over the pebbles carefully, watching where to tread. Suddenly her eye caught something glittering in the gravel. She stooped and her fingers closed around a small bright lump, perhaps the size of a walnut. She examined it and gave a gasp. Surely it was gold!

'These are my people, and this my land'

Events moved swiftly after that. While his wife roamed about the compound in the glow of late afternoon, thrilling to the birdsong and watching the parrots dart in and out of the trees in a dazzling blur of blues and reds and greens, General Nicolson began to plan his campaign. His eyes gleamed with the feverish light that Lister Kaye had known so well to exploit and, what with diagrams and thoughts of gold concessions, by evening he seemed almost to have forgotten that Violet was there. His preoccupation continued over dinner and at bedtime he announced his decision: he was off to the coast to see to his gold-washing permit. He should be able to get down and back before the season changed, he added.

To Violet's murmured, 'Shall I come with you tomorrow, Malcolm?' he replied vaguely, 'Oh, if you like, dear, but perhaps you'd rather stay here till I get back? I'm sure Peters will look after you,' and early next morning after a hurried goodbye he set off for Ariakode and Calicut with Henry Wilson while Violet went back to sit alone in the verandah, with the sambur horns on the walls for company, and the whisper of the *tattie* screens for conversation.

It did not take her long to realise she wouldn't feel lonely. There was Nilambur to explore and the river, while the uncanny shrieks of the peacocks called her towards the jungle. But she was older now, and wiser, and while she was debating whether Padmanabhan, or little Ravi even, would act as her guide she saw Tom Peters crossing the compound towards her, with a stout balding white-haired man, whom he introduced as Dr Tindall from the local hospital.

'You must tell me,' the doctor said, 'if you want for anything. My wife is away at present, but I'd be only be too happy to help.'

Violet smiled and thanked him for his kindness. Perhaps she would care to join him for dinner that evening? he asked. Tom, too, of course, he added.

When Dr Tindall went back to his patients, Peters stayed. Tentatively, he suggested Mrs Nicolson might like to see the elephants working by the river and Violet agreed. If Malcolm returned in his present mood, and brought the monsoon with him, there would be precious little opportunity for such diversions!

When Peters took her past the huts where the women were working he affected not to notice them. Was he really so indifferent to those shapely amber breasts, his companion wondered as he hurried her on, and for the first time the familiar sight made her feel uncomfortable. They followed a well-trodden track into the government plantation where Peters was clearly more at ease. Taking his time, he identified each and every species: the exotic mahogany and rubber trees; the sandalwood and blackwood; the rare and highly prized Indian rosewood—he even pointed out the small white flowers and soft purple berries of the ipecacuanha bush, grown commercially for its medicinal properties. With obvious pride he pointed out the strong and durable teak tree *Tectona grandis*, supreme among Indian timbers and the most valued of them all.

A further ten-minute walk brought them to an open area where felled trees were being roughly squared, or waited to be shifted. Peters led the way towards the river, where a team of elephants was dragging the timber into the water to be floated downstream for sale. There they stopped and Peters fell silent.

Violet had been correct, When the Tiyah women walked past daily, he longed to finger their smooth firm golden flesh. At night he lay sleepless while the incessant beat of the tom-toms echoed the desperate pulsing of his blood. And now he was alone with an attractive young woman of his own kind and he wanted to touch her too. His eyes were drawn to the white curve of her throat, and on to where he could see the soft swell of her breasts beneath her shirt.

Intent on watching the elephants sort the massive tree trunks lying in untidy piles by the water's edge, Violet was unaware of Peters' scrutiny and she was disappointed when he abruptly suggested they return to the settlement. Once on their way back to the village, he took her arm in warning when a large olive-green rat snake sidled across her path and she wondered why he accepted her thanks so tersely.

Dinner with the doctor that evening proved a delight, and when he walked her home he suggested she meet some of the village women. He believed she would thoroughly enjoy their company. Next morning she communicated so well and stayed so long in the huts that Peters, who was lingering in the compound for a word, was thwarted and spent a thoroughly bad-tempered few hours down by the river with his elephants.

HEART, my heart, thou hast found thy home!
From gloom and sorrow thou hast come forth,
Thou who wast foolish, and sought to roam
'Neath the cruel stars of the frozen North.

Thou hast returned to thy dear delights;
The golden glow of the quivering days,
The silver silence of tropical nights,
No more to wander in alien ways.

Here, each star is a well-loved friend,
To me and my heart at the journey's end.

These are my people, and this my land,
I hear the pulse of her secret soul.
This is the life that I understand,
Savage and simple and sane and whole.

Washed in the light of a clear fierce sun,—
Heart, my heart, the journey is done ...

Here, 'neath the arch of the vast, clear sky,
Where range upon range the remote grey hills
Far in the distance recede and die,
There is no space for thy trivial ills.

On the low horizon towards the sea,
Faint yet vivid, the lightnings play,
The lucid air is kind as a kiss,
The falling twilight is cool and grey.
What has sorrow to do with thee?
Love was cruel? thou now art free.
Life unkind? it has given thee this!

Violet put down her pen with a sigh of satisfaction. Yes, that should give Blanche some idea of her growing joy in her surroundings. She wondered how to go on. Blanche was no more interested than Isabel in the jungle (in fact Izzie these days seemed to have little interest in the Nicolsons at all) but the Tiyah women—now that was a different matter! She must explain to Blanche how much better it was to be a woman in Malabar than Mhow! She picked up her pen again.

Blanche, these Tiyah women are perfect. Naked above the waist and below the knee, and unselfconscious and proud in their movements, particularly when in 'an interesting condition' (as our own society would say). Inheritance is through the female line, which must be unique in India, and almost everywhere else, but then, polyandry has existed here for generations. There are mothers here but no acknowledged fathers. It is truly a paradise for women! Violet decided to say nothing of the gold. *We are more than happy with our decision to return to India,* she concluded, *and although, of course, I miss my son and my friends, Malabar is where I wish to live …*

'The Furtive sense of Jungle Fear'

Although there were to be no more forest walks with Tom Peters while the general was away, the forest officer missed no opportunity to make contact with the general's wife. Whenever he could, he would stop at Mrs Nicolson's door to pass the time of day (although to his regret he was never asked inside) and many was the time he waylaid her in the compound. One evening when Malcolm had been absent for over a week, Violet and Peters dined with Dr Tindall. The conversation flowed freely against a background of tom-toms, and when Violet rose to her feet at nine o'clock Peters stood up too.

'There's absolutely no need for you to put yourself out, Doctor,' he said. 'I'm going that way and I'll see Mrs Nicolson safely to her door.' So Dr Tindall showed his guests out and bade them both goodnight.

Outside in the compound the noise of the drums was more insistent, and the night smelt fresh after the day's single heavy shower. Peters took Violet's arm to guide her past the worst of the puddles and as he felt her warm flesh through the thin fabric of her dress a dreadful feeling of loneliness pierced his heart. He had sat opposite this woman all evening. He had seen her lips curve in amusement and her eyes shine with laughter. He had watched the glow of the lamplight caress her skin …

All this warmth was surely wasted on an old man, he reasoned, and as they neared the bungalow a kind of desperation seized him. He followed Violet into the verandah and stood behind her as she put her hand to the door and opened it. When she turned to say goodnight he pulled her to him, fumbling with the buttons of her dress.

Horrified, she tried to push him away, only to feel his burning lips against her throat and his frantic fingers tugging at the neck of her gown.

'Let me come in with you,' he pleaded hoarsely. 'Mrs Nicolson—*Violet*—I beg you!' Then he was forcing kisses on her mouth.

With a wrench Violet tore herself free. 'Mr Peters,' she said in a shaking voice, 'please go.'

He did not seem to hear her; he obviously intended to follow her inside. She went in and shut the door quickly. She leaned against it. The handle turned once, then Peters must have gone. Where was the key? she thought wildly. Was there a key? She hadn't felt the need of one before and couldn't find one now. She heard footsteps outside—*he was coming back*! She took a chair and wedged it under the door handle. The footsteps halted and the handle turned again. She sat down on the chair. It wasn't comfortable but she felt safer.

'Mrs Nicolson,' came a thick voice. 'I'm so sorry. Please forgive me.'

Violet said nothing.

'May I come in and apologise?'

'*Goodnight, Mr Peters*,' she said in as firm a voice as she could muster and to her great relief the man said goodnight in his turn, and she heard him walk away.

This was no callow youth to be dominated, nor one of Malcolm's junior officers so easily put in his place. Violet was too nervous to go to bed in case Tom Peters returned. She rummaged in a bag and found what she wanted—her fingers closed around cold metal and she drew out Malcolm's service revolver. She loaded it with a single ball—if Peters returned she would frighten him away. Then she straightened the chair, sat down again with the weapon in her lap, leaned her head against the back and tried to ignore the pounding of her heart.

Some time later she woke in alarm. The door was slowly being pushed open and her weight on the chair was having no effect at all. She clutched the revolver and jumped to her feet.

'Go away,' she said in a voice that was barely more than a croak, 'go away or I promise I'll shoot!'

Her warning had no effect. The door flew open and the chair crashed to the ground.

'Don't come any nearer,' she repeated in a whisper. 'I mean it—I'll shoot.'

'Violet, what on earth are you up to?' Malcolm Nicolson took the gun from his suddenly speechless wife, closed the door, righted the chair and lit a lamp.

'You couldn't shoot anyone with that, you silly girl. It isn't cocked.' The hands that took hold of her were gentle, and the voice amused. 'I hope this sort of behaviour hasn't been going on every night?' he asked. Something had obviously happened; she was trembling and trying not to lose control. 'Sit down, sweetheart and tell me what's wrong.'

'Oh, Malcolm, I'm so pleased to see you, you've no idea!'

'You must forgive me, darling, but in the circumstances that's hard to believe.'

His tone was still light, but the look he gave her was searching. He knelt beside her and she told him what had happened. 'Are you hurt?' he asked. Violet shook her head, but instinctively put her hand to her throat. Nicolson moved the lamp nearer and saw the beginnings of a cruel bruise. He stifled a curse. 'It was Peters, of course,' and she nodded.

'We'd been to dinner with the doctor, and when he brought me back he just seemed to go mad.' She shivered as she remembered the intrusive hands and the hard hungry mouth.

'Are you sure you're all right?'

She nodded again.

'What absolute lunacy to put a young unmarried man up here with all those naked women,' he exclaimed. 'And then expect him to act like a monk! And what an idiot I was to leave you here alone! I blame myself as much as him, poor devil.'

Violet gave a shaky little laugh. 'You gave me more of a fright than he did. I'm glad I didn't shoot you.'

'So am I!' Not that she could have done any such thing—it was one thing to kill an anonymous tribesman, another to target someone you had believed a friend.

Malcolm helped her to her feet. His news, he decided, could wait until the morning.

General Nicolson had not wasted his time at the coast. He had brought back a document granting them surface rights over the reaches of the Chellambore immediately above Nilambur. It had been a rather complicated process, he told Violet, but with patience and Henry Wilson's help, and the added weight of his military rank—'You see, it can still be of use'—the complex tangle of legal niceties had been unravelled. They could, he said, make a start straight away. Violet looked up from unpacking the contents of her husband's portmanteau with a squeal of surprise.

'Malcolm Nicolson, have you quite taken leave of your senses?'

The last time it had been wooden *maravis* used by the natives for panning gold, now it was thermometers. Six of them. She straightened up, demanding an explanation.

Malcolm gave a boyish grin. 'Yes, I suppose it must look a bit odd, but we have to be prepared. When the natives wash the sand and gravel the gold will be left behind and we need to collect it.'

'If there is any,' she remarked, and immediately bit her tongue. 'I'm sorry, darling. I don't mean to be a wet blanket. Go on.'

'Well, Grant explained to me how difficult it was to collect the gold. Sometimes nuggets get washed down in the water and that's easy—you just pick them out of the pan. But usually you're left with grains, scales, or dust. The thing to do, apparently, is to mix all that with mercury and you get what is called an amalgam. It's then heated over a retort, the mercury is burned off—'

'And we have a lump of gold,' she finished for him. 'It sounds wonderful. But why the thermometers?'

So he explained the impossibility of finding mercury as such in Malabar, or just about anywhere outside a mining area. Now at least they would have enough from the thermometers to allow an experiment with amalgamation. 'Mercury is also known as quicksilver—in a moment you'll see why.'

Carefully Nicolson broke each thermometer open in turn and the small spherical drops of metal ran all over the table top.

'Don't get too close,' he cautioned, as he quickly collected them in a small bottle. 'Mercury isn't very nice at the best of times.' In its various forms it could be very useful about the house, he explained, for ointments and the like. Sublimate of mercury was invaluable as an insecticide.

'But,' and he gave a sudden grim smile, 'it should be treated with great respect—accidental poisoning is not a pretty death. So, be careful,' he warned again, and put the stopper firmly back in the bottle.

'Remembering ancient crimes'

A day after Nicolson's return Doctor Tindall came over from the hospital to meet him. With him he brought news of Tom Peters' sudden summons south to the government forest in the hills near the Palghat Gap. In a month or so he would go on to Europe, to take some well-earned leave.

'The poor fellow's been overdoing things lately,' the doctor remarked. 'The change will do him good.'

Violet glanced at Malcolm. His expression hadn't changed at the mention of Peter's name and neither of them referred to the incident again. Overnight the monsoon burst and the relentless rain beat down in heavy sheets. The gaunt forest trees bent under the onslaught of the weather and the slightest stream became a torrent. The goldwashing began in earnest and Violet, if not Malcolm, dismissed Peters from her mind.

The villagers worked away steadily, panning the gravels of the stream rhythmically, or rocking the heavy wooden cradles that had been sent up from Calicut. Sometimes tiny flecks of gold could be seen at the bottom of the pans or caught in the cradles' riffles. It all took a great deal of time.

'What we should really do,' Nicolson told his wife after a few days of supervising his small group of Tiyahs, 'is get in touch with your uncle.' He eyed the outcrop overlooking the torrent in a speculative way. 'Panning is all very well and the villagers are used to it, but he has just the expertise we need.'

Uncle Heneage Griffin, thought Violet, considering Malcolm's suggestion. Would he want to get involved in mining again? Surely not—it was eight years since he had sold the Seven-Thirty Mine in Colorado, and he had been back in Europe for two. She shook her head over Malcolm's eternal optimism, Malcolm who never seemed to tire of the hunt.

Henry Wilson had resumed his official duties and Violet often stayed behind in the village with her newfound friends. As the monsoon lessened in intensity and the weather fluctuated between deluge and sunshine, she wandered further and further from the compound. One day she came across a lonely grave. She carefully freed it of its pall of mauve-flowered creeper and found the lichen-covered headstone of a British soldier.

To the memory of Samuel Robert Clogstoun, she made out, *Lieutenant in the 23rd Regiment, M.N.I. He was born on the 26th January 1824 and drowned in the Chellambore river (Nilambur) near this spot on the 13th August 1843*.

How poignant, this lad lost in the very waters where Malcolm was standing now, when Malcolm himself was two months old. She imagined the nineteen-year-old lieutenant larking about in the river and drowning. *Generous, high spirited and of great promise*, the inscription went on, *he died deeply regretted*.

How many hearts had been broken as a result of the young man's death? She thought of her husband, equally high-spirited, stepping from crocodile to crocodile all those years ago. What if *he* had slipped? Violet felt a cold, sick feeling grip the pit of her stomach with icy fingers, and with difficulty overcame the impulse to dog his footsteps for the rest of the day.

While the general directed his workforce his wife sometimes played with little Ravi. The boy was oblivious to the dangers lurking in the undergrowth, and no one else seemed to care about them either. There were snakes everywhere: black, red and green, and while not all of them were poisonous, and she was used to them from Mhow—*such a snaky place*, as Violet Jacob once said—she feared for her small companion. Thank goodness her own child wasn't here, for how could they have made him understand the dangers of these beautifully speckled and banded creatures? And the alligators in the Beypore River, and the water snakes—the list was endless. Not to mention the insects, and she brushed them repeatedly away from her face. And the blood-sucking leeches of which she had learned to be wary. At last Violet Nicolson could bring herself to admit that her son was better off where he was.

She confided her change of heart to Malcolm one afternoon when they were relaxing in the verandah after work. But why did he look at her like that when surely he should have been pleased?

'Darling,' he confessed gravely, 'I've had something on my conscience since Cannanore.'

'Since Cannanore?'

Violet thought back to when he had been so neglectful and offhand.

'Was there a woman?' was all she could find to say.

'Violet Nicolson, how could you think such a thing?'

'What else could there possibly be?'

Malcolm took her hand. His face was serious and his eyes were as apprehensive as hers.

'Sweetheart,' he began at last, 'do you remember what you said my mother told you—about my health and the doctors' opinion? When I was so very angry?'

Violet nodded and wondered what was coming next.

'It was all a pack of lies, I'm afraid, and I should have told you as soon as I found out. But I thought you'd had enough to put up with.'

He hardly dared look at her while her hand remained in his, unmoving.

'Until now, when you thought I was ready. Am I right?'

'Yes.'

Violet's own anger at the revelation was tempered by a surge of relief. Now she understood why Malcolm had never dwelt on the subject of their little boy—it was not through indifference at all!

'So your mother tricked me.'

Nicolson was taken aback by the calmness of her voice.

'And our son could have been with us all this time. I see.'

Violet considered for a moment and then her eyes held his.

'Well,' she said bluntly, 'I've always thought your mother was an abominable old witch but I've done my best to get on with her—because she *was* your mother.'

She paused while the numerous small rebuffs and humiliations she had been made to suffer came to mind.

'Now at least I don't have to pretend any more, and that's something in itself! Your sisters are kind and decent women,' she continued, 'and they will look after Malcolm far better than I can at present—I should worry all the time if he were with us, and so would you.'

She paused before adding: 'But don't expect me ever to see or speak of your mother again.' The candid eyes were unusually hard and implacable and they did not waver from his face.

'Violet, I'm so sorry.'

'Don't be—she won't mind in the least and neither shall I! And something else, Malcolm—' Violet's expression softened and her fingers moved to squeeze his briefly.

'Thank you for not telling me sooner, it can't have been easy to keep all this to yourself.'

God bless the woman; would she never cease to amaze him?

*'The golden treasure of unhewn rocks
And the loose gold in the stream'*

At the end of each day the precious residue was collected from the bottom of each pan and stored in an earthenware vessel. One month after the general's return from Calicut he judged that enough particles had been amassed to warrant an experiment. He announced he was ready to try and Dr Tindall, who had shown great interest in the operation from the beginning, immediately offered his help.

So one afternoon in mid-July the *chatti*'s contents were carefully panned once more. With a flourish Violet produced the bottle of mercury, and its contents were poured into the sand, fine gravel and grains of gold. The pan was stirred from time to time and gradually the gold and the mercury separated from the rest.

Heads together like conspirators, the doctor and the Nicolsons leaned forward and watched the dull, heavy-looking lump of amalgam form. It was placed in muslin, strained to remove any excess metal, and left for twenty-four hours.

The next evening Dr Tindall joined them for dinner. He brought with him a porcelain retort and a small spirit burner from the hospital dispensary, and once the meal was over—and despite Violet's protestations that 'Surely it could have waited till the morning'—the three of them repaired outside, lamps in hand, to brave the mosquitoes and try their luck. Malcolm placed the amalgam in the crucible and balanced the spirit lamp carefully on a small pile of stones.

'You must remember to stand well back, General, you too, my dear,' the doctor warned. 'The fumes are highly poisonous, as I'm sure you both know.'

Malcolm lit the lamp and the trio waited with mounting excitement. After what seemed an interminable age, the doctor indicated that it was safe and the three moved forward as one. When each peered into the crucible and saw a tiny lump of gold, it was left to Violet to speak.

'Well,' she said, her surprise mingled with delight, 'so it really works!'

'I never doubted it.' Her husband's satisfaction knew no bounds. 'Doctor, I think it's time for a small celebration!'

Violet pleaded tiredness and left the men alone. She woke in the night to find the bed beside her still empty. She sat up with a start and made out her husband's figure by the window, outlined by the moonlight.

'Malcolm, what's wrong?' she asked in a loud whisper and he turned and came over to her.

'I'm sorry I woke you. I've been having a bad night. It's the old trouble, I'm afraid.' He sat down on the bed. 'It seems a little worse this time.'

She could see beads of sweat on his brow and gave a little cry of distress. 'Oh, Malcolm, what are we going to do?'

Nicolson managed a smile. 'You are going back to sleep and I shall join you as soon as I can.'

He pushed her gently back against the pillow and smoothed the sheet. Then he resumed his vigil at the window. He remained there long after the pain subsided, thinking of his state of health. And more than that, he was thinking of his age. Until two years ago he would have considered himself remarkably fit. Apart from the recurrent bouts of fever that every Frontier man came to regard as a normal part of life, he had almost never been unwell. But now Nicolson knew it was a different matter. Fever was an old enemy; here was an unknown foe. The year before, he had made his will in London as the result of an affliction that had first been an irritation only, then a cause of some concern. Medication had helped, but the real tonic had seemed a return to India.

Tonight the pain had been bad, but seeing the worry on Violet's face had been far worse. He suspected that to his wife he was still the athletic forty-six-year-old she had married, and how to convince her that he was more than middle-aged? (He mocked himself for his reluctance to use the word *old*.)

Malcolm Nicolson was nothing if not a realist: in the natural order of things he would be the first to die. He had tried to prepare her—indeed had he not strongly resisted their marriage on the grounds of their disparity in age? If Violet had thought all that irrelevant then, how could he make her face the facts now, when the intervening years had apparently proved her right and him wrong? And what could he do to prolong their life together?

When morning came and he told Violet he would consult Dr Tindall rather than waiting for Madras, she was relieved beyond words. She invited the doctor over to dinner and again retired to bed early, giving the same excuse.

Tindall thought that of the two the husband looked the wearier, and over a glass of brandy he broached the subject of the general's state of health. His kindly, professional manner made it easy for Malcolm to describe his symptoms. 'Yes,' said the doctor, when he had finished, 'that certainly fits what you were told in London. As for the rest, my dear fellow, men of your age—and mine—should expect certain inconveniences. Usually we put up with them well enough.' Tindall's eyes twinkled in sympathy and they both sipped their brandy.

In the comfortable silence that followed the doctor found himself reflecting on the woman who shared the general's life. If anyone ever asked him to define happiness in human form he would answer *Violet Nicolson.* He often met her returning arm in arm with her husband from mornings spent by the Chellambore stream, or from afternoons wandering the fringes of the forest with young Ravi; he had heard her talk with ever-increasing fluency to the Tiyah women. And always her eyes glowed with unspoken content.

'I know of no recipe for eternal youth, my friend, and the man who finds one will surely make his fortune,' Tindall remarked after a while. 'Given your wife's devotion, I would say, General Nicolson, that you must stand a better chance than most.'

The doctor's words stayed with Malcolm as he bade his guest goodnight, and he also thought of his final meeting with Tom Peters. He would never tell Violet of his personal intervention, nor of the observations the younger man had made before agreeing to leave forthwith—cruel observations that still made Malcolm smart. He stood in the verandah for a while, and then with a sigh went in to join his sleeping wife.

11

'Neath alien stars'

MADRAS. INDIA: 29 JULY–7 AUGUST 1904

Sir Norman Stewart was a sociable man, and when he received a telegram from Malcolm Nicolson announcing his arrival in Madras in two days' time he was delighted. 'He'll stay with us, of course.'

Ada Stewart looked up from her needlework. 'It's been a long time since we've seen him,' she remarked. 'When was the last time? Certainly not since he married. I suppose she's coming with him.' She resumed her petit point with no further comment.

Stewart sat down opposite his wife and the couple lapsed into a companionable silence. It would be good to see Nick again, thought General Stewart. They had first met in December 1878 in the biting cold beyond Quetta, when Nicolson, aged thirty-four, and Stewart, twenty-seven, were *en route* for Afghanistan and war. By the time their respective divisions were encamped outside Kandahar the acquaintance had strengthened into friendship. When Nicolson joined Sir Donald Stewart's Second Brigade in August the following year they met again, and together had faced the murderous Afghan knives at the battle of Ahmed Khel. But after the war they had gone their separate ways, meeting by chance once or twice, at a hill-station perhaps, but had lost touch since Nicolson's marriage.

As if reading her husband's mind, Lady Stewart raised her head from her needlework again. 'I'm surprised that marriage lasted,' she said.

'Are you, Ada? I can't say I am, but then I know Nick rather better than you. Oh, I know that when Malcolm Nicolson married, the whole frontier was rocked—he was the archetypal bachelor, of course, and you and your friends thought the marriage doomed to failure from the start. What was it all you women said—that he had taken a young bride for what, I suppose, is increasingly becoming known as *Sex*.'

Sir Norman gave a hearty guffaw at his wife's expression. 'Nick didn't need to marry for *that*. I know any number of officers' wives who would have been happy to oblige—and so, probably, do you!'

Nick at the time, his friend went on, was neither young enough nor old enough to make a fool of himself over a pretty face or figure. Given all the subsequent stories, there was clearly more to his Violet than that.

'No, no, Ada, I think we're both about to meet a rather unusual woman.' Sir Norman spoke with relish, while his wife, recalling the nature of some of those stories, stabbed her needle into the canvas and summoned a servant to bring them tea.

After arriving early in the morning and standing on the platform for what seemed a very long time, and just as Violet was wondering whether they really were expected, she heard a hearty shout. A short, stocky man in his mid-fifties was hurrying towards them.

'Nick? I say, is that you, old fellow? Sorry I wasn't here when you got in—the traffic's frightful!'

Violet stood back as the two men greeted each other, then Sir Norman Stewart addressed her equally warmly while assessing her with a pair of extremely shrewd brown eyes.

'I'm delighted to meet you, Mrs Nicolson. We were so glad you were able to come too. My wife is waiting for us in the carriage.'

He turned back to Malcolm and with a laugh gestured to the few items at his feet. 'Still travelling light I see, Nick—I take it this is all you've brought?'

General Stewart looked round with an imperious sweep of the hand and a red-turbaned coolie appeared as if from nowhere. He swooped on the stout wicker picnic hamper provided by Mrs Walter, and the small trunk that with Violet's carpetbag, Malcolm's trusty portmanteau, and the inevitable rolls of travel bedding comprised the Nicolsons' luggage. Violet gripped the carpetbag obstinately, despite the man's objections voiced in a language that even Malcolm did not understand. It contained all her unpublished poetry and she glared at him until he gave up. As he set off at a trot towards the exit, their belongings balanced miraculously on his head, Nicolson strode along behind. Stewart, meanwhile, gallantly offered his arm to his old friend's wife.

By the time the pair left the red brick railway station and reached the carriage, Nicolson was in animated conversation with a faded sharp-faced woman whom Sir Norman introduced to Violet as his wife. As thin as her husband was rotund, Lady Stewart responded warily to the introductions. In her plain dress of heavy maroon cotton with its long sleeves and buttons to the neck, she presented a sharp contrast to Violet Nicolson whom she looked up and down in ill-concealed disapproval. Mrs Nicolson must feel exceptionally cool in her light blue low-necked muslin gown, but she would soon learn the sense in wearing darker colours in Madras! The laterite streets seemed pleasant enough and smooth when traversed in a carriage, but the fine red dust thrown up by the constant passage of so many wheels stained any light-coloured material that came its way. Nick's wife would find that out to her cost if she chose to walk any distance at all!

When Lady Stewart made room beside her for General Nicolson Violet felt the familiar little pang: Lady Stewart and Malcolm clearly knew each other well. When she heard the older woman say, 'I do hope you will stay with us, Nick, and for as long as you like,' the equally familiar streak of perversity made Violet quickly reply in his stead.

'Actually, Lady Stewart, we intended staying in a hotel.'

And she, at least, still wanted to. Violet looked across at Malcolm, hoping against hope that he would support her. He did not.

Nicolson knew perfectly well what had prompted his wife's response. 'We would very much like to accept your kind invitation, Ada—wouldn't we, Violet?' he said, trusting that the demon of perversity, having had its say, was silenced.

To his relief she agreed. 'But only for a few days,' he added. 'I know how very busy you both must be, with your time here coming to an end.'

The streets they passed were a heaving mass of colour. Basketfuls of fruit and vegetables, gleaming brass pots and pans, all—like their luggage earlier—impossibly balanced on a noisy multitude of heads, bobbed their way to and from the native bazaars, while holy cows and calves roamed through the narrow streets at will, and created anarchy among the traffic. It took an hour for the Stewarts' carriage to cross The Island by which time the conversation was flagging. In Mount Road, the great thoroughfare leading to St Thomas's Mount, old Madras met the new. Lumbering bullock carts, box-like *jutkas* and luxurious gentlemen's carriages advanced, side by side and wheel by wheel, to the rattle and clank of trams. There was even the occasional motorcar.

'Confounded newfangled contraptions,' grumbled Sir Norman. 'Always getting in the way—and probably French. Damned subversive nation, that! I hope you don't mind, Nick,' he went on, his irritation quickly forgotten, 'but I've taken the liberty of arranging an appointment for you on Monday, with a Dr Blackett. He's a good man, or so I believe. I'll take you past his place on the way to Dunmore House.'

As they proceeded along Mount Road, Lady Stewart pointed out buildings she considered of interest to the other woman in the party: Whiteway Laidlaw's, the noted haberdashers; Higginbotham's iconic bookshop; Spencer and Company's vibrant Indo-Saracenic premises dating from 1882.

They passed the handsome grounds of what Sir Norman told them was the Madras Club and then he said, 'We've come a little bit out of our way—that's Mackay's Gardens Nursing Home over there.'

Violet just had time to glimpse a building at the end of a long gravel drive. She was reminded of the purpose of their visit and hardly heard Lady Stewart promise to take her shopping—*Madras is famous for its department stores, don't you know, my dear?*

Almost immediately the carriage turned into a pleasant tree-lined street whose aspect was almost rural, and where homes were set in grounds as big as public parks. Now and then, white facades sparkled in the brilliant morning sun as they came in and out of view. Violet was finding the niceties of conversation increasingly tiresome—the journey was taking so long—but at last the carriage turned through a set of tall cast-iron gates, and advanced slowly through extensive tree-filled grounds to stop before the Stewarts' rented home.

Dunmore House was an opulent house, created for opulent times. It was built in the flat-roof garden style made famous by the eighteenth-century English 'nabobs' of Madras. Plastered in dazzling white, it was surrounded by the classical pillars of a deep verandah and from a fine portico a broad sweep of stone steps led to the first-floor entrance.

They had been leasing Dunmore House for the past few weeks, Lady Stewart explained. It actually belonged to Mr Norton, a resident of long standing, and it was, of course, far too big.

The garden-house was certainly grand. Violet looked past the great portico to the glistening polished *chunam* of the walls. It looked like white marble, and who would guess that underneath the pulverised seashells there was only brick? Yes, appearances could be deceptive, and she only hoped that Lady Stewart was not as unpleasantly overbearing as she seemed.

'Affection's altar'

The private and public rooms were situated on the first floor of Dunmore House, and it was to the grand drawing room that Violet later retreated before the rising tide of reminiscence. She was unlikely to be disturbed for quite some time, so she installed herself in a blackwood chair of European design and examined her surroundings.

Mr Norton, whoever he was, had excellent taste. Her feet rested on an exquisite Persian rug and there were others of equal quality scattered over the shining teak floor. Several rosewood armchairs were set apart at regular intervals, and photographs of what must be the Stewarts' son and two daughters adorned various occasional tables. Against one of the walls, painted pale blue to resemble stucco, stood an impressive-looking bookcase.

Violet opened the glass-panelled doors and eyed the disappointing contents. Balfour's *Botany*, Lyell's *Geology*, *Tea Districts of China & India*, a life of Oliver Cromwell, another of George III ... They all smacked of the schoolroom and Mr Norton must have removed the best books for himself. She scowled at her reflection in the glass. She was bored. All Malcolm wanted to do was talk over old times with Sir Norman, and Lady Stewart was egging them on!

She made her way through to the dining room with its heavy mahogany furniture and great chandeliers and out into the upper verandah. There were the usual rattan chairs and couches along its length, and the blinds were down and stirring in the slightest of breezes. She peered through a gap in one. Her husband and Sir Norman were strolling through the grounds, deep in conversation. Violet sighed. The solemn look returned as she resigned herself to seeing precious little of her husband for the next few days, at least!

Lady Stewart was well aware of Violet's strategic withdrawal, and as both men plunged deeper and deeper into the past and disappeared into the garden she went off to find Nick's wife. Just as she reached the drawing room Violet, who had been leafing idly through an ancient copy of *Chambers's Magazine*, threw it down on the dainty table beside her in disgust. She was getting to her feet when she noticed Lady Stewart and sent her an uncertain smile.

'May I join you, Mrs Nicolson? I'm afraid all this nostalgia must be a little tedious for an outsider.' Ada Stewart sat down.

'I did feel a little *de trop*,' Violet confessed as she resumed her seat.

'I'm afraid we Indian Army wives all feel that way, some time or another. Of course, there are ways of dealing with it,' and Lady Stewart glanced at the photographs that Violet had spotted earlier. 'I've known many mothers take the children back to school in England and never return to be with their husbands. It's a question of divided loyalty, of course, but I never hesitated an instant to send them home alone. I understand you made a similar decision recently, Mrs Nicolson.'

Violet nodded. 'Yes, we decided to leave our son with Malcolm's family in the South of England. It wasn't at all easy, Lady Stewart, but Malcolm has and always will come first.'

'You must have had a difficult time of it, Mrs Nicolson, when your husband was promoted general. After the freedom of the frontier, I mean. A cantonment such as Mhow can be a difficult kind of place—especially when the senior lady takes precedence because of her husband's rank, and despite her tender years.'

Violet eyed her hostess suspiciously. Was she referring to anything in particular, or was she simply making conversation?

'Mhow was difficult for *both of us*,' she replied. 'Frankly, Lady Stewart, it was a tragedy that Malcolm didn't succeed Sir George White at Quetta. He has always been devoted to Baluchistan.'

'But, Mrs Nicolson, Mhow is the most prestigious appointment in all India!' exclaimed Ada Stewart (who privately deplored that Madras was only a *second-class* district).

'I know, Lady Stewart, but that sort of thing has never meant much to my husband. And certainly not to me! In fact,' Violet confessed, for the woman probably knew it anyway, 'I behaved very badly at first. It reflected on Malcolm, as I realised afterwards—when it was, of course, too late. But he forgave me.' Violet shrugged when Lady Stewart offered no comment. 'He understands that I do so hate it when I'm bored.'

'So you went shopping, after all?'

'As you see.' Violet walked towards her husband, wearing the spoils of the expedition. She pirouetted around him until he caught hold of her and brought the giddy dance to a halt. Then he slowly surveyed her from head to toe.

'I'm sorry, Malcolm. I shouldn't have bought it.'

It did seem to Nicolson that the less there was of a lady's garment, the more it cost, but in the case of his wife's latest acquisition he considered the expense well worthwhile. The rich navy of the silk suited her colouring, and the low-cut design showed off her figure to perfection. Her hair was swept up, and she was wearing a heavy silver necklace of Kashmiri design.

'Don't apologise,' he said. 'I told you to enjoy yourself.'

'It was hardly enjoyable,' she retorted. 'Well, not at first, anyway. But I could see that Ada Stewart was quite shocked, and that's when I decided you'd like it.'

She surveyed herself in the mirror and looked up into his appreciative eyes reflected in the glass.

'*Do* you like it?'

General Nicolson did not reply. Instead he bent and pressed a kiss into the soft hollow between her neck and shoulder. She turned, he kissed her mouth, and for the first time since their arrival in Madras, Violet Nicolson felt happy.

'Pale days and a league of laws'

That night Sir Norman waxed lyrical over the Madras Club, the premier club in the city, its main virtues being (according to Violet later) 'the exclusion of Indians, women and dogs, and in that order, I suppose.'

Lady Stewart unwittingly made matters worse. How wonderfully convenient it was, she said, now that the club had added a 'Ladies Pavilion' to its amenities.

'I often go to the *Morghi Khana* and wait there for my husband,' she told them, and Sir Norman beamed over his lemon sponge pudding. Apparently he accepted this wifely devotion as quite normal. Nicolson saw the colour rise rapidly to Violet's cheeks and the gleam of battle to her eyes, and ever the diplomat where his own wife's sensibilities were concerned, quickly diverted the imminent storm. Were there other clubs in town, he asked.

'Oh yes,' Sir Norman replied. 'We sometimes go to the Adyar Club. It's open to the ladies. We'll go there next week,' he promised. 'Can't go tomorrow, can we, Nick? We're dining at the Mount.'

When the Nicolsons were alone at last, Violet gave vent to the feelings she had somehow managed to suppress throughout the evening.

'The Madras Club—no, what did Sir Norman say? Yes, that's it—*We call it the Ace of Clubs*!' and she gave more than a passable imitation of Stewart's voice. 'How can you even *think* of going there?' she exploded, facing her husband across the bed as she struggled with the catch of her necklace.

'And the *Morghi Khana*—doesn't she know it means "the hen house"!' Violet snorted in disgust. 'The British are always criticising the Indians for their caste system,' she went on, 'and for keeping their women in purdah, and what happens? I'll tell you what happens! They do exactly the same when it suits them, with their clubs, and their officers' mess! Calling it the *Morghi Khana*, indeed! It's so—so—' she searched for the right word.

'British?' Malcolm suggested.

'Now you're laughing at me! You know exactly what I mean! It's *hypocritical*! They say they're preparing the country for independence, as well—but not yet! Not ever!'

'I'm not quite sure how we've moved on to that particular subject,' Nicolson observed calmly, 'but shall I help you with that before it breaks?'

He came round to her side of the bed and rescued the catch, and then he rested his hands lightly on her shoulders.

'Things *will* change,' he told her. 'I used not to think so, but now I do. Not in my lifetime—but maybe in yours. These things take time. You know that. The Indians are a patient lot—pray God they are patient enough.'

His voice was so serious that Violet's anger subsided.

'I'm sorry, darling.' She turned to look at him. 'But you know how angry these things always make me.'

'I do, I do,' he murmured, and he put his arms around her. The room was only dimly lit by lamplight, but he could imagine the heightened colour in her cheeks and he could feel the agitation of her breathing. He held her against him, saying nothing more.

When at last Violet reached up and touched his cheek his patience was rewarded.

'I love you so very much, Malcolm Nicolson,' she said, and her voice was vibrant with passion.

Over the crisp white linen of the breakfast table next morning Sir Norman enthusiastically outlined his plans for his friend. They were to spend the evening at the officers' mess at St Thomas's Mount, he said, and they would take tiffin at the Madras Club. It was a marvellous building, and the facilities were first rate. It was, of course, the oldest club in India and Nick was bound to come across some excellent people.

'And each one an Englishman,' Violet murmured. Only Nicolson heard the remark. About to raise a forkful of kedgeree to his lips, he paused to frown in warning at his wife, and so Violet silently resigned herself to another day spent with—or avoiding—Lady Stewart.

Ada Stewart, for her part, smiled outwardly and sighed inwardly. What to do with her difficult guest? She had quickly discovered that Mrs Nicolson had no time for the normal pursuits open to an Anglo-Indian woman: she was not at all interested in gossiping about other people's husbands and reluctant to spend the money of her own. But after all, the woman *wrote poetry* and what could you expect? Not that she had read any of it herself, of course, but she did know people who had—and very strange stuff it was, they told her. So very *Indian*, they said, and so very *sensual* …

After breakfast Violet used her correspondence as an excuse to make good her escape, taking the stairs from the drawing room down to the floor below. She knew that the ground floor was mainly reserved for the go-downs, the kitchen and the servants' quarters, but found her way out to the garden across the tessellated central hall. She wandered restlessly over the coarse, cropped grass then returned to the verandah to begin a letter to Isabel. She poured out her frustrations on sheet after sheet of paper, and then tore up every one.

Feeling better she drifted back outside. Whoever designed the garden half a century before had made provision for the heat of an Indian summer, as well as having a care to please the senses. Magnificent *gul mohur* trees shaded the walks and scattered their orange-red petals over the sere brown lawn that was beginning to show tinges of green. Among the pale leaves of the frangipani a few sweet-scented blossoms still lingered. They would all be dead in a week or two, Violet thought regretfully. Nothing ever lasted long.

She idly shredded a piece of peeling bark as she looked around her. The champak trees were covered in the yellow flowers she loved, their fragrance muted in the hot sun of morning. Evening was the best time, she reflected. What could compare with their perfume coming to you on the evening breeze? Unless it was the heady *moghra* … A squirrel scampered over her feet and brought her reverie to an end. Reluctantly, she turned back towards the house. It must be nearly time for tiffin and she did not want Lady Stewart—so determinedly punctual always—looking for her in the garden and spoiling its charm.

'The painful riddle of identity'

That afternoon Ada Stewart and her guest sat sipping tea, and the time was passing slowly, very slowly indeed. The loud ticking of the longcase clock filled the drawing room, while outside, one of Madras's famous downpours rattled insistently on the flagstones. While Violet was desperately thinking of something else to say, wheels came crunching to a halt in the driveway and someone ran noisily up the steps. Then a loud voice addressed the uniformed *chowkidar* on duty at the front door.

'Dear me,' Lady Stewart said, a trifle nervously. 'I do believe it's Mr Norton come to visit.'

She stood up looking flustered as the servant brought in a card. The visitor, a tall, dark-haired man of perhaps fifty, followed closely without waiting to be announced. When he reached Lady Stewart, he bowed slightly and raised her hand gallantly to his lips.

'Dear lady,' he murmured and straightened.

Ada Stewart blushed, and when she made her introductions Violet realised at last who the owner of Dunmore House must be.

This man was Eardley Norton, the defender of Indian rights and aspirations, the barrister dubbed 'a veiled seditionist' by his enemies for his addresses to the Indian National Congress. *If it be sedition to insist that the people should have a fair share in the administration of their own country and affairs, if it be sedition to resist tyranny, to raise my voice against oppression …to uphold the liberties of the individual …I am right glad to be called a 'seditionist'* … Recalling the impassioned phrases that had moved her to tears as a girl in Karachi—and her father to paroxysms of rage—Violet gave Norton her full attention. The force of his personality was undeniable, and his face, with its strong clean-cut lines, and firm mouth was, she decided, exceedingly handsome.

Norton was aware of the candid eyes that never wavered from his, and rather than repeat his extravagant greeting, he contented himself with shaking the younger woman's hand. He expressed the usual pleasantries in a beautifully modulated voice, then sat down in an armchair opposite. The conversation that followed covered a vast range of topics, but none in any depth. Eardley Norton was a man of many parts and interests, but he had learned from experience that Ada Stewart's views were narrow and that there were some topics best left alone. Anything to do with India, for one thing; literature, for another. He supposed that Mrs Nicolson would be much the same. Wasn't she some visiting general's wife? He had been told of the expected guests on an earlier visit, and now he was sorry he hadn't taken more notice.

Lady Stewart sent for more tea. As she did so she deplored the decline in standards among native servants; things had changed so much since her childhood in Bombay, she lamented.

'It was ever thus,' sympathised the visitor. '*Où sont les neiges d'antan*? As my old friend François Villon once asked.'

Lady Stewart looked blank and Violet gave a chuckle.

'You enjoy poetry, Mrs Nicolson? *French* poetry?' Norton asked. If so, this woman was a rare find to be treasured.

'Oh, but Mrs Nicolson *writes* poetry,' interjected Lady Stewart. 'She has published two books of her own.'

Now Norton remembered—Ada Stewart had told him so in a hushed tone, as if it were something scandalous, to be talked of only in whispers. But she had not been able to recall either of the titles.

'What are they called, dear?' she asked her guest indulgently.

When Violet told her, Norton had to prevent himself from sitting up in surprise. This woman was *Laurence Hope*? He stared at her and Violet who was used to such a reaction—if no longer amused—stared back.

When the barrister rose to take his leave, Lady Stewart pressed him to return later to dine. Norton readily agreed and suggested a drive before dinner.

'Why, how kind of you, Mr Norton!' Ada Stewart exclaimed. 'I have a thousand and one little things I must do, but I'm sure Mrs Nicolson would be delighted. She arrived only yesterday and has had no chance to see the sights. What do you say, dear?'

Anything would be better than a repetition of that dreadful afternoon, thought Violet, so it was arranged that the barrister would come for her a little before six o'clock, the fashionable hour for a drive.

Shortly after Norton's departure, Sir Norman and Malcolm returned. They seemed very pleased with themselves, as was only to be expected, Violet supposed, after several hours spent among the cream of Madras society.

'Have you had a good day, ladies?' Malcolm asked, as he sank into the chair so recently vacated by the barrister.

'Well, we did have a visit from Mr Norton this afternoon,' Violet replied.

'Our landlord, Nick, remember,' put in Sir Norman. 'You must meet him. Ada, why don't you invite him to dinner sometime next week?'

Lady Stewart smiled. 'Why, he's joining us tonight, since you two gentlemen insist on deserting us again. And he's taking Mrs Nicolson for a drive along the Marina beforehand. Nick, you've been neglecting your wife most shamefully!'

Far from being abashed at this playful criticism, Malcolm considered it a splendid idea, although when he heard what Stewart had to say later, he felt less nonchalant about the whole business.

Violet Nicolson sat opposite Eardley Norton, her hands demurely folded in her lap. Outwardly, nothing hinted at the passionate woman who had penned the verse of 'Laurence Hope', but Norton knew from his courtroom experience how deceptive appearances could be—the most villainous exterior often hiding the docility of a lamb, and an angelic countenance the vice of the devil incarnate. He pointed out first one sight then another, and Violet turned her head obediently in whichever direction was required.

'Now, to our left, Mrs Nicolson, the house you can just make out through the trees is the celebrated Capper House Hotel.' Violet looked but could see little. How nice it would have been to stay there, she thought, and she told Norton that they had almost taken rooms in a hotel.

'I suppose the Stewarts insisted you stay with them,' Norton said. 'They're seeing everyone they can before they go back to England—you didn't know about that?'

'I think Malcolm may have said something but I'm afraid I wasn't really listening. I find talk of his old friends a little boring.'

'Yes, they go home at the end of September. Sir Norman has just relinquished the Madras Command. Not that there's much to command these days—it's more like organising a picnic, really, and you'll certainly find the old boy a gregarious fellow. I gather that your husband has known the Stewarts for some considerable time?'

Violet nodded. 'I've never met them before, but Sir Norman and Malcolm served in Afghanistan together, under Sir Norman's father. They have a lot to talk about.' A wistful note crept into her voice.

Trained to detect the slightest nuance, Norton looked at his companion more carefully. Could she be lonely? If her husband was neglecting her, then the man was a fool. He had caught sight of him earlier. Grey-haired and elderly, he seemed unlikely to satisfy the woman seated opposite. But then, Eardley Norton added in all fairness, once General Nicolson was in his bedroom and out of his uniform, perhaps it was a case of like meeting like ...

He suggested they take a stroll through the Marina Gardens. How pleasant, murmured Mrs Nicolson, and he came round to her side of the carriage to help her down. The rain had freshened the air, and somewhere a band was playing a lively waltz. Violet and her escort mingled with the crowds of Europeans who strolled among the ornamental beds planted in strong lines along the promenade. The beach was filled with Indians, walking, talking, enjoying themselves singly or in groups; some were splashing in the water. When she saw the fishing boats putting out to sea Violet slowed her step, then stopped. Lost in memories, she saw a ruined fort framed in brightest gold against the evening sky. And other sands. And other sunsets.

Standing at her side, forgotten, Norton considered her face. It was too full of character to be merely pretty, but not classic enough in profile for conventional beauty. For him its appeal lay in its mobility, the expressiveness of the features, where a variety of emotions were passing even now in swift succession. In repose such a face might seem petulant, but as the sensual lips curved dreamily and the intelligent eyes lost themselves in the distance he felt its full appeal. Politeness, however, called a halt to his self-indulgence.

'I'm sorry, Mr Norton.' Violet turned to her companion. 'What did you say?'

'I think perhaps we should go back to the carriage,' he repeated. 'It wouldn't do to keep Lady Stewart's dinner waiting.'

On their way back to Dunmore House Norton pointed out the curious Ice House on the foreshore. With its curved frontage it resembled a tiered cake, didn't she think? One abandoned half-consumed by wedding guests who found it little to their taste. His companion smiled at his whimsy and Norton could think of nothing more to say. Violet was sorry when the glorious voice (an asset that he surely exploited in court) fell silent. But were his good looks an advantage or a disadvantage in his profession? So much of his life must be spent in playing a role, she mused, and did he see her as a woman or an audience?

When Norton became aware of her scrutiny his eyes held hers boldly until Violet found herself blushing.

'Oh dear,' she said in sudden confusion. 'You must find me very rude. I was thinking, you see, how like the stage the High Court must be. Do you find it odd, Mr Norton, to be forced to dissemble in order to reach the truth?'

Thus encouraged, Norton began to relate some of his more unusual cases, and in Violet Nicolson he found the perfect listener, one who chuckled appreciatively and offered apposite comments of her own in a slightly husky voice. Rarely had he spent a more enjoyable evening—an evening, he reminded himself, that was not yet over.

'Loth to listen'

'Did you enjoy your evening, darling?' Violet asked Malcolm as they prepared to go to breakfast next day. He had returned late and not woken her.

'Well, yes, I did,' he replied. 'There was no one there I knew, of course, apart from Stewart, but that never seems to matter at these things. Yes, it was all most agreeable.' He smiled at her. 'And how was yours? You had your drive with Norton, I suppose?'

'Yes. I found him charming.'

Perhaps now was the moment to tell Violet of Eardley Norton's past. Not that Malcolm felt her to be in any way at risk—the man was a figure of some repute. And Ada obviously thought well of him, or she would not have encouraged Violet to go driving with him in the first place.

'Stewart was telling me last night that ten years ago Norton was involved in a divorce case,' he offered casually. 'He was named as co-respondent. It created quite a furore at the time and nearly wrecked his career, Stewart said.'

'Oh, Malcolm,' Violet teased, 'and I thought you never listened to gossip!'

Nicolson frowned. He had expected his wife to be a little more impressed by his revelations. 'I simply thought you should know, as he's a visitor to this house,' he told her.

Violet laughed a little mockingly. 'General Nicolson, do you realise just how pompous you sometimes sound? I like Mr Norton. He's interesting to talk to. He loves poetry. And he offered last night to take me to the Connemara Public Library. No doubt he married the lady in question, and has been devoted to her ever since—and most likely has been forgiven by all and sundry. But I promise to be very, very careful, nonetheless. There, will that do?'

Damn, thought Nicolson, a man who rarely swore. Now I've antagonised her, and that wasn't at all my intention. I would have done better to leave well alone.

'So Mr Norton has had an amorous career? I'm glad of it,' his wife went on, laughter still dancing deep in her violet eyes. 'It possibly explains his love of poetry, don't you think? I doubt very much that we'll see him at church this morning, but you can talk to him about it tonight, if you like—he's invited us to dine at Norton's Gardens.'

Since church-going was a weekly ritual with the Stewarts, it was taken for granted that the Nicolsons would wish to attend mattins that Sunday with their hosts. Violet felt no such compulsion, but after breakfast she rammed the only remotely fashionable hat she possessed—and which her husband had had the foresight to include in her luggage—onto her rebellious head and followed the party downstairs.

They drove along Mount Road and across The Island to Fort St George. The barracks were modern, and the rest of the Fort was given over to Government offices and the arsenal. Apart from the church of St Mary's, few of the original buildings still existed. St Mary's spire, like the rest of the building, was clad in *chunam*, and it rose in stark silhouette against a cloudless sky. The rest of the church was in depressing contrast. From the moment the worshippers passed the ancient cracked tombstones and went inside, death embraced them. Why did the British always worship in the dark, wondered the mutinous Mrs Nicolson—by doing so they proclaimed the finality of the tomb, and surely contradicted all hope of resurrection. She paid scant attention to the Anglican ritual, standing and kneeling as required, and listening to the sermon not at all. She read the nearest memorial tablets to while away the time, although placed next to Sir Norman, she was aware of his pleasant baritone praising the Almighty earnestly in song and beseeching Him equally sincerely in prayer. Out in the sunshine at last, the Reverend Goss shook hands and welcomed the Nicolsons to Madras. Would they care for a guided tour of the oldest Anglican church in Asia, he wondered.

Sir Norman, who had sensed Violet's restlessness, tactfully came to the rescue. Nick wouldn't mind missing the tour, either, he reflected. It was always difficult to guess what *he* thought about religion. Why, even after that narrow escape at Ahmed Khel, he had been more concerned about his bloodied uniform than the wound to his jaw, and the deferred meeting with his Maker! It was even rumoured that the man was not totally indifferent to Islam, but what did it matter? In the end, God was God, by whatever name you addressed Him.

Promising the vicar to return another day, Sir Norman took his guests across the bridge onto the plain embraced by the two arms of the Cooum River. The Island, as it was known, had once been a peninsula, Lady Stewart explained, determined that Violet should have a secular tour, at least. A channel cut in the early days of the city had turned it into an island, which nowadays provided the troops with a parade ground, the officers with a gymkhana club, and everyone else with open space for their enjoyment. In the northwest area was St Mary's cemetery.

'*Such* a depressing place, I always think—but necessary, of course,' and Ada Stewart gave an affected little laugh.

'Perhaps the Parsees have the right idea,' Violet remarked laconically, and she looked up at the scavenging kites flying overhead. 'It saves a deal of trouble!'

'Oh, Mrs Nicolson, *how could you—*' Ada Stewart's laugh this time was one of genuine shock. Really, Nick's wife was quite impossible! Violet's words, and the images they evoked of dead flesh laid out to be torn by avid beaks, stayed with her and totally spoiled tiffin.

That afternoon Violet sat in the verandah outside her room. She was alone. The three others were in the drawing room, and the Stewarts had barely noticed her go.

She was looking through a pile of papers. Some were covered with poems; some held ideas or drafts. Before leaving Feroke Malcolm had suggested she prepare another book, and today seemed a good time to make a start.

The papers reflected her experiences as Malcolm's companion, or the influence of their travels together. Some dated from Baluchistan; others from the first heady contact with Hindu life in Deesa and Mhow. Then there were her recent verses written in Malabar. Would there be any, though, from this present visit? In the elegant surroundings afforded by Madras Malcolm had found it so easy to slip back into the old Anglo-Indian ways, while she felt more than ever the outsider. No, she was unlikely to find inspiration here.

The papers had fallen to the floor by the time Nicolson came to find her, all save one that she still held in her hand. The most desperate heat of the afternoon was over so he lifted one of the blinds a fraction. Violet looked tired and there were faint shadows beneath her eyes. She must have sat up late the night before, hoping to see him. But it was so easy to delay one's departure indefinitely when one was the centre of attention. And Stewart had been no help.

Poor lass! To come all this way to be a grass widow again. He gently woke her.

'And the gay guest-faces and flowers'

The banyan trees lining the road to Norton's Gardens were huge. Their aerial roots rose up to meet the branches hanging down, and together they formed a cool thick leafy tunnel. While the rays of the setting sun flashed in and out of the tangle above their heads, Sir Norman told the Nicolsons about their evening's host. Eardley Norton, he said, was a brilliant fellow. Not only was he the leading barrister in Madras, whose aggressive cross-examinations in the criminal court were legendary and whose quick wit and repartee were respected by all (and dreaded by not a few), but he was also a scholar, and widely read in both English and French literature.

'You're bound to get on with him, Mrs Nicolson,' Sir Norman continued. 'He could introduce you to the Literary Society, for example. They have a library with forty-five thousand volumes—or so they tell me. Never been there myself.'

That was all very interesting, Malcolm said, but *he* expected to escort his wife to such places. Violet smiled in the half-light; it was unlike Malcolm to be proprietorial. Lady Stewart also noticed the hint of reproof, but Sir Norman was quite oblivious.

'The man's an amazing fund of knowledge,' he went on. 'Medical science, engineering, technology—there seems to be nothing he doesn't know about.'

'Quite the Renaissance Man, in fact,' Nicolson observed dryly. Sir Norman, to whom the term meant little if anything, supposed so in a mumble and the quartet fell silent.

Near the Adyar River there were fewer European houses and more rice fields. Violet was reminded of Feroke, and she missed Malabar more than ever. Then Moubrays's Road came to an abrupt end and the carriage swung left, parallel to the river, and soon afterwards turned into a long driveway. At the end stood a typical garden house before which Eardley Norton was waiting to greet his guests.

'Welcome!' The mellifluous voice reverberated through the deep downstairs verandah. 'Come in, come in!' He greeted Lady Stewart in his usual extravagant manner, and with distaste Nicolson watched him also press the tips of Violet's fingers to his clean-shaven lips.

'Delighted to meet you, General Nicolson!' Not waiting for Stewart's formal introductions, Norton turned his attention to the one guest he had not already met. The two men, who were almost of a height, eyed each other in silence for a moment. Nicolson saw a supremely confident man ten years or so his junior; Norton, a military gentleman of dignified bearing whose gaze appeared to search one's very soul. The barrister's eyes were the first to look away.

It was a long time since Norton had felt such strong antagonism, and never in a total stranger—unless one counted the feeling coming from the dock. He supposed that old Stewart (who he would have been surprised to learn was his senior by very few years) had blown the gaff about the divorce. It would certainly explain everything. Whether Nicolson in turn had told his wife, he would probably never know, and either way it did not bother Norton in the least. In Mrs Nicolson he recognised a fierce spirit of independence, and he believed she would not allow anything to spoil their burgeoning friendship.

Eardley Norton rarely dined at home during the absence of his wife, but when he did, he did so in style. Servants in white uniforms were lined up against the wall under the steely eye of a red-and-gold turbaned butler as he ushered his guests into a dining room whose table was set with glittering crystal and silver, and ornamented with fruit and exquisitely scented flowers. Norton placed Violet, as the senior lady, on his right and Lady Stewart opposite him. They were both wearing silk, Violet in her new gown, Ada in dark red, and both looked to advantage in the soft light of numerous candelabra.

Although Norton turned to Violet in intimate asides whenever the occasion allowed, he did not neglect her husband. He engaged him in conversation about the current conflict between the Viceroy and his Commander in Chief. He asked him about the changes to the army. He discussed the situation in Afghanistan. Norton's intellect proclaimed itself with every word he spoke, and, as always, Malcolm Nicolson found himself responding to the owner of a fine mind. Despite himself, he found himself warming to a man he had been ready to dislike.

When Norton asked, 'And what took you to Malabar, General Nicolson?' and continued, 'an odd choice, surely, for someone of your background?' Nicolson was at an immediate loss as to what to reply. *A culmination of foolish failures, of disappointments, a desire to live out one's natural term as cheaply as possible?* Violet saw Malcolm's discomfiture and considered the question impertinent.

'Allow me to answer for my husband,' she said. 'You see, Mr Norton, we first visited Malabar in 1900, and after five years in Central India it seemed a second paradise. While we were there we learned I was carrying our child. How my husband indulged me in those happy, happy days! And now by taking me back, he is indulging me again. Isn't that so, darling?' She sent Malcolm an affectionate smile and he took up the story.

'What my wife says of my good nature is a little exaggerated, perhaps, but otherwise she is perfectly correct. What she *hasn't* told you, Norton, is that once we return to Feroke we intend to prospect for gold.'

The Stewarts, who already knew, showed no surprise. Eardley Norton, on the other hand, was taken aback. That General Nicolson, who appeared a sensible kind of a fellow, should indulge in such quixotic schemes seemed slightly shocking. That he should involve his wife was utterly reprehensible.

'I suppose you've gone into this thoroughly? There's a long history of failure in the South-East Wynaad gold fields, after all.'

'Yes, I know,' his guest admitted, 'but we've had promising signs.'

Oh, Malcolm, Malcolm—how could you? One chance nugget and a few grains of gold hardly constituted a sound basis for an enterprise, but Violet said nothing.

Norton searched his prodigious memory for ways of discouraging his guest. He told of the early days in the 1860s, when Australian miners had tried the luck that had deserted them in Ballarat, and how the prestigious Madras firm of Parry and Co. had lent their support to two unsuccessful ventures.

'In 1881 there were over forty companies in the Wynaad and Nilgiris, and by 1886 all except four had folded. They've *all* gone now. It's a good thing for Parry's that they pulled out when they did. Let me tell you, General Nicolson, that there are firms in this city that overreached themselves in the eighties and haven't recovered yet!'

He looked around the table as he would a courtroom, and Violet could imagine him saying, *I rest my case.*

'You won't change my husband's mind, Mr Norton,' she said. 'He's absolutely determined to go ahead. And so, of course, am I.'

Violet gave the barrister the full force of her smile, and then—human nature being what it was—Eardley Norton determined to offer Mrs Nicolson's husband all the support and advice that he could. With that in mind, he immediately set about winning the general's approval.

After the meal Norton suggested the gentlemen forego their port and cigars. 'It would be a shame to leave such charming ladies on their own,' he submitted, and with both Mrs Nicolson and Lady Stewart silently blessing him for the break with tradition, they all went up onto the flat roof to take coffee.

When John Bruce Norton built the house in 1853, a year after the birth of his son, Eardley John, he created a 'white' garden in the Indian style. The pattern of stone paths, all slightly raised above ground level, could be clearly seen in the moonlight, and in all directions ghostly flowers shone out from the darkness of the parent trees and shrubs.

'Perhaps, ladies, you would care to take a turn with me outside? The fragrance at this time of night is quite remarkable.'

'Why, I should love that, Mr Norton,' Violet said immediately.

'And so should I,' concurred Lady Stewart, who felt that a chaperone for Mrs Nicolson might perhaps be wise. She seemed to have eyes only for her husband, but who knew what such a night might not produce in Mr Norton—reformed character though he apparently was? Ada Stewart rose to her feet, and Violet followed.

'Perhaps we might have our port and cigars, after all,' Stewart suggested slyly, when the three walkers left them to go downstairs.

Norton, with a lady on either arm, contentedly showed off his domain. From all sides came the scent of a thousand flowers, and while at first it seemed possible to distinguish champak from tuberose, tuberose from jasmine, jasmine from stephanotis, soon all were intermingled in one single heady fragrance which, under other circumstances, might well have caused the barrister to commit some indiscretion.

As they passed a little isolated pavilion Norton looked down at the younger woman. The fireflies were dancing about her face and naked shoulders, and he imagined her some marble Galatea, waiting to be drawn inside and wakened by his kiss. Violet noticed nothing, but Lady Stewart who had been watching their host gave an exaggerated shiver.

'Perhaps we might join our husbands now, Mr Norton,' she suggested. 'It's getting a little chilly, don't you think?'

Politeness necessitated agreement, and the barrister led his charges back inside. Much later Eardley John Norton waved his guests farewell, and as they made their way back to Dunmore House the moon shone through the banyans, weaving fantastic patterns over the road ahead. All four were silent: Sir Norman thinking with satisfaction of the success of the evening, with everyone getting on so well; Violet recalling the glory of the garden; Lady Stewart thinking of Eardley Norton; and Malcolm Nicolson remembering his appointment with Dr Blackett.

'We have no idle self-deceiving'

Violet insisted on going with Malcolm next morning, and he was glad of her company. He had no doubt that all was far from well. The attacks of excruciating pain had passed—Malabar seemed to have been some kind of turning point in that respect—but other problems were manifesting themselves, problems he found difficult to discuss even with his wife.

Violet took his hand. 'Don't worry, darling. I'm sure all will be well.'

'Of course it will,' he replied automatically, 'and we'll soon know for certain.'

Mackay's Gardens turned out to be another typical Madras 'flat top', this one pre-dating Norton's Gardens by possibly some fifty or sixty years. The flaking *chunam* gave the house an uncared-for appearance, excusable, perhaps, in a nursing home whose concerns must lie elsewhere. Malcolm and Violet walked up the broad flight of shallow steps, lined on each side with pots of straggly plants, and rang the bell. Almost immediately a Eurasian girl in white, who was presumably some kind of nurse, ushered them inside.

'Dr Blackett will be with you shortly,' Miss Jones told them in her sing-song voice, and she showed them into a small dark waiting room to the left of the entrance.

They did not have long to wait. The doctor, who was possibly the same age as the general, bustled into the room, and his bland nondescript features expressed surprise at seeing the general was not alone. He shook hands with Violet upon Nicolson's introduction, and then turned his attention to her husband.

'I'm pleased to meet you, General Nicolson. How are you enjoying Madras?'

Before Malcolm could answer, the doctor said, 'I'm sure you won't mind, Mrs Nicolson, if I see your husband alone?'

That was what they had expected, and it was certainly what she wanted, Violet answered evenly. She was very happy to wait—all day if necessary—and she settled down to read the volume of Mr Hardy's *Wessex Poems* that she had had the foresight to bring.

Once in his consulting room, Blackett invited Malcolm to take a seat. He installed himself at a large desk opposite, between two windows with a view onto the gardens, and then looked across at his patient.

'So, General Nicolson, I understand that you've been having problems of a urinary nature? Perhaps you would tell me exactly what you've been experiencing?'

Malcolm repeated what he had told the doctors in London the year before: of the dull pains in the loins, with the occasional sharper twinges, and the occasional passing of blood.

'I see,' said Blackett. 'I take it, then, that you were treated for stone.' Yes, agreed Malcolm, and medication had brought some relief.

'Do you have those symptoms now?' asked the doctor. Before he arrived in Malabar, Malcolm explained, the symptoms had been fewer, in fact at times there had been nothing. Then he had begun to experience a burning sensation after emptying the bladder, and on one occasion about a month ago, he said, the pain on passing water had been almost unbearable. Since then, amazingly, he had felt no pain at all.

'Well, General Nicolson, it appears to me that your problems could be over. Did Sir Norman remind you to bring a sample of urine?'

He had. Malcolm smiled at the memory of his friend's slight awkwardness in relaying the instruction. Blackett put the bottle on his desk.

'We'll let it settle,' he said. 'Now you say you've had no pain recently, so I would suggest that you have passed the stone that's been causing all the trouble. We'll know in a moment whether there's an indication of more. If not, I think we can pronounce you clear.'

Blackett stood up and went over to the window. 'Without going into unnecessary detail, General,' he said after holding the bottle to the light, 'your urine seems perfectly normal. There's a slight cloudiness, admittedly, but no sign of what we call "gravel"; I imagine they told you all about that in London?'

They had, and it should have been easy to get up, reclaim Violet, and leave. But that was not the case.

'Is there something else?'

'Yes, Doctor, I'm afraid there is. Now I find that occasionally I have a certain difficulty in passing any water at all.'

Blackett frowned. This was more serious. 'I see. Then I'm afraid I shall have to give you an examination.'

He indicated a screen behind which there was a couch. Malcolm went behind it, undressed and lay down.

After twenty unpleasant minutes they emerged to resume their respective seats by the desk. Doctor Blackett wasted no time in saying that there might be another stone in the bladder causing a partial blockage, but without surgery he couldn't say for sure. What he *could* tell the general, however, was that he suffering from an enlarged prostate gland and that this would in time cause problems in itself—if it wasn't already responsible for the present trouble.

'We can draw off the urine if your symptoms persist, as I'm certain they will—' he paused, 'but if this should prove impossible, then I'm afraid it all becomes rather more complicated.' The doctor paused again.

'What I would suggest, General, and it is only a suggestion—what I would suggest is that I deal with any calculus by surgery and then proceed to removal of the prostate gland. And then I can guarantee you total relief. With, very probably,' and Blackett thought of the much younger woman waiting outside and the fears Nicolson had also confided, 'the prospect of a full sexual life for many years to come.' He stopped and waited for a reaction.

Malcolm cleared his throat. 'I see. What are the risks of such an operation, would you say?'

'In your case, General Nicolson, I envisage none. In a patient with any element of heart disease, it would be very risky indeed. But you are fit and strong, your heart is sound as a bell and I see no reason at all for alarm. And from what you have told me of your future plans, I would think the operation highly advisable. I have, of course, carried out the procedure often. Look, sir, there's no need at all for you to decide immediately. Why don't you talk it over with your wife and let me know later in the week? We would admit you the day before operating, and it would all be pretty straightforward from then on.'

When Malcolm rejoined Violet he gave her a reassuring smile and they went down the steps arm in arm. The carriage had been sent back to Dunmore House and they walked towards Mount Road. They needed to talk but didn't know the city. Where should they go?

At that moment Violet was finding the dusty street every bit as unpleasant as her hostess had envisaged, and it was a very relieved Mrs Nicolson who followed her husband into the Elphinstone Hotel.

Violet poured the tea, put down the teapot, and looked across at her husband expectantly. 'Well?' was all she said. Malcolm thought for a moment, then he sipped his tea. Where should he begin?

'Was it so awful?' she asked, as the silence continued.

'It certainly wasn't pleasant,' he admitted. 'Look, Vi,' suddenly the words started coming in a rush. 'Blackett thinks I should have an operation—it's a straightforward business and would make life a lot easier for me. I asked him about risks and he said that in my case there shouldn't be any.' He stopped as abruptly as he had begun.

For a moment Violet said nothing. Then, 'I suppose it's one of those terribly intimate masculine things that women aren't supposed to know about, but do?' she asked.

Nicolson found himself laughing. 'Yes,' he replied, 'I suppose it is. Well then, since you know so much, what do you think?'

'Darling,' she said, after she had listened for a while, 'you know that as far as I'm concerned all that matters is your health.'

Of course he knew! Hadn't she shown that time and time again? But he did not tell her of his other preoccupations. She would have gently mocked him for his fears, calling them ridiculous, and she would have probably been right. She took his hand in hers and raised it to her lips and then her cheek. 'If this operation means that your health and comfort are assured then you must go ahead,' she told him earnestly. 'I simply cannot bear to think of you in any kind of pain, but—' and Violet's voice trailed away.

'But?'

'Darling, what if something went wrong?'

'Nothing will go wrong. *Nothing will go wrong*,' he repeated emphatically.

Violet smiled at him trustingly. 'In that case, yes. We'll tell Dr Blackett that you're ready to have the operation.'

Her husband smiled back. 'Now, Violet,' he said, squeezing the hand that still held his. 'We've stayed with the Stewarts long enough and I think it's time for us to move.'

'Well, *I* certainly think so! However,' and Violet gave him a long level look, 'I've no intention of languishing in a hotel room while you go off carousing with Sir Norman. Is that clear?'

Nicolson returned her gaze somewhat guiltily. 'I've neglected you, I know. And you've been on my conscience.'

'I don't want to be on your conscience, Malcolm Nicolson; I want to be in your company! If Mr Norton hadn't saved me from Ada Stewart, your Afghan War would have paled into insignificance, believe me! So if we go to a hotel, will I see more of you—or less?'

'Oh dear, you sound like a tyrant.' And she looked like one. Gone for ever the girl who would have followed him blindly, no matter what! The great eyes watched him uncompromisingly with no trace of humour while she waited for his reply. He thought of the suavely handsome Eardley Norton, who with his wit and obvious culture was quite unlike anyone of their acquaintance. Had there been a veiled threat in Violet's remark? If he saw less of his wife, would the barrister see more?

'Well?'

'Sweetheart,' he assured her, 'I'll never let you out of my sight!'

'He advances, she retreating'

The Stewarts took them to the Adyar Club that afternoon. It was set in extensive grounds on the banks of the Adyar River, not far from Norton's Gardens. The dazzling white of the former Moubray House, built for a servant of the East India Company in the 1770s, was stunning, and above the main body of the building rose an unusual and dramatic cupola, octagonal in shape. The club had occupied the premises since 1890.

There were few Europeans in the central octagonal hall. Everyone who could had long since followed the governor of Madras to his summer capital of Ootacamund in the Nilgiri Hills. Those Europeans still in evidence were far outnumbered by the Indian bearers who hovered attentively to one side, immaculate in their white tunics and turbans, or bustled hither and thither on errands.

As Sir Norman pointed out the club's various attractions, someone advanced purposefully towards them through an archway and Violet recognised their host of the night before. It soon became clear that it was her husband's company he was seeking. Almost simultaneously Sir Norman was claimed by a red-faced acquaintance, Lady Stewart was swept away by a loud-voiced matron of uncertain age, and Violet was suddenly alone.

Giving her husband a gay little wave (which he may or may not have noticed) Violet went out through a verandah and down a flight of shallow steps onto the lawn. The grounds sloped away to the river, and as she walked towards it, she twirled her borrowed parasol with a nonchalance she was far from feeling.

The sun was hot, but not oppressive, and there was ample shade. For a while Violet followed the bank of the smoothly flowing river, and when she came to a stone seat beneath the leafy branches of a champak tree she sat down with a sigh of pure pleasure. She had escaped—but not, it seemed, for long. As she watched a bright blue kingfisher darting over the water she heard her name and looked up. Eardley Norton had come soundlessly over the grass to join her.

'We've been sadly neglecting you, I fear, Mrs Nicolson. Your husband suggested I keep you company.'

That hardly rang true, but Violet let it pass.

'May I?' and without waiting for a reply the barrister sat down at her feet. 'I was hoping you'd be here this afternoon. I've been giving General Nicolson the names of people he might find helpful to your enterprise.'

He stopped, waiting perhaps for her approval. She said nothing.

'I'm taking him to Best and Company tomorrow morning,' he continued. 'They have dealings with the Kolar goldfields and are bound to give useful advice.'

'Why, thank you, Mr Norton. That is kind of you. And I'm sure my husband thinks so too.' She smiled at him, and then looked back towards the river, where the kingfisher plunged once more in a sudden murderous flash.

'A handsome bird,' remarked her companion. 'But the pied kingfisher—the white and black ones—are the most beautiful. Or so I think. You know the Greek legend, perhaps?' Norton's splendid voice began to tell her of lonely Alcyone, who, mourning her lost husband, flies forever over the face of the waters in an endless unavailing quest.

'How cruel,' Violet exclaimed, a catch in her voice. 'Whenever I see a kingfisher I shall remember.'

She was so sensitive, so appealing … And so important to him, for all that he had known her but a few days. *Remember me, too,* he pleaded silently, *when you have gone away, back to that forsaken backwater they call Feroke.* The blossoms stirred overhead and Violet, face uplifted, breathed in avidly. For a moment he watched the faint pulse beating in her throat.

'I've read your poetry,' said Eardley Norton. 'You love India greatly, Mrs Nicolson.'

'Oh, yes,' she replied with deep feeling. 'We went back to Europe a few years ago and it nearly killed me.'

It was no exaggeration, thought her companion. This woman was surely made to live—and love—under Eastern skies. 'Let me read you some of the work of a man who felt for the Orient as you do,' he said.

When he left her husband in the smoking room surrounded by a group of admiring younger men, Norton had looked into the library and borrowed a slim volume from its shelves. Now, as Violet gave him her full attention he produced it and began to read:

Voici venir les temps où vibrant sur sa tige
Chaque fleur s'évapore ainsi qu'un encensoir;
Les sons et les parfums tournent dans l'air du soir—

Violet's eyes opened wide as the beautiful voice continued to the end. Sound, movement, colours, scent—all were there, whirling and swirling in a bloody sunset and a broken heart. When he had finished, her lips silently framed the question: *Who*?

'Charles Baudelaire,' Norton told her. 'Packed off to Calcutta by his stepfather in 1841. He got as far as Mauritius and Reunion then came back, but the exotic had marked him for life.' Also the fact that he had a mulatto mistress in Paris, he reflected, but he had no intention of telling his listener *that*. Turning the pages, he selected another poem then another, pausing here and there for effect, and looking up at the general's wife who returned his look with no trace of embarrassment, simply smiling and saying nothing.

But as he continued, a suspicion began to form in Violet's mind, crystallising into certain knowledge with a sudden shock—this man was using the power of his remarkable voice in a bid to seduce her! She made a helpless little gesture with her hand and stood up. Eardley Norton looked at her in surprise.

'Please don't go on,' she said. 'I really don't think I should listen to any more, do you? Although,' and she could not help telling him, 'you do read so beautifully.'

Norton's first reaction was of amused satisfaction. He had partially achieved his aim by unsettling this woman's composure. Then to his dismay he saw that Violet was truly distressed.

'I'm sorry if you feel I have given you any encouragement,' she added unhappily. 'If so, it was quite unintentional.'

'No, no,' he said, rising to his feet in a single graceful movement. 'It was entirely my fault! I'm afraid I find wit, charm and poetry an intoxicating combination. Do please forgive me.'

He grinned disarmingly, reminding Violet of a schoolboy caught out in some minor misdemeanour, then he closed the book and slipped it into his pocket. 'Mrs Nicolson, if I promise to behave myself, will you stay?'

Violet shook her head and he wondered desperately what he might do to preserve their fragile relationship. He watched her walk back to the club building, a small resolute figure who, had he but known it, was already regretting her decision to go.

Norton came across her again shortly afterwards in the now much busier Octagon Room. He had not tarried by the river, but had returned the book to the shelf where he had found it and was preparing to leave when he caught sight of her forlorn figure standing quite alone. So she had lost her husband, had she? Perhaps he might redeem himself in some small way.

'Can I be of service, Mrs Nicolson?'

'Mr Norton! I seem to have mislaid Malcolm and the Stewarts, and I've no idea where to start looking.'

'May I suggest we let them look for you instead? Come and sit down.' He drew her into an open area where people were standing, sitting, and talking. 'You'll be quite safe here, I assure you.' The smile he gave her was still amused.

'Thank you, you're very kind,' she said, smiling back.

'May I keep you company?'

'Of course.'

It became clear to the barrister over the next half an hour that Mrs Nicolson considered the matter of his earlier behaviour closed. He was sure, too, that she wouldn't mention it to her husband. They talked easily of his connection with the Indian National Congress, and when they shook hands in farewell later her manner was perfectly friendly. Perhaps he would see her when he called for the general next morning, but there would, he realised, be little chance of a moment alone.

The galling thing, reflected Norton, was that Violet Nicolson was completely unaware of the effect she had on a man. She looked at you frankly with those marvellous eyes, talked without affectation—and completely undermined all your good intentions.

Eardley John Norton spent the evening in the magnificent library created by his father and augmented by him.

I would have squandered Youth for you, he read, *and its hope and its promise, Before you wandered, careless, away from my useless passion—*

He closed *The Garden of Kama* at last, and proceeded to indulge in a severe bout of extreme self-pity.

'A fruit with bitter aftertaste'

While Violet was sitting by the river Malcolm had managed to have a word with his hostess alone, tentatively suggesting that it was time for him and his wife to move to a hotel. He had anticipated strong objections, but to his surprise Lady Stewart did not demur in the least. She had been steeling herself to warn her husband's old friend of possible dangers in Violet's continued association with the owner of Dunmore House, but now it seemed quite unnecessary. She breathed a sigh of relief and agreed that the Connemara Hotel would be ideal for the couple: it was modern, comfortable and—most importantly—near the nursing home. Also, thought Lady Stewart privately, it might be easier to get on with Mrs Nicolson when she was no longer a guest under her roof.

When Sir Norman heard that his guests were leaving he was most distressed, until his wife made plain to him in private that it was *for the best*.

'Good Lord, Ada,' Stewart said when she finished. 'Do you really think Norton's up to his old tricks?' He found his friend's pretty wife refreshing to talk to; as he told his wife on more than one occasion: 'You know where you are with Violet Nicolson. She gives you a straight answer to a question and she'll put you right, if she thinks you need it! In the pleasantest possible way, of course.' And therein, he suggested, might lie her appeal for someone like their landlord.

Ada Stewart sniffed. 'I imagine it would very much depend on whether he got any encouragement,' she said. 'A hotel would give less scope for that sort of thing than a house where the man is far too much at home.'

'It *is* his home,' Stewart pointed out, and Ada sniffed again.

'And perhaps Nick will give Violet more attention if he's away from *you*,' she pointed out in her turn, determined that no one should escape her censure. 'It would serve him right if she *did* get up to mischief! He's been neglecting her disgracefully!'

For Ada Stewart had not failed to notice the yearning look when Violet's husband told her he was about to spend another morning—and very likely the afternoon too, if *she* were any judge of things—away from her side. 'Well,' thought Lady Stewart with the determination that had helped her solve many a tricky problem in the past, 'we'll see about that!'

So when Norton, rather less ebullient than usual, arrived soon after breakfast to spirit Nicolson away to the premises of Best and Company in North Beach Road, he was delighted to find himself invited to return with the general for tiffin.

'Shall we say twelve-thirty, gentlemen? That should give you ample time for your business, don't you think? And then we can settle the Nicolsons into the Connemara Hotel.'

Norton shot a look at Violet. Why were they going? Had she told her husband after all? No, of course not; the old boy was being perfectly friendly and so was Lady Stewart, and he knew what a stickler *she* was for the proprieties. He lingered behind as they were leaving and held out a small package to Violet.

'I thought you might enjoy reading these for yourself. Please accept the book as a gift.'

He looked tired, thought Violet, little suspecting that the barrister had hardly slept at all, reading late into the night and then finding sleep almost impossible. When the two men had gone, she opened the package to reveal Norton's own copy of *Les Fleurs du Mal*. His name was written in bold characters on the flyleaf and beneath he had added:

> *—Alas what can I do for thee?*
> *By Fate, and thine own beauty, set above*
> *The need of all or any aid from me,*
> *Too high for service, as too far for love—*

Violet could not help but be touched by the tribute—but the irony of such a deliberate use of her own words did not escape her. Did this mean that Norton had accepted her reproof, or had decided to ignore it totally? Time perhaps would tell.

It proved impossible to move to the Connemara Hotel that afternoon. Not even Ada Stewart's determination could control the weather and it rained heavily for several hours. Norton stayed for tiffin, then made his excuses and braved the downpour to return to his home.

Violet was not sorry to see him leave. Earlier she had dipped into the volume of Baudelaire's poems he had given her, and found her cheeks burning at the thought that he might have presumed to address some of these verses to her in person, had she not spoken out when she did. And, honest with herself as always, she wondered what—given his glorious voice and the nature of the words—her own response might have been. So when Norton got up to go, hers was the only voice not raised in protest, and he had taken his leave feeling rebuked all over again.

'There is no barrier now, 'twixt me and thee'

Once Malcolm Nicolson decided to have his operation, time flew past. On Wednesday morning, after booking in at the Connemara Hotel in Binnie's Road, husband and wife spoke to Dr Blackett again. It was arranged that Nicolson would be admitted on Saturday morning, and the operation would take place early on Sunday. In only a few days, Blackett said, General Nicolson would be back on his feet, a new man—and in no time at all they would be able to pick up their life in Malabar.

It was a very optimistic couple that made its way back to the Connemara Hotel. The hotel was comfortable without being over ostentatious: modern amenities combined with the charm of the old. They could be hermits if they wished, or wander through the public rooms or outside in the courtyards and gardens. It was ideal, Violet thought happily; no Sir Norman to whisk Malcolm away, no Lady Stewart to eye her up and down in silent disapproval. And no Eardley Norton …

She watched Malcolm checking and writing lists in anticipation of their return to Feroke, and she dropped a kiss on his head as she went outside. He looked up and smiled before returning to his task. After a while he stopped writing. He could see Violet sitting in the verandah, her face turned away towards the garden. It was strange, he mused, that their once wide horizons should have narrowed down to this—one man and one woman in a suite of rented rooms. She wouldn't be truly happy, he supposed, until they were back in Malabar. Well, they should be ready to leave in about three weeks, providing his convalescence went according to plan. And there was no reason why it should not, he told himself firmly.

'Do you know,' he said, when Violet came in and joined him, 'this week has taught me a lesson and finally I'm tired of looking back!' A steady supply of mercury was assured, thanks to Best and Company, he continued, so prospecting could soon begin in earnest. With Heneage's help the enterprise was bound to prosper and in two years at the very most, he promised Violet, they would return to England to see their son.

He left the desk, went over to an armchair and pulled Violet onto his lap. 'I suppose I should thank our friend Norton. He's been tremendously helpful and generous with his time, and he's really made me feel that we can get somewhere in Nilambur. And,' he added, 'he's good company. As you said.'

Violet frowned. The barrister was the last person she wanted to talk about at present.

'He suggested you might like to visit Huddleston's Gardens. Apparently that fellow Olcott has built up a marvellous library over the years. What do you think?'

Violet said nothing. Although she had heard of the Theosophical Society library from Blanche, who had sung its praises in several letters, she had no wish for another tête-à-tête with Eardley Norton.

'I told him I'd take you tomorrow morning,' Malcolm went on, and he saw Violet's face light up with pleasure, in complete contrast to the fleeting shadow of only a moment before. 'Has anything happened between you and Norton?' he asked. There had been the farewell yesterday as well, he remembered, when Violet had seemed almost relieved to see the man go.

She hesitated before replying 'No …o.'

'You don't seem too sure,' he remarked with some amusement, and by way of answer she went into the bedroom and returned with Eardley Norton's book. 'He gave me this.' She handed it to him and Malcolm looked at the title.

'*Les Fleurs du Mal*. An odd choice, surely,' was his only comment.

'Look inside.'

He did and read the dedication aloud. 'I see.' He thought for a moment before saying dryly, 'Well, as long as he continues to think you *too far for love* I don't suppose there's any problem. Is there?' He looked at Violet more keenly and her eyes still did not waver.

'Aren't you in the least bit annoyed?' she eventually asked.

'Well,' he said, 'if you hadn't told me and I'd found out later, I suppose I would have been upset, and I might have wondered what else you'd been hiding.

But you've told me, and I'm sure you can handle Mr Norton on your own.'

A sudden thought struck him. 'Was he reading from this—when you were down by the river?'

Violet was surprised. 'You knew we were there? He *said* you had sent him to keep me company.'

'Hardly,' and her husband snorted. 'I wondered where you were, and saw you both from the terrace. Then Stewart and some others grabbed me, and I couldn't escape.' He grinned ruefully at Violet's expression. 'I'm sorry, I didn't even try,' he corrected, and once again drew her down onto his knees. 'So what happened?'

'Well, he did read to me, and I gradually realised that he was leading up to some kind of declaration—so I stopped him.'

'Poor fellow,' Nicolson remarked. 'I hope he wasn't too put out!'

'I don't imagine so—if anything, I was the more upset. Darling, I found it all very unsettling,' she admitted frankly, 'and I wish he hadn't given me the book. I read some of it while you were out with him yesterday and it doesn't seem quite the thing to read to another man's wife.'

Nicolson handed back the little volume. 'Keep it if you want to. Why not?'

But Violet had already decided to return it to its owner, when next they met.

'Are you happy, sweetheart?' Malcolm asked her later.

'Oh course I'm happy. Why do you ask?'

'I can't read you French love poetry, or write sonnets to your glorious eyes,' he said sombrely, 'but I do love you.'

'I know you do. Malcolm, is all this because of Mr Norton yesterday?'

'Yes, I suppose it is. He has a most wonderful voice.'

'Which he exploits.'

'And he's very handsome.'

'So are you.'

'He's ten years younger than I am—'

'What on earth has that to do with anything?'

'He's everything I'm not.'

'And you are everything *he*'s not—and I know which I prefer! Malcolm Nicolson, please will you stop this? Darling, sometimes you are so very, very silly!'

She kissed him in a way that quite dispelled his fears and then with a little laugh he freed himself. It must be the operation, he confided. He supposed anxiety was making him gloomy.

Violet looked at him. She had never seen him so unsettled. 'Is it absolutely necessary?' she asked unhappily.

'Blackett says so, yes.'

'But what about you, Malcolm? What do *you* think?'

Nicolson swallowed. Violet's eyes were luminous pools of unshed tears. He knew what she was going to ask, and how could he resist her if she did?

'Darling—' she began.

No!' he said. 'No—this is the only way. You know it is.'

Her lips parted again, and he touched them lightly with gentle fingers.

'*No*,' he repeated firmly, and the words of entreaty died away.

'No others sing as you have sung'

'Do you know,' Violet said next morning, 'Lady Stewart was almost glad to get rid of us yesterday. Did you notice?'

'Yes,' agreed her husband. 'She probably thinks there's less chance of my neglecting you now that I'm out of her husband's clutches.'

Violet said nothing; there was more than an element of truth in that. But they were alone together now and the whole day stretched ahead. She settled back in the carriage and watched the banyan trees go by. She recognised the entrance to the Adyar Club, as they turned left into Chamier's Road and on into Greenway's Road past the drive to Norton's Gardens. They exchanged a look but neither said a word. Then past another compound to the Elphinstone Bridge, where mangroves sent their twisted roots down into the water and the Adyar flowed sluggishly between sandbanks to the sea. Huddleston's Gardens, home of the Theosophical Movement, could be seen rising through the trees to the south.

Ibises and cranes strutted undisturbed beside the quiet waters, and the peace of the estuary was echoed by the serenity of the library they entered. Row upon row of bookshelves filled with volumes of many colours and sizes met their appreciative eyes and a bird-like little man, the librarian surely, came towards them with a smile of welcome.

He showed them Persian manuscripts whose exquisite calligraphy recalled for Violet the ancient tombs of Lahore and Hyderabad, and she listened spellbound as Malcolm traced for her the epic tale of Rustam. Then Moghul miniatures, which took her breath away, their cruel cold stylised faces redeemed by the flowers depicted so delicately in the gardens and the brightly plumaged birds in the trees; by the tiny details of the borders and their opulent gold surrounds. Now and then she and Malcolm would laugh over an imagined resemblance to some Baluch chieftain met in years gone by, before falling silent as another page was turned.

At last the librarian left them. They were, please, to remain and explore the contents of the room for as long as they wished, and with a little bow to Violet he fluttered away.

Husband and wife looked at one other and Malcolm was the first to speak. Who would have thought there were so many treasures here—where should they begin to look for more? Violet looked along the shelves then pointed; he reached up obediently and left her with her haul.

'Had enough?' he asked, when at last she came over to where he had been sitting watching her. 'You look as if you've been in your element—' Violet grinned back. She was dishevelled, her face bore a large orange smudge from some old calfskin binding and she was, thought Malcolm, quite enchanting. He stood up and produced his handkerchief. 'There, that's better,' he said at last, kissing the tip of her nose. 'Shall we go to the Adyar Club?'

This time the general did not leave her side. As they moved towards the dining room a familiar voice hailed them, as it had in the Central Railway Station almost a week before. 'Nicolson, I say, Nick! Over here, old man!' It was Norman Stewart with Ada by his side.

'We were just about to take tiffin. You're in time to join us. How are you, my dear?' and turning to Violet Sir Norman planted a kiss on her cheek. Violet was surprised but not at all annoyed; she had not taken long to come to an appreciation of Stewart's kind uncomplicated nature. She included his wife in her answering smile.

'We've had such a wonderful morning, Lady Stewart,' she explained. 'In the library at Huddleston's Gardens.'

Ada Stewart smiled warmly back.

Violet's pleasure in her prawn curry was a little marred by the sight of Eardley Norton, glimpsed through the pillars smoking in the verandah. *If only you don't disappear, Malcolm Nicolson*, she thought, *I shall be all right*. Nicolson, who had also spotted the barrister, had no intention of doing any such thing. He saw no point in putting his wife to any kind of test; he accepted her explanation, and that was that. And he had no wish to embarrass her—or Norton either. So he repulsed Stewart's determined efforts to include him in a four at bridge, and when Ada Stewart saw friends in the distance and made her excuses he settled down contentedly to enjoy an afternoon alone with his wife.

'Excuse me, General Nicolson.' Malcolm looked up at the man standing diffidently by his chair. 'We haven't met,' the stranger said apologetically, 'but I saw you this morning in the library. My name is Francis Grahame.' He turned to Violet with a smile.

'My wife, Mr Grahame,' said Malcolm Nicolson. 'Won't you join us?'

Francis Grahame sat down and began to talk. He was a retired civilian, he explained, and had lived in Madras for the last twenty years. He had seen General Nicolson in the Madras Club on Saturday with Sir Norman Stewart and had hoped to introduce himself, but it had proved impossible in the crush. Then this morning at Huddleston's Gardens he had seen him again and he had been reluctant to impose himself—Mrs Nicolson had been enjoying herself so much. Here he twinkled at Violet. Fortunately, he continued, he had heard their destination and had followed them here.

'You see, Mrs Nicolson,' and the words came tumbling out, 'I do so admire your poetry. And when I realised you were here in Madras, I simply had to meet you and tell you so. I do hope you don't mind, General Nicolson.'

'Not at all,' Malcolm replied affably. 'I'm a great admirer of my wife's work as well. In fact, she's presently preparing a third book—at my request.'

Indeed, Grahame murmured politely; as yet he had been unable to read the second. But he had *Stars of the Desert* on order at Higginbotham's, and they had promised to let him know the minute it arrived. Violet was touched: she didn't often meet a genuine admirer of her poetry.

Mr Grahame spoke again. 'Perhaps I might call when the book arrives, and we might discuss it together?' he shyly suggested. Violet said she would be delighted, explained that they were staying at the Connemara, and Grahame took his leave.

'So, Mrs Nicolson, you've made another conquest in Madras,' her husband remarked as the slightly stooping figure walked away. 'What an agreeable fellow—I'm sure he meant every word he said. Ah, here come the Stewarts.'

Norton was not one of those who stopped by to chat, and as the pleasant afternoon drew to a close everyone felt far too idle to move.

'So convenient to be able to dine here,' said Sir Norman.

'You'll get a chance to see the sunset,' said his wife. Sunsets on the Adyar were unsurpassed, she added, implying that the sunset that night would be the best of its kind—or she would know the reason why!

So, as the sun began to sink in the western sky, Malcolm Nicolson dutifully rose to his feet. With an old world courtesy that met with Lady Stewart's total approval, he offered his arm to his wife and led her to the very seat she had occupied the Monday before, and sat down at her side. The last rowing boat had long since gone when the sun sank out of sight. A chill little wind sprang up off the water. Disappointed, they were about to go in when an orange light appeared in the west. Imperceptibly the colour deepened and changed until the sky had turned to purest rose.

'Ada was right,' Violet whispered after a while. 'It truly is superb—' Malcolm drew her closer. Suddenly a kingfisher swooped, then soared aloft. They watched in silence until the speck of white and black had vanished, then they turned away.

'Be still, my heart, and listen'

Malcolm tossed and turned all night, finding it impossible to settle. Violet became increasingly exasperated as she lay awake beside him. Her repeated enquiries of, 'Are you all right, darling?' or, 'Do you want to talk?' were met either with silence, or an exhortation for her to stop worrying and go back to sleep. Finally she managed to drop off for an hour or so.

When she awoke her husband was already up and dressed, so she flung the mosquito net aside and got out of bed. He looked at her apologetically.

'I'm sorry, Vi,' he said, 'you must have had a rotten night. I simply couldn't get to sleep.'

'I know,' she answered. 'You're worrying about Sunday, aren't you?'

He nodded. 'I suppose it's only natural, but the thing has to be done.'

Violet said nothing. After all, what was there left to say? He had made his determination absolutely clear. 'I think I'll go down and take a turn in the garden,' he added. 'Why don't you dress and join me?'

Malcolm walked gloomily along the garden paths. Yes, he was worried. In fact, although he would never have admitted it to anyone, he was afraid; afraid for the first time for many years—on his own account, that was. He remembered the dreadful hours in Bombay when he had feared for Violet's life, when he had been forced to face up to the appalling possibility that she might die.

His fear this time was different: this time of his own free will he was preparing to place his life in the hands of another. Malcolm Nicolson was no coward, but during the night he had felt a strong temptation to cancel the whole undertaking, despite the subsequent loss of face. He wondered what his reaction would be if Violet tried again to make him change his mind, and he hoped he wouldn't have to find out.

Violet put the finishing touches to her toilette and went out into the verandah. She spotted Malcolm by a great banyan tree, moodily kicking at one of the roots. Then she saw someone walking to join him. Surely that was Mr Norton, dressed for riding?

From her vantage point Violet saw the two men shake hands, exchange a few words, and then turn and look in her direction. Another few words, then her husband began to walk back. She guessed that Norton had come with an invitation to go riding in the cool hours before breakfast when Anglo-India chose to exercise, and she felt nothing but relief. Thank goodness that Malcolm would have something to do this morning other than prowl around like some great caged beast—today Eardley John Norton seemed a blessing sent from heaven!

'Darling, Norton's brought a horse for me. Would you mind very much if I went off for a while?'

Her answer came immediately: 'Go! You'd be frightful company if you stayed.' She softened the words with a kiss. 'I'll go and keep Mr Norton company while you get ready,' she said generously, knowing her husband, usually the most organised of men, hated to rush. 'Take your time, darling. I'm sure I can keep him at bay!'

Violet glanced at Norton's book on the small table where she had tossed it the day before, but did not pick it up. Not today, she thought, when she had reason to be grateful to the man. She checked her hair in the mirror and passed out into the garden. The barrister was strolling to and fro across the lawn as he waited and his face lit up at her approach.

'Why, good morning, Mrs Nicolson. I didn't expect to see you so early.' But he had hoped to, nonetheless.

'Good morning, Mr Norton. My husband won't be long. It's really very good of you to think of him. It will do him no end of good to get out.'

For once Norton could think of little to say. The silence lengthened as she walked beside him, and he was unexpectedly relieved to see the general advancing towards them across the lawns.

Norton found Malcolm Nicolson every bit as silent as his wife. He looked at the older man as they headed down Moubray's Road towards the river. The general's face was tired and preoccupied.

'I'm sorry, Norton,' he said, aware of his companion's glance. 'I'm poor company today; perhaps my wife has warned you?'

'No, indeed,' and Eardley said no more, not wishing to pry, but waiting to see if the man would take him into his confidence. The silence fell again. 'Look, sir,' he said at last in a tone of some concern, 'if there's something worrying you, I do wish you would tell me. Perhaps I could be of service?'

Nicolson looked across at his companion. 'You're very kind,' he said eventually, 'but I wouldn't want to bore you with my problems.'

He was obviously used to keeping his worries to himself, thought the barrister, who was equally used to eliciting the confidences of others. He knew from his considerable experience that it would probably do Nicolson the world of good to talk to an outsider, and accordingly he set about penetrating his defences. So successful was he that the general agreed to stop at Norton's Gardens for breakfast.

When Malcolm was still not back by eight o'clock, Violet grew increasingly concerned. She told herself not to worry, that he was bound to be all right. Hadn't she herself said that the exercise was the very thing he needed? She returned anxiously to the hotel entrance again and again, and when the barrister's carriage at last swept into the drive she flew down the steps to meet it.

'Is anything wrong?' she cried.

Nicolson jumped down nimbly in reply. 'Steady on, darling,' he said, when he saw she was almost in tears. 'Come on, Violet, my little love,' and he smiled apologetically over her head at the barrister. 'Pull yourself together. You'll upset Mr Norton.'

'I'm sorry—it's just that you didn't come back for such ages, and when you did, you came by carriage. I thought—' Violet gave a slightly hysterical laugh.

'Stupid of me *not* to think,' Malcolm said gruffly, his arm still around her. 'Of course you were worried, sweetheart. But I'm fine.'

'I'm so sorry.' She apologised again, this time to Eardley Norton. 'I'm a little overwrought today—perhaps Malcolm has told you about Sunday?'

Norton nodded sympathetically. 'Look, Nicolson,' he said, 'perhaps I should leave now and call back this afternoon. What do you think?'

'Yes, perhaps that would be best.' Malcolm thanked him and took Violet off to their rooms. 'Darling, we have things to discuss when you're feeling better,' he said, once they were inside.

Violet looked at her husband's serious face. 'What things?' she asked immediately.

'I have all my papers with me,' he said. 'I want to go over them with you, and make sure you understand.'

She opened her mouth in protest, but saw it would be of no use. She swallowed and sat down. 'Very well,' she answered meekly. 'Then you'd better show me now!'

Nicolson wasted no time. He went to his portmanteau and produced several buff-coloured envelopes and took out a document from one. 'This you know about already; it's my will. All the debts mentioned here were paid before we left England. The other provisions you haven't seen.'

'Do I need to?'

'No, not if you don't want to.'

He had never forgotten the night in Central India when Violet had made a solemn undertaking in the event of his death. He had made his provisions accordingly, but this was no time or place for excessive emotion and he was thankful for her lack of curiosity.

He replaced the will, and opened another envelope. 'Here are details of the voluntary pension subscriptions I've been making on your behalf since we were married.'

She nodded.

'There's an ordinary pension, too. As my widow,' he affected not to see her flinch at the word and continued in a detached voice, 'you will receive one-hundred-and-twenty pounds per annum and young Malcolm twenty pounds, until he reaches eighteen years of age. It's not a fortune, but with my other expectations—they're all in the will, as well—you should be comfortable enough.'

He refused to look at her, for fear of what he might see. 'My pay goes into an account with Grindlay and Company. You can draw money from the branch on Mount Road, where I've made an arrangement. The details are here—' he tapped another envelope. 'The London branch holds the Life Assurance Policy—it's all made clear in the will.'

Then he saw her frozen face. Quickly he went and knelt beside her. 'My own dearest girl,' he said urgently, taking her cold hands in his, 'I would be failing in my duty and my love if I didn't tell you these things. I *have* to do this, don't you understand?'

'Of course I understand,' she answered fiercely, 'but it isn't easy.'

No, it wasn't easy for either of them, he pointed out. 'Now,' he went on after a moment, 'do you have any questions about anything at all?'

'Good,' he said, when she shook her head. He got to his feet. 'Norton has been more than kind. He's coming here this afternoon and I'm going to show him all this,' and he indicated the papers on the table with a sweep of his hand. 'Should the worst come to the worst—no, no, darling, let me finish—should the worst come to the worst, then he will know what to do and he will advise you. You can trust him to do what is best for you and our son. And Stewart will help, of course. He may not have a great deal of imagination, but he's dependable.'

God in Heaven, thought Violet hysterically, *don't talk as if you were dead already*! She took a deep breath and managed to regain control. 'I understand perfectly,' she said with an obvious effort. 'I shall do as you wish.'

'Good lass,' her husband said in relief. The first of the ordeals he had been dreading was over.

Mrs Nicolson left, looking white and drawn, as soon as Norton arrived. She was going shopping, she said. Not that she wanted to, she added with a tight little smile, but it would give her something to do while they were busy. Norton gazed after her with some concern and turned to her husband with a question in his eyes.

'I'm afraid she's extremely upset by the talk we had this morning,' Nicolson explained. 'She doesn't realise that this is simply a precaution.'

'A very wise one,' murmured the lawyer. 'Far too many people tend to ignore these things—and end up making the fortunes of people like me!' The two men settled down to business with a laugh.

It was a pensive Eardley Norton who returned to his home later that afternoon. He was a fool, he acknowledged, and he had made the mistake that he supposed others had made before him—that of assuming Malcolm and Violet Nicolson to be an ill-matched couple. The disparity in age was obvious; there must be a good twenty years between the general and his vivacious young-looking wife. But they had been married for fifteen years and anyone could see the marriage was still sound. The man was full of love and concern for his wife, and that she returned his love—and was still in love with him—any idiot could see, even if it took some of them longer than others!

'So sweet it was in the Times that Were'

When the Stewarts invited them to dine with them at Dunmore House, Violet wanted to refuse but Malcolm insisted. 'I know you're tired but a change of scene will do us both good. Hotels are all very well, but they're never the same, are they? Come on, darling—we'll enjoy it.'

Their hosts were so pleased to see them that perhaps, thought Violet, the effort had been worthwhile, after all. During the meal Malcolm regaled his friends with stories of Violet's adventures in Baluchistan, which to the Stewarts had only been rumours.

Norman Stewart studied each of the faces in turn: his own wife, giving the raconteur her full attention, hardly daring to believe her ears; Violet, looking quite lovely as she laughed at her husband's sallies; and Nick himself, his face alight with humour, his long fingers disposing of the cruets to emphasise some point in his story. Now and again the couple's eyes would meet and a silence would fall as they remembered. Then the merry voice drawled on, interrupted by Violet's frequent protests of 'Please don't believe him—Malcolm, tell them it wasn't like that at all!' Ignoring her interventions, Nicolson would only laugh and cap one unlikely tale with another, and then move on to equally improbable tales of Malabar.

Later Lady Stewart, who was unwilling to see the evening come to an end, suggested a game of bridge.

'No, no, never bridge, I beg you, Ada!' Nicolson exclaimed in mock horror. 'Violet has absolutely no understanding at all of bidding and has a quite devastating effect on any rubber she ever plays—isn't that so, darling?'

He turned to Violet who this time made no protest. 'I'm afraid it's absolutely true,' she admitted. 'But I do think I'm a little better at whist.'

Nicolson agreed that perhaps they might risk whist instead, so Sir Norman and Violet found themselves paired against the sharp wits of the others. Stewart proved the perfect partner. He gallantly covered up for Violet's mistakes and refused to let her ineptitude annoy him. It wasn't a question of ability, Sir Norman soon realised—Nick's wife was simply incapable of taking the game seriously. He watched her carelessly discard card after card, but what did it matter? He found his partner's insouciance delightful. It all ended in laughing disorder, with Nicolson apologising for his flushed and sleepy wife and taking her back to the Connemara Hotel.

'Never again,' he groaned, as he closed the door behind them. 'Poor Stewart—when you trumped his ace I thought he was going to have a fit! You are the most abominable player I have ever seen!'

'I know, I know,' she said, 'and I don't suppose they'll ever ask us to play again. But wasn't it fun?'

And it had quite taken their minds off what lay ahead.

'Will you be able to sleep tonight, do you think?' Violet went to a drawer in her dressing table and took out the pretty papier mâché box they had found in Kashmir. 'Would one of these help, do you think?'

Malcolm looked at the contents. 'Good God, Violet,' he exclaimed, 'you've enough opium there to finish off an army! How long have you had all that?'

'I'm not sure. I've always kept some for your fevers, and I suppose I was afraid of running out. I stocked up before we left Mhow, just in case.'

'You certainly did, but I won't be needing any tonight, neither will you!'

Around three in the morning Malcolm Nicolson woke briefly. Beside him Violet was muttering in her sleep. The moon was high over the gardens and a shaft of light played on the pillows beside him, turning her loosened hair to palest gold. After the operation was over, he promised himself, they would begin anew. There would be no further selfishness on his part, no more neglect. He would show her how much she meant to him, more than life itself. With infinite tenderness Malcolm Nicolson drew Violet closer to him, and drifted back into sleep.

'Fate Knows no Tears'

The moment of parting came later the following afternoon at Mackay's Gardens. 'You must go now, sweetheart,' Malcolm said with difficulty. 'I don't want you walking back to the hotel in the dark.'

'Let me stay a little longer,' Violet pleaded and she clung to him. 'Malcolm, please—I can't, not yet.'

'Silly girl,' he said, stroking her hair. 'Of course you must go. Oh, sweetheart, don't cry. Smile for me—please.' With a visible effort she blinked her tears away and forced a tremulous smile to her lips.

'That's better,' he said. 'Now remember, darling, I want yours to be the first face I see tomorrow morning when I wake up. Promise me, now.'

Violet nodded her head and her lip began to quiver. Nicolson kissed her on the brow, then on the lips. He hugged her, and with difficulty made himself take her to the door.

'Don't come down,' she said resolutely, 'I'll be all right.' She reached up and briefly touched his cheek. 'I love you,' she whispered once and was gone.

The staff of the nursing home was up and about early next morning. Miss Jones checked the operating room. Everything was in order; someone had even brought the chloroform bottle in readiness. Good, she thought. That would save her from struggling with the heavy winchester in the downstairs store. She placed the light green bottle on the table beside the narrow bed, alongside the surgical instruments meticulously prepared by Dr Blackett himself, and went to tell him that everything was ready.

Malcolm Nicolson's wife was awake early as well. She walked restlessly in the hotel garden for a while and wandered towards the shrubbery, a haven for jays, golden orioles and the vivid parakeets she loved. She startled them as she approached but not for long; the preoccupied woman presented no threat and they took up their song once more. Violet found she had no appetite for breakfast. She tried to pass the time in reading, but found herself walking down Mount Road and into Mackay's Gardens sooner than she intended.

She rang the bell. When no one came in answer she pushed the door and went in. On the ground floor all was quiet. She crossed the hall to the stairs and put her foot on the bottom tread. She hesitated. Should she perhaps wait a little longer? The operation should be over by now, so Violet made up her mind and continued.

She found her way to Malcolm's room. It was empty. She went out again and looked up and down the corridor. As she hovered indecisively, wondering in which direction to go, and thinking she should perhaps go downstairs and ring the bell again, she saw Dr Blackett emerge from a room a little way ahead. With a sigh of relief she hurried forward to greet him.

When she reached him she was shocked at his appearance. He was ashen-faced and beads of sweat stood out on his brow.

'Mrs Nicolson,' was all he said. His voice was barely audible.

'My husband?' asked Violet, moving towards the room the doctor had just left.

'No, no,' he said, and his voice was a little stronger, 'don't go in. You must not go in. We're—we're not ready for you—'

But Violet pushed past the arm intended to detain her. A nurse was busy putting some semblance of order to the sheets on the bed where Malcolm was lying asleep. She looked up and Violet recognised her. Miss Jones gave a gasp and hurried forward, taking her back to the door.

'I'm so sorry, Mrs Nicolson,' she said in a broken whisper, 'we did all we could. There just wasn't enough oxygen.'

'What do you mean—there wasn't enough oxygen? What are you talking about?' Violet's relentless fingers in the woman's arm made her wince with pain. 'If you need more oxygen, then get it! Or tell me where to go and I will!'

She turned to Dr Blackett who was now standing beside her. 'Where shall I go—a chemist's, a hospital? *For God's sake tell me!*' Her voice was shrill in its urgency.

'I'm afraid you don't understand, Mrs Nicolson.' Blackett forced himself to stay calm. 'There is nothing you or anyone else can do. General Nicolson died some time before you arrived.'

Violet rushed back into the room, but as she neared the bed she stopped in horror. She looked at Malcolm and even as she watched he seemed to change; before her shocked eyes the living colour was fading from his face.

She threw herself down by his side and gripped his shoulders, pressing her head to his breast, but try as she might she could detect no heart beat. She drew back and looked at his face again. There could be no doubt: Malcolm Nicolson's life was over.

General Stewart reached Mackay's Gardens Nursing Home thirty minutes later in prompt response to the terse note saying that his friend was dead. He had told his wife to stay at home.

'Wait here, my love,' he said in a voice made even gruffer by shock. 'She'll need you later, but I think it best that I go alone. I'll bring her back to you as soon as I can.'

The staff was not communicative, and Dr Blackett was nowhere to be seen. Stewart went upstairs, and found Violet still kneeling motionless by the bed, holding her husband's lifeless hand in hers and gazing into his face.

'We can't move her,' said Miss Jones. 'We've tried but she insists her place is by his side. Oh sir, I don't know what to do.' The dark eyes that met Stewart's were full of tears.

'All right, my dear,' he said. 'Leave this to me. Her husband and I are—that is, we were—old friends.' Sir Norman cleared his throat noisily.

Gratefully, the nurse left him to his task and Stewart looked down at the dead man's face. It was calm and absolutely at peace. Right, he vowed, later he would find out exactly what went wrong. At present, the living needed him more.

'Violet,' he used her name for the first time. '*Violet*—'

After what seemed an interminable age she looked at him, her eyes larger than ever in her white and haggard face. 'He's dead, Sir Norman,' she said. 'Malcolm is dead,' and she turned back to the bed.

'Now, my dear,' Stewart's voice was kindly but firm. 'We need to leave him for a little while. You can come back to him later.'

As he hoped, Violet Nicolson responded to the voice of quiet authority. She let him help her to her feet and support her, until the circulation returned to her cramped limbs and she could walk.

'No, no—he'll be all right till we come back,' the calm voice assured her, and at last Stewart was able to draw the unwilling woman from the room. He told the waiting nurse that they would be taking a little turn in the garden. 'We'll be back to see the general in a little while—you understand?' and a relieved Miss Jones nodded.

'I'll come and tell you when we're ready, sir,' she promised, and hurried off to find Dr Blackett.

Violet Nicolson couldn't think and couldn't feel. Her whole being was numb with shock. All she knew was that last night Malcolm had been alive and this morning he was dead. He had left her.

Norman Stewart walked with her in the garden, saying nothing and with his arm around her. It was impossible to believe what had happened. Nick had been so fit, active and full of life. And now he was gone. He looked at Violet. Poor little lady, so ill-prepared for widowhood. What would she do? I must get her back to Dunmore House and Ada, he thought. Once the shock passes, she'll need another woman. And there's the funeral to organise—it'll have to be tomorrow, I suppose.

Shaking his head, he tightened his grip on Violet's shoulders as the only comfort he could think to give.

She hardly noticed as Miss Jones came hurrying across the grass towards them. 'We can go to your husband now,' Sir Norman told her. 'Come this way, Violet, my dear.'

Malcolm Nicolson was back in his room. The bamboo screens were down and stirring slightly in the remains of the morning breeze and the room was cool. The dead man's features seemed carved from stone as he lay in fresh white sheets with his hands crossed on his chest. Stewart thought of the fine sensitive fingers so full of life only two days before, and the animated face laughing over dinner.

He stood back and let Violet go in alone. There was a chair by the bed and she resumed her place by the body.

This is my husband. My husband is dead. The words repeated themselves relentlessly in her brain, but even when Stewart came to fetch her their meaning failed to sink in.

'Say goodbye, Violet. We have to leave him now,' said the gentle voice. Her lips formed a silent plea of *no, not yet*, but Norman Stewart was adamant. 'Say goodbye to him, my dear,' he repeated.

So Violet Nicolson took one last look at the man who had given her life its meaning for so many years. Would she never see him again? She reached forward and touched his cheek, and then she allowed Malcolm's friend to take her from the room.

12

'I, who am strange to tears'

MADRAS: 8 AUGUST—4 OCTOBER 1904

The news spread through Madras like wildfire. The accounts varied greatly, from the factual (in so far as the facts were known, that is) to the sensational, but they all agreed on one point: Nicolson of Baluchistan was dead.

Those who expected Norman Stewart to clarify the details looked for him in vain. General Stewart had abandoned the clubrooms, and was busy arranging his friend's funeral and seeing to his wife.

Not that he was able to do much for Nicolson's widow. Violet sat in the drawing room at Dunmore House, pleating the folds of her dress mindlessly or twisting her handkerchief through her fingers, and always staring towards the door. In the face of such muted grief both Stewarts felt totally helpless.

'It's as if she expects Nick to walk in at any moment,' Ada Stewart whispered. 'I can't bear it. If only she would cry.' But the tears refused to come.

Of course she would go to the funeral, Violet told Stewart. Malcolm would expect his wife to be there and she would not fail him. Would Sir Norman please send for a *dhirzi*—she had nothing black to wear. To someone who had expected hysterics at the very least, this show of total calm was unnerving. In relaying the conversation to his wife some time later, Sir Norman said as much.

When Lady Stewart learned of Violet's stated intention, her voice was raised in anxious protest. 'Never mind the tailor, Norman; I really don't see how you can expect her to be there! Are you quite sure she realises what's involved? It won't be some quiet family affair, after all, and you know how she values her privacy. I can't imagine she'll want any part of it—and remember, if she gets caught up in it, there'll be no escape!'

Stewart's face grew increasingly serious as he listened to his wife's arguments, and he readily admitted she was right. He would explain it all to Violet right away, he said.

Before he could carry out his intention Eardley Norton arrived on horseback and sent in his card. Perhaps Mrs Nicolson would receive him—if she felt able. Otherwise he would return another day.

Mrs Nicolson was quite prepared to see him, came the answer, and Norton made his way into the drawing room. Violet was standing in the centre and he was struck by how very small she looked. She invited him to sit and then sat down opposite. Her hands clasped in her lap, she waited quietly for him to speak.

She was very composed, was his first thought. She was far too composed, was the second; she must still be in a state of very deep shock. He cleared his throat with difficulty and began.

'I was so sorry to hear about General Nicolson,' he said.

Violet looked at him with leaden gaze. Her voice, as she thanked him for his kindness, was low and dull. Was there anything he could do for her? Norton asked.

Thank you, but no. No one could do a thing.

Later, he said, there would be matters for them to discuss—of a legal nature.

Of course, she replied. He should come again—after the funeral. She would see to everything—after the funeral.

It seemed to Norton that she could see no further than what was to happen later that day. As if she were clinging to the fact that her husband would be with her until then; that until then she was still part of him, and he of her. How would she feel, he wondered, once the realisation struck her that from now on she would be alone—horribly alone. How old was she? He didn't know exactly, but she could live for as many years again.

'How is she?' Stewart asked when he met Norton on his way out.

Norton shook his head. 'I don't think she fully understands what has happened. When she does, it will be dreadful. Look, Stewart, she can't possibly put herself on show.'

Stewart nodded gloomily. 'You're right. Ada thinks so, too. But will *she* agree? I'll see what I can do.'

When at five-fifteen that afternoon the firing party lined up in front of Mackay's Gardens and the mourners, bearers and pallbearers went inside, the widow was not to be seen. Shortly afterwards the mortal remains of Malcolm Nicolson were brought out, placed on a gun carriage and covered with the Union Flag. The firing party presented arms, the officers saluted and the general's last journey began.

In the short time available to him, Norman Stewart had managed to do his late friend proud. The procession was headed by the wing of the 1st Leicester

Regiment and No. 52 Company of the Royal Garrison Artillery with their full complement of officers. The gun carriage, provided by the Royal Artillery at St Thomas's Mount and drawn by seven horses, followed. A number of military officers, including Stewart and his successor, marched behind the coffin. But there was one thing Sir Norman Stewart hadn't been able to manage: the cortege made its solemn way towards The Island with no accompanying music. The Leicesters' band was absent in Bellary, and Lieutenant General Malcolm Hassells Nicolson—who in life had so loved the sound of the bagpipes—was taken to his final resting place in heart-rending silence.

'Here on the Island of my Desolation'

Up Mount Road went the cortege, with only the rhythm of footfalls and the clinking of harness to mark the passing of the dead. Trust Norton to come up with the answer, thought Norman Stewart who was finding the whole business quite unnerving, and thank God Violet had finally agreed to go directly to the cemetery with him and Ada! Thirteen minute-guns were to be fired from the ramparts of the Fort when the procession reached Government House Bridge, and this would serve as a signal to Norton to take the women in. The first gun fired and General Stewart heaved a mighty sigh of relief.

When the procession halted at the mock-Gothic gates of St Mary's cemetery, Violet and her companions had been waiting at the graveside for ten minutes. During that time Violet had not spoken. Dressed in the severest of mourning, she simply looked straight ahead at the gaping wound in the rich red earth. 'They're here,' said Eardley Norton. He was standing to Violet's left, and Lady Stewart to her right. The orders to 'inwards turn' and 'rest on arms reversed' came to them clearly, before the gun carriage passed slowly through the ranks and the six non-commissioned officers appointed to the task stepped forward. They raised the coffin to their shoulders, the flag was removed and the garrison chaplain led the way to the grave.

Violet gave a sharp intake of breath when the coffin came into sight, but she still said nothing, and she did not move as the troops lined up and the committal service began.

Neither of Violet's two companions took in much, if anything, of the eulogy or the prayers that followed. They were too intent on Violet. She stood motionless between them, apparently hearing nothing—until the coffin was lowered into the ground and the handful of earth thrown by Sir Norman rattled down on its lid. Then she took a sudden step forward. The first of a further thirteen guns sounded from the Fort as Eardley Norton gripped her arm and pulled her back. 'No, Violet, dear, no!'

He held her until the gunfire faded, but she made no further movement until the Last Post pierced the sudden silence round the grave. Then memory struck, sharp as any sword. Recalling other bugles of long ago, she began to tremble. In a rare moment of helplessness Norton sent a silent appeal to Lady Stewart who proved equal to the occasion. Relentless fingernails digging into tender flesh kept hysteria at bay, and only when the troops had cleared the cemetery did the resourceful Ada release her charge.

Violet again moved forward and this time they did not stop her. She stood at the foot of the grave, looking down. *Is this how it all must end? We loved each other so much, you and I; how could you leave me? How can I let you go?*

Malcolm would never hold her again, in comfort or in love. At last she understood. It was over and she was alone. The bitter tears so long denied at last were flowing, and Violet sank to the earth in despair.

This time Ada Stewart, herself overcome by the sight of such total misery, could do nothing. It was left to Eardley Norton to raise the grieving woman to her feet and hold her in silent compassion until the storm of sobs should pass. At last he let her go. She took his proffered handkerchief with murmured thanks and he turned to his other companion, whose eyes were red but who was once more in command.

'Say goodbye to him now, Violet dear,' Lady Stewart said in an unconscious echo of Sir Norman's words the day before, and again Violet Nicolson obeyed. Her lips moved silently as she looked down at her husband's coffin. Again it proved too much, and Eardley Norton, visibly overcome himself, half led, half carried her to the waiting vehicle.

At Dunmore House they sent for a doctor.

'Let Mrs Nicolson cry,' was all he said. Norton opened his mouth to protest. 'I don't mean to be callous,' the man explained, 'although it must seem so. In my experience, the more crying she does, the more exhausted she'll be. And then she'll sleep. And once she sleeps, she'll be on the way to recovery.'

Norton doubted it, but he did not feel up to arguing with such heartless logic. He was exhausted and so were the occupants of Dunmore House.

For the widow's grief appeared to have no bounds. Curled up on her bed, she hugged her pillow for comfort like a child, while Ada sat watching. At last the hacking sobs died away into silence and Ada returned to the drawing room.

'She's sleeping,' she announced. 'But I don't know for how long. Oh dear, I feel so very helpless.' She looked from her husband to the barrister and was shocked by what she saw. 'I'd ask you to join us for dinner, Mr Norton, but you really look as if you'd be better off in bed yourself!'

Norton managed a travesty of a laugh. 'You're quite right, as usual, Lady Stewart! It's been a distressing few hours for us all, so I'll be off. I'll call tomorrow, if I may.'

As he was leaving he turned and said, 'I know you'll take good care of her. Goodnight.'

'What a strange man,' Sir Norman's wife observed afterwards. 'To see him in court you'd think the man was a monster of arrogance, and quite unfeeling, to boot. But today at the cemetery he was so gentle with her, and so patient. I cannot understand it.'

From the depths of an armchair, where he was achieving the seemingly impossible by nursing his aching feet and a much-needed whisky at one and the same time, Sir Norman answered. 'Can't you, Ada?' he said wearily. 'Why, the man's in love with her—has been ever since he first saw her. I should have thought it was as plain as the nose on your face.'

'Heart, my heart, the journey is done'

After the funeral the Stewarts tried to discuss her future with their guest, a future in which she showed scant interest. What would she do now? they wanted to know. They were happy to give her a home for as long as they were in Madras, of course, and they could delay their departure a little. Would she sail with them at the beginning of October—to England, to her son?

Try as they might, Violet's reply was always the same: 'Later—I'll think about it later.'

'Don't keep pressing her,' Sir Norman told his wife. 'She'll end up by saying no, and then you'll never get her to change her mind!'

Lady Stewart looked at him earnestly. In the weeks following Malcolm Nicolson's death he continued to surprise her, and she found herself increasingly deferring to his judgement. 'Do you really think so?' she asked.

'Yes I do. Leave her be, Ada. There's plenty of time—let her get over the shock.'

So they left Violet to spend most of her time in the garden where, in the cool of the evening, she would wander from tree to tree like some forlorn disembodied ghost until the sunset faded. Then Ada would coax her inside to sit with them in the drawing room until it was time for bed.

She asked her if she would like another room, thinking she might sleep more easily elsewhere. 'I should have known better than make such a suggestion,' she told her husband afterwards, when her guest had politely but firmly refused. Violet Nicolson had no intention of abandoning the bed where she and her husband had slept together and if memories threatened at times to drive her mad, then sobeit. There she would stay.

Eardley Norton became a frequent visitor to Dunmore House. He returned the day after the funeral to see how Mrs Nicolson fared, but waited for a week before mentioning the general's affairs to his widow. He, too, was met with vague replies to suggestions that they begin to put things into some kind of order. But, unlike the Stewarts, he persisted, and hit upon the magical formula of preceding everything with *Now, Violet, this is what Malcolm wanted.* And then she would listen.

The earlier formality between them had gone. After his kindness it seemed natural that he should call her by the name that Malcolm had given her all those years ago. And she was finding it easier to address the barrister not always as 'Mr Norton', but more frequently as 'Eardley'.

'Do you think it wise for the man to spend so much time with her alone?' Ada Stewart asked her husband in the beginning. 'Especially if what you tell me is true?'

'Can't see any harm in it at all,' grunted Sir Norman. 'She's perfectly safe with him; why, he's devoted to her. All he wants is to help in any way he can. Nick trusted him, after all, and *he* was nobody's fool.'

His wife sniffed. 'And what about Marie Norton? What will she think?'

'She's not due back from Europe for months and we'll all be gone by then. Look, my dear, all Violet wants is Nick—I don't imagine she'll ever look at another man. I know you always thought her flighty, but you have to admit that events have proved you wrong.'

'Yes, I was wrong, quite wrong.' After her unusual admission Ada Stewart looked at her husband with tears in her eyes. 'I've grown so fond of her, Norman. If only there were something we could do.'

Stewart was quite right. When Eardley Norton looked at Violet Nicolson these days, at the pale face in which the dark eyes seemed preternaturally large, she appeared absolutely sexless. Like some mediaeval lady who has taken vows at the death of her lord, he thought, and he mocked himself for his flight of fancy; and I her knight, to serve her faithfully till death, with no hope of earthly reward—unless one day I can hear her laugh again. And that, he admitted, seemed a forlorn hope indeed.

One day, when they walked together in the grounds of Dunmore House, she told him of how she had walked in another garden early on the morning Malcolm died, and how she remembered every blue jay, golden oriole and green parrot that had flown overhead. 'But now,' she said, with the sad little smile that always tore at his heart, 'the colours have all gone. They seem dark and dull, and even the flowers have lost their fragrance. When I lost Malcolm, I lost India too. What is there left for me, Eardley? Tell me, what is there left?'

Later they looked at the general's will together. Norton had had to persuade her, but now she listened thoughtfully while the barrister commented on the points he thought of most importance. 'Malcolm has bequeathed the sum of sixty pounds to his sisters towards your son's expenses over the coming year, but that won't be necessary, will it, Violet? You'll be going home soon. Going home to your son.'

A little smile played about her lips, but she said nothing.

'Malcolm leaves everything else to you, with remainder to your son.' Here he paused and looked at her again. The smile was still there.

He now came to the section that he had thought unusual when he had first seen the document. 'You will have plenty of support,' he observed, before handing her a list of five people Nicolson had appointed as co-guardians to their child.

'Yes, Malcolm seems to have thought of everything,' Violet murmured, as she scanned the paper. She read the names out loud: '*Miss Mary Nicolson, Miss Caroline Nicolson, Mrs Henry Steel, Major Arthur Legge, Col. Alfred Sinclair* ... I didn't know about this, Eardley, but Malcolm was always so thorough in everything he did. In fact,' she remarked, 'it's almost as if he thought I needn't be here at all.'

Norton watched the smile deepen until it reached her eyes.

'I keep your memory near my heart'

'I really do think it's time Violet pulled herself together.' Ada Stewart looked at her husband in some annoyance. 'Why, she won't even discuss Nick's tombstone! The man has been dead and buried for two weeks now, and the grave is still unmarked—and likely to remain so, if you ask my opinion.'

General Stewart said nothing. From a long experience going back almost thirty years he knew that his wife's opinions were always freely given and need never be requested.

'It's not *Christian*,' Ada continued. 'I've tried to get her interested, and do you know what she said?' She paused and Stewart waited for the enlightenment he knew would follow. 'She said that *she* knew where he was and *that* was all that mattered!'

'Well, she does have a point, you know,' Sir Norman countered. 'But you think everyone else might think it lacks respect. Is that it?'

'Precisely!' agreed his wife. 'So what are *you* going to do about it?' she asked, as she gladly passed the thorny problem on.

⁂

Eardley Norton, too, was concerned about Violet Nicolson. She was doing herself no good by wandering around all day, refusing to talk about the future and doing nothing but dwell on the past. He cast around for a solution to something that would only get worse if unaddressed. Violet must be given some aim—but what?

Then he recalled something Ada Stewart had said a few days earlier, when at her wits' end and exasperated with both Violet and Sir Norman; something to do with Malcolm Nicolson's grave. And he thought of a touching encounter he had had only the day before. Yes, thought Eardley Norton, yes, perhaps it would serve.

'I met an admirer of yours yesterday,' he said casually, when he called at Dunmore House.

'Oh?' Violet wasn't interested but Norton told her nonetheless.

'Yes. A retired civil servant called Francis Grahame. He said he'd had quite a talk with you and Malcolm one day in the Adyar Club. Perhaps you remember him?'

'Why, yes,' she said, with a little more interest, 'I do remember,' and she pictured the stooped elderly man who had introduced himself so diffidently, and whom Malcolm had said he liked.

'Mr Grahame was so sorry to hear of your husband's death,' Eardley continued. 'He said he had asked to call, to discuss your poetry with you'—here Violet made an impatient gesture with her hand—'and regretted that, of course, this was no longer possible.'

No, she agreed flatly, it was not; her poetry was totally irrelevant these days.

Norton, however, was not so easily deterred. 'Mr Grahame said how proud your husband was of your work; that you were preparing a third book of poetry at Malcolm's request—'

He watched her face brighten at the mention of Nicolson's interest. 'He said he thought how very much Malcolm had been looking forward to its publication,' and the barrister hid his satisfaction as Violet rose to the bait.

'Why, yes,' she said, 'how strange! I had quite forgotten, and yet we talked about the book so often. I'd even started on it here. Malcolm—' the word as she said it was like a caress, 'Malcolm would want me to finish it.'

Norton breathed a sigh of relief. Perhaps this would prove to be the turning point, he thought, as a little light returned to Violet's eyes.

'I must finish it, Eardley, don't you think?'

Norton nodded. 'And perhaps Mr Grahame might call, after all?' he suggested. 'He seems such a pleasant man.'

'Yes, yes,' she said instantly, 'I should like that.'

❧

So in the unlikely person of W. Francis Grahame, ICS (retired), a second *parfit gentil knight* came into the widow's life. At last Grahame felt able to produce his copy of *Stars of the Desert* (collected from Higginbotham's some weeks earlier), and he asked Violet to read from it. He became a frequent and welcome visitor, and between them he and Norton pulled her back from the brink of self-destruction. The work on the third volume was resumed, and as interest returned to her life, so did the colour to her cheeks.

But first she gave herself one other task, although once again she failed to suspect Norton's hand in her decision. For he never told her of Grahame's sad comment to him at the end of their first meeting, but encouraged the retired civil servant to tell her for himself.

'Violet, my dear,' Francis Grahame said one day, 'I went to The Island recently, to pay my respects at General Nicolson's grave. I hope you don't mind?'

She smiled. 'Mr Grahame, of course I don't mind!'

'Well, you see, my dear, I had such great difficulty in finding him—it was such a hot day, too. I'm afraid I had to give up and I was so very disappointed.'

Violet felt a pang of guilt at the thought of this dear old man wandering through the cemetery on a fruitless search for an unmarked grave. A week later Malcolm Nicolson had his headstone.

'Turn sleep to Death in some mysterious way'

The letters of condolence began to arrive. Her family—and his—asked when she was coming home. Heneage, asking the same, made no mention of Malcolm's letter. He was right, of course, thought his niece. With Malcolm dead, the golden dream was over.

The pert, fluffy-haired woman who had intercepted that letter, and read it with a derisive laugh before consigning it to the flames, wrote to her widowed sister not at all.

Flora Steel sent an irritatingly self-centred missive in which she lamented the long-standing friendship so tragically brought to a close. When would Violet be home? she asked. They had so much to talk about, so many memories of Malcolm to share. Violet answered the letter dutifully, and then destroyed it.

Mrs Crackanthorpe endeavoured over many pages to help her friend through what she called *these sad dark days*. Have courage, she exhorted. The day would come when she would be reunited with her loved one in the next world, but meantime she must live on in this—live for the sake of her child, and *for herself*.

You see, my dear, Blanche wrote in conclusion, *you have so much to live for*. Violet disagreed, but answered the letter—as she had all the others—briefly. She would be writing again soon, she promised, and at far greater length.

And Isabel … Isabel, stoically coming to terms with her own tragic loss, told her sister to do the same. She must come to Karachi as soon as she was able, Isabel urged, and not stay brooding in Madras where she could change nothing … Had her sister meant to be so blunt? It hardly mattered. *No*, Violet replied, *I don't intend to stay here much longer but, as you yourself once said, Karachi holds too many memories. So I won't be coming, even to visit. Don't worry about me, Izzie. I shall be all right.*

And so the weeks went by. Violet worked daily on what she never failed to call 'Malcolm's Book' and September drew to a close. Eardley Norton and Francis Grahame continued their regular visits, separately and sometimes together. They showed interest in her work always, but now and again a silence would fall and they knew she was far away. As the book neared completion Norton felt an almost overwhelming dread.

It seemed to him that Violet was more depressed and more inward looking with the conclusion of each day. Hint as he might, she would not confide in him and he refused to pry. Grahame, less scrupulous perhaps, or using the privilege conferred by age, managed to find the answer. 'For some reason or other,' he told the younger man, 'she's started to blame herself for General Nicolson's death. I don't know why, but there it is. And she's not sleeping either.'

That was obvious. The dark shadows had returned and the face had taken on a deathly pallor. After Grahame's revelation Norton confronted her. 'Violet, you're being quite ridiculous. How could you possibly be responsible?'

She raised her weary face and she expressed her relentless logic in a voice devoid of all emotion. 'If I had insisted, he wouldn't have had the operation and he would be alive today. I killed him.'

'Violet, that's utter nonsense *and you know it*. Malcolm needed surgery—why, without the operation his condition would have worsened. He would have been in great pain and he might have died. Yes, the operation was risky perhaps, but it was a risk he was prepared to take—he told me so.

'Tragically, he failed to recover from the anaesthetic—because they'd given him too much of the stuff. If you really must blame someone, don't blame yourself, blame the doctor, blame the staff!' Norton paused, but his words had no effect.

⁂

When Sir Norman visited Mackay's Gardens after the funeral he found Blackett and his staff both furtive and unhelpful. He had drawn his own conclusions from their behaviour and shared them with Eardley Norton—who in turn shared them with the dead man's widow. Both men, in fact, were right in apportioning blame to the nursing home, but for all the wrong reasons.

The patient had survived the surgery. The amount of anaesthetic had been correct, and Nicolson should easily have regained consciousness. It was a combination of carelessness, laziness, bad luck and sunlight that did for Malcolm Nicolson. The light-coloured bottle of chloroform used for the operation had been sitting near the windowsill for days, and the slow build-up of phosgene gas within it rendered it deadly. No man, however strong his heart or his will to live, could ever have survived.

Miss Jones, who had been so happy to save herself some trouble, may or may not have realised her mistake; Dr Blackett most probably suspected. But no one explained the facts to Violet, for no one outside the nursing home knew anything about them. And so Malcolm Nicolson's widow—reproaching herself bitterly for her husband's death—moved inexorably towards her rendezvous with Fate.

'Love has no future, but to die'

The Stewarts' last week in Madras was exceptionally busy. The governor was down from 'Ooty', and with his return the social season was under way with a swing. Everyone wished to say goodbye to the couple and Violet was often left to her own devices. It meant that for a short time she was free—free of Ada's incessant enquiries as to whether she was intending to accompany them, free of kind Sir Norman's own entreaties added at long last to those of his wife. *God in Heaven, would they never leave her alone?* In the end, to silence them, she had implied that she would be leaving India too, and allowed most of her few belongings to be packed in readiness. But she could still feel the Stewarts watching her, and wondering.

But they could not watch her all the time. The nights were the worst, when they saw the quiet, uncomplaining little figure take herself off to her lonely bed, and it was with relief that they saw her reappear each morning. She refused absolutely to accompany them to engagements where she would have been welcome, pleading, not bereavement, but the necessity of putting the finishing touches to Malcolm's book.

And this to some degree was true. Her decision to dedicate the book to her husband meant that the sorrowful outpourings—scribbled down in those desolate days when she had first begun to blame herself for his death—must be revised and polished to be worthy of him.

The Stewarts went out that afternoon of Monday the third of October, allowing Violet to finish writing out a second copy of the poem that brought the book to its conclusion. 'Vayu the Wind' was her recognition of everything India had brought her, as girl and woman, in life and in love. As well as making a fitting end to the volume, the poem would be her farewell. As Violet read it through, her lips curved in a reminiscent smile. The pictures she had conjured up brought a distant look to her eyes, and she sat with her memories for company until Mr Grahame arrived at Dunmore House a little after three.

He was surprised when Violet produced a sheet of paper that she pronounced to be her will and asked him to be a witness. He didn't ask why Norton hadn't taken care of it for her, although he did think it strange. It was a sudden impulse, he decided, to cover herself for her journey tomorrow. For he, unlike the Stewarts, was sure she would return to England. At her request he fetched the *khitmatgar*, and they wrote their signatures under hers at the foot of the paper. She thanked them both, put the paper to one side, and seemed to forget about it.

They spent a pleasant hour together. The manuscript was ready, she told him, and she would arrange for him to receive a copy of the book. She told him a little of the first appearance of *The Garden of Kama* and the excitement she had felt at seeing her poetry in print. It had opened a new world for her, she said; why, she had even met Thomas Hardy! And Malcolm had met him too ... Grahame, a great admirer of the writer, wanted to know more, and Violet became almost animated as she talked of Hardy's work and fetched the book the poet had given her. She read to him from it, and when he rose reluctantly to go she pressed it into his hands.

'Dear Francis,' she said, 'please take it. Keep it in memory of me when I'm gone.'

He might not have thought that odd—after all, she was sailing for England the following day—but the strange little smile that accompanied the gift and the words she murmured so low as he took his leave brought a sudden fear to the old man's heart. For she had quoted Hardy: 'I am *the vane that cankers on its point*, Francis. Like it, my direction is fixed, and I have no further need of the *Wessex Poems*.'

Norton met him at the end of the drive. 'How is she today?' he asked.

'I'm not sure, Eardley. In good spirits outwardly, I suppose. But that's strange in itself, wouldn't you say?' Grahame did not share his fears, which were beginning to seem far-fetched, but he did tell Norton that Violet had made her will. The barrister frowned, quickly said goodbye and hurried up to the house.

He found Violet in the upstairs verandah where Grahame had left her. She sent for tea and as she poured for them he thought how very composed she was looking. 'I've finished,' she announced, almost happily, 'just this morning. Would you like to see the final poem? I've made a copy—I thought you might like to keep it.'

He took the paper held out to him and read it silently. When he had finished, he looked at her long and hard.

'It's very fine,' he said, 'but do you mean this?'

Her eyes, beautiful still, and serene, held his. 'I do.'

And then Eardley John Norton, who had graced the High Court of Madras for years and held many a jury spellbound with the sharpness of his intellect and the sonorous eloquence of his voice, began his fight to convince Violet Nicolson of her need to live. And failed.

'You have a child and a family to go to. Violet, my dearest woman, you are young. You have no right to throw your life away!'

'Eardley, dear friend, I have every right.' Her head was high, her gaze almost mocking.

'All this will pass, this despair, this bitter grief—if only you will give yourself time!'

'Ah, yes, *time*—but the Stewarts leave tomorrow. *And I have no intention of going with them*!'

'Then stay! This house is yours for as long as you wish. You need want for nothing.'

'Oh Eardley, whatever are you suggesting?' The mockery reached her lips and as quickly died away. She touched his hand in apology. 'Forgive me, dear. I've no wish to hurt you, but can't you see? The world would judge you harshly—one divorce, a re-marriage, and now, they would say, a mistress—'

'Violet!' Anger blazed briefly in his eyes then died. 'One day you may love again and re-marry—how old are you?' He had never known.

'Too old, and do you really think I could ever feel for another man what I feel for Malcolm?' She shook her head. 'I fought so hard for the right to be myself and he helped me. But who *is* Violet Nicolson, after all? Without Malcolm, I am nothing, *nothing*. Even my very names were his gift!' Her yearning for the dead man throbbed in her voice as she went on: 'I have known the best, Eardley Norton, and I could never settle for less. Would you really condemn me to life, knowing that?'

No, he supposed he couldn't. He produced one more argument nonetheless. 'What of your son, Violet? Will you not go home to *him*?'

She flinched. For a moment, as he watched a solitary tear trace its way down one gaunt cheek, he thought he had won. 'Do you think I don't love him?' she cried. 'I carried that child in joy for nine long months. I bore him in agony and I nearly died to give him life. I love him. God knows how I love him! But,' and her mouth hardened, 'others took pains to replace me. I can't even be sure he remembers me.'

'Of course he remembers you, Violet! You've not been gone a year even!'

'Then let him remember me as I was—laughing at his father's side. Not mourning him ceaselessly.' Her thin hands fluttered white and birdlike against the severe black of her gown. She thought of her mother-in-law dressed in her eternal weeds, her widowed mother, the ageing maiden aunts … How could she add herself to the dismal throng, dragging her life out to its weary conclusion and afflicting the child with her grief?

'Violet, no—you are wrong! You *will* recover; you *will* forget the desperate grief; you *will* be happy. That is what Malcolm would have wanted.'

'No, Eardley, dear friend, *you* are wrong! If I had stopped him, Malcolm would be with me still—' It was a devastating reprise of the theme she had harped upon some weeks before. 'Now he expects me to join him. Otherwise,' and the look she gave him was triumphant, 'why did he put the five names in his will to take my place? I have done everything he wanted, Eardley. Malcolm's book is finished. I am ready to go.'

'All Farewells should be gently spoken'

Lady Stewart, home early from her engagement and about to join the couple in the verandah, heard Violet's very last words and she gave a profound sigh as tears of relief sprang to her eyes. So Francis Grahame was right—Violet was going home! She paused unseen a moment longer to compose herself and then Norton began to read:

And now I almost foresee the place and the hour
When I shall open my dying lips to thee
And receive a last cool kiss.
Afterwards, Wind, since I have always loved thee,—
Whirl my dust to the scented heart of a moghra flower
His *flower, but, ah, thou knowest,—*
So often thy kisses have mingled with his and mine.

'So, you mean it?' Norton went on. 'And how do you propose to do it?' His voice was low and subdued as he conceded Violet Nicolson's right to take her life—for what could reason do for her now?

'It will be easy,' she murmured. 'I shall take *the poppied drink that brings me endless rest.*'

'Opium—you have *opium*?' Eardley's voice was raised in surprise and Ada Stewart stifled a gasp. Where they had been indistinct before, she now caught every word.

'Oh, yes,' said Malcolm Nicolson's widow, 'I have opium.' *Enough to finish off an army*. 'And I intend to use it.'

Lady Stewart did not join them after all. With her hand to her mouth and horrified, she rushed away.

'I suppose,' Norton said, as a cold chill settled round his heart, 'you've taken the drug before.'

Violet nodded. 'Yes, in Mhow. For a while when I couldn't sleep. Malcolm made me stop.'

'And not since then?' Norton asked grimly.

'I took some a few weeks ago,' she admitted.

Yes, thought her companion, that would make sense. That would account for the despondency and the depression—and the self-recrimination that refused to go away. 'But not now?'

She looked at him and shook her head and he saw that her eyes were perfectly clear. 'And—?' he prompted.

'At first it was wonderful,' she said. 'I could sleep, and I had such beautiful dreams. But in the morning they were gone—' *He* was gone, leaving her without a backward glance. 'At first I thought I could bear the waking for the sake of the dreams, but it became too much—so I stopped.'

Her next words tightened the icy grip, making it painful for Norton to breathe. 'Yes, Eardley, I decided to wait—until I had finished Malcolm's book, you understand. And then I would take enough, enough to send me to sleep forever, so that the dream would never end. Or perhaps—' here she paused, and a radiant look such as he had never seen before stole over her face, 'perhaps I shall wake, and *he'll* be there, waiting for me.' She looked at her companion with those wondrous eyes. 'I'm ready now,' she said simply. 'And no one shall stop me.'

Norton said nothing. He, for one, would not even try.

'Eardley, will you take me to The Island, please? I want to show you Malcolm's grave.'

Norton had not been back to the cemetery since the day of the funeral. He knew, of course, that the headstone was in place—Grahame had taken Violet to see it and had later described it to him. So touching, Grahame said, in its simplicity, but still, he thought, a trifle difficult to find. 'I don't think she wants anyone to know he's there,' had been the old man's final comment.

While Norton was waiting for her to get ready Sir Norman appeared. 'I'm taking Violet to the cemetery,' the barrister explained. 'Please tell Lady Stewart; I wouldn't want her to be anxious.'

'Understood, my dear fellow,' replied Stewart. 'We're very worried about her, you know.'

'We all are,' Norton said, and said nothing more.

Violet came back wearing white. Both men were accustomed to the unrelieved black she had favoured since Nicolson's death, and her gown, together with the white scarf she had tossed over her head, had a startling effect. To them she seemed more insubstantial than ever, and if they thought her attire quite unsuitable for walking through the dusty cemetery, they kept their opinions to themselves—Sir Norman having learnt from experience that ladies always knew best on matters of dress, and Norton because this woman knew and didn't care.

How much of that harrowing August afternoon did Violet remember, Eardley wondered, as they passed through the Gothic arch. And how often had she been there since? She guided him confidently past the headstones until, 'Here we are,' she said and stopped.

The site was transformed. The grave was enclosed with a simple granite border and there was a plinth bearing a cross at its head. Not the usual cross, such as he could see all around them, but the heraldic *cross patée*, adopted by the most noble Order of the Bath. Only the initials *MHN* and a simple text marked the final resting place of Lieutenant General Malcolm Hassells Nicolson, BI, CB. The grave itself stood apart from the others. Yes, Norton saw exactly what Francis Grahame meant—it would be difficult to find.

The souls of the righteous are in the hands of God. The words she had chosen were very fine, Norton told Violet, quite befitting the soldier and the man. He cleared his throat and wondered what else to say.

'I've never thanked you for what you did for me that day,' Violet's voice was tender. So she *did* remember. 'You were so kind. It all seems a long, long time ago.'

Only two months, he thought.

'I wanted to come here again with you to show you that I'm better.' She looked down at her husband's grave. 'I really can't believe that Malcolm is dead, even now. I come here sometimes, you know, to talk to him and tell him it won't be long. I feel him here with me, waiting— No,' she repeated, turning back to her companion, 'it won't be long,' and her face was alight with joy.

As he listened to her Norton felt the hot tears blind his eyes. Violet touched his arm gently. 'Don't be sad for me, Eardley,' she murmured in her soft, sweet voice. 'Come here sometimes—afterwards—and stay with us awhile.'

He promised, and brushed away the tears.

She knelt by the cross and touched her lips to it in farewell. 'Do you see?' she said finally, pointing. 'I've planted a *moghra.* We loved its perfume so.'

The small bush would probably die, thought Eardley Norton. But he could always plant another, by this grave that would soon be her grave too. He took her arm but this time it was she who comforted him as they walked away.

Tuesday morning dawned and the occupants of Dunmore House were all busy in their different ways: Lady Stewart with her lists and final packing, Sir Norman checking the travel arrangements for the umpteenth time and receiving the frequent callers, and Violet in her room. The manuscript was ready, the pages in order and tied up in a neat parcel addressed to William Heinemann. Her letter to Blanche Crackanthorpe was written, requesting her to deliver the package in person.

Finally Violet wrote to Isabel in Karachi and asked her to explain her reasons to their family, the same reasons she had given Eardley Norton. *How can I possibly leave India?* she asked her sister. *And how can I stay, alone with all the memories? All I ever wanted was here, with him, and he has gone. So I shall join him. Please understand. And little Malcolm must understand it, too. Let him remember me as I was—his father's loving wife, not his grieving widow—if he can remember me at all. But tell him how much his parents always loved him.* She sealed the note, placed it with her will beside the bed, and went to find her host.

Sir Norman was alone in the drawing room. Violet handed over the parcel and the letter, explaining what they were, and entrusting them to his care. Frowning, and with reservations, he agreed. There were things he felt should be brought out into the open, and he would have done so then and there in a confrontation with his trying guest, had not two of his oldest friends in India been announced. Torn between his desire to settle Violet Nicolson's affairs once and for all, and his wish to do justice to his visitors and bid them farewell in the proper fashion, he murmured his excuses and turned away.

Violet made good her escape and returned to her room. She must be quick. She went to Malcolm's old battered portmanteau and looked inside. The Kashmiri box was no longer there! She tried desperately to remember; when had she seen it last? Yesterday, the day before? She couldn't recall—anything—and she couldn't think!

Don't panic, she told herself. Stay calm, where might it be? Look, look. It must be here, it *has* to be here ... But search as she might, it was nowhere to be found. Had it been packed by mistake?

Malcolm, Malcolm, she appealed, *tell me what to do*! She looked in the bag again, as if by some miracle the box would re-appear, and as she thrust her shaking fingers into a corner she felt something smooth and hard. Retrieving it, she saw a shell, with spirals like a markhor's horn. Baluchistan and Malcolm's gift!

She had forgotten, but he had kept it all this time!

One day it will remind us of happy times together, he had told her long ago in Zhob, but she had no time to sit and grieve—the memory of his words made her all the more determined to join him. *Where was that box?*

She rummaged again and felt something else wedged in and overlooked. When she withdrew her hand she was holding a small irregular nugget of gold. She held it to her cheek, and slowly at first, then in a rush, it all came flooding back. She remembered the thermometers, the capricious beads of metal—and Malcolm talking about the properties of mercury. He seemed to be talking to her now … *And she knew exactly what to do*!

Norman Stewart's hurried note contained enough detail to bring Eardley Norton rushing to Dunmore House. When he left Violet the previous evening she had said goodbye to him so sweetly that he had been convinced he would never see her alive again. And now this. What had happened to make her inflict this atrocity upon herself? He cast his mind back, and there was nothing—nothing. Why, they had even seen a kingfisher on the way back from the cemetery, and she had reminded him of the legend he had told her. 'Soon *my* quest will be over,' she had said so tranquilly, following the bird with her eyes long after it had disappeared. He had been so certain she would take an overdose of opium, and that her passing would be equally tranquil.

So why use sublimate of mercury? he kept asking himself. Why this obscenity? *Violet, Violet, don't go till I get there*, he implored silently as his carriage turned into the drive.

If the barrister was unable to explain Violet Nicolson's change of heart then someone else knew the answer. As she sat by the dying woman's bed, Ada Stewart's mind was in turmoil. By taking away the widow's opium she had acted for the best, hoping to remove all temptation and thus ensure her safe return to England. Instead, she had condemned Violet to an agonising death.

Sir Norman's two friends had stayed for tiffin. Lady Stewart returned from her engagement, but Violet had kept to her room. The animated meal had taken up more time than he had intended but with his visitors gone, Stewart could at last give Violet his full attention. It was two o'clock already. He felt his irritation rise as the *khitmatgar* came hurrying into the room, his usual dignity in shreds. What next? the general thought in exasperation, but soon he was listening to the garbled tale with mounting horror.

'Ada,' he cried, 'come with me!'

As they ran towards Violet's room he tried to explain what he had just been told. Their guest had gone to the kitchen and demanded insecticide. She had spoken to a new boy, who had trustingly handed over a full bottle of tablets. Only later had he thought to ask the identity of the *mem* who was so anxious to kill white ants …

'Please God we're not too late!' Stewart muttered as he threw open the unlocked door. But the memory of what they had found would never cease to haunt them: Violet, lying vomiting on the floor in the verandah, clutching her abdomen and crying out with the pain.

The Stewarts both did what they could. Sir Norman sent for a doctor, and Lady Stewart, recovering from the initial shock that threatened to paralyse her, sent to the kitchen for all the whites of egg available, forcing them down the unresisting woman's throat. The vomiting did not stop but they seemed to lessen the burning pain. Ada cradled the tiny figure in her arms while she waited for the doctor and blessed her husband's thoroughness when not one, but two, arrived.

And here was Violet now, lying back against the pillows, her face hardly less white, surrounded by strangers and friends, and slowly slipping away—not in the drugged and happy sleep she had planned, but in pain-racked agony. Her cheeks were sunken and her eyes hollow, her body drenched in sweat. Would it never, never end?

While Ada Stewart continued to bathe Violet's face and wipe her swollen mouth, Surgeon-Major Smith consulted briefly with his colleague, Major Giffard of the IMS. Then he gave the patient morphine to help the pain.

'How do you feel now, Mrs Nicolson?' he asked. Her pulse was faint, frequent and irregular.

It was difficult to answer, but Violet replied in a hoarse, husky whisper that it was a little better, thank you.

She was still conscious when they brought in Eardley Norton. Lady Stewart relinquished her seat and he sat down and took Violet's hand. She seemed to recognise him, and her cracked lips attempted a smile.

'Is there nothing you can do for her?' he asked Giffard in great distress.

'We've given her morphine,' came the reply.

'Well,' he retorted, 'it obviously wasn't enough—she's still in fearful pain!' Violet's face was almost unrecognisable, her body racked with convulsions as Eardley Norton got to his feet and advanced purposefully on the major. 'Give her more, for pity's sake!' It was hardly a request.

'I'm not sure about that, sir,' Major Giffard replied. The barrister's tall authoritative figure commanded respect, but there were certain ethical considerations that would worry him in increasing the dose.

Norton read his mind. 'In God's name,' he exploded, 'what difference does it make—she'll die anyway! But it will make all the difference in the world *to her*.'

The doctor glanced at his colleague then deferred to the passionate eyes. He reached into his bag and moved towards the bed while Norton bent over the dying woman. 'Violet,' he told her urgently, taking her hand again, 'we've given you more morphine. It will help you to sleep—dearest Violet, *do you understand?*'

Let it finish soon, he prayed, *and let her have her dreams*.

He felt a slight pressure from her fingers; she was looking at him. He smiled reassuringly. She pressed his hand again then closed her eyes.

The pain was gone, and Violet Nicolson was drifting away towards her endless rest. Gradually the voices around her became fainter until only one remained.

Wake up, my dearest girl, it seemed to be saying, *Violet, wake up*.

She forced her eyes open. Someone was standing by her bed, leaning over her. It was Malcolm, she realised joyously, and this time she knew he wouldn't go away without her.

Come away, sweetheart, she heard him say in the voice she loved so well. *Come away home to the hills*.

He held out his hand, and waited.

Those watching saw her lips move silently and her hand stir on the sheet. An ethereal glow spread over her face and she tried to rise. Then with a barely audible sigh she fell back against the pillows. Violet Nicolson was dead.

One of the first tasks Sir Norman Stewart set himself when he reached London was to call on Mrs Crackanthorpe at her home in Rutland Square. Blanche listened gravely to all he had to say, and then astounded her visitor by her response.

'I imagine Anglo-India thinks she let the side down,' she said with a grim little laugh. 'But do you know, General Stewart, I've been told that Hindus think Violet Nicolson a true and loyal wife; that by becoming *sati* she has bestowed countless blessings on her husband.'

Stewart replied gruffly that he knew nothing of such things, but he *could* say it had been a terrible, terrible way to die. His eyes were suspiciously bright as he handed over Violet's parcel and letter and said a swift goodbye. When he had gone Blanche put the package to one side and sat down to read the many requests and instructions contained in Violet's letter. Finally came an explanation.

Blanche, I am exercising my right to follow the man I love and I know you will not judge me—only God can do that and I know He will be merciful. Let Malcolm be remembered for his goodness, and me for the undying love I bore him. For that reason, would Blanche please ensure that the dedication to her husband had pride of place in the book?

Blanche leaned back and in her mind she reached out to her friend. *Oh, my dear Violet, you will truly be remembered for your love—just as you will always be remembered for your poetry. You were your poetry, how could it be otherwise? And your poetry is you: your spirit shines through it all. And you do yourself so little justice in the dedication; you are too harsh when you say you were of small joy to your husband—for we all knew the great happiness you brought him. And now, dear Violet, you surely know it, too …*

Mrs Crackanthorpe gathered up the manuscript purposefully and set off to visit William Heinemann. She had brought Laurence Hope's final book of poetry, she told him, and it was to be called *Indian Love*.

Epilogue

There was a Door to which I found no Key:
There was a Veil past which I could not see:
Some little Talk of ME and THEE
There seem'd - and then no more of THEE and ME.

The Rubáiyát of Omar Khayyám, ed. 1, xxxii

THE ISLAND, MADRAS: MID 1960s

The young man passed through the Gothic archway and paused. He looked around him and wondered which direction to take, for the cemetery was far bigger than he had expected. He took the wide path straight ahead, but after a few moments was forced to stop. Twenty years after the British had left the country, India was reclaiming her own. The graves nearest the path were still visible, but everywhere else the railings, tombstones and mausoleums were engulfed by brilliant creepers and rampant roses. Not that the Nicolsons would have minded, by all accounts—from what he had heard they were hardly ones for order and regimentation! The visitor turned back towards the entrance. He had promised his grandmother he would find them and it would be unkind to abandon his search so soon.

'Do go to St Mary's cemetery on The Island,' she had begged him, when he told her of his plan to visit Madras. 'And find the Nicolsons' grave. Oh, do say you will! You see, they were such a splendid couple, not that I ever met them, of course. But *my* grandmother knew them slightly, and she had such tales to tell—Oh, yes, they were legendary figures, even in their lifetime. Although British India didn't take to Mrs Nick at all,' and the old lady's eyes twinkled. Unwilling to disappoint her, her grandson had agreed, but without help it was obviously going to be impossible. He headed for the caretaker's lodge he had spotted earlier.

At last the *chowkidar* answered his summons. Yes, he said in impeccable English at odds with his unkempt appearance. Yes, he knew the grave in question. Did the *sahib* wish to see it? Biting back an impatient reply, the young man nodded.

Then please to come this way, said the *chowkidar*, and setting off at a brisk pace the old fellow made his way unerringly to a plot indistinguishable from its neighbours. There, he said, with a confident sweep of a claw-like hand—the general *sahib* and the general *sahib*'s wife. There was nothing but weeds to be seen.

The Indian waited, moving his open hand a little in the young man's direction until at last the latter understood. With a grin he brought out his wallet, produced a note, and the *chowkidar* set to work.

The inscription rapidly emerged.

LT GENL MALCOLM NICOLSON BI, CB
DIED 7TH AUGUST 1904
'WHOSE SOUL WAS NOBLE'

AND HIS WIFE
ADELA FLORENCE
DIED 4TH OCTOBER 1904
AGED 39 YEARS

So there they lay, the eccentric couple British India had dubbed 'The Nicks'. The plain English on the even plainer headstone was disappointing. Uninformative as it was, it hardly did their reputation justice. And there was no mention of the poet 'Laurence Hope'. He stood with head bowed for a moment recalling what his grandmother had told him: the adventures, the scandals, the untimely deaths; the books that were bestsellers into the nineteen-forties … How strange, he thought, that nowadays no one seemed to remember the Nicolsons at all.

From behind him came a cough and he turned his head. The caretaker had finished his work. From the look of it, the splendidly proportioned cross the old fellow had just revealed at the foot of the grave must have been covered for quite some time. 'How strange, it would have made a much finer headstone,' he muttered, and was surprised to get an answer.

'Yes, *sahib*,' and the *chowkidar* shook his head in agreement, Indian fashion. 'The grave of the general *sahib* and his wife looked different many years ago. Then the cross was standing upright at the head. It was moved many years ago.'

'When was it moved?'

'One November,' the old man thought it had been. 'Yes, it happened in November.'

'In which year was that?'

Surely the *sahib* didn't expect him to remember? It was many years ago, when he was only a boy and his grandfather was the *chowkidar*.

How could he be so sure of the month, if he couldn't remember the year?

Because it was raining, *sahib*, raining heavily like it always did in November—if the *sahib* ever visited Madras in November then he would understand why he remembered!

The young man conceded defeat and told the caretaker to go on.

One day, the old man said, the cross was at the head, the next day it lay quite flat upon the grave. Later on the workmen came, to put the headstone where he saw it now, the *new* headstone of the general *sahib* and his wife.

And the words on the cross—there must have been words. What had happened to the words?

The old man spread his hands. He didn't know, he said. The words had disappeared, all gone, vanished. A miracle, *sahib*, it was a miracle. Soft brown eyes invited the young man to share his sense of wonder, but the young man stooped to take a closer look.

It was no miracle. There were still traces of an inscription to be seen. And others could be felt if he ran his fingers over the roughened granite of the cross. Someone had taken a chisel and tried to efface the lot!

He squinted, but try as he might *MHN* was all he managed to decipher. But why hadn't they done a proper job?

He thought he knew. It was India, after all, and it had been raining. Whoever was responsible hadn't come back to check—and the workmen had taken advantage. And now *he* was faced with this enigma. Who could have carried out what was surely an act of desecration?

The Englishman pressed more notes into the old man's waiting hand and walked away. His grandmother perhaps would have the answer.

Acknowledgements

for the 1996 publication of

Fate Knows no Tears

My thanks to Reed International, holder of the copyright of Gertrude Bell's translations from the poetry of Hafiz, originally published by William Heinemann in 1897, for permission to quote from her work; quotations used as section headings are taken from Laurence Hope's three books of poetry: *The Garden of Kama* (1901), *Stars of the Desert* (1903), and *Indian Love* (1905), also published by Heinemann.

My original intention was to write a biography of Adela Florence Nicolson ('Laurence Hope'). When, however, my attempts to communicate with the descendants of some of the main protagonists met with silence, a biographer's nightmare rapidly turned into a novelist's dream, and for the past five years I have relied instead upon my own research and intuition in creating what I hope is a credible—if often fictional—account of the poet's life set against authentic events of the age in which she lived. In doing this I acknowledge my debt to Lesley Blanch's chapter on Laurence Hope in *Under a Lilac-Bleeding Star* (1963, John Murray, London); this was a useful starting point, drawing as it does on an unpublished memoir written by the poet's son, although tantalisingly vague on detail. Other memoirs and personal writings of the period helped shed more light on the poet's persona, but it was Violet Jacob's *Diaries and Letters from India* (1990, C. Anderson. ed., Canongate, Edinburgh), written in Mhow in the years 1895–1900, which brought the Nicolsons and their milieu to life, and my debt to these and to Violet Jacob's later, unpublished, Indian diary and papers held in the National Library of Scotland, Edinburgh, is considerable. Captain Crawford

McFall's *With the Zhob Field Force* (Heinemann 1895) gives a day-by-day account of the expedition's manoeuvres, and interesting details of the Griffin family and Heneage's mining ventures are contained in Maryjoy Martin's *Suicide Legends, Homicide Rumors* (1986, Spes in Deo Publications, Montrose, Colorado). But it is Laurence Hope's poetry that provided many of the clues, both to the poet's personality and life, and to her travels in the Indian sub-continent, Europe and North Africa.

I am grateful for the opportunity to research at the following institutions: the Australian National Library, Canberra; the Borchardt Library of La Trobe University, Melbourne; the British Library, London; the Edsell Ford Library, Lakeville, Connecticut, USA; Emory University and Georgia State University, Atlanta, Georgia, USA; the *Malayala Manorama* newspaper of Kerala, India; the Kipling Collection, University of Sussex; the Mitchell Library, Sydney; the National Army Museum, London; the National Library of Scotland, Edinburgh; the Oriental and India Office Collections of the British Library, London; the Library of the Royal Botanic Gardens, Edinburgh; the State Library of Victoria, Melbourne, and I would like to thank the staff of the above for their help, particularly the staff of the Borchardt and Victoria State Libraries. My thanks to the staff of the many libraries, archives and other institutions with whom I have been in written contact over the past five years, particularly the following: the BBC Archives; the British Library Newspaper Library, London; Debrett's Peerage; Octopus Library (William Heinemann); Richmond Library, Richmond, Sussex; the Archives of the Royal Opera House, Covent Garden; Shropshire County Library; Trinity College, Bristol.

I am very grateful for the opportunity to visit the cantonment at Mhow, Indore State, India, and greatly appreciate the hospitality and help afforded me by the General and Staff of the Infantry School.

I should also like to thank the following individuals: Frederick B. Adams; Michael Barthorp; Kathleen Cory; H. Colin Davis; Vin D'Cruz; Prya D'Cruz; R.G. Harris; Marion Harding and Angela Kelsall; Lieutenant Colonel C. Kannan (retd.); Professor E. Karim; Dr G. Krishnamurti; Margaret MacMillan; Edward Marx; Elise May; Professor Michael Millgate; S. Muthiah; Professor Harold Orel; Professor Emeritus A. Paneerselvam; Professor Thomas Pinney; Elisabeth Purbrick; Tim Thomas; the Webster family; Beryl and Malcolm Williams, and many others besides.

Special thanks are due to Valerie Hiley for her enthusiastic research at the India Office Library, which set me on the right road, and her interest and support throughout the project, and to Melvyn Hiley; to Pauline March, whose invaluable research in the National Archives of Pakistan, Islamabad, has thrown light on much that was hitherto unknown and greatly enriched the novel; to John

Jealous of Books about India and editor of the *Laurence Hope Newsletter* whose enthusiasm and help have been an inspiration, and to him and Dr Helen Ross for their hospitality on several occasions; to Donald Morrison for his generous gift of original manuscript letters from Blanche Alethea Crackanthorpe; to William Jacob for the opportunity to study the Jacob family papers and to him and Mrs Jacob for their kindness; to Michael and Frances Cory for their help and hospitality; to my family and friends for their interest, suggestions and practical assistance; finally my love and thanks to Roger, without whom nothing at all would have been possible—let alone finished—and who has provided never-failing encouragement and support throughout.

Wakefield Press is an independent publishing and
distribution company based in Adelaide, South Australia.
We love good stories and publish beautiful books.
To see our full range of books, please visit our website at
www.wakefieldpress.com.au
where all titles are available for purchase.
To keep up with our latest releases, news and events,
subscribe to our newsletter.

Find us!

Facebook: www.facebook.com/wakefield.press
Twitter: www.twitter.com/wakefieldpress
Instagram: www.instagram.com/wakefieldpress

www.ingramcontent.com/pod-product-compliance
Lightning Source LLC
LaVergne TN
LVHW030913080826
845145LV00011B/2877

* 9 7 8 1 8 6 2 5 4 7 8 5 8 *